THREE EIGHTEENTH CENTURY ROMANCES

THE CASTLE OF OTRANTO
VATHEK
THE ROMANCE OF THE FOREST

THREE EIGHTEENTH CENTURY ROMANCES

THE CASTLE OF OTRANTO
VATHEK
THE ROMANCE OF THE FOREST

WITH AN INTRODUCTION BY

HARRISON R. STEEVES

CHARLES SCRIBNER'S SONS
NEW YORK

CONTENTS

INTRODUCTION

In many respects the great and positive literary achievement of the eighteenth century was the English novel. With its roots in the journalistic narrative of Defoe, and its growth in emotional sensibility with Richardson, in worldly humor with Fielding, and in Frances Burney's quaint but wise scrutiny of contemporary manners, it had reached by the last quarter of the century a plane of manifest artistic fitness. In the hands of Defoe, Richardson, Fielding, and Miss Burney, the clear and studied purpose of the novel had been truth to life, and in a large way this purpose was expressly opposed to the romantic moods and attitudes of those who wrote fiction before 1700. Yet even with the advance of the realistic novel, a steady stream of romantic fiction continued to flow in more or less traditional channels throughout the eighteenth century—and beyond it.

These two obvious and distinct drifts in the fiction of the eighteenth century are only one evidence of the interesting duality of the period, its rational side seen in Locke, Voltaire, Franklin and Paine, its romantic side in Steele, Rousseau, Goldsmith, and in the general tendency of poetry throughout the last three quarters of the century. In poetry the romantic mood gradually displaced the realistic, the literal, the objective—whatever we may prefer to call it—but in fiction romanticism itself had been rather outworn when the eighteenth century opened; and the singular success of Defoe and Fielding in creating an interest in the contemporary and the probable rather than the sentimental or the bizarre, left the field of romantic fiction in the main to inferior writers who must have appealed to the less critical readers of their time.

Yet if the struggle between realistic and romantic aims in fiction was one-sided, it was far from conclusive, for it was concerned not only with questions of literary taste, but with questions of ethical aim. The realists faced a "resistance" on the part of readers who not only preferred the kaleidoscope to the microscope, but felt a moral glow in that preference. Even Defoe, accomplished realist as he was, confessed a certain shame in the picturing of the common and sordid details of contemporary life. A half-century later Clara Reeve drew an interesting and characteristic, though probably misleading, distinction between the realistic, which she felt must in its mere adherence to fact lack inspiriting ideality, and the romantic, which by its stress upon what she called the finer and nobler sides of life, offers something for encouragement and emulation. And throughout the century there was a somewhat pharisaical suspicion of the kind of truth that Fielding was able to convey. If Tom Jones and Captain Booth were real men, then it were better not to discuss the qualities of real men too frankly. But whether because of the moral force that Miss Reeve argued for romantic fiction, or because of the unstifled romantic predilections of the age, at any rate the century is dotted with curious fictions that have little kinship with the great novels.

The ideas and feelings that underlay these romantic stories are the familiar concepts of romanticism generally: love of the moods of nature, the sentimental attitude, the relish for antiquity and the exotic, and the melancholic strain that gives its tone to the poetry of Collins, Young, Gray, and Cowper. In the direct

stream of fiction, some of these influences had already
been felt before or during the earlier part of the century. Courtly and idyllic romances had been popular
for hundreds of years, though the worldliness of the
Restoration and the age of Anne had weakened their
vogue. The spirit and flavor of the Orient were brought
to Europe by Antoine Galland's French translation of
the *Arabian Nights,* completed in 1717. Richardson
had given England its first novel of sentiment in
Pamela (1740). The first historical novel—Charles
Leland's *Longsword*—was written in 1762; but this
was simply an expression in fiction of the "medieval-
ism" that had been gathering momentum from the beginning of the century. The cult of nature, on the other
hand, found its way rather late into prose fiction, after
it had struck its distinctive note in painting and poetry.
These were the spiritual forces at work in literature
during the period, and singly or collectively they are
found in those notable though secondary fictions that
appeared from the publication of Dr. Johnson's *Rasselas,* in 1759, on to the end of the century, when romantic fiction was temporarily submerged by the first
tide of modern realism in the social satires of Jane
Austen. Of these numerous romances, we have taken
three as representing the character and historical de-
velopment of the type.

The first of these tales, *The Castle of Otranto,* is
to-day somewhat difficult to take seriously. Its portentous mysteries and exaggerated terrors seem to us
both cheap and trivial. Yet it is the ancient head—
now fallen into disrepute—of an entire family of stories
of its kind, good, bad and indifferent, which includes
the work of as reputable authors as Poe, the Brontë
sisters, and Stevenson.

The author, Horace Walpole, was the son of Sir

Robert Walpole, one of the dominant figures in English political life in the early eighteenth century. The elder Walpole, who was an indefatigable collector, trained his son as a connoisseur; and Walpole's personal temper lent itself readily to this career. Walpole was educated at Eton and King's College, Cambridge, and was then sent with the young poet Gray to make the "grand tour" of the continent. Throughout his life he cultivated assiduously his interests in painting, literature, and antiquities, supported by the proceeds of political sinecures secured through family influence. The notable and picturesque occupation of his middle years was his rebuilding of his villa "Strawberry Hill," which he took in 1747, in the "Gothic" style, and the housing of his collections there. He also established at Strawberry Hill a private press from which were issued a number of books, including the poems of his friend Gray. Here he spent a long and leisured life as society man and wit, producing from time to time a variety of writings of greater or less importance.

In its day, *The Castle of Otranto* seemed absorbing and skilfully made, if not a great work of imagination. Even Sir Walter Scott admitted its spell. And obvious as it is in theme and treatment, its vogue is not difficult to understand. It appeared at a time (1764) when the literary world had looked too long and familiarly at reflections of its own social life, and was ready to find its escape in one of the characteristic forms of other-world interest. The particular color of this interest in Walpole's story was determined by the antiquarian tastes of the time, in combination with the charm of ancientry and the growing vogue of mystery and the mystical. *The Castle of Otranto* is unqualifiedly, undilutedly, romantic; so much so that it recognizes none of the checks of reason upon invention, but is for its time almost the absolute expression of imaginative freedom. The real artistic explanation of *The Castle of Otranto*, however, is that it is a *tour de force*, a display of virtuosity. Undoubtedly Walpole wrote it with his tongue in his cheek. He was too much a person of the world to be insensible of its extravagance and its emotional pose. To him the story was simply "a Gothic tale," and in the preface to the book he ingeniously excuses its excesses on the ground that they were the product of the credulity of the period in which he pretends the story was written.

Readers liked it, however, and it was published many times. Yet for a while it had no imitators. Twelve years later, in 1775, Clara Reeve wrote her *Old English Baron*, a very prosy story in which she tried to demonstrate that the terrors and mysteries of the Gothic type need not outrage the reader's common sense. She utilized much of Walpole's "machinery," but brought into her story no wonders, no apparitions, that could not be explained—after the fact, at least—in a perfectly reasonable way. A gap of another dozen years followed in which Walpole's supremacy was still unchallenged, when Ann Radcliffe brought out in 1789 a meagre and modest story, *The Castles of Athlyn and Dunbayne*, which set in motion her great though short-lived reputation.

Not very much is known of Mrs. Radcliffe (1764-1823). In the case of a writer who reflects so slightly the social concepts of her time, that matters relatively little. She had means, social contacts, leisure, and some acquaintance with the intellectual figures of her time; but she was not particularly a social spirit. She had an evident fondness for simple and leisurely travel, but never far from the shores of England. She did visit the Low Countries and the German frontier, and took carriage trips in England with her husband. Curiously enough, she appears not to have known at first hand either Italy or Southern France, the scenes of her most discussed novels, but gathered her color and atmosphere largely from books of travel—a fact which may account for the sometimes strongly geological and botanical savor of her description of landscape, as well as for her excess of scenic effects. With the close of her literary career, which extended over the early years of her married life, she retired not only from literature, but from public notice.

Mrs. Radcliffe's Gothic romances are the best of the pure type. She published five of them between 1789 and 1797, and her posthumous *Gaston de Blondeville* has a general relation to the genre. Of these, three—*The Romance of the Forest* (1791), *The Mysteries of Udolpho* (1794), and *The Italian* (1797), are still distinctly readable. *The Mysteries of Udolpho* is in a way the archetype of the species; but it is very long, thin and transparent in plot, and encumbered with meaningless terrors and mysteries. *The Italian* has more literary maturity than the others. But *The Romance of the Forest* is probably as clear, natural and intrinsically entertaining a piece as anything Mrs. Radcliffe wrote.

In pattern Mrs. Radcliffe's romances are curiously alike. The story is built typically about the misadventures and mishaps of a heroine of gentle and sensitive nature, in the background of whose history is some deep, and generally irrelevant, mystery. She is thrown into the power of sinister villains, and exposed continuously to both real and fancied terrors. But although she is constantly threatened with death—"or worse," as Mrs. Radcliffe puts it—her virtue and a certain blind but lucky courage carry her through the

perils of her situation.   In the end she is found affectionately but modestly united to the genteel young
lover from whom destiny has separated her in her
moments of trial.   This heroine is, in the eighteenth
century tradition, an object of great sentimental solicitude, and a model of feminine deportment.   Her emotional life is troubled and even melancholy, but her
outward poise reflects the best of breeding.   She
sketches, paints, plays the lute, embroiders, sings, reads
romances, walks—but not beyond the limitations of an
interestingly fragile constitution; and in her most exalted moments she writes poetry, specimens of which,
hopelessly pedestrian, Mrs. Radcliffe gives us in all her
stories.   This heroine is a skilled casuist in the pro-
prieties, too.   Witness the episode in *The Italian* in
which Ellena questions whether she should permit her
affianced lover to lead her from urgent danger, or even
death, except with proper chaperonage.

With this uniformity of general design, Mrs. Radcliffe's novels differ from one another only in detailed
handling.   And her details are in the main unessential
and episodic, her artistic resources always limited.   The
machinery of her stories maintains its uninterrupted
motion without much visible effect.   We find her heroine running away from threatened dangers with about
the same resultless persistency as in an artless moving-
picture serial of a few years ago.   Mrs. Radcliffe is
tediously circumstantial; and her plots are not merely
loose, but from the point of view of a real social import, generally meaningless.   She was, indeed, a poetical
spirit working in prose—and not in good prose, either.
Like Scott, she was both facile and careless.   Her
works abound in inconsistencies and anachronisms.   She
is redundant beyond belief.   In her earliest narrative,
The Castles of Athlin and Dunbayne, little more than

a short story, her heroine faints eight times; and in the description of a second fair damsel, we are told over and over again, with only the slightest variations of phrase, that "the bloom of her youth was shaded by a soft and pensive melancholy which communicated an extremely interesting expression to her fine blue eyes." Her phrase is impoverished, her invention limited, her characters and situations taken from an extremely small stock in trade. Her art lies simply in the accumulation of effects without proportion or reason, rarely with adequate phrase, rarely with restraint, never with more than the most elementary sense of literary architecture. In fact, any thoughtful criticism of Mrs. Radcliffe amounts to a general indictment of literary incapacity.

It is needless to say that Mrs. Radcliffe was in no sense a student of life, but merely the docile pupil of her sentimental age. She shares all the amiable errors of her time—a belief in the "natural breeding" of the rustic, in the charm of a delicate physique in a woman, in the logic of feminine inferiority, and generally in the fascination of the neurotic temper. Her historical perspective is similarly prejudiced and distorted, and her political and religious views (particularly apparent in *The Italian*) are insular, and even childish. Her morality is strictly conformist, set forth in placidly repeated commonplaces. In none of those matters in which we expect the novelist to be a critical observer of life has she any appeal for the reader of to-day.

And yet, her work has done indisputable service for imaginative vigor and romantic beauty in prose fiction. If she did not have art in any comprehensive sense, at any rate she had artistic cunning. This is evident principally in her partly new, and certainly effectual, use of romantic color and atmosphere. Everything in her stories contributes to their mood, and this mood is always sombre, agitated, pervasive. Her range in this respect is great. She can find the precise background for tender and pensive thoughts. But her great effects are gained by a wild and lavishly fashioned romantic imagery, often symbolic, and for the most part scenic—craggy castles, ruined abbeys, mouldering cloisters and tombs, midnight bells, black forests, impenetrable gorges, stretches of sea, moonlit vistas, picturesque ruffians, the dust of long-closed chambers, the dampness of the charnel-house; all of them external but highly useful furnishings for the familiar emotional appeal. These effects dominate the psychology of the moment, create its suspense, and surround even a trivial incident with a vivid if factitious interest. To be sure, she overdoes it; but that is to admit that she does it.

We must concede, however, that our interest in Mrs. Radcliffe is the interest of the curious. After all, the credulity of her readers, their pathetic willingness to be perturbed and mystified, is a revealing commentary upon the sentimental bias of her age. Fiction ran for the moment in a shallow and muddy stream, and Mrs. Radcliffe's transient reputation was challenged by no contemporary novelist of real strength or significance. But we may be sure that she was read, probably surreptitiously and nervously, by thousands of young ladies seeking emotional escape from the sheltered tranquillity of provincial and middle-class domesticity. Jane Austen ridicules it all in *Northanger Abbey*, adding her conviction that these mean cravings for the sensational in fiction were not only silly but somewhat base. It is hard now to believe that Mrs. Radcliffe was ever in good taste, despite her undoubted popularity.

With the publication of *The Italian*, Mrs. Radcliffe abruptly stopped writing. Why? Possibly she felt her own limitations. Possibly she was convinced of the

dubiety of much in the social and ethical points of view
of her novels. In this connection, there are two passages of instructive discourse in *The Mysteries of
Udolpho* in which the father of the heroine cautions her
against "sensibility (by which he means temperamental
susceptibility)—the romantic error of amiable minds."
Probably Mrs. Radcliffe anticipated in her own judgment the ridicule which Jane Austen poured upon her
heroines and her most moving situations. At any rate
the time was ripe for a fiction which should deal more
faithfully and soberly with life and people as they are,
and from 1795 on there were many writers able and
anxious to accomplish that aim.

Before the Gothic tradition was quite worn out, there
appeared even more striking examples of the type than
Mrs. Radcliffe herself had produced, and from the late
1790's on there was an epidemic of shorter Gothic
stories, many of them published as chap-books. The
most stirring of all the Gothics was Matthew Gregory
Lewis's violent and rather wicked *Monk* (1795). Probably the one most commended to-day is Charles Ma-
turin's lengthy *Melmoth the Wanderer*, published
strangely late in 1820, after Scott had brought new and
vigorous life into the historical-romantic novel. But the
peak of popularity of the Gothic novel had been reached
in those lean years from 1790 to 1800. Its real triumph and its fall came within that decade.

Where did the "influence" of these fictions lead?
Their most immediate and visible effect on literature of
any importance was to furnish the romantic mechanism
for the narrative verse of Scott and Byron. But beyond
this, the qualities of the Gothic romance filtered through
readable fiction during much of the nineteenth century.
Its influence, in common with that of German romanticism, passed through the American Charles Brockden

Brown to both Poe and Hawthorne. In Emily Brontë's *Wuthering Heights* we see its effect in a novel with more human characters and more credible social relations. In her sister Charlotte Brontë's *Jane Eyre* there is a similar use of uncouth mystery with eerie setting and electric atmosphere to maintain it. The violent storm that rises and breaks as Rochester proposes to Jane, and the voice of Rochester heard by Jane miles across the moors, are recognizably Gothic effects. Stevenson's *Markheim, The Pavilion on the Links, The Beach at Falesa,* and *Weir of Hermiston* all have a manifest strain of Gothic in them, though attenuated and rationalized. Even to-day we hear the echoes of the genre in the stories of Algernon Blackwood and Walter de la Mare.

Beckford's *Vathek* is quite another sort of thing. First of all, its background is not Gothic, but oriental, and it is quite free from the complacent imitativeness of the later Gothic romanticists. There is no doubt of its lasting and intrinsic merit. In its vigor, its profusion of color and its audacity of effect it is unquestionably a work of art. It is, too, one of the great literary burlesques, taking a place probably somewhat lower than Voltaire's *Candide*, Meredith's *Shaving of Shagpat*, and Max Beerbohm's *Zuleika Dobson*.

William Beckford was the descendant of a very old English family, which within the hundred years before his birth (1760) had become fabulously wealthy from great estates in the West Indies. Beckford's education, which was entirely under private direction, gave him wide cultivation and contacts, but his cultural interests were too scattered to be profound, and he was always volatile, fanciful, and so extravagant in his tastes that his contemporaries regarded him as a good deal of an oddity. He wrote rather industriously, but published grudgingly, for he affected a contempt for applause. But in spite of his touch of intellectual snobbery, Beckford showed both wit and understanding of aesthetic values in almost everything to which he set his hand.

Vathek is Beckford's one indisputable claim to literary note. The rest of his career is without interest except as the record of the fantastic doings of a man of enormous wealth and capricious tastes. After years spent largely in travel abroad, he returned in 1796 to the family seat at Fonthill to embark upon a vast scheme of lavish building and landscaping. He is one of the great subjects of contemporary anecdote, most of which illustrates the queer and unexpected sides of a character that the age never quite succeeded in appraising.

Vathek was written for the most part in 1782, not, however, in the "three days and two nights of hard labor" in which Beckford later said he had composed it. Possibly the first draft of the story was so written, but it is certain from Beckford's letters that he was at work upon the tale for the best part of a year, and it was in process of revision still longer. The tale was written in French, a language which Beckford, like his contemporaries Chesterfield and Gibbon, affected.

Beckford's first idea of writing an oriental romance came from his friend the Rev. Samuel Henley, a master at Harrow and a well informed orientalist. Henley's judgment was consulted upon countless literary, historical, linguistic and antiquarian problems connected with the book. In addition, Henley, apparently at Beckford's instance, translated the work from Beckford's manuscript, with the evident understanding that he should be allowed to publish this translation. Through an imperfect sense, however, of what his relations and agreements with the author implied, Henley published the English version in 1786, although the book was not yet finished to Beckford's satisfaction. He also unaccountably omitted to credit the book to Beckford, but stated that it was "adapted from the Arabic." Beckford brought out his French version as promptly as possible in the following year in two editions, one printed at Lausanne, the other at Paris. Probably Beckford's haste to issue in self-defense the original French version prevented him from publishing the romance in as lengthy a form as he had planned it. In any event, three "Episodes" from *Vathek*—the tales of the three princes encountered in the closing passage of the story—were not printed by Beckford, and for many years were thought to have been lost. These were found and separately published in 1912. The English version of Henley has always been regarded, rather curiously, as *the* book. This version appeared with labored notes upon oriental costume, folklore, geography, social habits and the like, which Beckford had attached to his tale. These notes Beckford at one time regarded as "certainly necessary," but probably he took altogether too serious a view of their value. In the present edition they are omitted, or where plainly necessary, are compressed into the briefest foot-notes.

Vathek shows artistic consistency. It is surprisingly like what it pretends to be. It has undeniably the oriental air—that arch blending of sobriety and wit, that interweaving of hard humor and emotional fervor, that the Western World knows chiefly through *The Thousand and One Nights*. In atmosphere it is probably less convincing, Beckford's anxiety to document his social life and customs giving the work a strain of pedantry. But with all that, it seems to be neither imitative nor labored. Once again, it is an artist's creation, free in spirit, but, in the good eighteenth-century sense of things, worshipful of form; for all its exoticism, a very typical thing.

As burlesque, *Vathek* ridicules the romantic vogue by accentuating the romantic styles. Its exaggerations—such as the slaughter of the fifty innocents, and the frantic chase of the Giaour—are purposely top-heavy. Its sentiment, too, is designedly affected, and furnishes a deliberate contrast to the actual fatuity and brutalism of the characters. Even its lavishness of image and of phrase is (for all it is admired) simply a gorgeous exercise in "fine writing," and it may even be questioned whether its pious conclusion—an amazing *non-sequitur* —is not intended as an anti-climax, possibly as a travesty upon the didactic conclusions of such tales as Johnson's *Rasselas*. There is, too, an obvious touch of satire in *Vathek*, the more notable because of its rather superficial relation to Voltaire's, Montesquieu's, and Goldsmith's satirical depiction of oriental customs, both in parallel and in contrast to those of Europe. But we may be tempted to draw too profound conclusions upon this point, for Beckford was scarcely by literary constitution a satirist. His tonic sense took in the ironies of the contemporary social system, but there is in his make-up little of that warmth of moral indignation combined with comic perception that makes the satirist's temper.

Possibly the most significant thing about the writing of *Vathek* is Beckford's quite characteristic nonchalance—his preoccupation with the game, so to speak, and his indifference to anything but a personally satisfying result. Indeed, were it not that the publication of the book was forced, it might never have seen the light; or almost as bad, it might have been still-born in that half-adequate French in which Beckford wrote it. In a word, such a piece of literary dilettantism as *Vathek* has no serious artistic relations, however we may calculate learnedly its sources and its influence. Beckford's admiration for the *Arabian Nights*, his interest in oriental lore, the mock gravity of his other writings, his imagined indebtedness to Voltaire, may explain certain aspects of his performance, but they are far from explaining an intrinsically brilliant and largely original work.

At any rate the result is unmistakable; *Vathek* could have been produced only by mature wit keenly awake to the incongruities of things, conjoined with literary connoisseurship. It is an unusual combination of qualities in the Englishman, as Meredith has pointed out; and it is therefore doubly prized because it *is* English.

HARRISON R. STEEVES

EDITOR'S NOTE

The early copies of the three texts in this volume, particularly of the last two, show many instances of either careless writing or faulty printing. In a few cases of obvious error the editor has ventured to make corrections; but even in the present text the meticulous reader will discover anomalies of phrase and syntax that reflect the fact that not all eighteenth century prose was as fair as Johnson's or Gibbon's. The punctuation in all three romances has also been somewhat modernized, but in such a way as to preserve as far as possible the rather unwieldy sentence structure of the originals.

Two fairly substantial cuts have been made in the text of *The Romance of the Forest*, both of them prolonged incidents of only secondary importance to the action of the story. The two episodes are summarized in their proper place (pp. 457–9 and 501–3 following). Without these cuts, the volume would scarcely have been possible; with them, the story is, if anything, more readable.

All editions of *The Romance of the Forest* which I have seen give two chapters X in succession, with a consequent error in the numbering of all the following chapters. In the present edition the second chapter X is numbered X².

THE CASTLE OF OTRANTO

A Gothic Story

BY

HORACE WALPOLE

1764

PREFACE

TO THE FIRST EDITION.*

THE following work was found in the library of an
ancient Catholic family in the north of England. It
was printed at Naples, in the black letter, in the year
1529. How much sooner it was written does not appear. The principal incidents are such as were believed
in the darkest ages of Christianity; but the language
and conduct have nothing that savours of barbarism.
The style is the purest Italian. If the story was written near the time when it is supposed to have happened,
it must have been between 1095, the era of the first
crusade, and 1243, the date of the last, or not long
afterwards. There is no other circumstance in the
work that can lead us to guess at the period in which
the scene is laid: the names of the actors are evidently
fictitious, and probably disguised on purpose; yet the
Spanish names of the domestics seem to indicate that
this work was not composed until the establishment of
the Arragonian kings in Naples had made Spanish ap-
pellations familiar in that country. The beauty of the
diction and the zeal of the author (moderated, however,
by singular judgment) concur to make me think that
the date of the composition was little antecedent to that

* The Preface to the Second Edition, often reprinted in
later editions, is omitted from this one. It is in large part a
labored defence of Walpole's use of low comedy scenes in
conjunction with a "tragic" theme, justified by him on the
authority of Shakespeare's practice, and challenging Voltaire's condemnation of it. The First Preface, printed here,
is plainly a part of the actual structure of the story.

of the impression. Letters were then in the most flourishing state in Italy, and contributed to dispel the empire of superstition, at that time so forcibly attacked
by the reformers. It is not unlikely that an artful
priest might endeavour to turn their own arms on the
innovators; and might avail himself of his abilities as
an author to confirm the populace in their ancient errors
and superstitions. If this was his view, he has certainly
acted with signal address. Such a work as the following would enslave a hundred vulgar minds beyond half
the books of controversy that have been written from
the days of Luther to the present hour.

This solution of the author's motives is, however, offered as a mere conjecture. Whatever his views were,
or whatever effects the execution of them might have,
his work can only be laid before the public at present as
a matter of entertainment. Even as such, some apology
for it is necessary. Miracles, visions, necromances,
dreams, and other preternatural events, are exploded
now even from romances. That was not the case when
our author wrote; much less when the story itself is
supposed to have happened. Belief in every kind of
prodigy was so established in those dark ages that an
author would not be faithful to the manners of the
times who should omit all mention of them. He is
not bound to believe them himself, but he must represent his actors as believing them.

If this air of the miraculous is excused, the reader
will find nothing else unworthy of his perusal. Allow
the possibility of the facts, and all the actors comport
themselves as persons would do in their situation.
There is no bombast, no similes, flowers, digressions,
or unnecessary descriptions. Everything tends directly
to the catastrophe. Never is the reader's attention re-

laxed. The rules of the drama are almost observed throughout the conduct of the piece. The characters are well drawn, and still better maintained. Terror, the author's principal engine, prevents the story from ever languishing; and it is so often contrasted by pity that the mind is kept up in a constant vicissitude of interesting passions.

Some persons may, perhaps, think the characters of the domestics too little serious for the general cast of the story; but, besides their opposition to the principal personages, the art of the author is very observable in his conduct of the subalterns. They discover many passages essential to the story, which could not be well brought to light but by their *naïveté* and simplicity: in particular, the womanish terror and foibles of Bianca in the last chapter conduce essentially towards advancing the catastrophe.

It is natural for a translator to be prejudiced in favour of his adopted work. More impartial readers may not be so much struck with the beauties of this piece as I was. Yet I am not blind to my author's defects. I could wish he had grounded his plan on a more useful moral than this: that *the sins of the fathers are visited on their children to the third and fourth generation.* I doubt whether in his time, any more than at present, ambition curbed its appetite of dominion from the dread of so remote a punishment. And yet this moral is weakened by that less direct insinuation, that even such anathema may be diverted by devotion to St. Nicholas. Here the interest of the monk plainly gets the better of the judgment of the author. However, with all its faults, I have no doubt but the English reader will be pleased with a sight of this performance. The piety that reigns throughout, the lessons of

virtue that are inculcated, and the rigid purity of the
sentiments, exempt this work from the censure to which
romances are but too liable.   Should it meet with the
success I hope for, I may be encouraged to reprint the
original Italian, though it will tend to depreciate my
own labour.   Our language falls far short of the charms
of the Italian, both for variety and harmony.   The
latter is peculiarly excellent for simple narrative.   It
is difficult in English to relate without falling too low or
rising too high, a fault obviously occasioned by the
little care taken to speak pure language in common
conversation.   Every Italian or Frenchman of any rank
piques himself on speaking his own tongue correctly
and with choice.   I cannot flatter myself with having
done justice to my author in this respect; his style is
as elegant, as his conduct of the passions is masterly.
It is pity that he did not apply his talents to what they
were evidently proper for—the theatre.

I will detain the reader no longer, but to make one
short remark.   Though the machinery is invention, and
the names of the actors imaginary, I cannot but believe
that the groundwork of the story is founded on truth.
The scene is undoubtedly laid in some real castle.   The
author seems frequently, without design, to describe
particular parts, "The chamber," says he, "on the right
hand; the door on the left hand; the distance from the
chapel to Conrad's apartment."   These, and other passages, are strong presumptions that the author had some
certain building in his eye.   Curious persons, who have
leisure to employ in such researches, may possibly discover in the Italian writers the foundation on which our
author has built.   If a catastrophe at all resembling
that which he describes, is believed to have given rise
to this work, it will contribute to interest the reader,

and will make THE CASTLE OF OTRANTO a still more moving story.

CHAPTER I

MANFRED, Prince of Otranto, had one son and one daughter: the latter, a most beautiful virgin, aged eighteen, was called Matilda. Conrad, the son, was three years younger, a homely youth, sickly, and of no promising disposition; yet he was the darling of his father, who never showed any symptoms of affection to Matilda. Manfred had contracted a marriage for his son with the Marquis of Vicenza's daughter, Isabella; and she had already been delivered by her guardians into the hands of Manfred, that he might celebrate the wedding as soon as Conrad's infirm state of health would permit. Manfred's impatience for this ceremonial was remarked by his family and neighbours. The former, indeed, apprehending the severity of their prince's disposition, did not dare to utter their surmises on this precipitation. Hippolita, his wife, an amiable lady, did sometimes venture to represent the danger of marrying their only son so early, considering his great youth, and greater infirmities; but she never received any other answer than reflections on her own sterility, who had given him but one heir. His tenants and subjects were less cautious in their discourses: they attributed this hasty wedding to the prince's dread of seeing accomplished an ancient prophecy, which was said to have pronounced that *the Castle and Lordship of Otranto should pass from the present family whenever the real owner should be grown too large to inhabit it.* It was difficult to make any sense of this prophecy,

and still less easy to conceive what it had to do with
the marriage in question. Yet these mysteries, or contradictions, did not make the populace adhere the less
to their opinion.

Young Conrad's birthday was fixed for his espousals.
The company was assembled in the chapel of the castle,
and everything ready for beginning the divine office,
when Conrad himself was missing. Manfred, impatient
of the least delay, and who had not observed his son
retire, despatched one of his attendants to summon the
young prince. The servant, who had not stayed long
enough to have crossed the court to Conrad's apartment, came running back breathless, in a frantic manner, his eyes staring, and foaming at the mouth. He
said nothing, but pointed to the court. The company
were struck with terror and amazement. The Princess
Hippolita, without knowing what was the matter, but
anxious for her son, swooned away. Manfred, less apprehensive than enraged at the procrastination of the
nuptials, and at the folly of his domestic, asked imperiously what was the matter? The fellow made no
answer, but continued pointing towards the court-yard;
and, at last, after repeated questions put to him, cried
out,—

"Oh! the helmet! the helmet!"

In the meantime, some of the company had run into
the court, from whence was heard a confused noise of
shrieks, horror, and surprise. Manfred, who began to
be alarmed at not seeing his son, went himself to get
information of what occasioned this strange confusion.
Matilda remained endeavouring to assist her mother,
and Isabella stayed for the same purpose, and to avoid
showing any impatience for the bridegroom, for whom,
in truth, she had conceived little affection.

The first thing that struck Manfred's eyes was a

group of his servants endeavouring to raise something that appeared to him a mountain of sable plumes. He gazed without believing his sight. "What are ye doing?" cried Manfred, wrathfully. "Where is my son?" A volley of voices replied, "Oh! my lord! the prince! the prince! the helmet! the helmet!"

Shocked with these lamentable sounds, and dreading he knew not what, he advanced hastily—but, what a sight for a father's eyes!—he beheld his child dashed to pieces, and almost buried under an enormous helmet, a hundred times more large than any casque ever made for human being, and shaded with a proportionable quantity of black feathers.

The horror of the spectacle, the ignorance of all around how this misfortune had happened, and, above all, the tremendous phenomenon before him, took away the prince's speech. Yet his silence lasted longer than even grief could occasion. He fixed his eyes on what he wished in vain to believe a vision; and seemed less attentive to his loss than buried in meditation on the stupendous object that had occasioned it. He touched, he examined, the fatal casque; nor could even the bleeding mangled remains of the young prince divert the eyes of Manfred from the portent before him. All who had known his partial fondness for young Conrad were as much surprised at their prince's insensibility as thunderstruck themselves at the miracle of the helmet. They conveyed the disfigured corpse into the hall, without receiving the least direction from Manfred. As little was he attentive to the ladies who remained in the chapel; on the contrary, without mentioning the unhappy princesses, his wife and daughter, the first sounds that dropped from Manfred's lips were, "Take care of the Lady Isabella."

The domestics, without observing the singularity of

this direction, were guided by their affection to their mistress, to consider it as peculiarly addressed to her situation, and flew to her assistance. They conveyed her to her chamber more dead than alive, and indifferent to all the strange circumstances she heard, except the death of her son. Matilda, who doted on her mother, smothered her own grief and amazement, and thought of nothing but assisting and comforting her afflicted parent. Isabella, who had been treated by Hippolita like a daughter, and who returned that tenderness with equal duty and affection, was scarce less assiduous about the princess; at the same time endeavouring to partake and lessen the weight of sorrow which she saw Matilda strove to suppress, for whom she had conceived the warmest sympathy of friendship. Yet her own situation could not help finding its place in her thoughts. She felt no concern for the death of young Conrad, except commiseration; and she was not sorry to be delivered from a marriage which had promised her little felicity, either from her destined bridegroom, or from the severe temper of Manfred, who, though he had distinguished her by great indulgence, had impressed her mind with terror, from his causeless rigour to such amiable princesses as Hippolita and Matilda.

While the ladies were conveying the wretched mother to her bed, Manfred remained in the court, gazing on the ominous casque, and regardless of the crowd which the strangeness of the event had now assembled around him. The few words he articulated tended solely to enquiries whether any man knew from whence it could have come? Nobody could give him the least information. However, as it seemed to be the sole object of his curiosity, it soon became so to the rest of the spectators, whose conjectures were as absurd and improbable as the catastrophe itself was unprecedented. In the midst of their senseless guesses, a young peasant, whom rumour had drawn thither from a neighbouring village, observed that the miraculous helmet was exactly like that on the figure in black marble of Alfonso the Good, one of their former princes, in the church of St. Nicholas.

"Villain! what sayest thou?" cried Manfred, starting from his trance in a tempest of rage, and seizing the young man by the collar. "How darest thou utter such treason? Thy life shall pay for it."

The spectators, who as little comprehended the cause of the prince's fury as all the rest they had seen, were at a loss to unravel this new circumstance. The young peasant himself was still more astonished, not conceiving how he had offended the prince; yet recollecting himself, with a mixture of grace and humility, he disengaged himself from Manfred's gripe, and then, with an obeisance which discovered more jealousy of innocence than dismay, he asked with respect of what he was guilty? Manfred, more enraged at the vigour, however decently exerted, with which the young man had shaken off his hold, than appeased by his submission, ordered his attendants to seize him, and if he had not been withheld by his friends, whom he had invited to the nuptials, would have poniarded the peasant in their arms.

During this altercation, some of the vulgar spectators had run to the great church, which stood near the castle, and came back open-mouthed, declaring that the helmet was missing from Alfonso's statue. Manfred, at this news, grew perfectly frantic; and, as if he sought a subject on which to vent the tempest within him, he rushed again on the young peasant, crying, "Villain! monster! sorcerer! 'tis thou hast done this! 'tis thou hast slain my son!"

The mob, who wanted some object within the scope of their capacities on whom they might discharge their bewildered reasonings, caught the words from the mouth of their lord, and re-echoed, "Ay, ay; 'tis he, 'tis he! He has stolen the helmet from good Alfonso's tomb, and dashed out the brains of our young prince with it," never reflecting how enormous the disproportion was between the marble helmet that had been in the church, and that of steel before their eyes; nor how impossible it was for a youth, seemingly not twenty, to wield a piece of armour of so prodigious a weight.

The folly of these ejaculations brought Manfred to himself: yet, whether provoked at the peasant having observed the resemblance between the two helmets, and thereby led to the farther discovery of the absence of that in the church, or wishing to bury any fresh rumour under so impertinent a supposition, he gravely pronounced that the young man was certainly a necromancer, and that till the church could take cognisance of the affair, he would have the magician whom they had thus detected, kept prisoner under the helmet itself, which he ordered his attendants to raise, and place the young man under it; declaring he should be kept there without food, with which his own infernal art might furnish him.

It was in vain for the youth to represent against this preposterous sentence; in vain did Manfred's friends endeavour to divert him from this savage and ill-grounded resolution. The generality were charmed with their lord's decision, which to their apprehensions carried great appearance of justice, as the magician was to be punished by the very instrument with which he had offended; nor were they struck with the least compunction at the probability of the youth being starved,

for they firmly believed that by his diabolical skill he
could easily supply himself with nutriment.

Manfred thus saw his commands even cheerfully
obeyed, and appointing a guard, with strict orders to
prevent any food being conveyed to the prisoner, he
dismissed his friends and attendants and retired to his
own chamber, after locking the gates of the castle, in
which he suffered none but his domestics to remain.

In the mean time, the care and zeal of the young
ladies had brought the Princess Hippolita to herself,
who, amidst the transports of her own sorrow, frequently demanded news of her lord, would have dismissed her attendants to watch over him, and at last
enjoined Matilda to leave her, and visit and comfort
her father. Matilda, who wanted not affectionate duty
to Manfred, though she trembled at his austerity,
obeyed the orders of Hippolita, whom she tenderly
recommended to Isabella; and enquiring of the domestics of her father, was informed that he was retired
to his chamber, and had commanded that nobody should
have admittance to him. Concluding that he was immersed in sorrow for the death of her brother, and
fearing to renew his tears by the sight of his sole remaining child, she hesitated whether she should break
in upon his affliction: yet solicitude for him, backed by
the commands of her mother, encouraged her to venture
disobeying the orders he had given; a fault she had
never been guilty of before. The gentle timidity of her
nature made her pause for some minutes at his door.
She heard him traverse his chamber backwards and forwards, with disordered steps; a mood which increased
her apprehensions. She was however just going to
beg admittance, when Manfred suddenly opened the
door; and as it was now twilight, concurring with the
disorder of his mind, he did not distinguish the person,

but asked angrily who it was. Matilda replied, trembling, "My dearest father, it is I, your daughter."

Manfred, stepping back hastily, cried, "Begone, I do not want a daughter;" and, flinging back abruptly, clapped the door against the terrified Matilda.

She was too well acquainted with her father's impetuosity to venture a second intrusion. When she had a little recovered the shock of so bitter a reception, she wiped away her tears, to prevent the additional stab that the knowledge of it would give to Hippolita, who questioned her in the most anxious terms on the health of Manfred, and how he bore his loss. Matilda assured her he was well, and supported his misfortune with manly fortitude.

"But will he not let me see him?" said Hippolita, mournfully; "will he not permit me to blend my tears with his, and shed a mother's sorrows in the bosom of her lord? Or do you deceive me, Matilda? I know how Manfred doted on his son; is not the stroke too heavy for him? has he not sunk under it? You do not answer me:—alas! I dread the worst!—raise me, my maidens; I will, I will see my lord. Bear me to him instantly. He is dearer to me even than my children."

Matilda made signs to Isabella to prevent Hippolita's rising; and both those lovely young women were using their gentle violence to stop and calm the princess, when a servant, on the part of Manfred, arrived and told Isabella that his lord demanded to speak with her.

"With me!" cried Isabella.

"Go," said Hippolita, relieved by a message from her lord: "Manfred cannot support the sight of his own family. He thinks you less disordered than we are, and dreads the shock of my grief. Console him, dear Isabella, and tell him I will smother my own anguish rather than add to his."

As it was now evening, the servant who conducted
Isabella bore a torch before her. When they came to
Manfred, who was walking impatiently about the gal-
lery, he started and said hastily,—

"Take away that light, and begone." Then shutting
the door impetuously, he flung himself upon a bench
against the wall and bade Isabella sit by him. She
obeyed trembling.

"I sent for you, lady," said he, and then stopped,
under great appearance of confusion.

"My lord!"

"Yes, I sent for you on a matter of great moment,"
resumed he. "Dry your tears, young lady:—you have
lost your bridegroom. Yes, cruel fate! and I have lost
the hopes of my race! but Conrad was not worthy of
your beauty."

"How! my lord," said Isabella; "sure you do not
suspect me of not feeling the concern I ought! my
duty and affection would have always ——"

"Think no more of him," interrupted Manfred: "he
was a sickly, puny child; and Heaven has perhaps
taken him away that I might not trust the honours of
my house on so frail a foundation. The line of Manfred calls for numerous supports. My foolish fondness
for that boy blinded the eyes of my prudence—but it
is better as it is. I hope in a few years to have reason
to rejoice at the death of Conrad."

Words cannot paint the astonishment of Isabella. At
first she apprehended that grief had disordered Manfred's understanding. Her next thought suggested that
this strange discourse was designed to ensnare her: she
feared that Manfred had perceived her indifference for
his son; and in consequence of that idea she replied,—

"Good my lord, do not doubt my tenderness: my
heart would have accompanied my hand. Conrad would

have engrossed all my care; and wherever fate shall dispose of me, I shall always cherish his memory, and regard your highness and the virtuous Hippolita as my parents."

"Curse on Hippolita!" cried Manfred: "forget her from this moment, as I do. In short, lady, you have missed a husband undeserving of your charms: they shall now be better disposed of. Instead of a sickly boy, you shall have a husband in the prime of his age, who will know how to value your beauties, and who may expect a numerous offspring."

"Alas! my lord," said Isabella, "my mind is too sadly engrossed by the recent catastrophe in your family to think of another marriage. If ever my father returns, and it shall be his pleasure, I shall obey, as I did when I consented to give my hand to your son; but until his return permit me to remain under your hospitable roof, and employ the melancholy hours in assuaging yours, Hippolita's, and the fair Matilda's affliction."

"I desired you once before," said Manfred, angrily, "not to name that woman. From this hour she must be a stranger to you, as she must be to me:—in short, Isabella, since I cannot give you my son, I offer you myself."

"Heavens!" cried Isabella, waking from her delusion, "what do I hear? You, my lord! You! my father-in-law, the father of Conrad! the husband of the virtuous and tender Hippolita!"

"I tell you," said Manfred imperiously, "Hippolita is no longer my wife; I divorce her from this hour. Too long has she cursed me by her unfruitfulness. My fate depends on having sons, and this night I trust will give a new date to my hopes."

At those words he seized the cold hand of Isabella, who was half dead with fright and horror. She shrieked and started from him. Manfred rose to pursue her, when the moon, which was now up and gleamed in at the opposite casement, presented to his sight the plumes of the fatal helmet, which rose to the height of the windows, waving backwards and forwards in a tempestuous manner and accompanied with a hollow and rustling sound. Isabella, who gathered courage from her situation, and who dreaded nothing so much as Manfred's pursuit of his declaration, cried,—

"Look, my lord! see, Heaven itself declares against your impious intentions!"

"Heaven nor hell shall impede my designs," said Manfred, advancing again to seize the princess. At that instant the portrait of his grandfather, which hung over the bench where they had been sitting, uttered a deep sigh and heaved its breast. Isabella, whose back was turned to the picture, saw not the motion, nor whence the sound came, but started and said,—"Hark, my lord! what sound was that?" and at the same time made towards the door. Manfred, distracted between the flight of Isabella, who had now reached the stairs, and yet unable to keep his eyes from the picture, which began to move, had, however, advanced some steps after her, still looking backwards on the portrait, when he saw it quit its panel, and descend on the floor with a grave and melancholy air.

"Do I dream?" cried Manfred, returning; "or are the devils themselves in league against me? Speak, infernal spectre! or, if thou art my grandsire, why dost thou too conspire against thy wretched descendant, who too dearly pays for ——" Ere he could finished the sentence, the vision sighed again, and made a sign to Manfred to follow him.

"Lead on!" cried Manfred: "I will follow thee to the gulf of perdition." The spectre marched sedately, but dejected, to the end of the gallery, and turned into a chamber on the right hand. Manfred accompanied him at a little distance, full of anxiety and horror, but resolved. As he would have entered the chamber, the door was clapped to with violence by an invisible hand. The prince, collecting courage from this delay, would have forcibly burst open the door with his foot, but found that it resisted his utmost efforts.

"Since hell will not satisfy my curiosity," said Manfred, "I will use the human means in my power for preserving my race; Isabella shall not escape me."

That lady, whose resolution had given way to terror the moment she had quitted Manfred, continued her flight to the bottom of the principal staircase. There she stopped, not knowing whither to direct her steps, nor how to escape from the impetuosity of the prince. The gates of the castle she knew were locked, and guards placed in the court. Should she, as her heart prompted her, go and prepare Hippolita for the cruel destiny that awaited her, she did not doubt but Manfred would seek her there, and that his violence would incite him to double the injury he meditated, without leaving room for them to avoid the impetuosity of his passions. Delay might give him time to reflect on the horrid measures he had conceived, or produce some circumstance in her favour, if she could for that night at least avoid his odious purpose. Yet where conceal herself? how avoid the pursuit he would infallibly make throughout the castle? As these thoughts passed rapidly through her mind, she recollected a subterraneous passage which led from the vaults of the castle to the church of St. Nicholas. Could she reach the altar before she was overtaken, she knew even Manfred's violence would not dare to profane the sacredness of the place; and she determined, if no other means of deliverance offered, to shut herself up for ever among the holy virgins, whose convent was contiguous to the cathedral. In this resolution she seized a lamp that burned at the foot of the staircase, and hurried towards the secret passage.

The lower part of the castle was hollowed into several intricate cloisters; and it was not easy for one under so much anxiety to find the door that opened into the cavern. An awful silence reigned throughout those subterraneous regions, except now and then some blasts of wind that shook the doors she had passed, and which, grating on the rusty hinges, were re-echoed through that long labyrinth of darkness. Every murmur struck her with new terror;—yet more she dreaded to hear the wrathful voice of Manfred urging his domestics to pursue her. She trod as softly as impatience would give her leave,—yet frequently stopped and listened to hear if she was followed. In one of those moments she thought she heard a sigh. She shuddered and recoiled a few paces. In a moment she thought she heard the step of some person. Her blood curdled: she concluded it was Manfred. Every suggestion that horror could inspire rushed into her mind. She condemned her rash flight, which had thus exposed her to his rage in a place where her cries were not likely to draw anybody to her assistance. Yet the sound seemed not to come from behind: if Manfred knew where she was, he must have followed her: she was still in one of the cloisters, and the steps she had heard were too distinct to proceed from the way she had come. Cheered with this reflection, and hoping to find a friend in whoever was not the prince, she was going to advance, when a door that stood ajar at some distance to the left was opened gently; but ere her lamp, which she held up, could discover who opened it, the person retreated precipitately on seeing the light.

Isabella, whom every incident was sufficient to dismay, hesitated whether she should proceed. Her dread of Manfred soon outweighed every other terror. The very circumstance of the person avoiding her, gave her a sort of courage. It could only be, she thought, some domestic belonging to the castle. Her gentleness had never raised her an enemy, and conscious innocence made her hope that, unless sent by the prince's order to seek her, his servants would rather assist than prevent her flight. Fortifying herself with these reflections, and believing, by what she could observe, that she was near the mouth of the subterraneous cavern, she approached the door that had been opened; but a sudden gust of wind that met her at the door extinguished her lamp, and left her in total darkness.

Words cannot paint the horror of the princess's situation. Alone, in so dismal a place, her mind impressed with all the terrible events of the day, hopeless of escaping, expecting every moment the arrival of Manfred, and far from tranquil on knowing she was within reach of somebody, she knew not whom, who for some cause seemed concealed thereabouts; all these thoughts crowded on her distracted mind, and she was ready to sink under her apprehensions. She addressed herself to every saint in heaven, and inwardly implored their assistance. For a considerable time she remained in an agony of despair. At last, as softly as was possible, she felt for the door, and having found it, entered trembling into the vault from whence she had heard the sigh and steps. It gave her a kind of momentary joy to perceive an imperfect ray of clouded moonshine gleam from the roof of the vault, which seemed to be fallen in, and from whence hung a fragment of earth or building, she could not distinguish which, that appeared to have been crushed inwards. She advanced eagerly towards this chasm, when she discerned a human form standing close against the wall.

She shrieked, believing it the ghost of her betrothed Conrad. The figure, advancing, said in a submissive voice, "Be not alarmed, lady; I will not injure you."

Isabella, a little encouraged by the words and tone of voice of the stranger, and recollecting that this must be the person who had opened the door, recovered her spirits enough to reply, "Sir, whoever you are, take pity on a wretched princess standing on the brink of destruction; assist me to escape from this fatal castle, or, in a few moments I may be made miserable for ever."

"Alas!" said the stranger, "what can I do to assist you? I will die in your defence, but I am unacquainted with the castle, and want ——"

"Oh!" said Isabella, hastily interrupting him, "help me but to find a trap-door that must be hereabout, and it is the greatest service you can do me, for I have not a minute to lose." Saying these words, she felt about on the pavement, and directed the stranger to search likewise, for a smooth piece of brass enclosed in one of the stones. "That," said she, "is the lock, which opens with a spring of which I know the secret. If we can find that, I may escape; if not, alas courteous stranger, I fear I shall have involved you in my misfortunes. Manfred will suspect you for the accomplice of my flight, and you will fall a victim to his resentment."

"I value not my life," said the stranger; "and it will be some comfort to lose it in trying to deliver you from his tyranny."

"Generous youth!" said Isabella, "how shall I ever requite ——"

As she uttered these words, a ray of moonshine, streaming through a cranny of the ruin above, shone directly on the lock they sought.—"Oh! transport!" said Isabella, "here is the trap-door;" and, taking out the key, she touched the spring, which, starting aside, discovered an iron ring. "Lift up the door," said the princess. The stranger obeyed, and beneath appeared some stone steps descending into a vault totally dark. "We must go down here," said Isabella; "follow me; dark and dismal as it is, we cannot miss our way. It leads directly to the church of St. Nicholas—but, perhaps," added the princess, modestly, "you have no reason to leave the castle, nor have I farther occasion for your service; in a few minutes I shall be safe from Manfred's rage—only let me know to whom I am so much obliged."

"I will never quit you," said the stranger eagerly, "until I have placed you in safety—nor think me, princess, more generous than I am; though you are my principal care ——"

The stranger was interrupted by a sudden noise of voices that seemed approaching, and they soon distinguished these words:—"Talk not to me of necromancers; I tell you she must be in the castle; I will find her in spite of enchantment."

"Oh, heavens!" cried Isabella, "it is the voice of Manfred; make haste, or we are ruined! and shut the trap-door after you." Saying this, she descended the steps precipitately; and, as the stranger hastened to follow her, he let the door slip out of his hands: it fell, and the spring closed over it. He tried in vain to open it, not having observed Isabella's method of touching the spring; nor had he many moments to make an essay. The noise of the falling door had been heard by Manfred, who, directed by the sound, hastened thither, attended by his servants with torches.

"It must be Isabella," cried Manfred, before he entered the vault: "she is escaping by the subterraneous passage, but she cannot have got far." What was the astonishment of the prince, when, instead of Isabella, the light of the torches discovered to him the young peasant, whom he thought confined under the fatal helmet. "Traitor!" said Manfred, "how camest thou here? I thought thee in durance above in the court."

"I am no traitor," replied the young man boldly, "nor am I answerable for your thoughts."

"Presumptuous villain!" cried Manfred, "dost thou provoke my wrath? Tell me; how hast thou escaped from above? Thou hast corrupted thy guards, and their lives shall answer it."

"My poverty," said the peasant calmly, "will disculpate them: though the ministers of a tyrant's wrath, to thee they are faithful, and but too willing to execute the orders which you unjustly imposed upon them."

"Art thou so hardy as to dare my vengeance?" said the prince; "but tortures shall force the truth from thee. Tell me; I will know thy accomplices."

"There was my accomplice!" said the youth, smiling and pointing to the roof.

Manfred ordered the torches to be held up, and perceived that one of the cheeks of the enchanted casque had forced its way through the pavement of the court, as his servants had let it fall over the peasant, and had broken through into the vault, leaving a gap through which the peasant had pressed himself some minutes before he was found by Isabella. "Was that the way by which thou didst descend?" said Manfred.

"It was," said the youth.

"But what noise was that," said Manfred, "which I heard, as I entered the cloister?"

"A door clapped," said the peasant; "I heard it as well as you."

"What door?" said Manfred hastily.

"I am not acquainted with your castle," said the peasant: "this is the first time I ever entered it; and this vault the only part of it within which I ever was."

"But I tell thee," said Manfred, wishing to find out if the youth had discovered the trap-door, "it was this way I heard the noise; my servants heard it too."

"My lord," interrupted one of them officiously, "to be sure it was the trap-door, and he was going to make his escape."

"Peace! blockhead," said the prince, angrily; "if he was going to escape, how should he come on this side? I will know from his own mouth what noise it was I heard. Tell me truly; thy life depends on thy veracity."

"My veracity is dearer to me than my life," said the peasant; "nor would I purchase the one by forfeiting the other."

"Indeed, young philosopher!" said Manfred, contemptuously; "tell me, then, what was that noise I heard?"

"Ask me what I can answer," said he, "and put me to death instantly, if I tell you a lie."

Manfred, growing impatient at the steady valour and indifference of the youth, cried,—"Well then, thou man of truth! answer; was it the fall of the trap-door that I heard?"

"It was," said the youth.

"It was!" said the prince; "and how didst thou come to know there was a trap-door here?"

"I saw the plate of brass by a gleam of moonshine," replied he.

"But what told thee it was a lock?" said Manfred; "how didst thou discover the secret of opening it?"

"Providence, that delivered me from the helmet, was able to direct me to the spring of a lock," said he.

"Providence should have gone a little farther, and have placed thee out of the reach of my resentment," said Manfred: "when Providence had taught thee to open the lock, it abandoned thee for a fool, who did not know how to make use of its favours. Why didst thou not pursue the path pointed out for thy escape? Why didst thou shut the trap-door before thou hadst descended the steps?"

"I might ask you, my lord," said the peasant, "how I, totally unacquainted with your castle, was to know that those steps led to any outlet? but I scorn to evade your questions. Wherever those steps led to, perhaps I should have explored the way. I could not be in a worse situation than I was. But the truth is, I let the trap-door fall: your immediate arrival followed. I had given the alarm—what imported it to me whether I was seized a minute sooner or a minute later?"

"Thou art a resolute villain for thy years," said Manfred; "yet on reflection I suspect thou dost but trifle with me; thou hast not yet told me how thou didst open the lock."

"That I will show you, my lord," said the peasant; and, taking up a fragment of stone that had fallen from above, he laid himself on the trap-door, and began to beat on the piece of brass that covered it, meaning to gain time for the escape of the princess. This presence of mind, joined to the frankness of the youth, staggered Manfred. He even felt a disposition towards pardoning one who had been guilty of no crime. Man-

fred was not one of those savage tyrants who wanton
in cruelty unprovoked. The circumstances of his fortune had given an asperity to his temper, which was
naturally humane; and his virtues were always ready
to operate when his passions did not obscure his reason.
While the prince was in this suspense, a confused
noise of voices echoed through the distant vaults. As
the sound approached, he distinguished the clamours of
some of his domestics, whom he had dispersed through
the castle in search of Isabella, calling out, "Where is
my lord? where is the prince?"

"Here I am," said Manfred, as they came nearer;
"have you found the princess?"

The first that arrived replied, "Oh, my lord, I am
glad we have found you."

"Found me!" said Manfred; "have you found the
princess?"

"We thought we had, my lord," said the fellow,
looking terrified, "but ——"

"But what?" cried the prince; "has she escaped?"

"Jaquez and I, my lord ——"

"Yes, I and Diego," interrupted the second, who
came up in still greater consternation.

"Speak one of you at a time," said Manfred; "I ask
you, where is the princess?"

"We do not know," said they both together; "but we
are frightened out of our wits."

"So I think, blockheads," said Manfred; "what is it
has scared you thus?"

"Oh, my lord," said Jaquez, "Diego has seen such a
sight! your highness would not believe your eyes."

"What new absurdity is this?" cried Manfred; "give
me a direct answer, or by heaven ——"

"Why, my lord, if it please your highness to hear
me," said the poor fellow, "Diego and I ——"

"Yes, I and Jaquez," cried his comrade.

"Did not I forbid you to speak both at a time?" said the prince: "you, Jaquez, answer; for the other fool seems more distracted than thou art: what is the matter?"

"My gracious lord," said Jaquez, "if it please your highness to hear me. Diego and I, according to your highness's orders, went to search for the young lady; but being apprehensive that we might meet the ghost of my young lord, your highness's son, God rest his soul! as he has not received Christian burial ——"

"Sot!" cried Manfred, in a rage, "is it only a ghost, then, that thou hast seen?"

"Oh, worse! worse! my lord," cried Diego: "I had rather have seen ten whole ghosts."

"Grant me patience!" said Manfred; "those blockheads distract me. Out of my sight, Diego; and thou, Jaquez, tell me, in one word, art thou sober? art thou raving? thou wast wont to have some sense; has the other sot frightened himself and thee too? speak; what is it he fancies he has seen?"

"Why, my lord," replied Jaquez, trembling, "I was going to tell your highness that since the calamitous misfortune of my young lord, God rest his precious soul! not one of us, your highness's faithful servants, indeed we are, my lord, though poor men; I say, not one of us has dared to set a foot about the castle, but two together: so Diego and I, thinking that my young lady might be in the great gallery, went up there to look for her, and tell her your highness wanted something to impart to her."

"O blundering fools!" cried Manfred; "and in the mean time she has made her escape, because you were afraid of goblins! Why, thou knave! she left me in the gallery; I came from thence myself."

"For all that, she may be there still for aught I know," said Jaquez; "but the devil shall have me before I seek her there again: poor Diego! I do not believe he will ever recover it."

"Recover what?" said Manfred; "am I never to learn what it is has terrified these rascals? But I lose my time; follow me, slave; I will see if she is in the gallery."

"For heaven's sake, my dear good lord," cried Jaquez, "do not go to the gallery! Satan himself, I believe, is in the chamber next to the gallery."

Manfred, who hitherto had treated the terror of his servants as an idle panic, was struck at this new circumstance. He recollected the apparition of the portrait, and the sudden closing of the door at the end of the gallery—his voice faltered, and he asked with disorder, "What is in the great chamber?"

"My lord," said Jaquez, "when Diego and I came into the gallery, he went first, for he said he had more courage than I;—so, when we came into the gallery, we found nobody. We looked under every bench and stool; and still we found nobody."

"Were all the pictures in their places?" said Manfred.

"Yes, my lord," answered Jaquez; "but we did not think of looking behind them."

"Well, well," said Manfred, "proceed."

"When we came to the door of the great chamber," continued Jaquez, "we found it shut."

"And could not you open it?" said Manfred.

"Oh yes, my lord; would to heaven we had not!" replied he: "nay, it was not I neither, it was Diego: he was grown foolhardy, and would go on, though I advised him not. If ever I open a door that is shut again!"

"Trifle not," said Manfred, shuddering, "but tell me

what you saw in the great chamber on opening the
door."

"I! my lord!" said Jaquez, "I saw nothing: I was
behind Diego; but I heard the noise."

"Jaquez," said Manfred, in a solemn tone of voice;
"tell me, I adjure thee by the souls of my ancestors,
what was it thou sawest? what was it thou heardest?"

"It was Diego saw it my lord, it was not I," replied
Jaquez; "I only heard the noise. Diego had no
sooner opened the door, than he cried out, and ran back
—I ran back too, and said, 'Is it the ghost?'—'The
ghost! no, no,' said Diego, and his hair stood on end;
'it is a giant, I believe; he is all clad in armour, for I
saw his foot and part of his leg, and they are as large
as the helmet below in the court.' As he said these
words, my lord, we heard a violent motion and the rattling of armour, as if the giant was rising, for Diego
has told me since that he believes the giant was lying
down, for the foot and leg were stretched at length on
the floor. Before we could get to the end of the gallery, we heard the door of the great chamber clap
behind us, but we did not dare turn back to see if the
giant was following us—yet, now I think on it, we
must have heard him if he pursued us; but for heaven's
sake, good my lord, send for the chaplain and have the
castle exorcised, for for certain it is enchanted."

"Ay, pray do, my lord," cried all the servants at
once, "or we must leave your highness's service."

"Peace, dotards!" said Manfred, "and follow me;
I will know what all this means."

"We! my lord?" cried they, with one voice; "we
would not go up to the gallery for your highness's
revenue."

The young peasant, who had stood silent, now spoke.
"Will your highness," said he, "permit me to try this

adventure? my life is of consequence to nobody; I fear no bad angel and have offended no good one."

"Your behaviour is above your seeming," said Manfred, viewing him with surprise and admiration; "hereafter I will reward your bravery; but now," continued he with a sigh, "I am so circumstanced that I dare trust no eyes but my own. However, I give you leave to accompany me."

Manfred, when he first followed Isabella from the gallery, had gone directly to the apartment of his wife, concluding the princess had retired thither. Hippolita, who knew his step, rose with anxious fondness to meet her lord, whom she had not seen since the death of her son. She would have flown in a transport, mixed of joy and grief, to his bosom, but he pushed her rudely off and said, "Where is Isabella?"

"Isabella, my lord!" said the astonished Hippolita.

"Yes, Isabella," cried Manfred imperiously; "I want Isabella."

"My lord," replied Matilda, who perceived how much his behaviour had shocked her mother, "she has not been with us since your highness summoned her to your apartment."

"Tell me where she is," said the prince; "I do not want to know where she has been."

"My good lord," says Hippolita, "your daughter tells you the truth. Isabella left us by your command, and has not returned since; but, my good lord, compose yourself; retire to your rest; this dismal day has disordered you. Isabella shall wait your orders in the morning."

"What, then, you know where she is?" cried Manfred. "Tell me directly, for I will not lose an instant; and you, woman," speaking to his wife, "order your chaplain to attend me forthwith."

"Isabella," said Hippolita, calmly, "is retired, I suppose to her chamber; she is not accustomed to watch at this late hour. Gracious my lord," continued she, "let me know what has disturbed you. Has Isabella offended you?"

"Trouble me not with questions," said Manfred, "but tell me where she is."

"Matilda shall call her," said the princess. "Sit down, my lord, and resume your wonted fortitude."

"What! art thou jealous of Isabella?" replied he, "that you wish to be present at our interview?"

"Good heavens! my lord," said Hippolita; "what is it your highness means?"

"Thou wilt know ere many minutes are passed," said the cruel prince. "Send your chaplain to me, and wait my pleasure here." At these words he flung out of the room in search of Isabella, leaving the amazed ladies thunderstruck with his words and frantic deportment, and lost in vain conjectures on what he was meditating.

Manfred was now returning from the vault, attended by the peasant and a few of his servants whom he had obliged to accompany him. He ascended the staircase without stopping till he arrived at the gallery, at the door of which he met Hippolita and her chaplain. When Diego had been dismissed by Manfred, he had gone directly to the princess's apartment with the alarm of what he had seen. That excellent lady, who no more than Manfred doubted of the reality of the vision, yet affected to treat it as a delirium of the servants. Willing, however, to save her lord from any additional shock, and prepared by a series of grief not to tremble at any accession to it, she determined to make herself the first sacrifice, if fate had marked the present hour for their destruction. Dismissing the reluctant Matilda to her rest, who in vain sued for leave to accompany her

mother, and attended only by her chaplain, Hippolita
had visited the gallery and great chamber; and now,
with more serenity of soul than she had felt for many
hours, she met her lord and assured him that the vision
of the gigantic leg and foot was all a fable, and no
doubt an impression made by fear and the dark and
dismal hour of the night on the minds of his servants.
She and the chaplain had examined the chamber, and
found every thing in the usual order.

Manfred, though persuaded, like his wife, that the
vision had been no work of fancy, recovered a little
from the tempest of mind into which so many strange
events had thrown him. Ashamed, too, of his inhuman
treatment of a princess who returned every injury with
new marks of tenderness and duty, he felt returning
love forcing itself into his eyes; but not less ashamed
of feeling remorse towards one against whom he was
inwardly meditating a yet more bitter outrage, he
curbed the yearnings of his heart and did not dare to
lean even towards pity. The next transition of his
soul was to exquisite villainy. Presuming on the un-
shaken submission of Hippolita, he flattered himself
that she would not only acquiesce with patience to a
divorce, but would obey, if it was his pleasure, in endeavouring to persuade Isabella to give him her hand—
but ere he could indulge this horrid hope, he reflected
that Isabella was not to be found. Coming to himself,
he gave orders that every avenue to the castle should
be strictly guarded, and charged his domestics, on pain
of their lives, to suffer nobody to pass out. The young
peasant, to whom he spoke favourably, he ordered to
remain in a small chamber on the stairs, in which there
was a pallet-bed, and the key of which he took away
himself, telling the youth he would talk with him in the
morning. Then dismissing his attendants, and bestow-

ing a sullen kind of half-nod on Hippolita, he retired
to his own chamber.

CHAPTER II

MATILDA, who by Hippolita's order had retired to her
apartment, was ill-disposed to take any rest. The
shocking fate of her brother had deeply affected her.
She was surprised at not seeing Isabella; but the
strange words which had fallen from her father, and
his obscure menace to the princess, his wife, accompanied by the most furious behaviour, had filled her
gentle mind with terror and alarm. She waited anxiously for the return of Bianca, a young damsel that
attended her, whom she had sent to learn what was
become of Isabella. Bianca soon appeared, and informed her mistress of what she had gathered from the
servants, that Isabella was nowhere to be found. She
related the adventure of the young peasant who had
been discovered in the vault, though with many simple
additions from the incoherent accounts of the domestics; and she dwelt principally on the gigantic leg and
foot which had been seen in the gallery-chamber. This
last circumstance had terrified Bianca so much that she
was rejoiced when Matilda told her that she would not
go to rest, but would watch till the princess should rise.

The young princess wearied herself in conjectures on
the flight of Isabella, and on the threats of Manfred
to her mother. "But what business could he have so
urgent with the chaplain?" said Matilda. "Does he intend to have my brother's body interred privately in
the chapel?"

"Oh, madam," said Bianca, "now I guess. As you

are become his heiress, he is impatient to have you married. He has always been raving for more sons; I warrant he is now impatient for grandsons. As sure as I live, madam, I shall see you a bride at last. Good madam, you won't cast off your faithful Bianca: you won't put Donna Rossara over me, now you are a great princess!"

"My poor Bianca," said Matilda, "how fast your thoughts ramble! I a great princess! What hast thou seen in Manfred's behaviour since my brother's death that bespeaks any increase of tenderness to me? No, Bianca; his heart was ever a stranger to me—but he is my father, and I must not complain. Nay, if Heaven shuts my father's heart against me, it overpays my little merit in the tenderness of my mother.—O that dear mother! Yes, Bianca, 'tis there I feel the rugged temper of Manfred. I can support·his harshness to me with patience, but it wounds my soul when I am witness to his causeless severity towards her."

"Oh, madam," said Bianca, "all men use their wives so when they are weary of them."

"And yet you congratulated me but now," said Matilda, "when you fancied my father intended to dispose of me!"

"I would have you a great lady," replied Bianca, "come what will. I do not wish to see you moped in a convent, as you would be if you had your will, and if my lady, your mother, who knows that a bad husband is better than no husband at all, did not hinder you.— Bless me! what noise is that? St. Nicholas forgive me! I was but in jest."

"It is the wind," said Matilda, "whistling through the battlements in the tower above. You have heard it a thousand times."

"Nay," said Bianca, "there was no harm neither in

what I said; it is no sin to talk of matrimony—and so, madam, as I was saying, if my Lord Manfred should offer you a handsome young prince for a bridegroom, you would drop him a courtesy, and tell him you would rather take the veil?"

"Thank Heaven! I am in no such danger," said Matilda: "you know how many proposals for me he has rejected."

"And you thank him like a dutiful daughter, do you, madam?—but come, madam; suppose to-morrow morning he was to send for you to the great council-chamber, and there you should find at his elbow a lovely young prince with large black eyes, a smooth white forehead, and manly curling locks like jet; in short, madam, a young hero resembling the picture of the good Alfonso in the gallery, which you sit and gaze at for hours together."

"Do not speak lightly of that picture," interrupted Matilda, sighing: "I know the adoration with which I look at that picture is uncommon—but I am not in love with a coloured panel. The character of that virtuous prince, the veneration with which my mother has inspired me for his memory, the orisons which, I know not why, she has enjoined me to pour forth at his tomb, all have concurred to persuade me that somehow or other my destiny is linked with something relating to him."

"Lord, madam! how should that be?" said Bianca: "I have always heard that your family was no way related to his; and I am sure I cannot conceive why my lady, the princess, sends you in a cold morning or a damp evening to pray at his tomb; he is no saint by the almanack. If you must pray, why does she not bid you address yourself to our great St. Nicholas? I am sure he is the saint I pray to for a husband."

"Perhaps my mind would be less affected," said Matilda, "if my mother would explain her reasons to me; but it is the mystery she observes that inspires me with this—I know not what to call it. As she never acts from caprice, I am sure there is some fatal secret at bottom—nay, I know there is. In her agony of grief for my brother's death she dropped some words that intimated as much."

"Oh, dear madam," cried Bianca, "what were they?"

"No," said Matilda, "if a parent lets fall a word, and wishes it recalled, it is not for a child to utter it."

"What! was she sorry for what she had said?" asked Bianca. "I am sure, madam, you may trust me."

"With my own little secrets, when I have any, I may," said Matilda; "but never with my mother's. A child ought to have no ears or eyes but as a parent directs."

"Well, to be sure, madam, you was born to be a saint," said Bianca, "and there is no resisting one's vocation: you will end in a convent at last. But there is my Lady Isabella would not be so reserved to me: she will let me talk to her of young men; and when a handsome cavalier has come to the castle, she has owned to me that she wished your brother Conrad resembled him."

"Bianca," said the princess, "I do not allow you to mention my friend disrespectfully. Isabella is of a cheerful disposition, but her soul is as pure as virtue itself. She knows your idling, babbling humour, and perhaps has now and then encouraged it to divert melancholy and enliven the solitude in which my father keeps us."

"Blessed Mary!" said Bianca, starting, "there it is again! Dear madam, do you hear nothing? This castle is certainly haunted!"

"Peace!" said Matilda, "and listen! I did think I heard a voice—but it must be fancy; your terrors, I suppose, have infected me."

"Indeed! indeed! madam," said Bianca, half weeping with agony, "I am sure I heard a voice."

"Does anybody lie in the chamber beneath?" said the princess.

"Nobody has dared to lie there," answered Bianca, "since the great astrologer, that was your brother's tutor, drowned himself. For certain, madam, his ghost and the young prince's are now met in the chamber below; for Heaven's sake let us fly to your mother's apartment!"

"I charge you not to stir," said Matilda. "If they are spirits in pain, we may ease their sufferings by questioning them. They can mean no hurt to us, for we have not injured them; and if they should, shall we be more safe in one chamber than in another? Reach me my beads; we will say a prayer and then speak to them."

"Oh, dear lady, I would not speak to a ghost for the world," cried Bianca. As she said these words, they heard the casement of the little chamber below Matilda's open. They listened attentively, and in a few minutes thought they heard a person sing, but could not distinguish the words.

"This can be no evil spirit," said the princess, in a low voice: "it is undoubtedly one of the family—open the window and we shall know the voice."

"I dare not, indeed, madam," said Bianca.

"Thou art a very fool," said Matilda, opening the window gently herself. The noise that the princess made was, however, heard by the person beneath, who stopped, and they concluded had heard the casement open.

"Is any body below?" said the princess: "if there is, speak."

"Yes," said an unknown voice.

"Who is it?" said Matilda.

"A stranger," replied the voice.

"What stranger?" said she, "and how didst thou come here at this unusual hour, when all the gates of the castle are locked?"

"I am not here willingly," answered the voice; "but pardon me, lady, if I have disturbed your rest: I knew not that I was overheard. Sleep had forsaken me: I left a restless couch and came to waste the irksome hours with gazing on the fair approach of morning, impatient to be dismissed from this castle."

"Thy words and accents," said Matilda, "are of a melancholy cast: if thou art unhappy, I pity thee. If poverty afflicts thee, let me know it: I will mention thee to the princess, whose beneficent soul ever melts for the distressed, and she will relieve thee."

"I am, indeed, unhappy," said the stranger, "and I know not what wealth is, but I do not complain of the lot which Heaven has cast for me. I am young and healthy, and am not ashamed of owing my support to myself; yet think me not proud, or that I disdain your generous offers. I will remember you in my orisons, and I will pray for blessings on your gracious self and your noble mistress—if I sigh, lady, it is for others, not for myself."

"Now I have it, madam," said Bianca, whispering the princess. "This is certainly the young peasant; and, by my conscience, he is in love:—well, this is a charming adventure! Do, madam, let us sift him. He does not know you, but takes you for one of my Lady Hippolita's women."

"Art thou not ashamed, Bianca?" said the princess.

"What right have we to pry into the secrets of this young man's heart? He seems virtuous and frank, and tells us he is unhappy. Are those circumstances that authorise us to make a property of him? How are we entitled to his confidence?"

"Lord! madam, how little you know of love!" replied Bianca: "why, lovers have no pleasure equal to talking of their mistress."

"And would you have me become a peasant's confidante?" said the princess.

"Well, then, let me talk to him," said Bianca: "though I have the honour of being your highness's maid of honour, I was not always so great. Besides, if love levels ranks, it raises them too: I have a respect for a young man in love."

"Peace, simpleton," said the princess. "Though he said he was unhappy, it does not follow that he must be in love. Think of all that has happened to-day, and tell me if there are no misfortunes but what love causes. —Stranger," resumed the princess, "if thy misfortunes have not been occasioned by thy own fault, and are within the compass of the Princess Hippolita's power to redress, I will take upon me to answer that she will be thy protectress. When thou art dismissed from this castle, repair to holy father Jerome at the convent adjoining to the church of St. Nicholas, and make thy story known to him as far as thou thinkest meet. He will not fail to inform the princess, who is the mother of all that want her assistance. Farewell! It is not seemly for me to hold farther converse with a man at this unwonted hour."

"May the saints guard thee, gracious lady!" replied the peasant; "but, oh! if a poor and worthless stranger might presume to beg a minute's audience farther—am

I so happy?—the casement is not shut—might I venture to ask ——"

"Speak quickly," said Matilda; "the morning dawns apace; should the labourers come into the fields and perceive us—what wouldst thou ask?"

"I know not how—I know not if I dare," said the young stranger, faltering; "yet the humanity with which you have spoken to me emboldens—lady, dare I trust you?"

"Heavens," said Matilda, "what dost thou mean? with what wouldst thou trust me—speak boldly, if thy secret is fit to be intrusted to a virtuous breast."

"I would ask," said the peasant, recollecting himself, "whether what I have heard from the domestics is true, that the princess is missing from the castle?"

"What imports it to thee to know?" replied Matilda: "thy first words bespoke a prudent and becoming gravity. Dost thou come hither to pry into the secrets of Manfred? Adieu. I have been mistaken in thee." Saying these words, she shut the casement hastily, without giving the young man time to reply.

"I had acted more wisely," said the princess to Bianca, with some sharpness, "if I had let thee converse with this peasant; his inquisitiveness seems of a piece with thy own."

"It is not fit for me to argue with your highness," replied Bianca; "but perhaps the questions I should have put to him would have been more to the purpose than those you have been pleased to ask him."

"Oh, no doubt," said Matilda; "you are a very discreet personage! may I know what you would have asked him?"

"A by-stander often sees more of the game than those that play," answered Bianca. "Does your highness think, madam, that his question about my Lady Isabella

was the result of mere curiosity? No, no, madam; there
is more in it than you great folks are aware of. Lopez
told me, that all the servants believe this young fellow
contrived my Lady Isabella's escape—now, pray,
madam, observe—you and I both know that my Lady
Isabella never much fancied the prince your brother—
well, he is killed just in the critical minute—I accuse
nobody. A helmet falls from the moon—so my lord,
your father, says; but Lopez and all the servants say
that this young spark is a magician, and stole it from
Alfonso's tomb."

"Have done with this rhapsody of impertinence,"
said Matilda.

"Nay, madam, as you please," cried Bianca; "yet it
is very particular, though, that my Lady Isabella should
be missing the very same day, and that this young
sorcerer should be found at the mouth of the trap-door
—I accuse nobody—but if my young lord came honestly
by his death ——"

"Dare not, on thy duty," said Matilda, "to breathe
a suspicion on the purity of my dear Isabella's fame."

"Purity or not purity," said Bianca, "gone she is—
a stranger is found that nobody knows. You question
him yourself. He tells you he is in love, or unhappy,
it is the same thing—nay, he owned he was unhappy
about others; and is anybody unhappy about another
unless they are in love with them? and at the very next
word he asks innocently, poor soul, if my Lady Isabella
is missing."

"To be sure," said Matilda, "thy observations are not
totally without foundation; Isabella's flight amazes me.
The curiosity of the stranger is very particular; yet Isabella never concealed a thought from me."

"So she told you," said Bianca, "to fish out your
secrets; but who knows, madam, but this stranger may

be some prince in disguise? Do, madam, let me open
the window and ask him a few questions."

"No," replied Matilda, "I will ask him myself; if he
knows aught of Isabella, he is not worthy that I should
converse farther with him." She was going to open the
casement, when they heard the bell ring at the postern
gate of the castle, which is on the right hand of the
tower where Matilda lay. This prevented the princess
from renewing the conversation with the stranger.

After continuing silent for some time, "I am persuaded," said she to Bianca, "that whatever be the cause
of Isabella's flight, it had no unworthy motive. If this
stranger was accessory to it, she must be satisfied of
his fidelity and worth. I observed, did not you, Bianca?
that his words were tinctured with an uncommon in-
fusion of piety. It was no ruffian's speech; his phrases
were becoming a man of gentle birth."

"I told you, madam," said Bianca, "that I was sure
he was some prince in disguise."

"Yet," said Matilda, "if he was privy to her escape,
how will you account for his not accompanying her in
her flight? Why expose himself unnecessarily and
rashly to my father's resentment?"

"As for that, madam," replied she, "if he could get
from under the helmet, he will find ways of eluding your
father's anger. I do not doubt but he has some talisman
or other about him."

"You resolve everything into magic," said Matilda;
"but a man who has any intercourse with infernal spirits
does not dare to make use of those tremendous and holy
words which he uttered. Didst thou not observe with
what fervour he vowed to remember me to Heaven in
his prayers? yes, Isabella was undoubtedly convinced
of his piety."

"Commend me to the piety of a young fellow and a

damsel that consult to elope!" said Bianca. "No, no, madam; my Lady Isabella is of another guess mould than you take her for. She used, indeed, to sigh and lift up her eyes in your company, because she knows you are a saint; but when your back was turned——"

"You wrong her," said Matilda. "Isabella is no hypocrite: she has a due sense of devotion, but never affected a call she has not. On the contrary, she always combated my inclination for the cloister; and though I own the mystery she has made to me of her flight confounds me—though it seems inconsistent with the friendship between us—I cannot forget the disinterested warmth with which she always opposed my taking the veil: she wished to see me married, though my dower would have been a loss to her and my brother's children. For her sake I will believe well of this young peasant."

"Then you do think there is some liking between them?" said Bianca. While she was speaking, a servant came hastily into the chamber, and told the princess that the Lady Isabella was found.

"Where?" said Matilda.

"She has taken sanctuary in St. Nicholas's church," replied the servant: "Father Jerome has brought the news himself; he is below with his highness."

"Where is my mother?" said Matilda.

"She is in her own chamber, madam, and has asked for you."

Manfred had risen at the first dawn of light, and gone to Hippolita's apartment to enquire if she knew aught of Isabella. While he was questioning her, word was brought that Jerome demanded to speak with him. Manfred, little suspecting the cause of the friar's arrival, and knowing he was employed by Hippolita in her charities, ordered him to be admitted, intending to

leave them together while he pursued his search. after
Isabella.

"Is your business with me or the princess?" said
Manfred.

"With both," replied the holy man. "The Lady Isabella ——"

"What of her?" interrupted Manfred, eagerly.

"Is at St. Nicholas's altar," replied Jerome.

"That is no business of Hippolita's," said Manfred
with confusion: "let us retire to my chamber, father,
and inform me how she came thither."

"No, my lord," replied the good man with an air of
firmness and authority, that daunted even the resolute
Manfred, who could not help revering the saint-like
virtues of Jerome, "my commission is to both; and, with
your highness's good liking, in the presence of both I
shall deliver it: but first, my lord, I must interrogate the
princess whether she is acquainted with the cause of
the Lady Isabella's retirement from your castle."

"No, on my soul," said Hippolita: "does Isabella
charge me with being privy to it?"

"Father," interrupted Manfred, "I pay due reverence
to your holy profession; but I am sovereign here, and
will allow no meddling priest to interfere in the affairs
of my domestic. If you have aught to say, attend me to
my chamber. I do not use to let my wife be acquainted
with the secret affairs of my state; they are not within
a woman's province."

"My lord," said the holy man, "I am no intruder into
the secrets of families. My office is to promote peace, to
heal divisions, to preach repentance, and teach mankind
to curb their headstrong passions. I forgive your highness's uncharitable apostrophe; I know my duty, and
am the minister of a mightier prince than Manfred.
Hearken to him who speaks through my organs."

Manfred trembled with rage and shame. Hippolita's countenance declared her astonishment and impatience to know where this would end. Her silence more strongly spoke her observance of Manfred.

"The Lady Isabella," resumed Jerome, "commends herself to both your highnesses. She thanks both for the kindness with which she has been treated in your castle; she deplores the loss of your son and her own misfortune in not becoming the daughter of such wise and noble princes, whom she shall always respect as parents; she prays for uninterrupted union and felicity between you (Manfred's colour changed); but, as it is no longer possible for her to be allied to you, she entreats your consent to remain in sanctuary till she can learn news of her father, or, by the certainty of his death, be at liberty by the approbation of her guardians to dispose of herself in suitable marriage."

"I shall give no such consent," said the prince; "but insist on her return to the castle without delay. I am answerable for her person to her guardians, and will not brook her being in any hands but my own."

"Your highness will recollect whether that can any longer be proper," replied the friar.

"I want no monitor," said Manfred, colouring: "Isabella's conduct leaves room for strange suspicions; and that young villain, who was at least the accomplice of her flight, if not the cause of it——"

"The cause!" interrupted Jerome; "was a *young* man the cause?"

"This is not to be borne!" cried Manfred. "Am I to be bearded in my own palace by an insolent monk? Thou art privy, I guess, to their amours."

"I would pray to Heaven to clear up your uncharitable surmises," said Jerome, "if your highness were not satisfied in your conscience how unjustly you accuse me. I do pray to Heaven to pardon that uncharitableness; and I implore your highness to leave the princess at peace in that holy place, where she is not liable to be disturbed by such vain and worldly fantasies as discourses of love from any man."

"Cant not to me," said Manfred, "but return and bring the princess to her duty."

"It is my duty to prevent her return hither," said Jerome. "She is where orphans and virgins are safest from the snares and wiles of this world; and nothing but a parent's authority shall take her thence."

"I am her parent," cried Manfred, "and demand her."

"She wished to have you for her parent," said the friar: "but Heaven, that forbade that connection, has for ever dissolved all ties betwixt you, and I announce to your highness ——"

"Stop! audacious man," said Manfred, "and dread my displeasure."

"Holy father," said Hippolita, "it is your office to be no respecter of persons: you must speak as your duty prescribes; but it is my duty to hear nothing that it pleases not my lord I should hear. Attend the prince to his chamber. I will retire to my oratory, and pray to the blessed Virgin to inspire you with her holy counsels, and to restore the heart of my gracious lord to its wonted peace and gentleness."

"Excellent woman!" said the friar.—"My lord, I attend your pleasure."

Manfred, accompanied by the friar, passed to his own apartment, where, shutting the door, "I perceive, father," said he, "that Isabella has acquainted you with my purpose. Now hear my resolve, and obey. Reasons of state, most urgent reasons, my own and the safety of my people, demand that I should have a son.

It is in vain to expect an heir from Hippolita; *I* have made choice of Isabella. You must bring her back, and you must do more. I know the influence you have with Hippolita: her conscience is in your hands. She is, I allow, a faultless woman: her soul is set on Heaven, and scorns the little grandeur of this world; you can withdraw her from it entirely. Persuade her to consent to the dissolution of our marriage, and to retire into a monastery; she shall endow one if she will, and shall have the means of being as liberal to your order as she or you can wish. Thus you will divert the calamities that are hanging over our heads, and have the merit of saving the principality of Otranto from destruction. You are a prudent man, and though the warmth of my temper betrayed me into some unbecoming expressions, I honour your virtue and wish to be indebted to you for the repose of my life and the preservation of my family."

"The will of Heaven be done," said the friar. "I am but its worthless instrument. It makes use of my tongue to tell thee, prince, of thy unwarrantable designs. The injuries of the virtuous Hippolita have mounted to the throne of pity. By me thou art reprimanded for thy adulterous intention of repudiating her; by me thou art warned not to pursue the incestuous design on thy contracted daughter. Heaven, that delivered her from thy fury when the judgments so recently fallen on thy house ought to have inspired thee with other thoughts, will continue to watch over her. Even I, a poor and despised friar, am able to protect her from thy violence. I, sinner as I am, and uncharitably reviled by your highness as an accomplice of I know not what amours, scorn the allurements with which it has pleased thee to tempt mine honesty. I love my order; I honour devout souls; I respect the piety of thy princess; but I

will not betray the confidence she reposes in me, nor
serve even the cause of religion by foul and sinful
compliances.   But, forsooth, the welfare of the state
depends on your highness having a son!   Heaven mocks
the short-sighted views of man.   But yester-morn, whose
house was so great, so flourishing as Manfred's?   Where
is young Conrad now?   My lord, I respect your tears,
but I mean not to check them; let them flow, prince!
they will weigh more with Heaven towards the welfare
of thy subjects than a marriage which, founded on lust
or policy, could never prosper.   The sceptre which
passed from the race of Alfonso to thine cannot be preserved by a match which the church will never allow.
If it is the will of the Most High that Manfred's name
must perish, resign yourself, my lord, to its decrees;
and thus deserve a crown that can never pass away.
Come, my lord, I like this sorrow; let us return to the
princess; she is not apprised of your cruel intentions;
nor did I mean more than to alarm you.   You saw with
what gentle patience, with what efforts of love, she
heard, she rejected hearing, the extent of your guilt.   I
know she longs to fold you in her arms and assure you
of her unalterable affection."

"Father," said the prince, "you mistake my compunction.   True, I honour Hippolita's virtues; I think her a
saint; and wish it were for my soul's health to tie faster
the knot that has united us.   But, alas, father, you know
not the bitterest of my pangs; it is some time that I
have had scruples on the legality of our union: Hippolita is related to me in the fourth degree—it is true,
we had a dispensation, but I have been informed that
she had also been contracted to another.   This it is that
sits heavy at my heart; to this state of unlawful wed-
lock I impute the visitation that has fallen on me in
the death of Conrad.   Ease my conscience of this

burden, dissolve our marriage, and accomplish the work of godliness which your divine exhortations have commenced in my soul."

How cutting was the anguish which the good man felt when he perceived this turn in the wily prince. He trembled for Hippolita, whose ruin he saw was determined; and he feared if Manfred had no hope of recovering Isabella, that his impatience for a son would direct him to some other object who might not be equally proof against the temptation of Manfred's rank. For some time the holy man remained absorbed in thought. At length, conceiving some hopes from delay, he thought the wisest conduct would be to prevent the prince from despairing of recovering Isabella. Her the friar knew he could dispose, from her affection to Hippolita, and from the aversion she had expressed to him for Manfred's addresses, to second his views till the censures of the church could be fulminated against a divorce. With this intention, as if struck with the prince's scruples, he at length said,—

"My lord, I have been pondering on what your highness has said; and if in truth it is delicacy of conscience that is the real motive of your repugnance to your virtuous lady, far be it from me to endeavour to harden your heart. The church is an indulgent mother; unfold your griefs to her; she alone can administer comfort to your soul, either by satisfying your conscience, or, upon examination of your scruples, by setting you at liberty and indulging you in the lawful means of continuing your lineage. In the latter case, if the Lady Isabella can be brought to consent——"

Manfred, who concluded that he had either overreached the good man or that his first warmth had been but a tribute paid to appearance, was overjoyed at his sudden turn, and repeated the most magnificent promises, if he should succeed by the friar's mediation. The well-meaning priest suffered him to deceive himself, fully determined to traverse his views instead of seconding them.

"Since we now understand one another," resumed the prince, "I expect, father, that you satisfy me in one point. Who is the youth that I found in the vault? He must have been privy to Isabella's flight. Tell me truly, is he her lover? or is he an agent for another's passion? I have often suspected Isabella's indifference to my son; a thousand circumstances crowd on my mind that confirm that suspicion. She herself was so conscious of it that while I discoursed with her in the gallery she outran my suspicions, and endeavoured to justify herself from coolness to Conrad."

The friar, who knew nothing of the youth but what he had learnt occasionally from the princess, ignorant what was become of him, and not sufficiently reflecting on the impetuosity of Manfred's temper, conceived that it might not be amiss to sow the seeds of jealousy in his mind. They might be turned to some use hereafter, either by prejudicing the prince against Isabella, if he persisted in that union, or by diverting his attention to a wrong scent, and employing his thoughts on a visionary intrigue, prevent his engaging in any new pursuit. With this unhappy policy, he answered in a manner to confirm Manfred in the belief of some connection between Isabella and the youth. The prince, whose passions wanted little fuel to throw them into a blaze, fell into a rage at the idea of what the friar had suggested.

"I will fathom to the bottom of this intrigue," cried he; and quitting Jerome abruptly, with a command to remain there till his return, he hastened to the great hall of the castle, and ordered the peasant to be brought before him.

"Thou hardened young impostor," said the prince, as soon as he saw the youth; "what becomes of thy boasted veracity now? It was Providence, was it, and the light of the moon, that discovered the lock of the trap-door to thee? Tell me, audacious boy, who thou art, and how long thou hast been acquainted with the princess; and take care to answer with less equivocation than thou didst last night, or tortures shall wring the truth from thee."

The young man, perceiving that his share in the flight of the princess was discovered, and concluding that anything he should say could no longer be of service or detriment to her, replied, "I am no impostor, my lord, nor have I deserved opprobrious language. I answered to every question your highness put to me last night with the same veracity that I shall speak now; and that will not be from fear of your tortures, but because my soul abhors a falsehood. Please to repeat your questions, my lord; I am ready to give you all the satisfaction in my power."

"You know my questions," replied the prince, "and only want time to prepare an evasion. Speak directly; who art thou, and how long hast thou been known to the princess?"

"I am a labourer at the next village," said the peasant; "my name is Theodore. The princess found me in the vault last night; before that hour I never was in her presence."

"I may believe as much or as little as I please of this," said Manfred; "but I will hear thy own story before I examine into the truth of it. Tell me, what reason did the princess give thee for making her escape? Thy life depends on thy answer."

"She told me," replied Theodore, "that she was on the brink of destruction, and that if she could not escape from the castle, she was in danger in a few moments of being made miserable for ever."

"And on this slight foundation, on a silly girl's report," said Manfred, "thou didst hazard my displeasure!"

"I fear no man's displeasure," said Theodore, "when a woman in distress puts herself under my protection."

During this examination Matilda was going to the apartment of Hippolita. At the upper end of the hall, where Manfred sat, was a boarded gallery, with latticed windows, through which Matilda and Bianca were to pass. Hearing her father's voice, and seeing the servants assembled round him, she stopped to learn the occasion. The prisoner soon drew her attention: the steady and composed manner in which he answered, and the gallantry of his last reply, which were the first words she heard distinctly, interested her in his favour. His person was noble, handsome and commanding, even in that situation, but his countenance soon engrossed her whole care.

"Heavens! Bianca," said the princess softly, "do I dream, or is not that youth the exact resemblance of Alfonso's picture in the gallery?" She could say no more, for her father's voice grew louder at every word.

"This bravado," said he, "surpasses all thy former insolence. Thou shalt experience the wrath with which thou darest to trifle. Seize him," continued Manfred, "and bind him—the first news the princess hears of her champion shall be that he has lost his head for her sake."

"The injustice of which thou art guilty towards me," said Theodore, "convinces me that I have done a good deed in delivering the princess from thy tyranny. May she be happy, whatever becomes of me!"

"This is a lover," cried Manfred, in a rage; "a

peasant within sight of death is not animated by such sentiments. Tell me, tell me, rash boy, who thou art, or the rack shall force thy secret from thee."

"Thou hast threatened me with death already," said the youth, "for the truth I have told thee; if that is all the encouragement I am to expect for sincerity, I am not tempted to indulge thy vain curiosity farther."

"Then thou wilt not speak?" said Manfred.

"I will not," replied he.

"Bear him away into the court-yard," said Manfred; "I will see his head this instant severed from his body."

Matilda fainted at hearing those words. Bianca shrieked and cried, "Help, help! the princess is dead!" Manfred started at this ejaculation and demanded what was the matter. The young peasant, who heard it too, was struck with horror, and asked eagerly the same question; but Manfred ordered him to be hurried into the court, and kept there for execution, till he had informed himself of the cause of Bianca's shrieks. When he learned the meaning, he treated it as a womanish panic, and ordering Matilda to be carried to her apartment, he rushed into the court, and calling for one of his guards, bade Theodore kneel down and prepare to receive the fatal blow.

The undaunted youth received the bitter sentence with a resignation that touched every heart but Manfred's. He wished earnestly to know the meaning of the words he had heard relating to the princess; but fearing to exasperate the tyrant more against her, he desisted. The only boon he deigned to ask was that he might be permitted to have a confessor, and make his peace with Heaven. Manfred, who hoped by the confessor's means to come at the youth's history, readily granted his request; and being convinced that Father Jerome was now in his interest, he ordered him to be called and shrive the prisoner. The holy man, who had little foreseen the catastrophe that his imprudence occasioned, fell on his knees to the prince, and adjured him in the most solemn manner not to shed innocent blood. He accused himself in the bitterest terms for his indiscretion, endeavoured to exculpate the youth, and left no method untried to soften the tyrant's rage. Manfred, more incensed than appeased by Jerome's intercession, whose retraction now made him suspect he had been imposed upon by both, commanded the friar to do his duty, telling him he would not allow the prisoner many minutes for confession.

"Nor do I ask many, my lord," said the unhappy young man. "My sins, thank Heaven, have not been numerous; nor exceed what might be expected at my years. Dry your tears, good father, and let us despatch; this is a bad world, nor have I had cause to leave it with regret."

"Oh, wretched youth!" said Jerome, "how canst thou bear the sight of me with patience? I am thy murderer! It is I have brought this dismal hour upon thee!"

"I forgive thee from my soul," said the youth, "as I hope Heaven will pardon me. Hear my confession, father, and give me thy blessing."

"How can I prepare thee for thy passage as I ought?" said Jerome. "Thou canst not be saved without pardoning thy foes, and canst thou forgive that impious man there?"

"I can," said Theodore; "I do."

"And does not this touch thee, cruel prince?" said the friar.

"I sent for thee to confess him," said Manfred, sternly; "not to plead for him. Thou didst first incense me against him; his blood be upon thy head."

"It will, it will!" said the good man, in an agony of sorrow. "Thou and I must never hope to go where this blessed youth is going."

"Despatch," said Manfred; "I am no more to be moved by the whining of priests than by the shrieks of women."

"What!" said the youth; "is it possible that my fate could have occasioned what I heard? Is the princess, then, again in thy power?"

"Thou dost but remember me of my wrath," said Manfred; "prepare thee, for this moment is thy last."

The youth, who felt his indignation rise, and who was touched with the sorrow which he saw he had infused into all the spectators, as well as into the friar, suppressed his emotions, and putting off his doublet, and unbuttoning his collar, knelt down to his prayers. As he stooped, his shirt slipped down below his shoulder and discovered the mark of a bloody arrow.

"Gracious Heaven!" cried the holy man, starting, "what do I see? It is my child, my Theodore!"

The passions that ensued must be conceived; they cannot be painted. The tears of the assistants were suspended by wonder rather than stopped by joy. They seemed to enquire into the eyes of their lord what they ought to feel. Surprise, doubt, tenderness, respect, succeeded each other in the countenance of the youth. He received with modest submission the effusion of the old man's tears and embraces; yet, afraid of giving a loose to hope, and suspecting from what had passed the inflexibility of Manfred's temper, he cast a glance towards the prince as if to say, canst thou be unmoved at such a scene as this?

Manfred's heart was capable of being touched. He forgot his anger in his astonishment; yet his pride for-

bade his owning himself affected. He even doubted
whether this discovery was not a contrivance of the
friar to save the youth. "What may this mean?" said
he; "how can he be thy son? Is it consistent with thy
profession or reputed sanctity to avow a peasant's offspring for the fruit of thy irregular amours?"

"Oh God!" said the holy man, "dost thou question
his being mine? Could I feel the anguish I do, if I
were not his father? Spare him, good prince! spare
him! and revile me as thou pleasest."

"Spare him! spare him!" cried the attendants, "for
this good man's sake."

"Peace!" said Manfred, sternly; "I must know, ere
I am disposed to pardon. A saint's bastard may be no
saint himself."

"Injurious lord!" said Theodore; "add not insult to
cruelty. If I am this venerable man's son, though no
prince, as thou art, know, the blood that flows in my
veins ——"

"Yes," said the friar, interrupting him, "his blood is
noble; nor is he that abject thing, my lord, you speak
him. He is my lawful son; and Sicily can boast of few
houses more ancient than that of Falconara—but, alas!
my lord, what is blood? what is nobility? We are all
reptiles, miserable, sinful creatures. It is piety alone
that can distinguish us from the dust whence we sprung
and whither we must return."

"Truce to your sermon," said Manfred; "you forget
you are no longer Friar Jerome, but the Count of Falconara. Let me know your history: you will have time
enough to moralise hereafter, if you should not happen
to obtain the grace of that sturdy criminal there."

"Mother of God!" said the friar, "is it possible my
lord can refuse a father the life of his only, his long-

lost child? Trample me, my lord, scorn, afflict me, accept my life for his, but spare my son!"

"Thou canst feel, then," said Manfred, "what it is to lose an only son! A little hour ago thou didst preach up resignation to me: *my* house, if fate so pleased, must perish—but the Count of Falconara ——"

"Alas! my lord," said Jerome, "I confess I have offended; but aggravate not an old man's sufferings. I boast not of my family nor think of such vanities; it is nature that pleads for this boy; it is the memory of the dear woman that bore him—is she, Theodore, is she dead?"

"Her soul has long been with the blessed," said Theodore.

"Oh! how?" cried Jerome; "tell me—no—she is happy! Thou art all my care now. Most dread lord! will you—will you grant me my poor boy's life?"

"Return to thy convent," answered Manfred; "conduct the princess hither; obey me in what else thou knowest, and I promise thee the life of thy son."

"Oh, my lord!" said Jerome, "is my honesty the price I must pay for this dear youth's safety?"

"For me!" cried Theodore; "let me die a thousand deaths rather than stain thy conscience. What is it the tyrant would exact of thee? Is the princess still safe from his power? Protect her, thou venerable old man, and let all the weight of his wrath fall on me."

Jerome endeavoured to check the impetuosity of the youth; and ere Manfred could reply, the trampling of horses was heard, and a brazen trumpet which hung without the gate of the castle was suddenly sounded. At the same instant the sable plumes on the enchanted helmet, which still remained at the other end of the court, were tempestuously agitated, and nodded thrice, as if bowed by some invisible wearer.

CHAPTER III

MANFRED'S heart misgave him when he beheld the
plumage on the miraculous casque shaken in concert
with the sounding of the brazen trumpet. "Father,"
said he to Jerome, whom he now ceased to treat as
Count of Falconara, "what mean these portents? If I
have offended"—the plumes were shaken with greater
violence than before. "Unhappy prince that I am!"
cried Manfred. "Holy father, will you not assist me
with your prayers?"

"My lord," replied Jerome, "Heaven is no doubt
displeased with your mockery of its servants. Submit
yourself to the church, and cease to persecute her ministers. Dismiss this innocent youth, and learn to re-
pect the holy character I wear: Heaven will not be
trifled with. You see"—the trumpet sounded again.

"I acknowledge I have been too hasty," said Manfred. "Father, do you go to the wicket and demand
who is at the gate."

"Do you grant me the life of Theodore?" replied
the friar.

"I do," said Manfred; "but enquire who is without."

Jerome, falling on the neck of his son, discharged a
flood of tears that spoke the fulness of his soul.

"You promised to go to the gate," said Manfred.

"I thought," replied the friar, "your highness would
excuse my thanking you first in this tribute of my
heart."

"Go, dearest sir," said Theodore, "obey the prince;
I do not deserve that you should delay his satisfaction
for me."

Jerome, enquiring who was without, was answered,
"A herald."

"From whom?" said he.

"From the Knight of the Gigantic Sabre," said the herald; "and I must speak with the usurper of Otranto."

Jerome returned to the prince, and did not fail to repeat the message in the very words it had been uttered. The first sounds struck Manfred with terror; but when he heard himself styled usurper, his rage rekindled, and all his courage revived.

"Usurper!—insolent villain!" cried he; "who dares to question my title? Retire, father; this is no business for monks; I will meet this presumptuous man myself. Go to your convent and prepare the princess's return. Your son shall be a hostage for your fidelity; his life depends on your obedience."

"Good Heaven! my lord," cried Jerome, "your highness did but this instant freely pardon my child. Have you so soon forgot the interposition of Heaven?"

"Heaven," replied Manfred, "does not send heralds to question the title of a lawful prince. I doubt whether it even notifies its will through friars; but that is your affair, not mine. At present you know my pleasure; and it is not a saucy herald that shall save your son, if you do not return with the princess."

It was in vain for the holy man to reply. Manfred commanded him to be conducted to the postern gate and shut out from the castle; and he ordered some of his attendants to carry Theodore to the top of the Black Tower, and guard him strictly, scarce permitting the father and son to exchange a hasty embrace at parting. He then withdrew to the hall, and seating himself in princely state, ordered the herald to be admitted to his presence.

"Well, thou insolent!" said the prince, "what wouldst thou with me?"

"I come," replied he, "to thee, Manfred, usurper of the principality of Otranto, from the renowned and invincible knight, the Knight of the Gigantic Sabre: in the name of his lord, Frederic Marquis of Vicenza, he demands the Lady Isabella, daughter of that prince, whom thou hast basely and traitorously got into thy power, by bribing her false guardians during his absence; and he requires thee to resign the principality of Otranto, which thou hast usurped from the said Lord Frederic, the nearest of blood to the last rightful lord, Alfonso the Good. If thou dost not instantly comply with these just demands, he defies thee to single combat to the last extremity." And so saying, the herald cast down his warder.

"And where is this braggart who sends thee?" said Manfred.

"At the distance of a league," said the herald: "he comes to make good his lord's claim against thee, as he is a true knight, and thou an usurper and ravisher."

Injurious as this challenge was, Manfred reflected that it was not his interest to provoke the marquis. He knew how well founded the claim of Frederic was, nor was this the first time he had heard of it. Frederic's ancestors had assumed the style of Princes of Otranto, from the death of Alfonso the Good without issue; but Manfred, his father, and grandfather, had been too powerful for the house of Vicenza to dispossess them. Frederic, a martial and amorous young prince, had married a beautiful young lady, of whom he was enamoured. and who had died in childbed of Isabella. Her death affected him so much that he had taken the cross and gone to the Holy Land, where he was wounded in an engagement against the infidels, made prisoner, and reported to be dead. When the news reached Manfred's ears, he bribed the guardians of the Lady Isabella to deliver her up to him as a bride for his son Conrad, by which alliance he had proposed to unite the claims of the two houses. This motive, on Conrad's death, had cooperated to make him so suddenly resolve on espousing her himself; and the same reflection determined him now to endeavour at obtaining the consent of Frederic to this marriage. A like policy inspired him with the thought of inviting Frederic's champion into his castle, lest he should be informed of Isabella's flight, which he strictly enjoined his domestics not to disclose to any of the knight's retinue.

"Herald," said Manfred, as soon as he had digested these reflections, "return to thy master, and tell him, ere we liquidate our differences by the sword, Manfred would hold some converse with him. Bid him welcome to my castle, where, by my faith, as I am a true knight, he shall have courteous reception and full security for himself and followers. If we cannot adjust our quarrel by amicable means, I swear he shall depart in safety, and shall have full satisfaction according to the laws of arms. So help me God and his Holy Trinity!" The herald made three obeisances, and retired.

During this interview, Jerome's mind was agitated by a thousand contrary passions. He trembled for the life of his son, and his first thought was to persuade Isabella to return to the castle. Yet he was scarce less alarmed at the thought of her union with Manfred. He dreaded Hippolita's unbounded submission to the will of her lord; and though he did not doubt but he could alarm her piety not to consent to a divorce, if he could get access to her, yet, should Manfred discover that the obstruction came from him, it might be equally fatal to Theodore. He was impatient to know whence came the herald, who with so little management had questioned the title of Manfred; yet he did not dare absent himself from the convent lest Isabella should leave it and her flight be imputed to him. He returned disconsolately to the monastery, uncertain on what conduct to resolve. A monk, who met him in the porch and observed his melancholy air, said, "Alas! brother, is it then true that we have lost our excellent Princess Hippolita?"

The holy man started, and cried, "What meanest thou, brother? I came this instant from the castle, and left her in perfect health."

"Martelli," replied the other friar, "passed by the convent but a quarter of an hour ago, on his way from the castle, and reported that her highness was dead. All our brethren are gone to the chapel to pray for her happy transit to a better life, and willed me to wait thy arrival. They know thy holy attachment to that good lady, and are anxious for the affliction it will cause thee—indeed we have all reason to weep; she was a mother to our house. But this life is but a pilgrimage; we must not murmur—we shall all follow her: may our end be like hers!"

"Good brother, thou dreamest," said Jerome; "I tell thee I come from the castle, and left the princess well: —where is the Lady Isabella?"

"Poor gentlewoman," replied the friar, "I told her the sad news, and offered her spiritual comfort; I reminded her of the transitory condition of mortality, and advised her to take the veil: I quoted the example of the holy Princess Sanchia of Arragon."

"Thy zeal was laudable," said Jerome, impatiently; "but at present it was unnecessary. Hippolita is well —at least I trust in the Lord she is; I heard nothing to the contrary—yet methinks, the prince's earnestness —well, brother, but where is the Lady Isabella?"

"I know not," said the friar: "she wept much, and said she would retire to her chamber."

Jerome left his comrade abruptly, and hastened to the princess, but she was not in her chamber. He enquired of the domestics of the convent, but could learn no news of her. He searched in vain throughout the monastery and the church, and despatched messengers round the neighbourhood, to get intelligence if she had been seen, but to no purpose. Nothing could equal the good man's perplexity. He judged that Isabella, suspecting Manfred of having precipitated his wife's death, had taken the alarm, and withdrawn herself to some more secret place of concealment. This new flight would probably carry the prince's fury to the height. The report of Hippolita's death, though it seemed almost incredible, increased his consternation; and though Isabella's escape bespoke her aversion of Manfred for a husband, Jerome could feel no comfort from it while it endangered the life of his son. He determined to return to the castle, and made several of his brethren accompany him to attest his innocence to Manfred, and, if necessary, join their intercessions with his for Theodore.

The prince, in the mean time, had passed into the court, and ordered the gates of the castle to be flung open for the reception of the stranger knight and his train. In a few minutes the cavalcade arrived. First came two harbingers with wands; next a herald, followed by two pages and two trumpeters; then a hundred foot guards. These were attended by as many horse. After them fifty footmen, clothed in scarlet and black, the colours of the knight; then a led horse. Two heralds on each side of a gentleman on horseback, bearing a banner with the arms of Vicenza and Otranto quarterly—a circumstance that much offended Man-

fred, but he stifled his resentment. Two more pages;
the knight's confessor telling his beads; fifty more footmen, clad as before; two knights habited in complete
armour, their beavers down, comrades to the principal
knight; the squires of the two knights, carrying their
shields and devices; the knight's own squire; a hundred
gentlemen bearing an enormous sword, and seeming to
faint under the weight of it. The knight himself, on a
chestnut steed, in complete armour, his lance in the
rest, his face entirely concealed by his visor, which was
surmounted by a large plume of scarlet and black feathers. Fifty foot guards, with drums and trumpets,
closed the procession, which wheeled off to the right
and left to make room for the principal knight.

As soon as he approached the gate, he stopped; and
the herald advancing, read again the words of the
challenge. Manfred's eyes were fixed on the gigantic
sword, and he scarce seemed to attend to the cartel;
but his attention was soon diverted by a tempest of
wind that rose behind him. He turned, and beheld the
plumes of the enchanted helmet agitated in the same
extraordinary manner as before. It required intrepidity
like Manfred's not to sink under a concurrence of circumstances that seemed to announce his fate. Yet
scorning in the presence of strangers to betray the
courage he had always manifested, he said boldly,—

"Sir Knight, whoever thou art, I bid thee welcome.
If thou art of mortal mould, thy valour shall meet its
equal; and if thou art a true knight, thou wilt scorn to
employ sorcery to carry thy point. Be these omens
from Heaven or Hell, Manfred trusts to the righteousness of his cause and to the aid of St. Nicholas, who
has ever protected his house. Alight, Sir Knight, and
repose thyself; tomorrow thou shalt have a fair field;
and Heaven befriend the juster side!"

The knight made no reply, but dismounting, was conducted by Manfred to the great hall of the castle. As they traversed the court, the knight stopped to gaze on the miraculous casque; and, kneeling down, seemed to pray inwardly for some minutes. Rising, he made a sign to the prince to lead on. As soon as they entered the hall, Manfred proposed to the stranger to disarm, but the knight shook his head in token of refusal. "Sir Knight," said Manfred, "this is not courteous: but by my good faith I will not cross thee; nor shalt thou have cause to complain of the Prince of Otranto. No treachery is designed on my part; I hope none is intended on thine; here, take my gauge (giving him his ring), your friends and you shall enjoy the laws of hospitality. Rest here until refreshments are brought; I will but give orders for the accommodation of your train, and return to you."

The three knights bowed, as accepting his courtesy. Manfred directed the stranger's retinue to be conducted to an adjacent hospital, founded by the Princess Hippolita for the reception of pilgrims. As they made the circuit of the court to return towards the gate, the gigantic sword burst from the supporters, and falling to the ground opposite to the helmet, remained immovable. Manfred, almost hardened to preternatural appearances, surmounted the shock of this new prodigy; and returning to the hall, where by this time the feast was ready, he invited his silent guests to take their places. Manfred, however ill his heart was at ease, endeavoured to inspire the company with mirth. He put several questions to them, but was answered only by signs. They raised their visors but sufficiently to feed themselves, and that but sparingly.

"Sirs," said the prince, "ye are the first guests I ever treated within these walls, who scorned to hold any in-

tercourse with me; nor has it oft been customary, I
ween, for princes to hazard their state and dignity
against strangers and mutes. You say you come in
the name of Frederic of Vicenza; I have ever heard
that he was a gallant and courteous knight; nor would
he, I am bold to say, think it beneath him to mix in
social converse with a prince who is his equal and not
unknown by deeds in arms.—Still ye are silent—well,
be it as it may, by the laws of hospitality and chivalry
ye are masters under this roof: ye shall do your pleasure—but come, give me a goblet of wine; ye will not
refuse to pledge me to the healths of your fair mis-
tresses." The principal knight sighed and crossed himself, and was rising from the board. "Sir Knight," said
Manfred, "what I said was but in sport; I shall con-
strain you in nothing. Use your good liking; since
mirth is not your mood, let us be sad. Business may
hit your fancies better; let us withdraw, and hear if
what I have to unfold may be better relished than the
vain efforts I have made for your pastime."

Manfred then conducting the three knights into an
inner chamber, shut the door, and inviting them to be
seated, began thus, addressing himself to the chief
personage:—

"You come, Sir Knight, as I understand it, in the
name of the Marquis of Vicenza, to redemand the Lady
Isabella, his daughter, who has been contracted, in the
face of holy church, to my son, by the consent of her
legal guardians; and to require me to resign my dominions to your lord, who gives himself for the nearest
of blood to Prince Alfonso, whose soul God rest! I
shall speak to the latter article of your demands first.
You must know, your lord knows, that I enjoy the
principality of Otranto from my father Don Manuel,
as he received it from his father Don Ricardo. Alfonso,

their predecessor, dying childless in the Holy Land,
bequeathed his estates to my grandfather, Don Ricardo,
in consideration of his faithful services."—The stranger
shook his head.—"Sir Knight," said Manfred, warmly,
"Ricardo was a valiant and upright man; he was a
pious man; witness his munificent foundation of the adjoining church and two convents. He was peculiarly
patronised by St. Nicholas—my grandfather was incapable—I say, sir, Don Ricardo was incapable—
excuse me, your interruption has disordered me.—I
venerate the memory of my grandfather.—Well! sirs,
he held this estate; he held it by his good sword
and by the favour of St. Nicholas—so did my father;
and so, sirs, will I, come what come will.—But Frederic,
my lord, is nearest in blood.—I have consented to put
my title to the issue of the sword—does that imply a
vicious title?—I might have asked, where is Frederic,
your lord? Report speaks him dead in captivity. You
say, your actions say, he lives—I question it not—I
might, sirs; I might, but I do not. Other princes would
bid Frederic take his inheritance by force if he can:
they would not stake their dignity on a single combat:
they would not submit it to the decision of unknown
mutes!—Pardon me, gentlemen, I am too warm. But
suppose yourselves in my situation: as ye are stout
knights, would it not move your choler to have your
own and the honour of your ancestors called in question?—But to the point: ye require me to deliver up the
Lady Isabella.—Sirs, I must ask if ye are authorised
to receive her?"—The knight nodded—"Receive her!"
continued Manfred; "well, you are authorised to receive her—but, gentle knight, may I ask if you have
full powers?"—The knight nodded.—" 'T is well," said
Manfred. "Then hear what I have to offer.—Ye see,
gentlemen, before you the most unhappy of men (he

began to weep); afford me your compassion; I am entitled to it; indeed I am.   Know, I have lost my only
hope, my joy, the support of my house—Conrad died
yestermorning."—The knights discovered signs of surprise.—"Yes, sirs, fate has disposed of my son. Isabella is at liberty."

"Do you then restore her?" cried the chief knight,
breaking silence.

"Afford me your patience," said Manfred. "I rejoice
to find, by this testimony of your good will, that this
matter may be adjusted without bloodshed. It is no
interest of mine dictates what little I have farther to
say. Ye behold in me a man disgusted with the world;
the loss of my son has weaned me from earthly cares.
Power and greatness have no longer any charms in my
eyes. I wished to transmit the sceptre I had received
from my ancestors with honour to my son—but that is
over! Life itself is so indifferent to me that I accepted
your defiance with joy; a good knight cannot go to the
grave with more satisfaction than when falling in his
vocation. Whatever is the will of Heaven I submit;
for, alas! sirs, I am a man of many sorrows. Manfred
is no object of envy—but no doubt you are acquainted
with my story."—The knight made signs of ignorance,
and seemed curious to have Manfred proceed.—"Is it
possible, sirs," continued the prince, "that my story
should be a secret to you? Have you heard nothing
relating to me and the Princess Hippolita?"—They
shook their heads.—"No! thus then, sirs, it is. You
think me ambitious: ambition, alas! is composed of more
rugged materials. If I were ambitious, I should not for
so many years have been a prey to all the hell of con-
scientious scruples—but I weary your patience: I will
be brief. Know, then, that I have long been troubled
in mind on my union with the Princess Hippolita.—Oh,

sirs, if ye were acquainted with that excellent woman! if ye knew that I adore her like a mistress, and cherish her as a friend—but man was not born for perfect happiness! She shares my scruples, and with her consent I have brought this matter before the church, for we are related within the forbidden degrees. I expect every hour the definitive sentence that must separate us for ever—I am sure you feel for me—I see you do— pardon these tears!"—The knights gazed on each other, wondering where this would end. Manfred continued: —"The death of my son betiding while my soul was under this anxiety, I thought of nothing but resigning my dominions, and retiring for ever from the sight of mankind. My only difficulty was to fix on a successor, who would be tender of my people, and to dispose of the Lady Isabella, who is dear to me as my own blood. I was willing to restore the line of Alfonso, even in his most distant kindred; and though, pardon me, I am satisfied it was his will that Ricardo's lineage should take place of his own relations, yet where was I to search for those relations? I knew of none but Frederic, your lord: he was a captive to the infidels, or dead; and were he living, and at home, would he quit the flourishing state of Vicenza for the inconsiderable principality of Otranto? If he would not, could I bear the thought of seeing a hard unfeeling viceroy set over my poor faithful people?—for, sirs, I love my people, and, thank Heaven, am beloved by them.

"But ye will ask, whither tends this long discourse? briefly, then, thus, sirs. Heaven in your arrival seems to point out a remedy for these difficulties and my misfortunes. The Lady Isabella is at liberty; I shall soon be so—I would submit to any thing for the good of my people—were it not the best, the only way to extinguish the feuds between our families if I was to take the Lady

Isabella to wife—you start—but though Hippolita's
virtues will ever be dear to me, a prince must not consider himself; he is born for his people.''—A servant
at that instant entering the chamber, apprised Manfred
that Jerome and several of his brethren demanded immediate access to him.

The prince, provoked at this interruption, and fearing
that the friar would discover to the strangers that Isabella had taken sanctuary, was going to forbid Jerome's
entrance. But recollecting that he was certainly arrived
to notify the princess's return, Manfred began to excuse himself to the knights for leaving them for a few
moments, but was prevented by the arrival of the
friars. Manfred angrily reprimanded them for their
intrusion, and would have forced them back from the
chamber, but Jerome was too much agitated to be re-
pulsed. He declared aloud the flight of Isabella, with
protestations of his own innocence.

Manfred, distracted at the news, and not less at its
coming to the knowledge of the strangers, uttered nothing but incoherent sentences, now upbraiding the friar,
now apologising to the knights; earnest to know what
was become of Isabella, yet equally afraid of their knowing; impatient to pursue her, yet dreading to have them
join in the pursuit. He offered to despatch messengers in
quest of her,—but the chief knight, no longer keeping
silence, reproached Manfred in bitter terms for his dark
and ambiguous dealing, and demanded the cause of Isabella's first absence from the castle. Manfred, casting
a stern look at Jerome, implying a command of silence,
pretended that on Conrad's death he had placed her in
sanctuary until he could determine how to dispose of
her. Jerome, who trembled for his son's life, did not
dare contradict this falsehood, but one of his brethren,
not under the same anxiety, declared frankly that she

had fled to their church in the preceding night. The prince in vain endeavoured to stop this discovery, which overwhelmed him with shame and confusion.

The principal stranger, amazed at the contradictions he heard, and more than half persuaded that Manfred had secreted the princess, notwithstanding the concern he expressed at her flight, rushing to the door, said, —"Thou traitor-prince! Isabella shall be found." Manfred endeavoured to hold him, but the other knights assisting their comrade, he broke from the prince, and hastened into the court, demanding his attendants. Manfred, finding it vain to divert him from the pursuit, offered to accompany him, and summoning his attendants, and taking Jerome and some of the friars to guide them, they issued from the castle, Manfred privately giving orders to have the knight's company secured, while to the knight he affected to despatch a messenger to require their assistance.

The company had no sooner quitted the castle than Matilda, who felt herself deeply interested for the young peasant, since she had seen him condemned to death in the hall, and whose thoughts had been taken up with concerting measures to save him, was informed by some of the female attendants that Manfred had despatched all his men various ways in pursuit of Isabella. He had in his hurry given this order in general terms, not meaning to extend it to the guard he had set upon Theodore, but forgetting it. The domestics, officious to obey so peremptory a prince, and urged by their own curiosity and love of novelty to join in any precipitate chase, had to a man left the castle. Matilda disengaged herself from her women, stole up to the Black Tower, and unbolting the door, presented herself to the astonished Theodore.

"Young man," said she, "though filial duty and

womanly modesty condemn the step I am taking, yet
holy charity, surmounting all over ties, justifies this act.
Fly; the doors of thy prison are open; my father and his
domestics are absent; but they may soon return. Begone
in safety, and may the angels of heaven direct thy
course!"

"Thou art surely one of those angels!" said the enraptured Theodore; "none but a blessed saint could
speak, could act, could look like thee! May I not know
the name of my divine protectress? Methought thou
namedst thy father. Is it possible? Can Manfred's
blood feel holy pity? Lovely lady, thou answerest not
—but how art thou here thyself? Why dost thou neglect
thy own safety, and waste a thought on a wretch like
Theodore? Let us fly together. The life thou bestowest
shall be dedicated to thy defence."

"Alas! thou mistakest," said Matilda, sighing: "I am
Manfred's daughter, but no dangers await me."

"Amazement!" said Theodore; "but last night I
blessed myself for yielding thee the service thy gracious
compassion so charitably returns me now."

"Still thou art in error," said the princess; "but this
is no time for explanation. Fly, virtuous youth, while
it is in my power to save thee. Should my father return, thou and I both should indeed have cause to
tremble."

"How?" said Theodore, "thinkest thou, charming
maid, that I will accept of life at the hazard of aught
calamitous to thee? Better I endure a thousand deaths."

"I run no risk," said Matilda, "but by thy delay.
Depart; it cannot be known that I assisted thy flight."

"Swear by the saints above," said Theodore, "that
thou canst not be suspected; else here I vow to wait
whatever can befall me."

"Oh, thou art too generous," said Matilda; "but rest assured that no suspicion can alight on me."

"Give me thy beauteous hand in token that thou dost not deceive me," said Theodore; "and let me bathe it with the warm tears of gratitude."

"Forbear," said the princess; "this must not be."

"Alas!" said Theodore, "I have never known but calamity until this hour—perhaps shall never know other fortune again: suffer the chaste raptures of holy gratitude. 'Tis my soul would print its effusions on thy hand."

"Forbear, and be gone," said Matilda; "how would Isabella approve of seeing thee at my feet?"

"Who is Isabella?" said the young man with surprise.

"Ah me! I fear," said the princess, "I am serving a deceitful one;—hast thou forgot thy curiosity this morning?"

"Thy looks, thy actions, all thy beauteous self, seem an emanation of divinity," said Theodore; "but thy words are dark and mysterious:—speak, lady; speak to thy servant's comprehension."

"Thou understandest but too well!" said Matilda. "But once more, I command thee to be gone. Thy blood, which I may preserve, will be on my head if I waste the time in vain discourse."

"I go, lady," said Theodore, "because it is thy will, and because I would not bring the grey hairs of my father with sorrow to the grave. Say but, adored lady, that I have thy gentle pity."

"Stay," said Matilda; "I will conduct thee to the subterraneous vault by which Isabella escaped; it will lead thee to the church of St. Nicholas, where thou mayest take sanctuary."

"What!" said Theodore, "was it another, and not thy

lovely self, that I assisted to find the subterraneous passage?"

"It was," said Matilda; "but ask no more. I tremble to see thee still abide here; fly to the sanctuary."

"To sanctuary!" said Theodore; "no, princess, sanctuaries are for helpless damsels, or for criminals. Theodore's soul is free from guilt, nor will wear the appearance of it. Give me a sword, lady, and thy father shall learn that Theodore scorns an ignominious flight."

"Rash youth!" said Matilda, "thou wouldst not dare to lift thy presumptuous arm against the Prince of Otranto?"

"Not against thy father; indeed, I dare not," said Theodore. "Excuse me, lady; I had forgotten—but could I gaze on thee, and remember thou art sprung from the tyrant Manfred?—but he is thy father, and from this moment my injuries are buried in oblivion." A deep and hollow groan, which seemed to come from above, startled the princess and Theodore. "Good Heaven! we are overheard!" said the princess. They listened, but perceived no farther noise. They both concluded it the effect of pent-up vapours. And the princess, preceding Theodore softly, carried him to her father's armoury, where equipping him with a complete suit, he was conducted by Matilda to the postern-gate.

"Avoid the town," said the princess, "and all the western side of the castle. 'Tis there the search must be making by Manfred and the strangers; but hie thee to the opposite quarter. Yonder, behind that forest to the east, is a chain of rocks, hollowed into a labyrinth of caverns that reach to the sea-coast. There thou mayest lie concealed till thou canst make signs to some vessel to put on shore and take thee off. Go; Heaven be thy guide!—and sometimes in thy prayers remember —Matilda!"

Theodore flung himself at her feet, and seizing her lily hand, which with struggles she suffered him to kiss, he vowed on the earliest opportunity to get himself knighted, and fervently entreated her permission to swear himself eternally her knight. Ere the princess could reply, a clap of thunder was suddenly heard that shook the battlements. Theodore, regardless of the tempest, would have urged his suit, but the princess, dismayed, retreated hastily into the castle, and commanded the youth to be gone with an air that would not be disobeyed. He sighed and retired, but with eyes fixed on the gate, until Matilda closing it put an end to an interview in which the hearts of both had drunk so deeply of a passion which both now tasted for the first time.

Theodore went pensively to the convent, to acquaint his father with his deliverance. There he learned the absence of Jerome, and the pursuit that was making after the Lady Isabella, with some particulars of whose story he now first became acquainted. The generous gallantry of his nature prompted him to wish to assist her; but the monks could lend him no lights to guess at the route she had taken. He was not tempted to wander far in search of her, for the idea of Matilda had imprinted itself so strongly on his heart that he could not bear to absent himself at much distance from her abode. The tenderness Jerome had expressed for him concurred to confirm this reluctance; and he even persuaded himself that filial affection was the chief cause of his hovering between the castle and monastery until Jerome should return at night. Theodore at length determined to repair to the forest that Matilda had pointed out to him. Arriving there, he sought the gloomiest shades, as best suited to the pleasing melancholy that reigned in his mind. In this mood he roved insensibly to the caves which had formerly served as a retreat to hermits and were now reported round the country to be haunted by evil spirits. He recollected to have heard this tradition; and being of a brave and adventurous disposition, he willingly indulged his curiosity in exploring the secret recesses of this labyrinth. He had not penetrated far before he thought he heard the steps of some person who seemed to retreat before him.

Theodore, though firmly grounded in all our holy faith enjoins to be believed, had no apprehension that good men were abandoned without cause to the malice of the powers of darkness. He thought the place more likely to be infested by robbers than by those infernal agents who are reported to molest and bewilder travellers. He had long burned with impatience to approve his valour. Drawing his sabre, he marched sedately onwards, still directing his steps as the imperfect rustling sound before him led the way. The armour he wore was a like indication to the person who avoided him. Theodore, now convinced that he was not mistaken, redoubled his pace, and evidently gained on the person that fled, whose haste increasing, Theodore came up just as a woman fell breathless before him. He hasted to raise her; but her terror was so great that he apprehended she would faint in his arms. He used every gentle word to dispel her alarms, and assured her that far from injuring, he would defend her at the peril of his life. The lady recovering her spirits from his courteous demeanour, and gazing on her protector, said, "Sure, I have heard that voice before!"

"Not to my knowledge," replied Theodore, "unless, as I conjecture, thou art the Lady Isabella."

"Merciful Heaven!" cried she, "thou art not sent in quest of me, art thou?" And saying these words she threw herself at his feet, and besought him not to deliver her up to Manfred.

"To Manfred!" cried Theodore; "no, lady, I have once already delivered thee from his tyranny, and it shall fare hard with me now but I will place thee out of the reach of his daring."

"Is it possible," said she, "that thou shouldst be the generous unknown whom I met last night in the vault of the castle? Sure thou art not a mortal, but my guardian angel. On my knees let me thank——"

"Hold, gentle princess," said Theodore, "nor demean thyself before a poor and friendless young man. If Heaven has selected me for thy deliverer, it will accomplish its work, and strengthen my arm in thy cause. But come, lady, we are too near the mouth of the cavern; let us seek its inmost recesses; I can have no tranquillity till I have placed thee beyond the reach of danger."

"Alas, what mean you, sir?" said she. "Though all your actions are noble, though your sentiments speak the purity of your soul, is it fitting that I should accompany you alone in these perplexed retreats? Should we be found together, what would a censorious world think of my conduct?"

"I respect your virtuous delicacy," said Theodore; "nor do you harbour a suspicion that wounds my honour. I meant to conduct you into the most private cavity of these rocks, and then, at the hazard of my life, to guard their entrance against every living thing. Besides, lady," continued he, drawing a deep sigh, "beauteous and all perfect as your form is, and though my wishes are not guiltless of aspiring, know, my soul is dedicated to another; and although——" A sudden noise prevented Theodore from proceeding. They soon distinguished these sounds, "Isabella! what ho! Isabella!"

The trembling princess relapsed into her former agony of fear. Theodore endeavoured to encourage her, but in vain. He assured her he would rather die than suffer her to return under Manfred's power, and begging her to remain concealed, he went forth to prevent the person in search of her from approaching.

At the mouth of the cavern he found an armed knight discoursing with a peasant, who assured him he had seen a lady enter the passes of the rock. The knight was preparing to seek her, when Theodore, placing himself in his way, with his sword drawn, sternly forbade him at his peril to advance.

"And who art thou who darest to cross my way?" said the knight haughtily.

"One who does not dare more than he will perform," said Theodore.

"I seek the Lady Isabella," said the knight, "and understand she has taken refuge among these rocks. Impede me not, or thou wilt repent having provoked my resentment."

"Thy purpose is as odious as thy resentment is contemptible," said Theodore. "Return whence thou camest, or we shall soon know whose resentment is most terrible."

The stranger, who was the principal knight that had arrived from the Marquis of Vicenza, had galloped from Manfred as he was busied in getting information of the princess and giving various orders to prevent her falling into the power of the three knights. Their chief had suspected Manfred of being privy to the princess's absconding, and this insult from a man who, he concluded, was stationed by that prince to secrete her, confirming his suspicions, he made no reply, but discharging a blow with his sabre at Theodore, would soon have removed all obstruction, if Theodore, who took him for one of Manfred's captains, and who had no sooner given the provocation than he prepared to support it, had not received the stroke on his shield. The valour that had so long been smothered in his breast broke forth at once; and he rushed impetuously on the knight, whose pride and wrath were not less powerful incentives to hardy deeds. The combat was furious, but not long: Theodore wounded the knight in three several places, and at last disarmed him, as he fainted by the loss of blood.

The peasant, who had fled on the first onset, had given the alarm to some of Manfred's domestics, who by his orders were dispersed through the forest in pursuit of Isabella. They came up as the knight fell, whom they soon discovered to be the noble stranger. Theodore, notwithstanding his hatred to Manfred, could not behold the victory he had gained without emotions of pity and generosity. But he was more touched when he learned the quality of his adversary, and was informed that he was no retainer, but an enemy of Manfred. He assisted the servants of the latter in disarming the knight, and in endeavouring to stanch the blood that flowed from his wounds. The knight recovering his speech, said, in a faint and faltering voice, "Generous foe, we have both been in an error: I took thee for an instrument of the tyrant. I perceive thou hast made the like mistake: it is too late for excuses—I faint—if Isabella is at hand, call her; I have important secrets to ——"

"He is dying," said one of the attendants. "Has nobody a crucifix about them? Andrea, do thou pray over him."

"Fetch some water," said Theodore, "and pour it

down his throat, while I hasten to the princess." Saying this, he flew to Isabella, and in few words told her modestly that he had been so unfortunate by mistake as to wound a gentleman from her father's court, who wished ere he died to impart something of consequence to her. The princess, who had been transported at hearing the voice of Theodore, as he called to her to come forth, was astonished at what she heard. Suffering herself to be conducted by Theodore, the new proof of whose valour recalled her dispersed spirits, she came where the bleeding knight lay speechless on the ground —but her fears returned when she beheld the domestics of Manfred. She would again have fled if Theodore had not made her observe that they were unarmed, and had not threatened them with instant death if they should dare to seize the princess. The stranger, opening his eyes, and beholding a woman, said, "Art thou— pray tell me truly—art thou Isabella of Vicenza?"

"I am," said she. "Good Heaven restore thee!"

"Then thou —— then thou ——" said the knight, struggling for utterance, "seest—thy father. Give me one ——"

"Oh, amazement! horror! What do I hear? What do I see?" cried Isabella. "My father! you my father! How came you here, sir? For Heaven's sake speak!— Oh, run for help, or he will expire!"

" 'Tis most true," said the wounded knight, exerting all his force; "I am Frederic thy father—yes, I came to deliver thee—it will not be.—Give me a parting kiss, and take ——"

"Sir," said Theodore, "do not exhaust yourself; suffer us to convey you to the castle."

"To the castle!" said Isabella; "is there no help nearer than the castle? Would you expose my father to the tyrant? If he goes thither, I cannot accompany him—and yet, can I leave him?"

"My child," said Frederic, "it matters not to me whither I am carried; a few minutes will place me beyond danger—but while I have eyes to dote on thee, forsake me not, dear Isabella! This brave knight, I know not who he is, will protect thy innocence.—Sir, you will not abandon my child, will you?"

Theodore, shedding tears over his victim, and vowing to guard the princess at the expense of his life, persuaded Frederic to suffer himself to be conducted to the castle. They placed him on a horse belonging to one of the domestics, after binding up his wounds as well as they were able. Theodore marched by his side, and the afflicted Isabella, who could not bear to quit him, followed mournfully behind.

CHAPTER IV

THE sorrowful troop no sooner arrived at the castle than they were met by Hippolita and Matilda, whom Isabella had sent one of the domestics before to advertise of their approach. The ladies causing Frederic to be conveyed into the nearest chamber, retired, while the surgeons examined his wounds. Matilda blushed at seeing Theodore and Isabella together, but endeavoured to conceal it by embracing the latter, and condoling with her on her father's mischance. The surgeons soon came to acquaint Hippolita that none of the marquis's wounds were dangerous, and that he was desirous of seeing his daughter and the princesses. Theodore, under pretence of expressing his joy at being freed from his apprehensions of the combat being fatal to Frederic, could not resist the impulse of following Matilda. Her eyes were so often cast down on meeting his that Isabella, who regarded Theodore as attentively as he gazed on Matilda, soon divined who the object was that he had told her in the cave engaged his affections. While this mute scene passed, Hippolita demanded of Frederic the cause of his having taken that mysterious course for reclaiming his daughter, and threw in various apologies to excuse her lord for the match contracted between their children. Frederic, however incensed against Manfred, was not insensible to the courtesy and benevolence of Hippolita, but he was still more struck with the lovely form of Matilda. Wishing to detain them by his bedside, he informed Hippolita of his story. He told her that while prisoner to the infidel, he had dreamed that his daughter, of whom he had learned no news since his captivity, was detained in a castle where she was in danger of the most dreadful misfortunes; and that if he obtained his liberty, and repaired to a wood near Joppa, he would learn more. Alarmed at this dream, and incapable of obeying the direction given by it, his chains became more grievous than ever. But while his thoughts were occupied on the means of obtaining his liberty, he received the agreeable news that the confederate princes, who were warring in Palestine, had paid his ransom. He instantly set out for the wood that had been marked in his dream. For three days he and has attendants had wandered in the forest without seeing a human form, but on the evening of the third they came to a cell in which they found a venerable hermit in the agonies of death. Applying rich cordials, they brought the saint-like man to his speech. "My sons," said he, "I am bounden to your charity—but it is in vain—I am going to my eternal rest—yet I die with the satisfaction of performing the will of Heaven.

When first I repaired to this solitude, after seeing my country become a prey to unbelievers—it is, alas! above fifty years since I was witness to that dreadful scene—St. Nicholas appeared to me and revealed a secret which he bade me never disclose to mortal man but on my death-bed. This is that tremendous hour, and ye are no doubt the chosen warriors to whom I was ordered to reveal my trust. As soon as ye have done the last offices to this wretched corse, dig under the seventh tree on the left hand of this poor cave, and your pains will —— Oh, good Heaven, receive my soul!" With those words the devout man breathed his last.

"By break of day," continued Frederic, "when we had committed the holy relics to earth, we dug according to direction; but what was our astonishment, when, about the depth of six feet, we discovered an enormous sabre—the very weapon yonder in the court. On the blade, which was then partly out of the scabbard, though since closed by our efforts in removing it, were written the following lines—No; excuse me, madam," added the marquis, turning to Hippolita, "if I forbear to repeat them; I respect your sex and rank, and would not be guilty of offending your ear with sounds injurious to aught that is dear to you."

He paused—Hippolita trembled. She did not doubt but Frederic was destined by Heaven to accomplish the fate that seemed to threaten her house. Looking with anxious fondness at Matilda, a silent tear stole down her cheek; but recollecting herself, she said, "Proceed, my lord, Heaven does nothing in vain; mortals must receive its divine behests with lowliness and submission. It is our part to deprecate its wrath, or bow to its decrees. Repeat the sentence, my lord; we listen resigned."

Frederic was grieved that he had proceeded so far. The dignity and patient firmness of Hippolita penetrated him with respect; and the tender, silent affection with which the princess and her daughter regarded each other melted him almost to tears. Yet apprehensive that his forbearance to obey would be more alarming, he repeated in a faltering and low voice the following lines:—

> Where'er a casque that suits this sword is found,
> With perils is thy daughter compass'd round;
> Alfonso's blood alone can save the maid,
> And quiet a long restless prince's shade.

"What is there in these lines," said Theodore, impatiently, "that affects these princesses? Why were they to be shocked by a mysterious delicacy that has so little foundation?"

"Your words are rude, young man," said the marquis; "and though fortune has favoured you once ——"

"My honoured lord," said Isabella, who resented Theodore's warmth, which she perceived was dictated by his sentiments for Matilda, "discompose not yourself for the glozing of a peasant's son. He forgets the reverence he owes you, but he is not accustomed ——"

Hippolita, concerned at the heat that had arisen, checked Theodore for his boldness, but with an air acknowledging his zeal, and changing the conversation, demanded of Frederic where he had left her lord?

As the marquis was going to reply, they heard a noise without, and rising to enquire the cause, Manfred, Jerome, and part of the troop, who had met an imperfect rumour of what had happened, entered the chamber. Manfred advanced hastily towards Frederic's bed to condole with him on his misfortune and to learn the

circumstances of the combat, when, starting in an agony
of terror and amazement, he cried,—

"Ah! what are thou? Thou dreadful spectre! Is my
hour come?"

"My dearest, gracious lord," cried Hippolita, clasp-
ing him in her arms, "what is it you see? Why do you
fix your eyeballs thus?"

"What," cried Manfred, breathless, "dost thou see
nothing, Hippolita? Is this ghastly phantom sent to
me alone—to me, who did not——"

"For mercy's sweetest self, my lord," said Hippolita,
"resume your soul; command your reason. There are
none here but us, your friends."

"What, is not that Alfonso?" cried Manfred; "dost
thou not see him? Can it be my brain's delirium?"

"This! my lord," said Hippolita: "this is Theodore,
the youth who has been so unfortunate."

"Theodore," said Manfred mournfully, and striking
his forehead—"Theodore, or a phantom, he has un-
hinged the soul of Manfred. But how comes he here?
and how comes he in armour?"

"I believe he went in search of Isabella," said Hippolita.

"Of Isabella," said Manfred, relapsing into rage.
"Yes, yes, that is not doubtful—but how did he escape
from durance, in which I left him? Was it Isabella or
this hypocritical old friar that procured his enlarge-
ment?"

"And would a parent be criminal, my lord," said
Theodore, "if he meditated the deliverance of his child?"

Jerome, amazed to hear himself in a manner accused
by his son, and without foundation, knew not what to
think. He could not comprehend how Theodore had
escaped, how he came to be armed and to encounter
Frederic. Still he would not venture to ask any ques-

tions that might tend to inflame Manfred's wrath against his son. Jerome's silence convinced Manfred that he had contrived Theodore's release.

"And is it thus, thou ungrateful old man," said the prince, addressing himself to the friar, "that thou repayest mine and Hippolita's bounties? And not content with traversing my heart's nearest wishes, thou armest thy bastard and bringest him into my own castle to insult me!"

"My lord," said Theodore, "you wrong my father; nor he nor I are capable of harbouring a thought against your peace. Is it insolence thus to surrender myself to your highness's pleasure?" added he, laying his sword respectfully at Manfred's feet. "Behold my bosom; strike, my lord, if you suspect that a disloyal thought is lodged there. There is not a sentiment engraven on my heart that does not venerate you and yours."

The grace and fervour with which Theodore uttered these words interested every person present in his favour. Even Manfred was touched; yet still possessed with his resemblance to Alfonso, his admiration was dashed with secret horror.

"Rise," said he; "thy life is not my present purpose. But tell me thy history, and how thou camest connected with this old traitor here."

"My lord——" said Jerome, eagerly.

"Peace! imposter," said Manfred; "I will not have him prompted."

"My lord," said Theodore, "I want no assistance; my story is very brief. I was carried at five years of age to Algiers with my mother, who had been taken by corsairs from the coast of Sicily. She died of grief in less than a twelvemonth." The tears gushed from Jerome's eyes, on whose countenance a thousand anxious passions stood expressed. "Before she died," continued Theodore, "she bound a writing about my arm under my garments, which told me I was the son of the Count Falconara."

"It is most true," said Jerome; "I am that wretched father."

"Again I enjoin thee silence," said Manfred. "Proceed."

"I remained in slavery," said Theodore, "until within these two years, when, attending on my master in his cruises, I was delivered by a Christian vessel which overpowered the pirate, and discovering myself to the captain, he generously put me on shore in Sicily. But, alas! instead of finding a father, I learned that his estate, which was situated on the coast, had during his absence been laid waste by the rover who had carried my mother and me into captivity; that his castle had been burnt to the ground, and that my father, on his return, had sold what remained, and was retired into religion in the kingdom of Naples, but where, no man could inform me. Destitute and friendless, hopeless almost of attaining the transport of a parent's embrace, I took the first opportunity of setting sail for Naples, from whence, within these six days, I wandered into this province, still supporting myself by the labour of my hands; nor until yester-morn did I believe that Heaven had reserved any lot for me but peace of mind and contented poverty. This, my lord, is Theodore's story. I am blessed beyond my hope in finding a father; I am unfortunate beyond my desert in having incurred your highness's displeasure."

He ceased. A murmur of approbation gently arose from the audience.

"This is not all," said Frederic. "I am bound in honour to add what he suppresses. Though he is modest, I must be generous—he is one of the bravest youths on Christian ground. He is warm too; and from the short knowledge I have of him, I will pledge myself for his veracity; if what he reports of himself were not true, he would not utter it.—And for me, youth, I honour a frankness which becomes thy birth. But now, and thou didst offend me; yet the noble blood which flows in thy veins may well be allowed to boil out, when it has so recently traced itself to its source.—Come, my lord," turning to Manfred, "if I can pardon him, surely you may: it is not the youth's fault if you took him for a spectre."

This bitter taunt galled the soul of Manfred. "If beings from another world," replied he haughtily, "have power to impress my mind with awe, it is more than living man can do; nor could a stripling's arm ——"

"My lord," interrupted Hippolita, "your guest has occasion for repose; shall we not leave him to his rest?" Saying this, and taking Manfred by the hand, she took leave of Frederic and led the company forth. The prince, not sorry to quit a conversation which recalled to mind the discovery he had made of his most secret sensations, suffered himself to be conducted to his own apartment, after permitting Theodore, though under engagement to return to the castle on the morrow (a condition the young man gladly accepted), to retire with his father to the convent. Matilda and Isabella were too much occupied with their own reflections, and too little content with each other, to wish for farther converse that night. They separated, each to her chamber, with more expressions of ceremony and fewer of affection than had passed between them since their childhood.

If they parted with small cordiality, they did but meet with greater impatience, as soon as the sun was risen. Their minds were in a situation that excluded sleep, and each recollected a thousand questions which she wished she had put to the other over night. Matilda reflected that Isabella had been twice delivered by Theodore in very critical situations, which she could not believe accidental. His eyes, it was true, had been fixed on her in Frederic's chamber; but that might have been to disguise his passion for Isabella from the fathers of both. It were better to clear this up. She wished to know the truth, lest she should wrong her friend by entertaining a passion for Isabella's lover. Thus jealousy prompted, and at the same time borrowed, an excuse from friendship to justify its curiosity.

Isabella, not less restless, had better foundation for her suspicions. Both Theodore's tongue and eyes had told her his heart was engaged—it was true—yet perhaps Matilda might not correspond to his passion; she had ever appeared insensible to love: all her thoughts were set on Heaven. "Why did I dissuade her?" said Isabella to herself; "I am punished for my generosity. But when did they meet? where? It cannot be. I have deceived myself; perhaps last night was the first time they ever beheld each other; it must be some other object that has prepossessed his affections. If it is, I am not so unhappy as I thought. If it is not my friend Matilda—how! can I stoop to wish for the affection of a man who rudely and unnecessarily acquainted me with his indifference—and that at the very moment in which common courtesy demanded at least expressions of civility? I will go to my dear Matilda, who will confirm me in this becoming pride. Man is false—I will advise with her on taking the veil: she will rejoice to find me in this disposition, and I will acquaint her that I no longer oppose her inclination for the cloister." In this frame of mind, and determined to open her heart entirely to Matilda, she went to that princess's chamber,

whom she found already dressed, and leaning pensively
on her arm. This attitude, so correspondent to what
she felt herself, revived Isabella's suspicions, and destroyed the confidence she had purposed to place in her
friend. They blushed at meeting, and were too much
novices to disguise their sensations with address. After
some unmeaning questions and replies, Matilda demanded of Isabella the cause of her flight. The latter,
who had almost forgotten Manfred's passion, so entirely
was she occupied by her own, concluding that Matilda
referred to her last escape from the convent, which
had occasioned the events of the preceding evening,
replied, "Martelli brought word to the convent that your
mother was dead ———"

"Oh!" said Matilda, interrupting her, "Bianca has
explained that mistake to me: on seeing me faint, she
cried out, 'The princess is dead'; and Martelli, who had
come for the usual dole to the castle ———"

"And what made you faint?" said Isabella, indifferent
to the rest.

Matilda blushed, and stammered, "My father—he
was sitting in judgment on a criminal."

"What criminal?" said Isabella, eagerly.

"A young man," said Matilda:—"I believe—I think
it was that young man that ———"

"What, Theodore?" said Isabella.

"Yes," answered she; "I never saw him before; I
do not know how he had offended my father—but as he
has been of service to you, I am glad my lord has pardoned him."

"Served me!" replied Isabella; "do you term it serving me, to wound my father, and almost occasion his
death? Though it is but since yesterday that I am
blessed with knowing a parent, I hope Matilda does not
think I am such a stranger to filial tenderness as not to

resent the boldness of that audacious youth, and that it is impossible for me ever to feel any affection for one who dared to lift his arm against the author of my being. No, Matilda, my heart abhors him, and if you still retain the friendship for me that you have vowed from your infancy, you will detest the man who has been on the point of making me miserable for ever."

Matilda held down her head, and replied, "I hope my dearest Isabella does not doubt her Matilda's friendship. I never beheld that youth until yesterday; he is almost a stranger to me; but as the surgeons have pronounced your father out of danger, you ought not to harbour uncharitable resentment against one who, I am persuaded, did not know the marquis was related to you."

"You plead his cause very pathetically," said Isabella, "considering he is so much a stranger to you! I am mistaken, or he returns your charity."

"What mean you?" said Matilda.

"Nothing," said Isabella, repenting that she had given Matilda a hint of Theodore's inclination for her. Then, changing the discourse, she asked Matilda what occasioned Manfred to take Theodore for a spectre?

"Bless me," said Matilda, "did you not observe his extreme resemblance to the portrait of Alfonso in the gallery? I took notice of it to Bianca even before I saw him in armour; but with the helmet on he is the very image of that picture."

"I do not much observe pictures," said Isabella: "much less have I examined this young man so attentively as you seem to have done. Ah, Matilda, your heart is in danger; but let me warn you as a friend—he has owned to me that he is in love. It cannot be with you, for yesterday was the first time you ever met—was it not?"

"Certainly," replied Matilda; "but why does my dearest Isabella conclude from anything I have said that"—she paused—then continuing: "he saw you first, and I am far from having the vanity to think that my little portion of charms could engage a heart devoted to you—may you be happy, Isabella, whatever is the fate of Matilda!"

"My lovely friend," said Isabella, whose heart was too honest to resist a kind expression, "it is you that Theodore admires. I saw it; I am persuaded of it; nor shall a thought of my own happiness suffer me to interfere with yours." This frankness drew tears from the gentle Matilda, and jealousy, that for a moment had raised a coolness between these amiable maidens, soon gave way to the natural sincerity and candour of their souls. Each confessed to the other the impression that Theodore had made on her; and this confidence was followed by a struggle of generosity, each insisting on yielding her claim to her friend. At length the dignity of Isabella's virtue reminding her of the preference which Theodore had almost declared for her rival, made her determine to conquer her passion and cede the beloved object to her friend.

During this contest of amity, Hippolita entered her daughter's chamber.

"Madam," said she to Isabella, "you have so much tenderness for Matilda, and interest yourself so kindly in whatever affects our wretched house, that I can have no secrets with my child which are not proper for you to hear." The princesses were all attention and anxiety.

"Know then, madam," continued Hippolita, "and you, my dearest Matilda, that being convinced by all the events of these two last ominous days that Heaven purposes the sceptre of Otranto should pass from Manfred's hands into those of the Marquis Frederic; I have been perhaps inspired with the thought of averting our total destruction by the union of our rival houses. With this view I have been proposing to Manfred, my lord, to tender this dear, dear child to Frederic your father."

"Me to lord Frederic!" cried Matilda. "Good heavens! my gracious mother, and have you named it to my father?"

"I have," said Hippolita: "he listened benignly to my proposal, and is gone to break it to the marquis."

"Ah! wretched princess," cried Isabella, "what hast thou done? what ruin has thy inadvertent goodness been preparing for thyself, for me, and for Matilda!"

"Ruin for me, to you, and to my child!" said Hippolita; "what can this mean?"

"Alas!" said Isabella, "the purity of your own heart prevents your seeing the depravity of others. Manfred, your lord, that impious man ——"

"Hold!" said Hippolita, "you must not, in my presence, young lady, mention Manfred with disrespect; he is my lord and husband, and ——"

"Will not long be so," said Isabella, "if his wicked purposes can be carried into execution."

"This language amazes me," said Hippolita. "Your feeling, Isabella, is warm, but until this hour I never knew it betray you into intemperance. What deed of Manfred authorises you to treat him as a murderer, an assassin?"

"Thou virtuous, and too credulous princess!" replied Isabella; "it is not thy life he aims at—it is to separate himself from thee! to divorce thee! to ——"

"To divorce me!" "To divorce my mother!" cried Hippolita and Matilda at once.

"Yes," said Isabella; "and, to complete his crime, he meditates—I cannot speak it!"

"What can surpass what thou hast already uttered?" said Matilda.

Hippolita was silent. Grief choked her speech; and the recollection of Manfred's late ambiguous discourses confirmed what she heard.

"Excellent, dear lady!—madam! mother!" cried Isabella, flinging herself at Hippolita's feet in a transport of passion; "trust me, believe me, I will die a thousand deaths sooner than consent to injure you, than yield to so odious ——"

"Oh, this is too much!" cried Hippolita. "What crimes does one crime suggest! Rise, dear Isabella; I do not doubt your virtue. Oh, Matilda, this stroke is too heavy for thee! Weep not, my child; and not a murmur, I charge thee. Remember, he is *thy* father still!"

"But you are my mother, too," said Matilda, fervently; "and *you* are virtuous, *you* are guiltless! Oh, must not I, must not I complain?"

"You must not," said Hippolita; "come, all will be well. Manfred, in the agony for the loss of thy brother, knew not what he said; perhaps Isabella misunderstood him. His heart is good—and, my child, thou knowest not all. There is a destiny hangs over us; the hand of Providence is stretched out. Oh, could I but save thee from the wreck.—Yes," continued she, in a firmer tone, "perhaps the sacrifice of myself may atone for all; I will go and offer myself to this divorce—it boots not what becomes of me. I will withdraw into the neighbouring monastery and waste the remainder of life in prayers and tears for my child and—the prince."

"Thou art much too good for this world," said Isabella, "as Manfred is execrable—but think not, lady, that thy weakness shall determine for me. I swear, hear me all ye angels ——"

"Stop, I adjure thee," cried Hippolita; "remember

thou dost not depend on thyself; thou hast a
father ——"

"My father is too pious, too noble," interrupted Isabella, "to command an impious deed. But should he
command it, can a father enjoin a cursed act? I was
contracted to the son; can I wed the father?—No,
madam, no; force should not drag me to Manfred's
hated bed. I loathe him, I abhor him. Divine and
human laws forbid; and, my friend, my dearest Matilda,
would I wound her tender soul by injuring her adored
mother? my own mother—I never have known another."

"Oh, she is the mother of both," cried Matilda; "can
we, can we, Isabella, adore her too much?"

"My lovely children," said the touched Hippolita,
"your tenderness overpowers me; but I must not give
way to it. It is not ours to make election for ourselves;
Heaven, our fathers, and our husbands, must decide for
us. Have patience until you hear what Manfred and
Frederic have determined. If the marquis accepts Matilda's hand, I know she will readily obey. Heaven may
interpose and prevent the rest. What means my
child?" continued she, seeing Matilda fall at her feet
with a flood of speechless tears.—"But no; answer me
not, my daughter; I must not hear a word against the
pleasure of thy father."

"Oh, doubt not my obedience, my dreadful obedience
to him and to you!" said Matilda. "But can I, most
respected of women, can I experience all this tenderness, this world of goodness, and conceal a thought
from the best of mothers?"

"What art thou going to utter?" said Isabella, trembling. "Recollect thyself, Matilda."

"No, Isabella," said the princess, "I should not deserve this incomparable parent, if the inmost recesses
of my soul harboured a thought without her permission

—nay, I have offended her; I have suffered a passion to
enter my heart without her avowal; but here I disclaim
it; here I vow to Heaven and her——"

"My child! my child!" said Hippolita, "what words
are these? what new calamities has fate in store for us?
Thou, a passion! Thou, in this hour of destruction!"

"Oh, I see all my guilt," said Matilda. "I abhor
myself, if I cost my mother a pang; she is the dearest
thing I have on earth. Oh, I will never, never behold
him more!"

"Isabella," said Hippolita, "thou art conscious to this
unhappy secret, whatever it is. Speak!"

"What!" cried Matilda, "have I so forfeited my
mother's love, that she will not permit me even to speak
my own guilt? Oh, wretched, wretched Matilda!"

"Thou art too cruel," said Isabella to Hippolita;
"canst thou behold this anguish of a virtuous mind, and
not commiserate it?"

"Not pity my child!" said Hippolita, catching Matilda in her arms. "Oh, I know she is good; she is all
virtue, all tenderness and duty. I do forgive thee, my
excellent, my only hope!"

The princesses then revealed to Hippolita their mutual inclination for Theodore, and the purpose of Isabella to resign him to Matilda. Hippolita blamed their
imprudence, and showed them the improbability that
either father would consent to bestow his heiress on so
poor a man, though nobly born. Some comfort it gave
her to find their passion of so recent a date, and that
Theodore had had but little cause to suspect it in either.
She strictly enjoined them to avoid all correspondence
with him. This Matilda fervently promised; but Isabella, who flattered herself that she meant no more than
to promote his union with her friend, could not determine to avoid him, and made no reply.

"I will go to the convent," said Hippolita, "and order new masses to be said for a deliverance from these calamities."

"Oh, my mother," said Matilda, "you mean to quit us: you mean to take sanctuary, and to give my father an opportunity of pursuing his fatal intentions. Alas! on my knees I supplicate you to forbear. Will you leave me a prey to Frederic? I will follow you to the convent."

"Be at peace, my child," said Hippolita; "I will return instantly. I will never abandon thee until I know it is the will of Heaven, and for thy benefit."

"Do not deceive me," said Matilda. "I will not marry Frederic until thou commandest it. Alas! what will become of me?"

"Why that exclamation?" said Hippolita. "I have promised thee to return."

"Ah, my mother," replied Matilda; "stay and save me from myself. A frown from thee can do more than all my father's severity. I have given away my heart, and you alone can make me recall it."

"No more," said Hippolita; "thou must not relapse, Matilda."

"I can quit Theodore," said she, "but must I wed another? Let me attend thee to the altar, and shut myself from the world for ever."

"Thy fate depends on thy father," said Hippolita: "I have ill bestowed my tenderness if it has taught thee to revere aught beyond him. Adieu! my child, I go to pray for thee."

Hippolita's real purpose was to demand of Jerome whether in conscience she might not consent to the divorce. She had oft urged Manfred to resign the principality, which the delicacy of her conscience rendered an hourly burden to her. These scruples concurred to make the separation from her husband appear less dreadful to her than it would have seemed in any other situation.

Jerome, at quitting the castle overnight, had questioned Theodore severely why he had accused him to Manfred of being privy to his escape. Theodore owned it had been with design to prevent Manfred's suspicion from alighting on Matilda; and added, the holiness of Jerome's life and character secured him from the tyrant's wrath. Jerome was heartily grieved to discover his son's inclination for that princess, and leaving him to his rest, promised in the morning to acquaint him with important reasons for conquering his passion. Theodore, like Isabella, was too recently acquainted with parental authority to submit to its decisions against the impulse of his heart. He had little curiosity to learn the friar's reasons, and less disposition to obey them. The lovely Matilda had made stronger impressions on him than filial affection. All night he pleased himself with visions of love, and it was not till late after the morning-office that he recollected the friar's commands to attend him at Alfonso's tomb.

"Young man," said Jerome, when he saw him, "this tardiness does not please me. Have a father's commands already so little weight?"

Theodore made awkward excuses, and attributed his delay to having overslept himself.

"And on whom were thy dreams employed?" said the friar sternly. His son blushed. "Come, come," resumed the friar, "inconsiderate youth, this must not be; eradicate this guilty passion from thy breast."

"Guilty passion!" cried Theodore: "can guilt dwell with innocent beauty and virtuous modesty?"

"It is sinful," replied the friar, "to cherish those whom Heaven has doomed to destruction. A tyrant's

THE CASTLE OF OTRANTO 99

race must be swept from the earth to the third and fourth generation."

"Will Heaven visit the innocent for the crimes of the guilty?" said Theodore. "The fair Matilda has virtues enough ——"

"To undo thee," interrupted Jerome. "Hast thou so soon forgotten that twice the savage Manfred has pronounced thy sentence?"

"Nor have I forgotten, sir," said Theodore, "that the charity of his daughter delivered me from his power. I can forget injuries, but never benefits."

"The injuries thou hast received from Manfred's race," said the friar, "are beyond what thou canst conceive. Reply not, but view this holy image! Beneath this marble monument rest the ashes of the good Alfonso, a prince adorned with every virtue, the father of his people, the delight of mankind! Kneel, headstrong boy, and list while a father unfolds a tale of horror that will expel every sentiment from thy soul but sensations of sacred vengeance. Alfonso! much injured prince! let thy unsatisfied shade sit awful on the troubled air while these trembling lips —— Ha! who comes there?"

"The most wretched of women," said Hippolita, entering the choir. "Good father, art thou at leisure? But why this kneeling youth? What means the horror imprinted on each countenance? Why at this venerable tomb?—alas! hast thou seen aught?"

"We were pouring forth our orisons to Heaven," replied the friar, with some confusion, "to put an end to the woes of this deplorable province. Join with us, lady; thy spotless soul may obtain an exemption from the judgments which the portents of these days but too speakingly denounce against thy house."

"I pray fervently to Heaven to divert them," said the

pious princess. "Thou knowest it has been the occupation of my life to wrest a blessing for my lord and my harmless children. One, alas! is taken from me; would Heaven but hear me for my poor Matilda! Father, intercede for her."

"Every heart will bless her!" cried Theodore with rapture.

"Be dumb, rash youth," said Jerome. "And thou, fond princess, contend not with the powers above. The Lord giveth, and the Lord taketh away; bless his holy name, and submit to his decrees."

"I do most devoutly," said Hippolita; "but will he not spare my only comfort? Must Matilda perish too? —Ah, father, I came—but dismiss thy son. No ear but thine must hear what I have to utter."

"May Heaven grant thy every wish, most excellent princess!" said Theodore, retiring. Jerome frowned.

Hippolita then acquainted the friar with a proposal she had suggested to Manfred, his approbation of it, and the tender of Matilda that he was gone to make to Frederic. Jerome could not conceal his dislike of the motion, which he covered under pretence of the improbability that Frederic, the nearest of blood to Alfonso, and who was come to claim his succession, would yield to an alliance with the usurper of his right. But nothing could equal the perplexity of the friar, when Hippolita confessed her readiness not to oppose the separation, and demanded his opinion on the legality of her acquiescence. The friar catched eagerly at her request of his advice; and without explaining his aversion to the proposed marriage of Manfred and Isabella, he painted to Hippolita in the most alarming colours the sinfulness of her consent, denounced judgments against her if she complied, and enjoined her in the severest terms to treat any such proposition with every mark of indignation and refusal.

Manfred in the mean time had broken his purpose to Frederic, and proposed the double marriage. That weak prince, who had been struck with the charms of Matilda, listened but too eagerly to the offer. He forgot his enmity to Manfred, whom he saw but little hope of dispossessing by force; and flattering himself that no issue might succeed from the union of his daughter with the tyrant, he looked upon his own succession to the principality as facilitated by wedding Matilda. He made faint opposition to the proposal; affecting, for form only, not to acquiesce unless Hippolita should consent to the divorce. Manfred took that upon himself. Transported with his success, and impatient to see himself in a situation to expect sons, he hastened to his wife's apartment, determined to extort her compliance. He learned with indignation that she was absent at the convent. His guilt suggested to him that she had probably been informed by Isabella of his purpose. He doubted whether her retirement to the convent did not import an intention of remaining there until she could raise obstacles to their divorce; and the suspicions he had already entertained of Jerome made him apprehend that the friar would not only traverse his views, but might have inspired Hippolita with the resolution of taking sanctuary. Impatient to unravel this clue, and to defeat its success, Manfred hastened to the convent, and arrived there as the friar was earnestly exhorting the princess never to yield to the divorce.

"Madam," said Manfred, "what business drew you hither? why did you not await my return from the marquis?"

"I came to implore a blessing on your councils," replied Hippolita.

"My councils do not need a friar's intervention," said Manfred; "and of all men living is that hoary traitor the only one whom you delight to confer with?"

"Profane prince!" said Jerome; "is it at the altar thou choosest to insult the servants of the altar?—but, Manfred, thy impious schemes are known. Heaven and this virtuous lady know them:—nay, frown not, prince. The church despises thy menaces. Her thunders will be heard above thy wrath. Dare to proceed in thy cursed purpose of a divorce, until her sentence be known, and here I launch her anathema at thy head."

"Audacious rebel!" said Manfred, endeavouring to conceal the awe with which the friar's words inspired him; "dost thou presume to threaten thy lawful prince?"

"Thou art no lawful prince," said Jerome; "thou art no prince:—go, discuss thy claim with Frederic; and when that is done ——"

"It is done," replied Manfred: "Frederic accepts Matilda's hand, and is content to waive his claim, unless I have no male issue."—As he spoke those words, three drops of blood fell from the nose of Alfonso's statue. Manfred turned pale, and the princess sunk on her knees.

"Behold!" said the friar; "mark this miraculous indication that the blood of Alfonso will never mix with that of Manfred!"

"My gracious lord," said Hippolita, "let us submit ourselves to Heaven. Think not thy ever obedient wife rebels against thy authority. I have no will but that of my lord and the church. To that reverend tribunal let us appeal. It does not depend on us to burst the bonds that unite us. If the church shall approve the dissolution of our marriage, be it so—I have but few years, and those of sorrow, to pass. Where can they be worn away so well as at the foot of this altar, in prayers for thine and Matilda's safety?"

"But thou shalt not remain here until then," said Manfred. "Repair with me to the castle, and there I will advise on the proper measure for a divorce. But this meddling friar comes not thither: my hospitable roof shall never more harbour a traitor—and for thy reverence's offspring," continued he, "I banish him from my dominions. He, I ween, is no sacred personage, nor under the protection of the church. Whoever weds Isabella, it shall not be Father Falconara's started-up son."

"They start up," said the friar, "who are suddenly beheld in the seat of lawful princes; but they wither away like the grass, and their place knows them no more."

Manfred, casting a look of scorn at the friar, led Hippolita forth; but at the door of the church whispered one of his attendants to remain concealed about the convent, and bring him instant notice if any one from the castle should repair thither.

CHAPTER V

EVERY reflection which Manfred made on the friar's behaviour conspired to persuade him that Jerome was privy to an amour between Isabella and Theodore. But Jerome's new presumption, so dissonant from his former meekness, suggested still deeper apprehensions. The prince even suspected that the friar depended on some secret support from Frederic, whose arrival coinciding with the novel appearance of Theodore, seemed to bespeak a correspondence. Still more was he troubled

with the resemblance of Theodore to Alfonso's portrait.
The latter he knew had unquestionably died without
issue. Frederic had consented to bestow Isabella on
him. These contradictions agitated his mind with numberless pangs. He saw but two methods of extricating
himself from his difficulties. The one was to resign his
dominions to the marquis.—Pride, ambition, and his
reliance on ancient prophecies, which had pointed out
a possibility of his preserving them to his posterity,
combated that thought. The other was to press his
marriage with Isabella. After long ruminating on these
anxious thoughts as he marched silently with Hippolita
to the castle, he at last discoursed with that princess on
the subject of his disquiet, and used every insinuating
and plausible argument to extract her consent to, even
her promise of promoting, the divorce. Hippolita
needed little persuasion to bend her to his pleasure.
She endeavoured to win him over to the measure of
resigning his dominions, but finding her exhortations
fruitless, she assured him that, as far as her conscience
would allow, she would raise no opposition to a separation, though without better founded scruples than what
he yet alleged, she would not engage to be active in
demanding it.

This compliance, though inadequate, was sufficient to
raise Manfred's hopes. He trusted that his power and
wealth would easily advance his suit at the court of
Rome, whither he resolved to engage Frederic to take
a journey on purpose. That prince had discovered so
much passion for Matilda that Manfred hoped to obtain
all he wished by holding out or withdrawing his daughter's charms, according as the marquis should appear
more or less disposed to co-operate in his views. Even
the absence of Frederic would be a material point

gained, until he could take further measures for his
security.

Dismissing Hippolita to her apartment, he repaired
to that of the marquis, but crossing the great hall,
through which he was to pass, he met Bianca. The
damsel, he knew, was in the confidence of both the
young ladies. It immediately occurred to him to sift
her on the subject of Isabella and Theodore. Calling
her aside into the recess of the oriel window of the
hall, and soothing her with many fair words and promises, he demanded of her whether she knew aught of
the state of Isabella's affections.

"I! my lord! no, my lord—yes, my lord—poor lady!
she is wonderfully alarmed about her father's wounds!
but I tell her he will do well; don't your highness
think so?"

"I do not ask you," replied Manfred, "what she
thinks about her father; but you are in her secrets.
Come, be a good girl, and tell me; is there any young
man—ha!—you understand me."

"Lord bless me! understand your highness, no, not I:
I told her a few vulnerary herbs and repose ——"

"I am not talking," replied the prince, impatiently,
"about her father; I know he will do well."

"Bless me, I rejoice to hear your highness say so;
for though I thought it not right to let my young lady
despond, methought his greatness had a wan look, and
a something—I remember when young Ferdinand was
wounded by the Venetian ——"

"Thou answerest from the point," interrupted Manfred; "but here, take this jewel, perhaps that may fix
thy attention; nay, no reverences: my favour shall not
stop here—come, tell me truly, how stands Isabella's
heart."

"Well, your highness has such a way!" said Bianca,

"to be sure; but can your highness keep a secret? If it should ever come out of your lips ———"

"It shall not; it shall not," cried Manfred.

"Nay, but swear, your highness. By my halidame, if it should ever be known that I said it—why, truth is truth, I do not think my Lady Isabella ever much affectioned my young lord, your son—yet he was a sweet youth, as one should see. I am sure, if I had been a princess—but bless me! I must attend my Lady Matilda; she will marvel what is become of me."

"Stay!" cried Manfred, "thou hast not satisfied my question. Hast thou ever carried any message, any letter?"

"I! good gracious!" cried Bianca; "I carry a letter? I would not to be a queen. I hope your highness thinks, though I am poor, I am honest. Did your highness never hear what Count Marsigli offered me when he came a wooing to my Lady Matilda?"

"I have not leisure," said Manfred, "to listen to thy tales. I do not question thy honesty; but it is thy duty to conceal nothing from me. How long has Isabella been acquainted with Theodore?"

"Nay, there is nothing can escape your highness," said Bianca: "not that I know any thing of the matter. Theodore, to be sure, is a proper young man, and, as my Lady Matilda says, the very image of good Alfonso. Has not your highness remarked it?"

"Yes, yes,—no,—thou torturest me," said Manfred; "where did they meet? when?"

"Who? my Lady Matilda?" said Bianca.

"No, no, not Matilda; Isabella. When did Isabella first become acquainted with this Theodore?"

"Virgin Mary!" said Bianca, "how should I know?"

"Thou dost know," said Manfred, "and I must know; I will."

"Lord! your highness is not jealous of young Theodore!" said Bianca.

"Jealous! no, no: why should I be jealous? perhaps I mean to unite them, if I were sure Isabella would have no repugnance."

"Repugnance! no, I'll warrant her," said Bianca: "he is as comely a youth as ever trod on Christian ground. We are all in love with him; there is not a soul in the castle but would be rejoiced to have him for our prince—I mean, when it shall please Heaven to call your highness to itself."

"Indeed," said Manfred, "has it gone so far? oh, this cursed friar! but I must not lose time:—go, Bianca, attend Isabella; but I charge thee, not a word of what has passed. Find out how she is affected towards Theodore: bring me good news, and that ring has a companion. Wait at the foot of the winding staircase; I am going to visit the marquis, and will talk farther with thee at my return."

Manfred, after some general conversation, desired Frederic to dismiss the two knights his companions, having to talk with him on urgent affairs. As soon as they were alone, he began in artful guise to sound the marquis on the subject of Matilda; and finding him disposed to his wish, he let drop hints on the difficulties that would attend the celebration of their marriage, unless—at that instant Bianca burst into the room with a wildness in her look and gestures that spoke the utmost terror.

"Oh, my lord, my lord!" cried she; "we are all undone! It is come again! it is come again!"

"What is come again?" cried Manfred, amazed.

"Oh, the hand! the giant! the hand!—support me! I am terrified out of my senses," cried Bianca; "I will not sleep in the castle to-night. Where shall I go?

My things may come after me to-morrow—Would I had
been content to wed Francesco!—this comes of
ambition."

"What has terrified thee thus, young woman?" said
the marquis. "Thou art safe here; be not alarmed."

"Oh, your greatness is wonderfully good," said Bianca, "but I dare not—no, pray let me go. I had
rather leave everything behind me than stay another
hour under this roof."

"Go to; thou hast lost thy senses," said Manfred.
"Interrupt us not; we were communing on important
matters. My lord, this wench is subject to fits. Come
with me, Bianca."

"Oh, the saints, no," said Bianca; "for certain it
comes to warn your highness: why should it appear to
me else? I say my prayers morning and evening. Oh,
if your highness had believed Diego! 'Tis the same
hand that he saw the foot to in the gallery chamber.
Father Jerome has often told us the prophecy would be
out one of these days. 'Bianca,' said he, 'mark my
words ——' "

"Thou ravest!" said Manfred in a rage. "Begone,
and keep these fooleries to frighten thy companions."

"What, my lord!" cried Bianca, "do you think I have
seen nothing? Go to the foot of the great stairs yourself—as I live I saw it."

"Saw what? Tell us, fair maid, what thou hast
seen," said Frederic.

"Can your highness listen," said Manfred, "to the
delirium of a silly wench, who has heard stories of apparitions until she believes them?"

"This is more than fancy," said the marquis; "her
terror is too natural and too strongly impressed to be the
work of imagination. Tell us, fair maiden, what it is
has moved thee thus."

"Yes, my lord, thank your greatness," said Bianca. "I believe I look very pale; I shall be better when I have recovered myself. I was going to my Lady Isabella's chamber by his highness's order ——"

"We do not want the circumstances," interrupted Manfred. "Since his highness will have it so, proceed; but be brief."

"Lord! your highness thwarts one so!" replied Bianca. "I fear my hair—I am sure I never in my life— well, as I was telling your greatness, I was going, by his highness's order, to my Lady Isabella's chamber. She lies in the watchet-coloured chamber, on the right hand, one pair of stairs. So when I came to the great stairs, I was looking on his highness's present here ——"

"Grant me patience!" said Manfred; "will this wench never come to the point? What imports it to the marquis, that I gave thee a bauble for thy faithful attendance on my daughter; we want to know what thou sawest."

"I was going to tell your highness," said Bianca, "if you would permit me. So as I was rubbing the ring— I am sure I had not gone up three steps, but I heard the rattling of armour; for all the world such a clatter, as Diego says he heard when the giant turned him about in the gallery-chamber."

"What does she mean, my lord?" said the marquis: "is your castle haunted by giants and goblins?"

"Lord! what, has not your greatness heard the story of the giant in the gallery-chamber?" cried Bianca. "I marvel his highness has not told you—mayhap you do not know there is a prophecy ——"

"This trifling is intolerable," interrupted Manfred. "Let us dismiss this silly wench, my lord; we have more important affairs to discuss."

"By your favour," said Frederic, "these are no trifles.
The enormous sabre I was directed to in the wood, yon
casque, its fellow—are these visions of this poor maid-
en's brain?"

"So Jaquez thinks, may it please your greatness,"
said Bianca. "He says this moon will not be out without our seeing some strange revolution. For my part,
I should not be surprised if it was to happen to-morrow; for, as I was saying, when I heard the clattering
of armour, I was all in a cold sweat. I looked up, and,
if your greatness will believe me, I saw upon the upper-
most banister of the great stairs a hand in armour, as
big, as big—I thought I should have swooned—I never
stopped until I came hither. Would I were well out of
this castle! My Lady Matilda told me but yestermorning that her highness Hippolita knows something."

"Thou art an insolent!" cried Manfred. "Lord marquis, it much misgives me that this scene is concerted
to affront me. Are my own domestics suborned to
spread tales injurious to my honour? Pursue your
claim by manly daring; or let us bury our feuds, as
was proposed, by the intermarriage of our children.
But trust me, it ill becomes a prince of your bearing
to practise on mercenary wenches."

"I scorn your imputation," said Frederic: "until this
hour I never set eyes on this damsel. I have given her
no jewel! My lord, my lord, your conscience, your
guilt, accuses you, and would throw the suspicion on
me; but keep your daughter, and think no more of Isabella. The judgments already fallen on your house
forbid me matching into it."

Manfred, alarmed at the resolute tone in which Frederic delivered these words, endeavoured to pacify him.
Dismissing Bianca, he made such submissions to the
marquis, and threw in such artful encomiums on Ma-

tilda, that Frederic was once more staggered. However, as his passion was of so recent a date, it could not at once surmount the scruples he had conceived. He had gathered enough from Bianca's discourse to persuade him that Heaven declared itself against Manfred. The proposed marriages, too, removed his claim to a distance; and the principality of Otranto was a stronger temptation than the contingent reversion of it with Matilda. Still he would not absolutely recede from his engagements, but purposing to gain time, he demanded of Manfred if it was true in fact that Hippolita consented to the divorce. The prince, transported to find no other obstacle, and depending on his influence over his wife, assured the marquis it was so, and that he might satisfy himself of the truth from her own mouth.

As they were thus discoursing, word was brought that the banquet was prepared. Manfred conducted Frederic to the great hall, where they were received by Hippolita and the young princesses. Manfred placed the marquis next to Matilda, and seated himself between his wife and Isabella. Hippolita comported herself with an easy gravity; but the young ladies were silent and melancholy. Manfred, who was determined to pursue his point with the marquis in the remainder of the evening, pushed on the feast until it waxed late, affecting unrestrained gaiety, and plying Frederic with repeated goblets of wine. The latter, more upon his guard than Manfred wished, declined his frequent challenges on pretence of his late loss of blood, while the prince, to raise his own disordered spirits and to counterfeit unconcern, indulged himself in plentiful draughts, though not to the intoxication of his senses.

The evening being far advanced, the banquet concluded. Manfred would have withdrawn with Frederic; but the latter pleading weakness and want of repose, retired to his chamber, gallantly telling the prince that his daughter should amuse his highness until himself could attend him. Manfred accepted the party, and, to the no small grief of Isabella, accompanied her to her apartment. Matilda waited on her mother, to enjoy the freshness of the evening on the ramparts of the castle.

Soon as the company were dispersed their several ways, Frederic, quitting his chamber, enquired if Hippolita was alone, and was told by one of her attendants, who had not noticed her going forth, that at that hour she generally withdrew to her oratory, where he probably would find her. The marquis, during the repast, had beheld Matilda with increase of passion. He now wished to find Hippolita in the disposition her lord had promised. The portents that had alarmed him were forgotten in his desires. Stealing softly and unobserved to the apartment of Hippolita, he entered it with a resolution to encourage her acquiescence to the divorce, having perceived that Manfred was resolved to make the possession of Isabella an unalterable condition before he would grant Matilda to his wishes.

The marquis was not surprised at the silence that reigned in the princess's apartment. Concluding her, as he had been advertised, in her oratory, he passed on. The door was ajar, the evening gloomy and overcast. Pushing open the door gently, he saw a person kneeling before the altar. As he approached nearer, it seemed not a woman, but one in a long woollen weed, whose back was towards him. The person seemed absorbed in prayer. The marquis was about to return, when the figure, rising, stood some moments fixed in meditation, without regarding him. The marquis, expecting the holy person to come forth, and meaning to excuse his uncivil interruption, said,—

"Reverend father, I sought the Lady Hippolita."

"Hippolita!" replied a hollow voice; "camest thou to this castle to seek Hippolita?" And then the figure, turning slowly round, discovered to Frederic the fleshless jaws and empty sockets of a skeleton, wrapt in a hermit's cowl.

"Angels of peace protect me!" cried Frederic, recoiling.

"Deserve their protection," said the spectre.

Frederic, falling on his knees, adjured the phantom to take pity on him.

"Dost thou not remember me?" said the apparition. "Remember the wood of Joppa!"

"Art thou that holy hermit?" cried Frederic, trembling; "can I do ought for thy eternal peace?"

"Wast thou delivered from bondage," said the spectre, "to pursue carnal delights? Hast thou forgotten the buried sabre, and the behest of Heaven engraven on it?"

"I have not, I have not," said Frederic; "but say, blest spirit, what is thy errand to me? What remains to be done?"

"To forget Matilda," said the apparition, and vanished.

Frederic's blood froze in his veins. For some minutes he remained motionless. Then falling prostrate on his face before the altar, he besought the intercession of every saint for pardon. A flood of tears succeeded to this transport, and the image of the beauteous Matilda rushing, in spite of him, on his thoughts, he lay on the ground in a conflict of penitence and passion. Ere he could recover from this agony of his spirits, the Princess Hippolita, with a taper in her hand, entered the oratory alone. Seeing a man without motion on the floor, she gave a shriek, concluding him dead. Her fright brought Frederic to himself. Rising suddenly, his face bedewed with tears, he would have rushed from her presence; but Hippolita stopping him, conjured him in the most plaintive accents to explain the cause of his disorder, and by what strange chance she had found him there in that posture.

"Ah, virtuous princess!" said the marquis, penetrated with grief, and stopped.

"For the love of Heaven, my lord," said Hippolita, "disclose the cause of this transport! What mean these doleful sounds, this alarming exclamation on my name? What woes has Heaven still in store for the wretched Hippolita?—Yet silent! By every pitying angel, I adjure thee, noble prince," continued she, falling at his feet, "to disclose the purport of what lies at thy heart. I see thou feelest for me; thou feelest the sharp pangs that thou inflictest. Speak, for pity! Does aught thou knowest concern my child?"

"I cannot speak," cried Frederic, bursting from her. "Oh, Matilda!"

Quitting the princess thus abruptly, he hastened to his own apartment. At the door of it he was accosted by Manfred, who, flushed by wine and love, had come to seek him, and to propose to waste some hours of the night in music and revelling. Frederic, offended at an invitation so dissonant from the mood of his soul, pushed him rudely aside, and, entering his chamber, flung the door intemperately against Manfred, and bolted it inwards. The haughty prince, enraged at this unaccountable behaviour, withdrew in a frame of mind capable of the most fatal excesses. As he crossed the court, he was met by the domestic whom he planted at the convent as a spy on Jerome and Theodore. This man, almost breathless with the haste he had made, informed his lord that Theodore and some lady from the castle were at that instant in private conference at the tomb of Alfonso in St. Nicholas's church. He had dogged Theodore thither, but the gloominess of the night had prevented his discovering who the woman was.

Manfred, whose spirits were inflamed, and whom Isabella had driven from her on his urging his passion with too little reserve, did not doubt but the inquietude she had expressed had been occasioned by her impatience to meet Theodore. Provoked by this conjecture, and enraged at her father, he hastened secretly to the great church. Gliding softly between the aisles, and guided by an imperfect gleam of moonshine that shone faintly through the illuminated windows, he stole towards the tomb of Alfonso, to which he was directed by indistinct whispers of the persons he sought. The first sounds he could distinguish were,—

"Does it, alas! depend on me? Manfred will never permit our union."

"No, this shall prevent it!" cried the tyrant, drawing his dagger, and plunging it over her shoulder into the bosom of the person that spoke.

"Ah me, I am slain!" cried Matilda, sinking; "good Heaven receive my soul!"

"Savage, inhuman monster, what hast thou done?" cried Theodore, rushing on him and wrenching his dagger from him.

"Stop, stop thy impious hand!" cried Matilda; "it is my father!"

Manfred, waking as from a trance, beat his breast, twisted his hands in his locks, and endeavoured to recover his dagger from Theodore to despatch himself. Theodore, scarce less distracted, and only mastering the transports of his grief to assist Matilda, had now by his cries drawn some of the monks to his aid. While part of them endeavoured, in concert with the afflicted Theodore, to stop the blood of the dying princess, the rest prevented Manfred from laying violent hands on himself.

Matilda, resigning herself patiently to her fate, acknowledged with looks of grateful love the zeal of Theodore. Yet oft, as her faintness would permit her speech its way, she begged the assistants to comfort her father.

Jerome by this time had learnt the fatal news, and reached the church. His looks seemed to reproach Theodore, but turning to Manfred, he said, "Now, tyrant, behold the completion of woe fulfilled on thy impious and devoted head! The blood of Alfonso cried to Heaven for vengeance; and Heaven has permitted its altar to be polluted by assassination that thou mightest shed thy own blood at the foot of that prince's sepulchre!"

"Cruel man," cried Matilda, "to aggravate the woes of a parent! may Heaven bless my father, and forgive him as I do! My lord, my gracious sire, dost thou forgive thy child? Indeed I came not hither to meet Theodore. I found him praying at this tomb, whither my mother sent me to intercede for thee, for her—dearest father, bless your child, and say you forgive her."

"Forgive thee, murderous monster," cried Manfred; "can assassins forgive? I took thee for Isabella, but Heaven directed my bloody hand to the heart of my child—Oh, Matilda, I cannot utter it: canst thou forgive the blindness of my rage?"

"I can; I do; and may Heaven confirm it," said Matilda; "but while I have life to ask it—oh, my mother, what will she feel! Will you comfort her, my lord, will you not put her away? Indeed she loves you—oh, I am faint; bear me to the castle—can I live to have her close my eyes?"

Theodore and the monks besought her earnestly to suffer herself to be borne into the convent; but her instances were so pressing to be carried to the castle that, placing her on a litter, they conveyed her thither as she requested. Theodore supporting her head with his arm, and hanging over her in an agony of despairing love, still endeavoured to inspire her with hopes of life. Jerome on the other side comforted her with discourses of Heaven, and holding a crucifix before her, which she bathed with innocent tears, prepared her for her passage to immortality. Manfred, plunged in the deepest affliction, followed the litter in despair.

Ere they reached the castle, Hippolita, informed of the dreadful catastrophe, had flown to meet her murdered child; but when she saw the afflicted procession, the mightiness of her grief deprived her of her senses, and she fell lifeless to the earth in a swoon. Isabella and Frederic, who attended her, were overwhelmed in almost equal sorrow. Matilda alone seemed insensible to her own situation; every thought was lost in tenderness for her mother. Ordering the litter to stop, as soon as Hippolita was brought to herself, she asked for her father. He approached, unable to speak. Matilda, seizing his hand and her mother's, locked them in her own, and then clasped them to her heart. Manfred could not support this act of pathetic piety. He dashed himself on the ground, and cursed the day he was born. Isabella, apprehensive that these struggles of passion were more than Matilda could support, took upon herself to order Manfred to be borne to his apartment, while she caused Matilda to be conveyed to the nearest chamber. Hippolita, scarce more alive than her daughter, was regardless of everything but her; but

when the tender Isabella's care would have likewise
removed her, while the surgeons examined Matilda's
wound, she cried,—

"Remove me! never! never! I lived but in her, and
will expire with her." Matilda raised her eyes at her
mother's voice, but closed them again without speaking.
Her sinking pulse and the damp coldness of her hand
soon dispelled all hopes of recovery. Theodore followed the surgeons into the outer chamber, and heard
them pronounce the fatal sentence with a transport
equal to frenzy.

"Since she cannot live mine," cried he, "at least she
shall be mine in death! Father! Jerome! will you not
join our hands?" cried he to the friar, who with the
marquis had accompanied the surgeons.

"What means thy distracted rashness?" said Jerome;
"is this an hour for marriage?"

"It is, it is," cried Theodore; "alas! there is no
other!"

"Young man, thou art too unadvised," said Frederic:
"dost thou think we are to listen to thy fond transports
in this hour of fate? What pretensions hast thou to the
princess?"

"Those of a prince," said Theodore, "of the sovereign
of Otranto. This reverend man, my father, has informed me who I am."

"Thou ravest," said the marquis: "there is no prince
of Otranto but myself, now Manfred, by murder, by
sacrilegious murder, has forfeited all pretensions."

"My lord," said Jerome, assuming an air of command, "he tells you true. It was not my purpose the
secret should have been divulged so soon; but fate
presses onward to its work. What his hot-headed passion has revealed, my tongue confirms. Know, prince,
that when Alfonso set sail for the Holy Land——"

"Is this a season for explanations?" cried Theodore. "Father, come and unite me to the princess; she shall be mine—in every other thing I will dutifully obey you. My life! my adored Matilda!" continued Theodore, rushing back into the inner chamber, "will you not be mine? Will you not bless your ——" Isabella made signs to him to be silent, apprehending the princess was near her end. "What, is she dead?" cried Theodore; "is it possible?" The violence of his exclamations brought Matilda to herself. Lifting up her eyes, she looked around for her mother.

"Life of my soul! I am here," cried Hippolita; "think not I will quit thee!"

"Oh, you are too good," said Matilda; "but weep not for me, my mother! I am going where sorrow never dwells;—Isabella, thou hast loved me; wo't thou not supply my fondness to this dear, dear woman?—Indeed I am faint!"

"Oh, my child, my child!" said Hippolita, in a flood of tears, "can I not withhold thee a moment?"

"It will not be," said Matilda: "commend me to Heaven—where is my father? Forgive him, dearest mother—forgive him my death; it was an error. Oh, I had forgotten, dearest mother, I vowed never to see Theodore more—perhaps that has drawn down this calamity, but it was not intentional—can you pardon me?"

"Oh, wound not my agonising soul," said Hippolita; "thou never couldst offend me. Alas! she faints! help! help!"

"I would say something more," said Matilda, struggling, "but it wonnot be—Isabella—Theodore—for my sake—oh!" She expired. Isabella and her women tore Hippolita from the corse; but Theodore threatened destruction to all who attempted to remove him from it. He printed a thousand kisses on her clay-cold hands, and uttered every expression that despairing love could dictate.

Isabella in the mean time was accompanying the afflicted Hippolita to her apartment; but in the middle of the court they were met by Manfred, who, distracted with his own thoughts, and anxious once more to behold his daughter, was advancing towards the chamber where she lay. As the moon was now at its height, he read in the countenances of this unhappy company the event he dreaded.

"What! is she dead?" cried he in wild confusion. A clap of thunder at that instant shook the castle to its foundations; the earth rocked, and the clank of more than mortal armour was heard behind. Frederic and Jerome thought the last day was at hand. The latter, forcing Theodore along with them, rushed into the court. The moment Theodore appeared, the walls of the castle behind Manfred were thrown down with a mighty force, and the form of Alfonso, dilated to an immense magnitude, appeared in the centre of the ruins.

"Behold in Theodore the true heir of Alfonso!" said the vision; and having pronounced those words, accompanied by a clap of thunder, it ascended solemnly towards Heaven, where, the clouds parting asunder, the form of St. Nicholas was seen, and receiving Alfonso's shade, they were soon wrapt from mortal eyes in a blaze of glory.

The beholders fell prostrate on their faces, acknowledging the divine will. The first that broke silence was Hippolita.

"My lord," said she to the desponding Manfred, "behold the vanity of human greatness! Conrad is gone! Matilda is no more! In Theodore we view the true prince of Otranto. By what miracle he is so, I know not—suffice it to us, our doom is pronounced! Shall we

not—can we but—dedicate the few deplorable hours we
have to live in deprecating the farther wrath of Heaven?
Heaven ejects us; whither can we fly but to yon holy
cells that yet offer us a retreat?"

"Thou guiltless but unhappy woman! unhappy by my
crimes!" replied Manfred; "my heart at last is open to
thy devout admonitions. Oh, could—but it cannot be—
ye are lost in wonder,—let me at last do justice on
myself! To heap shame on my own head is all the satisfaction I have left to offer to offended Heaven. My
story has drawn down these judgments; let my confession atone—but ah! what can atone for usurpation
and a murdered child; a child murdered in a consecrated place? List, sirs, and may this bloody record
be a warning to future tyrants!

"Alfonso, ye all know, died in the Holy Land—ye
would interrupt me—ye would say he came not fairly
to his end—it is most true—why else this bitter cup
which Manfred must drink to the dregs? Ricardo, my
grandfather, was his chamberlain—I would draw a veil
over my ancestor's crimes, but it is in vain! Alfonso
died by poison. A fictitious will declared Ricardo his
heir. His crimes pursued him. Yet he lost no Conrad,
no Matilda! I pay the price of usurpation for all. A
storm overtook him. Haunted by his guilt, he vowed to
St. Nicholas to found a church and two convents, if he
lived to reach Otranto. The sacrifice was accepted;
the saint appeared to him in a dream, and promised
that Ricardo's posterity should reign in Otranto until
the rightful owner should be grown too large to inhabit
the castle, and as long as issue male from Ricardo's
loins should remain to enjoy it. Alas! alas! nor male
nor female, except myself, remains of all his wretched
race!—I have done—the woes of these three days speak
the rest. How this young man can be Alfonso's heir,

I know not—yet I do not doubt it. His are these dominions: I resign them—yet I knew not Alfonso had an heir—I question not the will of Heaven—poverty and prayer must fill up the woeful space until Manfred shall be summoned to Ricardo."

"What remains is my part to declare," said Jerome. "When Alfonso set sail for the Holy Land, he was driven by a storm to the coast of Sicily. The other vessel, which bore Ricardo and his train, as your *lordship* must have heard, was separated from him."

"It is most true," said Manfred; "and the title you give me is more than an outcast can claim—well! be it so—proceed."

Jerome blushed, and continued.

"For three months Lord Alfonso was wind-bound in Sicily. There he became enamoured of a fair virgin, named Victoria. He was too pious to tempt her to forbidden pleasures. They were married. Yet deeming this amour incongruous with the holy vow of arms by which he was bound, he determined to conceal their nuptials until his return from the crusade, when he purposed to seek and acknowledge her for his lawful wife. He left her pregnant. During his absence she was delivered of a daughter; but scarce had she felt a mother's pangs, ere she heard the fatal rumour of her lord's death, and the succession of Ricardo. What could a friendless, helpless woman do? Would her testimony avail?—yet, my lord, I have an authentic writing ——"

"It needs not," said Manfred; "the horrors of these days, the vision we have but now seen, all corroborate thy evidence beyond a thousand parchments. Matilda's death and my expulsion ——"

"Be composed, my lord," said Hippolita; "this holy man did not mean to recall your griefs."

Jerome proceeded.

"I shall not dwell on what is needless. The daughter of which Victoria was delivered was, at her maturity, bestowed in marriage on me. Victoria died; and the secret remained locked in my breast. Theodore's narrative has told the rest."

The friar ceased. The disconsolate company retired to the remaining part of the castle. In the morning, Manfred signed his abdication of the principality, with the approbation of Hippolita, and each took on them the habit of religion in the neighbouring convents. Frederic offered his daughter to the new prince, which Hippolita's tenderness for Isabella concurred to promote. But Theodore's grief was too fresh to admit the thought of another love; and it was not until after frequent discourses with Isabella of his dear Matilda, that he was persuaded he could know no happiness but in the society of one with whom he could for ever indulge the melancholy that had taken possession of his soul.

THE END

VATHEK

BY

WILLIAM BECKFORD

1786

Vathek, ninth caliph of the race of the Abassides, was the son of Motassem, and the grandson of Haroun al Raschid. From an early accession to the throne, and the talents he possessed to adorn it, his subjects were induced to expect that his reign would be long and happy. His figure was pleasing and majestic; but when he was angry, one of his eyes became so terrible that no person could bear to behold it; and the wretch upon whom it was fixed instantly fell backward, and sometimes expired. For fear, however, of depopulating his dominions and making his palace desolate, he but rarely gave way to his anger.

Being much addicted to woman and the pleasures of the table, he sought by his affability to procure agreeable companions, and he succeeded the better as his generosity was unbounded and his indulgences unrestrained; for he did not think, with the Caliph Omar Ben Abdalaziz, that it was necessary to make a hell of this world to enjoy paradise in the next.

He surpassed in magnificence all his predecessors. The palace of Alkoremi, which his father, Motassem, had erected on the hill of Pied Horses, and which commanded the whole city of Samarah, was, in his idea, far too scanty: he added, therefore, five wings, or rather other palaces, which he destined for the particular gratification of each of the senses.

In the first of these were tables continually covered with the most exquisite dainties, which were supplied both by night and by day, according to their constant consumption; whilst the most delicious wines and the choicest cordials flowed forth from a hundred fountains that were never exhausted. This palace was called *The Eternal or Unsatiating Banquet.*

The second was styled *The Temple of Melody,* or *The Nectar of the Soul.* It was inhabited by the most skilful musicians and admired poets of the time, who not only displayed their talents within, but dispersing in bands without, caused every surrounding scene to reverberate their songs, which were continually varied in the most delightful succession.

The palace named *The Delight of the Eyes,* or *The Support of Memory,* was one entire enchantment. Rarities collected from every corner of the earth were there found in such profusion as to dazzle and confound, but for the order in which they were arranged. One gallery exhibited the pictures of the celebrated Mani, and statues that seemed to be alive. Here a well managed perspective attracted the sight; there the magic of optics agreeably deceived it: whilst the naturalist, on his part, exhibited in their several classes the various gifts that Heaven had bestowed on our globe. In a word, Vathek omitted nothing in this palace that might gratify the curiosity of those who resorted to it, although he was not able to satisfy his own; for, of all men, he was the most curious.

The Palace of Perfumes, which was termed likewise *The Incentive to Pleasure,* consisted of various halls where the different perfumes which the earth produces were kept perpetually burning in censers of gold. Flambeaux and aromatic lamps were here lighted in open day. But the too powerful effects of this agreeable delirium might be alleviated by descending into an immense garden, where an assemblage of every fragrant flower diffused through the air the purest odours.

The fifth palace, denominated *The Retreat of Mirth,*

or the Dangerous, was frequented by troops of young
females, beautiful as the Houris, and not less seducing,
who never failed to receive with caresses all whom the
caliph allowed to approach them and enjoy a few hours
of their company.

Notwithstanding the sensuality in which Vathek indulged, he experienced no abatement in the love of his
people, who thought that a sovereign giving himself up
to pleasure was as able to govern as one who declared
himself an enemy to it. But the unquiet and impetuous
disposition of the caliph would not allow him to rest
there. He had studied so much for his amusement in
the lifetime of his father, as to acquire a great deal of
knowledge, though not a sufficiency to satisfy himself;
for he wished to know everything: even sciences that
did not exist. He was fond of engaging in disputes
with the learned, but did not allow them to push their
opposition with warmth. He stopped with presents the
mouths of those whose mouths could be stopped, whilst
others, whom his liberality was unable to subdue, he
sent to prison to cool their blood, a remedy that often
succeeded.

Vathek discovered also a predilection for theological
controversy, but it was not with the orthodox that he
usually held. By this means he induced the zealots to
oppose him, and then persecuted them in return; for he
resolved, at any rate, to have reason on his side.

The great prophet, Mahomet, whose vicars the caliphs
are, beheld with indignation from his abode in the seventh heaven, the irreligious conduct of such a vicegerent.
"Let us leave him to himself," said he to the Genii, who
are always ready to receive his commands: "let us see
to what lengths his folly and impiety will carry him; if
he run into excess, we shall know how to chastise him.
Assist him, therefore, to complete the tower which, in

imitation of Nimrod, he hath begun; not, like that great warrior, to escape being drowned, but from the insolent curiosity of penetrating the secrets of heaven:—he will not divine the fate that awaits him.''

The Genii obeyed, and when the workmen had raised their structure a cubit in the daytime, two cubits more were added in the night. The expedition with which the fabric arose, was not a little flattering to the vanity of Vathek: he fancied that even insensible matter showed a forwardness to subserve his designs, not considering that the successes of the foolish and wicked form the first rod of their chastisement.

His pride arrived at its height when having ascended for the first time the fifteen hundred stairs of his tower, he cast his eyes below, and beheld men not larger than pismires, mountains than shells, and cities than beehives. The idea which such an elevation inspired of his own grandeur completely bewildered him; he was almost ready to adore himself, till, lifting his eyes upward, he saw the stars as high above him as they appeared when he stood on the surface of the earth. He consoled himself, however, for this intruding and unwelcome perception of his littleness with the thought of being great in the eyes of others, and flattered himself that the light of his mind would extend beyond the reach of his sight and extort from the stars the decrees of his destiny.

With this view, the inquisitive prince passed most of his nights on the summit of his tower, till becoming an adept in the mysteries of astrology, he imagined that the planets had disclosed to him the most marvellous adventures, which were to be accomplished by an extraordinary personage from a country altogether unknown. Prompted by motives of curiosity, he had always been courteous to strangers; but from this instant he redoubled his attention, and ordered it to be announced by sound of trumpet through all the streets of Samarah that no one of his subjects, on peril of his displeasure, should either lodge or detain a traveller, but forthwith bring him to the palace.

Not long after this proclamation, arrived in his metropolis a man so abominably hideous that the very guards who arrested him were forced to shut their eyes as they led him along. The caliph himself appeared startled at so horrible a visage, but joy succeeded to this emotion of terror when the stranger displayed to his view such rarities as he had never before seen, and of which he had no conception.

In reality nothing was ever so extraordinary as the merchandise this stranger produced; most of his curiosities, which were not less admirable for their workmanship than splendour, had, besides, their several virtues described on a parchment fastened to each. There were slippers which, by spontaneous springs, enabled the feet to walk; knives that cut without motion of the hand; sabres that dealt the blow at the person they were wished to strike; and the whole enriched with gems that were hitherto unknown.

The sabres especially, the blades of which emitted a dazzling radiance, fixed more than all the rest the caliph's attention, who promised himself to decipher at his leisure the uncouth characters engraven on their sides. Without, therefore, demanding their price, he ordered all the coined gold to be brought from his treasury, and commanded the merchant to take what he pleased. The stranger obeyed, took little, and remained silent.

Vathek, imagining that the merchant's taciturnity was occasioned by the awe which his presence inspired, encouraged him to advance, and asked him with an air of condescension who he was, whence he came, and where he obtained such beautiful commodities. The man, or rather monster, instead of making a reply, thrice rubbed his forehead, which, as well as his body, was blacker than ebony; four times clapped his paunch, the projection of which was enormous; opened wide his huge eyes, which glowed like firebrands; began to laugh with a hideous noise, and discovered his long amber-coloured teeth, bestreaked with green.

The caliph, though a little startled, renewed his enquiries, but without being able to procure a reply. At which, beginning to be ruffled, he exclaimed,—"Knowest thou, wretch, who I am, and at whom thou art aiming thy gibes?" Then, addressing his guards,—"Have ye heard him speak?—Is he dumb?"—"He hath spoken," they replied, "but to no purpose."—"Let him speak then again," said Vathek, "and tell me who he is, from whence he came, and where he procured these singular curiosities; or I swear, by the ass of Balaam, that I will make him rue his pertinacity."

This menace was accompanied by one of the caliph's angry and perilous glances, which the stranger sustained without the slightest emotion; although his eyes were fixed on the terrible eye of the prince.

No words can describe the amazement of the courtiers when they beheld this rude merchant withstand the encounter unshocked. They all fell prostrate with their faces on the ground, to avoid the risk of their lives; and would have continued in the same abject posture, had not the caliph exclaimed, in a furious tone,—"Up, cowards! seize the miscreant! see that he be committed to prison, and guarded by the best of my soldiers! Let him, however, retain the money I gave him. It is not my intent to take from him his property; I only want him to speak."

No sooner had he uttered these words than the stranger was surrounded, pinioned, and bound with strong fetters, and hurried away to the prison of the great tower, which was encompassed by seven empalements of iron bars, and armed with spikes in every direction, longer and sharper than spits. The caliph, nevertheless, remained in the most violent agitation. He sat down indeed to eat, but, of the three hundred dishes that were daily placed before him, he could taste of no more than thirty-two.

A diet to which he had been so little accustomed, was sufficient of itself to prevent him from sleeping. What then must be its effect when joined to the anxiety that preyed upon his spirits? At the first glimpse of dawn he hastened to the prison, again to importune this intractable stranger; but the rage of Vathek exceeded all bounds on finding the prison empty, the grates burst asunder, and his guards lying lifeless around him. In the paroxysm of his passion he fell furiously on the poor carcasses, and kicked them till evening without intermission. His courtiers and vizirs exerted their efforts to soothe his extravagance; but finding every expedient ineffectual, they all united in one vociferation,—"The caliph is gone mad! the caliph is out of his senses!"

This outcry, which soon resounded through the streets of Samarah, at length reached the ears of Carathis, his mother, who flew in the utmost consternation to try her ascendency on the mind of her son. Her tears and caresses called off his attention; and he was prevailed upon by her entreaties to be brought back to the palace.

Carathis, apprehensive of leaving Vathek to himself, had him put to bed; and seating herself by him, endeavoured by her conversation to appease and compose him. Nor could any one have attempted it with better success, for the caliph not only loved her as a mother, but respected her as a person of superior genius. It was she who had induced him, being a Greek herself, to adopt the sciences and systems of her country which all good Mussulmans hold in such thorough abhorrence.

Judiciary astrology was one of those sciences in which Carathis was a perfect adept. She began, therefore, with reminding her son of the promise which the stars had made him, and intimated an intention of consulting them again. "Alas!" said the caliph as soon as he could speak, "what a fool I have been! not for having bestowed forty thousand kicks on my guards, who so tamely submitted to death, but for never considering that this extraordinary man was the same that the planets had foretold; whom, instead of ill-treating, I should have conciliated by all the arts of persuasion."

"The past," said Carathis, "cannot be recalled; but it behoves us to think of the future. Perhaps you may again see the object you so much regret. It is possible the inscriptions on the sabres will afford information. Eat, therefore, and take thy repose, my dear son. We will consider tomorrow in what manner to act."

Vathek yielded to her counsel as well as he could, and arose in the morning with a mind more at ease. The sabres he commanded to be instantly brought; and, poring upon them through a coloured glass, that their glittering might not dazzle, he set himself in earnest to decipher the inscriptions; but his reiterated attempts were all of them nugatory. In vain did he beat his head, and bite his nails; not a letter of the whole was he able to ascertain. So unlucky a disappointment would have undone him again, had not Carathis by good fortune entered the apartment.

"Have patience, my son!" said she: "you certainly are possessed of every important science; but the knowledge of languages is a trifle at best; and the accom-

plishment of none but a pedant. Issue a proclamation
that you will confer such rewards as become your greatness upon any one that shall interpret what you do not
understand, and what is beneath you to learn. You will
soon find your curiosity gratified."

"That may be," said the caliph; "but in the mean
time I shall be horribly disgusted by a crowd of smat-
terers, who will come to the trial as much for the pleasure of retailing their jargon, as from the hope of
gaining the reward. To avoid this evil, it will be proper
to add that I will put every candidate to death who
shall fail to give satisfaction; for, thank Heaven! I
have skill enough to distinguish whether one translates
or invents."

"Of that I have no doubt," replied Carathis; "but
to put the ignorant to death is somewhat severe, and
may be productive of dangerous effects. Content yourself with commanding their beards to be burnt; beards
in a state are not quite so essential as men."

The caliph submitted to the reasons of his mother;
and, sending for Morakanabad, his prime vizir, said,—
"Let the common criers proclaim, not only in Samarah,
but throughout every city in my empire, that whosoever
will repair hither and decipher certain characters which
appear to be inexplicable, shall experience that liberality for which I am renowned; but that all who fail
upon trial shall have their beards burnt off to the last
hair. Let them add also that I will bestow fifty beautiful slaves, and as many jars of apricots from the
Isle of Kirmith, upon any man that shall bring me intelligence of the stranger."

The subjects of the caliph, like their sovereign, being
great admirers of women and apricots from Kirmith,
felt their mouths water at these promises, but were

totally unable to gratify their hankering; for no one knew what had become of the stranger.

As to the caliph's other requisition, the result was different. The learned, the half learned, and those who were neither, but fancied themselves equal to both, came boldly to hazard their beards, and all shamefully lost them. The exaction of these forfeitures, which found sufficient employment for the eunuchs, gave them such a smell of singed hair as greatly to disgust the ladies of the seraglio, and to make it necessary that this new occupation of their guardians should be transferred to other hands.

At length, however, an old man presented himself whose beard was a cubit and a half longer than any that had appeared before him. The officers of the palace whispered to each other, as they ushered him in,— "What a pity, oh! what a great pity, that such a beard should be burnt!" Even the caliph, when he saw it, concurred with them in opinion, but his concern was entirely needless. This venerable personage read the characters with facility, and explained them verbatim as follows:—"We were made where every thing is well made: we are the least of the wonders of a place where all is wonderful, and deserving the sight of the first potentate on earth."

"You translate admirably!" cried Vathek; "I know to what these marvellous characters allude. Let him receive as many robes of honour and thousands of sequins of gold as he hath spoken words. I am in some measure relieved from the perplexity that embarrassed me!" Vathek invited the old man to dine, and even to remain some days in the palace.

Unluckily for him, he accepted the offer; for the caliph having ordered him next morning to be called, said,—"Read again to me what you have read already;

I cannot hear too often the promise that is made me—
the completion of which I languish to obtain." The
old man forthwith put on his green spectacles, but they
instantly dropped from his nose, on perceiving that
the characters he had read the day preceding had given
place to others of different import. "What ails you?"
asked the caliph; "and why these symptoms of wonder?"—"Sovereign of the world!" replied the old man,
"these sabres hold another language to-day from that
they yesterday held."—"How say you?" returned Vathek:—"but it matters not, tell me, if you can, what
they mean."—"It is this, my lord," rejoined the old
man:—"'Woe to the rash mortal who seeks to know
that of which he should remain ignorant, and to undertake that which surpasseth his power!'"—"And woe to
thee!" cried the caliph, in a burst of indignation:
"to-day thou art void of understanding: begone from
my presence, they shall burn but the half of thy beard,
because thou wert yesterday fortunate in guessing:—
my gifts I never resume." The old man, wise enough
to perceive he had luckily escaped, considering the
folly of disclosing so disgusting a truth, immediately
withdrew and appeared not again.

But it was not long before Vathek discovered abundant reason to regret his precipitation; for, though he
could not decipher the characters himself, yet, by constantly poring upon them, he plainly perceived that
they every day changed; and, unfortunately, no other
candidate offered to explain them. This perplexing
occupation inflamed his blood, dazzled his sight, and
brought on such a giddiness and debility that he could
hardly support himself. He failed not, however, though
in so reduced a condition, to be often carried to his
tower, as he flattered himself that he might there read
in the stars, which he went to consult, something more

congruous to his wishes. But in this his hopes were
deluded; for his eyes, dimmed by the vapours of his
head, began to subserve his curiosity so ill that he
beheld nothing but a thick dun cloud, which he took for
the most direful of omens.

Agitated with so much anxiety, Vathek entirely lost
all firmness; a fever seized him, and his appetite failed.
Instead of being one of the greatest eaters, he became
as distinguished for drinking. So insatiable was the
thirst which tormented him that his mouth, like a fun-
nel, was always open to receive the various liquors that
might be poured into it, and especially cold water,
which calmed him more than any other.

This unhappy prince, being thus incapacitated for
the enjoyment of any pleasure, commanded the palaces
of the five senses to be shut up, forebore to appear in
public, either to display his magnificence or administer
justice, and retired to the inmost apartment of his
harem. As he had ever been an excellent husband, his
wives, overwhelmed with grief at his deplorable situation, incessantly supplied him with prayers for his
health and water for his thirst.

In the mean time the Princess Carathis, whose affliction no words can describe, instead of confining herself
to sobbing and tears, was closeted daily with the vizir
Morakanabad, to find out some cure or mitigation of the
caliph's disease. Under the persuasion that it was
caused by enchantment, they turned over together, leaf
by leaf, all the books of magic that might point out a
remedy; and caused the horrible stranger, whom they
accused as the enchanter, to be everywhere sought for
with the strictest diligence.

At the distance of a few miles from Samarah stood a
high mountain, whose sides were swarded with wild
thyme and basil, and its summit overspread with so

VATHEK 139

delightful a plain that it might have been taken for the paradise destined for the faithful. Upon it grew a hundred thickets of eglantine and other fragrant shrubs; a hundred arbours of roses, entwined with jessamine and honeysuckle; as many clumps of orange trees, cedar, and citron, whose branches, interwoven with the palm, the pomegranate, and the vine, presented every luxury that could regale the eye or the taste. The ground was strewed with violets, harebells, and pansies, in the midst of which numerous tufts of jonquils, hyacinths, and carnations perfumed the air. Four fountains, not less clear than deep, and so abundant as to slake the thirst of ten armies, seemed purposely placed here, to make the scene more resemble the garden of Eden watered by four sacred rivers. Here, the nightingale sang the birth of the rose, her well beloved, and at the same time lamented its short-lived beauty, whilst the dove deplored the loss of more substantial pleasures, and the wakeful lark hailed the rising light that reanimates the whole creation. Here, more than anywhere, the mingled melodies of birds expressed the various passions which inspired them, and the exquisite fruits which they pecked at pleasure seemed to have given them a double energy.

To this mountain Vathek was sometimes brought for the sake of breathing a purer air, and especially to drink at will of the four fountains. His attendants were his mother, his wives, and some eunuchs, who assiduously employed themselves in filling capacious bowls of rock crystal, and emulously presenting them to him. But it frequently happened that his avidity exceeded their zeal, insomuch that he would prostrate himself upon the ground to lap the water, of which he could never have enough.

One day when this unhappy prince had been long

lying in so debasing a posture, a voice, hoarse but
strong, thus addressed him:—"Why dost thou assimilate
thyself to a dog, O caliph, proud as thou art of thy
dignity and power?" At this apostrophe he raised up
his head, and beheld the stranger that had caused him
so much affliction. Inflamed with anger at the sight, he
exclaimed,—"Accursed Giaour!* what comest thou
hither to do? Is it not enough to have transformed a
prince, remarkable for his agility, into a water budget?
Perceivest thou not that I may perish by drinking to
excess, as well as by thirst?"

"Drink, then, this draught," said the stranger, as he
presented to him a phial of a red and yellow mixture:
"and to satiate the thirst of thy soul as well as of thy
body, know that I am an Indian; but from a region of
India which is wholly unknown."

The caliph, delighted to see his desires accomplished
in part, and flattering himself with the hope of obtaining their entire fulfilment, without a moment's hesitation swallowed the potion, and instantaneously found
his health restored, his thirst appeased, and his limbs as
agile as ever. In the transports of his joy, Vathek
leaped upon the neck of the frightful Indian, and kissed
his horrid mouth and hollow cheeks as though they had
been the coral lips and the lilies and roses of his most
beautiful wives.

Nor would these transports have ceased had not the
eloquence of Carathis repressed them. Having prevailed upon him to return to Samarah, she caused a
herald to proclaim as loudly as possible,—"The wonderful stranger hath appeared again; he hath healed the
caliph; he hath spoken! he hath spoken!"

Forthwith all the inhabitants of this vast city quitted
their habitations, and ran together in crowds to see the

* An evil spirit; by implication an unbeliever.

procession of Vathek and the Indian, whom they now
blessed as much as they had before execrated, incessantly shouting,—"He hath healed our sovereign; he
hath spoken! he hath spoken!" Nor were these words
forgotten in the public festivals, which were celebrated
the same evening to testify the general joy; for the
poets applied them as a chorus to all the songs they
composed on this interesting subject.

The caliph in the meanwhile caused the palaces of
the senses to be again set open; and, as he found himself naturally prompted to visit that of taste in preference to the rest, immediately ordered a splendid
entertainment, to which his great officers and favourite
courtiers were all invited. The Indian, who was placed
near the prince, seemed to think that as a proper ac-
knowledgment of so distinguished a privilege, he could
neither eat, drink, nor talk too much. The various
dainties were no sooner served up than they vanished,
to the great mortification of Vathek, who piqued himself on being the greatest eater alive, and at this time
in particular was blessed with an excellent appetite.

The rest of the company looked round at each other
in amazement; but the Indian, without appearing to
observe it, quaffed large bumpers to the health of each
of them, sang in a style altogether extravagant, related
stories at which he laughed immoderately, and poured
forth extemporaneous verses, which would not have
been thought bad, but for the strange grimaces with
which they were uttered. In a word, his loquacity was
equal to that of a hundred astrologers; he ate as much
as a hundred porters, and caroused in proportion.

The caliph, notwithstanding the table had been thirty-
two times covered, found himself incommoded by the
voraciousness of his guest, who was now considerably
declined in the prince's esteem. Vathek, however, being

unwilling to betray the chagrin he could hardly disguise, said in a whisper to Bababalouk, the chief of his eunuchs,—"You see how enormous his performances are in every way. What would be the consequence should he get at my wives!—Go! redouble your vigilance, and be sure look well to my Circassians, who would be more to his taste than all of the rest."

The bird of the morning had thrice renewed his song when the hour of the divan was announced. Vathek, in gratitude to his subjects having promised to attend, immediately arose from table and repaired thither, leaning upon his vizir, who could scarcely support him; so disordered was the poor prince by the wine he had drunk, and still more by the extravagant vagaries of his boisterous guest.

The vizirs, the officers of the crown and of the law, arranged themselves in a semicircle about their sovereign, and preserved a respectful silence, whilst the Indian, who looked as cool as if he had been fasting, sat down without ceremony on one of the steps of the throne, laughing in his sleeve at the indignation with which his temerity had filled the spectators.

The caliph, however, whose ideas were confused, and whose head was embarrassed, went on administering justice at hap-hazard, till at length the prime vizir, perceiving his situation, hit upon a sudden expedient to interrupt the audience and rescue the honour of his master, to whom he said in a whisper,—"My lord, the Princess Carathis, who hath passed the night in consulting the planets, informs you that they portend you evil, and the danger is urgent. Beware lest this stranger, whom you have so lavishly recompensed for his magical gewgaws, should make some attempt on your life. His liquor, which at first had the appearance of effecting your cure, may be no more than a poison, the operation of which will be sudden. Slight not this surmise. Ask him, at least, of what it was compounded, whence he procured it; and mention the sabres, which you seem to have forgotten."

Vathek, to whom the insolent airs of the stranger became every moment less supportable, intimated to his vizir by a wink of acquiescence that he would adopt his advice; and at once turning towards the Indian, said,— "Get up, and declare in full divan of what drugs was compounded the liquor you enjoined me to take, for it is suspected to be poison. Give also that explanation I have so earnestly desired concerning the sabres you sold me, and thus show your gratitude for the favours heaped on you."

Having pronounced these words, in as moderate a tone as he well could, he waited in silent expectation for an answer. But the Indian, still keeping his seat, began to renew his loud shouts of laughter, and exhibit the same horrid grimaces he had shown them before, without vouchsafing a word in reply. Vathek, no longer able to brook such insolence, immediately kicked him from the steps; instantly descending, repeated his blow; and persisted with such assiduity as incited all who were present to follow his example. Every foot was up and aimed at the Indian, and no sooner had any one given him a kick than he felt himself constrained to reiterate the stroke.

The stranger afforded them no small entertainment; for being both short and plump, he collected himself into a ball and rolled round on all sides at the blows of his assailants, who pressed after him wherever he turned with an eagerness beyond conception, whilst their numbers were every moment increasing. The ball, indeed, in passing from one apartment to another, drew every person after it that came in its way; insomuch that the whole palace was thrown into confusion and resounded with a tremendous clamour. The women of the harem, amazed at the uproar, flew to their blinds to discover the cause; but no sooner did they catch a glimpse of the ball than, feeling themselves unable to refrain, they broke from the clutches of their eunuchs, who to stop their flight pinched them till they bled, but in vain; whilst themselves, though trembling with terror at the escape of their charge, were as incapable of resisting the attraction.

After having traversed the halls, galleries, chambers, kitchens, gardens, and stables of the palace, the Indian at last took his course through the courts; whilst the caliph, pursuing him closer than the rest, bestowed as many kicks as he possibly could; yet not without receiving now and then a few which his competitors, in their eagerness, designed for the ball.

Carathis, Morakanabad, and two or three old vizirs, whose wisdom had hitherto withstood the attraction, wishing to prevent Vathek from exposing himself in the presence of his subjects, fell down in his way to impede the pursuit: but he, regardless of their obstruction, leaped over their heads and went on as before. They then ordered the Muezins to call the people to prayers, both for the sake of getting them out of the way, and of endeavouring, by their petitions, to avert the calamity; but neither of these expedients was a whit more successful. The sight of this fatal ball was alone sufficient to draw after it every beholder. The Muezins themselves, though they saw it but at a distance, hastened down from their minarets and mixed with the crowd, which continued to increase in so surprising a manner that scarce an inhabitant was left in Samarah except the aged, the sick confined to their beds, and infants at the breast, whose nurses could run more nimbly

without them. Even Carathis, Morakanabad and the
rest were all become of the party. The shrill screams
of the females, who had broken from their apartments
and were unable to extricate themselves from the
pressure of the crowd, together with those of the
eunuchs jostling after them and terrified lest their
charge should escape from their sight; the execrations
of husbands, urging forward and menacing each other;
kicks given and received; stumblings and overthrows at
every step; in a word, the confusion that universally
prevailed, rendered Samarah like a city taken by storm
and devoted to absolute plunder. At last the cursed
Indian, who still preserved his rotundity of figure, after
passing through all the streets and public places, and
leaving them empty, rolled onwards to the plain of
Catoul, and entered the valley at the foot of the mountain of the four fountains.

As a continual fall of water had excavated an immense gulf in the valley, whose opposite side was closed
in by a steep acclivity, the caliph and his attendants
were apprehensive lest the ball should bound into the
chasm, and, to prevent it, redoubled their efforts, but
in vain. The Indian persevered in his onward direction, and, as had been apprehended, glancing from the
precipice with the rapidity of lightning, was lost in the
gulf below.

Vathek would have followed the perfidious Giaour,
had not an invisible agency arrested his progress. The
multitude that pressed after him were at once checked
in the same manner, and a calm instantaneously ensued.
They all gazed at each other with an air of astonishment; and notwithstanding that the loss of veils and
turbans, together with torn habits, and dust blended
with sweat, presented a most laughable spectacle, yet
there was not one smile to be seen. On the contrary,

all with looks of confusion and sadness returned in silence to Samarah, and retired to their inmost apartments, without ever reflecting that they had been impelled by an invisible power into the extravagance for which they reproached themselves; for it is but just that men, who so often arrogate to their own merit the good of which they are but instruments, should also attribute to themselves absurdities which they could not prevent.

The caliph was the only person who refused to leave the valley. He commanded his tents to be pitched there, and stationed himself on the very edge of the precipice, in spite of the representations of Carathis and Morakanabad, who pointed out the hazard of its brink giving way, and the vicinity to the magician that had so cruelly tormented him. Vathek derided all their remonstrances, and having ordered a thousand flambeaux to be lighted, and directed his attendants to proceed in lighting more, lay down on the slippery margin, and attempted by the help of this artificial splendour to look through that gloom which all the fires of the empyrean had been insufficient to pervade. One while he fancied to himself voices arising from the depth of the gulf; at another, he seemed to distinguish the accents of the Indian; but all was no more than the hollow murmur of waters and the din of the cataracts that rushed from steep to steep down the sides of the mountain.

Having passed the night in this cruel perturbation, the caliph at daybreak retired to his tent, where, without taking the least sustenance, he continued to doze till the dusk of evening began again to come on. He then resumed his vigils as before, and persevered in observing them for many nights together. At length, fatigued with so fruitless an employment, he sought re-

lief from change. To this end, he sometimes paced with
hasty strides across the plain, and as he wildly gazed
at the stars, reproached them with having deceived
him. But, lo! on a sudden the clear blue sky appeared
streaked over with streams of blood, which reached
from the valley even to the city of Samarah. As this
awful phenomenon seemed to touch his tower, Vathek at
first thought of repairing thither to view it more distinctly; but feeling himself unable to advance, and
being overcome with apprehension, he muffled up his face
in the folds of his robe.

Terrifying as these prodigies were, this impression
upon him was no more than momentary, and served only
to stimulate his love of the marvellous. Instead, therefore, of returning to his palace, he persisted in the
resolution of abiding where the Indian had vanished
from his view. One night, however, while he was walking as usual on the plain, the moon and stars were
eclipsed at once, and a total darkness ensued. The
earth trembled beneath him, and a voice came forth,
the voice of the Giaour, who in accents more sonorous
than thunder thus addressed him:—"Wouldest thou devote thyself to me, adore the terrestrial influences, and
abjure Mahomet? On these conditions I will bring
thee to the Palace of Subterranean Fire. There shalt
thou behold, in immense depositories, the treasures
which the stars have promised thee; and which will be
conferred by those intelligences whom thou shalt thus
render propitious. It was from thence I brought my
sabres, and it is there that Soliman Ben Daoud reposes,
surrounded by the talismans that control the world."

The astonished caliph trembled as he answered, yet
he answered in a style that showed him to be no novice
in preternatural adventures;—"Where art thou? Be
present to my eyes; dissipate the gloom that perplexes

me, and of which I deem thee the cause. After the many flambeaux I have burnt to discover thee, thou mayest, at least, grant a glimpse of thy horrible visage."—"Abjure then Mahomet!" replied the Indian, "and promise me full proofs of thy sincerity: otherwise, thou shalt never behold me again."

The unhappy caliph, instigated by insatiable curiosity, lavished his promises in the utmost profusion. The sky immediately brightened; and, by the light of the planets, which seemed almost to blaze, Vathek beheld the earth open; and, at the extremity of a vast black chasm, a portal of ebony, before which stood the Indian, holding in his hand a golden key, which he sounded against the lock.

"How," cried Vathek, "can I descend to thee? Come, take me, and instantly open the portal."—"Not so fast," replied the Indian, "impatient caliph!—Know that I am parched with thirst, and cannot open this door till my thirst be thoroughly appeased. I require the blood of fifty children. Take them from among the most beautiful sons of thy viziers and great men; or neither can my thirst nor thy curiosity be satisfied. Return to Samarah; procure for me this necessary libation; come back hither; throw it thyself into this chasm, and then shalt thou see!"

Having thus spoken, the Indian turned his back on the caliph, who, incited by the suggestions of demons, resolved on the direful sacrifice. He now pretended to have regained his tranquillity, and set out for Samarah amidst the acclamations of a people who still loved him, and forebore not to rejoice when they believed him to have recovered his reason. So successfully did he conceal the emotion of his heart that even Carathis and Morakanabad were equally deceived with the rest. Nothing was heard of but festivals and rejoicings. The fatal ball, which no tongue had hitherto ventured to mention, was brought on the tapis. A general laugh went round, though many, still smarting under the hands of the surgeon, from the hurts received in that memorable adventure, had no great reason for mirth.

The prevalence of this gay humour was not a little grateful to Vathek, who perceived how much it conduced to his project. He put on the appearance of affability to every one, but especially to his vizirs and the grandees of his court, whom he failed not to regale with a sumptuous banquet, during which he insensibly directed the conversation to the children of his guests. Having asked with a good-natured air which of them were blessed with the handsomest boys, every father at once asserted the pretensions of his own; and the contest imperceptibly grew so warm that nothing could have withholden them from coming to blows but their profound reverence for the person of the caliph. Under the pretence, therefore, of reconciling the disputants, Vathek took upon him to decide, and with this view commanded the boys to be brought.

It was not long before a troop of these poor children made their appearance, all equipped by their fond mothers with such ornaments as might give the greatest relief to their beauty or most advantageously display the graces of their age. But whilst this brilliant assemblage attracted the eyes and hearts of every one besides, the caliph scrutinised each in his turn with a malignant avidity that passed for attention, and selected from their number the fifty whom he judged the Giaour would prefer.

With an equal show of kindness as before, he proposed to celebrate a festival on the plain for the entertainment of his young favourites, who, he said, ought to rejoice still more than all at the restoration of his health, on account of the favours he intended for them.

The caliph's proposal was received with the greatest delight, and soon published through Samarah. Litters, camels, and horses were prepared. Women and children, old men and young, every one placed himself as he chose. The cavalcade set forward, attended by all the confectioners in the city and its precincts; the populace, following on foot, composed an amazing crowd, and occasioned no little noise. All was joy; nor did any one call to mind what most of them had suffered when they lately travelled the road they were now passing so gaily.

The evening was serene, the air refreshing, the sky clear, and the flowers exhaled their fragrance. The beams of the declining sun, whose mild splendour reposed on the summit of the mountain, shed a glow of ruddy light over its green declivity and the white flocks sporting upon it. No sounds were heard save the murmurs of the four fountains, and the reeds and voices of shepherds calling to each other from different eminences.

The lovely innocents, destined for the sacrifice, added not a little to the hilarity of the scene. They approached the plain full of sportiveness, some coursing butterflies, others culling flowers or picking up the shining little pebbles that attracted their notice. At intervals they nimbly started from each other for the sake of being caught again and mutually imparting a thousand caresses.

The dreadful chasm at whose bottom the portal of ebony was placed, began to appear at a distance. It looked like a black streak that divided the plain. Morakanabad and his companions took it for some work which the caliph had ordered. Unhappy men! little did they surmise for what it was destined. Vathek, unwilling that they should examine it too nearly, stopped the procession, and ordered a spacious circle to be formed on this side, at some distance from the accursed chasm. The body-guard of eunuchs was detached, to measure out the lists intended for the games and prepare the rings for the arrows of the young archers. The fifty competitors were soon stripped, and presented to the admiration of the spectators the suppleness and grace of their delicate limbs. Their eyes sparkled with a joy which those of their fond parents reflected. Every one offered wishes for the little candidate nearest his heart, and doubted not of his being victorious. A breathless suspense awaited the contests of these amiable and innocent victims.

The caliph, availing himself of the first moment to retire from the crowd, advanced towards the chasm, and there heard, yet not without shuddering, the voice of the Indian, who, gnashing his teeth, eagerly demanded,—"Where are they?—Where are they?—Perceivest thou not how my mouth waters?"—"Relentless Giaour!" answered Vathek, with emotion; "can nothing content thee but the massacre of these lovely victims? Ah! wert thou to behold their beauty, it must certainly move thy compassion."—"Perdition on thy compassion, babbler!" cried the Indian: "give them me; instantly give them, or my portal shall be closed against thee for ever!"—"Not so loudly," replied the caliph, blushing. —"I understand thee," returned the Giaour with the grin of an ogre; "thou wantest no presence of mind: I will, for a moment, forbear."

During this exquisite dialogue, the games went forward with all alacrity, and at length concluded just as the twilight began to overcast the mountains. Vathek, who was still standing on the edge of the chasm, called out with all his might,—"Let my fifty little favourites

approach me, separately; and let them come in the order
of their success. To the first, I will give my diamond
bracelet; to the second, my collar of emeralds; to the
third, my aigret of rubies; to the fourth, my girdle of
topazes; and to the rest, each a part of my dress, even
down to my slippers."

This declaration was received with reiterated acclamations; and all extolled the liberality of a prince who
would thus strip himself for the amusement of his subjects and the encouragement of the rising generation.
The caliph in the meanwhile undressed himself by
degrees, and, raising his arm as high as he was able,
made each of the prizes glitter in the air; but, whilst
he delivered it, with one hand, to the child, who sprung
forward to receive it, he with the other pushed the
poor innocent into the gulf, where the Giaour, with a
sullen muttering, incessantly repeated, "More! more!"

This dreadful device was executed with so much dex-
terity that the boy who was approaching him remained
unconscious of the fate of his forerunner, and as to the
spectators, the shades of evening, together with their
distance, precluded them from perceiving any object
distinctly. Vathek having in this manner thrown in the
last of the fifty, and expecting that the Giaour, on
receiving him, would have presented the key, already
fancied himself as great as Soliman, and consequently
above being amenable for what he had done; when to
his utter amazement the chasm closed, and the ground
became as entire as the rest of the plain.

No language could express his rage and despair. He
execrated the perfidy of the Indian, loaded him with
the most infamous invectives, and stamped with his foot
as resolving to be heard. He persisted in this till his
strength failed him, and then fell on the earth like one
void of sense. His vizirs and grandees, who were

nearer than the rest, supposed him at first to be sitting on the grass, at play with their amiable children; but at length, prompted by doubt, they advanced towards the spot and found the caliph alone, who wildly demanded what they wanted? "Our children! our children!" cried they. "It is, assuredly, pleasant," said he, "to make me accountable for accidents. Your children, while at play, fell from the precipice, and I should have experienced their fate had I not suddenly started back."

At these words, the fathers of the fifty boys cried out aloud, the mothers repeated their exclamations an octave higher, whilst the rest, without knowing the cause, soon drowned the voices of both with still louder lamentations of their own. "Our caliph," said they, and the report soon circulated, "our caliph has played us this trick, to gratify his accursed Giaour. Let us punish him for perfidy! Let us avenge ourselves! Let us avenge the blood of the innocent! Let us throw this cruel prince into the gulf that is near, and let his name be mentioned no more!"

At this rumour and these menaces, Carathis, full of consternation, hastened to Morakanabad, and said, "Vizir, you have lost two beautiful boys, and must necessarily be the most afflicted of fathers, but you are virtuous. Save your master."—"I will brave every hazard," replied the vizir, "to rescue him from his present danger; but, afterwards, will abandon him to his fate. Bababalouk," continued he, "put yourself at the head of your eunuchs; disperse the mob, and, if possible, bring back this unhappy prince to his palace." Bababalouk and his fraternity, felicitating each other in a low voice on their having been spared the cares as well as the honour of paternity, obeyed the mandate of the vizir, who, seconding their exertions to the utmost of his power, at length accomplished his generous enterprise, and retired, as he resolved, to lament at his leisure.

No sooner had the caliph re-entered his palace than Carathis commanded the doors to be fastened; but perceiving the tumult to be still violent, and hearing the imprecations which resounded from all quarters, she said to her son,—"Whether the populace be right or wrong, it behoves you to provide for your safety; let us retire to your own apartment, and from thence through the subterranean passage known only to ourselves, into your tower. There, with the assistance of the mutes who never leave it, we may be able to make a powerful resistance. Bababalouk, supposing us to be still in the palace, will guard its avenues, for his own sake; and we shall soon find, without the counsels of that blubberer Morakanabad, what expedient may be the best to adopt."

Vathek, without making the least reply, acquiesced in his mother's proposal, and repeated as he went, "Nefarious Giaour! where art thou? Hast thou not yet devoured those poor children? Where are thy sabres, thy golden key, thy talismans?" Carathis, who guessed from these interrogations a part of the truth, had no difficulty to apprehend in getting at the whole as soon as he should be a little composed in his tower. This princess was so far from being influenced by scruples that she was as wicked as woman could be, which is not saying a little; for the sex pique themselves on their superiority in every competition. The recital of the caliph, therefore, occasioned neither terror nor surprise to his mother. She felt no emotion but from the promises of the Giaour, and said to her son, "This Giaour, it must be confessed, is somewhat sanguinary in his taste; but the terrestrial powers are always terrible.

Nevertheless, what the one hath promised, and the others can confer, will prove a sufficient indemnification. No crimes should be thought too dear for such a reward; forbear, then, to revile the Indian; you have not fulfilled the conditions to which his services are annexed. For instance; is not a sacrifice to the subterranean Genii required, and should we not be prepared to offer it as soon as the tumult is subsided? This charge I will take on myself, and have no doubt of succeeding, by means of your treasures, which, as there are now so many others in store, may without fear be exhausted." Accordingly the princess, who possessed the most consummate skill in the art of persuasion, went immediately back through the subterranean passage, and presenting herself to the populace from a window of the palace, began to harangue them with all the address of which she was mistress; whilst Bababalouk showered money from both hands amongst the crowd, who by these united means were soon appeased. Every person retired to his home, and Carathis returned to the tower.

Prayer at break of day was announced, when Carathis and Vathek ascended the steps which led to the summit of the tower, where they remained for some time, though the weather was lowering and wet. This impending gloom corresponded with their malignant dispositions; but when the sun began to break through the clouds, they ordered a pavilion to be raised as a screen against the intrusion of his beams. The caliph, overcome with fatigue, sought refreshment from repose, at the same time hoping that significant dreams might attend on his slumbers, whilst the indefatigable Carathis, followed by a party of her mutes, descended to prepare whatever she judged proper for the oblation of the approaching night.

By secret stairs, contrived within the thickness of the wall, and known only to herself and her son, she first repaired to the mysterious recesses in which were deposited the mummies that had been wrested from the catacombs of the ancient Pharaohs. Of these she ordered several to be taken. From thence she resorted to a gallery where, under the guard of fifty female negroes, mute and blind of the right eye, were preserved the oil of the most venomous serpents, rhinoceros' horns, and woods of a subtle and penetrating odour procured from the interior of the Indies, together with a thousand other horrible rarities. This collection had been formed for a purpose like the present, by Carathis herself, from a presentiment that she might one day enjoy some intercourse with the infernal powers, to whom she had ever been passionately attached, and to whose taste she was no stranger.

To familiarise herself the better with the horrors in view, the princess remained in the company of her negresses, who squinted in the most amiable manner from the only eye they had, and leered with exquisite delight at the skulls and skeletons which Carathis had drawn forth from her cabinets, all of them making the most frightful contortions, and uttering such shrill chatterings that the princess, stunned by them and suffocated by the potency of the exhalations, was forced to quit the gallery, after stripping it of a part of its abominable treasures.

Whilst she was thus occupied, the caliph, who, instead of the visions he expected, had acquired in these unsubstantial regions a voracious appetite, was greatly provoked at the mutes. For having totally forgotten their deafness, he had impatiently asked them for food; and seeing them regardless of his demand, he began to cuff, pinch, and bite them, till Carathis arrived to terminate a scene so indecent, to the great content of these miserable creatures—"Son! what means all this?" said she, panting for breath. "I thought I heard as I came up the shrieks of a thousand bats, torn from their crannies in the recesses of a cavern; and it was the outcry only of these poor mutes, whom you were so unmercifully abusing. In truth, you but ill deserve the admirable provision I have brought you."—"Give it me instantly," exclaimed the caliph; "I am perishing for hunger!"—"As to that," answered she, "you must have an excellent stomach if it can digest what I have brought."—"Be quick," replied the caliph;—"but, oh heavens! what horrors! What do you intend?"— "Come, come," returned Carathis, "be not so squeamish, but help me to arrange everything properly, and you shall see that what you reject with such symptoms of disgust will soon complete your felicity. Let us get ready the pile for the·sacrifice of tonight, and think not of eating till that is performed. Know you not that all solemn rites ought to be preceded by a rigorous abstinence?"

The caliph, not daring to object, abandoned himself to grief and the wind that ravaged his entrails, whilst his mother went forward with the requisite operations. Phials of serpents' oil, mummies, and bones, were soon set in order on the balustrade of the tower. The pile began to rise, and in three hours was twenty cubits high. At length darkness approached, and Carathis, having stripped herself to her inmost garment, clapped her hands in an impulse of ecstasy. The mutes followed her example, but Vathek, extenuated with hunger and impatience, was unable to support himself, and fell down in a swoon. The sparks had already kindled the dry wood; the venomous oil burst into a thousand blue flames; the mummies, dissolving, emitted a thick dun vapour; and the rhinoceros' horns, beginning to consume, all together diffused such a stench that the caliph, recovering, started from his trance, and gazed wildly on the scene in full blaze around him. The oil gushed forth in a plenitude of streams, and the negresses, who supplied it without intermission, united their cries to those of the princess. At last the fire became so violent, and the flames reflected from the polished marble so dazzling, that the caliph, unable to withstand the heat and the blaze, effected his escape, and took shelter under the imperial standard.

In the meantime, the inhabitants of Samarah, scared at the light which shone over the city, arose in haste, ascended their roofs, beheld the tower on fire, and hurried half naked to the square. Their love for their sovereign immediately awoke; and apprehending him in danger of perishing in his tower, their whole thoughts were occupied with the means of his safety. Morakanabad flew from his retirement, wiped away his tears, and cried out for water like the rest. Bababalouk, whose olfactory nerves were more familiarised to magical odours, readily conjecturing that Carathis was engaged in her favourite amusements, strenuously exhorted them not to be alarmed. Him, however, they treated as an old poltroon, and styled him a rascally traitor. The camels and dromedaries were advancing with water, but no one knew by which way to enter the tower. Whilst the populace was obstinate in forcing the doors, a violent north-east wind drove an immense volume of flame against them. At first they recoiled, but soon came back with redoubled zeal. At the same time, the stench of the horns and mummies increasing, most of the crowd fell backward in a state of suffocation. Those that kept their feet mutually wondered at the cause of the smell, and admonished each other to retire. Morakanabad, more sick than the rest, remained in a piteous condition. Holding his nose with one hand, every one persisted in his efforts with the other to burst open the doors and obtain admission. A hundred and forty of the strongest and most resolute at length accomplished their purpose. Having gained the staircase, by their violent exertions they attained a great height in a quarter of an hour.

Carathis, alarmed at the signs of her mutes, advanced to the staircase, went down a few steps, and heard several voices calling out from below,—"You shall in a moment have water!" Being rather alert, considering her age, she presently regained the top of the tower, and bade her son suspend the sacrifice for some minutes, adding,—"We shall soon be enabled to render it more grateful. Certain dolts of your subjects, imagining, no doubt, that we were on fire, have been rash enough to break through those doors which had hitherto remained inviolate, for the sake of bringing up water. They are very kind, you must allow, so soon to forget the wrongs you have done them; but that is of little moment. Let us offer them to the Giaour. Let them come up. Our mutes, who neither want strength nor experience, will soon despatch them, exhausted as they are with fatigue."—"Be it so," answered the caliph, "provided we finish, and I dine." In fact, these good people, out of breath from ascending fifteen hundred stairs in such haste, and chagrined at having spilt by the way the water they had taken, were no sooner arrived at the top than the blaze of the flames and the fumes of the mummies at once overpowered their senses. It was a pity! for they beheld not the agreeable smile with which the mutes and negresses adjusted the cord to their necks. These amiable personages rejoiced, however, no less at the scene. Never before had the ceremony of strangling been performed with so much facility. They all fell, without the least resistance or struggle, so that Vathek, in the space of a few moments, found himself surrounded by the dead bodies of the most faithful of his subjects, all which were thrown on the top of the pile. Carathis, whose presence of mind never forsook her, perceiving that she had carcasses sufficient to complete her oblation, commanded the chains to be stretched across the staircase and the iron doors barricadoed that no more might come up.

No sooner were these orders obeyed, than the tower shook; the dead bodies vanished in the flames, which at once changed from a swarthy crimson to a bright rose colour; an ambient vapour emitted the most exquisite fragrance; the marble columns rang with harmonious sounds, and the liquefied horns diffused a delicious perfume. Carathis, in transports, anticipated the success of her enterprise; whilst her mutes and negresses, to whom these sweets had given the cholic, retired grumbling to their cells.

Scarcely were they gone when, instead of the pile, horns, mummies, and ashes, the caliph both saw and felt, with a degree of pleasure which he could not express, a table covered with the most magnificent repast: flagons of wine and vases of exquisite sherbet reposing on snow. He availed himself without scruple of such an entertainment, and had already laid hands on a lamb stuffed with pistachios, whilst Carathis was privately drawing from a filigree urn a parchment that seemed to be endless, and which had escaped the notice of her son. Totally occupied in gratifying an importunate appetite, he left her to peruse it without interruption; which having finished, she said to him in an authoritative tone, "Put an end to your gluttony, and hear the splendid promises with which you are favoured!" She

then read as follows:—"Vathek, my well beloved, thou
hast surpassed my hopes. My nostrils have been re-
galed by the savour of thy mummies, thy horns, and
still more by the lives devoted on the pile. At the full
of the moon, cause the bands of thy musicians and thy
tymbals to be heard; depart from thy palace, surrounded by all the pageants of majesty, thy most faithful slaves, thy best beloved wives, thy most magnificent
litters, thy richest loaden camels, and set forward on
thy way to Istakar. There I await thy coming. That
is the region of wonders; there shalt thou receive the
diadem of Gian Ben Gian, the talismans of Soliman,
and the treasures of the pre-adamite sultans.* There
shalt thou be solaced with all kinds of delight.—But
beware how thou enterest any dwelling on thy route,
or thou shalt feel the effects of my anger."

The caliph, notwithstanding his habitual luxury, had
never before dined with so much satisfaction. He gave
full scope to the joy of these golden tidings, and betook
himself to drinking anew. Carathis, whose antipathy
to wine was by no means insuperable, failed not to
pledge him at every bumper he ironically quaffed to
the health of Mahomet. This infernal liquor completed
their impious temerity and prompted them to utter a
profusion of blasphemies. They gave a loose to their
wit, at the expense of the ass of Balaam, the dog of the
seven sleepers, and the other animals admitted into the
paradise of Mahomet. In this sprightly humour they
descended the fifteen hundred stairs, diverting themselves, as they went, at the anxious faces they saw on
the square, through the barbicans and loopholes of the

*These were princes of evil and workers of magic in the
Arabian mythology. The original notes to Vathek discourse
spaciously on these and other legendary names found throughout the work.

tower, and at length arrived at the royal apartments by the subterranean passage. Bababalouk was parading to and fro, and issuing his mandates with great pomp to the eunuchs, who were snuffing the lights and painting the eyes of the Circassians. No sooner did he catch sight of the caliph and his mother, than he exclaimed, —"Hah! you have then, I perceive, escaped from the flames; I was not, however, altogether out of doubt."— "Of what moment is it to us what you thought or think?" cried Carathis: "go, speed, tell Morakanabad that we immediately want him; and take care not to stop by the way to make your insipid reflections."

Morakanabad delayed not to obey the summons, and was received by Vathek and his mother with great solemnity. They told him with an air of composure and commiseration that the fire at the top of the tower was extinguished, but that, it had cost the lives of the brave people who sought to assist them.

"Still more misfortunes!" cried Morakanabad, with a sigh. "Ah, commander of the faithful, our holy prophet is certainly irritated against us! it behoves you to appease him."—"We will appease him hereafter," replied the caliph, with a smile that augured nothing of good. "You will have leisure sufficient for your supplications during my absence, for this country is the bane of my health. I am disgusted with the mountain of the four fountains, and am resolved to go and drink of the stream of Rocnabad. I long to refresh myself in the delightful valleys which it waters. Do you, with the advice of my mother, govern my dominions, and take care to supply whatever her experiments may demand; for you well know that our tower abounds in materials for the advancement of science."

The tower but ill suited Morakanabad's taste. Immense treasures had been lavished upon it; and nothing

had he ever seen carried thither but female negroes,
mutes, and abominable drugs. Nor did he know well
what to think of Carathis, who, like a chameleon, could
assume all possible colours. Her cursed eloquence had
often driven the poor Mussulman to his last shifts. He
considered, however, that if she possessed but few good
qualities, her son had still fewer, and that the alternative on the whole would be in her favour. Consoled,
therefore, with this reflection, he went in good spirits
to soothe the populace and make the proper arrange-
ments for his master's journey.

Vathek, to conciliate the spirits of the subterranean
palace, resolved that his expedition should be uncommonly splendid. With this view he confiscated on all
sides the property of his subjects, whilst his worthy
mother stripped the seraglios she visited of the gems
they contained. She collected all the sempstresses and
embroiderers of Samarah and other cities to the distance
of sixty leagues to prepare pavilions, palanquins, sofas,
canopies, and litters for the train of the monarch.
There was not left in Masulipatan a single piece of
chintz; and so much muslin had been brought up to
dress out Bababalouk and the other black eunuchs that
there remained not an ell of it in the whole Irak of
Babylon.

During these preparations, Carathis, who never lost
sight of her great object, which was to obtain favour
with the powers of darkness, made select parties of the
fairest and most delicate ladies of the city, but in the
midst of their gaiety she contrived to introduce vipers
amongst them, and to break pots of scorpions under the
table. They all bit to a wonder; and Carathis would
have left her friends to die, were it not that, to fill
up the time, she now and then amused herself in cur-
ing their wounds with an excellent anodyne of her own

invention; for this good princess abhorred being indolent.

Vathek, who was not altogether so active as his mother, devoted his time to the sole gratification of his senses in the palaces which were severally dedicated to them. He disgusted himself no more with the divan, or the mosque. One half of Samarah followed his example, whilst the other lamented the progress of corruption.

In the midst of these transactions, the embassy returned which had been sent in pious times to Mecca. It consisted of the most reverend moullahs, who had fulfilled their commission and brought back one of those precious besoms which are used to sweep the sacred Cahaba;* a present truly worthy of the greatest potentate on earth!

The caliph happened at this instant to be engaged in an apartment by no means adapted to the reception of embassies. He heard the voice of Bababalouk calling out from between the door and the tapestry that hung before it,—"Here are the excellent Edris al Shafei, and the seraphic Al Mouhateddin, who have brought the besom from Mecca, and, with tears of joy, entreat they may present it to your majesty in person."—"Let them bring the besom hither; it may be of use," said Vathek. —"How!" answered Bababalouk, half aloud and amazed.—"Obey," replied the caliph, "for it is my sovereign will; go instantly, vanish! for here will I receive the good folk who have thus filled thee with joy."

The eunuch departed muttering, and bade the venerable train attend him. A sacred rapture was diffused amongst these reverend old men. Though fatigued with the length of their expedition, they followed Bababalouk

*Today generally spelled Kaaba. The most sacred portion of the temple at Mecca.

with an alertness almost miraculous, and felt themselves highly flattered as they swept along the stately
porticoes, that the caliph would not receive them like
ambassadors in ordinary in his hall of audience. Soon
reaching the interior of the harem, (where, through
blinds of Persian, they perceived large soft eyes, dark
and blue, that came and went like lightning,) penetrated
with respect and wonder, and full of their celestial mission, they advanced in procession towards the small
corridors that appeared to terminate in nothing, but
nevertheless led to the cell where the caliph expected
their coming.

"What! is the commander of the faithful sick?" said
Edris al Shafei, in a low voice to his companion.—"I
rather think he is in his oratory," answered Al Mouhateddin. Vathek, who heard the dialogue, cried out,—
"What imports it you, how I am employed? Approach
without delay." They advanced, whilst the caliph, without showing himself, put forth his hand from behind
the tapestry that hung before the door, and demanded
of them the besom. Having prostrated themselves as
well as the corridor would permit, and even in a tolerable semicircle, the venerable Al Shafei, drawing forth
the besom from the embroidered and perfumed scarves
in which it had been enveloped and secured from the
profane gaze of vulgar eyes, arose from his associates,
and advanced with an air of the most awful solemnity
towards the supposed oratory. But with what astonishment! with what horror was he seized! Vathek, bursting out with a villanous laugh, snatched the besom
from his trembling hand, and fixing upon some cobwebs
that hung from the ceiling, gravely brushed them away
till not a single one remained. The old men, overpowered with amazement, were unable to lift their
beards from the ground; for, as Vathek had carelessly

left the tapestry between them half drawn, they were witnesses of the whole transaction. Their tears bedewed the marble. Al Mouhateddin swooned through mortification and fatigue, whilst the caliph, throwing himself backward on his seat, shouted and clapped his hands without mercy. At last, addressing himself to Bababalouk,—"My dear black," said he, "go, regale these pious poor souls with my good wine from Schiraz, since they can boast of having seen more of my palace than any one besides." Having said this, he threw the besom in their faces, and went to enjoy the laugh with Carathis. Bababalouk did all in his power to console the ambassadors, but the two most infirm expired on the spot; the rest were carried to their beds, from whence, being heartbroken with sorrow and shame, they never arose.

The succeeding night, Vathek, attended by his mother, ascended the tower to see if everything were ready for his journey; for he had great faith in the influence of the stars. The planets appeared in their most favourable aspects. The caliph, to enjoy so flattering a sight, supped gaily on the roof, and fancied that he heard during his repast loud shouts of laughter resound through the sky, in a manner that inspired the fullest assurance.

All was in motion at the palace; lights were kept burning through the whole of the night; the sound of implements, and of artisans finishing their work, the voices of women, and their guardians, who sung at their embroidery, all conspired to interrupt the stillness of nature, and infinitely delighted the heart of Vathek, who imagined himself going in triumph to sit upon the throne of Soliman. The people were not less satisfied than himself; all assisted to accelerate the moment

which should rescue them from the wayward caprices
of so extravagant a master.

The day preceding the departure of this infatuated
prince was employed by Carathis in repeating to him
the decrees of the mysterious parchment, which she had
thoroughly gotten by heart, and in recommending him
not to enter the habitation of any one by the way:—
"For well thou knowest," added she, "how liquorish
thy taste is after good dishes and young damsels. Let
me therefore enjoin thee to be content with thy old
cooks, who are the best in the world, and not to forget
that in thy ambulatory seraglio there are at least three
dozen of pretty faces which Bababalouk has not yet
unveiled. I myself have a great desire to watch over
thy conduct and visit the subterranean palace, which,
no doubt, contains whatever can interest persons like
us. There is nothing so pleasing as retiring to caverns:
my taste for dead bodies, and everything like mummy,
is decided; and, I am confident, thou wilt see the most
exquisite of their kind. Forget me not then, but the
moment thou art in possession of the talismans which
are to open the way to the mineral kingdoms and the
centre of the earth itself, fail not to despatch some
trusty genius to take me and my cabinet; for the oil of
the serpents I have pinched to death will be a pretty
present to the Giaour, who cannot but be charmed with
such dainties."

Scarcely had Carathis ended this edifying discourse,
when the sun, setting behind the mountain of the four
fountains, gave place to the rising moon. This planet,
being that evening at full, appeared of unusual beauty
and magnitude in the eyes of the women, the eunuchs,
and the pages, who were all impatient to set forward.
The city re-echoed with shouts of joy and flourishing of
trumpets. Nothing was visible but plumes nodding on

pavilions, and aigrets shining in the mild lustre of the moon. The spacious square resembled an immense parterre variegated with the most stately tulips of the East.

Arrayed in the robes which were only worn at the most distinguished ceremonials, and supported by his vizir and Bababalouk, the caliph descended the great staircase of the tower in the sight of all his people. He could not forbear pausing at intervals to admire the superb appearance which everywhere courted his view; whilst the whole multitude, even to the camels with their sumptuous burdens, knelt down before him. For some time a general stillness prevailed, which nothing happened to disturb but the shrill screams of some eunuchs in the rear. These vigilant guards, having remarked certain cages of the ladies swagging somewhat awry, and discovered that a few adventurous gallants had contrived to get in, soon dislodged the enraptured culprits, and consigned them with good commendations to the surgeons of the serail. The majesty of so magnificent a spectacle was not, however, violated by incidents like these. Vathek, meanwhile, saluted the moon with an idolatrous air, that neither pleased Morakanabad nor the doctors of the law, any more than the vizirs and grandees of his court, who were all assembled to enjoy the last view of their sovereign.

At length the clarions and trumpets from the top of the tower announced the prelude of departure. Though the instruments were in unison with each other, yet a singular dissonance was blended with their sounds. This proceeded from Carathis, who was singing her direful orisons to the Giaour, while the negresses and mutes supplied thorough bass without articulating a word. The good Mussulmans fancied that they heard the sullen hum of those nocturnal insects which presage evil, and importuned Vathek to beware how he ventured his sacred person.

On a given signal the great standard of the Califat was displayed; twenty thousand lances shone around it, and the caliph, treading royally on the cloth of gold which had been spread for his feet, ascended his litter amidst the general acclamations of his subjects.

The expedition commenced with the utmost order, and so entire a silence that even the locusts were heard from the thickets on the plain of Catoul. Gaiety and good humour prevailing, they made full six leagues before the dawn; and the morning star was still glittering in the firmament when the whole of this numerous train had halted on the banks of the Tigris, where they encamped to repose for the rest of the day.

The three days that followed were spent in the same manner, but on the fourth the heavens looked angry. Lightnings broke forth in frequent flashes, re-echoing peals of thunder succeeded, and the trembling Circassians clung with all their might to their ugly guardians. The caliph himself was greatly inclined to take shelter in the large town of Ghulchissar, the governor of which came forth to meet him and tendered every kind of refreshment the place could supply. But, having examined his tablets, he suffered the rain to soak him almost to the bone, notwithstanding the importunity of his first favourites. Though he began to regret the palace of the senses, yet he lost not sight of his enterprise, and his sanguine expectation confirmed his resolution. His geographers were ordered to attend him, but the weather proved so terrible that these poor people exhibited a lamentable appearance; and their maps of the different countries, spoiled by the rain, were in a still worse plight than themselves. As no long journey had been undertaken since the time of Haroun al Raschid, every one was ignorant which way to turn, and Vathek, though well versed in the course of the heavens, no longer knew his situation on earth. He thundered even louder than the elements, and muttered forth certain hints of the bow-string which were not very soothing to literary ears. Disgusted at the toilsome weariness of the way, he determined to cross over the craggy heights and follow the guidance of a peasant, who undertook to bring him in four days to Rocnabad. Remonstrances were all to no purpose; his resolution was fixed.

The females and eunuchs uttered shrill wailings at the sight of the precipices below them, and the dreary prospects that opened in the vast gorges of the mountains. Before they could reach the ascent of the steepest rock, night overtook them, and a boisterous tempest arose which, having rent the awnings of the palanquins and cages, exposed to the raw gusts the poor ladies within, who had never before felt so piercing a cold. The dark clouds that overcast the face of the sky deepened the horrors of this disastrous night, insomuch that nothing could be heard distinctly but the mewling of pages and lamentations of sultanas.

To increase the general misfortune, the frightful uproar of wild beasts resounded at a distance; and there was soon perceived in the forest they were skirting the glaring of eyes which could belong only to devils or tigers. The pioneers, who as well as they could had marked out a track, and a part of the advanced guard, were devoured before they had been in the least apprised of their danger. The confusion that prevailed was extreme. Wolves, tigers and other carnivorous animals, invited by the howling of their companions, flocked together from every quarter. The crashing of bones was

heard on all sides, and a fearful rush of wings over-
head; for now vultures also began to be of the party.

The terror at length reached the main body of the
troops which surrounded the monarch and his harem at
the distance of two leagues from the scene. Vathek
(voluptuously reposed in his capacious litter upon
cushions of silk, with two little pages beside him of
complexions more fair than the enamel of Franguistan,
who were occupied in keeping off flies), was soundly
asleep, and contemplating in his dreams the treasures
of Soliman. The shrieks, however, of his wives awoke
him with a start; and, instead of the Giaour with his
key of gold, he beheld Bababalouk full of consternation.
"Sire," exclaimed this good servant of the most potent
of monarchs, "misfortune is arrived at its height; wild
beasts, who entertain no more reverence for your sacred
person than for a dead ass, have beset your camels and
their drivers. Thirty of the most richly laden are already become their prey, as well as your confectioners,
your cooks, and purveyors; and unless our holy Prophet
should protect us, we shall have all eaten our last
meal."

At the mention of eating, the caliph lost all patience.
He began to bellow, and even beat himself (for there
was no seeing in the dark). The rumour every instant
increased; and Bababalouk, finding no good could be
done with his master, stopped both his ears against the
hurlyburly of the harem, and called out aloud,—"Come,
ladies and brothers! all hands to work. Strike light in
a moment! Never shall it be said that the commander
of the faithful served to regale these infidel brutes."
Though there wanted not in this bevy of beauties a
sufficient number of capricious and wayward, yet on
the present occasion they were all compliance. Fires
were visible in a twinkling in all their cages. Ten thou-

sand torches were lighted at once. The caliph himself
seized a large one of wax; every person followed his
example; and by kindling ropes' ends dipped in oil and
fastened on poles, an amazing blaze was spread. The
rocks were covered with the splendour of sunshine. The
trails of sparks, wafted by the wind, communicated to
the dry fern, of which there was plenty. Serpents were
observed to crawl forth from their retreats with amazement and hissings, whilst the horses snorted, stamped
the ground, tossed their noses in the air, and plunged
about without mercy.

One of the forests of cedar that bordered their way
took fire; and the branches that overhung the path, extending their flames to the muslins and chintzes which
covered the cages of the ladies, obliged them to jump
out, at the peril of their necks. Vathek, who vented on
the occasion a thousand blasphemies, was himself compelled to touch with his sacred feet the naked earth.

Never had such an incident happened before. Full
of mortification, shame and despondence, and not knowing how to walk, the ladies fell into the dirt. "Must I
go on foot?" said one. "Must I wet my feet?" cried
another. "Must I soil my dress?" asked a third. "Execrable Bababalouk!" exclaimed all. "Outcast of hell!
what hast thou to do with torches? Better were it to be
eaten by tigers than to fall into our present condition!
we are for ever undone! Not a porter is there in the
army, nor a currier of camels, but hath seen some part
of our bodies, and, what is worse, our very faces!" On
saying this the most bashful amongst them hid their
foreheads on the ground, while such as had more boldness flew at Bababalouk; but he, well apprised of their
humour, and not wanting in shrewdness, betook himself to his heels along with his comrades, all dropping
their torches and striking their tymbals.

It was not less light than in the brightest of the dog-days, and the weather was hot in proportion; but how degrading was the spectacle to behold the caliph bespattered like an ordinary mortal! As the exercise of his faculties seemed to be suspended, one of his Ethiopian wives (for he delighted in variety) clasped him in her arms, threw him upon her shoulder like a sack of dates, and, finding that the fire was hemming them in, set off with no small expedition, considering the weight of her burden. The other ladies, who had just learned the use of their feet, followed her: their guards galloped after; and the camel-drivers brought up the rear as fast as their charge would permit.

They soon reached the spot where the wild beasts had commenced the carnage, but which they had too much good sense not to leave at the approaching of the tumult, having made besides a most luxurious supper. Bababalouk nevertheless seized on a few of the plumpest, which were unable to budge from the place, and began to flay them with admirable adroitness. The cavalcade having proceeded so far from the conflagration that the heat felt rather grateful than violent, it was immediately resolved on to halt. The tattered chintzes were picked up, the scraps left by the wolves and tigers interred, and vengeance was taken on some dozens of vultures that were too much glutted to rise on the wing. The camels, which had been left unmolested to make sal ammoniac, being numbered, and the ladies once more enclosed in their cages, the imperial tent was pitched on the levellest ground they could find.

Vathek, reposing upon a mattress of down, and tolerably recovered from the jolting of the Ethiopian, who to his feelings seemed the roughest trotting jade he had hitherto mounted, called out for something to eat.

But, alas! those delicate cakes which had been baked
in silver ovens for his royal mouth, those rich manchets,
amber comfits, flagons of Schiraz wine, porcelain vases
of snow, and grapes from the banks of the Tigris, were
all irremediably lost! And nothing had Bababalouk to
present in their stead but a roasted wolf, vultures à la
daube, aromatic herbs of the most acrid poignancy,
rotten truffles, boiled thistles, and such other wild plants
as must ulcerate the throat and parch up the tongue.
Nor was he better provided in the article of drink, for
he could procure nothing to accompany these irritating
viands but a few phials of abominable brandy which
had been secreted by the scullions in their slippers.
Vathek made wry faces at so savage a repast, and
Bababalouk answered them with shrugs and contortions. The caliph, however, eat with tolerable appetite, and fell into a nap that lasted six hours.

The splendour of the sun, reflected from the white
cliffs of the mountains, in spite of the curtains that
enclosed Vathek, at length disturbed his repose. He
awoke terrified, and stung to the quick by wormwood-
colour flies, which emitted from their wings a suffocat-
ing stench. The miserable monarch was perplexed how
to act, though his wits were not idle in seeking expedients; whilst Bababalouk lay snoring amidst a
swarm of those insects that busily thronged to pay court
to his nose. The little pages, famished with hunger,
had dropped their fans on the ground, and exerted their
dying voices in bitter reproaches on the caliph, who
now for the first time heard the language of truth.

Thus stimulated, he renewed his imprecations against
the Giaour, and bestowed upon Mahomet some soothing
expressions. "Where am I?" cried he; "what are
these dreadful rocks—these valleys of darkness? Are
we arrived at the horrible Kaf? Is the Simurgh com-

ing to pluck out my eyes, as a punishment for undertaking this impious enterprise?" Having said this he
turned himself towards an outlet in the side of his
pavilion; but, alas! what objects occurred to his view?
On one side a plain of blank sand that appeared to be
unbounded, and on the other perpendicular crags, bris-
tled over with those abominable thistles which had so
severely lacerated his tongue. He fancied, however,
that he perceived amongst the brambles and briars some
gigantic flowers, but was mistaken; for these were only
the dangling palampores and variegated tatters of his
gay retinue. As there were several clefts in the rock
from whence water seemed to have flowed, Vathek applied his ear with the hope of catching the sound of
some latent torrent, but could only distinguish the low
murmurs of his people, who were repining at their journey and complaining for the want of water. "To what
purpose," asked they, "have we been brought hither?
Hath our caliph another tower to build? or have the
relentless afrits whom Carathis so much loves fixed
their abode in this place?"

At the name of Carathis, Vathek recollected the tablets he had received from his mother, who assured him
they were fraught with preternatural qualities, and advised him to consult them as emergencies might require.
Whilst he was engaged in turning them over, he heard
a shout of joy and a loud clapping of hands. The
curtains of his pavilion were soon drawn back, and he
beheld Bababalouk followed by a troop of his favourites,
conducting two dwarfs, each a cubit high, who brought
between them a large basket of melons, oranges, and
pomegranates. They were singing in the sweetest tones
the words that follow:—"We dwell on the top of these
rocks, in a cabin of rushes and canes. The eagles envy
us our nests. A small spring supplies us with water

for the Abdest,* and we daily repeat prayers, which
the Prophet approves. We love you, O commander of
the faithful! Our master, the good Emir Fakreddin,
loves you also; he reveres, in your person, the vicegerent
of Mahomet. Little as we are, in us he confides: he
knows our hearts to be as good as our bodies are contemptible, and hath placed us here to aid those who
are bewildered on these dreary mountains. Last night,
whilst we were occupied within our cell in reading the
holy Koran, a sudden hurricane blew out our lights,
and rocked our habitation. For two whole hours a pal-
pable darkness prevailed, but we heard sounds at a distance which we conjectured to proceed from the bells
of a cafila,† passing over the rocks. Our ears were
soon filled with deplorable shrieks, frightful roarings,
and the sound of tymbals. Chilled with terror, we concluded that the Deggial, with his exterminating angels,
had sent forth his plagues on the earth. In the midst
of these melancholy reflections we perceived flames of
the deepest red glow in the horizon, and found ourselves
in a few moments covered with flakes of fire. Amazed
at so strange an appearance, we took up the volume
dictated by the blessed Intelligence, and kneeling, by
the light of the fire that surrounded us, we recited the
verse which says, 'Put no trust in anything but the
mercy of Heaven; there is no help save in the holy
Prophet: the mountain of Kaf, itself, may tremble; it
is the power of Allah only that cannot be moved.' After
having pronounced these words, we felt consolation,
and our minds were hushed into a sacred repose.
Silence ensued, and our ears clearly distinguished a
voice in the air saying,—'Servants of my faithful servant! go down to the happy valley of Fakreddin; tell

* The Mahometan ablutions before prayers.
† Caravan.

him that an illustrious opportunity now offers to satiate the thirst of his hospitable heart. The commander of true believers is this day bewildered amongst these mountains, and stands in need of thy aid.'—We obeyed, with joy, the angelic mission; and our master, filled with pious zeal, hath culled with his own hands these melons, oranges, and pomegranates. He is following us with a hundred dromedaries, laden with the purest waters of his fountains, and is coming to kiss the fringe of your consecrated robe, and implore you to enter his humble habitation, which, placed amidst these barren wilds, resembles an emerald set in lead." The dwarfs, having ended their address, remained still standing, and with hands crossed upon their bosoms, preserved a respectful silence.

Vathek, in the midst of this curious harangue, seized the basket, and long before it was finished, the fruits had dissolved in his mouth. As he continued to eat, his piety increased, and in the same breath he recited his prayers and called for the Koran and sugar.

Such was the state of his mind when the tablets, which were thrown by at the approach of the dwarfs, again attracted his eye. He took them up, but was ready to drop on the ground when he beheld, in large red characters, inscribed by Carathis, these words, which were, indeed, enough to make him tremble: "Beware of old doctors and their puny messengers of but one cubit high. Distrust their pious frauds, and instead of eating their melons, empale on a spit the bearers of them. Shouldest thou be such a fool as to visit them, the portal of the subterranean palace will shut in thy face with such force as shall shake thee asunder; thy body shall be spit upon, and bats will nestle in thy belly."

"To what tends this ominous rhapsody?" cries the

caliph; "and must I, then, perish in these deserts with thirst, whilst I may refresh myself in the delicious valley of melons and cucumbers? Accursed be the Giaour with his portal of ebony! he hath made me dance attendance too long already. Besides, who shall prescribe laws to me? I, forsooth, must not enter any one's habitation! Be it so; but what one can I enter that is not my own?" Bababalouk, who lost not a syllable of this soliloquy, applauded it with all his heart; and the ladies for the first time agreed with him in opinion.

The dwarfs were entertained, caressed, and seated with great ceremony on little cushions of satin. The symmetry of their persons was a subject of admiration; not an inch of them was suffered to pass unexamined. Knick-knacks and dainties were offered in profusion; but all were declined with respectful gravity. They climbed up the sides of the caliph's seat, and placing themselves each on one of his shoulders, began to whisper prayers in his ears. Their tongues quivered like aspen leaves; and the patience of Vathek was almost exhausted, when the acclamations of the troops announced the approach of Fakreddin, who was come with a hundred old grey-beards and as many Korans and dromedaries. They instantly set about their ablutions, and began to repeat the Bismillah. Vathek, to get rid of these officious monitors, followed their example, for his hands were burning.

The good emir, who was punctiliously religious, and likewise a great dealer in compliments, made an harangue five times more prolix and insipid than his little harbingers had already delivered. The caliph, unable any longer to refrain, exclaimed,—"For the love of Mahomet, my dear Fakreddin, have done! Let us proceed to your valley, and enjoy the fruits that Heaven hath vouchsafed you." The hint of proceeding put all

into motion. The venerable attendants of the emir set
forward somewhat slowly, but Vathek having ordered
his little pages in private to goad on the dromedaries,
loud fits of laughter broke forth from the cages; for the
unwieldy curvetting of these poor beasts, and the ridiculous distress of their superannuated riders, afforded
the ladies no small entertainment.

They descended, however, unhurt into the valley, by
the easy slopes which the emir had ordered to be cut in
the rock; and already the murmuring of streams and
the rustling of leaves began to catch their attention.
The cavalcade soon entered a path which was skirted
by flowering shrubs, and extended to a vast wood of
palm trees, whose branches overspread a vast building
of freestone. This edifice was crowned with nine domes,
and adorned with as many portals of bronze, on which
was engraven the following inscription:—"This is the
asylum of pilgrims, the refuge of travellers, and the
depositary of secrets from all parts of the world."

Nine pages, beautiful as the day, and decently clothed
in robes of Egyptian linen, were standing at each door.
They received the whole retinue with an easy and inviting air. Four of the most amiable placed the caliph on
a magnificent tecthtrevan;* four others, somewhat less
graceful, took charge of Bababalouk, who capered for
joy at the snug little cabin that fell to his share. The
pages that remained waited on the rest of the train.

Every man being gone out of sight, the gate of a large
enclosure on the right turned on its harmonious hinges;
and a young female of a slender form came forth. Her
light brown hair floated in the hazy breeze of the twilight. A troop of young maidens, like the Pleiades,
attended her on tiptoe. They hastened to the pavilions
that contained the sultanas, and the young lady, grace-

* Throne.

fully bending, said to them,—"Charming princesses! every thing is ready; we have prepared beds for your repose, and strewed your apartments with jasmine. No insects will keep off slumber from visiting your eyelids; we will dispel them with a thousand plumes. Come, then, amiable ladies! refresh your delicate feet and your ivory limbs in baths of rose-water, and, by the light of perfumed lamps your servants will amuse you with tales. The sultanas accepted with pleasure these obliging offers, and followed the young lady to the emir's harem, where we must, for a moment, leave them, and return to the caliph.

Vathek found himself beneath a vast dome, illuminated by a thousand lamps of rock crystal. As many vases of the same material, filled with excellent sherbet, sparkled on a large table, where a profusion of viands were spread. Amongst others were rice boiled in milk of almonds, saffron soups, and lamb à la crême, of all which the caliph was amazingly fond. He took of each as much as he was able, testified his sense of the emir's friendship by the gaiety of his heart, and made the dwarfs dance against their will,—for these little devotees durst not refuse the commander of the faithful. At last he spread himself on the sofa and slept sounder than he ever had before.

Beneath this dome a general silence prevailed; for there was nothing to disturb it but the jaws of Bababalouk, who had untrussed himself to eat with greater advantage, being anxious to make amends for his fast in the mountains. As his spirits were too high to admit of his sleeping, and hating to be idle, he proposed with himself to visit the harem, and repair to his charge of the ladies, to examine if they had been properly lubricated with the balm of Mecca, if their eyebrows and tresses were in order, and, in a word, to perform all the little offices they might need. He sought for a long time together, but without being able to find out the door. He durst not speak aloud, for fear of disturbing the caliph; and not a soul was stirring in the precincts of the palace. He almost despaired of effecting his purpose, when a low whispering just reached his ear. It came from the dwarfs, who were returned to their old occupation, and, for the nine hundred and ninety-ninth time in their lives, were reading over the Koran. They very politely invited Bababalouk to be of their party, but his head was full of other concerns. The dwarfs, though not a little scandalised at his dissolute morals, directed him to the apartments he wanted to find.

His way thither led through a hundred dark corridors, along which he groped as he went, and at last began to catch from the extremity of a passage the charming gossiping of the women, which not a little delighted his heart. "Ah, ha! what, not yet asleep?" cried he; and, taking long strides as he spoke, "did you not suspect me of abjuring my charge?" Two of the black eunuchs, on hearing a voice so loud, left their party in haste, sabre in hand, to discover the cause; but presently was repeated on all sides,—" 'Tis only Bababalouk! no one but Bababalouk!" This circumspect guardian, having gone up to a thin veil of carnation-colour silk that hung before the doorway, distinguished by means of the softened splendour that shone through it an oval bath of dark porphyry, surrounded by curtains festooned in large folds. Through the apertures between them, as they were not drawn close, groups of young slaves were visible, among whom Bababalouk perceived his pupils, indulgingly expanding their arms, as if to embrace the perfumed water and refresh themselves after their fatigues. The looks of tender languor, their confidential whispers, and the enchanting smiles with which they were imparted, the exquisite fragrance of the roses all combined to inspire a voluptuousness which even Bababalouk himself was scarce able to withstand.

He summoned up, however, his usual solemnity, and in the peremptory tone of authority commanded the ladies instantly to leave the bath. Whilst he was issuing these mandates, the young Nouronihar, daughter of the emir, who was as sprightly as an antelope, and full of wanton gaiety, beckoned one of her slaves to let down the great swing which was suspended to the ceiling by cords of silk, and whilst this was doing, winked to her companions in the bath, who, chagrined to be forced from so soothing a state of indolence, began to twist and entangle their hair to plague and detain Bababalouk, and teased him besides with a thousand vagaries.

Nouronihar, perceiving that he was nearly out of patience, accosted him with an arch air of respectful concern, and said,—"My lord! it is not by any means decent that the chief eunuch of the caliph, our sovereign, should thus continue standing; deign but to recline your graceful person upon this sofa, which will burst with vexation if it have not the honour to receive you." Caught by these flattering accents, Bababalouk gallantly replied,—"Delight of the apple of my eye! I accept the invitation of your honied lips; and, to say truth, my senses are dazzled with the radiance that beams from your charms."—"Repose, then, at your ease," replied the beauty, as she placed him on the pretended sofa, which, quicker than lightning, flew up all at once. The rest of the women, having aptly conceived her design, sprang naked from the bath, and plied the swing with such unmerciful jerks that it swept through the whole compass of a very lofty dome, and took from the poor victim all power of respiration. Sometimes his feet rased the surface of the water, and, at others, the skylight almost flattened his nose. In vain did he fill the air with the cries of a voice that resembled the ringing of a cracked jar; their peals of laughter were still predominant.

Nouronihar, in the inebriety of youthful spirits, being used only to eunuchs of ordinary harems, and having never seen any thing so eminently disgusting, was far more diverted than all of the rest. She began to parody some Persian verses, and sang, with an accent most demurely piquant,—"Oh, gentle white dove! as thou soar'st through the air, vouchsafe one kind glance on the mate of thy love. Melodious Philomel, I am thy rose; warble some couplet to ravish my heart!"

The sultanas and their slaves, stimulated by these pleasantries, persevered at the swing with such unremitted assiduity that at length the cord which had secured it snapped suddenly asunder, and Bababalouk fell, floundering like a turtle, to the bottom of the bath. This accident occasioned an universal shout. Twelve little doors, till now unobserved, flew open at once, and the ladies in an instant made their escape, but not before having heaped all the towels on his head and put out the lights that remained.

The deplorable animal, in water to the chin, overwhelmed with darkness, and unable to extricate himself from the wrappers that embarrassed him, was still doomed to hear for his further consolation the fresh bursts of merriment his disaster occasioned. He bustled, but in vain, to get from the bath, for the margin was become so slippery with the oil spilt in breaking the lamps, that at every effort he slid back with a plunge which resounded aloud through the hollow of the dome. These cursed peals of laughter were redoubled at every relapse, and he, who thought the place infested rather by devils than women, resolved to cease groping and abide in the bath, where he amused himself with soliloquies interspersed with imprecations, of which his malicious neighbours, reclining on down, suffered not an accent to escape. In this delectable plight the morning surprised him. The caliph, wondering at his absence, had caused him to be sought for everywhere. At last, he was drawn forth almost smothered from under the wisp of linen, and wet even to the marrow. Limping, and his teeth chattering with cold, he approached his master, who enquired what was the matter, and how he came soused in so strange a pickle?—"And why did you enter this cursed lodge?" answered Bababalouk, gruffly. "Ought a monarch like you to visit with his harem the abode of a grey-bearded emir, who knows nothing of life?—And with what gracious damsels doth the place too abound! Fancy to yourself how they have soaked me like a burnt crust, and made me dance like a jack-pudding, the livelong night through, on their damnable swing. What an excellent lesson for your sultanas, into whom I had instilled such reserve and decorum!" Vathek, comprehending not a syllable of all this invective, obliged him to relate minutely the transaction; but, instead of sympathising with the miserable sufferer, he laughed immoderately at the device of the swing and the figure of Bababalouk mounted upon it. The stung eunuch could scarcely preserve the semblance of respect. "Ay, laugh, my lord! laugh," said he; "but I wish this Nouronihar would play some trick on you; she is too wicked to spare even majesty itself." These words made for the present but a slight impression on the caliph; but they not long after recurred to his mind.

This conversation was cut short by Fakreddin, who

came to request that Vathek would join in the prayers
and ablutions to be solemnised on a spacious meadow
watered by innumerable streams. The caliph found
the waters refreshing, but the prayers abominably irksome. He diverted himself, however, with the multitude of calenders, santons, and derviches,* who were
continually coming and going; but especially with the
bramins, faquirs, and other enthusiasts, who had travelled from the heart of India and halted on their way
with the emir. These latter had each of them some
mummery peculiar to himself. One dragged a huge
chain wherever he went, another an ouran-outang, whilst
a third was furnished with scourges; and all performed
to a charm. Some would climb up trees, holding one
foot in the air; others poise themselves over a fire, and
without mercy fillip their noses. There were some
amongst them that cherished vermin, which were not ungrateful in requitting their caresses. These rambling
fanatics revolted the hearts of the derviches, the calenders, and santons. However, the vehemence of their
aversion soon subsided, under the hope that the presence of the caliph would cure their folly and convert
them to the Mussulman faith. But alas! how great
was their disappointment! for Vathek, instead of preach-
ing to them, treated them as buffoons, bade them present his compliments to Visnow and Ixhora, and discovered a predilection for a squat old man from the
Isle of Serendib who was more ridiculous than any of
the rest. "Come!" said he, "for the love of your gods,
bestow a few slaps on your chops to amuse me." The
old fellow, offended at such an address, began loudly
to weep; but as he betrayed a villanous drivelling in
shedding tears, the caliph turned his back and listened

* Calenders, sautons and dervishes were all Mahometan
ascetics, differing in their devoutness and their observances.

to Bababalouk, who whispered whilst he held the umbrella over him, "Your majesty should be cautious of this odd assembly, which hath been collected I know not for what. Is it necessary to exhibit such spectacles to a mighty potentate, with interludes of talapoins* more mangy than dogs? Were I you, I would command a fire to be kindled, and at once rid the estates of the emir, of his harem, and all his menagerie."— "Tush, dolt," answered Vathek, "and know that all this infinitely charms me. Nor shall I leave the meadow till I have visited every hive of these pious mendicants."

Wherever the caliph directed his course, objects of pity were sure to swarm round him: the blind, the purblind, smarts without noses, damsels without ears, each to extol the munificence of Fakreddin, who, as well as his attendant greybeards, dealt about gratis plasters and cataplasms to all that applied. At noon a superb corps of cripples made its appearance, and soon after advanced by platoons on the plain the completest association of invalids that had ever been embodied till then. The blind went groping with the blind, the lame limped on together, and the maimed made gestures to each other with the only arm that remained. The sides of a considerable waterfall were crowded by the deaf, amongst whom were some from Pegu, with ears uncommonly handsome and large, but who were still less able to hear than the rest. Nor were there wanting others in abundance with hump-backs, wenny necks, and even horns of an exquisite polish.

The emir, to aggrandise the solemnity of the festival, in honour of his illustrious visitant, ordered the turf to be spread on all sides with skins and table-cloths, upon which were served up for the good Mussulmans pilaus of every hue with other orthodox dishes; and, by the ex-

* Another Mahometan religious order.

press order of Vathek, who was shamefully tolerant, small plates of abominations were prepared, to the great scandal of the faithful. The holy assembly began to fall to. The caliph, in spite of every remonstrance from the chief of his eunuchs, resolved to have a dinner dressed on the spot. The complaisant emir immediately gave orders for a table to be placed in the shade of the willows. The first service consisted of fish, which they drew from a river flowing over sands of gold at the foot of a lofty hill. These were broiled as fast as taken, and served up with a sauce of vinegar and small herbs that grew on Mount Sinai; for everything with the emir was excellent and pious.

The dessert was not quite set on when the sound of lutes from the hill was repeated by the echoes of the neighbouring mountains. The caliph, with an emotion of pleasure and surprise, had no sooner raised up his head, than a handful of jasmine dropped on his face. An abundance of tittering succeeded the frolic, and instantly appeared through the bushes the elegant forms of several young females, skipping and bounding like roes. The fragrance diffused from their hair struck the sense of Vathek, who in an ecstasy, suspending his re-past, said to Bababalouk,—"Are the peries come down from their spheres? Note her in particular whose form is so perfect, venturously running on the brink of the precipice, and turning back her head as regardless of nothing but the graceful flow of her robe. With what captivating impatience doth she contend with the bushes for her veil? Could it be she who threw the jasmine at me?"—"Ay! she it was; and you too would she throw, from the top of the rock," answered Bababa-louk, "for that is my good friend Nouronihar, who so kindly lent me her swing. My dear lord and master," added he, wresting a twig from a willow, "let me cor-

rect her for her want of respect: the emir will have no
reason to complain, since (bating what I owe to his
piety) he is much to be blamed for keeping a troop of
girls on the mountains, where the sharpness of the air
gives their blood too brisk a circulation."

"Peace! blasphemer," said the caliph; "speak not thus
of her who over these mountains leads my heart a willing captive. Contrive, rather, that my eyes may be
fixed upon hers, that I may respire her sweet breath as
she bounds panting along these delightful wilds!" On
saying these words, Vathek extended his arms towards
the hill, and directing his eyes with an anxiety unknown
to him before, endeavoured to keep within view the object that enthralled his soul; but her course was as
difficult to follow as the flight of one of those beautiful
blue butterflies of Cachemire, which are at once so
volatile and rare.

The caliph, not satisfied with seeing, wished also to
hear Nouronihar, and eagerly turned to catch the sound
of her voice. At last he distinguished her whispering
to one of her companions behind the thicket from
whence she had thrown the jasmine,—"A caliph, it
must be owned, is a fine thing to see, but my little
Gulchenrouz is much more amiable; one lock of his
hair is of more value to me than the richest embroidery
of the Indies. I had rather that his teeth should mis-
chievously press my finger, than the richest ring of the
imperial treasure. Where have you left him, Sutlememe? and why is he not here?"

The agitated caliph still wished to hear more, but she
immediately retired with all her attendants. The fond
monarch pursued her with his eyes till she was gone
out of sight, and then continued like a bewildered and
benighted traveller from whom the clouds had obscured
the constellation that guided his way. The curtain of

night seemed dropped before him; everything appeared
discoloured. The falling waters filled his soul with
dejection, and his tears trickled down the jasmines he
had caught from Nouronihar and placed in his inflamed
bosom. He snatched up a few shining pebbles, to remind him of the scene where he felt the first tumults
of love. Two hours were elapsed and evening drew on
before he could resolve to depart from the place. He
often, but in vain, attempted to go; a soft languor enervated the powers of his mind. Extending himself on
the brink of the stream, he turned his eyes towards the
blue summits of the mountain and exclaimed,—"What
concealest thou behind thee, pitiless rock? What is
passing in thy solitudes? Whither is she gone? O
heaven! perhaps she is now wandering in thy grottoes
with her happy Gulchenrouz!"

In the mean time the damps began to descend, and
the emir, solicitous for the health of the caliph, ordered
the imperial litter to be brought. Vathek, absorbed in
his reveries, was imperceptibly removed and conveyed
back to the saloon that received him the evening before.
But let us leave the caliph immersed in his new passion,
and attend Nouronihar beyond the rocks, where she had
again joined her beloved Gulchenrouz.

This Gulchenrouz was the son of Ali Hassan, brother
to the emir, and the most delicate and lovely creature
in the world. Ali Hassan, who had been absent ten
years on a voyage to the unknown seas, committed at
his departure this child, the only survivor of many, to
the care and protection of his brother. Gulchenrouz
could write in various characters with precision, and
paint upon vellum the most elegant arabesques that
fancy could devise. His sweet voice accompanied the
lute in the most enchanting manner, and when he sang
the loves of Megnoun and Leilah, or some unfortunate

lovers of ancient days, tears insensibly overflowed the
cheeks of his auditors. The verses he composed (for,
like Megnoun, he too was a poet,) inspired that un-
resisting languor so frequently fatal to the female heart.
The women all doted upon him and, though he had
passed his thirteenth year, they still detained him in the
harem. His dancing was light as the gossamer waved
by the zephyrs of spring, but his arms, which twined
so gracefully with those of the young girls in the dance,
could neither dart the lance in the chase nor curb the
steeds that pastured in his uncle's domains. The bow,
however, he drew with a certain aim, and would have
excelled his competitors in the race, could he have
broken the ties that bound him to Nouronihar.

The two brothers had mutually engaged their children to each other, and Nouronihar loved her cousin
more than her own beautiful eyes. Both had the same
tastes and amusements, the same long, languishing looks,
the same tresses, the same fair complexions; and when
Gulchenrouz appeared in the dress of his cousin, he
seemed to be more feminine than even herself. If at
any time he left the harem to visit Fakreddin, it was
with all the bashfulness of a fawn that consciously ven-
tures from the lair of its dam. He was, however,
wanton enough to mock the solemn old greybeards,
though sure to be rated without mercy in return. Whenever this happened, he would hastily plunge into the
recesses of the harem, and sobbing, take refuge in the
fond arms of Nouronihar, who loved even his faults
beyond the virtues of others.

It fell out this evening that after leaving the caliph
in the meadow, she ran with Gulchenrouz over the
green sward of the mountain that sheltered the vale
where Fakreddin had chosen to reside. The sun was
dilated on the edge of the horizon, and the young peo-

ple, whose fancies were lively and inventive, imagined they beheld in the gorgeous clouds of the west the domes of Shaddukian and Ambreabad, where the peries have fixed their abode. Nouronihar, sitting on the slope of the hill, supported on her knees the perfumed head of Gulchenrouz. The unexpected arrival of the caliph, and the splendour that marked his appearance, had already filled with emotion the ardent soul of Nouronihar. Her vanity irresistibly prompted her to pique the prince's attention; and this she before took good care to effect, whilst he picked up the jasmine she had thrown upon him. But when Gulchenrouz asked after the flowers he had culled for her bosom, Nouronihar was all in confusion. She hastily kissed his forehead, arose in a flutter, and walked with unequal steps on the border of the precipice. Night advanced and the pure gold of the setting sun had yielded to a sanguine red, the glow of which, like the reflection of a burning furnace, flushed Nouronihar's animated countenance. Gulchenrouz, alarmed at the agitation of his cousin, said to her with a supplicating accent,—"Let us begone; the sky looks portentous, the tamarisks tremble more than common, and the raw wind chills my very heart. Come! let us begone; 'tis a melancholy night!" Then taking hold of her hand, he drew it towards the path he besought her to go. Nouronihar unconsciously followed the attraction, for a thousand strange imaginations occupied her spirits. She passed the large round of honeysuckles, her favourite resort, without ever vouchsafing it a glance; yet Gulchenrouz could not help snatching off a few shoots in his way, though he ran as if a wild beast were behind.

The young females seeing them approach in such haste, and, according to custom, expecting a dance, instantly assembled in a circle and took each other by the hand; but Gulchenrouz, coming up out of breath, fell down at once on the grass. This accident struck with consternation the whole of this frolicsome party, whilst Nouronihar, half distracted and overcome both by the violence of her exercise and the tumult of her thoughts, sunk feebly down at his side, cherished his cold hands in her bosom, and chafed his temples with a fragrant perfume. At length he came to himself, and wrapping up his head in the robe of his cousin, entreated that she would not return to the harem. He was afraid of being snapped at by Shaban his tutor, a wrinkled old eunuch of a surly disposition; for, having interrupted the wonted walk of Nouronihar, he dreaded lest the churl should take it amiss. The whole of this sprightly group, sitting round upon a mossy knoll, began to entertain themselves with various pastimes, whilst their superintendents, the eunuchs, were gravely conversing at a distance. The nurse of the emir's daughter, observing her pupil sit ruminating with her eyes on the ground, endeavoured to amuse her with diverting tales; to which Gulchenrouz, who had already forgotten his inquietudes, listened with a breathless attention. He laughed, he clapped his hands, and passed a hundred little tricks on the whole of the company, without omitting the eunuchs, whom he provoked to run after him in spite of their age and decrepitude.

During these occurrences the moon arose, the wind subsided, and the evening became so serene and inviting that a resolution was taken to sup on the spot. One of the eunuchs ran to fetch melons, whilst others were employed in showering down almonds from the branches that overhung this amiable party. Sutlememe, who excelled in dressing a salad, having filled large bowls of porcelain with eggs of small birds, curds turned with

citron juice, slices of cucumber, and the inmost leaves
of delicate herbs, handed it round from one to another
and gave each their shares with a large spoon of cock-
nos. Gulchenrouz, nestling as usual in the bosom of
Nouronihar, pouted out his vermilion little lips against
the offer of Sutlememe, and would take it only from
the hand of his cousin, on whose mouth he hung like a
bee inebriated with the nectar of flowers.

In the midst of this festive scene there appeared a
light on the top of the highest mountain which attracted
the notice of every eye. This light was not less bright
than the moon when at full, and might have been taken
for her, had not the moon already risen. The phenomenon occasioned a general surprise, and no one
could conjecture the cause. It could not be a fire, for
the light was clear and bluish; nor had meteors ever
been seen of that magnitude or splendour. This strange
light faded for a moment, and immediately renewed its
brightness. It first appeared motionless at the foot of
the rock, whence it darted in an instant to sparkle in a
thicket of palm-trees; from thence it glided along the
torrent, and at last fixed in a glen that was narrow and
dark. The moment it had taken its direction, Gulchenrouz, whose heart always trembled at any thing sudden or rare, drew Nouronihar by the robe, and anxiously
requested her to return to the harem. The women were
importunate in seconding the entreaty, but the curiosity of the emir's daughter prevailed. She not only
refused to go back, but resolved at all hazards to pursue the appearance.

Whilst they were debating what was best to be done,
the light shot forth so dazzling a blaze that they all fled
away shrieking. Nouronihar followed them a few steps,
but coming to the turn of a little by-path, stopped and
went back alone. As she ran with an alertness peculiar

to herself, it was not long before she came to the place where they had just been supping. The globe of fire now appeared stationary in the glen, and burned in majestic stillness. Nouronihar, pressing her hands upon her bosom, hesitated for some moments to advance. The solitude of her situation was new, the silence of the night awful, and every object inspired sensations which till then she never had felt. The affright of Gulchenrouz recurred to her mind, and she a thousand times turned to go back, but this luminous appearance was always before her. Urged on by an irresistible impulse, she continued to approach it, in defiance of every obstacle that opposed her progress.

At length she arrived at the opening of the glen, but instead of coming up to the light, she found herself surrounded by darkness, excepting that at a considerable distance a faint spark glimmered by fits. She stopped a second time; the sound of waterfalls mingling their murmurs, the hollow rustlings among the palm branches, and the funereal screams of the birds from their rifted trunks, all conspired to fill her soul with terror. She imagined every moment that she trod on some venomous reptile. All the stories of malignant dives and dismal ghouls thronged into her memory, but her curiosity was, notwithstanding, more predominant than her fears. She therefore firmly entered a winding track that led towards the spark, but being a stranger to the path, she had not gone far till she began to repent of her rashness. "Alas!" said she, "that I were but in those secure and illuminated apartments where my evenings glided on with Gulchenrouz! Dear child! how would thy heart flutter with terror wert thou wandering in these wild solitudes like me!" Thus speaking, she advanced, and coming up to steps hewn in the rock, ascended them undismayed. The light, which was now

gradually enlarging, appeared above her on the summit of the mountain, and as if proceeding from a cavern.
At length she distinguished a plaintive and melodious
union of voices that resembled the dirges which are
sung over tombs. A sound like that which arises from
the filling of baths struck her ear at the same time.
She continued ascending, and discovered large wax
torches in full blaze, planted here and there in the
fissures of the rock. This appearance filled her with
fear, whilst the subtle and potent odour which the
torches exhaled caused her to sink almost lifeless at
the entrance of the grot.

Casting her eyes within, in this kind of trance, she
beheld a large cistern of gold filled with a water the
vapour of which distilled on her face a dew of the essence of roses. A soft symphony resounded through the
grot. On the sides of the cistern she noticed ap-
pendages of royalty, diadems and feathers of the heron,
all sparkling with carbuncles. Whilst her attention was
fixed on this display of magnificence, the music ceased,
and a voice instantly demanded,—"For what monarch
are these torches kindled, this bath prepared, and these
habiliments which belong not only to the sovereigns of
the earth, but even to the talismanic powers?" To
which a second voice answered, "They are for the
charming daughter of the Emir Fakreddin."—"What,"
replied the first, "for that trifler, who consumes her
time with a giddy child, immersed in softness, and who
at best can make but a pitiful husband?"—"And can
she," rejoined the other voice, "be amused with such
empty toys, whilst the caliph, the sovereign of the
world, he who is destined to enjoy the treasures of the
pre-adamite sultans, a prince six feet high, and whose
eyes pervade the inmost soul of a female, is inflamed
with love for her? No! she will be wise enough to

answer that passion alone that can aggrandise her glory. No doubt she will, and despise the puppet of her fancy. Then all the riches this place contains, as well as the carbuncle of Giamschid, shall be hers."—"You judge right," returned the first voice; "and I haste to Istakar to prepare the palace of subterranean fire for the reception of the bridal pair."

The voices ceased; the torches were extinguished; the most entire darkness succeeded; and Nouronihar, recovering with a start, found herself reclined on a sofa in the harem of her father. She clapped her hands, and immediately came together Gulchenrouz and her women, who, in despair at having lost her, had despatched eunuchs to seek her in every direction. Shaban appeared with the rest, and began to reprimand her with an air of consequence:—"Little impertinent," said he, "have you false keys, or are you beloved of some genius that hath given you a picklock? I will try the extent of your power: come to the dark chamber, and expect not the company of Gulchenrouz. Be expeditious! I will shut you up, and turn the key twice upon you!" At these menaces, Nouronihar indignantly raised her head, opened on Shaban her black eyes, which since the important dialogue of the enchanted grot were considerably enlarged, and said,—"Go, speak thus to slaves, but learn to reverence her who is born to give laws, and subject all to her power."

Proceeding in the same style, she was interrupted by a sudden exclamation of "The caliph! the caliph!" All the curtains were thrown open, the slaves prostrated themselves in double rows, and poor little Gulchenrouz went to hide beneath the couch of a sofa. At first appeared a file of black eunuchs trailing after them long trains of muslin embroidered with gold, and holding in their hands censers, which dispensed, as they passed, the grateful perfume of the wood of aloes. Next marched Bababalouk with a solemn strut, and tossing his head, as not overpleased at the visit. Vathek came close after, superbly robed. His gait was unembarrassed and noble, and his presence would have engaged admiration, though he had not been the sovereign of the world. He approached Nouronihar with a throbbing heart, and seemed enraptured at the full effulgence of her radiant eyes, of which he had before caught but a few glimpses; but she instantly depressed them, and her confusion augmented her beauty.

Bababalouk, who was a thorough adept in coincidences of this nature, and knew that the worst game should be played with the best face, immediately made a signal for all to retire; and no sooner did he perceive beneath the sofa the little one's feet, than he drew him forth without ceremony, set him upon his shoulders, and lavished on him, as he went off, a thousand unwelcome caresses. Gulchenrouz cried out, and resisted till his cheeks became the colour of the blossom of pomegranates, and his tearful eyes sparkled with indignation. He cast a significant glance at Nouronihar, which the caliph noticing, asked, "Is that, then, your Gulchenrouz?"—"Sovereign of the world!" answered she, "spare my cousin, whose innocence and gentleness deserve not your anger!"—"Take comfort," said Vathek, with a smile: "he is in good hands. Bababalouk is fond of children, and never goes without sweetmeats and comfits." The daughter of Fakreddin was abashed, and suffered Gulchenrouz to be borne away without adding a word. The tumult of her bosom betrayed her confusion, and Vathek becoming still more impassioned, gave a loose to his frenzy, which had only not subdued the last faint strugglings of reluctance, when the emir suddenly bursting in, threw his face upon the ground at the feet of the caliph and said,—"Commander of the faithful! abase not yourself to the meanness of your slave."—"No, emir," replied Vathek, "I raise her to an equality with myself: I declare her my wife; and the glory of your race shall extend from one generation to another."—"Alas! my lord," said Fakreddin, as he plucked off a few grey hairs of his beard, "cut short the days of your faithful servant, rather than force him to depart from his word. Nouronihar is solemnly promised to Gulchenrouz, the son of my brother Ali Hassan. They are united also in heart; their faith is mutually plighted; and affiances so sacred cannot be broken."—"What then!" replied the caliph bluntly; "would you surrender this divine beauty to a husband more womanish than herself; and can you imagine that I will suffer her charms to decay in hands so inefficient and nerveless? No! she is destined to live out her life within my embraces. Such is my will. Retire, and disturb not the night I devote to the worship of her charms."

The irritated emir drew forth his sabre, presented it to Vathek, and stretching out his neck, said in a firm tone of voice, "Strike your unhappy host, my lord: he has lived long enough, since he hath seen the Prophet's vicegerent violate the rights of hospitality." At his uttering these words, Nouronihar, unable to support any longer the conflict of her passions, sunk down in a swoon. Vathek, both terrified for her life and furious at an opposition to his will, bade Fakreddin assist his daughter, and withdrew; darting his terrible look at the unfortunate emir, who suddenly fell backward, bathed in a sweat as cold as the damp of death.

Gulchenrouz, who had escaped from the hands of Bababalouk, and was at that instant returned, called out for help as loudly as he could, not having strength to afford it himself. Pale and panting, the poor child attempted to revive Nouronihar by caresses; and it happened that the thrilling warmth of his lips restored her to life. Fakreddin beginning also to recover from the look of the caliph, with difficulty tottered to a seat and after warily casting round his eye to see if this dangerous prince were gone, sent for Shaban and Sutlememe and said to them apart,—"My friends! violent evils require violent remedies. The caliph has brought desolation and horror into my family, and how shall we resist his power? Another of his looks will send me to the grave. Fetch, then, that narcotic powder which a dervich brought me from Aracan. A dose of it, the effect of which will continue three days, must be administered to each of these children. The caliph will believe them to be dead for they will have all the appearance of death. We shall go as if to inter them in the cave of Meimouné, at the entrance of the great desert of sand, and near the bower of my dwarfs. When all the spectators shall be withdrawn, you, Shaban, and four select eunuchs shall convey them to the lake, where provision shall be ready to support them a month; for one day allotted to the surprise this event will occasion, five to the tears, a fortnight to reflection, and the rest to prepare for renewing his progress, will, according to my calculation, fill up the whole time that Vathek will tarry; and I shall then be freed from his intrusion."

"Your plan is good," said Sutlememe, "if it can but be effected. I have remarked that Nouronihar is well able to support the glances of the caliph, and that he is far from being sparing of them to her. Be assured, therefore, that, notwithstanding her fondness for Gulchenrouz, she will never remain quiet while she knows him to be here. Let us persuade her that both herself and Gulchenrouz are really dead, and that they were conveyed to those rocks for a limited season to expiate the little faults of which their love was the cause. We will add that we killed ourselves in despair and that your dwarfs, whom they never yet saw, will preach to them delectable sermons. I will engage that everything shall succeed to the bent of your wishes."—"Be it so!" said Fakreddin: "I approve your proposal; let us lose not a moment to give it effect."

They hastened to seek for the powder, which, being mixed in a sherbet, was immediately administered to Gulchenrouz and Nouronihar. Within the space of an hour, both were seized with violent palpitations and a general numbness gradually ensued. They arose from the floor where they had remained ever since the caliph's departure and ascending to the sofa, reclined themselves upon it, clasped in each other's embraces. "Cherish me, my dear Nouronihar!" said Gulchenrouz: "put thy hand upon my heart; it feels as if it were frozen. Alas! thou art as cold as myself! Hath the caliph murdered us both with his terrible look?"—"I am dying!" cried she, in a faltering voice; "press me closer; I am ready to expire!"—"Let us die, then, together," answered the little Gulchenrouz; whilst his breast laboured with a convulsive sigh. "Let me at least breathe forth my soul on thy lips!" They spoke no more and became as dead.

Immediately the most piercing cries were heard through the harem whilst Shaban and Sutlememe personated with great adroitness the parts of persons in despair. The emir, who was sufficiently mortified to be forced into such untoward expedients, and had now for the first time made a trial of his powder, was under no necessity of counterfeiting grief. The slaves, who had flocked together from all quarters, stood motionless at the spectacle before them. All lights were extinguished save two lamps, which shed a wan glimmering over the faces of these lovely flowers, that seemed to be faded in the spring-time of life. Funeral vestments were prepared, their bodies were washed with rosewater, their beautiful tresses were braided and incensed, and they were wrapped in symars whiter than alabaster.

At the moment that their attendants were placing two wreaths of their favourite jasmines on their brows, the caliph, who had just heard the tragical catastrophe, arrived. He looked not less pale and haggard than the ghouls that wander at night among the graves. Forgetful of himself and every one else, he broke through the midst of the slaves, fell prostrate at the foot of the sofa, beat his bosom, called himself "atrocious murderer" and invoked upon his head a thousand imprecations. With a trembling hand he raised the veil that covered the countenance of Nouronihar, and uttering a loud shriek, fell lifeless on the floor. The chief of the eunuchs dragged him off with horrible grimaces, and repeated as he went, "Ay, I foresaw she would play you some ungracious turn!"

No sooner was the caliph gone than the emir commanded biers to be brought, and forbade that any one should enter the harem. Every window was fastened, all instruments of music were broken, and the imans began to recite their prayers. Towards the close of this melancholy day, Vathek sobbed in silence, for they had been forced to compose with anodynes his convulsions of rage and desperation.

At the dawn of the succeeding morning the wide folding doors of the palace were set open, and the funeral procession moved forward for the mountain. The wailful cries of "La Illah illa Allah!" reached the caliph, who was eager to cicatrise himself and attend the ceremonial; nor could he have been dissuaded, had not his excessive weakness disabled him from walking. At the few first steps he fell on the ground, and his people were obliged to lay him on a bed, where he remained many days in such a state of insensibility as excited compassion in the emir himself.

When the procession was arrived at the grot of Meimouné, Shaban and Sutlememe dismissed the whole of the train, excepting the four confidential eunuchs who were appointed to remain. After resting some moments near the biers, which had been left in the open air, they caused them to be carried to the brink of a small lake, whose banks were overgrown with a hoary moss. This was the great resort of herons and storks, which preyed continually on little blue fishes. The dwarfs, instructed by the emir, soon repaired thither and with the help of the eunuchs began to construct cabins of rushes and reeds, a work in which they had admirable skill. A magazine also was contrived for provisions, with a small oratory for themselves and a pyramid of wood, neatly piled, to furnish the necessary fuel; for the air was bleak in the hollows of the mountains.

At evening two fires were kindled on the brink of the lake, and the two lovely bodies, taken from their biers, were carefully deposited upon a bed of dried leaves within the same cabin. The dwarfs began to recite the Koran with their clear shrill voices, and Shaban and Sutlememe stood at some distance, anxiously waiting the effects of the powder. At length Nouronihar and Gulchenrouz faintly stretched out their arms and gradually opening their eyes, began to survey with looks of increasing amazement every object around them. They even attempted to rise, but for want of strength fell back again. Sutlememe, on this, administered a cordial which the emir had taken care to provide.

Gulchenrouz, thoroughly aroused, sneezed out aloud, and raising himself with an effort that expressed his surprise, left the cabin and inhaled the fresh air with the greatest avidity. "Yes," said he, "I breathe again! Again do I exist! I hear sounds! I behold a firmament spangled over with stars!"—Nouronihar, catching these beloved accents, extricated herself from the leaves and ran to clasp Gulchenrouz to her bosom. The first objects she remarked were their long simars, their garlands of flowers, and their naked feet. She hid her face in her hands to reflect. The vision of the enchanted bath, the despair of her father, and, more vividly than both, the majestic figure of Vathek, recurred to her memory. She recollected also that herself and Gulchenrouz had been sick and dying, but all these images bewildered her mind. Not knowing where she was, she turned her eyes on all sides as if to recognise the surrounding scene. This singular lake, those flames reflected from its glassy surface, the pale hues of its banks, the romantic cabins, the bulrushes that sadly waved their drooping heads, the storks whose melancholy cries blended with the shrill voices of the dwarfs, —everything conspired to persuade her that the angel of death had opened the portal of some other world.

Gulchenrouz on his part, lost in wonder, clung to the neck of his cousin. He believed himself in the region of phantoms and was terrified at the silence she preserved. At length addressing her. "Speak," said he; "where are we? Do you not see those spectres that are stirring the burning coals? Are they Monker and Nekir* who are come to throw us into them? Does the

* "Two black angels who examined the departed upon the subject of his faith."

fatal bridge cross this lake, whose solemn stillness, perhaps, conceals from us an abyss in which for whole ages we shall be doomed incessantly to sink?"

"No, my children," said Sutlememe, going towards them; "take comfort! the exterminating angel, who conducted our souls hither after yours, hath assured us that the chastisement of your indolent and voluptuous life shall be restricted to a certain series of years which you must pass in this dreary abode where the sun is scarcely visible and where the soil yields neither fruits nor flowers. These," continued she, pointing to the dwarfs, "will provide for our wants, for souls so mundane as ours retain too strong a tincture of their earthly extraction. Instead of meats, your food will be nothing but rice and your bread shall be moistened in the fogs that brood over the surface of the lake."

At this desolating prospect, the poor children burst into tears and prostrated themselves before the dwarfs, who perfectly supported their characters and delivered an excellent discourse of a customary length upon the sacred camel, which after a thousand years was to convey them to the paradise of the faithful.

The sermon being ended and ablutions performed, they praised Allah and the Prophet, supped very indifferently, and retired to their withered leaves. Nouronihar and her little cousin consoled themselves on finding that the dead might lie in one cabin. Having slept well before, the remainder of the night was spent in conversation on what had befallen them, and both, from a dread of apparitions, betook themselves for protection to one another's arms.

In the morning, which was lowering and rainy, the dwarfs mounted high poles like minarets and called them to prayers. The whole congregation, which consisted of Sutlememe, Shaban, the four eunuchs, and a

---

few storks that were tired of fishing, was already assembled. The two children came forth from their cabin with a slow and dejected pace. As their minds were in a tender and melancholy mood, their devotions were performed with fervour. No sooner were they finished than Gulchenrouz demanded of Sutlememe and the rest, how they happened to die so opportunely for his cousin and himself—"We killed ourselves," returned Sutlememe, "in despair at your death." On this, Nouronihar, who, notwithstanding what had passed, had not yet forgotten her vision, said,—"And the caliph, is he also dead of his grief, and will he likewise come hither?" The dwarfs, who were prepared with an answer, most demurely replied, "Vathek is damned beyond all redemption!"—"I readily believe so," said Gulchenrouz, "and am glad from my heart to hear it; for I am convinced it was his horrible look that sent us hither to listen to sermons and mess upon rice." One week passed away on the side of the lake, unmarked by any variety, Nouronihar ruminating on the grandeur of which death had deprived her, and Gulchenrouz applying to prayers and basket-making with the dwarfs, who infinitely pleased him.

Whilst this scene of innocence was exhibiting in the mountains, the caliph presented himself to the emir in a new light. The instant he recovered the use of his senses, with a voice that made Bababalouk quake he thundered out,—"Perfidious Giaour! I renounce thee for ever! It is thou who hast slain my beloved Nouronihar! and I supplicate the pardon of Mahomet, who would have preserved her to me had I been more wise. Let water be brought to perform my ablutions, and let the pious Fakreddin be called to offer up his prayers with mine, and reconcile me to him. Afterwards we will go together and visit the sepulchre of the unfortunate Nouronihar. I am resolved to become a hermit and consume the residue of my days on this mountain, in hope of expiating my crimes."—"And what do you intend to live upon there?" enquired Bababalouk.—"I hardly know," replied Vathek, "but I will tell you when I feel hungry—which, I believe, will not soon be the case."

The arrival of Fakreddin put a stop to this conversation. As soon as Vathek saw him, he threw his arms around his neck, bedewed his face with a torrent of tears, and uttered things so affecting, so pious, that the emir, crying for joy, congratulated himself in his heart upon having performed so admirable and unexpected a conversion. As for the pilgrimage to the mountain, Fakreddin had his reasons not to oppose it; therefore, each ascending his own litter, they started.

Notwithstanding the vigilance with which his attendants watched the caliph, they could not prevent his harrowing his cheeks with a few scratches when on the place where he was told Nouronihar had been buried; they were even obliged to drag him away by force of hands from the melancholy spot. However, he swore with a solemn oath that he would return thither every day. This resolution did not exactly please the emir—yet he flattered himself that the caliph might not proceed farther, and would merely perform his devotions in the cavern of Meimouné. Besides, the lake was so completely concealed within the solitary bosom of those tremendous rocks that he thought it utterly impossible any one could ever find it. This security of Fakreddin was also considerably strengthened by the conduct of Vathek, who performed his vow most scrupulously, and returned daily from the hill so devout and so contrite that all the grey beards were in a state of ecstasy on account of it.

Nouronihar was not altogether so content, for though
she felt a fondness for Gulchenrouz, who, to augment
the attachment, had been left at full liberty with her,
yet she still regarded him as but a bauble that bore no
competition with the carbuncle of Giamschid. At times
she indulged doubts on the mode of her being, and
scarcely could believe that the dead had all the wants
and the whims of the living. To gain satisfaction,
however, on so perplexing a topic, one morning whilst
all were asleep she arose with a breathless caution from
the side of Gulchenrouz, and, after having given him a
soft kiss, began to follow the windings of the lake till
it terminated with a rock, the top of which was accessi-
ble, though lofty. This she climbed with considerable
toil, and having reached the summit, set forward in a
run, like a doe before the hunter. Though she skipped
with the alertness of an antelope, yet at intervals she
was forced to desist, and rest beneath the tamarisks to
recover her breath. Whilst she, thus reclined, was occupied with her little reflections on the apprehension
that she had some knowledge of the place, Vathek, who,
finding himself that morning but ill at ease, had gone
forth before the dawn, presented himself on a sudden
to her view. Motionless with surprise, he durst not
approach the figure before him trembling and pale, but
yet lovely to behold. At length, Nouronihar, with a
mixture of pleasure and affliction raising her fine eyes
to him, said, "My lord! are you then come hither to eat
rice and hear sermons with me?"—"Beloved phantom!"
cried Vathek; "thou dost speak; thou hast the same
graceful form, the same radiant features; art thou pal-
pable likewise?" and eagerly embracing her, added,
"Here are limbs and a bosom animated with a gentle
warmth!—What can such a prodigy mean?"

Nouronihar with indifference answered,—"You know,

my lord, that I died on the very night you honoured me with your visit. My cousin maintains it was from one of your glances, but I cannot believe him, for to me they seem not so dreadful. Gulchenrouz died with me, and we were both brought into a region of desolation, where we are fed with a wretched diet. If you be dead also and are come hither to join us, I pity your lot, for you will be stunned with the clang of the dwarfs and the storks. Besides it is mortifying in the extreme that you as well as myself should have lost the treasures of the subterranean palace."

At the mention of the subterranean palace the caliph suspended his caresses, (which, indeed, had proceeded pretty far) to seek from Nouronihar an explanation of her meaning. She then recapitulated her vision, what immediately followed, and the history of her pretended death, adding also a description of the place of expiation from whence she had fled; and all in a manner that would have extorted his laughter had not the thoughts of Vathek been too deeply engaged. No sooner, however, had she ended, than he again clasped her to his bosom and said, "Light of my eyes, the mystery is unravelled; we both are alive! Your father is a cheat, who for the sake of dividing us hath deluded us both, and the Giaour, whose design, as far as I can discover, is that we shall proceed together, seems scarce a whit better. It shall be some time at least before he finds us in his palace of fire. Your lovely little person, in my estimation, is far more precious than all the treasures of the pre-adamite sultans, and I wish to possess it at pleasure, and in open day, for many a moon, before I go to burrow under ground like a mole. Forget this little trifler, Gulchenrouz, and ———" "Ah, my lord!" interposed Nouronihar, "let me entreat that you do him no evil."—"No, no!" replied Vathek; "I have al-

ready bid you forbear to alarm yourself for him. He
has been brought up too much on milk and sugar to
stimulate my jealousy. We will leave him with the
dwarfs, who, by the by, are my old acquaintances.
Their company will suit him far better than yours. As
to other matters, I will return no more to your father's.
I want not to have my ears dinned by him and his
dotards with the violation of the rights of hospitality,
as if it were less an honour for you to espouse the sovereign of the world than a girl dressed up like a boy."

Nouronihar could find nothing to oppose in a discourse so eloquent. She only wished the amorous monarch had discovered more ardour for the carbuncle of
Giamschid, but flattered herself it would gradually increase, and therefore yielded to his will with the most
bewitching submission.

When the caliph judged it proper, he called for Bababalouk, who was asleep in the cave of Meimouné and
dreaming that the phantom of Nouronihar, having
mounted him once more on her swing, had just given
him such a jerk that he one moment soared above the
mountains, and the next sunk into the abyss. Starting
from his sleep at the sound of his master, he ran, gasp-
ing for breath, and had nearly fallen backward at the
sight, as he believed, of the spectre by whom he had
so lately been haunted in his dream. "Ah, my lord!"
cried he, recoiling ten steps and covering his eyes with
both hands, "do you then perform the office of a ghoul?
Have you dug up the dead? Yet hope not to make her
your prey, for after all she hath caused me to suffer
she is wicked enough to prey even upon you."

"Cease to play the fool," said Vathek, "and thou
shalt soon be convinced that it is Nouronihar herself,
alive and well, whom I clasp to my breast. Go and
pitch my tents in the neighbouring valley. There will

I fix my abode with this beautiful tulip, whose colours I soon shall restore. There exert thy best endeavours to procure whatever can augment the enjoyments of life till I shall disclose to thee more of my will."

The news of so unlucky an event soon reached the ears of the emir, who abandoned himself to grief and despair, and began, as did his old greybeards, to begrime his visage with ashes. A total supineness ensued; travellers were no longer entertained; no more plasters were spread; and instead of the charitable activity that had distinguished this asylum, the whole of its inhabitants exhibited only faces of half a cubit long, and uttered groans that accorded with their forlorn situation.

Though Fakreddin bewailed his daughter as lost to him for ever, yet Gulchenrouz was not forgotten. He despatched immediate instructions to Sutlememe, Shaban, and the dwarfs, enjoining them not to undeceive the child in respect to his state, but under some pretence to convey him far from the lofty rock at the extremity of the lake, to a place which he should appoint as safer from danger, for he suspected that Vathek intended him evil.

Gulchenrouz in the mean while was filled with amazement at not finding his cousin; nor were the dwarfs less surprised. But Sutlememe, who had more penetration, immediately guessed what had happened. Gulchenrouz was amused with the delusive hope of once more embracing Nouronihar in the interior recesses of the mountains, where the ground, strewed over with orange blossoms and jasmines, offered beds much more inviting than the withered leaves in their cabin; where they might accompany with their voices the sounds of their lutes and chase butterflies. Sutlememe was far gone in this sort of description when one of the four eunuchs beckoned her aside to apprise her of the arrival of a

messenger from their fraternity who had explained the
secret of the flight of Nouronihar and brought the commands of the emir. A council with Shaban and the
dwarfs was immediately held. Their baggage being
stowed in consequence of it, they embarked in a shallop
and quietly sailed with the little one, who acquiesced
in all their proposals. Their voyage proceeded in the
same manner till they came to the place where the lake
sinks beneath the hollow of a rock; but as soon as the
bark had entered it, and Gulchenrouz found himself surrounded with darkness, he was seized with a dreadful
consternation and incessantly uttered the most piercing
outcries; for he now was persuaded he should actually
be damned for having taken too many little freedoms in
his lifetime with his cousin.

But let us return to the caliph, and her who ruled
over his heart. Bababalouk had pitched the tents, and
closed up the extremities of the valley with magnificent
screens of India cloth, which were guarded by Ethiopian
slaves with their drawn sabres. To preserve the ver-
dure of this beautiful enclosure in its natural freshness,
white eunuchs went continually round it with gilt water
vessels. The waving of fans was heard near the imperial pavilion, where, by the voluptuous light that
glowed through the muslins, the caliph enjoyed at full
view all the attractions of Nouronihar. Inebriated with
delight, he was all ear to her charming voice, which accompanied the lute; while she was not less captivated
with his descriptions of Samarah and the tower full of
wonders, but especially with his relation of the adventure of the ball, and the chasm of the Giaour with its
ebony portal.

In this manner they conversed the whole day, and at
night they bathed together in a basin of black marble,
which admirably set off the fairness of Nouronihar.

Bababalouk, whose good graces this beauty had re-gained, spared no attention that their repasts might be served up with the minutest exactness. Some exquisite rarity was ever placed before them; and he sent even to Schiraz for that fragrant and delicious wine which had been hoarded up in bottles prior to the birth of Ma-homet. He had excavated little ovens in the rock, to bake the nice manchets which were prepared by the hands of Nouronihar, from whence they had derived a flavour so grateful to Vathek that he regarded the rag-outs of his other wives as entirely mawkish; whilst they would have died of chagrin at the emir's, at finding themselves so neglected, if Fakreddin, notwithstanding his resentment, had not taken pity upon them.

The Sultana Dilara, who till then had been the favourite, took this dereliction of the caliph to heart with a vehemence natural to her character; for during her continuance in favour she had imbibed from Vathek many of his extravagant fancies, and was fired with impatience to behold the superb tombs of Istakar and the palace of forty columns. Besides, having been brought up amongst the magi, she had fondly cherished the idea of the caliph's devoting himself to the worship of fire; thus his voluptuous and desultory life with her rival was to her a double source of affliction. The transient piety of Vathek had occasioned her some seri-ous alarms, but the present was an evil of far greater magnitude. She resolved, therefore, without hesitation to write to Carathis and acquaint her that all things went ill; that they had eaten, slept, and revelled at an old emir's, whose sanctity was very formidable; and that after all the prospect of possessing the treasures of the pre-adamite sultans was no less remote than before. This letter was intrusted to the care of two woodmen, who were at work in one of the great forests of the mountains and who, being acquainted with the shortest cuts, arrived in ten days at Samarah.

The Princess Carathis was engaged at chess with Morakanabad when the arrival of these woodfellers was announced. She, after some weeks of Vathek's absence, had forsaken the upper regions of her tower, because everything appeared in confusion among the stars, which she consulted relative to the fate of her son. In vain did she renew her fumigations, and extend herself on the roof to obtain mystic visions; nothing more could she see in her dreams than pieces of brocade, nosegays of flowers, and other unmeaning gewgaws. These disappointments had thrown her into a state of dejection which no drug in her power was sufficient to remove. Her only resource was in Morakanabad, who was a good man and endowed with a decent share of confidence; yet whilst in her company he never thought himself on roses.

No person knew aught of Vathek, and of course a thousand ridiculous stories were propagated at his expense. The eagerness of Carathis may be easily guessed at receiving the letter, as well as her rage at reading the dissolute conduct of her son. "Is it so?" said she: "either I will perish, or Vathek shall enter the palace of fire. Let me expire in flames, provided he may reign on the throne of Soliman!" Having said this, and whirled herself round in a magical manner, which struck Morakanabad with such terror as caused him to recoil, she ordered her great camel Alboufaki to be brought, and the hideous Nerkes, with the unrelenting Cafour, to attend. "I require no other retinue," said she to Morakanabad; "I am going on affairs of emergency; a truce, therefore, to parade! Take you care of the people: fleece them well in my absence; for we shall expend large sums, and one knows not what may betide."

The night was uncommonly dark, and a pestilential blast blew from the plain of Catoul that would have deterred any other traveller, however urgent the call: but Carathis enjoyed most whatever filled others with dread. Nerkes concurred in opinion with her, and Cafour had a particular predilection for a pestilence. In the morning this accomplished caravan, with the woodfellers, who directed their route, halted on the edge of an extensive marsh from whence so noxious a vapour arose as would have destroyed any animal but Alboufaki, who naturally inhaled these malignant fogs with delight. The peasants entreated their convoy not to sleep in this place. "To sleep," cried Carathis, "what an excellent thought! I never sleep, but for visions; and as to my attendants, their occupations are too many to close the only eye they have." The poor peasants, who were not overpleased with their party, remained open-mouthed with surprise.

Carathis alighted, as well as her negresses; and severally stripping off their outer garments, they all ran to cull from those spots where the sun shone fiercest the venomous plants that grew on the marsh. This provision was made for the family of the emir; and whoever might retard the expedition to Istakar. The woodmen were overcome with fear when they beheld these three horrible phantoms run, and, not much relishing the company of Alboufaki, stood aghast at the command of Carathis to set forward, notwithstanding it was noon and the heat fierce enough to calcine even rocks. In spite, however, of every remonstrance, they were forced implicitly to submit.

Alboufaki, who delighted in solitude, constantly snorted whenever he perceived himself near a habita-

tion; and Carathis, who was apt to spoil him with indulgence, as constantly turned him aside: so that the
peasants were precluded from procuring subsistence;
for the milch goats and ewes, which Providence had
sent towards the district they traversed to refresh
travellers with their milk, all fled at the sight of the
hideous animal and his strange riders. As to Carathis,
she needed no common aliment, for her invention had
previously furnished her with an opiate to stay her
stomach, some of which she imparted to her mutes.

At dusk Alboufaki, making a sudden stop, stamped
with his foot, which to Carathis, who knew his ways,
was a certain indication that she was near the confines
of some cemetery. The moon shed a bright light on the
spot, which served to discover a long wall with a large
door in it, standing ajar, and so high that Alboufaki
might easily enter. The miserable guides, who perceived their end approaching, humbly implored Carathis, as she had now so good an opportunity, to inter
them, and immediately gave up the ghost. Nerkes and
Cafour, whose wit was of a style peculiar to themselves,
were by no means parsimonious of it on the folly of
these poor people; nor could anything have been found
more suited to their taste than the site of the burying-
ground and the sepulchres which its precincts contained.
There were at least two thousand of them on the declivity of a hill. Carathis was too eager to execute her
plan to stop at the view, charming as it appeared in
her eyes. Pondering the advantages that might accrue
from her present situation, she said to herself, "So
beautiful a cemetery must be haunted by ghouls! They
never want for intelligence. Having heedlessly suffered
my stupid guides to expire, I will apply for directions
to them, and, as an inducement, will invite them to regale on these fresh corpses." After this wise soliloquy,

she beckoned to Nerkes and Cafour, and made signs with her fingers, as much as to say, "Go; knock against the sides of the tombs, and strike up your delightful warblings."

The negresses, full of joy at the behests of their mistress, and promising themselves much pleasure from the society of the ghouls, went with an air of conquest and began their knockings at the tombs. As their strokes were repeated, a hollow noise was made in the earth, the surface hove up into heaps, and the ghouls, on all sides, protruded their noses to inhale the effluvia which the carcasses of the woodmen began to emit. They assembled before a sarcophagus of white marble, where Carathis was seated between the bodies of her miserable guides. The princess received her visitants with distinguished politeness, and supper being ended, they talked of business. Carathis soon learned from them everything she wanted to discover, and without loss of time prepared to set forward on her journey. Her negresses, who were forming tender connections with the ghouls, importuned her with all their fingers to wait at least till the dawn. But Carathis, being chastity in the abstract, and an implacable enemy to love intrigues and sloth, at once rejected their prayer, mounted Alboufaki, and commanded them to take their seats instantly. Four days and four nights she continued her route without interruption. On the fifth she traversed craggy mountains and half-burnt forests, and arrived on the sixth before the beautiful screens which concealed from all eyes the voluptuous wanderings of her son.

It was daybreak and the guards were snoring on their posts in careless security, when the rough trot of Alboufaki awoke them in consternation. Imagining that a group of spectres, ascended from the abyss, was approaching, they all without ceremony took to their heels.

Vathek was at that instant with Nouronihar in the bath,
hearing tales and laughing at Bababalouk, who related
them; but no sooner did the outcry of his guards reach
him, than he flounced from the water like a carp, and
as soon threw himself back at the sight of Carathis;
who, advancing with her negresses upon Alboufaki,
broke through the muslin awnings and veils of the
pavilion. At this sudden apparition, Nouronihar (for
she was not at all times free from remorse) fancied that
the moment of celestial vengeance was come, and clung
about the caliph in amorous despondence.

Carathis, still seated on her camel, foamed with indignation at the spectacle which obtruded itself on her
chaste view. She thundered forth without check or
mercy, "Thou double-headed and four-legged monster!
what means all this winding and writhing? Art thou
not ashamed to be seen grasping this limber sapling in
preference to the sceptre of the pre-adamite sultans?
Is it then for this paltry doxy that thou hast violated
the conditions in the parchment of our Giaour? Is it on
her thou hast lavished thy precious moments? Is this
the fruit of the knowledge I have taught thee? Is this
the end of thy journey? Tear thyself from the arms
of this little simpleton; drown her in the water before
me, and instantly follow my guidance."

In the first ebullition of his fury, Vathek had resolved
to rip open the body of Alboufaki, and to stuff it with
those of the negresses and of Carathis herself; but the
remembrance of the Giaour, the palace of Istakar, the
sabres, and the talismans, flashing before his imagination with the simultaneousness of lightning, he became
more moderate, and said to his mother in a civil but
decisive tone, "Dread lady, you shall be obeyed; but
I will not drown Nouronihar. She is sweeter to me
than a Myrabolan comfit, and is enamoured of carbun-

cles, especially that of Giamschid, which hath also been promised to be conferred upon her. She therefore shall go along with us, for I intend to repose with her upon the sofas of Soliman; I can sleep no more without her." "Be it so," replied Carathis, alighting and at the same time committing Alboufaki to the charge of her black women.

Nouronihar, who had not yet quitted her hold, began to take courage, and said with an accent of fondness to the caliph, "Dear sovereign of my soul, I will follow thee, if it be thy will, beyond the Kaf, in the land of the afrits. I will not hesitate to climb for thee the nest of the Simurgh, who, this lady excepted, is the most awful of created beings." "We have here, then," subjoined Carathis, "a girl both of courage and science!" Nouronihar had certainly both, but notwithstanding all her firmness, she could not help casting back a thought of regret upon the graces of her little Gulchenrouz, and the days of tender endearments she had participated with him. She even dropped a few tears, which the caliph observed; and inadvertently breathed out with a sigh, "Alas! my gentle cousin, what will become of thee?" Vathek, at this apostrophe, knitted up his brows, and Carathis enquired what it could mean. "She is preposterously sighing after a stripling with languishing eyes and soft hair, who loves her," said the caliph. "Where is he?" asked Carathis. "I must be acquainted with this pretty child, for," added she, lowering her voice, "I design, before I depart, to regain the favour of the Giaour. There is nothing so delicious, in his estimation, as the heart of a delicate boy palpitating with the first tumults of love."

Vathek, as he came from the bath, commanded Bababalouk to collect the women and other movables of his harem, embody his troops, and hold himself in readiness to march within three days, whilst Carathis retired alone to a tent, where the Giaour solaced her with encouraging visions. But at length waking, she found at her feet Nerkes and Cafour, who informed her by their signs that having led Alboufaki to the borders of a lake to browse on some grey moss that looked tolerably venomous, they had discovered certain blue fishes, of the same kind with those in the reservoir on the top of the tower. "Ah! ha!" said she, "I will go thither to them. These fish are, past doubt, of a species that by a small operation I can render oracular. They may tell me where this little Gulchenrouz is, whom I am bent upon sacrificing." Having thus spoken, she immediately set out with her swarthy retinue.

It being but seldom that time is lost in the accomplishment of a wicked enterprise, Carathis and her negresses soon arrived at the lake, where after burning the magical drugs with which they were always provided, they stripped themselves naked and waded to their chins, Nerkes and Cafour waving torches around them, and Carathis pronouncing her barbarous incantations. The fishes with one accord thrust forth their heads from the water, which was violently rippled by the flutter of their fins; and at length finding themselves constrained by the potency of the charm, they opened their piteous mouths and said, "From gills to tail, we are yours; what seek ye to know?"—"Fishes," answered she, "I conjure you, by your glittering scales, tell me where now is Gulchenrouz?"—"Beyond the rock," replied the shoal, in full chorus. "Will this content you? for we do not delight in expanding our mouths." "It will," returned the princess: "I am not to learn that you are not used to long conversations. I will leave you therefore to repose, though I had other questions to propound." The instant she had spoken the water became smooth, and the fishes at once disappeared.

Carathis, inflated with the venom of her projects, strode hastily over the rock, and found the amiable Gulchenrouz asleep in an arbour, whilst the two dwarfs were watching at his side and ruminating their accustomed prayers. These diminutive personages possessed the gift of divining whenever an enemy to good Mussulmans approached. Thus they anticipated the arrival of Carathis, who, stopping short, said to herself, "How placidly doth he recline his lovely little head! how pale and languishing are his looks! it is just the very child of my wishes!" The dwarfs interrupted this delectable soliloquy by leaping instantly upon her, and scratching her face with their utmost zeal. But Nerkes and Cafour, betaking themselves to the succour of their mistress, pinched the dwarfs so severely in return that they both gave up the ghost, imploring Mahomet to inflict his sorest vengeance upon this wicked woman and all her household.

At the noise which this strange conflict occasioned in the valley, Gulchenrouz awoke, and, bewildered with terror, sprung impetuously and climbed an old fig-tree that rose against the acclivity of the rocks, from thence he gained their summits and ran for two hours without once looking back. At last, exhausted with fatigue, he fell senseless into the arms of a good old genius, whose fondness for the company of children had made it his sole occupation to protect them. Whilst performing his wonted rounds through the air, he had pounced on the cruel Giaour at the instant of his growling in the horrible chasm, and had rescued the fifty little victims which the impiety of Vathek had devoted to his voracity. These the genius brought up in nests still higher than the clouds, and himself fixed his abode in a nest more

capacious than the rest, from which he had expelled the
Rocs that had built it.

These inviolable asylums were defended against the
dives and the afrits by waving streamers, on which
were inscribed in characters of gold that flashed like
lightning, the names of Allah and the Prophet. It was
there that Gulchenrouz, who as yet remained unde-
ceived with respect to his pretended death, thought
himself in the mansions of eternal peace. He admitted
without fear the congratulations of his little friends,
who were all assembled in the nest of the venerable
genius, and vied with each other in kissing his serene
forehead and beautiful eyelids. Remote from the inquietudes of the world, the impertinence of harems, the
brutality of eunuchs, and the inconstancy of women,
there he found a place truly congenial to the delights of
his soul. In this peaceable society his days, months,
and years glided on; nor was he less happy than the
rest of his companions. For the genius, instead of
burdening his pupils with perishable riches and vain
sciences, conferred upon them the boon of perpetual
childhood.

Carathis, unaccustomed to the loss of her prey, vented
a thousand execrations on her negresses for not seizing
the child, instead of amusing themselves with pinching
to death two insignificant dwarfs from which they
gained no advantage. She returned into the valley
murmuring, and finding that her son was not risen from
the arms of Nouronihar, discharged her ill humour upon
both. The idea, however, of departing next day for
Istakar, and of cultivating through the good offices of
the Giaour an intimacy with Eblis himself, at length
consoled her chagrin. But fate had ordained it
otherwise.

In the evening, as Carathis was conversing with

Dilara, who through her contrivance had become of the party, and whose taste resembled her own, Bababalouk came to acquaint her that the sky towards Samarah looked of a fiery red and seemed to portend some alarming disaster. Immediately recurring to her astrolabes and instruments of magic, she took the altitude of the planets, and discovered by her calculations, to her great mortification, that a formidable revolt had taken place at Samarah, that Motavakel, availing himself of the disgust which was inveterate against his brother, had incited commotions amongst the populace, made himself master of the palace, and actually invested the great tower, to which Morakanabad had retired with a handful of the few that still remained faithful to Vathek.

"What!" exclaimed she; "must I lose, then, my tower! my mutes! my negresses! my mummies! and, worse than all, the laboratory, the favourite resort of my nightly lucubrations, without knowing, at least, if my hair-brained son will complete his adventure? No! I will not be duped. Immediately will I speed to support Morakanabad. By my formidable art, the clouds shall pour grapeshot in the faces of the assailants, and shafts of red-hot iron on their heads. I will let loose my stores of hungry serpents and torpedoes from beneath them, and we shall soon see the stand they will make against such an explosion!"

Having thus spoken, Carathis hasted to her son, who was tranquilly banqueting with Nouronihar, in his superb carnation-coloured tent. "Glutton that thou art!" cried she; "were it not for me, thou wouldst soon find thyself the mere commander of savoury pies. Thy faithful subjects have abjured the faith they swore to thee. Motavakel, thy brother, now reigns on the hill of Pied Horses; and, had I not some slight resources in the tower, would not be easily persuaded to abdicate. But, that time may not be lost, I shall only add a few words:—Strike tent to-night, set forward, and beware how thou loiterest again by the way. Though thou hast forfeited the conditions of the parchment, I am not yet without hope; for it cannot be denied that thou hast violated to admiration the laws of hospitality by seducing the daughter of the emir after having partaken of his bread and his salt. Such a conduct cannot but be delightful to the Giaour; and if on thy march thou canst signalise thyself by an additional crime, all will still go well, and thou shalt enter the palace of Soliman in triumph. Adieu! Alboufaki and my negresses are waiting at the door."

The caliph had nothing to offer in reply: he wished his mother a prosperous journey, and ate on till he had finished his supper. At midnight the camp broke up amidst the flourishing of trumpets and other martial instruments. But loud indeed must have been the sound of the tymbals to overpower the blubbering of the emir and his greybeards, who by an excessive profusion of tears had so far exhausted the radical moisture that their eyes shrivelled up in their sockets and their hairs dropped off by the roots. Nouronihar, to whom such a symphony was painful, did not grieve to get out of hearing. She accompanied the caliph in the imperial litter, where they amused themselves with imagining the splendour which was soon to surround them. The other women, overcome with dejection, were dolefully rocked in their cages, whilst Dilara consoled herself with anticipating the joy of celebrating the rites of fire on the stately terraces of Istakar.

In four days they reached the spacious valley of Rocnabad. The season of spring was in all its vigour; and the grotesque branches of the almond trees in full blossom, fantastically checkered with hyacinths and jonquils, breathed forth a delightful fragrance. Myriads of bees, and scarce fewer of santons, had there taken up their abode. On the banks of the stream, hives and oratories were alternately ranged; and their neatness and whiteness were set off by the deep green of the cypresses that spired up amongst them. These pious personages amused themselves with cultivating little gardens that abounded with flowers and fruits, especially musk melons of the best flavour that Persia could boast. Sometimes, dispersed over the meadow, they entertained themselves with feeding peacocks whiter than snow and turtles more blue than the sapphire. In this manner were they occupied when the harbingers of the imperial procession began to proclaim, "Inhabitants of Rocnabad! prostrate yourselves on the brink of your pure waters; and tender your thanksgivings to Heaven, that vouchsafeth to show you a ray of its glory: for, lo! the commander of the faithful draws near."

The poor santons, filled with holy energy, having bustled to light up wax torches in their oratories, and expand the Koran on their ebony desks, went forth to meet the caliph with baskets of honeycomb, dates, and melons. But whilst they were advancing in solemn procession and with measured steps, the horses, camels, and guards wantoned over their tulips and other flowers and made a terrible havoc amongst them. The santons could not help casting from one eye a look of pity on the ravages committing around them; whilst the other was fixed upon the caliph and Heaven. Nouronihar, enraptured with the scenery of a place which brought back to her remembrance the pleasing solitudes where her infancy had passed, entreated Vathek to stop; but he, suspecting that these oratories might be

deemed by the Giaour an habitation, commanded his
pioneers to level them all. The santons stood motionless with horror at the barbarous mandate, and at last
broke out into lamentations; but these were uttered
with so ill a grace that Vathek bade his eunuchs to kick
them from his presence. He then descended from the
litter with Nouronihar. They sauntered together in the
meadow, and amused themselves with culling flowers
and passing a thousand pleasantries on each other. But
the bees, who were staunch Mussulmans, thinking it
their duty to revenge the insult offered to their dear
masters the santons, assembled so zealously to do it
with good effect that the caliph and Nouronihar were
glad to find their tents prepared to receive them.

Bababalouk, who in capacity of purveyor had acquitted himself with applause as to peacocks and turtles,
lost no time in consigning some dozens to the spit and
as many to be fricasseed. Whilst they were feasting,
laughing, carousing, and blaspheming at pleasure on
the banquet so liberally furnished, the moullahs, the
sheiks, the cadis, and imans of Schiraz (who seemed
not to have met the santons) arrived, leading by bridles
of riband, inscribed from the Koran, a train of asses
which were loaded with the choicest fruits the country
could boast. Having presented their offerings to the
caliph, they petitioned him to honour their city and
mosques with his presence.

"Fancy not," said Vathek, "that you can detain me.
Your presence I condescend to accept, but beg you will
let me be quiet, for I am not over-fond of resisting
temptation. Retire, then; yet, as it is not decent for
personages so reverend to return on foot, and as you
have not the appearance of expert riders, my eunuchs
shall tie you on your asses, with the precaution that
your backs be not turned towards me; for they under-

stand etiquette."—In this deputation were some high-stomached sheiks, who, taking Vathek for a fool, scrupled not to speak their opinion. These Bababalouk girded with double cords; and having well disciplined their asses with nettles behind, they all started with a preternatural alertness, plunging, kicking, and running foul of one another in the most ludicrous manner imaginable.

Nouronihar and the caliph mutually contended who should most enjoy so degrading a sight. They burst out in peals of laughter to see the old men and their asses fall into the stream. The leg of one was fractured, the shoulder of another dislocated, the teeth of a third dashed out, and the rest suffered still worse.

Two days more, undisturbed by fresh embassies, having been devoted to the pleasures of Rocnabad, the expedition proceeded, leaving Schiraz on the right, and verging towards a large plain from whence were discernible on the edge of the horizon the dark summits of the mountains of Istakar.

At this prospect the caliph and Nouronihar were unable to repress their transports. They bounded from their litter to the ground, and broke forth into such wild exclamations as amazed all within hearing. Interrogating each other, they shouted, "Are we not approaching the radiant palace of light? or gardens more delightful than those of Sheddad?"—Infatuated mortals! they thus indulged delusive conjecture, unable to fathom the decrees of the Most High!

The good genii, who had not totally relinquished the superintendence of Vathek, repairing to Mahomet in the seventh heaven, said, "Merciful Prophet! stretch forth thy propitious arms towards thy vicegerent; who is ready to fall irretrievably into the snare which his enemies, the dives, have prepared to destroy him. The

Giaour is awaiting his arrival in the abominable palace
of fire, where if he once set his foot, his perdition will
be inevitable." Mahomet answered with an air of indignation, "He hath too well deserved to be resigned to
himself, but I permit you to try if one effort more will
be effectual to divert him from pursuing his ruin."

One of these beneficent genii, assuming without delay
the exterior of a shepherd more renowned for his piety
than all the derviches and santons of the region, took
his station near a flock of white sheep on the slope of
a hill, and began to pour forth from his flute such airs
of pathetic melody as subdued the very soul and, wak-
ening remorse, drove far from it every frivolous fancy.
At these energetic sounds, the sun hid himself beneath
a gloomy cloud, and the waters of two little lakes, that
were naturally clearer than crystal, became of a colour
like blood. The whole of this superb assembly was involuntarily drawn towards the declivity of the hill.
With downcast eyes they all stood abashed, each upbraiding himself with the evil he had done. The heart
of Dilara palpitated, and the chief of the eunuchs, with
a sigh of contrition, implored pardon of the women,
whom for his own satisfaction he had so often
tormented.

Vathek and Nouronihar turned pale in their litter,
and, regarding each other with haggard looks, reproached themselves—the one with a thousand of the
blackest crimes, a thousand projects of impious ambition,—the other, with the desolation of her family and
the perdition of the amiable Gulchenrouz. Nouronihar
persuaded herself that she heard, in the fatal music, the
groans of her dying father, and Vathek, the sobs of the
fifty children he had sacrificed to the Giaour. Amidst
these complicated pangs of anguish, they perceived
themselves impelled towards the shepherd, whose coun-

tenance was so commanding that Vathek for the first
time felt overawed, whilst Nouronihar concealed her
face with her hands.

The music paused, and the genius, addressing the
caliph, said, "Deluded prince! to whom Providence hath
confided the care of innumerable subjects, is it thus
that thou fulfillest thy mission? Thy crimes are already completed, and art thou now hastening towards
thy punishment? Thou knowest that beyond these
mountains Eblis and his accursed dives hold their infernal empire, and seduced by a malignant phantom,
thou art proceeding to surrender thyself to them! This
moment is the last of grace allowed thee. Abandon thy
atrocious purpose, return, give back Nouronihar to her
father, who still retains a few sparks of life; destroy
thy tower with all its abominations; drive Carathis
from thy councils; be just to thy subjects; respect the
ministers of the Prophet; compensate for thy impieties
by an exemplary life; and instead of squandering thy
days in voluptuous indulgence, lament thy crimes on
the sepulchres of thy ancestors. Thou beholdest the
clouds that obscure the sun. At the instant he recovers
his splendour, if thy heart be not changed, the time of
mercy assigned thee will be past for ever."

Vathek, depressed with fear, was on the point of
prostrating himself at the feet of the shepherd, whom
he perceived to be of a nature superior to man; but his
pride prevailing, he audaciously lifted his head, and
glancing at him one of his terrible looks, said, "Whoever
thou art, withhold thy useless admonitions; thou wouldst
either delude me or art thyself deceived. If what I
have done be so criminal as thou pretendest, there remains not for me a moment of grace. I have traversed
a sea of blood to acquire a power which will make thy
equals tremble. Deem not that I shall retire when in

view of the port, or that I will relinquish her who is dearer to me than either my life or thy mercy. Let the sun appear! let them illume my career! it matters not where it may end." On uttering these words, which made even the genius shudder, Vathek threw himself into the arms of Nouronihar, and commanded that his horses should be forced back to the road.

There was no difficulty in obeying these orders, for the attraction had ceased: the sun shone forth in all his glory, and the shepherd vanished with a lamentable scream.

The fatal impression of the music of the genius remained, notwithstanding, in the heart of Vathek's attendants. They viewed each other with looks of consternation. At the approach of night almost all of them escaped, and of this numerous assemblage there only remained the chief of the eunuchs, some idolatrous slaves, Dilara, and a few other women who like herself were votaries of the religion of the Magi.

The caliph, fired with the ambition of prescribing laws to the powers of darkness, was but little embarrassed at this dereliction. The impetuosity of his blood prevented him from sleeping, nor did he encamp any more, as before. Nouronihar, whose impatience if possible exceeded his own, importuned him to hasten his march, and lavished on him a thousand caresses, to beguile all reflection. She fancied herself already more potent than Balkis, and pictured to her imagination the genii falling prostrate at the foot of her throne. In this manner they advanced by moonlight till they came within view of the two towering rocks that form a kind of portal to the valley, at the extremity of which rose the vast ruins of Istakar. Aloft on the mountain glimmered the fronts of various royal mausoleums, the horror of which was deepened by the shadows of night.

They passed through two villages almost deserted, the only inhabitants remaining being a few feeble old men, who at the sight of horses and litters fell upon their knees, and cried out, "O Heaven! is it then by these phantoms that we have been for six months tormented? Alas! it was from the terror of these spectres, and the noise beneath the mountains, that our people have fled, and left us at the mercy of the malificent spirits!" The caliph, to whom these complaints were but unpromising auguries, drove over the bodies of these wretched old men, and at length arrived at the foot of the terrace of black marble. There he descended from his litter, handing down Nouronihar. Both with beating hearts stared wildly around them, and expected with an apprehensive shudder the approach of the Giaour, but nothing as yet announced his appearance.

A death-like stillness reigned over the mountain and through the air. The moon dilated on a vast platform the shades of the lofty columns, which reached from the terrace almost to the clouds. The gloomy watch-towers, whose number could not be counted, were covered by no roof; and their capitals, of an architecture unknown in the records of the earth, served as an asylum for the birds of night, which, alarmed at the approach of such visitants, fled away croaking.

The chief of the eunuchs, trembling with fear, besought Vathek that a fire might be kindled. "No," replied he, "there is no time left to think of such trifles. Abide where thou art, and expect my commands." Having thus spoken, he presented his hand to Nouronihar; and ascending the steps of a vast staircase, reached the terrace, which was flagged with squares of marble, and resembled a smooth expanse of water upon whose surface not a blade of grass ever dared to vegetate. On the right rose the watch-towers, ranged before the ruins of an immense palace, whose walls were embossed with various figures. In front stood forth the colossal forms of four creatures, composed of the leopard and the griffin, and though but of stone, inspired emotions of terror. Near these were distinguished by the splendour of the moon, which streamed full on the place, characters like those on the sabres of the Giaour, and which possessed the same virtue of changing every moment. These, after vacillating for some time, fixed at last in Arabic letters, and prescribed to the caliph the following words:—"Vathek, thou hast violated the conditions of my parchment, and deservest to be sent back; but in favour to thy companion, and as the meed for what thou hast done to obtain it, Eblis permitteth that the portal of his palace shall be opened, and the subterranean fire will receive thee into the number of its adorers."

He scarcely had read these words before the mountain, against which the terrace was reared, trembled, and the watch-towers were ready to topple headlong upon them. The rock yawned, and disclosed within it a staircase of polished marble, that seemed to approach the abyss. Upon each stair were planted two large torches, like those Nouronihar had seen in her vision, the camphorated vapour of which ascended and gathered itself into a cloud under the hollow of the vault.

This appearance, instead of terrifying, gave new courage to the daughter of Fakreddin. Scarcely deigning to bid adieu to the moon and the firmament, she abandoned without hesitation the pure atmosphere, to plunge into these infernal exhalations. The gait of those impious personages was haughty and determined. As they descended by the effulgence of the torches, they gazed on each other with mutual admiration, and both appeared so resplendent that they already esteemed themselves spiritual intelligences. The only circumstance that perplexed them was their not arriving at the bottom of the stairs. On hastening their descent with an ardent impetuosity, they felt their steps accelerated to such a degree that they seemed not walking but falling from a precipice. Their progress, however, was at length impeded by a vast portal of ebony, which the caliph without difficulty recognised. Here the Giaour awaited them with the key in his hand. "Ye are welcome!" said he to them with a ghastly smile, "in spite of Mahomet and all his dependents. I will now usher you into that palace where you have so highly merited a place." Whilst he was uttering these words, he touched the enamelled lock with his key, and the doors at once flew open with a noise still louder than the thunder of the dog days, and as suddenly recoiled the moment they had entered.

The caliph and Nouronihar beheld each other with amazement at finding themselves in a place which, though roofed with a vaulted ceiling, was so spacious and lofty that at first they took it for an immeasurable plain. But their eyes at length growing familiar to the grandeur of the surrounding objects, they extended their view to those at a distance, and discovered rows of columns and arcades, which gradually diminished till they terminated in a point radiant as the sun when he darts his last beams athwart the ocean. The pavement, strewed over with gold dust and saffron, exhaled so subtle an odour as almost overpowered them. They, however, went on, and observed an infinity of censers in which ambergris and the wood of aloes were continually burning. Between the several columns were placed tables, each spread with a profusion of viands, and wines of every species sparkling in vases of crystal. A throng of genii and other fantastic spirits of either sex danced lasciviously at the sound of music which issued from beneath.

In the midst of this immense hall a vast multitude was incessantly passing, who severally kept their right hands on their hearts, without once regarding any thing around them; they had all the livid paleness of death. Their eyes, deep sunk in their sockets, resembled those phosphoric meteors that glimmer by night in places of interment. Some stalked slowly on, absorbed in profound reverie; some, shrieking with agony, ran furiously about like tigers wounded with poisoned arrows; whilst others, grinding their teeth in rage, foamed along more frantic than the wildest maniac. They all avoided each other; and though surrounded by a multitude that no one could number, each wandered at random unheedful of the rest, as if alone on a desert where no foot had trodden.

Vathek and Nouronihar, frozen with terror at a sight so baleful, demanded of the Giaour what these appearances might mean, and why these ambulating spectres never withdrew their hands from their hearts? "Perplex not yourselves with so much at once," replied he bluntly; "you will soon be acquainted with all. Let us haste, and present you to Eblis." They continued their way through the multitude; but notwithstanding their confidence at first, they were not sufficiently composed to examine with attention the various prospective of halls and of galleries that opened on the right hand and left, which were all illuminated by torches and braziers, whose flames rose in pyramids to the centre of the vault. At length they came to a place where long curtains, brocaded with crimson and gold, fell from all parts in solemn confusion. Here the choirs and dances were heard no longer. The light which glimmered came from afar.

After some time Vathek and Nouronihar perceived a gleam brightening through the drapery, and entered a vast tabernacle hung round with the skins of leopards. An infinity of elders with streaming beards and afrits in complete armour had prostrated themselves before the ascent of a lofty eminence, on the top of which, upon a globe of fire, sat the formidable Eblis.   His person was that of a young man, whose noble and regular features seemed to have been tarnished by malignant vapours.   In his large eyes appeared both pride and despair.   His flowing hair retained some resemblance to that of an angel of light.   In his hand, which thunder had blasted, he swayed the iron sceptre that causes the monster Ouranbad, the afrits, and all the powers of the abyss to tremble.   At his presence the heart of the caliph sunk within him; and he fell prostrate on his face.   Nouronihar, however, though greatly dismayed, could not help admiring the person of Eblis, for she expected to have seen some stupendous giant.

Eblis, with a voice more mild than might be imagined, but such as penetrated the soul and filled it with the deepest melancholy, said, "Creatures of clay, I receive you into mine empire: ye are numbered amongst my adorers.   Enjoy whatever this palace affords: the treasures of the pre-adamite sultans, their fulminating sabres, and those talismans that compel the dives to open the subterranean expanses of the mountain of Kaf, which communicate with these.   There, insatiable as your curiosity may be, shall you find sufficient objects to gratify it.   You shall possess the exclusive privilege of entering the fortresses of Aherman and the halls of Argenk, where are portrayed all creatures endowed with intelligence, and the various animals that inhabited the earth prior to the creation of that con-

temptible being whom ye denominate the father of
mankind."

Vathek and Nouronihar, feeling themselves revived
and encouraged by this harangue, eagerly said to the
Giaour, "Bring us instantly to the place which contains
these precious talismans."

"Come," answered this wicked dive, with his malignant grin,—"come and possess all that my sovereign
hath promised, and more." He then conducted them
into a long aisle adjoining the tabernacle; preceding
them with hasty steps, and followed by his disciples
with the utmost alacrity. They reached at length a
hall of great extent and covered with a lofty dome,
around which appeared fifty portals of bronze, secured
with as many fastenings of iron. A funereal gloom
prevailed over the whole scene. Here upon two beds
of incorruptible cedar lay recumbent the fleshless forms
of the pre-adamite kings, who had been monarchs of
the whole earth. They still possessed enough of life
to be conscious of their deplorable condition. Their
eyes retained a melancholy motion; they regarded one
another with looks of the deepest dejection, each holding his right hand motionless on his heart. At their
feet were inscribed the events of their several reigns,
their power, their pride, and their crimes: Soliman
Daki, and Soliman called Gian Ben Gian, who, after
having chained up the dives in the dark caverns of Kaf,
became so presumptuous as to doubt of the Supreme
Power. All these maintained great state, though not to
be compared with the eminence of Soliman Ben Daoud.

This king, so renowned for his wisdom, was on the
loftiest elevation, and placed immediately under the
dome. He appeared to possess more animation than
the rest. Though from time to time he laboured with
profound sighs, and like his companions, kept his right

hand on his heart, yet his countenance was more composed, and he seemed to be listening to the sullen roar of a cataract visible in part through one of the grated portals. This was the only sound that intruded on the silence of these doleful mansions. A range of brazen vases surrounded the elevation. "Remove the covers from these cabalistic depositaries," said the Giaour to Vathek, "and avail thyself of the talismans which will break asunder all these gates of bronze, and not only render the master of the treasures contained within them, but also of the spirits by which they are guarded."

The caliph, whom this ominous preliminary had entirely disconcerted, approached the vases with faltering footsteps, and was ready to sink with terror when he heard the groans of Soliman. As he proceeded, a voice from the livid lips of the prophet articulated these words:—"In my lifetime I filled a magnificent throne, having on my right hand twelve thousand seats of gold, where the patriarchs and the prophets heard my doctrines; on my left the sages and doctors, upon as many thrones of silver, were present at all my decisions. Whilst I thus administered justice to innumerable multitudes, the birds of the air, hovering over me, served as a canopy against the rays of the sun. My people flourished, and my palace rose to the clouds. I erected a temple to the Most High, which was the wonder of the universe; but I basely suffered myself to be seduced by the love of women, and a curiosity that could not be restrained by sublunary things. I listened to the counsels of Aherman, and the daughter of Pharaoh, and adored fire, and the hosts of heaven. I forsook the holy city, and commanded the genii to rear the stupendous palace of Istakar and the terrace of the watchtowers, each of which was consecrated to a star. There

for a while I enjoyed myself in the zenith of glory
and pleasure. Not only men but supernatural beings
were subject also to my will. I began to think, as
these unhappy monarchs around had already thought,
that the vengeance of Heaven was asleep, when at once
the thunder burst my structures asunder and precipitated me hither; where, however, I do not remain, like
the other inhabitants, totally destitute of hope, for an
angel of light hath revealed that in consideration of
the piety of my early youth my woes shall come to an
end when this cataract shall forever cease to flow. Till
then I am in torments, ineffable torments! An unrelenting fire preys on my heart."

Having uttered this exclamation, Soliman raised his
hands towards heaven, in token of supplication; and the
caliph discerned through his bosom, which was transparent as crystal, his heart enveloped in flames. At
a sight so full of horror, Nouronihar fell back like one
petrified into the arms of Vathek, who cried out with
a convulsive sob, "O Giaour! whither hast thou brought
us! Allow us to depart, and I will relinquish all thou
hast promised. O Mahomet! remains there no more
mercy?"

"None! none!" replied the malicious dive. "Know,
miserable prince, thou art now in the abode of vengeance and despair. Thy heart, also, will be kindled
like those of the other votaries of Eblis. A few days
are allotted thee previous to this fatal period. Employ
them as thou wilt; recline on these heaps of gold; command the infernal potentates; range at thy pleasure
through these immense subterranean domains; no bar-
rier shall be shut against thee. As for me, I have
fulfilled my mission: I now leave thee to thyself." At
these words he vanished.

The caliph and Nouronihar remained in the most abject affliction. Their tears were unable to flow, and scarcely could they support themselves. At length, taking each other despondingly by the hand, they went faltering from this fatal hall, indifferent which way they turned their steps. Every portal opened at their approach. The dives fell prostrate before them. Every reservoir of riches was disclosed to their view, but they no longer felt the incentives of curiosity, of pride, or avarice. With like apathy they heard the chorus of genii and saw the stately banquets prepared to regale them. They went wandering on from chamber to chamber, hall to hall, and gallery to gallery; all without bounds or limit; all distinguishable by the same lowering gloom; all adorned with the same awful grandeur; all traversed by persons in search of repose and consolation, but who sought them in vain; for every one carried within him a heart tormented in flames. Shunned by these various sufferers, who seemed by their looks to be upbraiding the partners of their guilt, they withdrew from them to wait in direful suspense the moment which should render them to each other the like objects of terror.

"What!" exclaimed Nouronihar; "will the time come when I shall snatch my hand from thine?"

"Ah!" said Vathek, "and shall my eyes ever cease to drink from thine long draughts of enjoyment? Shall the moments of our reciprocal ecstasies be reflected on with horror? It was not thou that broughtest me hither; the principles by which Carathis perverted my youth have been the sole cause of my perdition! It is but right she should have her share of it." Having given vent to these painful expressions, he called to an afrit, who was stirring up one of the braziers, and bade him fetch the Princess Carathis from the palace of Samarah.

After issuing these orders, the caliph and Nouronihar
continued walking amidst the silent crowd, till they
heard voices at the end of the gallery. Presuming them
to proceed from some unhappy beings who, like themselves, were awaiting their final doom, they followed
the sound, and found it to come from a small square
chamber, where they discovered sitting on sofas four
young men of goodly figure and a lovely female, who
were holding a melancholy conversation by the glimmering of a lonely lamp. Each had a gloomy and
forlorn air; and two of them were embracing each other
with great tenderness. On seeing the caliph and the
daughter of Fakreddin enter, they arose, saluted, and
made room for them. Then he who appeared the most
considerable of the group, addressed himself thus to
Vathek:—"Strangers! who doubtless are in the same
state of suspense with ourselves, as you do not yet bear
your hand on your heart, if you are come hither to pass
the interval allotted, previous to the infliction of our
common punishment, condescend to relate the adventures that have brought you to this fatal place; and we
in return will acquaint you with ours, which deserve
but too well to be heard. To trace back our crimes to
their source, though we are not permitted to repent, is
the only employment suited to wretches like us!"

The caliph and Nouronihar assented to the proposal;
and Vathek began, not without tears and lamentations,
a sincere recital of every circumstance that had passed.
When the afflicting narrative was closed, the young man
entered on his own.* Each person proceeded in order,
and when the third prince had reached the midst of his

* Here Beckford had intended inserting the three "Episodes" which were discovered and published later. See Introduction, p. xxi.

adventures, a sudden noise interrupted him, which caused the vault to tremble and to open.

Immediately a cloud descended, which gradually dissipating, discovered Carathis on the back of an afrit, who grievously complained of his burden. She, instantly springing to the ground, advanced towards her son, and said, "What dost thou here, in this little square chamber? As the dives are become subject to thy beck, I expected to have found thee on the throne of the preadamite kings."

"Execrable woman!" answered the caliph; "cursed be the day thou gavest me birth! Go, follow this afrit; let him conduct thee to the hall of the prophet Soliman. There thou wilt learn to what these palaces are destined, and how much I ought to abhor the impious knowledge thou hast taught me."

"Has the height of power to which thou art arrived turned thy brain?" answered Carathis; "but I ask no more than permission to show my respect for Soliman the prophet. It is, however, proper thou shouldst know that (as the afrit has informed me neither of us shall return to Samarah) I requested his permission to arrange my affairs, and he politely consented. Availing myself, therefore, of the few moments allowed me, I set fire to the tower, and consumed in it the mutes, negresses, and serpents which have rendered me so much good service; nor should I have been less kind to Morakanabad, had he not prevented me by deserting at last to thy brother. As for Bababalouk, who had the folly to return to Samarah, to provide husbands for thy wives, I undoubtedly would have put him to the torture, but being in a hurry, I only hung him, after having decoyed him in a snare, with thy wives, whom I buried alive by the help of my negresses, who thus spent their last moments greatly to their satisfaction.

With respect to Dilara, who ever stood high in my
favour, she hath evinced the greatness of her mind by
fixing herself near, in the service of one of the magi,
and, I think, will soon be one of our society."

Vathek, too much cast down to express the indignation excited by such a discourse, ordered the afrit to
remove Carathis from his presence, and continued immersed in thoughts which his companions durst not
disturb.

Carathis, however, eagerly entered the dome of Soliman, and without regarding in the least the groans of
the prophet, undauntedly removed the covers of the
vases and violently seized on the talismans. Then with
a voice more loud than had hitherto been heard within
these mansions, she compelled the dives to disclose to
her the most secret treasures, the most profound stores,
which the afrit himself had not seen. She passed by
rapid descents, known only to Eblis and his most
favoured potentates, and thus penetrated the very entrails of the earth, where breathes the sansar, or the
icy wind of death. Nothing appalled her dauntless
soul. She perceived, however, in all the inmates who
bore their hands on their hearts, a little singularity
not much to her taste.

As she was emerging from one of the abysses, Eblis
stood forth to her view; but notwithstanding he displayed the full effulgence of his infernal majesty, she
preserved her countenance unaltered, and even paid her
compliments with considerable firmness.

This superb monarch thus answered:—"Princess,
whose knowledge and whose crimes have merited a conspicuous rank in my empire, thou dost well to avail thyself of the leisure that remains; for the flames and torments, which are ready to seize on thy heart, will not

fail to provide thee soon with full employment." He said, and was lost in the curtains of his tabernacle.

Carathis paused for a moment with surprise, but, resolved to follow the advice of Eblis, she assembled all the choirs of genii and all the dives to pay her homage. Thus marched she in triumph through a vapour of perfumes, amidst the acclamations of all the malignant spirits, with most of whom she had formed a previous acquaintance. She even attempted to dethrone one of the Solimans, for the purpose of usurping his place, when a voice, proceeding from the abyss of death, proclaimed, "All is accomplished!" Instantaneously the haughty forehead of the intrepid princess became corrugated with agony; she uttered a tremendous yell, and fixed, no more to be withdrawn, her right hand upon her heart, which was become a receptacle of eternal fire.

In this delirium, forgetting all ambitious projects, and her thirst for that knowledge which should ever be hidden from mortals, she overturned the offerings of the genii; and, having execrated the hour she was begotten and the womb that had borne her, glanced off in a rapid whirl that rendered her invisible, and continued to revolve without intermission.

Almost at the same instant, the same voice announced to the caliph, Nouronihar, the four princes, and the princess, the awful and irrevocable decree. Their hearts immediately took fire, and they at once lost the most precious gift of heaven,—HOPE. These unhappy beings recoiled, with looks of the most furious distraction. Vathek beheld in the eyes of Nouronihar nothing but rage and vengeance; nor could she discern aught in his but aversion and despair. The two princes who were friends, and till that moment had preserved their attachment, shrunk back, gnashing their teeth with mutual and unchangeable hatred. Kalilah and his sister made reciprocal gestures of imprecation; all testified their horror for each other by the most ghastly convulsions, and screams that could not be smothered. All severally plunged themselves into the accursed multitude, there to wander in an eternity of unabating anguish.

Such was, and such should be, the punishment of unrestrained passions and atrocious deeds! Such shall be the chastisement of that blind curiosity which would transgress those bounds the wisdom of the Creator has prescribed to human knowledge; and such the dreadful disappointment of that restless ambition which, aiming at discoveries reserved for beings of a supernatural order, perceives not through its infatuated pride that the condition of man upon earth is to be—humble and ignorant.

Thus the caliph Vathek, who for the sake of empty pomp and forbidden power had sullied himself with a thousand crimes, became a prey to grief without end and remorse without mitigation; whilst the humble, the despised Gulchenrouz passed whole ages in undisturbed tranquillity, and in the pure happiness of childhood.

THE ROMANCE OF THE FOREST

BY

MRS. ANN RADCLIFFE

1791

CHAPTER I

"WHEN once sordid interest seizes on the heart, it freezes up the source of every warm and liberal feeling; it is an enemy alike to virtue and to taste—*this* it perverts, and *that* it annihilates. The time may come, my friend, when death shall dissolve the sinews of avarice, and justice be permitted to resume her rights."

Such were the words of the Advocate Nemours to Pierre de la Motte, as the latter stept at midnight into the carriage which was to bear him far from Paris, from his creditors and the persecution of the laws. La Motte thanked him for this last instance of his kindness, the assistance he had given him in escape; and when the carriage drove away, uttered a sad adieu! The gloom of the hour and the peculiar emergency of his circumstances sunk him in silent reverie.

Whoever has read Guyot de Pitaval, the most faithful of those writers who record the proceedings in the Parliamentary Courts of Paris during the seventeenth century, must surely remember the striking story of Pierre de la Motte and the Marquis Philippe de Montalt: let all such, therefore, be informed that the person here introduced to their notice was that individual Pierre de la Motte.

As Madame La Motte leaned from the coach window and gave a last look to the walls of Paris—Paris, the scene of her former happiness, and the residence of many dear friends—the fortitude which had till now supported her, yielded to the force of grief. "Farewell all!" sighed she, "this last look and we are separated for ever!" Tears followed her words, and, sinking back, she resigned herself to the stillness of sorrow. The recollection of former times pressed heavily upon her heart: a few months before and she was surrounded by friends, fortune, and consequence; now she was deprived of all, a miserable exile from her native place, without home, without comfort—almost without hope. It was not the least of her afflictions that she had been obliged to quit Paris without bidding adieu to her only son, who was now on duty with his regiment in Germany; and such had been the precipitancy of this removal that had she even known where he was stationed, she had no time to inform him of it, or of the alteration in his father's circumstances.

Pierre de la Motte was a gentleman descended from an ancient house of France. He was a man whose passions often overcame his reason, and for a time silenced his conscience; but though the image of virtue which Nature had impressed upon his heart was sometimes obscured by the passing influence of vice, it was never wholly obliterated. With strength of mind sufficient to have withstood temptation, he would have been a good man; as it was, he was always a weak and sometimes a vicious member of society; yet his mind was active and his imagination vivid, which, co-operating with the force of passion, often dazzled his judgment and subdued principle. Thus he was a man infirm in purpose and visionary in virtue: in a word, his conduct was suggested by feeling rather than principle; and his virtue, such as it was, could not stand the pressure of occasion.

Early in life he had married Constance Valentia, a beautiful and elegant woman, attached to her family and beloved by them. Her birth was equal, her fortune superior to his; and their nuptials had been celebrated under the auspices of an approving and flattering world. Her heart was devoted to La Motte, and, for some time she found in him an affectionate husband; but, allured by the gaieties of Paris, he was soon devoted to its luxuries, and in a few years his fortune and affection were equally lost in dissipation. A false pride had still operated against his interest, and withheld him from honourable retreat while it was yet in his power. The habits which he had acquired, enchained him to the scene of his former pleasure, and thus he had continued an expensive style of life till the means of prolonging it were exhausted. He at length awoke from this lethargy of security; but it was only to plunge into new error, and to attempt schemes for the reparation of his fortune, which served to sink him deeper in destruction. The consequence of a transaction in which he thus engaged, now drove him with the small wreck of his property into dangerous and ignominious exile.

It was his design to pass into one of the southern provinces, and there seek near the borders of the kingdom an asylum in some obscure village. His family consisted of his wife and two faithful domestics, a man and woman, who followed the fortunes of their master.

The night was dark and tempestuous, and at about the distance of three leagues from Paris, Peter, who now acted as postillion, having driven for some time over a wild heath where many ways crossed, stopped and acquainted La Motte with his perplexity. The sudden stopping of the carriage roused the latter from his reverie and filled the whole party with the terror of pursuit. He was unable to supply the necessary direction, and the extreme darkness made it dangerous to proceed without one. During this period of distress a light was perceived at some distance, and after much doubt and hesitation, La Motte, in the hope of obtaining assistance, alighted and advanced towards it; he proceeded slowly, from the fear of unknown pits. The light issued from the window of a small and ancient house, which stood alone on the heath at the distance of half a mile.

Having reached the door, he stopped for some moments, listening in apprehensive anxiety—no sound was heard but that of the wind, which swept in hollow gusts over the waste. At length he ventured to knock, and having waited some time, during which he indistinctly heard several voices in conversation, some one within inquired what he wanted? La Motte answered that he was a traveller who had lost his way, and desired to be directed to the nearest town. "That," said the person, "is seven miles off, and the road bad enough, even if you could see it. If you only want a bed, you may have it here, and had better stay."

The "pitiless pelting" of the storm, which at this time beat with increasing fury upon La Motte, inclined him to give up the attempt of proceeding farther till day-light, but, desirous of seeing the person with whom he conversed, before he ventured to expose his family by calling up the carriage, he asked to be admitted. The door was now opened by a tall figure with a light, who invited La Motte to enter. He followed the man through a passage into a room almost unfurnished, in one corner of which a bed was spread upon the floor. The forlorn and desolate aspect of this apartment made La Motte shrink involuntarily, and he was turning to go out when the man suddenly pushed him back, and he heard the door locked upon him. His heart failed, yet he made a desperate, though vain, effort to force the door and called loudly for release. No answer was returned, but he distinguished the voices of men in the room above, and not doubting but their intention was to rob and murder him, his agitation at first overcame his reason. By the light of some almost expiring embers, he perceived a window, but the hope which this discovery revived was quickly lost when he found the aperture guarded by strong iron bars. Such preparation for security surprised him, and confirmed his worst apprehensions. Alone, unarmed—beyond the chance of assistance, he saw himself in the power of people whose trade was apparently rapine!—murder their means! After revolving every possibility of escape, he endeavoured to await the event with fortitude, but La Motte could boast of no such virtue.

The voices had ceased, and all remained still for a quarter of an hour, when between the pauses of the wind he thought he distinguished the sobs and moaning of a female. He listened attentively and became confirmed in his conjecture; it was too evidently the accent of distress. At this conviction, the remains of his courage forsook him, and a terrible surmise darted with the rapidity of lightning across his brain. It was probable that his carriage had been discovered by the people of the house, who with a design of plunder had secured her servant and brought hither Madame La Motte. He was the more inclined to believe this by the stillness which had for some time reigned in the house previous to the sounds he now heard. Or it was possible that the inhabitants were not robbers, but persons to whom he had been betrayed by his friend or servant, and who were appointed to deliver him into the hands of justice. Yet he hardly dared to doubt the integrity of his friend, who had been intrusted with the secret of his flight and the plan of his route, and had procured him the carriage in which he had escaped. "Such depravity," exclaimed La Motte, "cannot surely exist in human nature; much less in the heart of Nemours!"

This ejaculation was interrupted by a noise in the passage leading to the room. It approached—the door was unlocked—and the man who had admitted La Motte into the house entered, leading, or rather forcibly dragging along, a beautiful girl, who appeared to be about eighteen. Her features were bathed in tears, and she seemed to suffer the utmost distress. The man fastened the lock and put the key in his pocket. He then advanced to La Motte, who had before observed other persons in the passage, and pointing a pistol to his breast, "You are wholly in our power," said he, "no assistance can reach you. If you wish to save your life, swear that you will convey this girl where I may never see her more; or rather consent to take her with you, for your oath I would not believe, and I can take care you shall not find me again.—Answer quickly, you have no time to lose."

He now seized the trembling hand of the girl, who shrunk aghast with terror, and hurried her towards La Motte, whom surprise still kept silent. She sunk at his feet, and with supplicating eyes that streamed with tears implored him to have pity on her. Notwithstanding his present agitation, he found it impossible to contemplate the beauty and distress of the object before him with indifference. Her youth, her apparent innocence, the artless energy of her manner, forcibly assailed his heart, and he was going to speak, when the ruffian, who mistook the silence of astonishment for that of hesitation, prevented him. "I have a horse ready to take you from hence," said he, "and I will direct you over the heath. If you return within an hour, you die; after then, you are at liberty to come here when you please."

La Motte, without answering, raised the lovely girl from the floor, and was so much relieved from his own apprehensions that he had leisure to attempt dissipating hers. "Let us be gone," said the ruffian, "and have no more of this nonsense; you may think yourself well off it's no worse. I'll go and get the horse ready."

The last words roused La Motte, and perplexed him with new fears. He dreaded to discover his carriage lest its appearance might tempt the banditti to plunder, and to depart on horseback with this man might produce a consequence yet more to be dreaded. Madame La Motte, wearied with apprehension, would probably send for her husband to the house, when all the former danger would be incurred, with the additional evil of being separated from his family and the chance of being detected by the emissaries of justice in endeavouring to recover them. As these reflections passed over his mind in tumultuous rapidity, a noise was again heard in the passage, an uproar and scuffle ensued, and in the same moment he could distinguish the voice of his servant, who had been sent by Madame La Motte in search of him. Being now determined to disclose what could not long be concealed, he exclaimed aloud that a horse was unnecessary, that he had a carriage at some distance which would convey them from the heath, the man who was seized being his servant.

The ruffian, speaking through the door, bade him be patient a while and he should hear more from him. La Motte now turned his eyes upon his unfortunate companion, who, pale and exhausted, leaned for support against the wall. Her features, which were delicately beautiful, had gained from distress an expression of captivating sweetness: she had

> An eye
> As when the blue sky trembles thro' a cloud
> Of purest white.

A habit of grey camlet, with short slashed sleeves, shewed, but did not adorn, her figure. It was thrown open at the bosom, upon which part of her hair had fallen in disorder, while the light veil hastily thrown on, had in her confusion been suffered to fall back. Every moment of farther observation heightened the surprise of La Motte, and interested him more warmly in her favour. Such elegance and apparent refinement, contrasted with the desolation of the house and the savage manners of its inhabitants, seemed to him like a romance of imagination rather than an occurrence of real life. He endeavoured to comfort her, and his sense of compassion was too sincere to be misunderstood. Her terror gradually subsided into gratitude and grief. "Ah, sir," said she, "heaven has sent you to my relief, and will surely reward you for your protection: I have no friend in the world if I do not find one in you."

La Motte assured her of his kindness, when he was interrupted by the entrance of the ruffian. He desired to be conducted to his family. "All in good time," replied the latter; "I have taken care of one of them, and will of you, please St. Peter; so be comforted." These *comfortable* words renewed the terror of La Motte, who now earnestly begged to know if his family were safe. "O! as for that matter, they are safe enough, and you will be with them presently; but don't stand *parlying* here all night. Do you choose to go or stay?

You know the conditions." They now bound the eyes of La Motte and of the young lady, whom terror had hitherto kept silent, and then placing them on two horses, a man mounted behind each and they immediately galloped off. They had proceeded in this way near half an hour when La Motte entreated to know whither he was going? "You will know that by and by," said the ruffian, "so be at peace." Finding interrogatories useless, La Motte resumed silence till the horses stopped. His conductor then hallooed, and being answered by voices at some distance, in a few moments the sound of carriage wheels was heard, and presently after, the words of a man directing Peter which way to drive. As the carriage approached, La Motte called, and, to his inexpressible joy, was answered by his wife.

"You are now beyond the borders of the heath, and may go which way you will," said the ruffian; "if you return within an hour, you will be welcomed by a brace of bullets." This was a very unnecessary caution to La Motte, whom they now released. The young stranger sighed deeply, as she entered the carriage, and the ruffian, having bestowed upon Peter some directions and more threats, waited to see him drive off. They did not wait long.

La Motte immediately gave a short relation of what had passed at the house, including an account of the manner in which the young stranger had been introduced to him. During this narrative her deep convulsive sighs frequently drew the attention of Madame La Motte, whose compassion became gradually interested in her behalf, and who now endeavoured to tranquillize her spirits. The unhappy girl answered her kindness in artless and simple expressions, and then relapsed into tears and silence. Madame forbore for the present to ask any questions that might lead to a discovery of her connections or seem to require an explanation of the late adventure, which now furnishing her with a new subject of reflection, the sense of her own misfortunes pressed less heavily upon her mind. The distress of La Motte was even for a while suspended; he ruminated on the late scene, and it appeared like a vision, or one of those improbable fictions that sometimes are exhibited in a romance. He could reduce it to no principles of probability, nor render it comprehensible by any endeavour to analyze it. The present charge, and the chance of future trouble brought upon him by this adventure, occasioned some dissatisfaction, but the beauty and seeming innocence of Adeline united with the pleadings of humanity in her favour, and he determined to protect her.

The tumult of emotions which had passed in the bosom of Adeline began now to subside; terror was softened into anxiety, and despair into grief. The sympathy so evident in the manners of her companions, particularly in those of Madame La Motte, soothed her heart and encouraged her to hope for better days.

Dismally and silently the night passed on, for the minds of the travellers were too much occupied by their several sufferings to admit of conversation. The dawn, so anxiously watched for, at length appeared, and introduced the strangers more fully to each other. Adeline derived comfort from the looks of Madame La Motte, who gazed frequently and attentively at her, and thought she had seldom seen a countenance so interesting or a form so striking. The languor of sorrow threw a melancholy grace upon her features that appealed immediately to the heart; and there was a penetrating sweetness in her blue eyes which indicated an intelligent and amiable mind.

La Motte now looked anxiously from the coach window, that he might judge of their situation and observe whether he was followed. The obscurity of the dawn confined his views, but no person appeared. The sun at length tinted the eastern clouds and the tops of the highest hills, and soon after burst in full splendour on the scene. The terrors of La Motte began to subside, and the griefs of Adeline to soften. They entered upon a lane confined by high banks and overarched by trees, on whose branches appeared the first green buds of spring glittering with dews. The fresh breeze of the morning animated the spirits of Adeline, whose mind was delicately sensible to the beauties of nature. As she viewed the flowery luxuriance of the turf, and the tender green of the trees, or caught between the opening banks a glimpse of the varied landscape, rich with wood, and fading into blue and distant mountains, her heart expanded in momentary joy. With Adeline the charms of external nature were heightened by those of novelty; she had seldom seen the grandeur of an extensive prospect, or the magnificence of a wide horizon— and not often the picturesque beauties of more confined scenery. Her mind had not lost by long oppression that elastic energy which resists calamity; else, however susceptible might have been her original taste, the beauties of nature would no longer have charmed her thus easily even to temporary repose.

The road, at length, wound down the side of a hill, and La Motte, again looking anxiously from the window, saw before him an open champaign country, through which the road, wholly unsheltered from observation, extended almost in a direct line. The danger of these circumstances alarmed him, for his flight might without difficulty be traced for many leagues from the hills he was now descending. Of the first peasant that passed, he inquired for a road among the hills, but heard of none. La Motte now sunk into his former terrors. Madame, notwithstanding her own apprehensions, endeavoured to reassure him, but finding her efforts ineffectual, she also retired to the contemplation of her misfortunes. Often, as they went on, did La Motte look back upon the country they had passed, and often did imagination suggest to him the sounds of distant pursuit.

The travellers stopped to breakfast in a village where the road was at length obscured by woods, and La Motte's spirits again revived. Adeline appeared more tranquil than she had yet been, and La Motte now asked for an explanation of the scene he had witnessed on the preceding night. The inquiry renewed all her distress, and with tears she entreated for the present to be spared on the subject. La Motte pressed it no farther, but he observed that for the greater part of the day she seemed to remember it in melancholy and dejection. They now travelled among the hills, and were therefore in less danger of observation; but La Motte avoided the great towns, and stopped in obscure ones no longer than to refresh the horses. About two hours after noon the road wound into a deep valley, watered by a rivulet and overhung with wood. La Motte called to Peter, and ordered him to drive to a thickly embowered spot that appeared on the left. Here he alighted with his family, and Peter having spread the provisions on the turf, they seated themselves and partook of a repast which in other circumstances would have been thought delicious. Adeline endeavoured to smile, but the languor of grief was now heightened by indisposition. The violent agitation of mind and fatigue of body which she had suffered for the last twenty-four hours had overpowered her strength, and when

La Motte led her back to the carriage, her whole frame trembled with illness. But she uttered no complaint, and having long observed the dejection of her companions, she made a feeble effort to enliven them. They continued to travel throughout the day without any accident or interruption, and, about three hours after sunset, arrived at Monville, a small town where La Motte determined to pass the night. Repose was, indeed, necessary to the whole party, whose pale and haggard looks, as they alighted from the carriage, were but too obvious to pass unobserved by the people of the inn. As soon as beds could be prepared, Adeline withdrew to her chamber, accompanied by Madame La Motte, whose concern for the fair stranger made her exert every effort to soothe and console her. Adeline wept in silence, and taking the hand of Madame, pressed it to her bosom. These were not merely tears of grief—they were mingled with those which flow from the grateful heart when unexpectedly it meets with sympathy. Madame La Motte understood them. After some momentary silence she renewed her assurances of kindness, and entreated Adeline to confide in her friendship; but she carefully avoided any mention of the subject which had before so much affected her. Adeline at length found words to express her sense of this goodness, which she did in a manner so natural and sincere, that Madame, finding herself much affected, took leave of her for the night.

In the morning, La Motte rose at an early hour, impatient to be gone. Everything was prepared for his departure, and the breakfast had been waiting some time, but Adeline did not appear. Madame La Motte went to her chamber, and found her sunk in a disturbed slumber. Her breathing was short and irregular—she frequently started or sighed, and sometimes she muttered an incoherent sentence. While Madame gazed with concern upon her languid countenance, she awoke, and, looking up, gave her hand to Madame La Motte, who found it burning with fever. She had passed a restless night, and as she now attempted to rise, her head, which beat with intense pain, grew giddy, her strength failed, and she sunk back.

Madame was much alarmed, being at once convinced that it was impossible she could travel, and that a delay might prove fatal to her husband. She went to inform him of the truth, and his distress may be more easily imagined than described. He saw all the inconvenience and danger of delay, yet he could not so far divest himself of humanity as to abandon Adeline to the care, or rather to the neglect, of strangers. He sent immediately for a physician, who pronounced her to be in a high fever, and said a removal in her present state must be fatal. La Motte now determined to wait the event, and endeavoured to calm the transports of terror which at times assailed him. In the meanwhile, he took such precautions as his situation admitted of, passing the greater part of the day out of the village, in a spot from whence he had a view of the road for some distance; yet to be exposed to destruction by the illness of a girl whom he did not know, and who had actually been forced upon him, was a misfortune to which La Motte had not philosophy enough to submit with composure.

Adeline's fever continued to increase during the whole day, and at night, when the physician took his leave, he told La Motte the event would very soon be decided. La Motte received this intelligence with real concern. The beauty and innocence of Adeline had overcome the disadvantageous circumstances under which she had been introduced to him, and he now gave less consideration to the inconvenience she might hereafter occasion him than to the hope of her recovery.

Madame La Motte watched over her with tender anxiety, and observed with admiration her patient sweetness and mild resignation. Adeline amply repaid her, though she thought she could not.—"Young as I am," she would say, "and deserted by those upon whom I have a claim for protection, I can remember no connection to make me regret life so much as that I hoped to form with you. If I live, my conduct will best express my sense of your goodness;—words are but feeble testimonies."

The sweetness of her manners so much attracted Madame La Motte that she watched the crisis of her disorder with a solicitude which precluded every other interest. Adeline passed a very disturbed night, and when the physician appeared in the morning, he gave orders that she should be indulged with whatever she liked, and answered the inquiries of La Motte with a frankness that left him nothing to hope.

In the meantime his patient, after drinking profusely of some mild liquids, fell asleep, in which she continued for several hours, and so profound was her repose that her breath alone gave sign of existence. She awoke free from fever, and with no other disorder than weakness, which in a few days she overcame so well as to be able to set out with La Motte for B——, a village out of the great road, which he thought it prudent to quit. There they passed the following night, and early the next morning commenced their journey upon a wild and woody tract of country. They stopped about noon at a solitary village, where they took refreshments and obtained directions for passing the vast forest of Fontanville, upon the borders of which they now were. La Motte wished at first to take a guide, but he apprehended more evil from the discovery he might make of his route, than he hoped for benefit from assistance in the wilds of this uncultivated tract.

La Motte now designed to pass on to Lyons, where he could either seek concealment in its neighbourhood, or embark on the Rhone for Geneva, should the emergency of his circumstances hereafter require him to leave France. It was about twelve o'clock at noon, and he was desirous to hasten forward, that he might pass the forest of Fontanville and reach the town on its opposite borders, before night-fall. Having deposited a fresh stock of provisions in the carriage, and received such directions as were necessary concerning the roads, they again set forward, and in a short time entered upon the forest. It was now the latter end of April, and the weather was remarkably temperate and fine. The balmy freshness of the air, which breathed the first pure essence of vegetation, and the gentle warmth of the sun, whose beams vivified every hue of nature and opened every floweret of spring, revived Adeline and inspired her with life and health. As she inhaled the breeze, her strength seemed to return, and as her eyes wandered through the romantic glades that opened into the forest, her heart was gladdened with complacent delight: but when from these objects she turned her regard upon Monsieur and Madame La Motte, to whose tender attentions she owed her life, and in whose looks she now read esteem and kindness, her bosom glowed with sweet affections, and she experienced a force of gratitude which might be called sublime.

For the remainder of the day they continued to travel without seeing a hut or meeting a human being. It was now near sunset, and the prospect being closed on all sides by the forest, La Motte began to have apprehensions that his servant had mistaken the way. The road, if a road it could be called which afforded only a slight track upon the grass, was sometimes overrun by luxuriant vegetation, and sometimes obscured by the deep shades, and Peter at length stopped, uncertain of the way. La Motte, who dreaded being benighted in a scene so wild and solitary as this forest, and whose apprehensions of banditti were very sanguine, ordered him to proceed at any rate, and if he found no track, to endeavour to gain a more open part of the forest. With these orders, Peter again set forwards, but having proceeded some way, and his views being still confined by woody glades and forest walks, he began to despair of extricating himself, and stopped for further orders. The sun was now set, but as La Motte looked anxiously from the window, he observed upon the vivid glow of the western horizon some dark towers rising from among the trees at a little distance, and ordered Peter to drive towards them.—"If they belong to a monastery," said he, "we may probably gain admittance for the night."

The carriage drove along under the shade of "melancholy boughs," through which the evening twilight, which yet coloured the air, diffused a solemnity that vibrated in thrilling sensations upon the hearts of the travellers. Expectation kept them silent. The present scene recalled to Adeline a remembrance of the late terrific circumstances, and her mind responded but too easily to the apprehension of new misfortunes. La Motte alighted at the foot of a green knoll, where the trees again opening to light, permitted a nearer though imperfect view of the edifice.

CHAPTER II

HE APPROACHED, and perceived the Gothic remains of
an abbey. It stood on a kind of rude lawn, overshad-
owed by high and spreading trees which seemed coeval
with the building and diffused a romantic gloom around.
The greater part of the pile appeared to be sinking into
ruins, and that which had withstood the ravages of
time showed the remaining features of the fabric more
awful in decay. The lofty battlements, thickly en-
wreathed with ivy, were half demolished, and become
the residence of birds of prey. Huge fragments of
the eastern tower, which was almost demolished, lay
scattered amid the high grass that waved slowly to the
breeze. "The thistle shook its lonely head; the moss
whistled to the wind." A Gothic gate richly ornamented with fret work, which opened into the main
body of the edifice, but which was now obstructed
with brush-wood, remained entire. Above the vast and
magnificent portal of this gate arose a window of the
same order, whose pointed arches still exhibited fragments of stained glass, once the pride of monkish devotion. La Motte, thinking it possible it might yet
shelter some human being, advanced to the gate and
lifted a massy knocker. The hollow sounds rung
through the emptiness of the place. After waiting a
few minutes, he forced back the gate, which was heavy
with iron-work and creaked harshly on its hinges.

He entered what appeared to have been the chapel
of the abbey, where the hymn of devotion had once
been raised and the tear of penitence had once been
shed: sounds which could now only be recalled by
imagination—tears of penitence which had been long
since fixed in fate. La Motte paused a moment, for he

felt a sensation of sublimity rising into terror—a suspension of mingled astonishment and awe! He surveyed the vastness of the place, and as he contemplated
its ruins, fancy bore him back to past ages.—"And these
walls," said he, "where once superstition lurked and
austerity anticipated an earthly purgatory, now tremble
over the mortal remains of the beings who reared
them!"

The deepening gloom now reminded La Motte that
he had no time to lose, but curiosity prompted him to
explore farther, and he obeyed the impulse. As he
walked over the broken pavement, the sound of his
steps ran in echoes through the place, and seemed like
the mysterious accents of the dead, reproving the sacrilegious mortal who thus dared to disturb their
precincts.

From this chapel he passed into the nave of the
great church, of which one window, more perfect than
the rest, opened upon a long vista of the forest, through
which was seen the rich colouring of evening, melting
by imperceptible gradations into the solemn grey of
upper air. Dark hills, whose outline appeared distinct
upon the vivid glow of the horizon, closed the perspective. Several of the pillars which had once supported the roof remained the proud effigies of sinking
greatness, and seemed to nod at every murmur of the
blast over the fragments of those that had fallen a little
before them. La Motte sighed. The comparison between himself and the gradation of decay which these
columns exhibited was but too obvious and affecting.
"A few years," said he, "and I shall become like the
mortals on whose reliques I now gaze, and, like them
too, I may be the subject of meditation to a succeeding
generation, which shall totter but a little while over

the object they contemplate, ere they also sink into the dust."

Retiring from this scene, he walked through the cloisters, till a door which communicated with the lofty part of the building attracted his curiosity. He opened this and perceived across the foot of the staircase, another door;—but now, partly checked by fear, and partly by the recollection of the surprise his family might feel in his absence, he returned with hasty steps to his carriage, having wasted some of the precious moments of twilight and gained no information.

Some slight answer to Madame La Motte's inquiries, and a general direction to Peter to drive carefully on and look for a road, was all that his anxiety would permit him to utter. The night shade fell thick around, which deepened by the gloom of the forest soon rendered it dangerous to proceed. Peter stopped, but La Motte, persisting in his first determination, ordered him to go on. Peter ventured to remonstrate, Madame La Motte entreated, but La Motte reproved—commanded, and at length repented; for the hind wheel rising upon the stump of an old tree, which the darkness had prevented Peter from observing, the carriage was in an instant overturned.

The party, as may be supposed, were much terrified, but no one was materially hurt, and having disengaged themselves from their perilous situation, La Motte and Peter endeavoured to raise the carriage. The extent of this misfortune was now discovered, for they perceived that the wheel was broke. Their distress was reasonably great, for not only was the coach disabled from proceeding, but it could not even afford a shelter from the cold dews of the night, it being impossible to preserve it in an upright situation. After a few moments' silence, La Motte proposed that they should return to the ruins which they had just quitted, which lay at a very short distance, and pass the night in the most habitable part of them; that when morning dawned Peter should take one of the coach horses and endeavour to find a road, and a town from whence assistance could be procured for repairing the carriage. This proposal was opposed by Madame La Motte, who shuddered at the idea of passing so many hours of darkness in a place so forlorn as the monastery. Terrors which she neither endeavoured to examine or combat, overcame her, and she told La Motte she had rather remain exposed to the unwholesome dews of night than encounter the desolation of the ruins. La Motte had at first felt an equal reluctance to return to this spot, but having subdued his own feelings, he resolved not to yield to those of his wife.

The horses being now disengaged from the carriage, the party moved towards the edifice. As they proceeded, Peter, who followed them, struck a light, and they entered the ruins by the flame of sticks which he had collected. The partial gleams thrown across the fabric seemed to make its desolation more solemn, with the obscurity of the greater part of the pile heightened its sublimity and led fancy on to scenes of horror. Adeline, who had hitherto remained in silence, now uttered an exclamation of mingled admiration and fear. A kind of pleasing dread thrilled her bosom and filled all her soul. Tears started into her eyes—she wished, yet feared to go on. She hung upon the arm of La Motte, and looked at him with a sort of hesitating interrogation.

He opened the door of the great hall, and they entered: its extent was lost in gloom.—"Let us stay here," said Madame La Motte, "I will go no farther." La Motte pointed to the broken roof, and was proceeding, when he was interrupted by an uncommon noise which passed along the hall. They were all silent—it was the silence of terror. Madame La Motte spoke first. "Let us quit this spot," said she, "any evil is preferable to the feeling which now oppresses me. Let us retire instantly." The stillness had for some time remained undisturbed, and La Motte, ashamed of the fear he had involuntarily betrayed, now thought it necessary to affect a boldness which he did not feel. He therefore opposed ridicule to the terror of Madame, and insisted upon proceeding. Thus compelled to acquiesce, she traversed the hall with trembling steps. They came to a narrow passage, and Peter's sticks being nearly exhausted, they awaited here while he went in search of more.

The almost expiring light flashed faintly upon the walls of the passage, showing the recess more horrible. Across the hall, the greater part of which was concealed in shadow, the feeble ray spread a tremulous gleam, exhibiting the chasm in the roof, while many nameless objects were seen imperfectly through the dusk. Adeline with a smile inquired of La Motte if he believed in spirits. The question was ill-timed, for the present scene impressed its terrors upon La Motte, and in spite of endeavour he felt a superstitious dread stealing upon him. He was now, perhaps, standing over the ashes of the dead. If spirits were ever permitted to revisit the earth, this seemed the hour and the place most suitable for their appearance. La Motte remaining silent, Adeline said, "Were I inclined to superstition"—she was interrupted by a return of the noise which had been lately heard. It sounded down the passage at whose entrance they stood, and sunk gradually away. Every heart palpitated, and they remained listening in silence. A new subject of apprehension seized La Motte:—the noise might proceed from banditti, and he hesitated whether it would be safe to proceed. Peter now came with the light. Madame refused to enter the passage— La Motte was not much inclined to it; but Peter, in whom curiosity was more prevalent than fear, readily offered his services. La Motte, after some hesitation, suffered him to go, while he awaited at the entrance the result of the inquiry. The extent of the passage soon concealed Peter from view, and the echoes of his footsteps were lost in a sound which rushed along the avenue and became fainter and fainter till it sunk into silence. La Motte now called aloud to Peter, but no answer was returned; at length, they heard the sound of a distant footstep, and Peter soon after appeared, breathless, and pale with fear.

When he came within hearing of La Motte, he called out, "An please your honour, I've done for them, I believe, but I've had a hard bout. I thought I was fighting with the devil."—"What are you speaking of?" said La Motte.

"They were nothing but owls and rooks after all," continued Peter; "but the light brought them all about my ears, and they made such a confounded clapping with their wings that I thought at first I had been beset with a legion of devils. But I have driven them all out, master, and you have nothing to fear now."

The latter part of the sentence, intimating a suspicion of his courage, La Motte could have dispensed with, and to retrieve in some degree his reputation, he made a point of proceeding through the passage. They now moved on with alacrity, for, as Peter said, they had nothing to fear.

The passage led into a large area, on one side of which, over a range of cloisters, appeared the west tower, and a lofty part of the edifice; the other side

was open to the woods. La Motte led the way to a door
of the tower, which he now perceived was the same he
had formerly entered; but he found some difficulty in
advancing, for the area was overgrown with brambles
and nettles, and the light which Peter carried afforded
only an uncertain gleam. When he unclosed the door,
the dismal aspect of the place revived the apprehensions
of Madame La Motte, and extorted from Adeline an
inquiry whither they were going. Peter held up the
light to shew the narrow staircase that wound round
the tower; but La Motte, observing the second door,
drew back the rusty bolts, and entered a spacious apartment which from its style and condition was evidently
of a much later date than the other part of the structure. Though desolate and forlorn, it was very little
impaired by time; the walls were damp, but not decayed; and the glass was yet firm in the windows.

They passed on to a suite of apartments resembling
the first they had seen, and expressed their surprise at
the incongruous appearance of this part of the edifice
with the mouldering walls they had left behind. These
apartments conducted them to a winding passage, that
received light and air through narrow cavities placed
high in the wall, and was at length closed by a door
barred with iron, which being with some difficulty
opened, they entered a vaulted room. La Motte surveyed it with a scrutinizing eye, and endeavoured to
conjecture for what purpose it had been guarded by a
door of such strength; but he saw little within to assist
his curiosity. The room appeared to have been built in
modern times upon a Gothic plan. Adeline approached
a large window that formed a kind of recess raised by
one step over the level of the floor. She observed to
La Motte that the whole floor was inlaid with Mosaic
work, which drew from him a remark that the style

of this apartment was not strictly Gothic. He passed on to a door which appeared on the opposite side of the apartment, and unlocking it, found himself in the great hall by which he had entered the fabric.

He now perceived, what the gloom had before concealed, a spiral staircase which led to a gallery above, and which from its present condition seemed to have been built with the more modern part of the fabric, though this also affected the Gothic mode of architecture. La Motte had little doubt that these stairs led to apartments corresponding with those he had passed below, and hesitated whether to explore them; but the entreaties of Madame, who was much fatigued, prevailed with him to defer all farther examination. After some deliberation in which of the rooms they should pass the night, they determined to return to that which opened from the tower.

A fire was kindled on a hearth which it is probable had not for many years before afforded the warmth of hospitality; and Peter having spread the provision he had brought from the coach, La Motte and his family encircling the fire, partook of a repast which hunger and fatigue made delicious. Apprehension gradually gave way to confidence, for they now found themselves in something like a human habitation, and they had leisure to laugh at their late terrors; but as the blast shook the doors, Adeline often started and threw a fearful glance around. They continued to laugh and talk cheerfully for a time; yet their merriment was transient, if not affected; for a sense of their peculiar and distressed circumstances pressed upon their recollection, and sunk each individual into languor and pensive silence. Adeline felt the forlornness of her condition with energy; she reflected upon the past with astonishment, and anticipated the future with fear. She found

herself wholly dependent upon strangers, with no other
claim than what distress demands from the common
sympathy of kindred beings. Sighs swelled her heart,
and the frequent tear started to her eye; but she
checked it ere it betrayed on her cheek the sorrow which
she thought it would be ungrateful to reveal.

La Motte at length broke this meditative silence by
directing the fire to be renewed for the night, and the
door to be secured. This seemed a necessary precaution even in this solitude, and was effected by means
of large stones piled against it, for other fastening there
was none. It had frequently occurred to La Motte
that this apparently forsaken edifice might be a place
of refuge to banditti. Here was solitude to conceal
them, and a wild and extensive forest to assist their
schemes of rapine, and to perplex with its labyrinths
those who might be bold enough to attempt pursuit.
These apprehensions, however, he hid within his own
bosom, saving his companions from a share of the
uneasiness they occasioned. Peter was ordered to watch
at the door, and having given the fire a rousing stir,
our desolate party drew round it and sought in sleep
a short oblivion of care.

The night passed on without disturbance. Adeline
slept, but uneasy dreams fleeted before her fancy, and
she awoke at an early hour. The recollection of her
sorrows arose upon her mind, and yielding to their
pressure, her tears flowed silently and fast. That she
might indulge them without restraint, she went to a
window that looked upon an open part of the forest.
All was gloom and silence. She stood for some time
viewing the shadowy scene.

The first tender tints of morning now appeared on
the verge of the horizon, stealing upon the darkness;—
so pure, so fine, so ætherial, it seemed as if heaven

was opening to the view. The dark mists were seen to roll off to the west as the tints of light grew stronger, deepening the obscurity of that part of the hemisphere, and involving the features of the country below. Meanwhile in the east the hues became more vivid, darting a trembling lustre far around, till a ruddy glow which fired all that part of the heavens announced the rising sun. At first, a small line of inconceivable splendour emerged on the horizon, which quickly expanding, the sun appeared in all his glory, unveiling the whole face of nature, vivifying every colour of the landscape, and sprinkling the dewy earth with glittering light. The low and gentle responses of birds, awakened by the morning ray, now broke the silence of the hour; their soft warbling rising by degrees till they swelled the chorus of universal gladness. Adeline's heart swelled too with gratitude and adoration.

The scene before her soothed her mind and exalted her thoughts to the great Author of Nature. She uttered an involuntary prayer: "Father of good, who made this glorious scene! I resign myself to thy hands; thou wilt support me under my present sorrows and protect me from future evil."

Thus confiding in the benevolence of God, she wiped the tears from her eyes, while the sweet union of conscience and reflection rewarded her trust; and her mind, losing the feelings which had lately oppressed it, became tranquil and composed.

La Motte awoke soon after, and Peter prepared to set out on his expedition. As he mounted his horse, "An' please you, master," said he, "I think we had as good look no farther for an habitation till better times turn up; for nobody will think of looking for us here; and when one sees the place by daylight, it's none so bad but what a little patching up would make it comfortable enough." La Motte made no reply, but he thought of Peter's words. During the intervals of the night, when anxiety had kept him waking, the same idea had occurred to him; concealment was his only security, and this place afforded it. The desolation of the spot was repulsive to his wishes, but he had only a choice of evils—a forest with liberty was not a bad home for one who had too much reason to expect a prison. As he walked through the apartments and examined their condition more attentively, he perceived they might easily be made habitable; and now surveying them under the cheerfulness of morning, his design strengthened, and he mused upon the means of accomplishing it, which nothing seemed so much to obstruct as the apparent difficulty of procuring food.

He communicated his thoughts to Madame La Motte, who felt repugnance to the scheme. La Motte, however, seldom consulted his wife till he had determined how to act, and he had already resolved to be guided in this affair by the report of Peter. If he could discover a town in the neighbourhood of the forest where provisions and other necessaries could be procured, he would seek no farther for a place of rest.

In the mean time he spent the anxious interval of Peter's absence in examining the ruin and walking over the environs. They were sweetly romantic, and the luxuriant woods with which they abounded seemed to sequester this spot from the rest of the world. Frequently a natural vista would yield a view of the country, terminated by hills which, retiring in distance, faded into the blue horizon. A stream, various and musical in its course, wound at the foot of the lawn on which stood the abbey. Here it silently glided beneath the shades, feeding the flowers that bloomed on its banks, and diffusing dewy freshness around; there it spread in broad expanse to day, reflecting the sylvan scene and the wild deer that tasted its waves. La Motte observed everywhere a profusion of game; the pheasants scarcely flew from his approach, and the deer gazed mildly at him as he passed. They were strangers to man!

On his return to the abbey, La Motte ascended the stairs that led to the tower. About half way up, a door appeared in the wall. It yielded without resistance to his hand; but a sudden noise within, accompanied by a cloud of dust, made him step back and close the door. After waiting a few minutes, he again opened it, and perceived a large room of the more modern building. The remains of tapestry hung in tatters upon the walls, which were become the residence of birds of prey, whose sudden flight on the opening of the door had brought down a quantity of dust and occasioned the noise. The windows were shattered, and almost without glass; but he was surprised to observe some remains of furniture: chairs whose fashion and condition bore the date of their antiquity, a broken table, and an iron gate almost consumed by rust.

On the opposite side of the room was a door which led to another apartment, proportioned like the first, but hung with arras somewhat less tattered. In one corner stood a small bedstead, and a few shattered chairs were placed round the walls. La Motte gazed with a mixture of wonder and curiosity. " 'Tis strange," said he, "that these rooms, and these alone, should bear the marks of inhabitation. Perhaps some wretched wanderer like myself may have here sought refuge from a persecuting world, and here, perhaps, laid down the load of existence. Perhaps, too, I have followed his footsteps but to mingle my dust with his! He turned suddenly and was about to quit the room, when he per-

ceived a small door near the bed. It opened into a
closet, which was lighted by one small window and was
in the same condition as the apartments he had passed,
except that it was destitute even of the remains of furniture. As he walked over the floor, he thought he felt
one part of it shake beneath his steps, and examining,
found a trap door. Curiosity prompted him to explore
farther, and with some difficulty he opened it. It disclosed a staircase which terminated in darkness. La
Motte descended a few steps, but was unwilling to
trust the abyss, and after wondering for what purpose
it was so secretly constructed, he closed the trap and
quitted this suite of apartments.

The stairs in the tower above were so much decayed
that he did not attempt to ascend them. He returned
to the hall, and by the spiral staircase which he had
observed the evening before, reached the gallery and
found another suite of apartments entirely unfurnished,
very much like those below.

He renewed with Madame La Motte his former conversation respecting the abbey, and she exerted all her
endeavours to dissuade him from his purpose, acknowledging the solitary security of the spot, but pleading
that other places might be found equally well adapted
for concealment and more for comfort. This La Motte
doubted; besides, the forest abounded with game, which
would at once afford him amusement and food, a circumstance, considering his small stock of money, by no
means to be overlooked; and he had suffered his mind
to dwell so much upon the scheme that it was become a
favourite one. Adeline listened in silent anxiety to the
discourse, and waited the issue of Peter's report.

The morning passed, but Peter did not return. Our
solitary party took their dinner of the provision they
had fortunately brought with them, and afterwards

walked forth into the woods. Adeline, who never suffered any good to pass unnoticed because it came attended with evil, forgot for a while the desolation of
the abbey in the beauty of the adjacent scenery. The
pleasantness of the shades soothed her heart and the
varied features of the landscape amused her fancy; she
almost thought she could be contented to live here. Already she began to feel an interest in the concerns of
her companions, and for Madame La Motte she felt
more: it was the warm emotion of gratitude and
affection.

The afternoon wore away, and they returned to the
abbey. Peter was still absent, and his absence now
began to excite surprise and apprehension. The approach of darkness also threw a gloom upon the hopes
of the wanderers. Another night must be passed under
the same forlorn circumstances as the preceding one,
and, what was still worse, with a very scanty stock of
provisions. The fortitude of Madame La Motte now
entirely forsook her, and she wept bitterly. Adeline's
heart was as mournful as Madame's, but she rallied
her drooping spirits and gave the first instance of her
kindness by endeavouring to revive those of her friend.

La Motte was restless and uneasy, and leaving the
abbey, he walked along the way which Peter had taken.
He had not gone far when he perceived him between
the trees, leading his horse.—"What news, Peter?" hallooed La Motte. Peter came on, panting for breath,
and said not a word, till La Motte repeated the question in a tone of somewhat more authority. "Ah, bless
you, master!" said he, when he had taken breath to
answer, "I am glad to see you; I thought I should never
have got back again; I've met with a world of misfortunes."

"Well, you may relate them hereafter; let me hear whether you have discovered ——"

"Discovered?" interrupted Peter, "yes, I am discovered with a vengeance! If your honour will look at my arms, you'll see how I am discovered."

"Discoloured! I suppose you mean," said La Motte. "But how came you in this condition?"

"Why, I'll tell you how it was, sir; your honour knows I learned a smack of boxing of that Englishman that used to come with his master to our house."

"Well, well—tell me where you have been."

"I scarcely know myself, master; I've been where I got a sound drubbing, but then it was in your business, and so I don't mind. But if ever I meet with that rascal again! ——"

"You seem to like your first drubbing so well that you want another, and unless you speak more to the purpose, you shall soon have one."

Peter was now frightened into method, and endeavoured to proceed: "When I left the old abbey," said he, "I followed the way you directed, and turning to the right of that grove of trees yonder, I looked this way and that to see if I could see a house, or a cottage, or even a man, but not a *soul* of them was to be seen, and so I jogged on near the value of a league, I warrant, and then I came to a track. 'Oh! oh!' says I, 'we have you now; this will do—paths can't be made without feet.' However, I was out in my reckoning, for the devil a bit of a *soul* could I see, and after following the track this way and that way, for the third of a league, I lost it and had to find out another."

"Is it impossible for you to speak to the point?" said La Motte; "omit these foolish particulars, and tell whether you have succeeded."

"Well, then, master, to be short, for that's the nearest

way after all, I wandered a long while at random, I
do not know where, all through a forest like this, and
I took special care to note how the trees stood, that I
might find my way back. At last I came to another
path, and was sure I should find something now, though
I had found nothing before, for I could not be mistaken twice. So peeping between the trees, I spied
a cottage, and I gave my horse a lash that sounded
through the forest, and I was at the door in a minute.
They told me there was a town about half a league
off, and bade me follow the track and it would bring
me there. So it did; and my horse, I believe, smelt the
corn in the manger by the rate he went at. I inquired
for a wheelwright, and was told there was but one
in the place, and he could not be found. I waited and
waited, for I knew it was in vain to think of returning
without doing my business. The man at last came
home from the country, and I told him how long I had
waited; 'for,' says I, 'I knew it was in vain to return
without my business.' "

"Do be less tedious," said La Motte, "if it is in thy
nature."

"It is in my nature," answered Peter, "and if it was
more in my nature your honour should have it all.
Would you think it, sir, the fellow had the impudence
to ask a louis d'or for mending the coach wheel! I
believe in my conscience he saw I was in a hurry and
could not do without him. 'A louis d'or!' says I, 'my
master shall give no such price; he sha'n't be imposed
upon by no such rascal as you.' Whereupon the fellow
looked glum, and gave me a douse o' the chops. With
this, I up with my fist and gave him another, and
should have beat him presently if another man had
not come in, and then I was obliged to give up."

"And so you are returned as wise as you went?"

"Why, master, I hope I have too much spirit to submit to a rascal, or let you submit to one either. Besides, I have bought some nails to try if I can't mend the wheel myself—I had always a hand at carpentry."

"Well, I commend your zeal in my cause, but on this occasion it was rather ill-timed. And what have you got in that basket?"

"Why, master, I bethought me that we could not get away from this place till the carriage was ready to draw us, 'and in the mean time,' says I, 'nobody can live without victuals, so I'll e'en lay out the little money I have and take a basket with me.'"

"That's the only wise thing you have done yet, and this, indeed, redeems your blunders."

"Why now, master, it does my heart good to hear you speak; I knew I was doing for the best all the while. But I've had a hard job to find my way back; and here's another piece of ill luck, for the horse has got a thorn in his foot."

La Motte made inquiries concerning the town, and found it was capable of supplying him with provision, and what little furniture was necessary to render the abbey habitable. This intelligence almost settled his plans, and he ordered Peter to return on the following morning and make inquiries concerning the abbey. If the answers were favourable to his wishes, he commissioned him to buy a cart and load it with some furniture and some materials necessary for repairing the modern apartments. Peter stared: "What, does your honour mean to live here?"

"Why, suppose I do?"

"Why, then your honour has made a wise determination, according to my hint; for your honour knows I said ——"

"Well, Peter, it is not necessary to repeat what you

said; perhaps I had determined on the subject before."

"Egad, master, you're in the right, and I'm glad of it, for I believe we shall not quickly be disturbed here, except by the rooks and owls. Yes, yes—I warrant I'll make it a place fit for a king; and as for the town, one may get anything, I'm sure of that; though they think no more about this place than they do about India or England, or any of those places."

They now reached the abbey, where Peter was received with great joy; but the hopes of his mistress and Adeline were repressed when they learned that he returned without having executed his commission, and heard his account of the town. La Motte's orders to Peter were heard with almost equal concern by Madame and Adeline; but the latter concealed her uneasiness and used all her efforts to overcome that of her friend. The sweetness of her behaviour and the air of satisfaction she assumed sensibly affected Madame, and discovered to her a source of comfort which she had hitherto overlooked. The affectionate attentions of her young friend promised to console her for the want of other society, and her conversation to enliven the hours which might otherwise be passed in painful regret.

The observations and general behaviour of Adeline already bespoke a good understanding and an amiable heart, but she had yet more—she had genius. She was now in her nineteenth year; her figure of the middling size, and turned to the most exquisite proportion; her hair was dark auburn, her eyes blue, and whether they sparkled with intelligence, or melted with tenderness, they were equally attractive. Her form had the airy lightness of a nymph, and when she smiled, her countenance might have been drawn for the younger sister of Hebe. The captivations of her beauty were heightened by the grace and simplicity of her manners, and confirmed by the intrinsic value of a heart

> That might be shrin'd in crystal,
> And have all its movements scann'd.

Annette now kindled the fire for the night; Peter's basket was opened, and supper prepared. Madame La Motte was still pensive and silent. "There is scarcely any condition so bad," said Adeline, "but we may one time or other wish we had not quitted it. Honest Peter, when he was bewildered in the forest, or had two enemies to encounter instead of one, confesses he wished himself at the abbey. And I am certain there is no situation so destitute but comfort may be extracted from it. The blaze of this fire shines yet more cheerfully from the contrasted dreariness of the place; and this plentiful repast is made yet more delicious from the temporary want we have suffered. Let us enjoy the good and forget the evil."

"You speak, my dear," replied Madame La Motte, "like one whose spirits have not been often depressed by misfortune (Adeline sighed) and whose hopes are therefore vigorous."

"Long suffering," said La Motte, "has subdued in our minds that elastic energy which repels the pressure of evil and dances to the bound of joy. But I speak in rhapsody, though only from the remembrance of such a time. I once, like you, Adeline, could extract comfort from most situations."

"And may now, my dear sir," said Adeline. "Still believe it possible, and you will find it is so."

"The illusion is gone—I can no longer deceive myself."

"Pardon me, sir, if I say it is now only you deceive yourself, by suffering the cloud of sorrow to tinge every object you look upon."

"It may be so," said La Motte, "but let us leave the subject."

After supper the doors were secured, as before, for the night, and the wanderers resigned themselves to repose.

On the following morning Peter again set out for the little town of Auboine, and the hours of his absence were again spent by Madame La Motte and Adeline in much anxiety and some hope, for the intelligence he might bring concerning the abbey might yet release them from the plans of La Motte. Towards the close of day he was descried coming slowly on and the cart which accompanied him too certainly confirmed their fears. He brought materials for repairing the place and some furniture.

Of the abbey he gave an account of which the following is the substance:—It belonged, together with a large part of the adjacent forest, to a nobleman who now resided with his family on a remote estate. He inherited it, in right of his wife, from his father-in-law, who had caused the more modern apartments to be erected, and had resided in them some part of every year for the purpose of shooting and hunting. It was reported that some person was soon after it came to the present possessor brought secretly to the abbey and confined in these apartments. Who or what he was had never been conjectured, and what became of him nobody knew. The report died gradually away, and many persons entirely disbelieved the whole of it. But however this affair might be, certain it was, the present owner had visited the abbey only two summers since his succeeding to it, and the furniture after some time was removed.

This circumstance had at first excited surprise, and various reports arose in consequence, but it was difficult to know what ought to be believed. Among the rest, it was said, that strange appearances had been observed at the abbey, and uncommon noises heard; and though this report had been ridiculed by sensible persons as the idle superstition of ignorance, it had fastened so strongly upon the minds of the common people that for the last seventeen years none of the peasantry had ventured to approach the spot. The abbey was now, therefore, abandoned to decay.

La Motte ruminated upon this account. At first it called up unpleasant ideas, but they were soon dismissed, and considerations more interesting to his welfare took place. He congratulated himself that he had now found a spot where he was not likely to be either discovered or disturbed; yet it could not escape him that there was a strange coincidence between one part of Peter's narrative and the condition of the chambers that opened from the tower above stairs. The remains of furniture, of which the other apartments were void, the solitary bed, the number and connection of the rooms, were circumstances that united to confirm his opinion. This, however, he concealed in his own breast, for he already perceived that Peter's account had not assisted in reconciling his family to the necessity of dwelling at the abbey.

But they had only to submit in silence, and whatever disagreeable apprehension might intrude upon them, they now appeared willing to suppress the expression of it. Peter, indeed, was exempt from any evil of this kind; he knew no fear, and his mind was now wholly occupied with his approaching business. Madame La Motte, with a placid kind of despair, endeavoured to reconcile herself to that which no effort of understanding could teach her to avoid, and which an indulgence in lamentation could only make more intolerable. Indeed, though a sense of the immediate inconveniences to be endured at the abbey had made her oppose the scheme of living there, she did not really know how their situation could be improved by removal. Yet her thoughts often wandered towards Paris, and reflected the retrospect of past times with the images of weeping friends, left, perhaps, forever. The affectionate endearments of her only son, whom from the danger of his situation and the obscurity of hers, she might reasonably fear never to see again, arose upon her memory and overcame her fortitude. "Why —why was I reserved for this hour?" would she say, "and what will be my years to come?"

Adeline had no retrospect of past delight to give emphasis to present calamity—no weeping friends—no dear regretted objects to point the edge of sorrow and throw a sickly hue upon her future prospects. She knew not yet the pangs of disappointed hope or the acuter sting of self-accusation; she had no misery but what patience could assuage or fortitude overcome.

At the dawn of the following day Peter arose to his labour. He proceeded with alacrity, and in a few days two of the lower apartments were so much altered for the better that La Motte began to exult, and his family to perceive that their situation would not be so miserable as they had imagined. The furniture Peter had already brought was disposed in these rooms, one of which was the vaulted apartment. Madame La Motte furnished this as a sitting room, preferring it for its large Gothic window, that descended almost to the floor, admitting a prospect of the lawn and the picturesque scenery of the surrounding woods.

Peter having returned to Auboine for a farther supply, all the lower apartments were in a few weeks not only habitable but comfortable. These, however, being insufficient for the accommodation of the family, a room above stairs was prepared for Adeline. It was the chamber that opened immediately from the tower, and she preferred it to those beyond because it was less distant from the family, and the windows fronting an avenue of the forest afforded a more extensive prospect. The tapestry, that was decayed and hung loosely from the walls, was now nailed up and made to look less desolate; and though the room had still a solemn aspect, from its spaciousness and the narrowness of the windows, it was not uncomfortable.

The first night that Adeline retired hither, she slept little. The solitary air of the place affected her spirits; the more so, perhaps, because she had with friendly consideration endeavoured to support them in the presence of Madame La Motte. She remembered the narrative of Peter, several circumstances of which had impressed her imagination in spite of her reason, and she found it difficult wholly to subdue apprehension. At one time, terror so strongly seized her mind that she had even opened the door with an intention of calling Madame La Motte; but, listening for a moment on the stairs of the tower, everything seemed still. At length, she heard the voice of La Motte speaking cheerfully, and the absurdity of her fears struck her forcibly; she blushed that she had for a moment submitted to them, and returned to her chamber wondering at herself.

CHAPTER III

LA MOTTE arranged his little plan of living. His mornings were usually spent in shooting or fishing, and the dinner thus provided by his industry he relished with a keener appetite than had ever attended him at the luxurious tables of Paris. The afternoons he passed with his family. Sometimes he would select a book from the few he had brought with him, and endeavour to fix his attention to the words his lips repeated. But his mind suffered little abstraction from its own cares, and the sentiment he pronounced left no trace behind it. Sometimes he conversed, but oftener sat in gloomy silence, musing upon the past or anticipating the future.

At these moments Adeline, with a sweetness almost irresistible, endeavoured to enliven his spirits and to withdraw him from himself. Seldom she succeeded, but when she did, the grateful looks of Madame La Motte and the benevolent feelings of her own bosom realized the cheerfulness she had at first only assumed. Adeline's mind had the happy art, or perhaps it were more just to say, the happy nature, of accommodating itself to her situation. Her present condition, though forlorn, was not devoid of comfort, and this comfort was confirmed by her virtues. So much she won upon the affections of her protectors that Madame La Motte loved her as her child, and La Motte himself, though a man little susceptible of tenderness, could not be insensible to her solicitudes. Whenever he relaxed from the sullenness of misery, it was at the influence of Adeline.

Peter regularly brought a weekly supply of provisions from Auboine, and on those occasions always quitted the town by a route contrary to that leading to the abbey. Several weeks having passed without molestation, La Motte dismissed all apprehension of pursuit, and at length became tolerably reconciled to the complexion of his circumstances. As habit and effort strengthened the fortitude of Madame La Motte, the features of misfortune appeared to soften. The forest, which at first seemed to her a frightful solitude, had lost its terrific aspect, and that edifice whose half-demolished walls and gloomy desolation had struck her mind with the force of melancholy and dismay, was now beheld as a domestic asylum and a safe refuge from the storms of power.

She was a sensible and highly accomplished woman, and it became her chief delight to form the rising graces of Adeline, who had, as has been already shown, a sweetness of disposition which made her quick to repay instruction with improvement and indulgence with love. Never was Adeline so pleased as when she anticipated her wishes, and never so diligent as when she was employed in her business. The little affairs of the household she overlooked and managed with such admirable exactness that Madame La Motte had neither anxiety nor care concerning them. And Adeline formed for herself in this barren situation many amusements that occasionally banished the remembrance of her misfortunes. La Motte's books were her chief consolation. With one of these she would frequently ramble into the forest, where the river, winding through a glade, diffused coolness, and with its murmuring accents invited repose. There she would seat herself, and resigned to the illusions of the page, pass many hours in oblivion of sorrow.

Here too, when her mind was tranquillized by the surrounding scenery, she wooed the gentle muse, and indulged in ideal happiness. The delight of these moments she commemorated in the following address:

To the Visions of Fancy.

Dear, wild illusions of creative mind!
  Whose varying hues arise to Fancy's art,
And by her magic force are swift combin'd
  In forms that please, and scenes that touch the heart:
Oh! whether at her voice ye soft assume
  The pensive grace of sorrow drooping low:
Or rise sublime on terror's lofty plume,
  And shake the soul with wildly thrilling woe;
Or, sweetly bright, your gayer tints ye spread,
  Bid scenes of pleasure steal upon my view,
Love wave his purple pinions o'er my head,
  And wake the tender thought to passion true
O! still—ye shadowy forms! attend my lonely hours,
Still chase my real cares with your illusive powers!

Madame La Motte had frequently expressed curiosity concerning the events of Adeline's life, and by what circumstances she had been thrown into a situation so perilous and mysterious as that in which La Motte had found her. Adeline had given a brief account of the manner in which she had been brought thither, but had always with tears entreated to be spared for that time from a particular relation of her history. Her spirits were not then equal to retrospection, but now that they were soothed by quiet and strengthened by confidence, she one day gave Madame La Motte the following narration.

"I am the only child," said Adeline, "of Louis de St. Pierre, a chevalier of reputable family, but of small fortune, who for many years resided at Paris. Of my mother I have a faint remembrance: I lost her when I was only seven years old, and this was my first misfortune. At her death my father gave up housekeeping, boarded me in a convent, and quitted Paris. Thus was I at this early period of my life abandoned to strangers. My father came sometimes to Paris; he then visited me, and I well remember the grief I used to feel when he bade me farewell. On these occasions, which wrung my heart with grief, he appeared unmoved, so that I often thought he had little tenderness for me. But he was my father, and the only person to whom I could look up for protection and love.

"In this convent I continued till I was twelve years old. A thousand times I had entreated my father to take me home, but at first motives of prudence, and afterwards of avarice, prevented him. I was now removed from this convent, and placed in another, where I learned my father intended I should take the veil. I will not attempt to express my surprise and grief on this occasion. Too long I had been immured in the walls of a cloister, and too much had I seen of the sullen misery of its votaries, not to feel horror and disgust at the prospect of being added to their number.

"The Lady Abbess was a woman of rigid decorum and severe devotion, exact in the observance of every detail of form, and never forgave an offence against ceremony. It was her method, when she wanted to make converts to her order, to denounce and terrify rather than to persuade and allure. Hers were the arts of cunning practised upon fear, not those of sophistication upon reason. She employed numberless stratagems to gain me to her purpose, and they all wore the complexion of her character. But in the life to which she would have devoted me I saw too many forms of real terror to be overcome by the influence of her ideal host, and was resolute in rejecting the veil. Here I passed several years of miserable resistance against cruelty and superstition. My father I seldom saw. When I did, I entreated him to alter my destination, but he objected that his fortune was insufficient to support me in the world, and at length denounced vengeance on my head if I persisted in disobedience.

"You, my dear madam, can form little idea of the wretchedness of my situation, condemned to perpetual imprisonment, and imprisonment of the most dreadful kind, or to the vengeance of a father, from whom I had no appeal. My resolution relaxed—for some time I paused upon the choice of evils—but at length the horrors of the monastic life rose so fully to my view that fortitude gave way before them. Excluded from the cheerful intercourse of society—from the pleasant view of nature—almost from the light of day—condemned to silence—rigid formality—abstinence and penance—condemned to forego the delights of a world which imagination painted in the gayest and most alluring colours, and whose hues were, perhaps, not the less captivating because they were only ideal:—such was the state to which I was destined. Again my resolution was invigorated; my father's cruelty subdued tenderness, and roused indignation. 'Since he can forget,' said I, 'the affection of a parent, and condemn his child without remorse to wretchedness and despair, the bond of filial and parental duty no longer subsists between us—he has himself dissolved it, and I will yet struggle for liberty and life.'

"Finding me unmoved by menace, the Lady Abbess had now recourse to more subtle measures. She condescended to smile, and even to flatter; but hers was the distorted smile of cunning, not the gracious emblem of kindness; it provoked disgust, instead of inspiring affection. She painted the character of a vestal in the most beautiful tints of art—its holy innocence—its mild dignity—its sublime devotion. I sighed as she spoke. This she regarded as a favourable symptom, and proceeded on her picture with more animation. She described the serenity of a monastic life—its security from the seductive charms, restless passions, and sorrowful vicissitudes of the world—the rapturous delights of religion, and the sweet reciprocal affection of the sisterhood.

"So highly she finished the piece that the lurking lines of cunning would to an inexperienced eye have escaped detection. Mine was too sorrowfully informed. Too often had I witnessed the secret tear and bursting sigh of vain regret, the sullen pinings of discontent, and the mute anguish of despair. My silence and my manner assured her of my incredulity, and it was with difficulty that she preserved a decent composure.

"My father, as may be imagined, was highly incensed at my perseverance, which he called obstinacy, but, what will not be so easily believed, he soon after relented, and appointed a day to take me from the convent. O! judge of my feelings when I received this intelligence. The joy it occasioned awakened all my gratitude; I forgot the former cruelty of my father, and that the present indulgence was less the effect of his kindness than of my resolution. I wept that I could not indulge his every wish.

"What days of blissful expectation were those that preceded my departure! The world from which I had been hitherto secluded—the world in which my fancy had been so often delighted to roam—whose paths were strewn with fadeless roses—whose every scene smiled in beauty and invited to delight—where all the people were good, and all the good happy—Ah! *then* that world was bursting upon my view. Let me catch the rapturous remembrance before it vanish! It is like the passing lights of autumn, that gleam for a moment on a hill and then leave it to darkness. I counted the days and hours that withheld me from this fairy land. It was in the convent only that people were deceitful and cruel; it was there only that misery dwelt. I was quitting it all! How I pitied the poor nuns that were to be left behind. I would have given half that world I prized so much, had it been mine, to have taken them out with me.

"The long wished for day at last arrived. My father came, and for a moment my joy was lost in the sorrow of bidding farewell to my poor companions, for whom I had never felt such warmth of kindness as at this instant. I was soon beyond the gates of the convent. I looked around me, and viewed the vast vault of heaven no longer bounded by monastic walls, and the green earth extended in hill and dale to the round verge of the horizon! My heart danced with delight, tears swelled in my eyes, and for some moments I was unable to speak. My thoughts rose to heaven in sentiments of gratitude to the Giver of all good!

"At length I returned to my father. 'Dear sir,' said I, 'how I thank you for my deliverance, and how I wish I could do every thing to oblige you.'

" 'Return, then, to your convent,' said he, in a harsh accent. I shuddered; his look and manner jarred the tone of my feelings; they struck discord upon my heart, which had before responded only to harmony. The ardour of joy was in a moment repressed, and every object around me was saddened with the gloom of disappointment. It was not that I suspected my father

would take me back to the convent, but that his feelings
seemed so very dissonant to the joy and gratitude which
I had but a moment before felt and expressed to him.
—Pardon, madam, a relation of these trivial circumstances; the strong vicissitudes of feeling which they
impressed upon my heart make me think them important, when they are perhaps only disgusting."

"No, my dear," said Madame La Motte, "they are
interesting to me; they illustrate little traits of character which I love to observe. You are worthy of all
my regards, and from this moment I give my tenderest
pity to your misfortunes, and my affection to your
goodness."

These words melted the heart of Adeline; she kissed
the hand which Madame held out, and remained a few
minutes silent. At length she said, "May I deserve
this goodness! and may I ever be thankful to God, who,
in giving me such a friend, has raised me to comfort
and hope!

"My father's house was situated a few leagues on
the other side of Paris, and in our way to it we passed
through that city. What a novel scene! Where were
now the solemn faces, the demure manners I had been
accustomed to see in the convent? Every countenance
was here animated, either by business or pleasure;
every step was airy, and every smile was gay. All the
people appeared like friends; they looked and smiled
at me; I smiled again, and wished to have told them
how pleased I was. 'How delightful,' said I, 'to live
surrounded by friends!'

"What crowded streets! What magnificent hotels!
What splendid equipages! I scarcely observed that the
streets were narrow or the way dangerous. What
bustle, what tumult, what delight! I could never be
sufficiently thankful that I was removed from the con-

vent. Again I was going to express my gratitude to my father, but his looks forbade me, and I was silent. I am too diffuse; even the faint forms which memory reflects of passed delight are grateful to the heart. The shadow of pleasure is still gazed upon with a melancholy enjoyment, though the substance is fled beyond our reach.

"Having quitted Paris, which I left with many sighs, and gazed upon till the towers of every church dissolved in distance from my view, we entered upon a gloomy and unfrequented road. It was evening when we reached a wild heath. I looked round in search of a human dwelling, but could find none; and not a human being was to be seen. I experienced something of what I used to feel in the convent; my heart had not been so sad since I left it. Of my father, who still sat in silence, I inquired if we were near home. He answered in the affirmative. Night came on, however, before we reached the place of our destination; it was a lone house on the waste. But I need not describe it to you, madam. When the carriage stopped, two men appeared at the door and assisted us to alight; so gloomy were their countenances, and so few their words, I almost fancied myself again in the convent. Certain it is, I had not seen such melancholy faces since I quitted it. 'Is this a part of the world I have so fondly contemplated?' said I.

"The interior appearance of the house was desolate and mean; I was surprised that my father had chosen such a place for his habitation, and also that no woman was to be seen; but I knew that inquiry would only produce a reproof, and was therefore silent. At supper the two men I had before seen sat down with us; they said little, but seemed to observe me much. I was confused and displeased, which my father noticing, he frowned at them with a look which convinced me he meant more than I comprehended. When the cloth was drawn, my father took my hand and conducted me to the door of my chamber; having set down the candle and wished me good night, he left me to my own solitary thoughts.

"How different were they from those I had indulged a few hours before! Then expectation, hope, delight, danced before me; now melancholy and disappointment chilled the ardour of my mind and discoloured my future prospect. The appearance of everything around conduced to depress me. On the floor lay a small bed without curtains or hangings; two old chairs and a table were all the remaining furniture in the room. I went to the window with an intention of looking out upon the surrounding scene, and found it was grated. I was shocked at this circumstance, and, comparing it with the lonely situation and the strange appearance of the house, together with the countenances and behaviour of the men who had supped with us, I was lost in a labyrinth of conjecture.

"At length I lay down to sleep; but the anxiety of my mind prevented repose; gloomy unpleasing images flitted before my fancy, and I fell into a sort of waking dream. I thought that I was in a lonely forest with my father; his looks were severe, and his gestures menacing. He upbraided me for leaving the convent, and while he spoke, drew from his pocket a mirror which he held before my face; I looked in it and saw, (my blood now thrills as I repeat it) I saw myself wounded, and bleeding profusely. Then I thought myself in the house again; and suddenly heard these words in accents so distinct that for some time after I awoke, I could scarcely believe them ideal, 'Depart this house, destruction hovers here.'

"I was awakened by a footstep on the stairs; it was my father retiring to his chamber. The lateness of the hour surprised me, for it was past midnight.

"On the following morning the party of the preceding evening assembled at breakfast, and were as gloomy and silent as before. The table was spread by a boy of my father's, but the cook and the house-maid, whatever they might be, were invisible.

"The next morning I was surprised, on attempting to leave my chamber, to find the door locked. I waited a considerable time before I ventured to call. When I did, no answer was returned. I then went to the window and called more loudly, but my own voice was still the only sound I heard. Near an hour I passed in a state of surprise and terror not to be described. At length I heard a person coming up stairs, and I renewed the call. I was answered that my father had that morning set off for Paris, whence he would return in a few days; in the meanwhile he had ordered me to be confined in my chamber. On my expressing surprise and apprehension at this circumstance, I was assured I had nothing to fear, and that I should live as well as if I was at liberty.

"The latter part of this speech seemed to contain an odd kind of comfort; I made little reply, but submitted to necessity. Once more I was abandoned to sorrowful reflection. What a day was the one I now passed! alone and agitated with grief and apprehension. I endeavoured to conjecture the cause of this harsh treatment, and at length concluded it was designed by my father, as a punishment for my former disobedience. But why abandon me to the power of strangers, to men whose countenances bore the stamp of villainy so strongly as to impress even my inexperienced mind with terror! Surmise involved me only deeper in perplexity, yet I found it impossible to forbear pursuing the subject; and the day was divided between lamentation and conjecture. Night at length came, and such a night! Darkness brought new terrors: I looked round the chamber for some means of fastening my door on the inside, but could perceive none. At last I contrived to place the back of a chair in an oblique direction, so as to render it secure.

"I had scarcely done this, and lain down upon my bed in my clothes, not to sleep, but to watch, when I heard a rap at the door of the house, which was opened and shut so quickly that the person who had knocked seemed only to deliver a letter or message. Soon after I heard voices at intervals in a room below stairs, sometimes speaking very low, and sometimes rising all together as if in dispute. Something more excusable than curiosity made me endeavour to distinguish what was said, but in vain. Now and then a word or two reached me, and once I heard my name repeated, but no more.

"Thus passed the hours till midnight, when all became still. I had lain for some time in a state between fear and hope, when I heard the lock of my door gently moved backward and forward. I started up and listened; for a moment it was still, then the noise returned, and I heard a whispering without. My spirits died away, but I was yet sensible. Presently an effort was made at the door, as if to force it; I shrieked aloud, and immediately heard the voices of the men I had seen at my father's table. They called loudly for the door to be opened, and on my returning no answer, uttered dreadful execrations. I had just strength sufficient to move to the window, in the desperate hope of escaping thence, but my feeble efforts could not even shake the bars. O! how can I recollect these moments of horror, and be sufficiently thankful that I am now in safety and comfort!

"They remained some time at the door. Then they quitted it and went down stairs. How my heart revived at every step of their departure; I fell upon my knees, thanked God that he had preserved me this time, and implored his farther protection. I was rising from this short prayer when suddenly I heard a noise in a different part of the room, and on looking round I perceived the door of a small closet open, and two men enter the chamber.

"They seized me, and I sunk senseless in their arms. How long I remained in this condition I know not, but on reviving, I perceived myself again alone, and heard several voices from below stairs. I had presence of mind to run to the door of the closet, my only chance of escape; but it was locked! I then recollected it was possible that the ruffians might have forgot to turn the key of the chamber door, which was held by the chair; but here also I was disappointed. I clasped my hands in an agony of despair, and stood for some time immovable.

"A violent noise from below roused me, and soon after I heard people ascending the stairs: I now gave myself up for lost. The steps approached, the door of the closet was again unlocked. I stood calmly and again saw the men enter the chamber. I neither spoke, nor resisted: the faculties of my soul were wrought up beyond the power of feeling, as a violent blow on the body stuns for a while the sense of pain. They led me down stairs; the door of a room below was thrown open, and I beheld a stranger. It was then that my senses returned; I shrieked and resisted, but was forced along. It is unnecessary to say that this stranger was

Monsieur La Motte, or to add that I shall for ever bless him as my deliverer."

Adeline ceased to speak; Madame La Motte remained silent. There were some circumstances in Adeline's narrative which raised all her curiosity. She asked if Adeline believed her father to be a party in this mysterious affair. Adeline, though it was impossible to doubt that he had been principally and materially concerned in some part of it, thought, or said she thought, he was innocent of any intention against her life. "Yet what motive," said Madame La Motte, "could there be for a degree of cruelty so apparently unprofitable?" Here the inquiry ended, and Adeline confessed she had pursued it till her mind shrunk from all farther research.

The sympathy which such uncommon misfortune excited, Madame La Motte now expressed without reserve, and this expression of it strengthened the tie of mutual friendship. Adeline felt her spirits relieved by the disclosure she had made to Madame La Motte; and the latter acknowledged the value of the confidence by an increase of affectionate attentions.

CHAPTER IV

La Motte had now passed above a month in this seclusion and his wife had the pleasure to see him recover tranquillity and even cheerfulness. In this pleasure Adeline warmly participated; and she might justly have congratulated herself as one cause of his restoration. Her cheerfulness and delicate attention had effected what Madame La Motte's greater anxiety had failed to accomplish. La Motte did not seem regardless of her amiable disposition, and sometimes thanked her in a manner more earnest than was usual with him. She in her turn considered him as her only protector, and now felt towards him the affection of a daughter.

The time she had spent in this peaceful retirement had softened the remembrance of past events, and restored her mind to its natural tone; and when memory brought back to her view her former short and romantic expectations of happiness, though she gave a sigh to the rapturous illusion, she less lamented the disappointment than rejoiced in her present security and comfort.

But the satisfaction which La Motte's cheerfulness diffused around him was of short continuance. He became suddenly gloomy and reserved; the society of his family was no longer grateful to him; and he would spend whole hours in the most secluded parts of the forest, devoted to melancholy and secret grief. He did not, as formerly, indulge the humour of his sadness without restraint in the presence of others; he now evidently endeavoured to conceal it, and affected a cheerfulness that was too artificial to escape detection.

His servant Peter, either impelled by curiosity or kindness, sometimes followed him unseen into the forest. He observed him frequently retire to one particular spot in a remote part, which having gained, he always disappeared before Peter, who was obliged to follow at a distance, could exactly notice where. All his endeavours, now prompted by wonder and invigorated by disappointment, were unsuccessful, and he was at length compelled to endure the tortures of unsatisfied curiosity.

This change in the manners and habits of her husband was too conspicuous to pass unobserved by Madame La Motte, who endeavoured by all the stratagems which affection could suggest or female invention supply, to win him to her confidence. He seemed insensible to the influence of the first, and withstood the wiles of the latter. Finding all her efforts insufficient to dissipate the glooms which overhung his mind or to penetrate their secret cause, she desisted from farther attempt and endeavoured to submit to this mysterious distress.

Week after week elapsed, and the same unknown cause sealed the lips and corroded the heart of La Motte. The place of his visitation in the forest had not been traced. Peter had frequently examined round the spot where his master disappeared, but had never discovered any recess which could be supposed to conceal him. The astonishment of the servant was at length raised to an insupportable degree, and he communicated to his mistress the subject of it.

The emotion which this information excited she disguised from Peter, and reproved him for the means he had taken to gratify his curiosity. But she revolved this circumstance in her thoughts, and comparing it with the late alteration in his temper, her uneasiness was renewed and her perplexity considerably increased. After much consideration, being unable to assign any other motive for his conduct, she began to attribute it to the influence of illicit passion; and her heart, which now outran her judgment, confirmed the supposition and roused all the torturing pangs of jealousy.

Comparatively speaking, she had never known affliction till now. She had abandoned her dearest friends and connections—had relinquished the gaieties, the luxuries, and almost the necessaries of life; fled with her family into exile, an exile the most dreary and comfortless, experiencing the evils of reality, and those of apprehension, united. All these she had patiently endured, supported by the affection of him for whose sake

she suffered. Though that affection, indeed, had for
some time appeared to be abated, she had borne its
decrease with fortitude;, but the last stroke of calamity,
hitherto withheld, now came with irresistible force—
the love, of which she lamented the loss, she now believed was transferred to another.

The operation of strong passion confuses the powers
of reason and warps them to its own particular direction. Her usual degree of judgment, unopposed by
the influence of her heart, would probably have pointed
out to Madame La Motte some circumstances upon the
subject of her distress, equivocal, if not contradictory
to her suspicions. No such circumstances appeared to
her, and she did not long hesitate to decide that Adeline
was the object of her husband's attachment. Her
beauty out of the question, who else, indeed, could it be
in a spot thus secluded from the world?

The same cause destroyed almost at the same moment
her only remaining comfort; and, when she wept that
she could no longer look for happiness in the affection
of La Motte, she wept also that she could no longer seek
solace in the friendship of Adeline. She had too great
an esteem for her to doubt at first the integrity of her
conduct, but in spite of reason, her heart no longer
expanded to her with its usual warmth of kindness. She
shrunk from her confidence; and as the secret broodings
of jealousy cherished her suspicions, she became less
kind to her, even in manner.

Adeline, observing the change, at first attributed it
to accident, and afterwards to a temporary displeasure
arising from some little inadvertency in her conduct.
She therefore increased her assiduities; but perceiving,
contrary to all expectation, that her efforts to please
failed of their usual consequence, and that the reserve
of Madame's manner rather increased than abated, she

became seriously uneasy, and resolved to seek an explanation. This Madame La Motte as sedulously avoided, and was for some time able to prevent. Adeline, however, too much interested in the event to yield to delicate scruples, pressed the subject so closely that Madame, at first agitated and confused, at length invented some idle excuse, and laughed off the affair.

She now saw the necessity of subduing all appearance of reserve towards Adeline; and though her art could not conquer the prejudices of passion, it taught her to assume with tolerable success the aspect of kindness. Adeline was deceived, and was again at peace. Indeed, confidence in the sincerity and goodness of others was her weakness. But the pangs of stifled jealousy struck deeper to the heart of Madame La Motte, and she resolved at all events to obtain some certainty upon the subject of her suspicions.

She now condescended to a meanness which she had before despised, and ordered Peter to watch the steps of his master, in order to discover, if possible, the place of his visitation! So much did passion win upon her judgment, by time and indulgence, that she sometimes ventured even to doubt the integrity of Adeline, and afterwards proceeded to believe it possible that the object of La Motte's rambles might be an assignation with her. What suggested this conjecture was that Adeline frequently took long walks alone in the forest, and sometimes was absent from the abbey for many hours. This circumstance, which Madame La Motte had at first attributed to Adeline's fondness for the picturesque beauties of nature, now operated forcibly upon her imagination, and she could view it in no other light than as affording an opportunity for secret conversation with her husband.

Peter obeyed the orders of his mistress with alacrity,

for they were warmly seconded by his own curiosity. All his endeavours were, however, fruitless; he never dared to follow La Motte near enough to observe the place of his last retreat. Her impatience thus heightened by delay, and her passion stimulated by difficulty, Madame La Motte now resolved to apply to her husband for an explanation of his conduct.

After some consideration, concerning the manner most likely to succeed with him, she went to La Motte, but when she entered the room where he sat, forgetting all her concerted address, she fell at his feet, and was for some moments lost in tears. Surprised at her attitude and distress, he inquired the occasion of it, and was answered that it was caused by his own conduct. "My conduct! What part of it, pray?" inquired he.

"Your reserve, your secret sorrow, and frequent absence from the abbey."

"Is it then so wonderful that a man who has lost almost everything, should sometimes lament his misfortunes, or so criminal to attempt concealing his grief that he must be blamed for it by those whom he would save from the pain of sharing it?"

Having uttered these words, he quitted the room, leaving Madame La Motte lost in surprise, but somewhat relieved from the pressure of her former suspicions. Still, however, she pursued Adeline with an eye of scrutiny; and the mask of kindness would sometimes fall off and discover the features of distrust. Adeline, without exactly knowing why, felt less at ease and less happy in her presence than formerly. Her spirits drooped, and she would often, when alone, weep at the forlornness of her condition. Formerly her remembrance of past sufferings was lost in the friendship of Madame La Motte; now, though her behaviour was too guarded to betray any striking instances of unkindness,

there was something in her manner which chilled the
hopes of Adeline, unable as she was to analyze it. But
a circumstance which soon occurred, suspended for a
while the jealousy of Madame La Motte, and roused
her husband from his state of gloomy stupefaction.

Peter, having been one day to Auboine, for the weekly
supply of provisions, returned with intelligence that
awakened in La Motte new apprehension and anxiety.

"Oh, sir! I've heard something that has astonished
me, as well it may," cried Peter, "and so it will you
when you come to know it. As I was standing in the
blacksmith's shop, while the smith was driving a nail
into the horse's shoe (by the bye, the horse lost it in an
odd way, I'll tell you, sir, how it was.)—"

"Nay, prithee leave it till another time, and go on
with your story."

"Why then, sir, as I was standing in the blacksmith's shop, comes in a man with a pipe in his mouth,
and a large pouch of tobacco in his hand—"

"Well—what has the pipe to do with the story?"

"Nay, sir, you put me out; I can't go on unless you
let me tell it my own way. As I was saying—with a
pipe in his mouth—I think I was there, your honour!"

"Yes, yes."

"He sets himself down on the bench, and, taking the
pipe from his mouth, says to the blacksmith—'Neighbour, do you know anybody of the name of La Motte
hereabouts?'—Bless your honour, I turned all of a cold
sweat in a minute!—Is not your honour well, shall I
fetch you any thing?"

"No—but be short in your narrative."

"'La Motte! La Motte!' said the blacksmith, 'I
think I've heard the name.'—'Have you?' said I, 'you're
cunning then, for there's no such person hereabouts, to
my knowledge.'"

"Fool!—why did you say that?"

"Because I did not want them to know your honour
was here; and if I had not managed very cleverly,
they would have found me out. 'There is no such person, hereabouts, to my knowledge,' says I,—'Indeed!'
says the blacksmith, 'you know more of the neighbourhood than I do then.'—'Aye,' says the man with the
pipe, 'that's very true. How came you to know so
much of the neighbourhood? I came here twenty-six
years ago, come next St. Michael, and you know more
than I do. How came you to know so much?'"

"With that he put his pipe in his mouth, and gave
a whiff full in my face. Lord! your honour, I trembled
from head to foot. 'Nay, as for that matter,' says I,
'I don't know more than other people, but I'm sure I
never heard of such a man as that.'—'Pray,' says the
blacksmith, staring me full in the face, 'an't you the
man that was inquiring some time since about St. Clair's
Abbey?'—'Well, what of that?' says I, 'what does that
prove?'—'Why, they say somebody lives in the abbey
now,' said the man, turning to the other; 'and, for
aught I know, it may be this same La Motte.'—'Aye,
or for aught I know either,' says the man with the pipe,
getting up from the bench, 'and you know more of this
than you'll own. I'll lay my life on't, this Monsieur
La Motte lives at the abbey.'—'Aye,' says I, 'you are
out there, for he does not live at the abbey now.'"

"Confound your folly!" cried La Motte, "but be
quick—how did the matter end?"

"'My master does not live there now,' said I.—'Oh!
oh!' said the man with the pipe; 'he is your master,
then? And pray how long has he left the abbey—and
where does he live now?' 'Hold,' said I, 'not so fast—I
know when to speak and when to hold my tongue—but
who has been inquiring for him?'"

" 'What! he expected somebody to inquire for him?'
says the man.—'No,' says I, 'he did not, but if he did,
what does that prove;—that argues nothing.' With
that he looked at the blacksmith, and they went out of
the shop together, leaving my horse's shoe undone.
But I never minded that, for the moment they were
gone I mounted and rode away as fast as I could. But
in my fright, your honour, I forgot to take the round-
about way, and so came straight home."

La Motte, extremely shocked at Peter's intelligence,
made no other reply than by cursing his folly, and
immediately went in search of Madame, who was walking with Adeline on the banks of the river. La Motte
was too much agitated to soften his information by
preface. "We are discovered!" said he, "the king's
officers have been inquiring for me at Auboine, and
Peter has blundered upon my ruin. He then informed
her of what Peter had related, and bade her prepare
to quit the abbey."

"But whither can we fly?" said Madame La Motte,
scarcely able to support herself. "Anywhere!" said
he, "to stay here is certain destruction. We must take
refuge in Switzerland, I think. If any part of France
would have concealed me, surely it had been this!"

"Alas, how are we persecuted!" rejoined Madame.
"This spot is scarcely made comfortable before we are
obliged to leave it and go we know not whither."

"I wish we may not yet know whither," replied La
Motte; "that is the least evil that threatens us. Let
us escape a prison, and I care not whither we go. But
return to the abbey immediately and pack up what
movables you can." A flood of tears came to the relief
of Madame La Motte, and she hung upon Adeline's arm
silent and trembling. Adeline, though she had no
comfort to bestow, endeavoured to command her feel-

ings and appear composed. "Come," said La Motte, "we waste time; let us lament hereafter, but at present prepare for flight. Exert a little of that fortitude which is so necessary for our preservation. Adeline does not weep, yet her state is as wretched as your own, for I know not how long I shall be able to protect her."

Notwithstanding her terror, this reproof touched the pride of Madame La Motte, who dried her tears, but disdained to reply, and looked at Adeline with a strong expression of displeasure. As they moved silently toward the abbey, Adeline asked La Motte if he was sure they were the king's officers who inquired for him. "I cannot doubt it," he replied, "who else could possibly inquire for me? Besides, the behaviour of the man who mentioned my name puts the matter beyond a question."

"Perhaps not," said Madame La Motte; "let us wait till morning ere we set off. We may then find it will be unnecessary to go."

"We may, indeed; the king's officers would probably by that time have told us as much." La Motte went to give orders to Peter. "Set off in an hour," said Peter, "Lord bless you, master! only consider the coach wheel; it would take me a day at least to mend it, for your honour knows I never mended one in my life."

This was a circumstance which La Motte had entirely overlooked. When they settled at the abbey, Peter had at first been too busy in repairing the apartments to remember the carriage, and afterwards, believing it would not quickly be wanted, he had neglected to do it. La Motte's temper now entirely forsook him, and with many execrations he ordered Peter to go to work immediately; but on searching for the materials formerly bought, they were nowhere to be found, and Peter at length remembered, though he was prudent enough to conceal this circumstance, that he had used the nails in repairing the abbey.

It was now, therefore, impossible to quit the forest that night, and La Motte had only to consider the most probable plan of concealment, should the officers of justice visit the ruin before the morning; a circumstance which the thoughtlessness of Peter in returning from Auboine by the straight way made not unlikely.

At first, indeed, it occurred to him that though his family could not be removed, he might himself take one of the horses and escape from the forest before night. But he thought there would still be some danger of detection in the towns through which he must pass, and he could not well bear the idea of leaving his family unprotected, without knowing when he could return to them or whither he could direct them to follow him. La Motte was not a man of very vigorous resolution, and he was perhaps rather more willing to suffer in company than alone.

After much consideration he recollected the trap-door of the closet belonging to the chambers above. It was invisible to the eye, and, whatever might be its direction, it would securely shelter *him* at least from discovery. Having deliberated farther upon the subject, he determined to explore the recess to which the stairs led, and thought it possible that for a short time his whole family might be concealed within it. There was little time between the suggestion of the plan and the execution of his purpose, for darkness was spreading around, and in every murmur of the wind he thought he heard the voices of his enemies.

He called for a light and ascended alone to the chamber. When he came to the closet, it was some time before he could find the trap-door, so exactly did it correspond with the boards of the floor. At length he found and raised it. The chill damps of long confined air rushed from the aperture, and he stood for a moment to let them pass ere he descended. As he stood looking down the abyss, he recollected the report which Peter had brought concerning the abbey, and it gave him an uneasy sensation. But this soon yielded to more pressing interests.

The stairs were steep, and in many places trembled beneath his weight. Having continued to descend for some time, his feet touched the ground, and he found himself in a narrow passage; but as he turned to pursue it, the damp vapours curled round him and extinguished the light. He called aloud for Peter, but could make nobody hear, and after some time he endeavoured to find his way up the stairs. In this with difficulty he succeeded, and passing the chambers with cautious steps, descended the tower.

The security which the place he had just quitted seemed to promise was of too much importance to be slightly rejected, and he determined immediately to make another experiment with the light;—having now fixed it in a lanthorn, he descended a second time to the passage. The current of vapours occasioned by the opening of the trap-door was abated, and the fresh air thence admitted had begun to circulate. La Motte passed on unmolested.

The passage was of considerable length, and led him to a door which was fastened. He placed the lanthorn at some distance to avoid the current of air, and applied his strength to the door. It shook under his hands, but did not yield. Upon examining it more closely, he perceived the wood round the lock was decayed, probably by the damps, and this encouraged him to proceed.

After some time it gave way to his effort, and he found himself in a square stone room.

He stood for some time to survey it. The walls, which were dripping with unwholesome dews, were entirely bare and afforded not even a window. A small iron grate alone admitted the air. At the further end, near a low recess, was another door. La Motte went towards it, and as he passed, looked into the recess. Upon the ground within it stood a large chest, which he went forward to examine, and, lifting the lid, he saw the remains of a human skeleton. Horror struck upon his heart, and he involuntary stept back. During a pause of some moments his first emotion subsided. That thrilling curiosity which objects of terror often excite in the human mind, impelled him to take a second view of this dismal spectacle.

La Motte stood motionless as he gazed. The object before him seemed to confirm the report that some person had formerly been murdered in the abbey. At length he closed the chest and advanced to the second door, which also was fastened, but the key was in the lock. He turned it with difficulty, and then found the door was held by two strong bolts. Having undrawn these, it disclosed a flight of steps, which he descended. They terminated in a chain of low vaults, or rather cells, that from the manner of their construction and present condition seemed to be coeval with the most ancient parts of the abbey. La Motte in his then depressed state of mind thought them the burial places of the monks who formerly inhabited the pile above; but they were more calculated for places of penance for the living than of rest for the dead.

Having reached the extremity of these cells, the way was again closed by a door. La Motte now hesitated whether he should attempt to proceed any farther. The present spot seemed to afford the security he sought. Here he might pass the night unmolested by apprehension of discovery, and it was most probable that if the officers arrived in the night and found the abbey vacated, they would quit it before morning, or at least before he could have any occasion to emerge from concealment. These considerations restored his mind to a state of greater composure. His only immediate care was to bring his family as soon as possible to this place of security, lest the officers should come unawares upon them; and while he stood thus musing, he blamed himself for delay.

But an irresistible desire of knowing to what this door led, arrested his steps, and he turned to open it. The door, however, was fastened, and as he attempted to force it, he suddenly thought he heard a noise above. It now occurred to him that the officers might already have arrived, and he quitted the cells with precipitation, intending to listen at the trap-door.

"There," said he, "I may wait in security, and perhaps hear something of what passes. My family will not be known, or at least not hurt, and their uneasiness on my account they must learn to endure."

These were the arguments of La Motte, in which, it must be owned, selfish prudence was more conspicuous than tender anxiety for his wife. He had by this time reached the bottom of the stairs, when on looking up, he perceived the trap-door was left open, and ascending in haste to close it, he heard footsteps advancing through the chambers above. Before he could descend entirely out of sight, he again looked up and perceived through the aperture the face of a man looking down upon him. "Master," cried Peter.—La Motte was somewhat relieved at the sound of his voice, though angry that he had occasioned him so much terror.

"What brings you here, and what is the matter below?"

"Nothing, sir; nothing's the matter, only my mistress sent me to see after your honour."

"There's nobody there then," said La Motte, setting his foot upon the step.

"Yes, sir, there is my mistress and Mademoiselle Adeline and ——"

"Well—well"—said La Motte briskly—"go your ways. I am coming."

He informed Madame La Motte where he had been and of his intention of secreting himself, and deliberated upon the means of convincing the officers, should they arrive, that he had quitted the abbey. For this purpose he ordered all the movable furniture to be conveyed to the cells below. La Motte himself assisted in this business, and every hand was employed for dispatch. In a very short time the habitable part of the fabric was left almost as desolate as he had found it. He then bade Peter take the horses to a distance from the abbey, and turn them loose. After farther consideration, he thought it might contribute to mislead them if he placed in some conspicuous part of the fabric an inscription signifying his condition, and mentioning the date of his departure from the abbey. Over the door of the tower, which led to the habitable part of the structure, he therefore cut the following lines:

O ye! whom misfortune may lead to this spot,
Learn that there are others as miserable as yourselves.

P——L—M—— a wretched exile, sought within these walls a refuge from persecution, on the 27th of April 1658, and quitted them on the 12th of July in the same year, in search of a more convenient asylum.

After engraving these words with a knife, the small stock of provisions remaining from the week's supply (for Peter, in his fright, had returned unloaded from his last journey) was put into a basket, and, La Motte having assembled his family, they all ascended the stairs of the tower and passed through the chambers to the closet. Peter went first with a light, and with some difficulty found the trap-door. Madame La Motte shuddered as she surveyed the gloomy abyss; but they were all silent.

La Motte now took the light and led the way. Madame followed, and then Adeline. "These old monks loved good wine as well as other people," said Peter, who brought up the rear, "I warrant your honour, now, this was their cellar; I smell the casks already."

"Peace," said La Motte; "reserve your jokes for a proper occasion."

"There is no harm in loving good wine, as your honour knows."

"Have done with this buffoonery," said La Motte, in a tone more authoritative, "and go first." Peter obeyed.

They came to the vaulted room. The dismal spectacle he had seen here deterred La Motte from passing the night in this chamber; and the furniture had by his own order been conveyed to the cells below. He was anxious that his family should not perceive the skeleton, an object which would probably excite a degree of horror not to be overcome during their stay. La Motte now passed the chest in haste; and Madame La Motte and Adeline were too much engrossed by their own thoughts to give minute attention to external circumstances.

When they reached the cells, Madame La Motte wept at the necessity which condemned her to a spot so dismal. "Alas," said she, "are we indeed thus reduced! The apartments above formerly appeared to me a deplorable habitation; but they are a palace compared to these."

"True, my dear," said La Motte, "and let the remembrance of what you once thought them soothe your discontent now; these cells are also a palace, compared to the Bicêtre or the Bastile, and to the terrors of further punishment which would accompany them. Let the apprehension of the greater evil teach you to endure the less; I am contented if we find here the refuge I seek."

Madame La Motte was silent, and Adeline, forgetting her late unkindness, endeavoured as much as she could to console her; while her heart was sinking with the misfortunes which she could not but anticipate, she appeared composed and even cheerful. She attended Madame La Motte with the most watchful solicitude, and felt so thankful that La Motte was now secreted within this recess that she almost lost her perception of its glooms and inconveniences.

This she artlessly expressed to him, who could not be insensible to the tenderness it discovered. Madame La Motte was also sensible of it, and it renewed a painful sensation. The effusions of gratitude she mistook for those of tenderness.

La Motte returned frequently to the trap-door, to listen if anybody was in the abbey; but no sound disturbed the stillness of night. At length they sat down to supper. The repast was a melancholy one. "If the officers do not come hither to-night," said Madame La Motte, sighing, "suppose, my dear, Peter returns to Auboine to-morrow. He may there learn something more of this affair, or at least he might procure a carriage to convey us hence."

"To be sure he might," said La Motte, peevishly, "and people to attend it also. Peter would be an excellent person to shew the officers the way to the abbey, and to inform them of what they might else be in doubt about, my concealment here."

"How cruel is this irony!" replied Madame La Motte, "I proposed only what I thought would be for our mutual good; my judgment was, perhaps, wrong, but my intention was certainly right." Tears swelled into her eyes as she spoke these words. Adeline wished to relieve her, but delicacy kept her silent. La Motte observed the effect of his speech, and something like remorse touched his heart. He approached, and taking her hand. "You must allow for the perturbation of my mind," said he, "I did not mean to afflict you thus. The idea of sending Peter to Auboine, where he has already done so much harm by his blunders, teased me, and I could not let it pass unnoticed. No, my dear, our only chance of safety is to remain where we are while our provisions last. If the officers do not come here to-night, they probably will to-morrow, or perhaps the next day. When they have searched the abbey without finding me, they will depart; we may then emerge from this recess and take measures for removing to a distant country."

Madame La Motte acknowledged the justice of his words, and her mind being relieved by the little apology he had made, she became tolerably cheerful. Supper being ended, La Motte stationed the faithful though simple Peter at the foot of the steps that ascended to the closet, there to keep watch during the night. Having done this, he returned to the lower cells, where he had left his little family. The beds were spread, and having mournfully bidden each other good night, they lay down and implored rest.

Adeline's thoughts were too busy to suffer her to repose, and when she believed her companions were sunk in slumbers, she indulged the sorrow which reflection brought. She also looked forward to the future with the most mournful apprehension. Should La Motte be seized, what was to become of her? She would then be a wanderer in the wide world, without friends to protect, or money to support her. The prospect was gloomy—was terrible! She surveyed it and shuddered! The distresses too of Monsieur and Madame La Motte, whom she loved with the most lively affection, formed no inconsiderable part of hers.

Sometimes she looked back to her father; but in him she only saw an enemy from whom she must fly. This remembrance heightened her sorrow; yet it was not the recollection of the suffering he had occasioned her by which she was so much afflicted, as by the sense of his unkindness. She wept bitterly. At length, with that artless piety which innocence only knows, she addressed the Supreme Being, and resigned herself to his care. Her mind then gradually became peaceful and reassured, and soon after she sunk to repose.

CHAPTER V

THE night passed without any alarm; Peter had remained upon his post, and heard nothing that prevented his sleeping. La Motte heard him, long before he saw him, most musically snoring, though it must be owned there was more of the bass than of any other part of the gamut in his performance. He was soon roused by the *bravura* of La Motte, whose notes sounded discord to his ears and destroyed the torpor of his tranquillity.

"God bless you, master, what's the matter?" cried Peter, waking; "are they come?"

"Yes, for aught you care, they might be come. Did I place you here to sleep, sirrah?"

"Bless you, master," returned Peter; "sleep is the only comfort to be had here; I'm sure I would not deny it to a dog in such a place as this."

La Motte sternly questioned him concerning any noise he might have heard in the night, and Peter full as solemnly protested he had heard none, an assertion which was strictly true, for he had enjoyed the comfort of being asleep the whole time.

La Motte ascended to the trap-door and listened attentively. No sounds were heard, and as he ventured to lift it, the full light of the sun burst upon his sight, the morning being now far advanced. He walked softly along the chambers, and looked through a window; no person was to be seen. Encouraged by this apparent security, he ventured down the stairs of the tower and entered the first apartment. He was proceeding towards the second when, suddenly recollecting himself, he first peeped through the crevice of the door, which stood half open. He looked, and distinctly saw a person sitting near the window, upon which his arm rested.

The discovery so much shocked him that for a moment he lost all presence of mind and was utterly unable to move from the spot. The person, whose back was towards him, arose and turned his head. La Motte now recovered himself, and quitting the apartment as quickly and at the same as silently as possible, ascended to the closet. He raised the trap-door, but before he closed it heard the footsteps of a person entering the outward chamber. Bolts or other fastening to the trap there was none; and his security depended solely upon the exact correspondence of the boards.

The outer door of the stone room had no means of
defence, and the fastenings of the inner one were on
the wrong side to afford security, even till some means
of escape could be found.

When he reached this room, he paused, and heard
distinctly persons walking in the closet above. While
he was listening, he heard a voice call him by name, and
he instantly fled to the cells below, expecting every
moment to hear the trap lifted, and the footsteps of
pursuit; but he was fled beyond the reach of hearing
either. Having thrown himself on the ground at the
farthest extremity of the vaults, he lay for some time
breathless with agitation. Madame La Motte and Adeline, in the utmost terror, inquired what had happened.
It was some time before he could speak. When he did,
it was almost unnecessary, for the distant noises which
sounded from above informed his family of a part of
the truth.

The sounds did not seem to approach, but Madame
La Motte, unable to command her terror, shrieked
aloud. This redoubled the distress of La Motte. "You
have already destroyed me," cried he; "that shriek
has informed them where I am." He traversed the
cells with clasped hands and quick steps. Adeline stood
pale and still as death, supporting Madame La Motte,
whom with difficulty she prevented from fainting. "O!
Dupras! Dupras! you are already avenged!" said he,
in a voice that seemed to burst from his heart. There
was a pause of silence. "But why should I deceive
myself with a hope of escaping?" he resumed; "why do
I wait here for their coming? Let me rather end these
torturing pangs by throwing myself into their hands
at once."

As he spoke, he moved towards the door, but the distress of Madame La Motte arrested his steps. "Stay,"

said she, "for my sake, stay; do not leave me thus, nor throw yourself voluntarily into destruction!"

"Surely, sir," said Adeline, "you are too precipitate; this despair is useless as it is ill-founded. We hear no person approaching; if the officers had discovered the trap-door, they would certainly have been here before now." The words of Adeline stilled the tumult of his mind; the agitation of terror subsided, and reason beamed a feeble ray upon his hopes. He listened attentively, and perceiving that all was silent, advanced with caution to the stone room, and thence to the foot of the stairs that led to the trap-door. It was closed; no sound was heard above.

He watched a long time, and the silence continuing, his hopes strengthened, and at length he began to believe that the officers had quitted the abbey. The day, however, was spent in anxious watchfulness. He did not dare to unclose the trap-door; and he frequently thought he heard distant noises. It was evident, however, that the secret of the closet had escaped discovery, and on this circumstance he justly founded his security. The following night was passed, like the day, in trembling hope and incessant watching.

But the necessities of hunger now threatened them. The provisions, which had been distributed with the nicest economy, were nearly exhausted, and the most deplorable consequences might be expected from their remaining longer in concealment. Thus circumstanced, La Motte deliberated upon the most prudent method of proceeding. There appeared no other alternative than to send Peter to Auboine, the only town from which he could return within the time prescribed by their necessities. There was game, indeed, in the forest, but Peter could neither handle a gun nor use a fishing rod to any advantage.

It was therefore agreed he should go to Auboine for a supply of provisions, and at the same time bring materials for mending the coach-wheel, that they might have some ready conveyance from the forest. La Motte forbade Peter to ask any questions concerning the people who had inquired for him, or take any methods for discovering whether they had quitted the country, lest his blunders should again betray him. He ordered him to be entirely silent as to these subjects, and to finish his business and leave the place with all possible dispatch.

A difficulty yet remained to be overcome—Who should first venture abroad into the abbey, to learn whether it was vacated by the officers of justice? La Motte considered that if he was again seen, he should be effectually betrayed; which would not be *so* certain if one of his family was observed; for they were all unknown to the officers. It was necessary, however, that the person he sent should have courage enough to go through with the inquiry, and wit enough to conduct it with caution. Peter, perhaps, had the first, but was certainly destitute of the last. Annette had neither. La Motte looked at his wife, and asked her if for his sake she dared to venture. Her heart shrunk from the proposal; yet she was unwilling to refuse, or appear indifferent upon a point so essential to the safety of her husband. Adeline observed in her countenance the agitation of her mind, and surmounting the fears which had hitherto kept her silent, she offered herself to go.

"They will be less likely to offend me," said she, "than a man." Shame would not suffer La Motte to accept her offer; and Madame, touched by the magnanimity of her conduct, felt a momentary renewal of all her former kindness. Adeline pressed her proposal so warmly and seemed so much in earnest that La Motte began to hesitate. "You, sir," said she, "once preserved me from the most imminent danger, and your kindness has since protected me. Do not refuse me the satisfaction of deserving your goodness by a grateful return of it. Let me go into the abbey, and if by so doing I should preserve you from evil, I shall be sufficiently rewarded for what little danger I may incur, for my pleasure will be at least equal to yours."

Madame La Motte could scarcely refrain from tears as Adeline spoke; and La Motte, sighing deeply, said, "Well, be it so; go, Adeline, and from this moment consider me as your debtor." Adeline staid not to reply, but taking a light, quitted the cells, La Motte following to raise the trap-door, and cautioning her to look if possible into every apartment before she entered it. "If you *should* be seen," said he, "you must account for your appearance so as not to discover me. Your own presence of mind may assist you; I cannot. God bless you!"

When she was gone, Madame La Motte's admiration of her conduct began to yield to other emotions. Distrust gradually undermined kindness, and jealousy raised suspicions. It must be a sentiment more powerful than gratitude, thought she, that could teach Adeline to subdue her fears. What but love could influence her to a conduct so generous. Madame La Motte, when she found it impossible to account for Adeline's conduct without alleging some interested motives for it, however her suspicions might agree with the practice of the world, had surely forgotten how much she once admired the purity and disinterestedness of her young friend.

Adeline meanwhile ascended to the chambers. The cheerful beams of the sun played once more upon her sight and re-animated her spirits; she walked lightly through the apartments, nor stopped till she came to the stairs of the tower. Here she stood for some time, but no sounds met her ear save the sighing of the wind among the trees, and at length she descended. She passed the apartments below without seeing any person; and the little furniture that remained seemed to stand exactly as she had left it. She now ventured to look out from the tower. The only animate objects that appeared were the deer quietly grazing under the shade of the woods. Her favourite little fawn distinguished Adeline, and came bounding towards her with strong marks of joy. She was somewhat alarmed lest the animal, being observed, should betray her, and walked swiftly away through the cloisters.

She opened the door that led to the great hall of the abbey, but the passage was so gloomy and dark that she feared to enter it, and started back. It was necessary, however, that she should examine farther, particularly on the opposite side of the ruin, of which she had hitherto had no view; but her fears returned when she recollected how far it would lead her from her only place of refuge, and how difficult it would be to retreat. She hesitated what to do; but when she recollected her obligations to La Motte, and considered this as perhaps her only opportunity of doing him a service, she determined to proceed.

As these thoughts passed rapidly over her mind, she raised her innocent looks to Heaven and breathed a silent prayer. With trembling steps she proceeded over fragments of the ruin, looking anxiously around, and often starting as the breeze rustled among the trees, mistaking it for the whisperings of men. She came to the lawn which fronted the fabric, but no person was to be seen, and her spirits revived. The great door of the hall she now endeavoured to open, but suddenly remembering that it was fastened by La Motte's orders, she proceeded to the north end of the abbey, and having surveyed the prospect around as far as the thick foliage of the trees would permit, without perceiving any person, she turned her steps to the tower from which she had issued.

Adeline was now light of heart, and returned with impatience to inform La Motte of his security. In the cloisters she was again met by her little favourite, and stopped for a moment to caress it. The fawn seemed sensible to the sound of her voice, and discovered new joy; but while she spoke, it suddenly started from her hand, and looking up, she perceived the door of the passage leading to the great hall open, and a man in the habit of a soldier issue forth.

With the swiftness of an arrow she fled along the cloisters, nor once ventured to look back; but a voice called to her to stop, and she heard steps advancing quick in pursuit. Before she could reach the tower, her breath failed her, and she leaned against a pillar of the ruin, pale and exhausted. The man came up, and gazing at her with a strong expression of surprise and curiosity, he assumed a gentle manner, assured her she had nothing to fear, and inquired if she belonged to La Motte. Observing that she still looked terrified and remained silent, he repeated his assurances and his question.

"I know that he is concealed within the ruin," said the stranger; "the occasion of his concealment I also know; but it is of the utmost importance I should see him, and he will then be convinced he has nothing to fear from me." Adeline trembled so excessively that it was with difficulty she could support herself. She hesitated, and knew not what to reply. Her manner seemed to confirm the suspicions of the stranger, and

her consciousness of this increased her embarrassment:
he took advantage of it to press her farther. Adeline
at length replied that La Motte had some time since
resided at the abbey. "And does still, madam," said
the stranger; "lead me to where he may be found—I
must see him, and ———"

"Never, sir," replied Adeline, "and I solemnly assure
you it will be in vain to search for him."

"That I must try," resumed he, "since you, madam,
will not assist me. I have already followed him to some
chambers above, where I suddenly lost him, thereabouts
he must be concealed, and it's plain, therefore, they
afford some secret passage."

Without waiting Adeline's reply, he sprung to the
door of the tower. She now thought it would betray a
consciousness of the truth of his conjecture to follow
him, and resolved to remain below. But, upon farther
consideration, it occurred to her that he might steal
silently into the closet, and possibly surprise La Motte
at the door of the trap. She therefore hastened after
him, that her voice might prevent the danger she apprehended. He was already in the second chamber when
she overtook him; she immediately began to speak aloud.

This room he searched with the most scrupulous
care, but finding no private door or other outlet, he
proceeded to the closet. Then it was that it required
all her fortitude to conceal her agitation. He continued
the search. "Within these chambers I know he is concealed," said he, "though hitherto I have not been able
to discover how. It was hither I followed a man whom
I believe to be him, and he could not escape without a
passage; I shall not quit the place till I have found it."

He examined the walls and the boards, but without
discovering the division of the floor, which, indeed, so
exactly corresponded that La Motte himself had not

perceived it by the eye, but by the trembling of the floor beneath his feet. "Here is some mystery," said the stranger, "which I cannot comprehend, and perhaps never shall." He was turning to quit the closet, when, who can paint the distress of Adeline upon seeing the trap-door gently raised, and La Motte himself appeared. "Hah!" cried the stranger, advancing eagerly to him. La Motte sprang forward, and they were locked in each other's arms.

The astonishment of Adeline for a moment surpassed even her former distress, but a remembrance darted across her mind which explained the present scene, and before La Motte could exclaim, "My son!" she knew the stranger as such. Peter, who stood at the foot of the stairs and heard what passed above, flew to acquaint his mistress with the joyful discovery, and in a few moments she was folded in the embrace of her son. This spot, so lately the mansion of despair, seemed metamorphosed into the palace of pleasure, and the walls echoed only to the accents of joy and congratulation.

The joy of Peter on this occasion was beyond expression. He acted a perfect pantomime—he capered about, clasped his hands, ran to his young master, shook him by the hand, in spite of the frowns of La Motte; ran everywhere, without knowing for what, and gave no rational answer to anything that was said to him.

After their first emotions were subsided, La Motte, as if suddenly recollecting himself, resumed his wonted solemnity: "I am to blame," said he, "thus to give way to joy, when I am still, perhaps, surrounded by danger. Let us secure a retreat while it is yet in our power," continued he; "in a few hours the king's officers may search for me again."

Louis comprehended his father's words, and immediately relieved his apprehensions by the following relation.

"A letter from Monsieur Nemours, containing an account of your flight from Paris, reached me at Peronne, where I was then upon duty with my regiment. He mentioned that you was gone towards the south of France, but as he had not since heard from you, he was ignorant of the place of your refuge. It was about this time that I was dispatched into Flanders, and, being unable to obtain farther intelligence of you, I passed some weeks of very painful solicitude. At the conclusion of the campaign I obtained leave of absence, and immediately set out for Paris, hoping to learn from Nemours where you had found an asylum.

"Of this, however, he was equally ignorant with myself. He informed me that you had once before written to him from D——, upon your second day's journey from Paris, under an assumed name, as had been agreed upon; and that you then said the fear of discovery would prevent your hazarding another letter. He therefore remained ignorant of your abode, but said he had no doubt you had continued your journey to the southward. Upon this slender information I quitted Paris in search of you, and proceeded immediately to V——, where my inquiries concerning your farther progress were successful as far as M——. There they told me you had staid some time on account of the illness of a young lady, a circumstance which perplexed me much, as I could not imagine what young lady would accompany you. I proceeded, however, to L——; but there all traces of you seemed to be lost. As I sat musing at the window of the inn, I observed some scribbling on the glass, and the curiosity of idleness prompted me to read it. I thought I knew the characters, and the lines

I read confirmed my conjecture, for I remembered to have heard you often repeat them.

"Here I renewed my inquiries concerning your route, and at length I made the people of the inn recollect you, and traced you as far as Auboine. There I again lost you, till upon my return from a fruitless inquiry in the neighbourhood, the landlord of the little inn where I lodged told me he believed he had heard news of you, and immediately recounted what had happened at a blacksmith's shop a few hours before.

"His description of Peter was so exact that I had not a doubt it was you who inhabited the abbey; and as I knew your necessity for concealment, Peter's denial did not shake my confidence. The next morning, with the assistance of my landlord, I found my way hither, and having searched every visible part of the fabric, I began to credit Peter's assertion. Your appearance, however, destroyed this fear, by proving that the place was still inhabited, for you disappeared so instantaneously that I was not certain it was you whom I had seen. I continued seeking you till near the close of day, and till then scarcely quitted the chambers whence you had disappeared. I called on you repeatedly, believing that my voice might convince you of your mistake. At length I retired to pass the night at a cottage near the border of the forest.

"I came early this morning to renew my inquiries, and hoped that, believing yourself safe, you would emerge from concealment. But how was I disappointed to find the abbey as silent and solitary as I had left it the preceding evening! I was returning once more from the great hall when the voice of this young lady caught my ear and effected the discovery I had so anxiously sought."

This little narrative entirely dissipated the late apprehensions of La Motte, but he now dreaded that the inquiries of his son and his own obvious desire of concealment might excite a curiosity amongst the people of Auboine and lead to a discovery of his true circumstances. However, for the present he determined to dismiss all painful thoughts, and endeavour to enjoy the comfort which the presence of his son had brought him. The furniture was removed to a more habitable part of the abbey, and the cells were again abandoned to their own glooms.

The arrival of her son seemed to have animated Madame La Motte with new life, and all her afflictions were for the present absorbed in joy. She often gazed silently on him with a mother's fondness, and her partiality heightened every improvement which time had wrought in his person and manner. He was now in his twenty-third year; his person was manly and his air military; his manners were unaffected and graceful, rather than dignified; and though his features were irregular, they composed a countenance which, having seen it once, you would seek again.

She made eager inquiries after the friends she had left at Paris, and learned that within the few months of her absence some had died and others quitted the place. La Motte also learned that a very strenuous search for him had been prosecuted at Paris; and though this intelligence was only what he had before expected, it shocked him so much that he now declared it would be expedient to remove to a distant country. Louis did not scruple to say that he thought he would be as safe at the abbey as at any other place, and repeated what Nemours had said, that the king's officers had been unable to trace any part of his route from Paris.

"Besides," resumed Louis, "this abbey is protected by

a supernatural power, and none of the country people dare approach it."

"Please you, my young master," said Peter, who was waiting in the room, "we were frightened enough the first night we came here, and I myself, God forgive me! thought the place was inhabited by devils, but they were only owls and such like after all."

"Your opinion was not asked," said La Motte, "learn to be silent."

Peter was abashed. When he had quitted the room, La Motte asked his son with seeming carelessness what were the reports circulated by the country people. "O! sir," replied Louis, "I cannot recollect half of them. I remember, however, they said that many years ago a person (but nobody had ever seen him, so we may judge how far the report ought to be credited) a person was privately brought to this abbey, and confined in some part of it, and that there were strong reasons to believe he came unfairly to his end."

La Motte sighed. "They farther said," continued Louis, "that the spectre of the deceased had ever since watched nightly among the ruins; and to make the story more wonderful, for the marvellous is the delight of the vulgar, they added that there was a certain part of the ruin from whence no person that had dared to explore it had ever returned. Thus people who have few objects of real interest to engage their thoughts, conjure up for themselves imaginary ones."

La Motte sat musing. "And what were the reasons," said he, at length awaking from his reverie, "they pretended to assign for believing the person confined here was murdered?"

"They did not use a term so positive as that," replied Louis.

"True," said La Motte, recollecting himself, "they only said he came unfairly to his end."

"That is a nice distinction," said Adeline.

"Why, I could not well comprehend what these reasons were," resumed Louis; "the people indeed say that the person who was brought here was never known to depart, but I do not find it certain that he ever arrived; that there was strange privacy and mystery observed while he was here, and that the abbey has never since been inhabited by its owner. There seems, however, to be nothing in all this that deserves to be remembered." La Motte raised his head as if to reply, when the entrance of Madame turned the discourse upon a new subject, and it was not resumed that day.

Peter was now dispatched for provisions, while La Motte and Louis retired to consider how far it was safe for them to continue at the abbey. La Motte, notwithstanding the assurances lately given him, could not but think that Peter's blunders and his son's inquiries might lead to a discovery of his residence. He revolved this in his mind for some time, but at length a thought struck him that the latter of these circumstances might considerably contribute to his security. "If you," said he to Louis, "return to the inn at Auboine, from whence you were directed here, and without seeming to intend giving intelligence, *do* give the landlord an account of your having found the abbey uninhabited, and then add that you had discovered the residence of the person you sought in some distant town, it would suppress any reports that may at present exist, and prevent the belief of any in future. And if, after all this, you can trust yourself for presence of mind and command of countenance, so far as to describe some dreadful apparition, I think these circumstances, together with the distance of the abbey and the intricacies of the forest, could entitle me to consider this place as my castle."

Louis agreed to all that his father had proposed, and, on the following day executed his commission with such success that the tranquillity of the abbey might be then said to have been entirely restored.

Thus ended this adventure, the only one that had occurred to disturb the family during their residence in the forest. Adeline, removed from the apprehension of those evils with which the late situation of La Motte had threatened her, and from the depression which her interest in his occasioned her, now experienced a more than usual complacency of mind. She thought too that she observed in Madame La Motte a renewal of her former kindness, and this circumstance awakened all her gratitude and imparted to her a pleasure as lively as it was innocent. The satisfaction with which the presence of her son inspired Madame La Motte, Adeline mistook for kindness to herself, and she exerted her whole attention in an endeavour to become worthy of it.

But the joy which his unexpected arrival had given to La Motte quickly began to evaporate, and the gloom of despondency again settled on his countenance. He returned frequently to his haunt in the forest—the same mysterious sadness tinctured his manner and revived the anxiety of Madame La Motte, who was resolved to acquaint her son with this subject of distress and solicit his assistance to penetrate its source.

Her jealousy of Adeline, however, she could not communicate, though it again tormented her and taught her to misconstrue with wonderful ingenuity every look and word of La Motte, and often to mistake the artless expressions of Adeline's gratitude and regard for those of warmer tenderness. Adeline had formerly accustomed herself to long walks in the forest, and the design Madame had formed of watching her steps, had been frustrated by the late circumstances, and was now entirely overcome by her sense of its difficulty and danger. To employ Peter in the affair would be to acquaint him with her fears, and to follow her herself, would most probably betray her scheme by making Adeline aware of her jealousy. Being thus restrained by pride and delicacy, she was obliged to endure the pangs of uncertainty concerning the greatest part of her suspicions.

To Louis, however, she related the mysterious change in his father's temper. He listened to her account with very earnest attention, and the surprise and concern impressed upon his countenance spoke how much his heart was interested. He was, however, involved in equal perplexity with herself upon this subject, and readily undertook to observe the motions of La Motte, believing his interference likely to be of equal service both to his father and his mother. He saw in some degree the suspicions of his mother, but as he thought she wished to disguise her feelings, he suffered her to believe that she succeeded.

He now inquired concerning Adeline, and listened to her little history, of which his mother gave a brief relation, with great apparent interest. So much pity did he express for her condition, and so much indignation at the unnatural conduct of her father, that the apprehensions which Madame La Motte began to form, of his having discovered her jealousy, yielded to those of a different kind. She perceived that the beauty of Adeline had already fascinated his imagination, and she feared that her amiable manners would soon impress his heart. Had her first fondness for Adeline continued, she would still have looked with displeasure upon their attachment, as an obstacle to the promotion and the fortune she hoped to see one day enjoyed by her son. On these she rested all her future hopes of prosperity, and regarded the matrimonial alliance which he might form as the only means of extricating his family from their present difficulties. She therefore touched lightly upon Adeline's merit, joined coolly with Louis in compassionating her misfortunes, and with her censure of the father's conduct mixed an implied suspicion of that of Adeline. The means she employed to repress the passions of her son had a contrary effect. The indifference which she expressed towards Adeline increased his pity for her destitute condition, and the tenderness with which she affected to judge the father heightened his honest indignation at his character.

As he quitted Madame La Motte, he saw his father cross the lawn and enter the deep shade of the forest on the left. He judged this to be a good opportunity of commencing his plan, and quitting the abbey, slowly followed at a distance. La Motte continued to walk straight forward, and seemed so deeply wrapt in thought that he looked neither to the right nor left and scarcely lifted his head from the ground. Louis had followed him near half a mile when he saw him suddenly strike into an avenue of the forest which took a different direction from the way he had hitherto gone. He quickened his steps that he might not lose sight of him, but having reached the avenue, found the trees so thickly interwoven that La Motte was already hid from his view.

He continued, however, to pursue the way before him. It conducted him through the most gloomy part of the forest he had yet seen, till at length it terminated in an obscure recess overarched with high trees whose interwoven branches secluded the direct rays of the sun and admitted only a sort of solemn twilight. Louis looked around in search of La Motte, but he was nowhere to be seen. While he stood surveying the place and considering what farther should be done, he observed through the gloom an object at some distance, but the deep shadow that fell around prevented his distinguishing what it was.

In advancing, he perceived the ruins of a small building which, from the traces that remained, appeared to have been a tomb. As he gazed upon it, "Here," said he, "are probably deposited the ashes of some ancient monk, once an inhabitant of the abbey; perhaps of the founder, who, after having spent a life of abstinence and prayer, sought in heaven the reward of his forbearance upon earth. Peace be to his soul! But did he think a life of mere negative virtue deserved an eternal reward? Mistaken man! Reason, had you trusted to its dictates, would have informed you that the active virtues, the adherence to the golden rule, 'Do as you would be done unto,' could alone deserve the favor of a Deity whose glory is benevolence."

He remained with his eyes fixed upon the spot, and presently saw a figure arise under the arch of the sepulchre. It started, as if on perceiving him, and immediately disappeared. Louis, though unused to fear, felt at that moment an uneasy sensation, but it almost immediately struck him that this was La Motte himself. He advanced to the ruin and called him. No answer was returned, and he repeated the call, but all was yet still as the grave. He then went up to the archway and endeavoured to examine the place where he had disappeared, but the shadowy obscurity rendered the attempt fruitless. He observed, however, a little to the right, an entrance to the ruin, and advanced some steps down a kind of dark passage, when, recollecting that this place might be the haunt of banditti, his danger alarmed him and he retreated with precipitation.

He walked towards the abbey by the way he came, and finding no person followed him, and believing himself again in safety, his former surmise returned, and he thought it was La Motte he had seen. He mused upon this strange possibility, and endeavoured to assign a reason for so mysterious a conduct, but in vain. Notwithstanding this, his belief of it strengthened, and he entered the abbey under as full a conviction as the circumstances would admit of, that it was his father who had appeared in the sepulchre. On entering what was now used as a parlour, he was much surprised to find him quietly seated there with Madame La Motte and Adeline, and conversing as if he had been returned some time.

He took the first opportunity of acquainting his mother with his late adventure, and of inquiring how long La Motte had been returned before him, when, learning that it was near half an hour, his surprise increased, and he knew not what to conclude.

Meanwhile a perception of the growing partiality of Louis co-operated with the canker of suspicion to destroy in Madame La Motte that affection which pity and esteem had formerly excited for Adeline. Her unkindness was now too obvious to escape the notice of her to whom it was directed, and being noticed, it occasioned an anguish which Adeline found it very difficult to endure. With the warmth and candour of youth, she sought an explanation of this change of behaviour and an opportunity of exculpating herself from any intention of provoking it. But this Madame La Motte artfully evaded, while at the same time she threw out hints that involved Adeline in deeper perplexity, and served to make her present affliction more intolerable.

"I have lost that affection," she would say, "which was my all. It was my only comfort—yet I have lost it—and this without even knowing my offence. But I am thankful I have not merited unkindness, and though *she* has abandoned *me*, I shall always love *her*."

Thus distressed, she would frequently leave the parlour, and retiring to her chamber, would yield to a despondency which she had never known till now.

One morning, being unable to sleep, she arose at a very early hour. The faint light of day now trembled through the clouds, and gradually spreading from the horizon, announced the rising sun. Every feature of the landscape was slowly unveiled, moist with the dews of night and brightening with the dawn, till at length the sun appeared and shed the full flood of day. The beauty of the hour invited her to walk, and she went forth into the forest to taste the sweets of morning. The carols of new-waked birds saluted her as she passed, and the fresh gale came scented with the breath of flowers, whose tints glowed more vivid through the dew drops that hung on their leaves.

She wandered on without noticing the distance, and following the windings of the river, came to a dewy glade whose woods, sweeping down to the very edge of the water, formed a scene so sweetly romantic that she seated herself at the foot of a tree to contemplate its beauty. These images insensibly soothed her sorrow and inspired her with that soft and pleasing melancholy so dear to the feeling mind. For some time she sat lost in a reverie, while the flowers that grew on the banks beside her seemed to smile in new life, and drew from her a comparison with her own condition. She

mused and sighed, and then in a voice whose charming
melody was modulated by the tenderness of her heart,
she sung the following words:

SONNET,*

To the Lily.

Soft silken flow'r! that in the dewy vale
   Unfoldst thy modest beauties to the morn,
And breath'st thy fragrance on her wand'ring gale,
   O'er earth's green hills and shadowy valley borne;

   When day has closed his dazzling eye
      And dying gales sink soft away;
   When eve steals down the western sky,
      And mountains, woods, and vales decay;

Thy tender cups, that graceful swell,
   Droop sad beneath her chilly dews;
Thy odours seek their silken cell,
   And twilight veils their languid hues.

But soon, fair flower! the morn shall rise,
   And rear again thy pensive head;
Again unveil thy snowy dyes,
   Again thy velvet foliage spread.

Sweet child of Spring! like thee, in sorrow's shade,
   Full oft I mourn in tears, and droop forlorn:
And O! like thine, may light *my* glooms pervade,
   And Sorrow fly before Joy's living morn!

A distant echo lengthened out her tones, and she sat
listening to the soft response, till repeating the last
* It need scarcely be noted that Mrs. Radcliffe's "sonnets"
are not technically sonnets at all in the modern sense.

stanza of the Sonnet, she was answered by a voice almost as tender, and less distant. She looked round in surprise, and saw a young man in a hunter's dress, leaning against a tree and gazing on her with that deep attention which marks an enraptured mind.

A thousand apprehensions shot athwart her busy thought; and she now first remembered her distance from the abbey. She rose in haste to be gone, when the stranger respectfully advanced; but observing her timid looks and retiring steps, he paused. She pursued her way towards the abbey; and, though many reasons made her anxious to know whether she was followed, delicacy forbade her to look back. When she reached the abbey, finding the family was not yet assembled to breakfast, she retired to her chamber, where her whole thoughts were employed in conjectures concerning the stranger. Believing that she was interested on this point, no farther than as it concerned the safety of La Motte, she indulged without scruple the remembrance of that dignified air and manner which so much distinguished the youth she had seen. After revolving the circumstance more deeply, she believed it impossible that a person of his appearance should be engaged in a stratagem to betray a fellow creature; and though she was destitute of a single circumstance that might assist her surmises of who he was, or what was his business in an unfrequented forest, she rejected unconsciously every suspicion injurious to his character. Upon farther deliberation, therefore, she resolved not to mention this little circumstance to La Motte; well knowing that though his danger might be imaginary, his apprehensions would be real, and would renew all the sufferings and perplexity from which he was but just released. She resolved, however, to refrain for some time walking in the forest.

When she came down to breakfast, she observed Madame La Motte to be more than usually reserved. La Motte entered the room soon after her, and made some trifling observations on the weather; and having endeavoured to support an effort at cheerfulness, sunk into his usual melancholy. Adeline watched the countenance of Madame with anxiety; and when there appeared in it a gleam of kindness, it was as sunshine to her soul. But she very seldom suffered Adeline thus to flatter herself. Her conversation was restrained, and often pointed at something more than could be understood. The entrance of Louis was a very seasonable relief to Adeline, who almost feared to trust her voice with a sentence, lest its trembling accents should betray her uneasiness.

"This charming morning drew you early from your chamber," said Louis, addressing Adeline. "You had, no doubt, a pleasant companion too," said Madame La Motte; "a solitary walk is seldom agreeable."

"I was alone, madam," replied Adeline.

"Indeed! your own thoughts must be highly pleasing then."

"Alas!" returned Adeline, a tear, spite of her efforts, starting to her eye, "there are now few subjects of pleasure left for them."

"That is very surprising," pursued Madame La Motte.

"Is it, indeed, surprising, madam, for those who have lost their last friend to be unhappy?"

Madame La Motte's conscience acknowledged the rebuke, and she blushed.

"Well," resumed she, after a short pause, "that is not your situation, Adeline;" looking earnestly at La Motte. Adeline, whose innocence protected her from suspicion, did not regard this circumstance; but smiling through her tears, said she rejoiced to hear her say so. During this conversation La Motte had remained absorbed in his own thoughts, and Louis, unable to guess at what it pointed, looked alternately at his mother and Adeline for an explanation. The latter he regarded with an expression so full of tender compassion that it revealed at once to Madame La Motte the sentiments of his soul; and she immediately replied to the last words of Adeline with a very serious air: "A friend is only estimable when our conduct deserves one; the friendship that survives the merit of its object is a disgrace, instead of an honour, to both parties."

The manner and emphasis with which she delivered these words again alarmed Adeline, who mildly said she hoped she should never deserve such censure. Madame was silent; but Adeline was so much shocked by what had already passed that tears sprung from her eyes and she hid her face with her handkerchief.

Louis now rose with some emotion; and La Motte, roused from his reverie, inquired what was the matter; but before he could receive an answer, he seemed to have forgotten that he had asked the question. "Adeline may give you her own account," said Madame La Motte. "I have not deserved this," said Adeline, rising, "but since my presence is displeasing, I will retire."

She moved towards the door, when Louis, who was pacing the room in apparent agitation, gently took her hand, saying, "Here is some unhappy mistake," and would have led her to the seat. But her spirits were too much depressed to endure longer restraint, and withdrawing her hand, "Suffer me to go," said she; "if there is any mistake, I am unable to explain it." Saying this, she quitted the room. Louis followed her with his eyes to the door; when, turning to his mother,

"Surely, madam," said he, "you are to blame. My life on it, she deserves your warmest tenderness."

"You are very eloquent in her cause, sir," said Madame, "may I presume to ask what has interested you thus in her favour."

"Her own amiable manners," rejoined Louis, "which no one can observe without esteeming them."

"But you may presume too much on your own observations. It is possible these amiable manners may deceive you."

"Your pardon, madam; I may without presumption affirm they cannot deceive me."

"You have no doubt good reasons for this assertion, and I perceive by your admiration of this artless *innocent*, she has succeeded in her design of entrapping your heart."

"Without designing it, she has won my admiration, which would not have been the case had she been capable of the conduct you mention."

Madame La Motte was going to reply, but was prevented by her husband, who, again roused from his reverie, inquired into the cause of dispute. "Away with this ridiculous behaviour," said he in a voice of displeasure. "Adeline has omitted some household duty I suppose, and an offence so heinous deserves severe punishment, no doubt; but let me be no more disturbed with your petty quarrels; if you must be tyrannical, madam, indulge your humour in private."

Saying this, he abruptly quitted the room, and Louis immediately following, Madame was left to her own unpleasant reflections. Her ill-humour proceeded from the usual cause. She had heard of Adeline's walk; and La Motte, having gone forth into the forest at an early hour, her imagination, heated by the broodings of jealousy, suggested that they had appointed a meeting.

This was confirmed to her by the entrance of Adeline, quickly followed by La Motte; and her perceptions thus jaundiced by passion, neither the presence of her son nor her usual attention to good manners had been able to restrain her emotions. The behaviour of Adeline in the late scene she considered as a refined piece of art; and the indifference of La Motte as affected.

So true is it, that

        —————— trifles, light as air,
Are, to the jealous, confirmations strong
As proofs of Holy Writ.

And so ingenious was she "to twist the true cause the wrong way."

Adeline had retired to her chamber to weep. When her first agitations were subsided, she took an ample view of her conduct, and perceiving nothing of which she could accuse herself, she became more satisfied, deriving her best comfort from the integrity of her intentions. In the moment of accusation, innocence may sometimes be oppressed with the punishment due only to guilt, but reflection dissolves the illusion of terror and brings to the aching bosom the consolations of virtue.

When La Motte quitted the room, he had gone into the forest, which Louis observing, he followed and joined him, with an intention of touching upon the subject of his melancholy. "It is a fine morning, sir," said Louis, "if you will give me leave, I will walk with you." La Motte, though dissatisfied, did not object; and after they had proceeded some way, he changed the course of his walk, striking into a path contrary to that which Louis had observed him take on the foregoing day.

Louis remarked that the avenue they had quitted was

more shady, and therefore more pleasant. La Motte not seeming to notice this remark, "It leads to a singular spot," continued he, "which I discovered yesterday." La Motte raised his head. Louis proceeded to describe the tomb, and the adventure he had met with. During this relation, La Motte regarded him with attention, while his own countenance suffered various changes. When he had concluded, "You were very daring," said La Motte, "to examine that place, particularly when you ventured down the passage. I would advise you to be more cautious how you penetrate the depths of this forest. I myself have not ventured beyond a certain boundary and am therefore uninformed what inhabitants it may harbour. Your account has alarmed me," continued he, "for if banditti are in the neighbourhood, I am not safe from their depredations; 'tis true, I have but little to lose, except my life."

"And the lives of your family," rejoined Louis.— "Of course," said La Motte.

"It would be well to have more certainty upon that head," rejoined Louis; "I am considering how we may obtain it."

" 'Tis useless to consider that," said La Motte, "the inquiry itself brings danger with it. Your life would perhaps be paid for the indulgence of your curiosity. Our only chance of safety is by endeavouring to remain undiscovered. Let us move towards the abbey."

Louis knew not what to think, but said no more upon the subject. La Motte soon after relapsed into a fit of musing, and his son now took occasion to lament that depression of spirits which he had lately observed in him. "Rather lament the cause of it," said La Motte with a sigh.

"That I do, most sincerely, whatever it may be. May I venture to inquire, sir, what is this cause?"

"Are, then, my misfortunes so little known to you," rejoined La Motte, "as to make that question necessary? Am I not driven from my home, from my friends, and almost from my country? And shall it be asked why I am afflicted?" Louis felt the justice of this reproof, and was a moment silent. "That you are afflicted, sir, does not excite my surprise," resumed he; "it would indeed be strange were you not."

"What then does excite your surprise?"

"The air of cheerfulness you wore when I first came hither."

"You lately lamented that I was afflicted," said La Motte, "and now seem not very well pleased that I once was cheerful. What is the meaning of this?"

"You much mistake me," said his son; "nothing could give me so much satisfaction as to see that cheerfulness renewed; the same cause of sorrow existed at that time, yet you was then cheerful."

"That I was then cheerful," said La Motte, "you might without flattery have attributed to yourself; your presence revived me, and I was relieved at the same time from a load of apprehensions."

"Why, then, as the same cause exists, are you not still cheerful?"

"And why do you not recollect that it is your father you thus speak to?"

"I do, sir, and nothing but anxiety for my father could have urged me thus far. It is with inexpressible concern I perceive you have some secret cause of uneasiness. Reveal it, sir, to those who claim a share in all your affliction, and suffer them by participation to soften its severity." Louis looked up, and observed the countenance of his father pale as death; his lips trembled while he spoke. "Your penetration, however you may rely upon it, has in the present instance deceived you. I have no subject of distress but what you are already acquainted with, and I desire this conversation may never be renewed."

"If it is your desire, of course, I obey," said Louis; "but, pardon me, sir, if ——"

"I will *not* pardon you, sir," interrupted La Motte; "let the discourse end here." Saying this, he quickened his steps, and Louis, not daring to pursue, walked quietly on till he reached the abbey.

Adeline passed the greatest part of the day alone in her chamber, where, having examined her conduct, she endeavoured to fortify her heart against the unmerited displeasure of Madame La Motte. This was a task more difficult than that of self-acquittance. She loved her, and had relied on her friendship, which, notwithstanding the conduct of Madame, still appeared valuable to her. It was true, she had not deserved to lose it, but Madame was so averse to explanation that there was little probability of recovering it, however ill-founded might be the cause of her dislike. At length she reasoned, or rather, perhaps, persuaded herself into tolerable composure; for to resign a real good with contentment is less an effort of reason than of temper.

For many hours she busied herself upon a piece of work which she had undertaken for Madame La Motte; and this she did without the least intention of conciliating her favour, but because she felt there was something in thus repaying unkindness which was suitable to her own temper, her sentiments, and her pride. Self-love *may* be the centre round which the human affections move, for whatever motive conduces to self-gratification may be resolved into self-love; yet some of these affections are in their nature so refined that though we cannot deny their origin, they almost deserve the name of virtue. Of this species was that of Adeline.

In this employment and in reading Adeline passed as much of the day as possible. From books, indeed, she had constantly derived her chief information and amusement. Those belonging to La Motte were few, but well chosen; and Adeline could find pleasure in reading them more than once. When her mind was discomposed by the behaviour of Madame La Motte, or by a retrospection of her early misfortunes, a book was the opiate that lulled it to repose. La Motte had several of the best English poets, a language which Adeline had learned in the convent; their beauties, therefore, she was capable of tasting, and they often inspired her with enthusiastic delight.

At the decline of day she quitted her chamber to enjoy the sweet evening hour, but strayed no farther than an avenue near the abbey, which fronted the west. She read a little, but finding it impossible any longer to abstract her attention from the scene around, she closed the book and yielded to the sweet complacent melancholy which the hour inspired. The air was still; the sun, sinking below the distant hill, spread a purple glow over the landscape, and touched the forest glades with softer light. A dewy freshness was diffused upon the air. As the sun descended, the dusk came silently on, and the scene assumed a solemn grandeur. As she mused, she recollected and repeated the following stanzas:

Night.

Now Ev'ning fades! her pensive step retires,
    And Night leads on the dews, and shadowy hours;
Her awful pomp of planetary fires,
    And all her train of visionary pow'rs.

These paint with fleeting shapes the dream of sleep,
  These swell the waking soul with pleasing dread;
These through the glooms in forms terrific sweep,
  And rouse the thrilling horrors of the dead!

Queen of the solemn thought—mysterious night!
  Whose step is darkness, and whose voice is fear!
Thy shades I welcome with severe delight,
  And hail thy hollow gales, that sigh so drear!

When, wrapt in clouds, and riding in the blast,
  Thou roll'st the storm along the sounding shore,
I love to watch the whelming billows cast
  On rocks below, and listen to the roar.

Thy milder terrors, Night, I frequent woo,
  Thy silent lightnings, and thy meteor's glare,
Thy northern fires, bright with ensanguine hue,
  That light in heaven's high vault the fervid air.

But chief I love thee, when thy lucid car
  Sheds through the fleecy clouds a trembling gleam,
And shews the misty mountain from afar,
  The nearer forest, and the valley's stream:

And nameless objects in the vale below,
  That floating dimly to the musing eye,
Assume, at Fancy's touch, fantastic shew,
  And raise her sweet romantic visions high.

Then let me stand amidst thy glooms profound
  On some wild woody steep, and hear the breeze
That swells in mournful melody around,
  And faintly dies upon the distant trees.

What melancholy charm steals o'er the mind!
  What hallow'd tears the rising rapture greet!
While many a viewless spirit in the wind,
  Sighs to the lonely hour in accents sweet!

Ah! who the dear illusions pleas'd would yield,
Which Fancy wakes from silence and from shades,
For all the sober forms of Truth reveal'd,
For all the scenes that Day's bright eye pervades!

On her return to the abbey she was joined by Louis,
who, after some conversation, said, "I am much grieved
by the scene to which I was witness this morning, and
have longed for an opportunity of telling you so. My
mother's behaviour is too mysterious to be accounted
for, but it is not difficult to perceive she labours under
some mistake. What I have to request is that whenever
I can be of service to you, you will command me."

Adeline thanked him for this friendly offer, which
she felt more sensibly than she chose to express. "I
am unconscious," said she, "of any offence that may
have deserved Madame La Motte's displeasure, and am
therefore totally unable to account for it. I have repeatedly sought an explanation, which she has as anxiously avoided. It is better, therefore, to press the
subject no farther. At the same time, sir, suffer me to
assure you I have a just sense of your goodness."
Louis sighed, and was silent. At length, "I wish you
would permit me," resumed he, "to speak with my
mother upon this subject. I am sure I could convince
her of her error."

"By no means," replied Adeline, "Madame La
Motte's displeasure has given me inexpressible concern; but to compel her to an explanation would only
increase this displeasure, instead of removing it. Let
me beg of you not to attempt it."

"I submit to your judgment," said Louis, "but for
once it is with reluctance. I should esteem myself
most happy if I could be of service to you." He spoke
this with an accent so tender that Adeline for the

first time perceived the sentiments of his heart. A mind more fraught with vanity than hers would have taught her long ago to regard the attentions of Louis as the result of something more than well-bred gallantry. She did not appear to notice his last words, but remained silent, and involuntarily quickened her pace. Louis said no more, but seemed sunk in thought; and this silence remained uninterrupted till they entered the abbey.

CHAPTER VI

NEAR a month elapsed without any remarkable occurrence. The melancholy of La Motte suffered little abatement, and the behaviour of Madame to Adeline, though somewhat softened, was still far from kind. Louis, by numberless little attentions, testified his growing affection for Adeline, who continued to treat them as passing civilities.

It happened one stormy night, as they were preparing for rest, that they were alarmed by a trampling of horses near the abbey. The sound of several voices succeeded, and a loud knocking at the great gate of the hall soon after confirmed the alarm. La Motte had little doubt that the officers of justice had at length discovered his retreat, and the perturbation of fear almost confounded his senses. He however ordered the lights to be extinguished and a profound silence to be observed, unwilling to neglect even the slightest possibility of security. There was a chance, he thought, that the persons might suppose the place uninhabited, and believe they had mistaken the object of their search. His orders were scarcely obeyed when the knocking

was renewed, and with increased violence. La Motte
now repaired to a small grated window in the portal of
the gate, that he might observe the number and appearance of the strangers.

The darkness of the night baffled his purpose. He
could only perceive a group of men on horseback; but
listening attentively, he distinguished a part of their
discourse. Several of the men contended that they had
mistaken the place, till a person who from his authoritative voice appeared to be their leader, affirmed
that the lights had issued from this spot, and he was
positive there were persons within. Having said this,
he again knocked loudly at the gate, and was answered
only by hollow echoes. La Motte's heart trembled at
the sound, and he was unable to move.

After waiting some time, the strangers seemed as if
in consultation, but their discourse was conducted in
such a low tone of voice that La Motte was unable to
distinguish its purport. They withdrew from the gate
as if to depart, but he presently thought he heard them
amongst the trees on the other side of the fabric, and
soon became convinced they had not left the abbey. A
few minutes held La Motte in a state of torturing suspense. He quitted the grate, where Louis now stationed himself, for that part of the edifice which overlooked the spot where he supposed them to be waiting.

The storm was now loud, and the hollow blasts which
rushed among the trees prevented his distinguishing any
other sound. Once in the pauses of the wind he thought
he heard distinct voices; but he was not long left to
conjecture, for the renewed knocking at the gate again
appalled him; and regardless of the terrors of Madame
La Motte and Adeline, he ran to try his last chance of
concealment by means of the trap-door.

Soon after, the violence of the assailants seeming to

increase with every gust of the tempest, the gate, which was old and decayed, burst from its hinges, and admitted them to the hall. At the moment of their entrance, a scream from Madame La Motte, who stood at the door of an adjoining apartment, confirmed the suspicions of the principal stranger, who continued to advance as fast as the darkness would permit him.

Adeline had fainted, and Madame La Motte was calling loudly for assistance, when Peter entered with lights, and discovered the hall filled with men, and his young mistress senseless upon the floor. A chevalier now advanced, and soliciting pardon of Madame for the rudeness of his conduct, was attempting an apology when, perceiving Adeline, he hastened to raise her from the ground; but Louis, who now returned, caught her in his arms, and desired the stranger not to interfere.

The person, to whom he spoke this, wore the star of one of the first orders in France, and had an air of dignity which declared him to be of superior rank. He appeared to be about forty, but perhaps the spirit and fire of his countenance made the impression of time upon his features less perceptible. His softened aspect and insinuating manners while, regardless of himself, he seemed attentive only to the condition of Adeline, gradually dissipated the apprehensions of Madame La Motte, and subdued the sudden resentment of Louis. Upon Adeline, who was yet insensible, he gazed with an eager admiration which seemed to absorb all the faculties of his mind. She was, indeed, an object not to be contemplated with indifference.

Her beauty, touched with the languid delicacy of illness, gained from sentiment what it lost in bloom. The negligence of her dress, loosened for the purpose of freer respiration, discovered those glowing charms which her auburn tresses, that fell in profusion over her bosom, shaded, but could not conceal.

There now entered another stranger, a young chevalier, who, having spoken hastily to the elder, joined the general group that surrounded Adeline. He was of a person in which elegance was happily blended with strength, and had a countenance animated but not haughty, noble, yet expressive of peculiar sweetness. What rendered it at present more interesting was the compassion he seemed to feel for Adeline, who now revived and saw him, the first object that met her eyes, bending over her in silent anxiety.

On perceiving him, a blush of quick surprise passed over her cheek, for she knew him to be the stranger she had seen in the forest. Her countenance instantly changed to the paleness of terror when she observed the room crowded with people. Louis now supported her into another apartment, where the two chevaliers, who followed her, again apologized for the alarm they had occasioned. The elder, turning to Madame La Motte, said, "You are no doubt, madam, ignorant that I am the proprietor of this abbey." She started. "Be not alarmed, madam; you are safe and welcome. This ruinous spot has been long abandoned by me and if it has afforded you a shelter, I am happy." Madame La Motte expressed her gratitude for this condescension, and Louis declared his sense of the politeness of the Marquis de Montalt, for that was the name of the noble stranger.

"My chief residence," said the Marquis, "is in a distant province, but I have a château near the borders of the forest, and in returning from an excursion I have been benighted and lost my way. A light which gleamed through the trees attracted me hither, and such was the darkness without that I did not know it pro-

ceeded from the abbey till I came to the door." The
noble deportment of the strangers, the splendour of
their apparel, and, above all, this speech, dissipated
every remaining doubt of Madame's, and she was giving
orders for refreshments to be set before them, when
La Motte, who had listened, and was now convinced
he had nothing to fear, entered the apartment.

He advanced towards the Marquis with a complacent
air, but as he would have spoke, the words of welcome
faltered on his lips, his limbs trembled, and a ghastly
paleness overspread his countenance. The Marquis was
little less agitated, and in the first moment of surprise,
put his hand upon his sword, but recollecting himself,
he withdrew it, and endeavoured to obtain a command
of features. A pause of agonizing silence ensued. La
Motte made some motion towards the door, but his agitated frame refused to support him, and he sunk into a
chair, silent and exhausted. The horror of his countenance, together with his whole behaviour, excited the
utmost surprise in Madame, whose eyes inquired of the
Marquis more than he thought proper to answer. His
looks increased, instead of explaining the mystery, and
expressed a mixture of emotions, which she could not
analyze. Meanwhile she endeavoured to soothe and
revive her husband, but he repressed her efforts, and
averting his face, covered it with his hands.

The Marquis, seeming to recover his presence of
mind, stepped to the door of the hall where his people
were assembled, when La Motte, starting from his seat,
with a frantic air called on him to return. The Marquis looked back and stopped, but still hesitating
whether to proceed. The supplications of Adeline, who
was now returned, added to those of La Motte, determined him, and he sat down. "I request of you, my

lord," said La Motte, "that we may converse for a few moments by ourselves."

"The request is bold, and the indulgence, perhaps, dangerous," said the Marquis; "it is more also than I will grant. You can have nothing to say with which your family are not acquainted—speak your purpose and be brief." La Motte's complexion varied to every sentence of this speech. "Impossible, my lord," said he; "my lips shall close forever ere they pronounce before another human being the words reserved for you alone. I entreat—I supplicate of you a few moments' private discourse." As he pronounced these words, tears swelled into his eyes, and the Marquis, softened by his distress, consented, though with evident emotion and reluctance, to his request.

La Motte took a light and led the Marquis to a small room in a remote part of the edifice, where they remained near an hour. Madame, alarmed by the length of their absence, went in quest of them. As she drew near, a curiosity in such circumstances perhaps not unjustifiable, prompted her to listen. La Motte just then exclaimed—"The phrenzy of despair!"—Some words followed, delivered in a low tone which she could not understand—"I have suffered more than I can express," continued he; "the same image has pursued me in my midnight dream, and in my daily wanderings. There is no punishment short of death which I would not have endured to regain the state of mind with which I entered this forest. I again address myself to your compassion."

A loud gust of wind that burst along the passage where Madame La Motte stood, overpowered his voice and that of the Marquis, who spoke in reply: but she soon after distinguished these words,—"Tomorrow, my lord, if you return to these ruins, I will lead you to the spot."

"That is scarcely necessary, and may be dangerous," said the Marquis. "From you, my lord, I can excuse these doubts," resumed La Motte; "but I will swear whatever you shall propose. Yes," continued he, "whatever may be the consequence, I will swear to submit to your decree!" The rising tempest again drowned the sound of their voices, and Madame La Motte vainly endeavoured to hear those words upon which probably hung the explanation of this mysterious conduct. They now moved towards the door, and she retreated with precipitation to the apartment where she had left Adeline with Louis and the young chevalier.

Hither the Marquis and La Motte soon followed, the first haughty and cool, the latter somewhat more composed than before, though the impression of horror was not yet faded from his countenance. The Marquis passed on to the hall where his retinue awaited. The storm was not yet subsided, but he seemed impatient to be gone, and ordered his people to be in readiness. La Motte observed a sullen silence, frequently pacing the room with hasty steps, and sometimes lost in reverie. Meanwhile the Marquis, seating himself by Adeline, directed to her his whole attention, except when sudden fits of absence came over his mind and suspended him in silence. At these times the young chevalier addressed Adeline, who with diffidence and some agitation shrunk from the observance of both.

The Marquis had been near two hours at the abbey, and the tempest still continuing, Madame La Motte offered him a bed. A look from her husband made her tremble for the consequence. Her offer was, however, politely declined, the Marquis being evidently as impatient to be gone as his tenant appeared distressed by

his presence. He often returned to the hall, and from
the gates raised a look of impatience to the clouds.
Nothing was to be seen through the darkness of night
—nothing heard but the howlings of the storm.

The morning dawned before he departed. As he
was preparing to leave the abbey, La Motte again drew
him aside and held him for a few moments in close
conversation. His impassioned gestures, which Madame
La Motte observed from a remote part of the room,
added to her curiosity a degree of wild apprehension
derived from the obscurity of the subject. Her endeavour to distinguish the corresponding words was
baffled by the low voice in which they were uttered.

The Marquis and his retinue at length departed, and
La Motte, having himself fastened the gates, silently
and dejectedly withdrew to his chamber. The moment
they were alone, Madame seized the opportunity of
entreating her husband to explain the scene she had
witnessed. "Ask me no questions," said La Motte
sternly, "for I will answer none. I have already forbidden your speaking to me on this subject."

"What subject?" said his wife. La Motte seemed
to recollect himself—"No matter—I was mistaken—
I thought you had repeated these questions before."

"Ah!" said Madame La Motte, "it is then as I suspected: your former melancholy and the distress of
this same night have the same cause."

"And why should you either suspect or inquire? Am
I always to be persecuted with conjectures?"

"Pardon me, I meant not to persecute you; but my
anxiety for your welfare will not suffer me to rest
under this dreadful uncertainty. Let me claim the
privilege of a wife and share the affliction which oppresses you. Deny me not."—La Motte interrupted her,
"Whatever may be the cause of the emotions which

you have witnessed, I swear that I will not now reveal it. A time may come when I shall no longer judge concealment necessary; till then be silent, and desist from importunity. Above all, forbear to remark to anyone what you may have seen uncommon in me. Bury your surmise in your own bosom, as you would avoid my curse and my destruction." The determined air with which he spoke this, while his countenance was overspread with a livid hue, made his wife shudder; and she forbore all reply.

Madame La Motte retired to bed, but not to rest. She ruminated on the past occurrence, and her surprise and curiosity concerning the words and behaviour of her husband were but more strongly stimulated by reflection. One truth, however, appeared: she could not doubt but the mysterious conduct of La Motte which had for so many months oppressed her with anxiety, and the late scene with the Marquis, originated from the same cause. This belief, which seemed to prove how unjustly she had suspected Adeline, brought with it a pang of self-accusation. She looked forward to the morrow, which would lead the Marquis again to the abbey, with impatience. Wearied nature at length resumed her rights and yielded a short oblivion of care.

At a late hour the next day the family assembled to breakfast. Each individual of the party appeared silent and abstracted, but very different was the aspect of their features, and still more the complexion of their thoughts. La Motte seemed agitated by impatient fear, yet the sullenness of despair overspread his countenance. A certain wildness in his eye at times expressed the sudden start of horror, and again his features would sink into the gloom of despondency.

Madame La Motte seemed harassed with anxiety;

she watched every turn of her husband's countenance, and impatiently awaited the arrival of the Marquis. Louis was composed and thoughtful. Adeline seemed to feel her full share of uneasiness. She had observed the behaviour of La Motte the preceding night with much surprise, and the happy confidence she had hitherto reposed in him was shaken. She feared also lest the exigency of his circumstances should precipitate him again into the world, and that he would be either unable or unwilling to afford her a shelter beneath his roof.

During breakfast La Motte frequently rose to the window, from whence he cast many an anxious look. His wife understood too well the cause of his impatience, and endeavoured to repress her own. In these intervals, Louis attempted by whispers to obtain some information from his father, but La Motte always returned to the table, where the presence of Adeline prevented farther discourse.

After breakfast, as he walked upon the lawn, Louis would have joined him, but La Motte peremptorily declared he intended to be alone, and soon after, the Marquis having not yet arrived, proceeded to a greater distance from the abbey.

Adeline retired into their usual working room with Madame La Motte, who affected an air of cheerfulness, and even of kindness. Feeling the necessity of offering some reason for the striking agitation of La Motte, and of preventing the surprise which the unexpected appearance of the Marquis would occasion Adeline, if she was left to connect it with his behaviour of the preceding night, she mentioned that the Marquis and La Motte had long been known to each other, and that this unexpected meeting after an absence of many years, and under circumstances so altered and humiliating on the part of the latter, had occasioned him much painful emotion. This had been heightened by a consciousness that the Marquis had formerly misinterpreted some circumstances in his conduct towards him which had caused a suspension of their intimacy.

This account did not bring conviction to the mind of Adeline, for it seemed inadequate to the degree of emotion which the Marquis and La Motte had mutually betrayed. Her surprise was excited and her curiosity awakened by the words, which were meant to delude them both. But she forbore to express her thoughts.

Madame, proceeding with her plan, said the Marquis was now expected, and she hoped whatever differences remained would be perfectly adjusted. Adeline blushed, and endeavouring to reply, her lips faltered. Conscious of this agitation and of the observance of Madame La Motte, her confusion increased, and her endeavours to suppress served only to heighten it. Still she tried to renew the discourse, and still she found it impossible to collect her thoughts. Shocked lest Madame should apprehend the sentiment which had till this moment been concealed almost from herself, her colour fled, she fixed her eyes on the ground, and, for some time found it difficult to respire. Madame La Motte inquired if she was ill, when Adeline, glad of the excuse, withdrew to the indulgence of her own thoughts, which were now wholly engrossed by the expectation of seeing again the young chevalier who had accompanied the Marquis.

As she looked from her room, she saw the Marquis on horseback, with several attendants, advancing at a distance, and she hastened to apprize Madame La Motte of his approach. In a short time he arrived at the gates, and Madame and Louis went out to receive him, La Motte being not yet returned. He entered the hall, followed by the young chevalier, and accosting Madame with a sort of stately politeness, inquired for La Motte, whom Louis now went to seek.

The Marquis remained for a few minutes silent, and then asked of Madame La Motte how her fair daughter did? Madame understood it was Adeline he meant; and having answered his inquiry, and slightly said that she was not related to them, Adeline, upon some indication of the Marquis's wish, was sent for. She entered the room with a modest blush and a timid air, which seemed to engage all his attention. His compliments she received with a sweet grace, but when the young chevalier approached, the warmth of his manner rendered hers involuntarily more reserved, and she scarcely dared to raise her eyes from the ground lest they should encounter his.

La Motte now entered and apologized for his absence, which the Marquis noticed only by a slight inclination of his head, expressing at the same time by his looks both distrust and pride. They immediately quitted the abbey together, and the Marquis beckoned his attendants to follow at a distance. La Motte forbade his son to accompany him, but Louis observed he took the way into the thickest part of the forest. He was lost in a chaos of conjecture concerning this affair, but curiosity and anxiety for his father induced him to follow at some distance.

In the meantime the young stranger, whom the Marquis addressed by the name of Theodore, remained at the abbey with Madame La Motte and Adeline. The former, with all her address, could scarcely conceal her agitation during this interval. She moved involuntarily to the door whenever she heard a footstep, and several times she went to the hall door in order to look into the forest, but as often returned, checked by disappointment. No person appeared. Theodore seemed to address as much of his attention to Adeline as politeness would allow him to withdraw from Madame La Motte. His manners, so gentle, yet dignified, insensibly subdued her timidity and banished her reserve. Her conversation no longer suffered a painful constraint, but gradually disclosed the beauties of her mind, and seemed to produce a mutual confidence. A similarity of sentiment soon appeared, and Theodore, by the impatient pleasure which animated his countenance, seemed frequently to anticipate the thought of Adeline.

To them the absence of the Marquis was short, though long to Madame La Motte, whose countenance brightened when she heard the trampling of horses at the gate.

The Marquis appeared but for a moment and passed on with La Motte to a private room, where they remained for some time in conference, immediately after which he departed. Theodore took leave of Adeline, who, as well as La Motte and Madame, attended them to the gates, with an expression of tender regret, and often as he went, looked back upon the abbey, till the intervening branches entirely excluded it from his view.

The transient glow of pleasure diffused over the cheek of Adeline disappeared with the young stranger, and she sighed as she turned into the hall. The image of Theodore pursued her to her chamber; she recollected with exactness every particular of his late conversation—his sentiments so congenial with her own, his manners so engaging, his countenance so animated, so ingenuous and so noble, in which manly dignity was blended with the sweetness of benevolence—these and every other grace she recollected, and a soft melancholy stole upon her. "I shall see him no more," said she. A sigh that followed told her more of her heart than she wished to know. She blushed, and sighed again, and then suddenly recollecting herself, she endeavoured to divert her thoughts to a different subject. La Motte's connection with the Marquis for some time engaged her attention, but unable to develop the mystery that attended it, she sought a refuge from her own reflections in the more pleasing ones to be derived from books.

During this time, Louis, shocked and surprised at the extreme distress which his father had manifested upon the first appearance of the Marquis, addressed him upon the subject. He had no doubt that the Marquis was intimately concerned in the event which made it necessary for La Motte to leave Paris, and he spoke his thoughts without disguise, lamenting at the same time the unlucky chance which had brought him to seek refuge in a place of all others the least capable of affording it—the estate of his enemy. La Motte did not contradict this opinion of his son's, and joined in lamenting the evil fate which had conducted him thither.

The term of Louis's absence from his regiment was now nearly expired, and he took occasion to express his sorrow that he must soon be obliged to leave his father in circumstances so dangerous as the present. "I should leave you, sir, with less pain," continued he, "was I sure I knew the full extent of your misfortunes. At present I am left to conjecture evils which perhaps do not exist. Relieve me, sir, from this state of painful uncertainty, and suffer me to prove myself worthy of your confidence."

"I have already answered you on this subject," said La Motte, "and forbade you to renew it. I am now obliged to tell you I care not how soon you depart if I am to be subjected to these inquiries." La Motte walked abruptly away and left his son to doubt and concern.

The arrival of the Marquis had dissipated the jealous fears of Madame La Motte, and she awoke to a sense of her cruelty towards Adeline. When she considered her orphan state—the uniform affection which had appeared in her behaviour—the mildness and patience with which she had borne her injurious treatment, she was shocked, and took an early opportunity of renewing her former kindness. But she could not explain this seeming inconsistency of conduct without betraying her late suspicions, which she now blushed to remember, nor could she apologize for her former behaviour without giving this explanation.

She contented herself, therefore, with expressing in her manner the regard which was thus revived. Adeline was at first surprised, but she felt too much pleasure at the change to be scrupulous in inquiring its cause.

But notwithstanding the satisfaction which Adeline received from the revival of Madame La Motte's kindness, her thoughts frequently recurred to the peculiar and forlorn circumstances of her condition. She could not help feeling less confidence than she had formerly done in the friendship of Madame La Motte, whose character now appeared less amiable than her imagination had represented it, and seemed strongly tinctured with caprice. Her thoughts often dwelt upon the strange introduction of the Marquis at the abbey, and on the mutual emotions and apparent dislike of La Motte and himself; and, under these circumstances it equally excited her surprise that La Motte should choose, and that the Marquis should permit him, to remain in his territory.

Her mind returned the oftener, perhaps, to this subject, because it was connected with Theodore; but it returned unconscious of the idea which attracted it. She attributed the interest she felt in the affair to her anxiety for the welfare of La Motte, and for her own future destination, which was now so deeply involved in his. Sometimes, indeed, she caught herself busy in conjecture as to the degree of relationship in which Theodore stood to the Marquis; but she immediately checked her thoughts, and severely blamed herself for having suffered them to stray to an object which she perceived was too dangerous to her peace.

CHAPTER VII

A FEW days after the occurrence related in the preceding chapter, as Adeline was alone in her chamber she was roused from a reverie by a trampling of horses near the gate. On looking from the casement she saw the Marquis de Montalt enter the abbey. This circumstance surprised her, and an emotion whose cause she did not trouble herself to inquire for, made her instantly retreat from the window. The same cause, however, led her thither again as hastily, but the object of her search did not appear, and she was in no haste to retire.

As she stood musing and disappointed, the Marquis came out with La Motte, and immediately looking up, saw Adeline and bowed. She returned his compliment respectfully, and withdrew from the window, vexed at having been seen there. They went into the forest, but the Marquis's attendants did not as before follow them thither. When they returned, which was

not till after a considerable time, the Marquis immediately mounted his horse and rode away.

For the remainder of the day, La Motte appeared
gloomy and silent, and was frequently lost in thought.
Adeline observed him with particular attention and
concern; she perceived that he was always more melancholy after an interview with the Marquis, and was
now surprised to hear that the latter had appointed to
dine the next day at the abbey.

When La Motte mentioned this, he added some high
eulogiums on the character of the Marquis, and particularly praised his generosity and nobleness of soul.
At this instant Adeline recollected the anecdotes she
had formerly heard concerning the abbey, and they
threw a shadow over the brightness of that excellence
which La Motte now celebrated. The account, however,
did not appear to deserve much credit, a part of it,
as far as a negative will admit of demonstration, having
been already proved false; for it had been reported
that the abbey was haunted, and no supernatural
appearance had ever been observed by the present inhabitants.

Adeline, however, ventured to inquire whether it was
the present Marquis of whom those injurious reports
had been raised? La Motte answered her with a smile
of ridicule. "Stories of ghosts and hobgoblins have
always been admired and cherished by the vulgar,"
said he. "I am inclined to rely upon my own experience, at least as much as upon the accounts of these
peasants. If you have seen anything to corroborate
these accounts, pray inform me of it, that I may establish my faith."

"You mistake me, sir," said she; "it was not concerning supernatural agency that I would inquire: I
alluded to a different part of the report, which hinted

that some person had been confined here by order of
the Marquis, who was said to have died unfairly. This
was alleged as a reason for the Marquis's having abandoned the abbey."

"All the mere coinage of idleness," said La Motte;
"a romantic tale to excite wonder. To see the Marquis
is alone sufficient to refute this; and if we credit half
the number of those stories that spring from the same
source, we prove ourselves little superior to the sim-
pletons who invent them. Your good sense, Adeline,
I think will teach you the merit of disbelief."

Adeline blushed and was silent; but La Motte's defence of the Marquis appeared much warmer and more
diffuse than was consistent with his own disposition or
required by the occasion. His former conversation with
Louis occurred to her, and she was the more surprised
at what passed at present.

She looked forward to the morrow with a mixture
of pain and pleasure; the expectation of seeing again
the young chevalier occupying her thoughts, and agi-
tating them with a various emotion: now she feared his
presence, and now she doubted whether he would come.
At length she observed this, and blushed to find how
much he engaged her attention. The morrow arrived
—the Marquis came—but he came alone; and the sunshine of Adeline's mind was clouded, though she was
able to wear her usual air of cheerfulness. The Marquis was polite, affable, and attentive; to manners the
most easy and elegant was added the last refinement of
polished life. His conversation was lively, amusing,
sometimes even witty, and discovered great knowledge
of the world, or, what is often mistaken for it, an
acquaintance with the higher circles and with the topics
of the day.

Here La Motte was also qualified to converse with

him, and they entered into a discussion of the characters and manners of the age with great spirit and some humour. Madame La Motte had not seen her husband so cheerful since they left Paris, and sometimes she could almost fancy she was there. Adeline listened till the cheerfulness which she had at first only assumed became real. The address of the Marquis was so insinuating and affable that her reserve insensibly gave way before it and her natural vivacity resumed its long lost empire.

At parting, the Marquis told La Motte he rejoiced at having found so agreeable a neighbour. La Motte bowed. "I shall sometimes visit you," continued he, "and I lament that I cannot at present invite Madame La Motte and her fair friend to my château, but it is undergoing some repairs which make it but an uncomfortable residence."

The vivacity of La Motte disappeared with his guest, and he soon relapsed into fits of silence and abstraction. "The Marquis is a very agreeable man," said Madame La Motte. "Very agreeable," replied he. "And seems to have an excellent heart," she resumed. "An excellent one," said La Motte.

"You seem discomposed, my dear; what has disturbed you?"

"Not in the least—I was only thinking that with such agreeable talents and such an excellent heart, it was a pity the Marquis should ——"

"What? my dear," said Madame with impatience.

"That the Marquis should—should suffer this abbey to fall into ruins," replied La Motte.

"Is that all?" said Madame with disappointment.

"That is all, upon my honour," said La Motte, and left the room.

Adeline's spirits, no longer supported by the animated conversation of the Marquis, sunk into languor, and when he departed she walked pensively into the forest. She followed a little romantic path that wound along the margin of the stream and was overhung with deep shades. The tranquillity of the scene, which autumn now touched with her sweetest tints, softened her mind to a tender kind of melancholy, and she suffered a tear which, she knew not wherefore, had stolen into her eye, to tremble there unchecked. She came to a little lonely recess formed by high trees. The wind sighed mournfully among the branches, and as it waved their lofty heads, scattered their leaves to the ground. She seated herself on a bank beneath, and indulged the melancholy reflections that pressed on her mind.

"Oh! could I dive into futurity and behold the events which await me!" said she; "I should perhaps by constant contemplation be enabled to meet them with fortitude. An orphan in this wide world—thrown upon the friendship of strangers for comfort, and upon their bounty for the very means of existence, what but evil have I to expect! Alas, my father! how could you thus abandon your child—how leave her to the storms of life—to sink perhaps beneath them? Alas, I have no friend!"

She was interrupted by a rustling among the fallen leaves; she turned her head, and perceiving the Marquis's young friend, arose to depart. "Pardon this intrusion," said he; "your voice attracted me hither, and your words detained me. My offence, however, brings with it its own punishment; having learned your sorrows—how can I help feeling them myself? Would that my sympathy or my suffering could rescue you from them!"—He hesitated.—"Would that I could deserve the title of your friend, and be thought worthy of it by yourself!"

The confusion of Adeline's thoughts could scarcely permit her to reply; she trembled, and gently withdrew her hand, which he had taken while he spoke. "You have, perhaps, heard, sir, more than is true: I am, indeed, not happy, but a moment of dejection has made me unjust, and I am less unfortunate than I have represented. When I said I had no friend, I was ungrateful to the kindness of Monsieur and Madame La Motte, who have been more than friends—have been as parents to me."

"If so, I honour them," cried Theodore with warmth; "and if I did not feel it to be presumption, I would ask why you are unhappy?—But"—he paused. Adeline, raising her eyes, saw him gazing upon her with intense and eager anxiety, and her looks were again fixed upon the ground. "I have pained you," said Theodore, "by an improper request. Can you forgive me, and also when I add that it was an interest in your welfare which urged my inquiry?"

"Forgiveness, sir, it is unnecessary to ask. I am certainly obliged by the compassion you express. But the evening is cold. If you please, we will walk towards the abbey." As they moved on, Theodore was for some time silent. At length, "It was but lately that I solicited your pardon," said he, "and I shall now, perhaps, have need of it again; but you will do me the justice to believe, that I have a strong and, indeed, a pressing reason to inquire how nearly you are related to Monsieur La Motte."

"We are not at all related," said Adeline; "but the service he has done me I can never repay, and I hope my gratitude will teach me never to forget it."

"Indeed!" said Theodore, surprised; "and may I ask how long you have known him?"

"Rather, sir, let me ask why these questions should be necessary."

"You are just," said he, with an air of self-condemnation; "my conduct has deserved this reproof; I should have been more explicit." He looked as if his mind was labouring with something which he was unwilling to express. "But you know not how delicately I am circumstanced," continued he, "yet I will aver that my questions are prompted by the tenderest interest in your happiness—and even by my fears for your safety." Adeline started. "I fear you are deceived," said he, "I fear there's danger near you."

Adeline stopped, and looking earnestly at him, begged he would explain himself. She suspected that some mischief threatened La Motte; and Theodore continuing silent, she repeated her request. "If La Motte is concerned in this danger," said she, "let me entreat you to acquaint him with it immediately. He has but too many misfortunes to apprehend."

"Excellent Adeline!" cried Theodore, "that heart must be adamant that would injure you. How shall I hint what I fear is too true, and how forbear to warn you of your danger without"—He was interrupted by a step among the trees, and presently after saw La Motte cross into the path they were in. Adeline felt confused at being thus seen with the chevalier, and was hastening to join La Motte, but Theodore detained her and entreated a moment's attention. "There is now no time to explain myself," said he; "yet what I would say is of the utmost consequence to *yourself.*"

"Promise, therefore, to meet me in some part of the forest at about this time to-morrow evening. You will then, I hope, be convinced that my conduct is directed neither by common circumstances nor common regard." Adeline shuddered at the idea of making an appointment; she hesitated, and at length entreated Theodore not to delay till to-morrow an explanation which appeared to be so important, but to follow La Motte and inform him of his danger immediately. "It is not with La Motte I would speak," replied Theodore; "I know of no danger that threatens him—but he approaches. Be quick, lovely Adeline, and promise to meet me."

"I do promise," said Adeline, with a faltering voice; "I will come to the spot where you found me this evening, an hour earlier to-morrow. Saying this, she withdrew her trembling hand, which Theodore had pressed to his lips in token of acknowledgement, and he immediately disappeared.

La Motte now approached Adeline, who, fearing that he had seen Theodore, was in some confusion. "Whither is Louis gone so fast?" said La Motte. She rejoiced to find his mistake, and suffered him to remain in it. They walked pensively towards the abbey, where Adeline, too much occupied by her own thoughts to bear company, retired to her chamber. She ruminated upon the words of Theodore, and the more she considered them, the more she was perplexed. Sometimes she blamed herself for having made an appointment, doubting whether he had not solicited it for the purpose of pleading a passion; and now delicacy checked this thought and made her vexed that she had presumed upon having inspired one. She recollected the serious earnestness of his voice and manner when he entreated her to meet him; and as they convinced her of the importance of the subject, she shuddered at a danger which she could not comprehend, looking forward to the morrow with anxious impatience.

Sometimes, too, a remembrance of the tender interest he had expressed for her welfare, and of his correspondent look and air, would steal across her memory, awakening a pleasing emotion and a latent hope that she was not indifferent to him. From reflections like these she was roused by a summons to supper. The repast was a melancholy one, it being the last evening of Louis's stay at the abbey. Adeline, who esteemed him, regretted his departure, while his eyes were often bent on her with a look which seemed to express that he was about to leave the object of his affection. She endeavoured by her cheerfulness to reanimate the whole party, and especially Madame La Motte, who frequently shed tears. "We shall soon meet again," said Adeline, "I trust, in happier circumstances." La Motte sighed. The countenance of Louis brightened at her words, "Do you wish it?" said he, with peculiar emphasis. "Most certainly I do," she replied. "Can you doubt my regard for my best friends?"

"I cannot doubt any thing that is good of you," said he.

"You forget you have left Paris," said La Motte to his son, while a faint smile crossed his face; "such a compliment would there be in character with the place —in these solitary woods it is quite *outré*."

"The language of admiration is not always that of compliment, sir," said Louis. Adeline, willing to change the discourse, asked to what part of France he was going. He replied that his regiment was now at Peronne, and he should go immediately thither. After some mention of indifferent subjects, the family withdrew for the night to their several chambers.

The approaching departure of her son occupied the thoughts of Madame La Motte, and she appeared at breakfast with eyes swollen with weeping. The pale countenance of Louis seemed to indicate that he had rested no better than his mother. When breakfast was over, Adeline retired for a while, that she might not interrupt by her presence their last conversation. As she walked on the lawn before the abbey she returned in thought to the occurrence of yesterday evening, and her impatience for the appointed interview increased. She was soon joined by Louis. "It was unkind of you to leave us," said he, "in the last moments of my stay. Could I hope that you would sometimes remember me when I am far away, I should depart with less sorrow." He then expressed his concern at leaving her, and though he had hitherto armed himself with a resolution to forbear a direct avowal of an attachment which must be fruitless, his heart now yielded to the force of passion, and he told what Adeline every moment feared to hear.

"This declaration," said Adeline, endeavouring to overcome the agitation it excited, "gives me inexpressible concern."

"O, say not so!" interrupted Louis, "but give me some slender hope to support me in the miseries of absence. Say that you do not hate me—Say ——"

"That I do most readily say," replied Adeline, in a tremulous voice; "if it will give you pleasure to be assured of my esteem and friendship—receive this assurance; as the son of my best benefactors, you are entitled to ——"

"Name not benefits," said Louis; "your merits outrun them all. And suffer me to hope for a sentiment less cool than that of friendship, as well as to believe that I do not owe your approbation of me to the actions of others. I have long borne my passion in silence because I foresaw the difficulties that would attend it; nay, I have even dared to endeavour to overcome it. I have dared to believe it possible, forgive the supposition, that I could forget you—and ——"

"You distress me," interrupted Adeline; "this is a

conversation which I ought not to hear. I am above
disguise, and therefore assure you that though your
virtues will always command my esteem, you have nothing to hope from my love. Were it even otherwise,
our circumstances would effectually decide for us. If
you are really my friend, you will rejoice that I am
spared this struggle between affection and prudence.
Let me hope also that time will teach you to reduce
love within the limits of friendship."

"Never," cried Louis vehemently. "Were this possible, my passion would be unworthy of its object."
While he spoke, Adeline's favourite fawn came bounding towards her. This circumstance affected Louis even
to tears. "This little animal," said he, after a short
pause, "first conducted me to you. It was witness to
that happy moment when I first saw you, surrounded
by attractions too powerful for my heart; that moment
is now fresh in my memory, and the creature comes
even to witness this sad one of my departure." Grief
interrupted his utterance.

When he recovered his voice, he said, "Adeline!
when you look upon your little favourite and caress it,
remember the unhappy Louis, who will then be far—
far from you. Do not deny me the poor consolation of
believing this!"

"I shall not require such a monitor to remind me of
you," said Adeline with a smile; "your excellent parents
and your own merits have sufficient claim upon my remembrance. Could I see your natural good sense resume its influence over passion, my satisfaction would
equal my esteem for you."

"Do not hope it," said Louis, "nor will I wish it—for
passion here is virtue." As he spoke he saw La Motte
turn round an angle of the abbey. "The moments are

precious," said he, "I am interrupted. O! Adeline, farewell! and say that you will sometimes think of me."

"Farewell," said Adeline, who was affected by his distress—"farewell! and peace attend you. I will think of you with the affection of a sister."—He sighed deeply and pressed her hands; when La Motte, winding round another projection of the ruin, again appeared. Adeline left them together and withdrew to her chamber, oppressed by the scene. Louis's passion and her esteem were too sincere not to inspire her with a strong degree of pity for his unhappy attachment. She remained in her chamber till he had quitted the abbey, unwilling to subject him or herself to the pain of a formal parting.

As evening and the hour of appointment drew nigh, Adeline's impatience increased; yet when the time arrived, her resolution failed, and she faltered from her purpose. There was something of indelicacy and dissimulation in an *appointed* interview on her part that shocked her. She recollected the tenderness of Theodore's manner, and several little circumstances which seemed to indicate that his heart was not unconcerned in the event. Again she was inclined to doubt whether he had not obtained her consent to this meeting upon some groundless suspicion, and she almost determined not to go. Yet it was possible Theodore's assertion might be sincere and her danger real. The chance of this made her delicate scruples appear ridiculous; she wondered that she had for a moment suffered them to weigh against so serious an interest, and, blaming herself for the delay they had occasioned, hastened to the place of appointment.

The little path which led to this spot was silent and solitary, and when she reached the recess Theodore had not arrived. A transient pride made her unwilling he should find that she was more punctual to his appointment than himself, and she turned from the recess into a track which wound among the trees to the right. Having walked some way without seeing any person or hearing a footstep, she returned; but he was not come, and she again left the place. A second time she came back, and Theodore was still absent. Recollecting the time at which she had quitted the abbey, she grew uneasy, and calculated that the hour appointed was now much exceeded. She was offended and perplexed, but she seated herself on the turf and was resolved to wait the event. After remaining here till the fall of twilight in fruitless expectation, her pride became more alarmed. She feared that he had discovered something of the partiality he had inspired, and believing that he now treated her with purposed neglect, she quitted the place with disgust and self-accusation.

When these emotions subsided and reason resumed its influence, she blushed for what she termed this childish effervescence of self-love. She recollected as if for the first time these words of Theodore: "I fear you are deceived, and that some danger is near you." Her judgment now acquitted the offender, and she saw only the friend. The import of these words, whose truth she no longer doubted, again alarmed her. Why did he trouble himself to come from the château on purpose to hint her danger, if he did not wish to preserve her? And if he wished to preserve her, what but necessity could have withheld him from the appointment?

These reflections decided her at once. She resolved to repair on the following day at the same hour to the recess, whither the interest which she believed him to take in her fate would no doubt conduct him in the hope of meeting her. That some evil hovered over her she could not disbelieve, but what it might be she was unable to guess. Monsieur and Madame La Motte were her friends, and who else, removed as she now thought herself beyond the reach of her father, could injure her? But why did Theodore say she was deceived? She found it impossible to extricate herself from the labyrinth of conjecture, but endeavoured to command her anxiety till the following evening. In the mean time she engaged herself in efforts to amuse Madame La Motte, who required some relief after the departure of her son.

Thus oppressed by her own cares and interested by those of Madame La Motte, Adeline retired to rest. She soon lost her recollection, but it was only to fall into harassed slumbers, such as but too often haunt the couch of the unhappy. At length her perturbed fancy suggested the following dream.

She thought she was in a large old chamber belonging to the abbey, more ancient and desolate, though in part furnished, than any she had yet seen. It was strongly barricadoed, yet no person appeared. While she stood musing and surveying the apartment, she heard a low voice call her, and looking towards the place whence it came, she perceived by the dim light of a lamp a figure stretched on a bed that lay on the floor. The voice called again, and approaching the bed, she distinctly saw the features of a man who appeared to be dying. A ghastly paleness overspread his countenance, yet there was an expression of mildness and dignity in it which strongly interested her.

While she looked on him, his features changed and seemed convulsed in the agonies of death. The spectacle shocked her and she started back, but he suddenly stretched forth his hand, and seizing hers, grasped it with violence. She struggled in terror to disengage herself, and again looking on his face, saw a man who appeared to be about thirty, with the same features, but in full health and of a most benign countenance. He smiled tenderly upon her and moved his lips as if to speak, when the floor of the chamber suddenly opened and he sunk from her view. The effort she made to save herself from following awoke her.— This dream had so strongly impressed her fancy that it was some time before she could overcome the terror it occasioned, or even be perfectly convinced she was in her own apartment. At length, however, she composed herself to sleep; again she fell into a dream.

She thought she was bewildered in some winding passages of the abbey, that it was almost dark and that she wandered about a considerable time without being able to find a door. Suddenly she heard a bell toll from above, and soon after a confusion of distant voices. She redoubled her efforts to extricate herself. Presently all was still, and at length, wearied with the search, she sat down on a step that crossed the passage. She had not been long here when she saw a light glimmer at a distance on the walls, but a turn in the passage, which was very long, prevented her seeing from what it proceeded. It continued to glimmer faintly for some time and then grew stronger, when she saw a man enter the passage habited in a long black cloak, like those usually worn by attendants at funerals, and bearing a torch. He called to her to follow him, and led her through a long passage to the foot of a staircase. Here she feared to proceed, and was running back, when the man suddenly turned to pursue her, and with the terror which this occasioned she awoke.

Shocked by these visions, and more so by their seeming connection, which now struck her, she endeavoured to continue awake, lest their terrific images should again haunt her mind. After some time, however, her harassed spirits again sunk into slumber, though not to repose.

She now thought herself in a large old gallery, and saw at one end of it a chamber door standing a little open, and a light within. She went towards it, and perceived the man she had before seen, standing at the door and beckoning her towards him. With the inconsistency so common in dreams, she no longer endeavoured to avoid him, but advancing, followed him into a suite of very ancient apartments hung with black and lighted up as if for a funeral. Still he led her on, till she found herself in the same chamber she remembered to have seen in her former dream. A coffin covered with a pall stood at the farther end of the room; some lights and several persons surrounded it, who appeared to be in great distress.

Suddenly she thought these persons were all gone, and that she was left alone; that she went up to the coffin, and while she gazed upon it, she heard a voice speak as if from within, but saw nobody. The man she had before seen soon after stood by the coffin, and lifting the pall, she saw beneath it a dead person, whom she thought to be the dying chevalier she had seen in her former dream. His features were sunk in death, but they were yet serene. While she looked at him, a stream of blood gushed from his side, and descending to the floor, the whole chamber was overflowed; at the same time some words were uttered in the voice she heard before; but the horror of the scene so entirely overcame her that she started and awoke.

When she had recovered her recollection, she raised herself in the bed, to be convinced it was a dream she had witnessed, and the agitation of her spirits was so great that she feared to be alone, and almost determined to call Annette. The features of the deceased person, and the chamber where he lay, were strongly impressed upon her memory, and she still thought she heard the voice and saw the countenance which her dream represented. The longer she considered these dreams, the more she was surprised; they were so very terrible, returned so often, and seemed to be so connected with each other, that she could scarcely think them accidental; yet why they should be supernatural she could not tell. She slept no more that night.

CHAPTER VIII

WHEN Adeline appeared at breakfast, her harassed and languid countenance struck Madame La Motte, who inquired if she was ill. Adeline, forcing a smile upon her features, said she had not rested well, for that she had had very disturbed dreams. She was about to describe them, but a strong and involuntary impulse prevented her. At the same time La Motte ridiculed her concern so unmercifully that she was almost ashamed to have mentioned it, and tried to overcome the remembrance of its cause.

After breakfast she endeavoured to employ her thoughts by conversing with Madame La Motte; but they were really engaged by the incidents of the last two days, the circumstance of her dreams, and her conjectures concerning the information to be communicated to her by Theodore. They had thus sat for some time when a sound of voices arose from the great gate of the abbey, and on going to the casement, Adeline saw the Marquis and his attendants on the lawn below. The portal of the abbey concealed several people from her view, and among these it was possible might be

Theodore, who had not yet appeared. She continued to look for him with great anxiety, till the Marquis entered the hall with La Motte and some other persons, soon after which Madame went to receive him, and Adeline retired to her own apartment.

A message from La Motte, however, soon called her to join the party, where she vainly hoped to find Theodore. The Marquis arose as she approached, and having paid her some general compliments, the conversation took a very lively turn. Adeline, finding it impossible to counterfeit cheerfulness while her heart was sinking with anxiety and disappointment, took little part in it: Theodore was not once named. She would have asked concerning him, had it been possible to inquire with propriety, but she was obliged to content herself with hoping, first, that he would arrive before dinner, and then before the departure of the Marquis.

Thus the day passed in expectation and disappointment. The evening was now approaching, and she was condemned to remain in the presence of the Marquis, apparently listening to a conversation which in truth she scarcely heard, while the opportunity was perhaps escaping that would decide her fate. She was suddenly relieved from this state of torture, and thrown into one if possible still more distressing.

The Marquis inquired for Louis, and being informed of his departure, mentioned that Theodore Peyrou had that morning set out for his regiment in a distant province. He lamented the loss he should sustain by his absence, and expressed some very flattering praise of his talents. The shock of this intelligence overpowered the long-agitated spirits of Adeline; the blood forsook her cheeks and a sudden faintness came over her, from which she recovered only to a consciousness of having discovered her emotion, and the danger of relapsing into a second fit.

She retired to her chamber, where, being once more alone, her oppressed heart found relief from tears, in which she freely indulged. Ideas crowded so fast upon her mind that it was long ere she could arrange them so as to produce anything like reasoning. She endeavoured to account for the abrupt departure of Theodore. "Is it possible," said she, "that he should take an interest in my welfare and yet leave me exposed to the full force of a danger which he himself foresaw? Or am I to believe that he has trifled with my simplicity for an idle frolic, and has now left me to the wondering apprehension he has raised? Impossible! a countenance so noble and a manner so amiable could never disguise a heart capable of forming so despicable a design. No!—whatever is reserved for me, let me not relinquish the pleasure of believing that he is worthy of my esteem."

She was awakened from thoughts like these by a peal of distant thunder, and now perceived that the gloominess of evening was deepened by the coming storm; it rolled onward, and soon after the lightning began to flash along the chamber. Adeline was superior to the affectation of fear, and was not apt to be terrified; but she now felt it unpleasant to be alone, and hoping that the Marquis might have left the abbey, she went down to the sitting-room. But the threatening aspect of the heavens had hitherto detained him, and now the evening tempest made him rejoice that he had not quitted a shelter. The storm continued, and night came on. La Motte pressed his guest to take a bed at the abbey, and he at length consented, a circumstance which threw Madame La Motte into some perplexity as to the accommodation to be afforded him. After some time she arranged the affair to her satisfaction, resigning her own apartment to the Marquis, and that of Louis to two of his superior attendants; Adeline, it was farther settled, should give up her room to Monsieur and Madame La Motte, and remove to an inner chamber, where a small bed, usually occupied by Annette, was placed for her.

At supper, the Marquis was less gay than usual; he frequently addressed Adeline, and his look and manner seemed to express the tender interest, which her indisposition, for she still appeared pale and languid, had excited. Adeline, as usual, made an effort to forget her anxiety and appear happy; but the veil of assumed cheerfulness was too thin to conceal the features of sorrow, and her feeble smiles only added a peculiar softness to her air. The Marquis conversed with her on a variety of subjects, and displayed an elegant mind. The observations of Adeline, which when called upon she gave with reluctant modesty, in words at once simple and forceful, seemed to excite his admiration, which he sometimes betrayed by an inadvertent expression.

Adeline retired early to her room, which adjoined on one side to Madame La Motte's, and on the other to the closet formerly mentioned. It was spacious and lofty, and what little furniture it contained was falling to decay; but perhaps the present tone of her spirits might contribute more than these circumstances to give that air of melancholy which seemed to reign in it. She was unwilling to go to bed, lest the dreams that had lately pursued her should return, and determined to sit up till she found herself oppressed by sleep, when it was probable her rest would be profound. She placed the light on a small table, and taking a book, continued to read for above an hour, till her mind refused any longer to abstract itself from its own cares, and she sat for some time leaning pensively on her arm.

The wind was high, and as it whistled through the desolate apartment and shook the feeble doors, she often started, and sometimes even thought she heard sighs between the pauses of the gust; but she checked these illusions, which the hour of the night and her own melancholy imagination conspired to raise. As she sat musing, her eyes fixed on the opposite wall, she perceived the arras with which the room was hung wave backwards and forwards; she continued to observe it for some minutes, and then rose to examine it farther. It was moved by the wind and she blushed at the momentary fear it had excited; but she observed that the tapestry was more strongly agitated in one particular place than elsewhere, and a noise that seemed something more than that of the wind issued thence. The old bedstead which La Motte had found in this apartment had been removed to accommodate Adeline, and it was behind the place where this had stood that the wind seemed to rush with particular force. Curiosity prompted her to examine still farther; she felt about the tapestry, and perceiving the wall behind shake under her hand, she lifted the arras and discovered a small door, whose loosened hinges admitted the wind and occasioned the noise she had heard.

The door was held only by a bolt, having undrawn which and brought the light, she descended by a few steps into another chamber. She instantly remembered her dreams. The chamber was not much like that in which she had seen the dying chevalier, and afterwards the bier; but it gave her a confused remembrance of one through which she had passed. Holding up the light to examine it more fully, she was convinced by its structure that it was part of the ancient foundation. A shattered casement, placed high from the floor, seemed to be the only opening to admit light. She observed a door on the opposite side of the apartment, and after some moments of hesitation gained courage and determined to pursue the inquiry. "A mystery seems to hang over these chambers," said she, "which it is perhaps my lot to develop; I will at least see to what that door leads."

She stepped forward, and having unclosed it, proceeded with faltering steps along a suite of apartments resembling the first in style and condition, and terminating in one exactly like that where her dream had represented the dying person. The remembrance struck so forcibly upon her imagination that she was in danger of fainting, and looking round the room, almost expected to see the phantom of her dream.

Unable to quit the place, she sat down on some old lumber to recover herself, while her spirits were nearly overcome by a superstitious dread such as she had never felt before. She wondered to what part of the abbey these chambers belonged, and that they had so long escaped detection. The casements were all too high to afford any information from without. When she was sufficiently composed to consider the direction of the rooms and the situation of the abbey, there appeared not a doubt that they formed an interior part of the original building.

As these reflections passed over her mind, a sudden gleam of moonlight fell upon some object without the casement. Being now sufficiently composed to wish to pursue the inquiry, and believing this object might afford her some means of learning the situation of these rooms, she combated her remaining terrors, and in order to distinguish it more clearly, removed the light to an outer chamber; but before she could return, a heavy cloud was driven over the face of the moon, and all without was perfectly dark. She stood for some moments waiting a returning gleam, but the obscurity continued. As she went softly back for the light, her foot stumbled over something on the floor, and while she stooped to examine it the moon again shone, so that she could distinguish through the casement the eastern towers of the abbey. This discovery confirmed her former conjectures concerning the interior situation of these apartments. The obscurity of the place prevented her discovering what it was that had impeded her steps, but having brought the light forward, she perceived on the floor an old dagger. With a trembling hand she took it up, and upon a closer view perceived that it was spotted and stained with rust.

Shocked and surprised, she looked round the room for some object that might confirm or destroy the dreadful suspicion which now rushed upon her mind, but she saw only a great chair with broken arms that stood in one corner of the room, and a table in a condition equally shattered, except that in another part lay a confused heap of things, which appeared to be old lumber. She went up to it and perceived a broken bedstead with some decayed remnants of furniture, covered with dust and cobwebs, and which seemed, indeed, as if they had not been moved for many years. Desirous, however, of examining farther, she attempted to raise what appeared to have been part of the bedstead, but it slipped from her hand and, rolling to the floor, brought with it some of the remaining lumber. Adeline started aside and saved herself, and when the noise it made had ceased, she heard a small rustling sound, and as she was about to leave the chamber saw something falling gently among the lumber.

It was a small roll of paper tied with a string and

covered with dust. Adeline took it up, and on opening it perceived an hand-writing. She attempted to read it, but the part of the manuscript she looked at was so much obliterated that she found this difficult, though what few words were legible impressed her with curiosity and terror, and induced her to return with it immediately to her chamber.

Having reached her own room, she fastened the private door and let the arras fall over it as before. It was now midnight. The stillness of the hour, interrupted only at intervals by the hollow sighings of the blast, heightened the solemnity of Adeline's feelings. She wished she was not alone, and before she proceeded to look into the manuscript, listened whether Madame La Motte was yet in her chamber. Not the least sound was heard, and she gently opened the door. The profound silence within almost convinced her that no person was there, but willing to be farther satisfied, she brought the light and found the room empty. The lateness of the hour made her wonder that Madame La Motte was not in her chamber, and she proceeded to the top of the tower stairs to hearken if any person was stirring.

She heard the sound of voices from below, and, amongst the rest that of La Motte speaking in his usual tone. Being now satisfied that all was well, she turned towards her room, when she heard the Marquis pronounce her name with very unusual emphasis. She paused. "I adore her," pursued he, "and by heaven"— He was interrupted by La Motte: "My lord, remember your promise."

"I do," replied the Marquis, "and I will abide by it. But we trifle. To-morrow I will declare myself, and I shall then know both what to hope and how to act." Adeline trembled so excessively that she could scarcely support herself. She wished to return to her chamber;

yet she was too much interested in the words she had heard not to be anxious to have them more fully explained. There was an interval of silence, after which they conversed in a lower tone. Adeline remembered the hints of Theodore, and determined if possible to be relieved from the terrible suspense she now suffered. She stole softly down a few steps that she might catch the accents of the speakers, but they were so low that she could only now and then distinguish a few words. "Her father, say you?" said the Marquis. "Yes, my lord, her father. I am well informed of what I say." Adeline shuddered at the mention of her father; a new terror seized her, and with increasing eagerness she endeavoured to distinguish their words, but for some time found this to be impossible. "Here is no time to be lost," said the Marquis; "to-morrow then."—She heard La Motte rise, and believing it was to leave the room, she hurried up the steps, and having reached her chamber, sunk almost lifeless in a chair.

It was her father only of whom she thought. She doubted not that he had pursued and discovered her retreat, and though this conduct appeared very inconsistent with his former behaviour in abandoning her to strangers, her fears suggested that it would terminate in some new cruelty. She did not hesitate to pronounce this the danger of which Theodore had warned her, but it was impossible to surmise how he had gained his knowledge of it, or how he had become sufficiently acquainted with her story, except through La Motte, her apparent friend and protector, whom she was thus, though unwillingly, led to suspect of treachery. Why, indeed, should La Motte conceal from her only his knowledge of her father's intention, unless he designed to deliver her into his hands? Yet it was long ere she could bring herself to believe this conclusion possible.

To discover depravity in those whom we have loved is one of the most exquisite tortures to a virtuous mind, and the conviction is often rejected before it is finally admitted.

The words of Theodore, which told her he was fearful she was deceived, confirmed this most painful apprehension of La Motte, with another yet more distressing, that Madame La Motte was also united against her. This thought for a moment subdued terror and left her only grief; she wept bitterly. "Is this human nature?" cried she. "Am I doomed to find everybody deceitful?" An unexpected discovery of vice in those whom we have admired inclines us to extend our censure of the individual to the species; we henceforth contemn appearances and too hastily conclude that no person is to be trusted.

Adeline determined to throw herself at the feet of La Motte on the following morning, and implore his pity and protection. Her mind was now too much agitated by her own interests to permit her to examine the manuscripts, and she sat musing in her chair till she heard the steps of Madame La Motte when she retired to bed. La Motte soon after came up to his chamber, and Adeline, the mild, persecuted Adeline, who had now passed two days of torturing anxiety and one night of terrific visions, endeavoured to compose her mind to sleep. In the present state of her spirits, she quickly caught alarm, and she had scarcely fallen into a slumber when she was roused by a loud and uncommon noise. She listened, and thought the sound came from the apartments below, but in a few minutes there was a hasty knocking at the door of La Motte's chamber.

La Motte, who had just fallen asleep, was not easily to be roused, but the knocking increased with such violence that Adeline, extremely terrified, arose and went to the door that opened from her chamber into his, with a design to call him. She was stopped by the voice of the Marquis, which she now clearly distinguished at the door. He called to La Motte to rise immediately, and Madame La Motte endeavoured at the same time to rouse her husband, who, at length, awoke in much alarm, and soon after joining the Marquis, they went down stairs together. Adeline now dressed herself as well as her trembling hands would permit, and went into the adjoining chamber, where she found Madame La Motte extremely surprised and terrified.

The Marquis in the mean time told La Motte with great agitation that he recollected having appointed some persons to meet him upon business of importance early in the morning, and it was therefore necessary for him to set off for his château immediately. As he said this, and desired that his servants might be called, La Motte could not help observing the ashy paleness of his countenance, or expressing some apprehension that his lordship was ill. The Marquis assured him he was perfectly well, but desired that he might set out immediately. Peter was now ordered to call the other servants, and the Marquis, having refused to take any refreshment, bade La Motte a hasty adieu, and as soon as his people were ready left the abbey.

La Motte returned to his chamber musing on the abrupt departure of his guest, whose emotion appeared much too strong to proceed from the cause assigned. He appeased the anxiety of Madame La Motte, and at the same time excited her surprise by acquainting her with the occasion of the late disturbance. Adeline, who had retired from the chamber on the approach of La Motte, looked out from her window on hearing the trampling of horses. It was the Marquis and his people, who just then passed at a little distance. Unable to distinguish who the persons were, she was alarmed at observing such a party about the abbey at that hour, and calling to inform La Motte of the circumstance, was made acquainted with what had passed.

At length she retired to her bed, and her slumbers were this night undisturbed by dreams.

When she arose in the morning, she observed La Motte walking alone in the avenue below, and she hastened to seize the opportunity which now offered of pleading her cause. She approached him with faltering steps, while the paleness and timidity of her countenance discovered the disorder of her mind. Her first words, without entering upon any explanation, implored his compassion. La Motte stopped, and looking earnestly in her face, inquired whether any part of his conduct towards her merited the suspicion which her request implied. Adeline for a moment blushed that she had doubted his integrity, but the words she had overheard returned to her memory.

"Your behaviour, sir," said she, "I acknowledge to have been kind and generous beyond what I had a right to expect, but"—and she paused. She knew not how to mention what she blushed to believe. La Motte continued to gaze on her in silent expectation, and at length desired her to proceed and explain her meaning. She entreated that he would protect her from her father. La Motte looked surprised and confused. "Your father!" said he. "Yes, sir," replied Adeline; "I am not ignorant that he has discovered my retreat. I have everything to dread from a parent who has treated me with such cruelty as you was witness of; and I again implore that you will save me from his hands."

La Motte stood fixed in thought, and Adeline continued her endeavours to interest his pity. "What reason have you to suppose, or, rather, how have you learned, that your father pursues you?" The question confused Adeline, who blushed to acknowledge that she had overheard his discourse, and disdained to invent or utter a falsity. At length she confessed the truth. The countenance of La Motte instantly changed to a savage fierceness, and sharply rebuking her for a conduct to which she had been rather tempted by chance than prompted by design, he inquired what she had overheard that could so much alarm her. She faithfully repeated the substance of the incoherent sentences that had met her ear. While she spoke he regarded her with a fixed attention. "And was this all you heard? Is it from these few words that you draw such a positive conclusion? Examine them, and you will find they do not justify it."

She now perceived, what the fervor of her fears had not permitted her to observe before, that the words, unconnectedly as she heard them, imported little, and that her imagination had filled up the void in the sentences so as to suggest the evil apprehended. Notwithstanding this, her fears were little abated. "Your apprehensions are doubtless now removed," resumed La Motte; "but to give you a proof of the sincerity which you have ventured to question, I will tell you they were just. You seem alarmed, and with reason. Your father has discovered your residence, and has already demanded you. It is true that from a motive of compassion I have refused to resign you, but I have neither authority to withhold nor means to defend you. When he comes to enforce his demand you will perceive this. Prepare yourself, therefore, for the evil which you see is inevitable."

Adeline for some time could speak only by her tears.

At length, with a fortitude which despair had roused, she said, "I resign myself to the will of heaven!" La Motte gazed on her in silence, and a strong emotion appeared in his countenance. He forbore, however, to renew the discourse, and withdrew to the abbey, leaving Adeline in the avenue absorbed in grief.

A summons to breakfast hastened her to the parlour, where she passed the morning in conversation with Madame La Motte, to whom she told all her apprehensions and expressed all her sorrow. Pity and superficial consolation was all that Madame La Motte could offer, though apparently much affected by Adeline's discourse. Thus the hours passed heavily away, while the anxiety of Adeline continued to increase and the moment of her fate seemed fast approaching. Dinner was scarcely over when Adeline was surprised to see the Marquis arrive. He entered the room with his usual ease, and apologizing for the disturbance he had occasioned on the preceding night, repeated what he had before told La Motte.

The remembrance of the conversation she had overheard at first gave Adeline some confusion, and withdrew her mind from a sense of the evils to be apprehended from her father. The Marquis, who was as usual attentive to Adeline, seemed affected by her apparent indisposition, and expressed much concern for that dejection of spirits which, notwithstanding every effort, her manner betrayed. When Madame La Motte withdrew, Adeline would have followed her, but the Marquis entreated a few moments' attention and led her back to her seat. La Motte immediately disappeared.

Adeline knew too well what would be the purport of the Marquis's discourse, and his words soon increased the confusion which her fears had occasioned. While he was declaring the ardour of his passion in such terms

as but too often make vehemence pass for sincerity,
Adeline, to whom this declaration, if honourable, was
distressing, and if dishonourable, was shocking, interrupted him and thanked him for the offer of a distinction, which, with a modest but determined air she said
she must refuse. She rose to withdraw. "Stay, too
lovely Adeline!" said he, "and if compassion for my
sufferings will not interest you in my favour, allow a
consideration of your own dangers to do so. Monsieur
La Motte has informed me of your misfortunes, and
of the evil that now threatens you; accept from me the
protection which he cannot afford."

Adeline continued to move towards the door, when
the Marquis threw himself at her feet, and seizing her
hand, impressed it with kisses. She struggled to disengage herself. "Hear me, charming Adeline! hear
me," cried the Marquis; "I exist but for you. Listen
to my entreaties and my fortune shall be yours. Do
not drive me to despair by ill-judged rigour, or because ———"

"My lord," interrupted Adeline, with an air of ineffable dignity, and still affecting to believe his proposal
honourable, "I am sensible of the generosity of your
conduct, and also flattered by the distinction you offer
me. I will therefore say something more than is necessary to a bare expression of the denial which I must
continue to give. *I can not* bestow my heart. *You can
not* obtain more than my esteem, to which, indeed, nothing can so much contribute as a forbearance from any
similar offers in future."

She again attempted to go, but the Marquis prevented
her, and after some hesitation again urged his suit,
though in terms that would no longer allow her to mis-
understand him. Tears swelled into her eyes, but she
endeavoured to check them, and with a look in which

grief and indignation seemed to struggle for preeminence she said, "My lord, this is unworthy of reply; let me pass."

For a moment, he was awed by the dignity of her manner, and he threw himself at her feet to implore forgiveness. But she waved her hand in silence and hurried from the room. When she reached her chamber, she locked the door, and sinking into a chair, yielded to the sorrow that pressed at her heart. And it was not the least of her sorrow to suspect that La Motte was unworthy of her confidence; for it was almost impossible that he could be ignorant of the real designs of the Marquis. Madame La Motte, she believed, was imposed upon by a specious pretence of honourable attachment; and thus was she spared the pang which a doubt of her integrity would have added.

She threw a trembling glance upon the prospect around her. On one side was her father, whose cruelty had already been but too plainly manifested, and on the other the Marquis pursuing her with insult and vicious passion. She resolved to acquaint Madame La Motte with the purport of the late conversation, and in the hope of her protection and sympathy she wiped away her tears, and was leaving the room just as Madame La Motte entered it. While Adeline related what had passed, her friend wept, and appeared to suffer great agitation. She endeavoured to comfort her and promised to use her influence in persuading La Motte to prohibit the addresses of the Marquis. "You know, my dear," added Madame, "that our present circumstances oblige us to preserve terms with the Marquis, and you will therefore suffer as little resentment to appear in your manner towards him as possible; conduct yourself with your usual ease in his presence and

I doubt not this affair will pass over without subjecting you to farther solicitation."

"Ah, madam!" said Adeline, "how hard is the task you assign me! I entreat you that I may never more be subjected to the humiliation of being in his presence, that whenever he visits the abbey I may be suffered to remain in my chamber."

"This," said Madame La Motte, "I would most readily consent to, would our situation permit it. But you well know our asylum in this abbey depends upon the good will of the Marquis, which we must not wantonly lose; and surely such a conduct as you propose would endanger this. Let us use milder measures, and we shall preserve his friendship without subjecting you to any serious evil. Appear with your usual complaisance; the task is not so difficult as you imagine."

Adeline sighed. "I obey you, madam," said she; "it is my duty to do so; but I may be pardoned for saying —it is with extreme reluctance." Madame La Motte promised to go immediately to her husband, and Adeline departed, though not convinced of her safety, yet somewhat more at ease.

She soon after saw the Marquis depart, and, as there now appeared to be no obstacle to the return of Madame La Motte, she expected her with extreme impatience. After thus waiting near an hour in her chamber, she was at length summoned to the parlour, and there found Monsieur La Motte alone. He arose upon her entrance, and for some minutes paced the room in silence. He then seated himself and addressed her: "What you have mentioned to Madame La Motte," said he, "would give me much concern, did I consider the behaviour of the Marquis in a light so serious as she does. I know that young ladies are apt to misconstrue the unmeaning gallantry of fashionable manners, and you, Adeline, can never be too cautious in distinguishing between a levity of this kind and a more serious address."

Adeline was surprised and offended that La Motte should think so lightly both of her understanding and disposition as his speech implied. "Is it possible, sir," said she, "that you have been apprized of the Marquis's conduct?"

"It is very possible, and very certain," replied La Motte with some asperity, "and very possible also that I may see this affair with a judgment less discoloured by prejudice than you do. But, however, I shall not dispute this point. I shall only request that since you are acquainted with the emergency of my circumstances, you will conform to them, and not by an ill timed resentment expose me to the enmity of the Marquis. He is now my friend, and it is necessary to my safety that he should continue such; but if I suffer any part of my family to treat him with rudeness, I must expect to see him my enemy. You may surely treat him with complaisance." Adeline thought the term *rudeness* a harsh one, as La Motte applied it, but she forbore from any expression of displeasure. "I could have wished, sir," said she, "for the privilege of retiring whenever the Marquis appeared, but since you believe this conduct would affect your interest, I ought to submit."

"This prudence and good will delights me," said La Motte, "and since you wish to serve me, know that you cannot more effectually do it than by treating the Marquis as a friend." The word *friend*, as it stood connected with the Marquis, sounded dissonantly to Adeline's ear; she hesitated and looked at La Motte. "As *your* friend, sir," said she, "I will endeavour to." "Treat him as mine," she would have said, but she found it impossible to finish the sentence. She entreated his protection from the power of her father.

"What protection I can afford is yours," said La Motte, "but you know how destitute I am both of the right and the means of resisting him, and also how much I require protection myself. Since he has discovered your retreat, he is probably not ignorant of the circumstances which detain me here, and if I oppose him, he may betray me to the officers of the law as the surest method of obtaining possession of you. We are encompassed with dangers," continued La Motte; "would I could see any method of extricating ourselves!"

"Quit this abbey," said Adeline, "and seek an asylum in Switzerland or Germany; you will then be freed from farther obligation to the Marquis and from the persecution you dread. Pardon me for thus offering advice which is certainly in some degree prompted by a sense of my own safety, but which at the same time seems to afford the only means of insuring yours."

"Your plan is reasonable," said La Motte, "had I money to execute it. As it is, I must be contented to remain here as little known as possible, and defend myself by making those who know me my friends. Chiefly I must endeavour to preserve the favour of the Marquis. He may do much, should your father even pursue desperate measures. But why do I talk thus? Your father may ere this have commenced these measures, and the effects of his vengeance may now be hanging over my head. My regard for you, Adeline, has exposed me to this; had I resigned you to his will, I should have remained secure."

Adeline was so much affected by this instance of La Motte's kindness, which she could not doubt, that she was unable to express her sense of it. When she could speak, she uttered her gratitude in the most lively terms. "Are you sincere in these expressions?" said La Motte. "Is it possible I can be less than sincere?" replied Adeline, weeping at the idea of ingratitude.—"Sentiments are easily pronounced," said La Motte, "though they may have no connection with the heart; I believe them to be sincere so far only as they influence our actions."

"What mean you, sir?" said Adeline with surprise.

"I mean to inquire whether if an opportunity should ever offer of thus proving your gratitude, you would adhere to your sentiments."

"Name one that I shall refuse," said Adeline with energy.

"If, for instance, the Marquis should hereafter avow a serious passion for you, and offer you his hand, would no petty resentment, no lurking prepossession for some more happy lover prompt you to refuse it?"

Adeline blushed and fixed her eyes on the ground. "You have, indeed, sir, named the only means I should reject of evincing my sincerity. The Marquis I can never love, nor, to speak sincerely, ever esteem. I confess the peace of one's whole life is too much to sacrifice even to gratitude."—La Motte looked displeased. "'Tis as I thought," said he; "these delicate sentiments make a fine appearance in speech, and render the person who utters them infinitely amiable; but bring them to the test of action and they dissolve into air, leaving only the wreck of vanity behind."

This unjust sarcasm brought tears to her eyes. "Since your safety, sir, depends upon my conduct," said she, "resign me to my father. I am willing to return to him, since my stay here must involve you in new misfortune. Let me not prove myself unworthy of the protection I have hitherto experienced by preferring my own welfare to yours. When I am gone, you will have no reason to apprehend the Marquis's displeasure, which you may probably incur if I stay here: for I feel it impossible that I could even consent to receive his addresses, however honourable were his views."

La Motte seemed hurt and alarmed. "This must not be," said he; "let us not harass ourselves by stating *possible* evils, and then, to avoid them, fly to those which are *certain*. No, Adeline, though you are ready to sacrifice yourself to my safety, I will not suffer you to do so. I will not yield you to your father but upon compulsion. Be satisfied therefore upon this point. The only return I ask is a civil deportment towards the Marquis."

"I will endeavour to obey you, sir," said Adeline.— Madame La Motte now entered the room and this conversation ceased. Adeline passed the evening in melancholy thoughts, and retired as soon as possible to her chamber, eager to seek in sleep a refuge from sorrow.

CHAPTER IX

The MS. found by Adeline the preceding night had several times occurred to her recollection in the course of the day, but she had then been either too much interested by the events of the moment, or too apprehensive of interruption, to attempt a perusal of it. She now took it from the drawer in which it had been deposited, and intending only to look cursorily over the few first pages, sat down with it by her bedside.

She opened it with an eagerness of inquiry which the discoloured and almost obliterated ink but slowly gratified. The first words on the page were entirely lost, but those that appeared to commence the narrative were as follows.

"O! ye, whoever ye are, whom chance or misfortune may hereafter conduct to this spot—to you I speak—to you reveal the story of my wrongs, and ask you to avenge them. Vain hope! yet it imparts some comfort to believe it possible that what I now write may one day meet the eye of a fellow-creature, that the words which tell my sufferings may one day draw pity from the feeling heart.

"Yet stay your tears—your pity now is useless. Long since have the pangs of misery ceased; the voice of complaining is passed away. It is weakness to wish for compassion which cannot be felt till I shall sink in the repose of death, and taste, I hope, the happiness of eternity!

"Know, then, that on the night of the twelfth of October, in the year 1642, I was arrested on the road to Caux, and on the very spot where a column is erected to the memory of the immortal Henry, by four ruffians who, after disabling my servant, bore me through wilds and woods to this abbey. Their demeanour was not that of common banditti, and I soon perceived they were employed by a superior power to perpetrate some dreadful purpose. Entreaties and bribes were vainly offered them to discover their employer and abandon their design. They would not reveal even the least circumstance of their intentions.

"But when after a long journey they arrived at this edifice, their base employer was at once revealed, and his horrid scheme but too well understood. What a moment was that! All the thunders of heaven seemed launched at this defenceless head! O! fortitude! nerve my heart to ——"

Adeline's light was now expiring in the socket, and the paleness of the ink, so feebly shone upon, baffled her efforts to discriminate the letters. It was impossible to procure a light from below without discovering that she was yet up; a circumstance which would excite surprise and lead to explanations such as she did not wish to enter upon. Thus compelled to suspend the inquiry which so many attendant circumstances had rendered awfully interesting, she retired to her humble bed.

What she had read of the MS. awakened a dreadful interest in the fate of the writer, and called up terrific images to her mind. "In these apartments!"—said she, and she shuddered and closed her eyes. At length she heard Madame La Motte enter her chamber, and the phantoms of fear beginning to dissipate, left her to repose.

In the morning she was awakened by Madame La Motte, and found to her disappointment that she had slept so much beyond her usual time as to be unable to renew the perusal of the MS.—La Motte appeared uncommonly gloomy, and Madame wore an air of melancholy which Adeline attributed to the concern she felt for her. Breakfast was scarcely over when the sound of horses' feet announced the arrival of a stranger, and Adeline, from the oriel recess of the hall, saw the Marquis alight. She retreated with precipitation, and forgetting the request of La Motte, was hastening to her chamber; but the Marquis was already in the hall, and seeing her leaving it, turned to La Motte with a look of inquiry. La Motte called her back, and by a frown too intelligent, reminded her of her promise. She summoned all her spirits to her aid, but advanced, notwithstanding, in visible emotion, while the Marquis addressed her as usual, the same easy gaiety playing upon his countenance and directing his manner.

Adeline was surprised and shocked at this careless confidence, which, however, by awakening her pride, communicated to her an air of dignity that abashed him. He spoke with hesitation, and frequently appeared abstracted from the subject of discourse. At length arising, he begged Adeline would favour him with a few moments' conversation. Monsieur and Madame La Motte were now leaving the room, when Adeline, turning to the Marquis, told him she would not hear any conversation except in the presence of her friends. But she said it in vain, for they were gone; and La Motte, as he withdrew, expressed by his looks how much an attempt to follow would displease him.

She sat for some time in silence and trembling expectation. "I am sensible," said the Marquis at length, "that the conduct to which the ardour of my passion lately betrayed me has injured me in your opinion, and that you will not easily restore me to your esteem, but I trust the offer which I now make you, both of my *title* and fortune, will sufficiently prove the sincerity of my attachment and atone for the transgression which love only prompted."

After this specimen of commonplace verbosity, which the Marquis seemed to consider as a prelude to triumph, he attempted to impress a kiss upon the hand of Adeline, who withdrawing it hastily, said, "You are already, my lord, acquainted with my sentiments upon this subject, and it is almost unnecessary for me now to repeat that I cannot accept the honour you offer me."

"Explain yourself, lovely Adeline! I am ignorant that till now I ever made you this offer."

"Most true, sir," said Adeline, "and you do well to remind me of this, since after having heard your former proposal, I can listen for a moment to any other." She rose to quit the room. "Stay, madam," said the Marquis, with a look in which offended pride struggled to conceal itself; "do not suffer an extravagant resentment to operate against your true interests; recollect the dangers that surround you, and consider the value of an offer which may afford you at least an honourable asylum."

"My misfortunes, my lord, whatever they are, I have never obtruded upon you; you will therefore excuse my observing that your present mention of them conveys a much greater appearance of insult than compassion." The Marquis, though with evident confusion, was going to reply, but Adeline would not be detained, and retired to her chamber. Destitute as she was, her heart revolted from the proposal of the Marquis, and she determined never to accept it. To her dislike of his general disposition and the aversion excited by his late offer, was added, indeed, the influence of a prior attachment, and of a remembrance which she found it impossible to erase from her heart.

The Marquis staid to dine, and in consideration of La Motte, Adeline appeared at table, where the former gazed upon her with such frequent and silent earnestness that her distress became insupportable, and when the cloth was drawn she instantly retired. Madame La Motte soon followed, and it was not till evening that she had an opportunity of returning to the MS. When Monsieur and Madame La Motte were in their chamber and all was still, she drew forth the narrative, and trimming her lamp, sat down to read as follows.

"The ruffians unbound me from my horse and led me through the hall up the spiral staircase of the abbey. Resistance was useless, but I looked around in the hope of seeing some person less obdurate than the men who brought me hither, some one who might be sensible to pity and capable at least of civil treatment. I looked in vain; no person appeared, and this circumstance confirmed my worst apprehensions. The secrecy of the business foretold a horrible conclusion. Having passed some chambers, they stopped in one hung with old tapestry. I inquired why we did not go on, and was told I should soon know.

"At that moment I expected to see the instrument of death uplifted, and silently recommended myself to God. But death was not then designed for me; they raised the arras and discovered a door, which they then opened. Seizing my arms, they led me through a suite of dismal chambers beyond. Having reached the farthest of these, they again stopped. The horrid gloom of the place seemed congenial to murder, and inspired deadly thoughts. Again I looked round for the instrument of destruction, and again I was respited. I supplicated to know what was designed me. It was now unnecessary to ask who was the author of the design. They were silent to my question, but at length told me this chamber was my prison. Having said this and set down a jug of water, they left the room, and I heard the door barred upon me.

"O sound of despair! O moment of unutterable anguish! The pang of death itself is surely not superior to that I then suffered. Shut out from day, from friends, from life—*for such I must foretell it*—in the prime of my years, in the height of my transgressions, and left to imagine horrors more terrible than any, perhaps, which certainty could give—I sink beneath the ——"

Here several pages of the manuscript were decayed with damp and totally illegible. With much difficulty Adeline made out the following lines:

"Three days have now passed in solitude and silence: the horrors of death are ever before my eyes, let me endeavour to prepare for the dreadful change! When I awake in the morning I think I shall not live to see another night; and when night returns, that I must never more unclose my eyes on morning. Why am I brought hither—why confined thus rigorously—but for death! Yet what action of my life has deserved this at the hand of a fellow creature?—Of ——"

.   .   .   .

"O my children! O friends far distant! I shall never see you more—never more receive the parting look of kindness—never bestow a parting blessing! Ye know not my wretched state—alas! ye cannot know it by human means. Ye believe me happy, or ye would fly to my relief. I know that what I now write cannot avail me, yet there is comfort in pouring forth my griefs; and I bless that man, less savage than his fellows, who has supplied me these means of recording them. Alas! he knows full well that from this indulgence he has nothing to fear. My pen can call no friends to succour me, nor reveal my danger ere it is too late. O! ye who may hereafter read what I now write, give a tear to my sufferings; I have wept often for the distresses of my fellow creatures!"

Adeline paused. Here the wretched writer appealed directly to her heart; he spoke in the energy of truth, and by a strong illusion of fancy it seemed as if his past sufferings were at this moment present. She was for some time unable to proceed, and sat in musing sorrow. "In these very apartments," said she, "this poor sufferer was confined—here he"—Adeline started, and thought she heard a sound, but the stillness of the night was undisturbed.—"In these very chambers," said she, "these lines were written—these lines, from which he then derived a comfort in believing they would hereafter be read by some pitying eye. This time is now come. Your miseries, O injured being! are lamented, where they were endured. *Here,* where you suffered, I weep for your sufferings!"

Her imagination was now strongly impressed, and to her distempered senses the suggestions of a bewildered mind appeared with the force of reality. Again she started and listened, and thought she heard *Here* distinctly repeated by a whisper immediately behind her. The terror of the thought, however, was but momentary; she knew it could not be. Convinced that her fancy had deceived her, she took up the MS. and again began to read.

"For what am I reserved! Why this delay? If I am to die—why not quickly? Three weeks have I now passed within these walls, during which time no look of pity has softened my afflictions; no voice save my own has met my ear. The countenances of the ruffians who attend me are stern and inflexible, and their silence is obstinate. This stillness is dreadful! O! ye who have known what it is to live in the depths of solitude, who have passed your dreary days without one sound to cheer you, ye, and ye only, can tell what now I feel; and ye may know how much I would endure to hear the accents of a human voice.

"O dire extremity! O state of living death! What dreadful stillness! All around me is dead; and do I really exist, or am I but a statue? Is this a vision? Are these things real? Alas, I am bewildered!—this death-like and perpetual silence, this dismal chamber, the dread of farther sufferings, have disturbed my fancy. O for some friendly breast to lay my weary head on! some cordial accents to revive my soul!

.   .   .   .

"I write by stealth. He who furnished me with the means, I fear, has suffered for some symptoms of pity he may have discovered for me; I have not seen him for several days. Perhaps he is inclined to help me, and for that reason is forbid to come. O that hope! but how vain. Never more must I quit these walls while life remains. Another day is gone, and yet I live; at this time tomorrow night my sufferings may be sealed in death. I will continue my journal nightly, till the hand that writes shall be stopped by death. When the journal ceases, the reader will know I am no more. Perhaps these are the last lines I shall ever write."

.   .   .   .

Adeline paused, while her tears fell fast. "Unhappy man!" she exclaimed, "and was there no pitying soul to save thee! Great God! thy ways are wonderful!" While she sat musing, her fancy, which now wandered in the regions of terror, gradually subdued reason. There was a glass before her upon the table, and she feared to raise her looks towards it, lest some other face than her own should meet her eyes: other dreadful ideas and strange images of fantastic thought now crossed her mind.

A hollow sigh seemed to pass near her. "Holy Virgin, protect me!" cried she, and threw a fearful glance round the room; "this is surely something more than fancy." Her fears so far overcame her that she was several times upon the point of calling up part of the family, but unwillingness to disturb them, and a dread of ridicule, withheld her. She was also afraid to move and almost to breathe. As she listened to the wind that murmured at the casement of her lonely chamber, she again thought she heard a sigh. Her imagination refused any longer the control of reason, and turning her eyes, a figure whose exact form she could not distinguish appeared to pass along an obscure part of the chamber; a dreadful chillness came over her, and she sat fixed in her chair. At length a deep sigh somewhat relieved her oppressed spirits, and her senses seemed to return.

All remaining quiet, after some time she began to question whether her fancy had not deceived her, and she so far conquered her terror as to desist from calling Madame La Motte. Her mind was, however, so much disturbed that she did not venture to trust herself that night again with the MS., but having spent some time in prayer and in endeavouring to compose her spirits, she retired to bed.

When she awoke in the morning, the cheerful sunbeams played upon the casements and dispelled the illusions of darkness. Her mind, soothed and invigorated by sleep, rejected the mystic and turbulent promptings of imagination. She arose refreshed and thankful, but upon going down to breakfast, this transient gleam of peace fled upon the appearance of the Marquis, whose frequent visits at the abbey, after what had passed, not only displeased but alarmed her. She saw that he was determined to persevere in addressing her, and the boldness and insensibility of this conduct, while it excited her indignation, increased her disgust. In pity to La Motte she endeavoured to conceal these emotions, though she now thought that he required too much from her complaisance, and began seriously to consider how she might avoid the necessity of continuing it. The Marquis behaved to her with the most respectful attention; but Adeline was silent and reserved, and seized the first opportunity of withdrawing.

As she passed up the spiral staircase, Peter entered the hall below, and seeing Adeline, he stopped and looked earnestly at her. She did not observe him, but he called her softly, and she then saw him make a signal as if he had something to communicate. In the next instant La Motte opened the door of the vaulted room, and Peter hastily disappeared. She proceeded to her chamber, ruminating upon this signal and the cautious manner in which Peter had given it.

But her thoughts soon returned to their wonted subjects. Three days were now passed, and she heard no intelligence of her father. She began to hope that he had relented from the violent measures hinted at by La Motte, and that he meant to pursue a milder plan; but when she considered his character, this appeared improbable, and she relapsed into her former fears. Her residence at the abbey was now become painful, from the perseverance of the Marquis and the conduct which La Motte obliged her to adopt; yet she could not think without dread of quitting it to return to her father.

The image of Theodore often intruded upon her busy thoughts, and brought with it a pang which his strange departure occasioned. She had a confused notion that his fate was somehow connected with her own; and her struggles to prevent the remembrance of him served only to shew how much her heart was his.

To divert her thoughts from these subjects, and gratify the curiosity so strongly excited on the preceding night, she now took up the MS., but was hindered from opening it by the entrance of Madame La Motte, who came to tell her the Marquis was gone. They passed their morning together in work and general conversation; La Motte not appearing till dinner, when he said little and Adeline less. She asked him, however, if he had heard from her father. "I have not heard from him," said La Motte; "but there is good reason, as I am informed by the Marquis, to believe he is not far off."

Adeline was shocked, yet she was able to reply with becoming firmness. "I have already, sir, involved you too much in my distress, and now see that resistance will destroy you without serving me; I am therefore contented to return to my father and thus spare you farther calamity."

"This is a rash determination," replied La Motte, "and if you pursue it, I fear you will severely repent. I speak to you as a friend, Adeline, and desire you will endeavour to listen to me without prejudice. The Marquis, I find, has offered you his hand. I know not which circumstance most excites my surprise, that a man of his rank and consequence should solicit a marriage with a person without fortune or ostensible connections, or that a person so circumstanced should even for a moment reject the advantages thus offered her. You weep, Adeline; let me hope that you are convinced of the absurdity of this conduct and will no longer trifle with your good fortune. The kindness I have shewn you must convince you of my regard, and that I have no motive for offering you this advice but your advantage. It is necessary, however, to say that, should your father not insist upon your removal, I know not how long my circumstances may enable me to afford even the humble pittance you receive here. Still you are silent."

The anguish which this speech excited suppressed her utterance, and she continued to weep. At length she said, "Suffer me, sir, to go back to my father; I should indeed make an ill return for the kindness you mention, could I wish to stay after what you now tell me; and to accept the Marquis, I feel to be impossible." The remembrance of Theodore arose to her mind, and she wept aloud.

La Motte sat for some time musing. "Strange infatuation," said he; "is it possible that you can persist in this heroism of romance, and prefer a father so inhuman as yours to the Marquis de Montalt, a destiny so full of danger to a life of splendour and delight!"

"Pardon me," said Adeline, "a marriage with the Marquis would be splendid, but never happy. His character excites my aversion, and I entreat, sir, that he may no more be mentioned."

CHAPTER X

THE conversation related in the last chapter was interrupted by the entrance of Peter, who as he left the room looked significantly at Adeline, and almost beckoned. She was anxious to know what he meant, and soon after went into the hall, where she found him loitering. The moment he saw her, he made a sign of silence, and beckoned her into the recess. "Well, Peter, what is it you would say?" said Adeline.

"Hush, ma'mselle; for heaven's sake speak lower: if we should be overheard, we are all blown up.—"Adeline begged him to explain what he meant. "Yes, ma'mselle, that is what I have wanted all day long. I have watched and watched for an opportunity, and looked and looked, till I was afraid my master himself would see me; but all would not do: you would not understand."

Adeline entreated he would be quick. "Yes, ma'am, but I'm so afraid we shall be seen; but I would do much to serve such a good young lady, for I could not bear to think of what threatened you without telling you of it."

"For God's sake," said Adeline, "speak quickly, or we shall be interrupted."

"Well, then; but you must first promise by the Holy Virgin never to say it was I that told you. My master would ——"

"I do, I do!" said Adeline.

"Well, then—on Monday evening as I—hark! did not I hear a step? Do, ma'mselle, just step this way to the cloisters. I would not for the world we should be seen. I'll go out at the hall door and you can go through the passage. I would not for the world we should be seen."—Adeline was much alarmed by Peter's words, and hurried to the cloisters. He quickly appeared, and looking cautiously round, resumed his discourse. "As I was saying, ma'mselle, Monday night when the Marquis slept here, you know he sat up very late, and I can guess, perhaps, the reason of that. Strange things came out, but it is not my business to tell all I think."

"Pray do speak to the purpose," said Adeline impatiently; "what is this danger which you say threatens me? Be quick, or we shall be observed."

"Danger enough, ma'mselle," replied Peter, "if you knew all, and when you do, what will it signify, for you can't help yourself. But that's neither here nor there; I was resolved to tell you, though I may repent it."

"Or rather you are resolved not to tell me," said Adeline; "for you have made no progress towards it.

But what do you mean? You was speaking of the Marquis."

"Hush, ma'am, not so loud. The Marquis, as I said, sat up very late and my master sat up with him. One of his men went to bed in the oak room, and the other staid to undress his lord. So as we were sitting together —Lord have mercy! it made my hair stand on end! I tremble yet. So as we were sitting together,—but as sure as I live yonder is my master; I caught a glimpse of him between the trees. If he sees me, it is all over with us. I'll tell you another time." So saying, he hurried into the abbey, leaving Adeline in a state of alarm, curiosity, and vexation. She walked out in the forest, ruminating upon Peter's words and endeavouring to guess to what they alluded; there Madame La Motte joined her, and they conversed on various topics till they reached the abbey.

Adeline watched in vain through that day for an opportunity of speaking with Peter. While he waited at supper, she occasionally observed his countenance with great anxiety, hoping it might afford her some degree of intelligence on the subject of her fears. When she retired, Madame La Motte accompanied her to her chamber and continued to converse with her for a considerable time, so that she had no means of obtaining an interview with Peter.—Madame La Motte appeared to labour under some great affliction, and when Adeline, noticing this, entreated to know the cause of her dejection, tears started into her eyes and she abruptly left the room.

This behaviour of Madame La Motte concurred with Peter's discourse to alarm Adeline, who sat pensively upon her bed, given up to reflection, till she was roused by the sound of a clock which stood in the room below, and which now struck twelve. She was preparing for rest, when she recollected the MS. and was unable to conclude the night without reading it. The first words she could distinguish were the following.

"Again I return to this poor consolation—again I have been permitted to see another day. It is now midnight! My solitary lamp burns beside me; the time is awful, but to me the silence of noon is as the silence of midnight: a deeper gloom is all in which they differ. The still, unvarying hours are numbered only by my sufferings! Great God! when shall I be released!

.   .   .   .

"But whence this strange confinement? I have nèver injured him. If death is designed me, why this delay; and for what but death am I brought hither? This abbey—alas!"—Here the MS. was again illegible, and for several pages Adeline could only make out disjointed sentences.

"O bitter draught! When, when shall I have rest! O my friends! will none of ye fly to aid me; will none of ye avenge my sufferings? Ah! when it is too late— when I am gone for ever, ye will endeavour to avenge them. .   .   .   .

"Once more is night returned to me. Another day has passed in solitude and misery. I have climbed to the casement, thinking the view of nature would refresh my soul, and somewhat enable me to support these afflictions. Alas! even this small comfort is denied me; the windows open towards other parts of this abbey, and admit only a portion of that day which I must never more fully behold. Last night! last night! O scene of horror!"

Adeline shuddered. She feared to read the coming

sentence, yet curiosity prompted her to proceed. Still she paused: an unaccountable dread came over her. "Some horrid deed has been done here," said she; "the reports of the peasants are true. Murder has been committed." The idea thrilled her with horror. She recollected the dagger which had impeded her steps in the secret chamber, and this circumstance served to confirm her most terrible conjectures. She wished to examine it, but it lay in one of these chambers, and she feared to go in quest of it.

"Wretched, wretched victim!" she exclaimed, "could no friend rescue thee from destruction! O that I had been near! yet what could I have done to save thee? Alas! nothing. I forget that even now, perhaps, I am like thee abandoned to dangers from which I have no friend to succour me. Too surely I guess the author of thy miseries!" She stopped, and thought she heard a sigh such as on the preceding night had passed along the chamber. Her blood was chilled, and she sat motionless. The lonely situation of her room, remote from the rest of the family, (for she was now in her old apartment, from which Madame La Motte had removed) who were almost beyond call, struck so forcibly upon her imagination that she with difficulty preserved herself from fainting. She sat for a considerable time, but all was still. When she was somewhat recovered, her first design was to alarm the family; but farther reflection again withheld her.

She endeavoured to compose her spirits, and addressed a short prayer to that Being who had hitherto protected her in every danger. While she was thus employed, her mind gradually became elevated and reassured; a sublime complacency filled her heart, and she sat down once more to pursue the narrative.

Several lines that immediately followed were obliterated.—

. . . .

"He had told me I should not be permitted to live long, not more than three days, and bade me choose whether I would die by poison or the sword. O the agonies of that moment! Great God! thou seest my sufferings! I often viewed, with a momentary hope of escaping, the high grated windows of my prison—all things within the compass of possibility I was resolved to try, and with an eager desperation I climbed towards the casements, but my foot slipped, and falling back to the floor, I was stunned by the blow. On recovering, the first sounds I heard were the steps of a person entering my prison. A recollection of the past returned, and deplorable was my condition. I shuddered at what was to come. The same man approached; he looked at me at first with pity, but his countenance soon recovered its natural ferocity. Yet he did not then come to execute the purposes of his employer. I am reserved to another day—Great God, thy will be done!"

Adeline could not go on. All the circumstances that seemed to corroborate the fate of this unhappy man crowded upon her mind:—the reports concerning the abbey, the dreams which had forerun her discovery of the private apartments, the singular manner in which she had found the MS., and the apparition, which she now believed she had really seen. She blamed herself for having not yet mentioned the discovery of the manuscript and chambers to La Motte, and resolved to delay the disclosure no longer than the following morning. The immediate cares that had occupied her mind, and a fear of losing the manuscript before she had read it, had hitherto kept her silent.

Such a combination of circumstances she believed could only be produced by some supernatural power operating for the retribution of the guilty. These reflections filled her mind with a degree of awe which the loneliness of the large old chamber in which she sat, and the hour of the night, soon heightened into terror. She had never been superstitious, but circumstances so uncommon had hitherto conspired in this affair that she could not believe them accidental. Her imagination, wrought upon by these reflections, again became sensible to every impression; she feared to look round lest she should again see some dreadful phantom, and she almost fancied she heard voices swell in the storm, which now shook the fabric.

Still she tried to command her feelings so as to avoid disturbing the family, but they became so painful that even the dread of La Motte's ridicule had hardly power to prevent her quitting the chamber. Her mind was now in such a state that she found it impossible to pursue the story in the MS., though, to avoid the tortures of suspense, she had attempted it. She laid it down again and tried to argue herself into composure. "What have I to fear?" said she; "I am at least innocent, and I shall not be punished for the crime of another."

The violent gust of wind that now rushed through the whole suite of apartments shook the door that led from her late bedchamber to the private rooms so forcibly that Adeline, unable to remain longer in doubt, ran to see from whence the noise issued. The arras which concealed the door was violently agitated, and she stood for a moment observing it in indescribable terror, till believing it was swayed by the wind, she made a sudden effort to overcome her feelings, and was stooping to raise it. At that instant she thought she

heard a voice. She stopped and listened, but every
thing was still; yet apprehension so far overcame her
that she had no power either to examine or to leave the
chambers.

In a few moments the voice returned. She was now
convinced she had not been deceived, for, though low,
she heard it distinctly, and was almost sure it repeated
her own name. So much was her fancy affected that
she even thought it was the same voice she had heard
in her dreams. This conviction entirely subdued the
small remains of her courage, and sinking into a chair,
she lost all recollection.

How long she remained in this state she knew not,
but when she recovered she exerted all her strength and
reached the winding staircase, where she called aloud.
No one heard her, and she hastened as fast as her
feebleness would permit to the chamber of Madame La
Motte. She tapped gently at the door and was answered by Madame, who was alarmed at being awakened at so unusual an hour, and believed that some
danger threatened her husband. When she understood
that it was Adeline, and that she was unwell, she
quickly came to her relief. The terror that was yet visible in Adeline's countenance excited her inquiries, and
the occasion of it was explained to her.

Madame was so much discomposed by the relation
that she called La Motte from his bed, who, more angry
at being disturbed than interested for the agitation he
witnessed, reproved Adeline for suffering her fancies
to overcome her reason. She now mentioned the discovery she had made of the inner chambers and the
manuscript, circumstances which roused the attention
of La Motte so much that he desired to see the MS.,
and resolved to go immediately to the apartments described by Adeline.

Madame La Motte endeavoured to dissuade him from his purpose; but La Motte, with whom opposition had always an effect contrary to the one designed, and who wished to throw farther ridicule upon the terrors of Adeline, persisted in his intention. He called to Peter to attend with a light, and insisted that Madame La Motte and Adeline should accompany him. Madame La Motte desired to be excused, and Adeline at first declared she could not go; but he would be obeyed.

They ascended the tower and entered the first chambers together, for each of the party was reluctant to be the last. In the second chamber all was quiet and in order. Adeline presented the MS. and pointed to the arras which concealed the door. La Motte lifted the arras, and opened the door, but Madame La Motte and Adeline entreated to go no farther. Again he called to them to follow. All was quiet in the first chamber; he expressed his surprise that the rooms should so long have remained undiscovered, and was proceeding to the second, but suddenly stopped. "We will defer our examination till to-morrow," said he; "the damps of these apartments are unwholesome at any time, but they strike one more sensibly at night. I am chilled. Peter, remember to throw open the windows early in the morning, that the air may circulate."

"Lord bless your honour," said Peter, "don't you see I can't reach them: besides, I don't believe they are made to open; see what strong iron bars there are; the room looks for all the world like a prison. I suppose this is the place the people meant when they said nobody that had been in ever came out." La Motte, who during this speech had been looking attentively at the high windows, which, if he had seen them at first, he had certainly not observed, now interrupted the eloquence of Peter and bade him carry the light before them. They all willingly quitted these chambers, and returned to the room below, where a fire was lighted and the party remained together for some time.

La Motte, for reasons best known to himself, attempted to ridicule the discovery and fears of Adeline till she, with a seriousness that checked him, entreated he would desist. He was silent, and soon after, Adeline, encouraged by the return of daylight, ventured to her chamber, and for some hours experienced the blessing of undisturbed repose.

On the following day Adeline's first care was to obtain an interview with Peter, whom she had some hopes of seeing as she went down stairs. He, however, did not appear, and she proceeded to the sitting-room, where she found La Motte apparently much disturbed. Adeline asked him if he had looked at the MS. "I have run my eye over it," said he, "but it is so much obscured by time that it can scarcely be deciphered. It appears to exhibit a strange romantic story; and I do not wonder that after you had suffered its terrors to impress your imagination, you fancied you saw spectres and heard wondrous noises."

Adeline thought La Motte did not choose to be convinced, and she therefore forbore reply. During breakfast she often looked at Peter (who waited) with anxious inquiry, and from his countenance was still more assured that he had something of importance to communicate. In the hope of some conversation with him, she left the room as soon as possible and repaired to her favourite avenue, where she had not long remained when he appeared. "God bless you! ma'mselle," said he, "I'm sorry I frighted you so last night."

"Frighted me," said Adeline; "how was you concerned in that?"

He then informed her that when he thought Monsieur and Madame La Motte were asleep, he had stolen to her chamber door with an intention of giving her the sequel of what he had begun in the morning; that he had called several times as loudly as he dared, but receiving no answer, he believed she was asleep or did not choose to speak with him, and he had therefore left the door. This account of the voice she had heard relieved Adeline's spirits; she was even surprised that she did not know it, till remembering the perturbation of her mind for some time preceding, this surprise disappeared.

She entreated Peter to be brief in explaining the danger with which she was threatened. "If you'll let me go on my own way, ma'am, you'll soon know it; but if you hurry me and ask me questions here and there, out of their places, I don't know what I am saying."

"Be it so," said Adeline; "only remember that we may be observed."

"Yes, ma'mselle, I'm as much afraid of that as you are, for I believe I should be almost as ill off; however, that is neither here nor there, but I'm sure if you stay in this old abbey another night, it will be worse for you; for as I said before, I know all about it."

"What mean you, Peter?"

"Why, about this scheme that's going on."

"What, then, is my father?"——"Your father," interrupted Peter; "Lord bless you, that is all fudge to frighten you; your father *nor nobody* else has ever sent after you. I dare say he knows no more of you than the pope does—not he." Adeline looked displeased. "You trifle," said she; "if you have anything to tell, say it quickly; I am in haste."

"Bless you, young lady, I meant no harm. I hope you're not angry; but I'm sure you can't deny that your

father is cruel. But, as I was saying, the Marquis de
Montalt likes you, and he and my master" (Peter looked
round) "have been laying their heads together about
you." Adeline turned pale—she comprehended a part
of the truth and eagerly entreated him to proceed.

"They have been laying their heads together about
you. This is what Jaques, the Marquis's man, tells
me. Says he, 'Peter, you little know what is going on—
I could tell all if I chose it, but it is not for those who
are trusted to tell again. I warrant now your master
is close enough with you.' Upon which I was piqued,
and resolved to make him believe I could be trusted as
well as he. 'Perhaps not,' says I, 'perhaps I know as
much as you, though I do not choose to brag on't;' and
I winked.—'Do you so?' says he, 'then you are closer
than I thought for. She is a fine girl,' says he, meaning
you, ma'mselle; 'but she is nothing but a poor found-
ling after all—so it does not much signify.' I had a
mind to know farther what he meant—so I did not
knock him down. By seeming to know as much as he,
I at last made him discover all, and he told me—but
you look pale, ma'mselle, are you ill?"

"No," said Adeline, in a tremulous accent, and
scarcely able to support herself; "pray proceed."

"And he told me that the Marquis had been courting
you a good while, but you would not listen to him, and
had even pretended he would marry you, and all would
not do. 'As for marriage,' says I, 'I suppose she knows
the Marchioness is alive; and I'm sure she is not one
for his turn upon other terms.'"

"The Marchioness is really living then!" said Adeline.

"O yes, ma'mselle! we all know that, and I thought
you had known it too.—'We shall see that,' replies
Jaques; 'at least, I believe that our master will outwit

her.'—I stared; I could not help it.—'Aye,' says he,
'you know your master has agreed to give her up to
my lord.'"

"Good God! what will become of me?" exclaimed
Adeline.

"Aye, ma'mselle, I am sorry for you; but hear me
out. When Jaques said this, I quite forgot myself.
'I'll never believe it,' said I, 'I'll never believe my
master would be guilty of such a base action: he'll not
give her up, or I'm no Christian.'—'Oh!' said Jaques,
'for that matter, I thought you'd known all, else I
should not have said a word about it. However, you
may soon satisfy yourself by going to the parlour door,
as I have done; they're in consultation about it now,
I dare say.'"

"You need not repeat any more of this conversation,"
said Adeline; "but tell me the result of what you heard
from the parlour."

"Why, ma'mselle, when he said this, I took him at
his word and went to the door, where, sure enough, I
heard my master and the Marquis talking about you.
They said a great deal, which I could make nothing of;
but, at last, I heard the Marquis say, 'You know the
terms; on these terms only will I consent to bury the
past in ob—ob—oblivion ——' that was the word. Monsieur La Motte then told the Marquis if he would return
to the abbey upon such a night, meaning this very
night, ma'mselle, everything should be prepared according to his wishes. 'Adeline shall then be yours,
my lord,' said he,—'you are already acquainted with
her chamber.'"

At these words Adeline clasped her hands and raised
her eyes to heaven in silent despair.—Peter went on.
"When I heard this, I could not doubt what Jaques had
said.—'Well,' said he, 'what do you think of it now?'

—'Why, that my master's a rascal,' says I.—'It's well you don't think mine one too,' says he.—'Why, as for that matter,' says I''—— Adeline, interrupting him, inquired if he had heard anything farther. "Just then," said Peter, "we heard Madame La Motte come out from another room, and so we made haste back to the kitchen."

"She was not present at this conversation then?" said Adeline. "No, ma'mselle, but my master has told her of it, I warrant." Adeline was almost as much shocked by this apparent perfidy of Madame La Motte as by a knowledge of the destruction that threatened her. After musing a few moments in extreme agitation, "Peter," said she, "you have a good heart, and feel a just indignation at your master's treachery—will you assist me to escape?"

"Ah, ma'mselle!" said he, "how can I assist you; besides, where can we go? I have no friends about here, no more than yourself."

"O!" replied Adeline in extreme emotion, "we fly from enemies; strangers may prove friends. Assist me but to escape from this forest, and you will claim my eternal gratitude. I have no fears beyond it."

"Why, as for this forest," replied Peter, "I am weary of it myself, though when we first came I thought it would be fine living here; at least I thought it was very different from any life I had ever lived before. But these ghosts that haunt the abbey—I am no more a coward than other men, but I don't like them. And then there *is* so many strange reports abroad; and my master—I thought I could have served him to the end of the world, but now I care not how soon I leave him, for his behaviour to you, ma'mselle."

"You consent, then, to assist me in escaping?" said Adeline with eagerness.

"Why as to that, ma'mselle, I would willingly if I knew where to go. To be sure, I have a sister lives in Savoy, but that is a great way off; and I have saved a little money out of my wages, but that won't carry us such a long journey."

"Regard not that," said Adeline; "if I was once beyond this forest, I would then endeavour to take care of myself, and repay you for your kindness."

"O! as for that, madam" ——

"Well, well, Peter, let us consider how we may escape. This night, say you, this night—the Marquis is to return?"

"Yes, ma'mselle, to-night, about dark. I have just thought of a scheme: my master's horses are grazing in the forest. We may take one of them and send it back from the first stage; but how shall we avoid being seen? Besides, if we go off in the day-light, he will soon pursue and overtake us; and if you stay till night, the Marquis will be come, and then there is no chance. If they miss us both at the same time, too, they'll guess how it is and set off directly. Could not you contrive to go first and wait for me till the hurly-burly's over? Then while they're searching in the place underground for you, I can slip away, and we should be out of their reach before they thought of pursuing us."

Adeline agreed to the truth of all this, and was somewhat surprised at Peter's sagacity. She inquired if he knew of any place in the neighbourhood of the abbey where she could remain concealed till he came with a horse. "Why yes, madam, there is a place, now I think of it, where you may be safe enough, for nobody goes near: but they say it's haunted, and perhaps you would not like to go there." Adeline, remembering the last night, was somewhat startled at this intelligence, but a sense of her present danger pressed again upon her mind and overcame every other apprehension. "Where is this place?" said she; "if it will conceal me, I shall not hesitate to go."

"It is an old tomb that stands in the thickest part of the forest about a quarter of a mile off the nearest way, and almost a mile the other. When my master used to hide himself so much in the forest, I have followed him somewhere thereabouts, but I did not find out the tomb till t'other day. However, that's neither here or there; if you dare venture to it, ma'mselle, I'll shew you the nearest way." So saying, he pointed to a winding path on the right. Adeline, having looked round without perceiving any person near, directed Peter to lead her to the tomb. They pursued the path, till turning into a gloomy, romantic part of the forest, almost impervious to the rays of the sun, they came to the spot whither Louis had formerly traced his father.

The stillness and solemnity of the scene struck awe upon the heart of Adeline, who paused and surveyed it for some time in silence. At length Peter led her into the interior part of the ruin, to which they descended by several steps. "Some old abbot," said he, "was formerly buried here, as the Marquis's people say; and it's like enough that he belonged to the abbey yonder. But I don't see why he should take it in his head to walk; *he* was not murdered, surely."

"I hope not," said Adeline.

"That's more than can be said for all that lies buried at the abbey though, and ——" Adeline interrupted him. "Hark! surely I hear a noise;" said she; "heaven protect us from discovery!" They listened, but all was still, and they went on. Peter opened a low door, and they entered upon a dark passage frequently obstructed by loose fragments of stone, and along which they moved with caution. "Whither are we going?"

said Adeline.—"I scarcely know myself," said Peter, "for I never was so far before; but the place seems quiet enough." Something obstructed his way. It was a door, which yielded to his hand and discovered a kind of cell, obscurely seen by the twilight admitted through a grate above. A partial gleam shot athwart the place, leaving the greatest part of it in shadow.

Adeline sighed as she surveyed it. "This is a frightful spot," said she, "but if it will afford me a shelter, it is a palace. Remember, Peter, that my peace and honour depend upon your faithfulness; be both discreet and resolute. In the dusk of the evening I can pass from the abbey with least danger of being observed, and in this cell I will wait your arrival. As soon as Monsieur and Madame La Motte are engaged in searching the vaults, you will bring here a horse. Three knocks upon the tomb shall inform me of your arrival. For heaven's sake be cautious, and be punctual."

"I will, ma'mselle, let come what may."

They reascended to the forest, and Adeline, fearful of observation, directed Peter to run first to the abbey and invent some excuse for his absence, if he had been missed. When she was again alone, she yielded to a flood of tears and indulged the excess of her distress. She saw herself without friends, without relations, destitute, forlorn, and abandoned to the worst of evils; betrayed by the very persons to whose comfort she had so long administered, whom she had loved as her protectors, and revered as her parents! These reflections touched her heart with the most afflicting sensations, and the sense of her immediate danger was for a while absorbed in the grief occasioned by a discovery of such guilt in others.

At length she roused all her fortitude, and turning towards the abbey, endeavoured to await with patience the hour of evening, and to sustain an appearance of composure in the presence of Monsieur and Madame La Motte. For the present she wished to avoid seeing either of them, doubting her ability to disguise her emotions. Having reached the abbey, she therefore passed on to her chamber. Here she endeavoured to direct her attention to indifferent subjects, but in vain; the danger of her situation and the severe disappointment she had received in the character of those whom she had so much esteemed, and even loved, pressed hard upon her thoughts. To a generous mind few circumstances are more afflicting than a discovery of perfidy in those whom we have trusted, even though it may fail of any absolute inconvenience to ourselves. The behaviour of Madame La Motte in thus, by concealment, conspiring to her destruction, particularly shocked her.

"How has my imagination deceived me!" said she; "What a picture did it draw of the goodness of the world! And must I then believe that everybody is cruel and deceitful? No—let me still be deceived and still suffer, rather than be condemned to a state of such wretched suspicion." She now endeavoured to extenuate the conduct of Madame La Motte by attributing it to a fear of her husband. "She dare not oppose his will," said she, "else she would warn me of my danger and assist me to escape from it. No—I will never believe her capable of conspiring my ruin. Terror alone keeps her silent."

Adeline was somewhat comforted by this thought. The benevolence of her heart taught her in this instance to sophisticate. She perceived not that by ascribing the conduct of Madame La Motte to terror, she only softened the degree of her guilt, imputing it to a motive less depraved but not less selfish. She remained in her chamber till summoned to dinner, when, drying her

tears, she descended with faltering steps and a palpitating heart to the parlour. When she saw La Motte,
in spite of all her efforts, she trembled and grew pale.
She could not behold even with apparent indifference the
man who she knew had destined her to destruction.
He observed her emotion, and inquiring if she was ill,
she saw the danger to which her agitation exposed her.
Fearful lest La Motte should suspect its true cause, she
rallied all her spirits, and with a look of complacency
answered she was well.

During dinner she preserved a degree of composure
that effectually concealed the varied anguish of her
heart. When she looked at La Motte, terror and indignation were her predominant feelings; but when she
regarded Madame La Motte, it was otherwise. Gratitude for her former tenderness had long been confirmed
into affection, and her heart now swelled with the bit-
terness of grief and disappointment. Madame La
Motte appeared depressed, and said little. La Motte
seemed anxious to prevent thought by assuming a fictitious and unnatural gaiety. He laughed and talked and
threw off frequent bumpers of wine; it was the mirth
of desperation. Madame became alarmed and would
have restrained him, but he persisted in his libations to
Bacchus till reflection seemed to be almost overcome.

Madame La Motte, fearful that in the carelessness of
the present moment he might betray himself, withdrew
with Adeline to another room. Adeline recollected the
happy hours she once passed with her, when confidence
banished reserve and sympathy and esteem dictated the
sentiments of friendship. Now those hours were gone
for ever; she could no longer unbosom her griefs to
Madame La Motte, no longer even esteem her. Yet
notwithstanding all the danger to which she was exposed by the criminal silence of the latter, she could not

converse with her, consciously for the last time, without feeling a degree of sorrow which wisdom may call weakness, but to which benevolence will allow a softer name.

Madame La Motte in her conversation appeared to labour under an almost equal oppression with Adeline. Her thoughts were abstracted from the subject of discourse, and there were long and frequent intervals of silence. Adeline more than once caught her gazing with a look of tenderness upon her, and saw her eyes fill with tears. By this circumstance she was so much affected that she was several times upon the point of throwing herself at her feet and imploring her pity and protection. Cooler reflection shewed her the extravagance and danger of this conduct. She suppressed her emotions, but they at length compelled her to withdraw from the presence of Madame La Motte.

CHAPTER X²*

ADELINE anxiously watched from her chamber window the sun set behind the distant hills, and the time of her departure draw nigh. It set with uncommon splendour and threw a fiery gleam athwart the woods and upon some scattered fragments of the ruins, which she could not gaze upon with indifference. "Never, probably, again shall I see the sun sink below those hills," said she, "or illumine this scene! Where shall I be when next it sets—where this time tomorrow? Sunk, perhaps, in misery!" She wept to the thought. "A few hours," resumed Adeline, "and the Marquis will arrive—a few hours, and this abbey will be a scene of confusion and tumult. Every eye will be in search of

* See the Editor's Note p. xxiv Ante.

me; every recess will be explored." These reflections
inspired her with new terror and increased her impatience to be gone.

Twilight gradually came on, and she now thought it
sufficiently dark to venture forth; but before she went,
she kneeled down and addressed herself to heaven. She
implored support and protection, and committed herself
to the care of the God of mercies. Having done this,
she quitted her chamber and passed with cautious steps
down the winding staircase. No person appeared, and
she proceeded through the door of the tower into the
forest. She looked around; the gloom of the evening
obscured every object.

With a trembling heart she sought the path pointed
out by Peter, which led to the tomb; having found it,
she passed along forlorn and terrified. Often did she
start as the breeze shook the light leaves of the trees,
or as the bat flitted by gamboling in the twilight, and
often as she looked back towards the abbey, thought
she distinguished amid the deepening gloom the figures
of men. Having proceeded some way, she suddenly
heard the feet of horses, and soon after a sound of
voices, among which she distinguished that of the Marquis. They seemed to come from the quarter she was
approaching, and evidently advanced. Terror for some
minutes arrested her steps; she stood in a state of
dreadful hesitation. To proceed was to run into the
hands of the Marquis; to return was to fall into the
power of La Motte.

After remaining for some time uncertain whither to
fly, the sounds suddenly took a different direction, and
wheeled towards the abbey. Adeline had a short cessation of terror. She now understood that the Marquis
had passed this spot only in his way to the abbey, and
she hastened to secrete herself in the ruin. At length

after much difficulty she reached it, the deep shades almost concealing it from her search. She paused at the entrance, awed by the solemnity that reigned within and the utter darkness of the place. At length she determined to watch without till Peter should arrive. "If any person approaches," said she, "I can hear them before they can see me, and I can then secrete myself in the cell."

She leaned against a fragment of the tomb in trembling expectation, and as she listened, no sound broke the silence of the hour. The state of her mind can only be imagined by considering that upon the present time turned the crisis of her fate. "They have now," thought she, "discovered my flight; even now they are seeking me in every part of the abbey. I hear their dreadful voices call me; I see their eager looks." The power of imagination almost overcame her. While she yet looked around, she saw lights moving at a distance; sometimes they glimmered between the trees and sometimes they totally disappeared.

They seemed to be in a direction with the abbey; and she now remembered that in the morning she had seen a part of the fabric through an opening in the forest. She had therefore no doubt that the lights she saw proceeded from people in search of her, who, she feared, not finding her at the abbey, might direct their steps towards the tomb. Her place of refuge now seemed too near her enemies to be safe, and she would have fled to a more distant part of the forest, but recollected that Peter would not know where to find her.

While these thoughts passed over her mind, she heard distant voices in the wind, and was hastening to conceal herself in the cell, when she observed the lights suddenly disappear. All was soon after hushed in silence and darkness; yet she endeavoured to find the way to the cell. She remembered the situation of the outward door and of the passage, and having passed these, she unclosed the door of the cell. Within it was utterly dark. She trembled violently, but entered; and, having felt about the walls, at length seated herself on a projection of stone.

She here again addressed herself to heaven, and endeavoured to reanimate her spirits till Peter should arrive. Above half an hour elapsed in this gloomy recess, and no sound foretold his approach. Her spirits sunk; she feared some part of their plan was discovered, or interrupted, and that he was detained by La Motte. This conviction operated sometimes so strongly upon her fears as to urge her to quit the cell alone, and seek in flight her only chance of escape.

While this design was fluctuating in her mind, she distinguished through the grate above a clattering of hoofs. The noise approached, and at length stopped at the tomb. In the succeeding moment she heard three strokes of a whip; her heart beat, and for some moments her agitation was such that she made no effort to quit the cell. The strokes were repeated: she now roused her spirits, and, stepping forward, ascended to the forest. She called Peter; for the deep gloom would not permit her to distinguish either man or horse. She was quickly answered: "Hush! ma'mselle, our voices will betray us."

They mounted and rode off as fast as the darkness would permit. Adeline's heart revived at every step they took. She inquired what had passed at the abbey, and how he had contrived to get away. "Speak softly, ma'mselle; you'll know all by and bye, but I can't tell you now." He had scarcely spoke ere they saw lights move along at a distance, and coming now to a more open part of the forest, he set off on a full gallop, and continued the pace till the horse could hold it no longer. They looked back, and no lights appearing, Adeline's terror subsided. She inquired again what had passed at the abbey when her flight was discovered. "You may speak without fear of being heard," said she; "we are gone beyond their reach I hope."

"Why, ma'mselle," said he, "you had not been gone long before the Marquis arrived, and Monsieur La Motte then found out you was fled. Upon this a great rout there was, and he talked a great deal with the Marquis."

"Speak louder," said Adeline; "I cannot hear you."

"I will, ma'mselle."—

"Oh! heavens!' interrupted Adeline, "what voice is this? It is not Peter's. For God's sake tell me who you are, and whither I am going?"

"You'll know that soon enough, young lady," answered the stranger, for it was indeed not Peter. "I am taking you where my master ordered." Adeline, not doubting he was the Marquis's servant, attempted to leap to the ground, but the man, dismounting, bound her to the horse. One feeble ray of hope at length beamed upon her mind: she endeavoured to soften the man to pity, and pleaded with all the genuine eloquence of distress; but he understood his interest too well to yield even for a moment to the compassion which, in spite of himself, her artless supplication inspired.

She now resigned herself to despair, and in passive silence submitted to her fate. They continued thus to travel till a storm of rain, accompanied by thunder and lightning, drove them to the covert of a thick grove. The man believed this a safe situation, and Adeline was now too careless of life to attempt convincing him of his error. The storm was violent and long, but as soon as it abated they set off on full gallop, and having continued to travel for about two hours, they came to the borders of the forest, and, soon after to a high lonely wall which Adeline could just distinguish by the moon-light which now streamed through the parting clouds.

Here they stopped. The man dismounted, and having opened a small door in the wall, he unbound Adeline, who shrieked, though involuntarily and in vain, as he took her from the horse. The door opened upon a narrow passage dimly lighted by a lamp which hung at the farther end. He led her on. They came to another door; it opened and disclosed a magnificent saloon, splendidly illuminated and fitted up in the most airy and elegant taste.

The walls were painted in fresco, representing scenes from Ovid, and hung above with silk drawn up in festoons and richly fringed. The sofas were of a silk to suit the hangings. From the centre of the ceiling, which exhibited a scene from the Armida of Tasso, descended a silver lamp of Etruscan form. It diffused a blaze of light that, reflected from large pier glasses, completely illuminated the saloon. Busts of Horace, Ovid, Anacreon, Tibullus, and Petronius Arbiter adorned the recesses, and stands of flowers, placed in Etruscan vases, breathed the most delicious perfume. In the middle of the apartment stood a small table spread with a collation of fruits, ices, and liquors. No person appeared. The whole seemed the works of enchantment, and rather resembled the palace of a fairy than anything of human conformation.

Adeline was astonished, and inquired where she was, but the man refused to answer her questions, and having desired her to take some refreshment, left her.

She walked to the windows, from which a gleam of moon-light discovered to her an extensive garden, where groves and lawns and water glittering in the moon-beam composed a scenery of varied and romantic beauty. "What can this mean!" said she: "Is this a charm to lure me to destruction?" She endeavoured with a hope of escaping to open the windows, but they were all fastened; she next attempted several doors, and found them also secured.

Perceiving all chance of escape was removed, she remained for some time given up to sorrow and reflection, but was at length drawn from her reverie by the notes of soft music, breathing such dulcet and entrancing sounds as suspended grief and waked the soul to tenderness and pensive pleasure. Adeline listened in surprise, and insensibly became soothed and interested; a tender melancholy stole upon her heart and subdued every harsher feeling. But the moment the strain ceased, the enchantment dissolved, and she returned to a sense of her situation.

Again the music sounded—music such as charmeth sleep—and again she gradually yielded to its sweet magic. A female voice, accompanied by a lute, a haut-boy, and a few other instruments, now gradually swelled into a tone so exquisite, as raised attention into ecstasy. It sunk by degrees, and touched a few simple notes with pathetic softness, when the measure was suddenly changed, and in a gay and airy melody Adeline distinguished the following words:

Song.

Life's a varied, bright illusion,
  Joy and sorrow—light and shade;
Turn from sorrow's dark suffusion,
  Catch the pleasures ere they fade.

Fancy paints with hues unreal,
    Smile of bliss, and sorrow's mood;
If they both are but ideal,
    Why reject the seeming good?

Hence! no more! 'tis wisdom calls ye,
    Bids ye court Time's present aid;
The future trust not—hope enthrals ye,
    "Catch the pleasures ere they fade."

The music ceased, but the sound still vibrated on her imagination, and she was sunk in the pleasing languor they had inspired when the door opened and the Marquis de Mońtalt appeared. He approached the sofa where Adeline sat, and addressed her, but she heard not his voice—she had fainted. He endeavoured to recover her, and at length succeeded; but when she unclosed her eyes and again beheld him, she relapsed into a state of insensibility, and having in vain tried various methods to restore her, he was obliged to call assistance. Two young women entered, and when she began to revive, he left them to prepare her for his reappearance. When Adeline perceived that the Marquis was gone, and that she was in the care of women, her spirits gradually returned; she looked at her attendants and was surprised to see so much elegance and beauty.

Some endeavour she made to interest their pity; but they seemed wholly insensible to her distress, and began to talk of the Marquis in terms of the highest admiration. They assured her it would be her own fault if she was not happy, and advised her to appear so in his presence. It was with the utmost difficulty that Adeline forbore to express the disdain which was rising to her lips, and that she listened to their discourse in silence. But she saw the inconvenience and fruitlessness of opposition, and she commanded her feelings.

They were thus proceeding in their praises of the Marquis, when he himself appeared, and waving his hand, they immediately quitted the apartment. Adeline beheld him with a kind of mute despair, while he approached and took her hand, which she hastily withdrew, and turning from him with a look of unutterable distress, burst into tears. He was for some time silent, and appeared softened by her anguish. But again approaching, and addressing her in a gentle voice, he entreated her pardon for the step which despair and, as he called it, love, had prompted. She was too much absorbed in grief to reply, till he solicited a return of his love, when her sorrow yielded to indignation and she reproached him with his conduct. He pleaded that he had long loved and sought her upon honourable terms, and his offer of those terms he began to repeat, but raising his eyes towards Adeline, he saw in her looks the contempt which he was conscious he deserved.

For a moment he was confused, and seemed to understand both that his plan was discovered and his person despised; but soon resuming his usual command of feature, he again pressed his suit and solicited her love. A little reflection shewed Adeline the danger of exasperating his pride by an avowal of the contempt which his pretended offer of marriage excited; and she thought it not improper upon an occasion in which the honour and peace of her life was concerned to yield somewhat to the policy of dissimulation. She saw that her only chance of escaping his designs depended upon delaying them, and she now wished him to believe her ignorant that the Marchioness was living and that his offers were delusive.

He observed her pause, and in the eagerness to turn her hesitation to his advantage, renewed his proposal with increased vehemence.—"To-morrow shall unite us,

lovely Adeline; to-morrow you shall consent to become
the Marchioness de Montalt. You will then return my
love and ——"

"You must first deserve my esteem, my lord."

"I will—I do deserve it. Are you not now in my
power, and do I not forbear to take advantage of
your situation? Do I not make you the most honourable proposals?"—Adeline shuddered. "If you wish
I should esteem you, my lord, endeavour if possible to
make me forget by what means I came into your power;
if your views are indeed honourable, prove them so by
releasing me from my confinement."

"Can you then wish, lovely Adeline, to fly from him
who adores you?" replied the Marquis, with a studied
air of tenderness. "Why will you exact so severe a
proof of my disinterestedness, a disinterestedness which
is not consistent with love? No, charming Adeline, let
me at least have the pleasure of beholding you till the
bonds of the church shall remove every obstacle to my
love. To-morrow ——"

Adeline saw the danger to which she was now exposed, and interrupted him. "*Deserve* my esteem, sir,
and then you will *obtain* it. As a first step towards
which, liberate me from a confinement that obliges me
to look on you only with terror and aversion. How can
I believe your professions of love while you shew that
you have no interest in my happiness?" Thus did
Adeline, to whom the arts and the practice of dissimulation were hitherto equally unknown, condescend to
make use of them in disguising her indignation and contempt. But though these arts were adopted only for
the purpose of self-preservation, she used them with
reluctance, and almost with abhorrence; for her mind
was habitually impregnated with the love of virtue in
thought, word, and action, and while her end in using

them was certainly good, she scarcely thought that end could justify the means.

The Marquis persisted in his sophistry. "Can you doubt the reality of that love which, to obtain you, has urged me to risk your displeasure? But have I not consulted your happiness even in the very conduct which you condemn? I have removed you from a solitary and desolate ruin to a gay and splendid villa, where every luxury is at your command and where every person shall be obedient to your wishes."

"My first wish is to go hence," said Adeline; "I entreat, I conjure you, my lord, no longer to detain me. I am a friendless and wretched orphan, exposed to many evils, and I fear abandoned to misfortune. I do not wish to be rude, but allow me to say that no misery can exceed that I shall feel in remaining here, or indeed in being anywhere pursued by the offers you make me!" Adeline had now forgot her policy. Tears prevented her from proceeding, and she turned away her face to hide her emotion.

"By heaven! Adeline, you do me wrong," said the Marquis, rising from his seat, and seizing her hand; "I love, I adore you; yet you doubt my passion, and are insensible to my vows. Every pleasure possible to be enjoyed within these walls you shall partake, but beyond them you shall not go." She disengaged her hand, and in silent anguish walked to a distant part of the saloon. Deep sighs burst from her heart, and almost fainting, she leaned on a window frame for support.

The Marquis followed her; "Why thus obstinately persist in refusing to be happy?" said he; "recollect the proposal I have made you, and accept it while it is yet in your power. To-morrow a priest shall join our hands—Surely, being, as you are, in my power, it must be your interest to consent to this?" Adeline could answer only by tears; she despaired of softening his heart to pity, and feared to exasperate his pride by disdain. He now led her, and she suffered him, to a seat near the banquet, at which he pressed her to partake of a variety of confectionaries, particularly of some liquors, of which he himself drank freely: Adeline accepted only of a peach.

And now the Marquis, who interpreted her silence into a secret compliance with his proposal, resumed all his gaiety and spirit, while the long and ardent regards he bestowed on Adeline, overcame her with confusion and indignation. In the midst of the banquet soft music again sounded the most tender and impassioned airs, but its effect on Adeline was now lost, her mind being too much embarrassed and distressed by the presence of the Marquis to admit even the soothings of harmony. A song was now heard written with that sort of impotent art by which some voluptuous poets believe they can at once conceal and recommend the principles of vice. Adeline received it with contempt and displeasure, and the Marquis, perceiving its effect, presently made a sign for another composition, which adding the force of poetry to the charms of music, might withdraw her mind from the present scene and enchant it in sweet delirium.

SONG OF A SPIRIT.

In sightless air I dwell,
　On the sloping sun-beams play;
Delve the cavern's inmost cell,
　Where never yet did day-light stray:

Dive beneath the green sea waves,
　And gambol in the briny deeps;

Skim every shore that Neptune laves,
  From Lapland's plains to India's steeps.

Oft I mount with rapid force
  Above the wide earth's shadowy zone;
Follow the day-star's flaming course
  Through realms of space to thought unknown:

And listen oft celestial sounds
  That swell the air unheard of men,
As I watch my nightly rounds
  O'er woody steep, and silent glen.

Under the shade of waving trees,
  On the green bank of fountain clear,
At pensive eve I sit at ease,
  While dying music murmurs near.

And oft on point of airy clift,
  That hangs upon the western main,
I watch the gay tints passing swift,
  And twilight veil the liquid plain.

Then, when the breeze has sunk away,
  And ocean scarce is heard to lave,
For me the sea-nymphs softly play
  Their dulcet shells beneath the wave.

Their dulcet shells! I hear them now,
  Slow swells the strain upon mine ear;
Now faintly falls—now warbles low,
  Till rapture melts into a tear.

The ray that silvers o'er the dew,
  And trembles through the leafy shade
And tints the scene with softer hue,
  Calls me to rove the lonely glade;

Or hie me to some ruin'd tower,
  Faintly shewn by moon-light gleam,
Where the lone wanderer owns my power
  In shadows dire that substance seem;

In thrilling sounds that murmur woe,
  And pausing silence make more dread;
In music breathing from below
  Sad solemn strains, that wake the dead.

Unseen I move—unknown am fear'd!
  Fancy's wildest dreams I weave;
And oft by bards my voice is heard
  To die along the gales of eve.

When the voice ceased, a mournful strain, played with exquisite expression, sounded from a distant horn. Sometimes the notes floated on the air in soft undulations—now they swelled into full and sweeping melody, and now died faintly into silence, when again they rose and trembled in sounds so sweetly tender as drew tears from Adeline and exclamations of rapture from the Marquis. He threw his arm round her, and would have pressed her towards him, but she liberated herself from his embrace, and with a look on which was impressed the firm dignity of virtue, yet touched with sorrow, she awed him to forbearance. Conscious of a superiority which he was ashamed to acknowledge, and endeavouring to despise the influence which he could not resist, he stood for a moment the slave of virtue, though the votary of vice. Soon, however, he recovered his confidence, and began to plead his love; when Adeline, no longer animated by the spirit she had lately shewn, and sinking beneath the languor and fatigue which the various and violent agitations of her mind produced, entreated he would leave her to repose.

The paleness of her countenance and the tremulous tone of her voice were too expressive to be misunderstood; and the Marquis, bidding her remember to-morrow, with some hesitation withdrew. The moment she was alone, she yielded to the bursting anguish of her heart, and was so absorbed in grief that it was some time before she perceived she was in the presence of the young women who had lately attended her, and had entered the saloon soon after the Marquis quitted it. They came to conduct her to her chamber. She followed them for some time in silence, till prompted by desperation, she again endeavoured to awaken their compassion. But again the praises of the Marquis were repeated, and perceiving that all attempts to interest them in her favour were in vain, she dismissed them. She secured the door through which they had departed, and then, in the languid hope of discovering some means of escape, she surveyed her chamber. The airy elegance with which it was fitted up and the luxurious accommodations with which it abounded seemed designed to fascinate the imagination and to seduce the heart. The hangings were of straw-coloured silk, adorned with a variety of landscapes and historical paintings, the subjects of which partook of the voluptuous character of the owner. The chimney-piece, of Parian marble, was ornamented with several reposing figures from the antique. The bed was of silk the colour of the hangings, richly fringed with purple and silver, and the head made in form of a canopy. The steps which were placed near the bed to assist in ascending it were supported by cupids, apparently of solid silver. China vases, filled with perfume, stood in several of the recesses upon stands of the same structure as the toilet, which was magnificent, and ornamented with a variety of trinkets.

Adeline threw a transient look upon these various objects, and proceeded to examine the windows, which descended to the floor and opened into balconies towards the garden she had seen from the saloon. They were now fastened, and her efforts to move them were ineffectual; at length she gave up the attempt. A door next attracted her notice, which she found was not fastened. It opened upon a dressing closet, to which she descended by a few steps. Two windows appeared; she hastened towards them. One refused to yield, but her heart beat with sudden joy when the other opened to her touch.

In the transport of the moment she forgot that its distance from the ground might yet deny the escape she meditated. She returned to lock the door of the closet to prevent a surprise, which, however, was unnecessary, that of the bed-room being already secured. She now looked out from the window. The garden lay before her, and she perceived that the window, which descended to the floor, was so near the ground that she might jump from it with ease. Almost in the moment she perceived this, she sprang forward and alighted safely in an extensive garden, resembling more an English pleasure ground than a series of French parterres.

Thence she had little doubt of escaping, either by some broken fence or low part of the wall; she tripped lightly along, for hope played round her heart. The clouds of the late storm were now dispersed, and the moon-light, which slept on the lawns and spangled the flowerets yet heavy with rain-drops, afforded her a distinct view of the surrounding scenery. She followed the direction of the high wall that adjoined the château, till it was concealed from her sight by a thick wilderness, so entangled with boughs and obscured by darkness that she feared to enter, and turned aside into a walk on the right. It conducted her to the margin of a lake overhung with lofty trees.

The moon-beams dancing upon the waters, that with gentle undulation played along the shore, exhibited a scene of tranquil beauty which would have soothed a heart less agitated than was that of Adeline. She sighed as she transiently surveyed it, and passed hastily on in search of the garden wall, from which she had now strayed a considerable way. After wandering for some time through alleys and over lawns without meeting with anything like a boundary to the grounds, she again found herself at the lake, and now traversed its border with the footsteps of despair. Tears rolled down her cheeks. The scene around exhibited only images of peace and delight; every object seemed to repose; not a breath waved the foliage; not a sound stole through the air; it was in her bosom only that tumult and distress prevailed. She still pursued the windings of the shore, till an opening in the woods conducted her up a gentle ascent; the path now wound along the side of a hill, where the gloom was so deep that it was with some difficulty she found her way. Suddenly, however, the avenue opened to a lofty grove, and she perceived a light issue from a recess at some distance.

She paused, and her first impulse was to retreat, but listening and hearing no sound, a faint hope beamed upon her mind that the person to whom the light belonged might be won to favour her escape. She advanced with trembling and cautious steps towards the recess, that she might secretly observe the person before she ventured to enter it. Her emotion increased as she approached, and having reached the bower, she beheld through an open window the Marquis reclining on a sofa, near which stood a table covered with fruit and wine. He was alone, and his countenance was flushed with drinking.

While she gazed, fixed to the spot by terror, he looked up towards the casement; the light gleamed full upon her face, but she stayed not to learn whether he had observed her, for with the swiftness of sound she left the place and ran without knowing whether she was pursued. Having gone a considerable way, fatigue at length compelled her to stop, and she threw herself upon the turf almost fainting with fear and languor. She knew if the Marquis detected her in an attempt to escape, he would probably burst the bounds which she had hitherto prescribed to himself, and that she had the most dreadful evils to expect. The palpitations of terror were so strong that she could with difficulty breathe.

She watched and listened in trembling expectation, but no form met her eye, no sound her ear. In this state she remained a considerable time. She wept, and the tears she shed relieved her oppressed heart. "O my father!" said she, "why did you abandon your child? If you knew the dangers to which you have exposed her, you would surely pity and relieve her. Alas! shall I never find a friend? Am I destined still to trust and be deceived?—Peter too, could he be treacherous?" She wept again, and then returned to a sense of her present danger and to a consideration of the means of escaping it—but no means appeared.

To her imagination the grounds were boundless; she had wandered from lawn to lawn and from grove to grove without perceiving any termination to the place; the garden wall she could not find, but she resolved neither to return to the château nor to relinquish her search. As she was rising to depart, she perceived a shadow move along at some distance; she stood still to

observe it. It slowly advanced and then disappeared,
but presently she saw a person emerge from the gloom
and approach the spot where she stood. She had no
doubt that the Marquis had observed her, and she ran
with all possible speed to the shade of some woods on
the left. Footsteps pursued her and she heard her
name repeated, while she in vain endeavoured to quicken
her pace.

Suddenly the sound of pursuit turned and sunk away
in a different direction. She paused to take breath;
she looked around and no person appeared. She now
proceeded slowly along the avenue, and had almost
reached its termination when she saw the same figure
emerge from the woods and dart across the avenue. It
instantly pursued her and approached. A voice called
her, but she was gone beyond its reach, for she had
sunk senseless upon the ground. It was long before
she revived; when she did, she found herself in the
arms of a stranger, and made an effort to disengage
herself.

"Fear nothing, lovely Adeline," said he; "fear nothing. You are in the arms of a friend who will encounter any hazard for your sake, who will protect you
with his life." He pressed her gently to his heart.
"Have you then forgot me?" continued he. She looked
earnestly at him, and was now convinced that it was
Theodore who spoke. Joy was her first emotion, but,
recollecting his former abrupt departure at a time so
critical to her safety, and that he was the friend of
the Marquis, a thousand mingled sensations struggled
in her breast and overwhelmed her with mistrust, apprehension, and disappointment.

Theodore raised her from the ground, and while he
yet supported her, "Let us immediately fly from this
place," said he; "a carriage waits to receive us; it

shall go wherever you direct, and convey you to your friends." This last sentence touched her heart: "Alas, I have no friend!" said she, "nor do I know whither to go." Theodore gently pressed her hand between his, and in a voice of the softest compassion, said, "*My* friends then shall be yours; suffer me to lead you to them. But I am in agony while you remain in this place; let us hasten to quit it." Adeline was going to reply, when voices were heard among the trees, and Theodore, supporting her with his arm, hurried her along the avenue. They continued their flight till Adeline, panting for breath, could go no farther.

Having paused a while, and heard no footsteps in pursuit, they renewed their course. Theodore knew that they were now not far from the garden wall; but he was also aware that in the intermediate space several paths wound from remote parts of the grounds into the walk he was to pass, from whence the Marquis's people might issue and intercept him. He, however, concealed his apprehensions from Adeline, and endeavoured to soothe and support her spirits.

At length they reached the wall, and Theodore was leading her towards a low part of it, near which stood the carriage, when again they heard voices in the air. Adeline's spirits and strength were nearly exhausted, but she made a last effort to proceed, and she now saw the ladder at some distance by which Theodore had descended to the garden. "Exert yourself yet a little longer," said he, "and you will be in safety." He held the ladder while she ascended; the top of the wall was broad and level, and Adeline, having reached it, remained there till Theodore followed and drew the ladder to the other side.

When they had descended, the carriage appeared in waiting, but without the driver. Theodore feared to call, lest his voice should betray him. He therefore put Adeline into the carriage and went himself in search of the postillion, whom he found asleep under a tree at some distance. Having awakened him, they returned to the vehicle, which soon drove furiously away. Adeline did not yet dare to believe herself safe, but after proceeding a considerable time without interruption, joy burst upon her heart and she thanked her deliverer in terms of the warmest gratitude. The sympathy expressed in the tone of his voice and manner proved that his happiness on this occasion almost equalled her own.

As reflection gradually stole upon her mind, anxiety superseded joy. In the tumult of the late moments she thought only of escape, but the circumstances of her present situation now appeared to her, and she became silent and pensive. She had no friends to whom she could fly, and was going with a young chevalier, almost a stranger to her, she knew not whither. She remembered how often she had been deceived and betrayed where she trusted most, and her spirits sunk. She remembered also the former attention which Theodore had shewn her, and dreaded lest his conduct might be prompted by a selfish passion. She saw this to be possible, but she disdained to believe it probable, and felt that nothing could give her greater pain than to doubt the integrity of Theodore.

He interrupted her reverie by recurring to her late situation at the abbey. "You would be much surprised," said he, "and, I fear, offended, that I did not attend my appointment at the abbey after the alarming hints I had given you in our last interview. That circumstance has perhaps injured me in your esteem, if indeed I was ever so happy as to possess it; but my designs were over-ruled by those of the Marquis de

Montalt, and I think I may venture to assert that my distress upon this occasion was at least equal to your apprehensions."

Adeline said she had been much alarmed by the hints he had given her, and by his failing to afford farther information, concerning the subject of her danger; and—She checked the sentence that hung upon her lips, for she perceived that she was unwarily betraying the interest he held in her heart. There were a few moments of silence, and neither party seemed perfectly at ease. Theodore at length renewed the conversation: "Suffer me to acquaint you," said he, "with the circumstances that withheld me from the interview I solicited; I am anxious to exculpate myself." Without waiting her reply, he proceeded to inform her that the Marquis had by some inexplicable means learned or suspected the subject of their last conversation, and perceiving his designs were in danger of being counteracted, had taken effectual means to prevent her obtaining farther intelligence of them. Adeline immediately recollected that Theodore and herself had been seen in the forest by La Motte, who had no doubt suspected their growing intimacy, and had taken care to inform the Marquis how likely he was to find a rival in his friend.

"On the day following that on which I last saw you," said Theodore, "the Marquis, who is my colonel, commanded me to prepare to attend my regiment, and appointed the following morning for my journey. This sudden order gave me some surprise, but I was not long in doubt concerning the motive for it. A servant of the Marquis who had been long attached to me entered my room soon after I had left his lord, and expressing concern at my abrupt departure, dropped some hints respecting it which excited my surprise. I inquired farther, and was confirmed in the suspicions I had for some time entertained of the Marquis's designs upon you.

"Jaques farther informed me that our late interview had been noticed and communicated to the Marquis. His information had been obtained from a fellow servant, and it alarmed me so much that I engaged him to send me intelligence from time to time concerning the proceedings of the Marquis. I now looked forward to the evening which would bring me again to your presence with increased impatience, but the ingenuity of the Marquis effectually counteracted my endeavours and wishes. He had made an engagement to pass the day at the villa of a nobleman some leagues distant and notwithstanding all the excuses I could offer, I was obliged to attend him. Thus compelled to obey, I passed a day of more agitation and anxiety than I had ever before experienced. It was midnight before we returned to the Marquis's château. I arose early in the morning to commence my journey, and resolved to seek an interview with you before I left the province.

"When I entered the breakfast room, I was much surprised to find the Marquis there already, who, commending the beauty of the morning, declared his intention of accompanying me as far as Chineau. Thus unexpectedly deprived of my last hope, my countenance, I believe, expressed what I felt, for the scrutinizing eye of the Marquis instantly changed from seeming carelessness to displeasure. The distance from Chineau to the abbey was at least twelve leagues; yet I had once some intention of returning from thence when the Marquis should leave me, till I recollected the very remote chance there would even then be of seeing you alone, and also that if I was observed by La Motte, it would awaken all his suspicions and caution him against any future plan I might see it expedient to attempt. I therefore proceeded to join my regiment.

"Jaques sent me frequent accounts of the operations of the Marquis, but his manner of relating them was so very confused that they only served to perplex and distress me. His last letter, however, alarmed me so much that my residence in quarters became intolerable, and as I found it impossible to obtain leave of absence, I secretly left the regiment and concealed myself in a cottage about a mile from the château, that I might obtain the earliest intelligence of the Marquis's plans. Jaques brought me daily information, and at last an account of the horrible plot which was laid for the following night.

"I saw little probability of warning you of your danger. If I ventured near the abbey, La Motte might discover me, and frustrate every attempt on my part to save you. Yet I determined to encounter this risk for the chance of seeing you, and towards evening I was preparing to set out for the forest, when Jaques arrived and informed me that you was to be brought to the château. My plan was thus rendered less difficult. I learned also that the Marquis, by means of those refinements in luxury with which he is but too well acquainted, designed, now that his apprehension of losing you was no more, to seduce you to his wishes and impose upon you by a fictitious marriage. Having obtained information concerning the situation of the room allotted you, I ordered a chaise to be in waiting, and with a design of scaling your window and conducting you thence, I entered the garden at midnight."

Theodore having ceased to speak:—"I know not how words can express my sense of the obligations I owe you," said Adeline, "or my gratitude for your generosity."

"Ah! call it not generosity," he replied; "it was love." He paused. Adeline was silent. After some moments of expressive emotion, he resumed: "But pardon this abrupt declaration. Yet why do I call it abrupt, since my actions have already disclosed what my lips have never till this instant ventured to acknowledge." He paused again. Adeline was still silent. "Yet do me the justice to believe that I am sensible of the impropriety of pleading my love at present, and have been surprised into this confession. I promise also to forbear from a renewal of the subject till you are placed in a situation where you may freely accept or refuse the sincere regards I offer you. If I could, however, now be certain that I possess your esteem, it would relieve me from much anxiety."

Adeline felt surprised that he should doubt her esteem for him, after the signal and generous service he had rendered her, but she was not yet acquainted with the timidity of love. "Do you then," said she, in a tremulous voice, "believe me ungrateful? It is impossible I can consider your friendly interference in my behalf without esteeming you." Theodore immediately took her hand and pressed it to his lips in silence. They were both too much agitated to converse, and continued to travel for some miles without exchanging a word.

CHAPTERS XI AND XII

[THESE two chapters (likewise Chapters XV to XVII in their proper place) are summarized. They are tedious and rather loosely integrated with the plot, and show the characters in no new or specially interesting light.

CHAPTER XI continues with the flight of Theodore and Adeline, who discover with the dawn that they are pursued by a body of horsemen. They are overtaken at an inn at which they had sought safety. Theodore is apprehended as a deserter from his regiment, which he had in fact left to aid Adeline, and an affray follows in which he is seriously wounded. When Theodore is partly recovered, he is told to be prepared to leave shortly, under arrest, and in the urgency of the moment he proposes to marry Adeline to protect her against the Marquis. Adeline, however, "though she had no friends to control and no contrariety of interests to perplex her, could not bring herself to consent thus hastily to a marriage with a man of whom she had little knowledge, and to whose family and connections she had no sort of introduction." She resolves to seek refuge in a neighbouring convent. These plans are interrupted, however, by the arrival of the Marquis himself. As Theodore is led off under arrest, in despair for Adeline he seizes a sword from one of his guards and dangerously wounds the Marquis. In the midst of her uncertainties as to the fate of either Theodore or the Marquis, Adeline is forced by the servants of the nobleman into a chaise and hurried from the village, ignorant of her destination.

CHAPTER XII gives a résumé of the steps by which the Marquis had been informed of Theodore's intervention in his plans, and the Marquis's consequent resolve to punish him for his presumption. Theodore's desperate situation excites the sympathy of the physician who has attended him, and who has been called to aid the Marquis in the later emergency. The physician therefore attempts to delay the Marquis's plans, by making him think that he is more dangerously injured than in fact he is. Meanwhile Theodore is sent off hurriedly

under guard, facing the prospect of death for assault
upon the Marquis, his superior officer.]

CHAPTER XIII

MEANWHILE the persecuted Adeline continued to travel
with little interruption all night. Her mind suffered
such a tumult of grief, regret, despair, and terror, that
she could not be said to think. The Marquis's valet,
who had placed himself in the chaise with her, at first
seemed inclined to talk, but her inattention soon silenced
him and left her to the indulgence of her own misery.

They seemed to travel through obscure lanes and by-
ways, along which the carriage drove as furiously as
the darkness would permit. When the dawn appeared,
she perceived herself on the borders of a forest, and
renewed her entreaties to know whither she was going.
The man replied he had no orders to tell, but she would
soon see. Adeline, who had hitherto supposed they
were carrying her to the villa, now began to doubt
it; and as every place appeared less terrible to her
imagination than that, her despair began to abate, and
she thought only of the devoted Theodore, whom she
knew to be the victim of malice and revenge.

They now entered upon the forest, and it occurred
to her that she was going to the abbey; for though she
had no remembrance of the scenery through which she
passed, it was not the less probable that this was the
forest of Fontanville, whose boundaries were by much
too extensive to have come within the circle of her
former walks. This conjecture revived a terror little
inferior to that occasioned by the idea of going to the
villa, for at the abbey she would be equally in the

power of the Marquis, and also in that of her cruel enemy La Motte. Her mind revolted at the picture her fancy drew, and as the carriage moved under the shades, she threw from the window a look of eager inquiry for some object which might confirm or destroy her present surmise. She did not long look, before an opening in the forest shewed her the distant towers of the abbey—"I am, indeed, lost then," said she, bursting into tears.

They were soon at the foot of the lawn, and Peter was seen running to open the gate, at which the carriage stopped. When he saw Adeline, he looked surprised and made an effort to speak, but the chaise now drove up to the abbey, where at the door of the hall La Motte himself appeared. As he advanced to take her from the carriage, an universal trembling seized her. It was with the utmost difficulty she supported herself, and for some moments she neither observed his countenance nor heard his voice. He offered his arm to assist her into the abbey, which she at first refused, but having tottered a few paces, was obliged to accept. They then entered the vaulted room, where, sinking into a chair, a flood of tears came to her relief. La Motte did not interrupt the silence, which continued for some time, but paced the room in seeming agitation. When Adeline was sufficiently recovered to notice external objects, she observed his countenance, and there read the tumult of his soul, while he was struggling to assume a firmness which his better feelings opposed.

La Motte now took her hand and would have led her from the room, but she stopped and with a kind of desperate courage made an effort to engage him to pity and to save her. He interrupted her: "It is not in my power," said he, in a voice of emotion; "I am not master of myself or my conduct; inquire no farther—

it is sufficient for you to know that I pity you; more
I cannot do." He gave her no time to reply, but taking her hand, led her to the stairs of the tower and
from thence to the chamber she had formerly occupied.

"Here you must remain for the present," said he,
"in a confinement which is perhaps almost as involuntary on my part as it can be on yours. I am willing
to render it as easy as possible, and have therefore
ordered some books to be brought you."

Adeline made an effort to speak, but he hurried
from the room, seemingly ashamed of the part he had
undertaken, and unwilling to trust himself with her
tears. She heard the door of the chamber locked, and
then looking towards the windows, perceived they were
secured. The door that led to the other apartments
was also fastened. Such preparation for security
shocked her, and hopeless as she had long believed
herself, she now perceived her mind sink deeper in
despair. When the tears she shed had somewhat relieved her and her thoughts could turn from the subjects of her immediate concern, she was thankful for
the total seclusion allotted her, since it would spare
her the pain she must feel in the presence of Monsieur
and Madame La Motte, and allow the unrestrained indulgence of her own sorrow and reflection; reflection
which, however distressing, was preferable to the agony
inflicted on the mind when, agitated by care and fear,
it is obliged to assume an appearance of tranquillity.

In about a quarter of an hour her chamber-door was
unlocked and Annette appeared with refreshments and
books. She expressed satisfaction at seeing Adeline
again, but seemed fearful of speaking, knowing, probably, that it was contrary to the orders of La Motte,
who she said was waiting at the bottom of the stairs.
When Annette was gone, Adeline took some refresh-

ment, which was indeed necessary; for she had tasted nothing since she left the inn. She was pleased but not surprised that Madame La Motte did not appear, who, it was evident, shunned her from a consciousness of her own ungenerous conduct, a consciousness which offered some presumption that she was still not wholly unfriendly to her. She reflected upon the words of La Motte: "I am not master of myself or my conduct," and though they afforded her no hope, she derived some comfort, poor as it was, from the belief that he pitied her. After some time spent in miserable reflection and various conjectures, her long-agitated spirits seemed to demand repose, and she lay down to sleep.

Adeline slept quietly for several hours, and awoke with a mind refreshed and tranquillized. To prolong this temporary peace, and to prevent therefore the intrusion of her own thoughts, she examined the books La Motte had sent her. Among these she found some that in happier times had elevated her mind and interested her heart. Their effect was now weakened; they were still, however, able to soften for a time the sense of her misfortunes.

But this Lethean medicine to a wounded mind was but a temporary blessing; the entrance of La Motte dissolved the illusions of the page and awakened her to a sense of her own situation. He came with food, and having placed it on the table, left the room without speaking. Again she endeavoured to read, but his appearance had broken the enchantment—bitter reflection returned to her mind, and brought with it the image of Theodore—of Theodore lost to her for ever!

La Motte, meanwhile, experienced all the terrors that could be inflicted by a conscience not wholly hardened to guilt. He had been led on by passion to dissipation—and from dissipation to vice; but having once

touched the borders of infamy, the progressive steps
followed each other fast, and he now saw himself the
pander of a villain and the betrayer of an innocent girl
whom every plea of justice and humanity called upon
him to protect. He contemplated his picture—he shrunk
from it, but he could change its deformity only by an
effort too nobly daring for a mind already effeminated
by vice. He viewed the dangerous labyrinth into which
he was led, and perceived, as if for the first time, the
progression of his guilt. From this labyrinth he weakly
imagined farther guilt could alone extricate him. Instead of employing his mind upon the means of saving
Adeline from destruction, and himself from being in-
strumental to it, he endeavoured only to lull the pangs
of conscience and to persuade himself into a belief that
he must proceed in the course he had begun. He knew
himself to be in the power of the Marquis, and he
dreaded that power more than the sure though distant
punishment that awaits upon guilt. The honour of
Adeline and the quiet of his own conscience he consented to barter for a few years of existence.

He was ignorant of the present illness of the Marquis, or he would have perceived that there was a chance
of escaping the threatened punishment at a price less
enormous than infamy, and he would perhaps have endeavoured to save Adeline and himself by flight. But
the Marquis, foreseeing the possibility of this, had ordered his servants carefully to conceal the circumstance
which detained him, and to acquaint La Motte that he
should be at the abbey in a few days, at the same time
directing his valet to await him there. Adeline, as he
expected, had neither inclination nor opportunity to
mention it, and thus La Motte remained ignorant of the
circumstance which might have preserved him from
farther guilt and Adeline from misery.

Most unwillingly had La Motte made his wife acquainted with the action which had made him absolutely dependent upon the will of the Marquis, but the perturbation of his mind partly betrayed him. Frequently in his sleep he muttered incoherent sentences, and frequently would start from his slumber and call in passionate exclamation upon Adeline. These instances of a disturbed mind had alarmed and terrified Madame La Motte, who watched while he slept and soon gathered from his words a confused idea of the Marquis's designs.

She hinted her suspicions to La Motte, who reproved her for having entertained them, but his manner, instead of repressing, increased her fears for Adeline, fears which the conduct of the Marquis soon confirmed. On the night that he slept at the abbey, it had occurred to her that whatever scheme was in agitation, it would now most probably be discussed, and anxiety for Adeline made her stoop to a meanness which in other circumstances would have been despicable. She quitted her room, and concealing herself in an apartment adjoining that in which she had left the Marquis and her husband, listened to their discourse. It turned upon the subject she had expected, and disclosed to her the full extent of their designs. Terrified for Adeline, and shocked at the guilty weakness of La Motte, she was for some time incapable of thinking or determining how to proceed. She knew her husband to be under great obligation to the Marquis, whose territory thus afforded him a shelter from the world, and that it was in the power of the former to betray him into the hands of his enemies. She believed also that the Marquis would do this, if provoked, yet she thought upon such an occasion La Motte might find some way of appeasing the Marquis without subjecting himself to dishonour. After some farther reflection her mind became more composed, and she returned to her chamber, where La Motte soon followed. Her spirits, however, were not now in a state to encounter either his displeasure or his opposition, which she had too much reason to expect, whenever she should mention the subject of her concern, and she therefore resolved not to notice it till the morrow.

On the morrow she told La Motte all he had uttered in his dreams, and mentioned other circumstances which convinced him it was in vain any longer to deny the truth of her apprehensions. His wife then represented to him how possible it was to avoid the infamy into which he was about to plunge by quitting the territories of the Marquis, and pleaded so warmly for Adeline that La Motte in sullen silence appeared to meditate upon the plan. His thoughts were, however, very differently engaged. He was conscious of having deserved from the Marquis a dreadful punishment, and knew that if he exasperated him by refusing to acquiesce with his wishes, he had little to expect from flight, for the eye of justice and revenge would pursue him with indefatigable research.

La Motte meditated how to break this to his wife, for he perceived that there was no other method of counteracting her virtuous compassion for Adeline, and the dangerous consequences to be expected from it, than by opposing it with terror for his safety, and this could be done only by shewing her the full extent of the evils that must attend the resentment of the Marquis. Vice had not yet so entirely darkened his conscience but that the blush of shame stained his cheek and his tongue faltered when he would have told his guilt. At length, finding it impossible to mention particulars, he told her that on account of an affair which no entreaties should ever induce him to explain, his life was in the power of the Marquis. "You see the alternative," said he; "take your choice of evils, and if you can, tell Adeline of her danger and sacrifice my life to save her from a situation which many would be ambitious to obtain." —Madame La Motte, condemned to the horrible alternative of permitting the seduction of innocence or of dooming her husband to destruction, suffered a distraction of thought which defied all control. Perceiving, however, that an opposition to the designs of the Marquis would ruin La Motte and avail Adeline little, she determined to yield and endure in silence.

At the time when Adeline was planning her escape from the abbey, the significant looks of Peter had led La Motte to suspect the truth and to observe them more closely. He had seen them separate in the hall with apparent confusion, and had afterwards observed them conversing together in the cloisters. Circumstances so unusual left him not a doubt that Adeline had discovered her danger and was concerting with Peter some means of escape. Affecting, therefore, to be informed of the whole affair, he charged Peter with treachery towards himself, and threatened him with the vengeance of the Marquis if he did not disclose all he knew. The menace intimidated Peter, and supposing that all chance of assisting Adeline was gone, he made a circumstantial confession and promised to forbear acquainting Adeline with the discovery of the scheme. In this promise he was seconded by inclination, for he feared to meet the displeasure which Adeline, believing he had betrayed her, might express.

On the evening of the day on which Adeline's intended escape was discovered, the Marquis designed to come to the abbey, and it had been agreed that he should then take Adeline to his villa. La Motte had immediately perceived the advantage of permitting Adeline to repair, in the belief of being undiscovered, to the tomb. It would prevent much disturbance and opposition, and spare himself the pain he must feel in her presence when she should know that he had betrayed her. A servant of the Marquis might go at the appointed hour to the tomb, and wrapt in the disguise of night, might take her quietly thence in the character of Peter. Thus without resistance she would be carried to the villa, nor discover her mistake till it was too late to prevent its consequence.

When the Marquis did arrive, La Motte, who was not so much intoxicated by the wine he had drank as to forget his prudence, informed him of what had happened and what he had planned, and the Marquis approving it, his servant was made acquainted with the signal which afterwards betrayed Adeline to his power.

A deep consciousness of the unworthy neutrality she had observed in Adeline's concerns, made Madame La Motte anxiously avoid seeing her now that she was again in the abbey. Adeline understood this conduct, and she rejoiced that she was spared the anguish of meeting her as an enemy, whom she had once considered as a friend. Several days now passed in solitude, in miserable retrospection and dreadful expectation. The perilous situation of Theodore was almost the constant subject of her thoughts. Often did she breathe an agonizing wish for his safety, and often look round the sphere of possibility in search of hope. But hope had almost left the horizon of her prospect, and when it did appear, it sprung only from the death of the Marquis, whose vengeance threatened most certain destruction.

The Marquis, meanwhile, lay at the inn at Caux in a state of very doubtful recovery. The physician and surgeon, neither of whom he would dismiss nor suffer to leave the village, proceeded upon contrary principles, and the good effect of what the one prescribed, was frequently counteracted by the injudicious treatment of the other. Humanity alone prevailed on the physician to continue his attendance. The malady of the Marquis was also heightened by the impatience of his temper, the terrors of death, and the irritation of his passions. One moment he believed himself dying, another he could scarcely be prevented from attempting to follow Adeline to the abbey. So various were the fluctuations of his mind and so rapid the schemes that succeeded each other, that his passions were in a continual state of conflict. The physician attempted to persuade him that his recovery greatly depended upon tranquillity, and to prevail upon him to attempt at least some command of his feelings, but he was soon silenced, in hopeless disgust, by the impatient answers of the Marquis.

At length the servant who had carried off Adeline returned, and the Marquis having ordered him into his chamber, asked so many questions in a breath that the man knew not which to answer. At length he pulled a folded paper from his pocket, which he said had been dropped in the chaise by Mademoiselle Adeline, and as he thought his lordship would like to see it, he had taken care of it. The Marquis stretched forth his hand with eagerness and received a note addressed to Theodore. On perceiving the superscription, the agitation of jealous rage for a moment overcame him, and he held it in his hand unable to open it.

He, however, broke the seal and found it to be a note of inquiry written by Adeline to Theodore during his illness, and which from some accident she had been prevented from sending him. The tender solicitude it expressed for his recovery stung the soul of the Mar-

quis and drew from him a comparison of her feelings
on the illness of his rival and that of himself. "She
could be solicitous for his recovery," said he, "but for
mine she only dreads it." As if willing to prolong the
pain this little billet had excited, he then read it again.
Again he cursed his fate and execrated his rival, giving
himself up as usual to the transports of his passion. He
was going to throw it from him, when his eyes caught
the seal, and he looked earnestly at it. His anger
seemed now to have subsided; he deposited the note
carefully in his pocket-book, and was for some time
lost in thought.

After many days of hopes and fears, the strength
of his constitution overcame his illness, and he was well
enough to write several letters, one of which he immediately sent off to prepare La Motte for his reception.
The same policy which had prompted him to conceal
his illness from La Motte, now urged him to say what
he knew would not happen, that he should reach the
abbey on the day after his servant. He repeated this
injunction, that Adeline should be strictly guarded, and
renewed his promises of reward for the future services
of La Motte.

La Motte, to whom each succeeding day had brought
new surprise and perplexity concerning the absence of
the Marquis, received this notice with uneasiness, for he
had begun to hope that the Marquis had altered his
intentions concerning Adeline, being either engaged in
some new adventure or obliged to visit his estates in
some distant province. He would have been willing
thus to have got rid of an affair which was to reflect so
much dishonour on himself.

This hope was now vanished, and he directed Madame
to prepare for the reception of the Marquis. Adeline
passed these days in a state of suspense which was now

cheered by hope and now darkened by despair. This delay, so much exceeding her expectation, seemed to prove that the illness of the Marquis was dangerous; and when she looked forward to the consequences of his recovery, she could not be sorry that it was so. So odious was the idea of him to her mind that she would not suffer her lips to pronounce his name, nor make the inquiry of Annette which was of such consequence to her peace.

It was about a week after the receipt of the Marquis's letter that Adeline one day saw from her window a party of horsemen enter the avenue, and knew them to be the Marquis and his attendants. She retired from the window in a state of mind not to be described, and sinking into a chair, was for some time scarcely conscious of the objects around her. When she had recovered from the first terror which his appearance excited, she again tottered to the window. The party was not in sight, but she heard the trampling of horses, and knew that the Marquis had wound round to the great gate of the abbey. She addressed herself to heaven for support and protection, and her mind being now somewhat composed, sat down to wait the event.

La Motte received the Marquis with expressions of surprise at his long absence, and the latter, merely saying he had been detained by illness, proceeded to inquire for Adeline. He was told she was in her chamber, from whence she might be summoned if he wished to see her. The Marquis hesitated, and at length excused himself, but desired she might be strictly watched. "Perhaps, my lord," said La Motte smiling, "Adeline's obstinacy has been too powerful for your passion; you seem less interested concerning her than formerly."

"O! by no means," replied the Marquis; "she interests me, if possible, more than ever; so much, indeed, that I cannot have her too closely guarded; and I therefore beg, La Motte, that you will suffer nobody to attend her but when you can observe them yourself. Is the room where she is confined sufficiently secure?" La Motte assured him it was, but at the same time expressed his wish that she was removed to the villa. "If by any means," said he, "she should contrive to escape, I know what I must expect from your displeasure; and this reflection keeps my mind in continual anxiety."

"This removal cannot be at present," said the Marquis; "she is safer here, and you do wrong to disturb yourself with any apprehension of her escape if her chamber is really so secure as you represent it."

"I can have no motive for deceiving you, my lord, in this point."

"I do not suspect you of any," said the Marquis; "guard her carefully, and trust me, she will not escape. I can rely upon my valet, and if you wish it, he shall remain here." La Motte thought there could be no occasion for him, and it was agreed that the man should go home.

The Marquis, after remaining about half an hour in conversation with La Motte, left the abbey, and Adeline saw him depart with a mixture of surprise and thankfulness that almost overcame her. She had waited in momentary expectation of being summoned to appear, and had been endeavouring to arm herself with resolution to support his presence. She had listened to every voice that sounded from below, and at every step that crossed the passage her heart had palpitated with dread lest it should be La Motte coming to lead her to the Marquis. This state of suffering had been prolonged almost beyond her power of enduring it, when she heard voices under her window, and rising, saw the Marquis ride away. After giving way to the joy of thankfulness that swelled her heart, she endeavoured to account for this circumstance, which, considering what had passed, was certainly very strange. It appeared, indeed, wholly inexplicable, and, after much fruitless inquiry, she quitted the subject, endeavouring to persuade herself that it could only portend good.

The time of La Motte's usual visitation now drew near, and Adeline expected it in the trembling hope of hearing that the Marquis had ceased his persecution; but he was, as usual, sullen and silent, and it was not till he was about to quit the room that Adeline had the courage to inquire when the Marquis was expected again? La Motte, opening the door to depart, replied, on the following day, and Adeline, whom fear and delicacy embarrassed, saw she could obtain no intelligence of Theodore but by a direct question. She looked earnestly, as if she would have spoke, and he stopped; but she blushed and was still silent, till upon his again attempting to leave the room, she faintly called him back.

"I would ask," said she, "after that unfortunate chevalier who has incurred the resentment of the Marquis by endeavouring to serve me. Has the Marquis mentioned him?"

"He has," replied La Motte; "and your indifference towards the Marquis is now fully explained."

"Since I must feel resentment towards those who injure me," said Adeline, "I may surely be allowed to be grateful towards those who serve me. Had the Marquis deserved my esteem, he would probably have possessed it."

"Well, well," said La Motte, "this young hero, who, it seems, has been brave enough to lift his arm against his colonel, is taken care of, and I doubt not will soon be sensible of the value of his quixotism." Indignation, grief, and fear struggled in the bosom of Adeline; she disdained to give La Motte an opportunity of again pronouncing the name of Theodore; yet the uncertainty under which she laboured, urged her to inquire whether the Marquis had heard of him since he left Caux? "Yes," said La Motte, "he has been safely carried to his regiment, where he is confined till the Marquis can attend to appear against him."

Adeline had neither power nor inclination to inquire farther, and La Motte quitting the chamber, she was left to the misery he had renewed. Though this information contained no new circumstance of misfortune, (for she now heard confirmed what she had always expected) a weight of new sorrow seemed to fall upon her heart, and she perceived that she had unconsciously cherished a latent hope of Theodore's escape before he reached the place of his destination. All hope was now, however, gone; he was suffering the miseries of a prison and the tortures of apprehension both for his own life and her safety. She pictured to herself the dark damp dungeon where he lay, loaded with chains and pale with sickness and grief; she heard him, in a voice that thrilled her heart, call upon her name and raise his eyes to heaven in silent supplication: she saw the anguish of his countenance, the tears that fell slowly on his cheek; and remembering at the same time the generous conduct that had brought him to this abyss of misery, and that it was for her sake he suffered, grief resolved itself into despair, her tears ceased to flow, and she sunk silently into a state of dreadful torpor.

On the morrow the Marquis arrived, and departed as before. Several days then elapsed, and he did not appear till one evening, as La Motte and his wife were in their usual sitting-room, he entered and conversed for some time upon general subjects, from which, however, he by degrees fell into a reverie, and after a pause of silence, he rose and drew La Motte to the window. "I would speak with you alone," said he, "if you are at leisure; if not, another time will do." La Motte, assuring him he was perfectly so, would have conducted him to another room, but the Marquis proposed a walk in the forest. They went out together, and when they had reached a solitary glade, where the spreading branches of the beech and oak deepened the shades of twilight and threw a solemn obscurity around, the Marquis turned to La Motte and addressed him:

"Your condition, La Motte, is unhappy; this abbey is a melancholy residence for a man like you fond of society, and like you also qualified to adorn it." La Motte bowed. "I wish it was in my power to restore you to the world," continued the Marquis; "perhaps if I knew the particulars of the affair which has driven you from it, I might perceive that my interest could effectually serve you. I think I have heard you hint it was an affair of honour." La Motte was silent. "I mean not to distress you, however; nor is it common curiosity that prompts this inquiry, but a sincere desire to befriend you. You have already informed me of some particulars of your misfortunes. I think the liberality of your temper led you into expenses which you afterwards endeavoured to retrieve by gaming."

"Yes, my lord," said La Motte, " 'tis true that I dissipated the greater part of an affluent fortune in luxurious indulgences, and that I afterwards took unworthy means to recover it; but I wish to be spared upon this subject. I would if possible lose the remembrance of a transaction which must forever stain my character, and the rigorous effect of which, I fear, it is not in your power, my lord, to soften."

"You may be mistaken on this point," replied the Marquis; "my interest at court is by no means inconsiderable. Fear not from me any severity of censure; I am not at all inclined to judge harshly of the faults of others. I well know how to allow for the emergency of circumstances; and I think, La Motte, you have hitherto found me your friend."

"I have, my lord."

"And when you recollect that I have forgiven a certain transaction of late date——"

"It is true, my lord; and allow me to say, I have a just sense of your generosity. The transaction you allude to is by far the worst of my life; and what I have to relate cannot therefore lower me in your opinion. When I had dissipated the greatest part of my property in habits of voluptuous pleasure, I had recourse to gaming to supply the means of continuing them. A run of good luck for some time enabled me to do this, and encouraging my most sanguine of expectations, I continued in the same career of success.

"Soon after this a sudden turn of fortune destroyed my hopes and reduced me to the most desperate extremity. In one night my money was lowered to the sum of two hundred louis. These I resolved to stake also, and with them my life; for it was my resolution not to survive their loss. Never shall I forget the horrors of that moment on which hung my fate, nor the deadly anguish that seized my heart when my last stake was gone. I stood for some time in a state of stupefaction, till roused to a sense of my misfortune, my passion made me pour forth execrations on my more fortunate rivals and act all the frenzy of despair. During this paroxysm of madness, a gentleman who had

been a silent observer of all that passed approached
me.—'You are unfortunate, sir,' said he.—'I need not
be informed of that, sir,' I replied.

"'You have perhaps been ill used,' resumed he.—
'Yes sir, I am ruined, and therefore it may be said I
am ill used.'

"'Do you know the people you have played with?'

"'No; but I have met them in the first circles.'

"'Then I am probably mistaken,' said he, and walked
away. His last words roused me and raised a hope
that my money had not been fairly lost. Wishing for
farther information, I went in search of the gentleman, but he had left the rooms; I, however, stifled my
transports, returned to the table where I had lost my
money, placed myself behind the chair of one of the
persons who had won it, and closely watched the game.
For some time I saw nothing that could confirm my
suspicions, but was at length convinced they were just.

"When the game was ended I called one of my ad-
versaries out of the room, and telling him what I had
observed, threatened instantly to expose him if he did
not restore my property. The man was for some time
as positive as myself, and assuming the bully, threatened me with chastisement for my scandalous assertions.
I was not, however, in a state of mind to be frightened,
and his manner served only to exasperate my temper,
already sufficiently inflamed by misfortune. After re-
torting his threats, I was about to return to the apartment we had left and expose what had passed when
with an insidious smile and a softened voice he begged
I would favour him with a few moments' attention, and
allow him to speak with the gentleman his partner. To
the latter part of his request I hesitated, but in the
mean time the gentleman himself entered the room. His
partner related to him in few words what had passed

between us, and the terror that appeared in his countenance sufficiently declared his consciousness of guilt.

"They then drew aside, and remained a few minutes
in conversation together, after which they approached
me with an offer, as they phrased it, of a compromise.
I declared, however, against any thing of this kind, and
swore nothing less than the whole sum I had lost should
content me.—Is it not possible, monsieur, that you may
be offered something as advantageous as the whole?—I
did not understand their meaning, but after they had
continued for some time to give distant hints of the
same sort, they proceeded to explain.

"Perceiving their characters wholly in my power,
they wished to secure my interest to their party, and
therefore informing me that they belonged to an association of persons who lived upon the folly and inex-
perience of others, they offered me a share in their
concern. My fortunes were desperate, and the proposal
now made me would not only produce an immediate
supply, but enable me to return to those scenes of
dissipated pleasure to which passion had at first, and
long habit afterwards, attached me. I closed with the
offer, and thus sunk from dissipation into infamy."

La Motte paused, as if the recollection of these times
filled him with remorse. The Marquis understood his
feelings. "You judge too rigorously of yourself," said
he; "there are few persons, let their appearance of
honesty be what it may, who in such circumstances
would have acted better than you have done. Had I
been in your situation, I know not how I might have
acted. That rigid virtue which shall condemn you may
dignify itself with the appellation of wisdom, but I
wish not to possess it; let it still reside, where it generally is to be found, in the cold bosoms of those who,

wanting feeling to be men, dignify themselves with the
title of philosophers.   But pray proceed."

"Our success was for some time unlimited, for we
held the wheel of fortune and trusted not to her caprice.
Thoughtless and voluptuous by nature, my expenses
fully kept pace with my income.   An unlucky discovery
of the practices of our party was at length made by a
young nobleman, which obliged us to act for some time
with the utmost circumspection.   It would be tedious
to relate the particulars which made us at length so
suspected that the distant civility and cold reserve of
our acquaintance rendered the frequenting public assem-
blies both painful and unprofitable.   We turned our
thoughts to other modes of obtaining money, and a
swindling transaction in which I engaged to a very large
amount soon compelled me to leave Paris.   You know
the rest, my lord."

La Motte was now silent, and the Marquis continued
for some time musing.   "You perceive, my lord," at
length resumed La Motte, "you perceive that my case
is hopeless."

"It is bad, indeed, but not entirely hopeless.   From
my soul I pity you.   Yet, if you should return to the
world, and incur the danger of prosecution, I think my
interest with the minister might save you from any
severe punishment.   You seem, however, to have lost
your relish for society, and perhaps do not wish to
return to it."

"Oh! my lord, can you doubt this?—But I am overcome with the excess of your goodness; would to heaven
it were in my power to prove the gratitude it inspires."

"Talk not of goodness," said the Marquis; "I will
not pretend that my desire of serving you is unalloyed
by any degree of self-interest.   I will not affect to be
more than man; and trust me, those who do are less.

It is in your power to testify your gratitude and bind me to your interest forever." He paused. "Name but the means," cried La Motte, "name but the means, and if they are within the compass of possibility they shall be executed." The Marquis was still silent. "Do you doubt my sincerity, my lord, that you are yet silent? Do you fear to repose a confidence in the man whom you have already loaded with obligation, who lives by your mercy, and almost by your means?" The Marquis looked earnestly at him, but did not speak. "I have not deserved this of you, my lord; speak, I entreat you."

"There are certain prejudices attached to the human mind," said the Marquis in a slow and solemn voice, "which it requires all our wisdom to keep from interfering with our happiness; certain set notions, acquired in infancy and cherished involuntarily by age, which grow up and assume a gloss so plausible that few minds in what is called a civilized country can afterwards overcome them. Truth is often perverted by education. While the refined Europeans boast a standard of honour and a sublimity of virtue which often leads them from pleasure to misery, and from nature to error, the simple uninformed American, follows the impulse of his heart and obeys the inspiration of wisdom." The Marquis paused, and La Motte continued to listen in eager expectation.

"Nature, uncontaminated by false refinement," resumed the Marquis, "everywhere acts alike in the great occurrences of life. The Indian discovers his friend to be perfidious, and he kills him; the wild Asiatic does the same; the Turk, when ambition fires or revenge provokes, gratifies his passion at the expense of life, and does not call it murder. Even the polished Italian, distracted by jealousy or tempted by a strong circumstance of advantage, draws his stilletto and accomplishes his purpose. It is the first proof of a superior mind to liberate itself from prejudices of country or of education. You are silent, La Motte; are you not of my opinion?"

"I am attending, my lord, to your *reasoning.*"

"There are, I repeat it," said the Marquis, "people of minds so weak as to shrink from acts they have been accustomed to hold wrong, however advantageous. They never suffer themselves to be guided by circumstances, but fix for life upon a certain standard from which they will on no account depart. Self preservation is the great law of nature; when a reptile hurts us, or an animal of prey threatens us, we think no farther, but endeavour to annihilate it. When my life, or what may be essential to my life, requires the sacrifice of another, or even if some passion, wholly unconquerable, requires it, I should be a madman to hesitate. La Motte, I think I may confide in you—there are ways of doing certain things—you understand me. There are times, and circumstances, and opportunities—you comprehend my meaning."

"Explain yourself, my lord."

"Kind services that—in short, there are services which excite all our gratitude, and which we can never think repaid. It is in your power to place me in such a situation."

"Indeed! my lord, name the means."

"I have already named them. This abbey well suits the purpose; it is shut up from the eye of observation; any transaction may be concealed within its walls; the hour of midnight may witness the deed, and the morn shall not dawn to disclose it. These woods tell no tales. Ah! La Motte, am I right in trusting this business with you; may I believe you are desirous of serving me, and of preserving yourself?" The Marquis paused, and looked steadfastly at La Motte, whose countenance was almost concealed by the gloom of evening.

"My lord, you may trust me in any thing. Explain yourself more fully."

"What security will you give me of your faithfulness?"

"My life, my lord; is it not already in your power?" The Marquis hesitated, and then said, "To-morrow about this time I shall return to the abbey, and will then explain my meaning, if, indeed, you shall not already have understood it. You in the meantime will consider your own powers of resolution, and be prepared either to adopt the purpose I shall suggest or to declare you will not." La Motte made some confused reply. "Farewell till to-morrow," said the Marquis; "remember that freedom and affluence are now before you." He moved towards the abbey, and mounting his horse, rode off with his attendants. La Motte walked slowly home, musing on the late conversation.

CHAPTER XIV

THE Marquis was punctual to the hour. La Motte received him at the gate, but he declined entering, and said he preferred a walk in the forest. Thither, therefore, La Motte attended him. After some general conversation, "Well," said the Marquis, "have you considered what I said, and are you prepared to decide?"

"I have, my lord, and will quickly decide, when you shall farther explain yourself. Till then I can form no resolution." The Marquis appeared dissatisfied, and was a moment silent. "Is it then possible," he at length resumed, "that you do not understand? This ignorance is surely affected. La Motte, I expect sincerity. Tell me, therefore, is it necessary I should say more?"

"It is, my lord," said La Motte, immediately. "If you fear to confide in me freely, how can I fully accomplish your purpose?"

"Before I proceed farther," said the Marquis, "let me administer some oath which shall bind you to secrecy. But this is scarcely necessary, for could I even doubt your word of honour, the remembrance of a certain transaction would point out to you the necessity of being as silent yourself as you must wish me to be." There was now a pause of silence, during which both the Marquis and La Motte betrayed some confusion. "I think, La Motte," said he, "I have given you sufficient proof that I can be grateful; the services you have already rendered me with respect to Adeline have not been unrewarded."

"True, my lord; I am ever willing to acknowledge this, and am sorry it has not been in my power to serve you more effectually. Your farther views respecting her I am ready to assist."

"I thank you.—Adeline"—the Marquis hesitated. "—Adeline," rejoined La Motte, eager to anticipate his wishes, "has beauty worthy of your pursuit. She has inspired a passion of which she ought to be proud, and at any rate she shall soon be yours. Her charms are worthy of ——"

"Yes, yes," interrupted the Marquis; "but" —— he paused.—"But they have given you too much trouble in the pursuit," said La Motte; "and to be sure, my lord, it must be confessed they have; but this trouble is all over—you may now consider her as your own."

"I would do so," said the Marquis, fixing an eye of earnest regard upon La Motte—"I would do so."

"Name your hour, my lord; you shall not be interrupted.—Beauty such as Adeline's ——"

"Watch her closely," interrupted the Marquis, "and on no account suffer her to leave her apartment. Where is she now?"

"Confined in her chamber."

"Very well. But I am impatient."

"Name your time, my lord—to-morrow night."

"*To-morrow* night," said the Marquis—"to-morrow night. Do you understand me now?"

"Yes, my lord, this night, if you wish it so. But had you not better dismiss your servants, and remain yourself in the forest. You know the door that opens upon the woods from the west tower. Come thither about twelve—I will be there to conduct you to her chamber. Remember, then, my lord, that to-night ——"

"Adeline dies!" interrupted the Marquis, in a low voice scarcely human. "Do you understand me now?"

La Motte shrunk aghast—"My lord!"

"La Motte!" said the Marquis.—There was a silence of several minutes, in which La Motte endeavoured to recover himself.—"Let me ask, my lord, the meaning of this?" said he, when he had breath to speak. "Why should you wish the death of Adeline—of Adeline, whom so lately you loved?"

"Make no inquiries for my motive," said the Marquis; "but it is as certain as that I live that she you name must die. This is sufficient." The surprise of La Motte equalled his horror. "The means are various," resumed the Marquis. "I could have wished that no blood might be spilt; and there are drugs sure and speedy in their effect, but they cannot be soon or safely procured. I also wish it over—it must be done quickly—this night."

"This night, my lord!"

"Aye, this night, La Motte; if it is to be, why not soon. Have you no convenient drug at hand?"

"None, my lord."

"I feared to trust a third person, or I should have been provided," said the Marquis. "As it is, take this poignard; use it as occasion offers, but be resolute." La Motte received the poignard with a trembling hand and continued to gaze upon it for some time, scarcely knowing what he did. "Put it up," said the Marquis, "and endeavour to recollect yourself." La Motte obeyed, but continued to muse in silence.

He saw himself entangled in the web which his own crimes had woven. Being in the power of the Marquis, he knew he must either consent to the commission of a deed from the enormity of which, depraved as he was, he shrunk in horror, or sacrifice fortune, freedom, probably life itself, to the refusal. He had been led on by slow gradations from folly to vice, till he now saw before him an abyss of guilt which startled even the conscience that so long had slumbered. The means of retreating were desperate—to proceed was equally so.

When he considered the innocence and the helplessness of Adeline, her orphan state, her former affectionate conduct, and her confidence in his protection, his heart melted with compassion for the distress he had already occasioned her, and shrunk in terror from the deed he was urged to commit. But when, on the other hand, he contemplated the destruction that threatened him from the vengeance of the Marquis, and then considered the advantages that were offered him of favour, freedom, and probably fortune, terror and temptation contributed to overcome the pleadings of humanity and silence the voice of conscience. In this state of tumultuous uncertainty he continued for some time silent, until the voice of the Marquis roused him to a convic-

tion of the necessity of at least appearing to acquiesce
in his designs.

"Do you hesitate?" said the Marquis.—"No, my lord,
my resolution is fixed—I will obey you. But methinks
it would be better to avoid bloodshed. Strange secrets
have been revealed by ——"

"Aye, but how avoid it?" interrupted the Marquis.—
"Poison *I* will not venture to procure. I have given
you one sure instrument of death. You also may find
it dangerous to inquire for a drug." La Motte perceived that he could not purchase poison without incur-
ring a discovery much greater than that he wished to
avoid. "You are right, my lord, and I will follow your
orders implicitly." The Marquis now proceeded in
broken sentences to give farther directions concerning
this dreadful scheme.

"In her sleep," said he, "at midnight; the family will
then be at rest." Afterwards they planned a story
which was to account for her disappearance, and by
which it was to seem that she had sought an escape
in consequence of her aversion to the addresses of the
Marquis. The doors of her chamber and of the west
tower were to be left open to corroborate this account,
and many other circumstances were to be contrived to
confirm the suspicion. They farther consulted how the
Marquis was to be informed of the event, and it was
agreed that he should come as usual to the abbey on
the following day. *"To-night, then,"* said the Marquis, "I may rely upon your resolution."

"You may, my lord."

"Farewell, then. When we meet again ——"

"When we meet again," said La Motte, "it will be
done." He followed the Marquis to the abbey, and
having seen him mount his horse and wished him a good

night, he retired to his chamber, where he shut himself up.

Adeline, meanwhile, in the solitude of her prison gave way to the despair which her condition inspired. She tried to arrange her thoughts and to argue herself into some degree of resignation, but reflection, by representing the past, and reason, by anticipating the future, brought before her mind the full picture of her misfortunes, and she sunk in despondency. Of Theodore, who by a conduct so noble had testified his attachment and involved himself in ruin, she thought with a degree of anguish infinitely superior to any she had felt upon any other occasion.

That the very exertions which had deserved all her gratitude and awakened all her tenderness should be the cause of his destruction, was a circumstance so much beyond the ordinary bounds of misery that her fortitude sunk at once before it. The idea of Theodore suffering—Theodore dying—was for ever present to her imagination, and frequently excluding the sense of her own danger, made her conscious only of his. Sometimes the hope he had given her of being able to vindicate his conduct, or at least to obtain a pardon, would return; but it was like the faint beam of an April morn, transient and cheerless. She knew that the Marquis, stung with jealousy and exasperated to revenge, would pursue him with unrelenting malice.

Against such an enemy what could Theodore oppose? Conscious rectitude would not avail him to ward off the blow which disappointed passion and powerful pride directed. Her distress was considerably heightened by reflecting that no intelligence of him could reach her at the abbey, and that she must remain she knew not how long in the most dreadful suspense concerning his fate. From the abbey she saw no possibility of escaping. She was a prisoner in a chamber inclosed at every avenue; she had no opportunity of conversing with any person who could afford her even a chance of relief; and she saw herself condemned to await in passive silence the impending destiny, infinitely more dreadful to her imagination than death itself.

Thus circumstanced, she yielded to the pressure of her misfortunes, and would sit for hours motionless and given up to thought. "Theodore!" she would frequently exclaim, "you cannot hear my voice; you cannot fly to help me; yourself a prisoner and in chains." The picture was too horrid. The swelling anguish of her heart would subdue her utterance—tears bathed her cheeks —and she became insensible to everything but the misery of Theodore.

On this evening her mind had been remarkably tranquil; and as she watched from her window with a still and melancholy pleasure the setting sun, the fading splendour of the western horizon, and the gradual approach of twilight, her thoughts bore her back to the time when in happier circumstances she had watched the same appearances. She recollected also the evening of her temporary escape from the abbey, when from this same window she had viewed the declining sun—how anxiously she had awaited the fall of twilight—how much she had endeavoured to anticipate the events of her future life—with what trembling fear she had descended from the tower and ventured into the forest. These reflections produced others that filled her heart with anguish and her eyes with tears.

While she was lost in her melancholy reverie she saw the Marquis mount his horse and depart from the gate. The sight of him revived in all its force a sense of the misery he inflicted on her beloved Theodore, and a consciousness of the evils which more immediately threatened herself. She withdrew from the window in an agony of tears, which continuing for a considerable time, her frame was at length quite exhausted, and she retired early to rest.

La Motte remained in his chamber till supper obliged him to descend. At table his wild and haggard countenance, which in spite of all his endeavours betrayed the disorder of his mind, and his long and frequent fits of abstraction surprised as well as alarmed Madame La Motte. When Peter left the room she tenderly inquired what had disturbed him, and he with a distorted smile tried to be gay, but the effort was beyond his art, and he quickly relapsed into silence. Or when Madame La Motte spoke, and he strove to conceal the absence of his thoughts, he answered so entirely from the purpose that his abstraction became still more apparent. Observing this, Madame La Motte appeared to take no notice of his present temper, and they continued to sit in uninterrupted silence till the hour of rest, when they retired to their chamber.

La Motte lay in a state of disturbed watchfulness for some time, and his frequent starts awoke Madame, who, however, being pacified by some trifling excuse, soon went to sleep again. This agitation continued till near midnight, when, recollecting that the time was now passing in idle reflection which ought to be devoted to action, he stole silently from his bed, wrapped himself in his night gown, and taking the lamp which burned nightly in his chamber, passed up the spiral staircase. As he went he frequently looked back, and often started and listened to the hollow sighings of the blast.

His hand shook so violently when he attempted to unlock the door of Adeline's chamber that he was obliged to set the lamp on the ground and apply both his hands. The noise he made with the key induced him to suppose he must have awakened her, but when he opened the door and perceived the stillness that reigned within, he was convinced she was asleep. When he approached the bed he heard her gently breathe, and soon after sigh—and he stopped; but silence returning, he again advanced, and then heard her sing in her sleep. As he listened he distinguished some notes of a melancholy little air which in her happier days she had often sung to him. The low and mournful accent in which she now uttered them expressed too well the tone of her mind.

La Motte now stepped hastily towards the bed, when, breathing a deep sigh, she was again silent. He undrew the curtain and saw her lying in a profound sleep, her cheek yet wet with tears, resting upon her arm. He stood a moment looking at her; and as he viewed her innocent and lovely countenance, pale in grief, the light of the lamp, which shone strong upon her eyes, awoke her, and perceiving a man, she uttered a scream. Her recollection returning, she knew him to be La Motte, and it instantly recurring to her that the Marquis was at hand, she raised herself in bed and implored pity and protection. La Motte stood looking eagerly at her, but without replying.

The wildness of his looks and the gloomy silence he preserved increased her alarm, and with tears of terror she renewed her supplication. "You once saved me from destruction," cried she; "O save me now! have pity upon me—I have no protector but you."

"What is it you fear?" said La Motte, in a tone scarcely articulate.—

"O save me—save me from the Marquis."

"Rise then," said he, "and dress yourself quickly—I shall be back again in a few minutes." He lighted a

candle that stood on the table, and left the chamber.
Adeline immediately arose and endeavoured to dress,
but her thoughts were so bewildered that she scarcely
knew what she did, and her whole frame so violently
agitated that it was with the utmost difficulty she preserved herself from fainting. She threw her clothes
hastily on, and then sat down to await the return of
La Motte. A considerable time elapsed, yet he did
not appear, and, having in vain endeavoured to compose
her spirits, the pain of suspense at length became so
insupportable that she opened the door of her chamber
and went to the top of the staircase to listen. She
thought she heard voices below; but considering that if
the Marquis was there, her appearance could only increase her danger, she checked the step she had almost
involuntarily taken to descend. Still she listened, and
still thought she distinguished voices. Soon after she
heard a door shut, and then footsteps, and she hastened
back to her chamber.

Near a quarter of an hour elapsed and La Motte did
not appear. When again she thought she heard a murmur of voices below, and also passing steps, and at
length her anxiety not suffering her to remain in her
room, she moved through the passage that communicated with the spiral staircase; but all was now still. In
a few moments, however, a light flashed across the hall,
and La Motte appeared at the door of the vaulted room.
He looked up, and seeing Adeline in the gallery, beckoned her to descend.

She hesitated and looked towards her chamber; but
La Motte now approached the stairs, and with faltering
steps she went to meet him. "I fear the Marquis may
see me," said she, whispering; "where is he?" La
Motte took her hand, and led her on, assuring her she
had nothing to fear from the Marquis. The wildness

of his looks, however, and the trembling of his hand, seemed to contradict this assurance, and she inquired whither he was leading her. "To the forest," said La Motte, "that you may escape from the abbey—a horse waits for you without. I can save you by no other means." New terror seized her. She could scarcely believe that La Motte, who had hitherto conspired with the Marquis and had so closely confined her, should now himself undertake her escape, and she at this moment felt a dreadful presentiment, which it was impossible to account for, that he was leading her out to murder her in the forest. Again shrinking back, she supplicated his mercy. He assured her he meant only to protect her, and desired she would not waste time.

There was something in his manner that spoke sincerity, and she suffered him to conduct her to a side door that opened into the forest, where she could just distinguish through the gloom a man on horseback. This brought to her remembrance the night in which she had quitted the tomb, when trusting to the person who appeared, she had been carried to the Marquis's villa. La Motte called, and was answered by Peter, whose voice somewhat reassured Adeline.

He then told her that the Marquis would return to the abbey on the following morning, and that this could be her only opportunity of escaping his designs; that she might rely upon his (La Motte's) word that Peter had orders to carry her wherever she chose; but as he knew the Marquis would be indefatigable in search of her, he advised her by all means to leave the kingdom, which she might do with Peter, who was a native of Savoy and would convey her to the house of his sister. There she might remain till La Motte himself, who did not now think it would be safe to continue much longer in France, should join her. He entreated her, whatever might happen, never to mention the events which had passed at the abbey. "To save you, Adeline, I have risked my life; do not increase my danger and your own by any unnecessary discoveries. We may never meet again, but I hope you will be happy; and remember when you think of me, that I am not quite so bad as I have been tempted to be."

Having said this, he gave her some money, which he told her would be necessary to defray the expenses of her journey. Adeline could no longer doubt his sincerity, and her transports of joy and gratitude would scarcely permit her to thank him. She wished to have bid Madame La Motte farewell, and indeed earnestly requested it, but he again told her she had no time to lose; and having wrapped her in a large cloak, he lifted her upon the horse. She bade him adieu with tears of gratitude, and Peter set off as fast as the darkness would permit.

When they were got some way, "I am glad with all my heart, ma'mselle," said he, "to see you again. Who would have thought, after all, that my master himself would have bid me take you away!—well, to be sure, strange things come to pass; but I hope we shall have better luck this time." Adeline, not choosing to reproach him with the treachery of which she feared he had been formerly guilty, thanked him for his good wishes, and said she hoped they should be more fortunate. But Peter, in his usual strain of eloquence, proceeded to undeceive her in this point, and to acquaint her with every circumstance which his memory, and it was naturally a strong one, could furnish.

Peter expressed such an artless interest in her welfare, and such a concern for her disappointment, that she could no longer doubt his faithfulness; and this conviction not only strengthened her confidence in the present undertaking, but made her listen to his conversation with kindness and pleasure. "I should never have staid at the abbey till this time," said he, "if I could have got away; but my master frighted me so about the Marquis, and I had not money enough to carry me into my own country, so that I was forced to stay. It's well we have got some solid louis d'ors now; for I question, ma'mselle, whether the people on the road would have taken those trinkets you formerly talked of for money."

"Possibly not," said Adeline: "I am thankful to Monsieur La Motte that we have more certain means of procuring conveniences. What route shall you take when we leave the forest, Peter?"—Peter mentioned very correctly a great part of the road to Lyons; "and then," said he, "we can easily get to Savoy, and that will be nothing. My sister, God bless her! I hope is living; I have not seen her many a year; but if she is not, all the people will be glad to see me, and you will easily get a lodging, ma'mselle, and everything you want."

Adeline resolved to go with him to Savoy. La Motte, who knew the character and designs of the Marquis, had advised her to leave the kingdom, and had told her, what her fears would have suggested, that the Marquis would be indefatigable in search of her. His motive for this advice must be a desire of serving her. Why else, when she was already in his power, should he remove her to another place, and even furnish her with money for the expenses of a journey?

At Leloncourt, where Peter said he was well known, she would be most likely to meet with protection and comfort, even should his sister be dead; and its distance and solitary situation were circumstances that pleased her. These reflections would have pointed out to her the prudence of proceeding to Savoy, had she been less destitute of resources in France; in her present situation they proved it to be necessary.

She inquired farther concerning the route they were to take, and whether Peter was sufficiently acquainted with the road. "When once I get to Thiers, I know it well enough," said Peter, "for I have gone it many a time in my younger days, and anybody will tell us the way there." They travelled for several hours in darkness and silence, and it was not till they emerged from the forest that Adeline saw the morning light streak the eastern clouds. The sight cheered and revived her, and as she travelled silently along, her mind revolved the events of the past night and meditated plans for the future. The present kindness of La Motte appeared so very different from his former conduct that it astonished and perplexed her, and she could only account for it by attributing it to one of those sudden impulses of humanity which sometimes operate even upon the most depraved hearts.

But when she recollected his former words, that he was not master of himself, she could scarcely believe that mere pity could induce him to break the bonds which had hitherto so strongly held him, and then considering the altered conduct of the Marquis, she was inclined to think that she owed her liberty to some change in his sentiments towards her. Yet the advice La Motte had given her to quit the kingdom, and the money with which he had supplied her for that purpose, seemed to contradict this opinion, and involved her again in doubt.

Peter now got directions to Thiers, which place they reached without any accident, and there stopped to refresh themselves. As soon as Peter thought the horse sufficiently rested, they again set forward, and from the rich plains of the Lyonnois, Adeline for the first time caught a view of the distant Alps, whose majestic heads, seeming to prop the vault of heaven, filled her mind with sublime emotions.

In a few hours they reached the vale in which stands the city of Lyons, whose beautiful environs, studded with villas and rich with cultivation, withdrew Adeline from the melancholy contemplation of her own circumstances and her more painful anxiety for Theodore.

When they reached that busy city, her first care was to inquire concerning the passage of the Rhone; but she forbore to make these inquiries of the people of the inn, considering that if the Marquis should trace her thither they might enable him to pursue her route. She therefore sent Peter to the quays to hire a boat, while she herself took a slight repast, it being her intention to embark immediately. Peter presently returned, having engaged a boat and men to take them up the Rhone to the nearest part of Savoy, from whence they were to proceed by land to the village of Leloncourt.

Having taken some refreshment, she ordered him to conduct her to the vessel. A new and striking scene presented itself to Adeline, who looked with surprise upon the river gay with vessels and the quay crowded with busy faces, and felt the contrast which the cheerful objects around bore to herself—to her, an orphan, desolate, helpless, and flying from persecution and her country. She spoke with the master of the boat, and having sent Peter back to the inn for the horse (La Motte's gift to Peter in lieu of some arrears of wages), they embarked.

As they slowly passed up the Rhone, whose steep banks, crowned with mountains, exhibited the most various, wild, and romantic scenery, Adeline sat in pensive reverie. The novelty of the scene through which she floated, now frowning with savage grandeur, and now smiling in fertility and gay with towns and villages, soothed her mind, and her sorrow gradually softened into a gentle and not unpleasing melancholy. She had seated herself at the head of the boat, where she watched its sides cleave the swift stream and listened to the dashing of the waters.

The boat, slowly opposing the current, passed along for some hours, and at length the veil of evening was stretched over the landscape. The weather was fine, and Adeline, regardless of the dews that now fell, remained in the open air observing the objects darken round her, the gay tints of the horizon fade away, and the stars gradually appear, trembling upon the lucid mirror of the waters. The scene was now sunk in deep shadow, and the silence of the hour was broken only by the measured dashing of the oars, and now and then by the voice of Peter speaking to the boatmen. Adeline sat lost in thought. The forlornness of her circumstances came heightened to her imagination.

She saw herself surrounded by the darkness and stillness of night, in a strange place, far distant from any friends, going she scarcely knew whither, under the guidance of strangers, and pursued, perhaps, by an inveterate enemy. She pictured to herself the rage of the Marquis now that he had discovered her flight, and though she knew it very unlikely he should follow her by water, for which reason she had chosen that manner of travelling, she trembled at the portrait her fancy drew. Her thoughts then wandered to the plan she should adopt after reaching Savoy; and much as her experience had prejudiced her against the manners of a convent, she saw no place more likely to afford her a proper asylum. At length she retired to the little cabin for a few hours repose.

She awoke with the dawn, and her mind being too much disturbed to sleep again, she rose and watched the gradual approach of day. As she mused, she expressed the feelings of the moment in the following

SONNET.

Morn's beaming eyes at length unclose,
And wake the blushes of the rose,
That all night long oppress'd with dews,
And veil'd in chilling shade its hues,
Reclin'd, forlorn, the languid head,
And sadly sought its parent bed;
Warmth from her ray the trembling flow'r derives,
And, sweetly blushing through its tears, revives.

"Morn's beaming eyes at length unclose,"
And melt the tears that bend the rose;
But can their charms suppress the sigh,
Or chase the tear from Sorrow's eye?
Can all their lustrous light impart
One ray of peace to Sorrow's heart?
Ah! no; their fires her fainting soul oppress—
Eve's pensive shades more soothe her meek distress!

When Adeline left the abbey, La Motte had remained for some time at the gate, listening to the steps of the horse that carried her till the sound was lost in distance; he then turned into the hall with a lightness of heart to which he had long been a stranger. The satisfaction of having thus preserved her, as he hoped, from the designs of the Marquis, overcame for a while all sense of the danger in which this step must involve him. But when he returned entirely to his own situation, the terrors of the Marquis's resentment struck their full force upon his mind, and he considered how he might best escape it.

It was now past midnight—the Marquis was expected early on the following day; and in this interval it at first appeared probable to him that he might quit the forest. There was only one horse; but he considered whether it would be best to set off immediately for Auboine, where a carriage might be procured to convey his family and his movables from the abbey, or quietly to await the arrival of the Marquis and endeavour to impose upon him by a forged story of Adeline's escape.

The time which must elapse before a carriage could reach the abbey would leave him scarcely sufficient to escape from the forest; what money he had remaining from the Marquis's bounty would not carry him far; and when it was expended he must probably be at a loss for subsistence, should he not before then be detected. By remaining at the abbey it would appear that he was unconscious of deserving the Marquis's resentment, and though he could not expect to impress a belief upon him that his orders had been executed, he might make it appear that Peter only had been accessary to the escape of Adeline; an account which would seem the more probable from Peter's having been formerly detected in a similar scheme. He believed also that if the Marquis should threaten to deliver him into the hands of justice, he might save himself by a menace of disclosing the crime he had commissioned him to perpetrate.

Thus arguing, La Motte resolved to remain at the abbey and await the event of the Marquis's disappointment.

When the Marquis did arrive, and was informed of Adeline's flight, the strong workings of his soul, which appeared in his countenance, for a while alarmed and

terrified La Motte. He cursed himself and her in terms
of such coarseness and vehemence as La Motte was
astonished to hear from a man whose *manners* were
generally amiable, whatever might be the violence and
criminality of his passions. To invent and express
these terms seemed to give him not only relief but delight; yet he appeared more shocked at the circumstance
of her escape than exasperated at the carelessness of
La Motte, and recollecting at length that he wasted
time, he left the abbey and dispatched several of his
servants in pursuit of her.

When he was gone, La Motte, believing his story
had succeeded, returned to the pleasure of considering
that he had done his duty, and to the hope that Adeline was now beyond the reach of pursuit. This calm
was of short continuance. In a few hours the Marquis
returned, accompanied by the officers of justice. The
affrighted La Motte, perceiving him approach, endeavoured to conceal himself, but was seized and carried to
the Marquis, who drew him aside.

"I am not to be imposed upon," said he, "by such a
superficial story as you have invented. You know your
life is in my hands; tell me instantly where you have
secreted Adeline, or I will charge you with the crime
you have committed against me; but upon your disclosing the place of her concealment, I will dismiss the
officers, and if you wish it, assist you to leave the kingdom. You have no time to hesitate, and may know that
I will not be trifled with." La Motte attempted to appease the Marquis, and affirmed that Adeline was really
fled he knew not whither. "You will remember, my
lord, that your character is also in my power, and that
if you proceed to extremities, you will compel me to
reveal in the face of day that you would have made me
a murderer."

"And who will believe you?" said the Marquis. "The crimes that banished you from society will be no testimony of your veracity, and that with which I now charge you will bring with it a sufficient presumption that your accusation is malicious. Officers, do your duty."

They entered the room and seized La Motte, whom terror now deprived of all power of resistance, could resistance have availed him, and in the perturbation of his mind he informed the Marquis that Adeline had taken the road to Lyons. This discovery, however, was made too late to serve himself; the Marquis seized the advantage it offered, but the charge had been given, and with the anguish of knowing that he had exposed Adeline to danger without benefiting himself, La Motte submitted in silence to his fate. Scarcely allowing him time to collect what little effects might easily be carried with him, the officers conveyed him from the abbey; but the Marquis, in consideration of the extreme distress of Madame La Motte, directed one of his servants to procure a carriage from Auboine, that she might follow her husband.

The Marquis in the meantime now acquainted with the route Adeline had taken, sent forward his faithful valet to trace her to her place of concealment, and return immediately with intelligence to the villa.

Abandoned to despair, La Motte and his wife quitted the forest of Fontanville, which had for so many months afforded them an asylum, and embarked once more upon the tumultuous world, where justice would meet La Motte in the form of destruction. They had entered the forest as a refuge rendered necessary by the former crimes of La Motte, and for some time found in it the security they sought; but other offences, for even in that sequestered spot there happened to be

temptation, soon succeeded, and his life, already sufficiently marked by the punishment of vice, now afforded
him another instance of this great truth, that "where
guilt is, there peace cannot enter."

CHAPTERS XV - XVII

[CHAPTERS XV, XVI, and XVII are summarized here.
They form what amounts to an independent episode
covering the weeks of Adeline's sojourn in Savoy and
Southern France, where, secure from the Marquis, she
awaits news of Theodore's fate. These chapters have
a certain idyllic attractiveness at times. Adeline is
among sympathetic friends, and except for her solicitude for Theodore, at peace with life. But the scene,
her life, and her feelings, are all so sentimentally depicted, and the incident is so protracted an interruption
to the course of the story, that, again, nothing of great
value is lost by the omission.

CHAPTER XV pictures Adeline's arrival with Peter
at the latter's native village of Leloncourt. Adeline
is placed in the simple cottage of Peter's sister, but the
journey and the stress of her anxiety for Theodore
bring about a dangerous fever. Her situation comes
to the attention of M. La Luc, the local "Minister,"
who takes her into his home in order that she may
have the attention of his sister and his daughter Clara.
Under their ministrations Adeline slowly recovers.
Something is told here of La Luc himself, a noble and
intelligent character, whose loss of his wife at Clara's
birth had thrown "a tincture of soft and interesting
melancholy over his character." La Luc's son (who
is discovered later in the story to be Theodore himself)

has been away from home for some years. La Luc's cottage is set in the midst of delightful Alpine scenery. The beauty of the surroundings raises the spirits of Adeline and helps in her recovery, but her happiness is always overcast by her fears for Theodore.

In CHAPTER XVI, Adeline is invited by La Luc to share his home as long as she will. She enters warmly into the life of the family, but her reticence prevents her telling them of the state of her heart or her fears for her lover. She passes her days in reading, in the enjoyment of the beauty of the country, and in half-repressed reflection, and finds relief "in the lute" and in writing poetry. The authoress finds occasion to note here that Adeline's "taste soon taught her to distinguish the superiority of the English poets from that of the French," an idea badly phrased, but unmistakably Radcliffian. On one of the family's excursions into the mountains Adeline's horse becomes unmanageable. She is rescued by "a gentleman," but both he and Adeline are injured. This M. Verneuil is taken to La Luc's house to recover, and a fine friendship grows up between the two men, sustained by much intellectual conversation.

CHAPTER XVII: Mr. Verneuil turns out to be a Frenchman of some fortune who has spent his time in travel. His stay with the La Lucs is prolonged through pure delight with the place and the people. When he leaves, La Luc, who is ageing, departs for Nice, in hope that a change of climate will improve his health. Clara and Adeline accompany him. Here they meet and cultivate the friendship of a chevalier, M. Armand, whose agreeable manners are (not unexpectedly) touched by a hidden sorrow. The cause of it is one evening confided to Adeline, who is "the very image" of his wife, lost to him some time before. Under the

stimulus of the climate and the beauty of the Riviera
Adeline rapidly recovers, but La Luc unfortunately
seems to decline even more noticeably. It is decided to
see what a sea voyage will do for him, and with Adeline and Clara he takes ship for Languedoc.]

CHAPTER XVIII

[CHAPTER XVIII opens with a rapid but solemn train
of memories and reflections as Adeline surveys the
sea at night. After a few days at sea, which "passed
with mingled pleasure and improvement," they land in
a small town in Southern France. The chapter continues.]

In the evening the beauty of the hour, and the desire of exploring new scenes, invited Adeline to walk.
La Luc was fatigued, and did not go out, and Clara
remained with him. Adeline took her way to the woods
that rose from the margin of the sea, and climbed the
wild eminence on which they hung. Often as she went
she turned her eyes to catch between the dark foliage
the blue waters of the bay, the white sail that flitted by,
and the trembling gleam of the setting sun. When she
reached the summit and looked down over the dark tops
of the woods on the wide and various prospect, she
was seized with a kind of still rapture impossible to be
expressed, and stood unconscious of the flight of time
till the sun had left the scene and twilight threw its
solemn shade upon the mountains. The sea alone reflected the fading splendour of the west; its tranquil
surface was partially disturbed by the low wind that
crept in tremulous lines along the waters, whence rising

to the woods, it shivered their light leaves and died away. Adeline, resigning herself to the luxury of sweet and tender emotions, repeated the following lines:

SUNSET.

Soft o'er the mountain's purple brow
   Meek Twilight draws her shadows gray;
From tufted woods, and valleys low,
   Light's magic colours steal away.
Yet still, amid the spreading gloom,
   Resplendent glow the western waves
   That roll o'er Neptune's coral caves,
A zone of light on Ev'ning's dome.
   On this lone summit let me rest,
And view the forms to Fancy dear,
   Till on the Ocean's darken'd breast
The stars of Ev'ning tremble clear;
Or the moon's pale orb appear,
   Throwing her line of radiance wide,
   Far o'er the lightly-curling tide,
That seems the yellow sands to chide.
No sounds o'er silence now prevail,
   Save of the dying wave below,
Or sailor's song borne on the gale,
   Or oar at distance striking slow.
So sweet! so tranquil! may my ev'ning ray
Set to this world—and rise in future day!

Adeline quitted the heights and followed a narrow path that wound to the beach below. Her mind was now particularly sensible to fine impressions, and the sweet notes of the nightingale amid the stillness of the woods again awakened her enthusiasm.

To the Nightingale.

Child of the melancholy song!
O yet that tender strain prolong!

Her lengthen'd shade, when Ev'ning flings,
    From mountain-cliffs and forests green,
And sailing slow on silent wings
    Along the glimm'ring West is seen;
I love o'er pathless hills to stray,
    Or trace the winding vale remote,
And pause, sweet Bird! to hear thy lay
    While moon-beams on the thin clouds float,
Till o'er the mountain's dewy head
Pale Midnight steals to wake the dead.

Far through the Heaven's ætherial blue,
    Wafted on Spring's light airs you come,
With blooms, and flow'rs, and genial dew,
    From climes where Summer joys to roam,
    O! welcome to your long-lost home!
"Child of the melancholy song!"
    Who lov'st the lonely woodland glade
To mourn, unseen, the boughs among,
    When Twilight spreads her pensive shade,
Again thy dulcet voice I hail!
    O! pour again the liquid note
That dies upon the ev'ning gale!
    For Fancy loves the kindred tone;
    Her griefs the plaintive accents own.
    She loves to hear thy music float
At solemn Midnight's stillest hour,
    And think on friends forever lost,
    On joys by disappointment crost,
And weep anew Love's charmful pow'r!

Then Memory wakes the magic smile,
  Th' impassion'd voice, the melting eye,
That wont the trusting heart beguile,
  And *wakes again* the hopeless sigh!

Her skill the glowing tints revive
  Of scenes that Time had bade decay;
She bids the soften'd Passions live—
  The Passions urge again their sway.
Yet o'er the long-regretted scene
  Thy song the grace of sorrow throws;
A melancholy charm serene,
  More rare than all that mirth bestows.
Then hail, sweet Bird! and hail, thy pensive tear!
To Taste, to Fancy, and to Virtue, dear!

The spreading dusk at length reminded Adeline of
her distance from the inn, and that she had her way
to find through a wild and lonely wood; she bade adieu
to the siren that had so long detained her, and pursued the path with quick steps. Having followed it for
some time, she became bewildered among the thickets,
and the increasing darkness did not allow her to judge
of the direction she was in. Her apprehensions heightened her difficulties; she thought she distinguished the
voices of men at some little distance, and she increased
her speed till she found herself on the sea-sands over
which the woods impended. Her breath was now exhausted—she paused a moment to recover herself, and
fearfully listened; but instead of the voices of men,
she heard faintly swelling in the breeze the notes of
mournful music.—Her heart, ever sensible to the impressions of melody, melted with the tones, and her
fears were for a moment lulled in sweet enchantment.
Surprise was soon mingled with delight when, as the

sounds advanced, she distinguished the tone of that instrument and the melody of that well-known air she had heard a few preceding evenings from the shores of Provence. But she had no time for conjecture—footsteps approached, and she renewed her speed. She was now emerged from the darkness of the woods, and the moon, which shone bright, exhibited along the level sands the town and port in the distance. The steps that had followed now came up with her, and she perceived two men, but they passed in conversation without noticing her, and as they passed she was certain she recollected the voice of him who was then speaking. Its tones were so familiar to her ear that she was surprised at the imperfect memory which did not suffer her to be assured by whom they were uttered. Another step now followed, and a rude voice called to her to stop. As she hastily turned her eyes she saw imperfectly by the moonlight a man in a sailor's habit pursuing, while he renewed the call. Impelled by terror, she fled along the sands, but her steps were short and trembling—those of her pursuer strong and quick.

She had just strength sufficient to reach the men who had before passed her, and to implore their protection, when her pursuer came up with them, but suddenly turned into the woods on the left and disappeared.

She had no breath to answer the inquiries of the strangers who supported her, till a sudden exclamation and the sound of her own name, drew her eyes attentively upon the person who uttered them, and in the rays which shone strong upon his features she distinguished M. Verneuil! Mutual satisfaction and explanation ensued, and when he learned that La Luc and his daughter were at the inn, he felt an increased pleasure in conducting her thither. He said that he had accidentally met with an old friend in Savoy, whom he now introduced by the name of Mauron, and who had prevailed on him to change his route and accompany him to the shores of the Mediterranean. They had embarked from the coast of Provence only a few preceding days, and had that evening landed in Languedoc on the estate of M. Mauron. Adeline had now no doubt that it was the flute of M. Verneuil, and which had so often delighted her at Leloncourt, that she had heard on the sea.

When they reached the inn they found La Luc under great anxiety for Adeline, in search of whom he had sent several people. Anxiety yielded to surprise and pleasure when he perceived her with M. Verneuil, whose eyes beamed with unusual animation on seeing Clara. After mutual congratulations, M. Verneuil observed, and lamented, the very indifferent accommodations which the inn afforded his friends, and M. Mauron immediately invited them to his château with a warmth of hospitality that overcame every scruple which delicacy or pride could oppose. The woods that Adeline had traversed formed a part of his domain, which extended almost to the inn; but he insisted that his carriage should take his guests to the château, and departed to give orders for their reception. The presence of M. Verneuil and the kindness of his friend gave to La Luc an unusual flow of spirits; he conversed with a degree of vigour and liveliness to which he had long been unaccustomed, and the smile of satisfaction that Clara gave to Adeline expressed how much she thought he was already benefited by the voyage. Adeline answered her look with a smile of less confidence, for she attributed his present animation to a more temporary cause.

About half an hour after the departure of M. Mauron, a boy who served as waiter brought a message from a chevalier then at the inn, requesting permission to speak with Adeline. The man who had pursued her along the sands instantly occurred to her, and she scarcely doubted that the stranger was some person belonging to the Marquis de Montalt, perhaps the Marquis himself, though that he should have discovered her accidentally, in so obscure a place and so immediately upon her arrival, seemed very improbable. With trembling lips, and a countenance pale as death, she inquired the name of the chevalier. The boy was not acquainted with it. La Luc asked what sort of a person he was, but the boy, who understood little of the art of describing, gave such a confused account of him that Adeline could only learn he was not large, but of a middle stature. This circumstance, however, convincing her it was not the Marquis de Montalt who desired to see her, she asked whether it would be agreeable to La Luc to have the stranger admitted. La Luc said by all means, and the waiter withdrew. Adeline sat in trembling expectation till the door opened, and Louis de la Motte entered the room. He advanced with an embarrassed and melancholy air, though his countenance had been enlightened with a momentary pleasure when he first beheld Adeline—Adeline, who was still the idol of his heart. After the first salutations were over, all apprehensions of the Marquis being now dissipated, she inquired when Louis had seen Monsieur and Madame La Motte.

"I ought rather to ask you that question," said Louis, in some confusion, "for I believe you have seen them since I have, and the pleasure of meeting you thus is equalled by my surprise. I have not heard from my father for some time, owing probably to my regiment being removed to new quarters."

He looked as if he wished to be informed with whom

Adeline now was; but as this was a subject upon which it was impossible she could speak in the presence of La Luc, she led the conversation to general topics, after having said that Monsieur and Madame La Motte were well when she left them. Louis spoke little, and often looked anxiously at Adeline, while his mind seemed labouring under strong oppression. She observed this, and recollecting the declaration he had made her on the morning of his departure from the abbey, she attributed his present embarrassment to the effect of a passion yet unsubdued, and did not appear to notice it. After he had sat near a quarter of an hour under a struggle of feelings which he could neither conquer or conceal, he rose to leave the room, and as he passed Adeline, said in a low voice, "Do permit me to speak with you alone for five minutes." She hesitated in some confusion, and then saying there were none but friends present, begged he would be seated.—"Excuse me," said he, in the same low accent; "what I would say nearly concerns you, and you only. Do favour me with a few moments' attention." He said this with a look that surprised her; and having ordered candles in another room, she went thither.

Louis sat for some moments silent, and seemingly in great perturbation of mind. At length he said, "I know not whether to rejoice or to lament at this unexpected meeting, though, if you are in safe hands, I ought certainly to rejoice, however hard the task that now falls to my lot. I am not ignorant of the dangers and persecutions you have suffered, and cannot forbear expressing my anxiety to know how you are now circumstanced. Are you indeed with friends?"—"I am," said Adeline; "M. La Motte has informed you ——" "No," replied Louis with a deep sigh, "not my father."—He paused.—"But I do indeed rejoice," resumed he, "O!

how sincerely rejoice! that you are in safety. Could you know, lovely Adeline, what I have suffered!"—— He checked himself.—"I understood you had something of importance to say, sir," said Adeline; "you must excuse me if I remind you that I have not many moments to spare."

"It is indeed of importance," replied Louis; "yet I know not how to mention it—how to soften —— This task is too severe. Alas! my poor friend!"

"Who is it you speak of, sir!" said Adeline, with quickness. Louis rose from his chair and walked about the room. "I would prepare you for what I have to say," he resumed, "but upon my soul I am not equal to it."

"I entreat you to keep me no longer in suspense," said Adeline, who had a wild idea that it was Theodore he would speak of. Louis still hesitated. "Is it—O is it?—I conjure you tell me the worst at once," said she, in a voice of agony. "I can bear it—indeed I can."

"My unhappy friend!" exclaimed Louis, "O Theodore!"——

"Theodore!" faintly articulated Adeline; "he lives then!"—— "He does," said Louis, "but—" He stopped. —"But what?" cried Adeline, trembling violently, "if he is living, you cannot tell me worse than my fears suggest; I entreat you, therefore, not to hesitate."—Louis resumed his seat, and endeavouring to assume a collected air, said, "He is living, madam, but he is a prisoner, and—for why should I deceive you?— I fear he has little to hope in this world."

"I have long feared so, sir," said Adeline, in a voice of forced composure; "you have something more terrible than this to relate, and I again entreat you will explain yourself."

"He has everything to apprehend from the Marquis

de Montalt," said Louis. "Alas! why do I say to apprehend? His judgment is already fixed—he is condemned to die."

At this confirmation of her fears a death-like paleness diffused itself over the countenance of Adeline; she sat motionless, and attempted to sigh, but seemed almost suffocated. Terrified at her situation, and expecting to see her faint, Louis would have supported her, but with her hand she waved him from her, and was unable to speak. He now called for assistance, and La Luc and Clara, with M. Verneuil, informed of Adeline's indisposition, were quickly by her side.

At the sound of their voices she looked up and seemed to recollect herself, when, uttering a heavy sigh, she burst into tears. La Luc rejoiced to see her weep, encouraged her tears, which after some time relieved her, and when she was able to speak, she desired to go back to La Luc's parlour. Louis attended her thither; when she was better he would have withdrawn, but La Luc begged he would stay.

"You are perhaps a relation of this young lady, sir," said he, "and may have brought news of her father."—"Not so, sir," replied Louis, hesitating.— "This gentleman," said Adeline, who had now recollected her dissipated thoughts, "is the son of the M. La Motte whom you may have heard me mention."— Louis seemed shocked to be declared the son of a man that had once acted so unworthily towards Adeline, who instantly perceiving the pain her words occasioned, endeavoured to soften their effect by saying that La Motte had saved her from imminent danger and had afforded her an asylum for many months. Adeline sat in a state of dreadful solicitude to know the particulars of Theodore's situation, yet could not acquire courage to renew the subject in the presence of La Luc; she ventured, however, to ask Louis if his own regiment was quartered in the town.

He replied that his regiment lay at Vaceau, a French town on the frontiers of Spain, that he had just crossed a part of the Gulf of Lyons, and was on his way to Savoy, whither he should set out early in the morning. "We are lately come from thence," said Adeline; "may I ask to what part of Savoy you are going?"— "To Leloncourt," he replied.—"To Leloncourt!" said Adeline in some surprise.—"I am a stranger to the country," resumed Louis; "but I go to serve my friend. You seem to know Leloncourt."—"I do indeed," said Adeline.—"You probably know then that M. La Luc lives there, and will guess the motive of my journey."

"O heaven! is it possible?" exclaimed Adeline—"is it possible that Theodore Peyrou is a relation of M. La Luc!"

"Theodore! what of my son?" asked La Luc in surprise and apprehension.—"Your son!" said Adeline, in a trembling voice, "your son!"—The astonishment and anguish depicted on her countenance increased the apprehensions of this unfortunate father, and he renewed his question. But Adeline was totally unable to answer him; and the distress of Louis on thus unexpectedly discovering the father of his unhappy friend, and knowing that it was his task to disclose the fate of his son, deprived him for some time of all power of utterance, and La Luc and Clara, whose fears were every instant heightened by this dreadful silence, continued to repeat their questions.

At length a sense of the approaching sufferings of the good La Luc overcoming every other feeling, Adeline recovered strength of mind sufficient to try to soften the intelligence Louis had to communicate, and to conduct Clara to another room. Here she collected resolution to tell her, and with much tender consideration, the circumstances of her brother's situation, concealing only her knowledge of his sentence being already pronounced. This relation necessarily included the mention of their attachment, and in the friend of her heart Clara discovered the innocent cause of her brother's destruction. Adeline also learned the occasion of that circumstance which had contributed to keep her ignorant of Theodore's relationship to La Luc; she was told the former had taken the name of Peyrou, with an estate which had been left him about a year before by a relation of his mother's, upon that condition. Theodore had been designed for the church, but his disposition inclined him to a more active life than the clerical habit would admit of, and on his accession to this estate he had entered into the service of the French king.

In the few and interrupted interviews which had been allowed them at Caux, Theodore had mentioned his family to Adeline only in general terms, and thus, when they were so suddenly separated, had without designing it, left her in ignorance of his father's name and place of residence.

The sacredness and delicacy of Adeline's grief, which had never permitted her to mention the subject of it even to Clara, had since contributed to deceive her.

The distress of Clara on learning the situation of her brother could endure no restraint; Adeline, who had commanded her feelings so as to impart this intelligence with tolerable composure, only by a strong effort of mind, was now almost overwhelmed by her own and Clara's accumulated suffering. While they wept forth the anguish of their hearts, a scene if possible more

affecting passed between La Luc and Louis, who perceived it was necessary to inform him, though cautiously and by degrees, of the full extent of his calamity.
He therefore told La Luc that though Theodore had
been first tried for the offence of having quitted his post,
he was now condemned on a charge of assault made upon
his general officer, the Marquis de Montalt, who had
brought witnesses to prove that his life had been endangered by the circumstance, and who, having pursued
the prosecution with the most bitter rancour, had at
length obtained the sentence which the law could not
withhold, but which every other officer in the regiment
deplored.

Louis added that the sentence was to be executed
in less than a fortnight, and that Theodore being very
unhappy at receiving no answers to the letters he had
sent his father, wishing to see him once more and
knowing that there was now no time to be lost, had
requested him to go to Leloncourt and acquaint his
father with his situation.

La Luc received the account of his son's condition
with a distress that admitted neither of tears nor complaint. He asked where Theodore was, and desiring
to be conducted to him, he thanked Louis for all his
kindness and ordered post-horses immediately.

A carriage was soon ready, and this unhappy father,
after taking a mournful leave of M. Verneuil, and sending a compliment to M. Mauron, attended by his family,
set out for the prison of his son. The journey was a
silent one; each individual of the party endeavoured,
in consideration of each other, to suppress the expression of grief, but was unable to do more. La Luc appeared calm and complacent; he seemed frequently to
be engaged in prayer; but a struggle for resignation

and composure was sometimes visible upon his countenance, notwithstanding the efforts of his mind.

CHAPTER XIX

WE NOW return to the Marquis de Montalt, who having seen La Motte safely lodged in the prison of D——y, and learning the trial would not come on immediately, had returned to his villa on the borders of the forest, where he expected to hear news of Adeline. It had been his intention to follow his servants to Lyons, but he now determined to wait a few days for letters, and he had little doubt that Adeline, since her flight had been so quickly pursued, would be overtaken, and probably before she could reach that city. In this expectation he had been miserably disappointed; for his servants informed him that though they traced her thither, they had neither been able to follow her route beyond nor to discover her at Lyons. This escape she probably owed to having embarked on the Rhone, for it does not appear that the Marquis's people thought of seeking her on the course of that river.

His presence was soon after required at Vaceau, where the court martial was then sitting; thither, therefore, he went, with passions still more exasperated by his late disappointment, and procured the condemnation of Theodore. The sentence was universally lamented, for Theodore was much beloved in his regiment, and the occasion of the Marquis's personal resentment towards him being known, every heart was interested in his cause.

Louis de la Motte happening at this time to be stationed in the same town, heard an imperfect account of

THE ROMANCE OF THE FOREST 517

the story, and being convinced that the prisoner was
the young chevalier whom he had formerly seen with
the Marquis at the abbey, he was induced partly from
compassion and partly with a hope of hearing of his
parents, to visit him. The compassionate sympathy
which Louis expressed, and the zeal with which he tendered his services, affected Theodore and excited in
him a warm return of friendship. Louis made him frequent visits, did everything that kindness could suggest
to alleviate his sufferings, and a mutual esteem and confidence ensued.

Theodore at length communicated the chief subject
of his concern to Louis, who discovered with inexpressible grief that it was Adeline whom the Marquis had
thus cruelly persecuted, and Adeline for whose sake the
generous Theodore was about to suffer. He soon perceived also that Theodore was his favoured rival, but
he generously suppressed the jealous pang this discovery occasioned, and determined that no prejudice of
passion should withdraw him from the duties of humanity and friendship. He eagerly inquired where
Adeline then resided. "She is yet, I fear, in the power
of the Marquis," said Theodore, sighing deeply. "O
God!—these chains!"—and he threw an agonizing
glance upon them. Louis sat silent and thoughtful; at
length starting from his reverie, he said he would go
to the Marquis, and immediately quitted the prison.
The Marquis was, however, already set off for Paris,
where he had been summoned to appear at the approaching trial of La Motte; and Louis, yet ignorant of the
late transactions at the abbey, returned to the prison,
where he endeavoured to forget that Theodore was the
favoured rival of his love, and to remember him only
as the defender of Adeline. So earnestly he pressed
his offers of service that Theodore, whom the silence

of his father equally surprised and afflicted, and who was very anxious to see him once again, accepted his proposal of going himself to Savoy. "My letters I strongly suspect to have been intercepted by the Marquis," said Theodore; "if so, my poor father will have the whole weight of this calamity to sustain at once, unless I avail myself of your kindness, and I shall neither see him nor hear from him before I die. Louis! there are moments when my fortitude shrinks from the conflict, and my senses threaten to desert me."

No time was to be lost; the warrant for his execution had already received the king's signature, and Louis immediately set forward for Savoy. The letters of Theodore had indeed been intercepted by order of the Marquis, who in the hope of discovering the asylum of Adeline, had opened and afterwards destroyed them.

But to return to La Luc, who now drew near Vaceau, and whom his family observed to be greatly changed in his looks since he had heard the late calamitous intelligence; he uttered no complaint; but it was too obvious that his disorder had made a rapid progress. Louis, who during the journey proved the goodness of his disposition by the delicate attentions he paid this unhappy party, concealed his observation of the decline of La Luc, and to support Adeline's spirits endeavoured to convince her that her apprehensions on this subject were groundless. Her spirits did indeed require support, for she was now within a few miles of the town that contained Theodore; and while her increasing perturbation almost overcame her, she yet tried to appear composed. When the carriage entered the town, she cast a timid and anxious glance from the window in search of the prison; but having passed through several streets without perceiving any building which corresponded with her idea of that she looked for, the coach stopped at the inn. The frequent changes in La Luc's countenance betrayed the violent agitation of his mind, and when he attempted to alight, feeble and exhausted, he was compelled to accept the support of Louis, to whom he faintly said as he passed to the parlour, "I am indeed sick at heart, but I trust the pain will not be long." Louis pressed his hand without speaking, and hastened back for Adeline and Clara, who were already in the passage. La Luc wiped the tears from his eyes (they were the first he had shed), as they entered the room. "I would go immediately to my poor boy," said he to Louis; "yours, sir, is a mournful office—be so good as to conduct me to him." He rose to go, but, feeble and overcome with grief, again sat down. Adeline and Clara united in entreating that he would compose himself, and take some refreshment, and Louis, urging the necessity of preparing Theodore for the interview, prevailed with him to delay it till his son should be informed of his arrival, and immediately quitted the inn for the prison of his friend. When he was gone, La Luc, as a duty he owed those he loved, tried to take some support, but the convulsions of his throat would not suffer him to swallow the wine he held to his parched lips, and he was now so much disordered that he desired to retire to his chamber, where alone and in prayer he passed the dreadful interval of Louis's absence.

Clara on the bosom of Adeline, who sat in calm but deep distress, yielded to the violence of her grief. "I shall lose my dear father too," said she; "I see it; I shall lose my father and my brother together." Adeline wept with her friend for some time in silence, and then attempted to persuade her that La Luc was not so ill as she apprehended.

"Do not mislead me with hope," she replied, "that

will not survive the shock of this calamity—I saw it
from the first." Adeline knowing that La Luc's distress would be heightened by the observance of his
daughter's, and that indulgence would only increase its
poignancy, endeavoured to rouse her to an exertion of
fortitude by urging the necessity of commanding her
emotion in the presence of her father. "This is possible," added she, "however painful may be the effort.
You must know, my dear, that my grief is not inferior
to your own, yet I have hitherto been enabled to support my sufferings in silence; for M. La Luc I do, indeed, love and reverence as a parent."

Louis meanwhile reached the prison of Theodore, who
received him with an air of mingled surprise and impatience. "What brings you back so soon," said he, "have
you heard news of my father?" Louis now gradually
unfolded the circumstances of their meeting, and La
Luc's arrival at Vaceau. A various emotion agitated
the countenance of Theodore on receiving this intelligence. "My poor father!" said he, "he has then followed his son to this ignominious place! Little did I
think when last we parted he would meet me in a prison
under condemnation!" This reflection roused an impetuosity of grief which deprived him for some time
of speech. "But where is he?" said Theodore, recovering himself; "now he is come, I shrink from the
interview I have so much wished for. The sight of
his distress will be dreadful to me. Louis! when I am
gone—comfort my poor father." His voice was again
interrupted by sobs; and Louis, who had been fearful
of acquainting him at the same time of the arrival of
La Luc and the discovery of Adeline, now judged it
proper to administer the cordial of this latter intelligence.

The glooms of a prison, and of calamity, vanished

for a transient moment; those who had seen Theodore would have believed this to be the instant which gave him life and liberty. When his first emotions subsided, "I will not repine," said he; "since I know that Adeline is preserved and that I shall once more see my father, I will endeavour to die with resignation." He inquired if La Luc was there in the prison; and was told he was at the inn with Clara and Adeline. "Adeline! Is Adeline there too!—This is beyond my hopes. Yet why do I rejoice? I must never see her more: this is no place for Adeline." Again he relapsed into an agony of distress, and again repeated a thousand questions concerning Adeline, till he was reminded by Louis that his father was impatient to see him—when, shocked that he had so long detained his friend, he entreated him to conduct La Luc to the prison, and endeavoured to recollect fortitude for the approaching interview.

When Louis returned to the inn La Luc was still in his chamber, and Clara quitting the room to call him, Adeline seized with trembling impatience the opportunity to inquire more particularly concerning Theodore than she chose to do in the presence of his unhappy sister. Louis represented him to be much more tranquil than he really was: Adeline was somewhat soothed by the account; and her tears, hitherto restrained, flowed silently and fast till La Luc appeared. His countenance had recovered its serenity, but was impressed with a deep and steady sorrow which excited in the beholder a mingled emotion of pity and reverence. "How is my son, sir?" said he as he entered the room. "We will go to him immediately."

Clara renewed the entreaties that had been already rejected, to accompany her father, who persisted in a refusal. "To-morrow you shall see him," added he; "but our first meeting must be alone. Stay with your

friend, my dear; she has need of consolation." When
La Luc was gone, Adeline, unable longer to struggle
against the force of grief, retired to her chamber and
her bed.

La Luc walked silently towards the prison, resting
on the arm of Louis. It was now night. A dim lamp
that hung above shewed them the gates, and Louis rung
a bell; La Luc, almost overcome with agitation, leaned
against the postern till the porter appeared. He inquired for Theodore, and followed the man; but when
he reached the second courtyard he seemed ready to
faint, and again stopped. Louis desired the porter
would fetch some water, but La Luc, recovering his
voice, said he should soon be better, and would not
suffer him to go. In a few minutes he was able to
follow Louis, who led him through several dark passages and up a flight of steps to a door, which being
unbarred, disclosed to him the prison of his son. He
was seated at a small table on which stood a lamp that
threw a feeble light across the place, sufficient only to
shew its desolation and wretchedness. When he perceived La Luc, he sprung from his chair and in the next
moment he was in his arms. "My father!" said he in a
tremulous voice. "My son!" exclaimed La Luc; and
they were for some time silent and locked in each other's
embrace. At length Theodore led him to the only chair
the room afforded, and seating himself with Louis at
the foot of the bed, had leisure to observe the ravages
which illness and calamity had made on the features of
his parent. La Luc made several efforts to speak, but
unable to articulate, laid his hand upon his breast and
sighed deeply. Fearful of the consequence of so affecting a scene on his shattered frame, Louis endeavoured
to call off his attention from the immediate object of his

distress, and interrupted the silence; but La Luc shuddering, and complaining he was very cold, sunk back in his chair. His condition roused Theodore from the stupor of despair; and while he flew to support his father, Louis ran out for other assistance.—"I shall soon be better, Theodore," said La Luc, unclosing his eyes, "the faintness is already going off. I have not been well of late; and this sad meeting!"——Unable any longer to command himself, Theodore wrung his hands, and the distress which had long struggled for utterance burst in convulsive sobs from his breast. La Luc gradually revived, and exerted himself to calm the transports of his son; but the fortitude of the latter had now entirely forsaken him and he could only utter exclamation and complaint. "Ah! little did I think we should ever meet under circumstances so dreadful as the present! But I have not deserved them, my father! the motives of my conduct have still been just."

"That is my supreme consolation," said La Luc, "and ought to support you in this hour of trial. The Almighty God, who is the judge of hearts, will reward you hereafter. Trust in him, my son; I look to him with no feeble hope, but with a firm reliance on his justice!" La Luc's voice faltered; he raised his eyes to heaven with an expression of meek devotion, while the tears of humanity fell slowly on his cheek.

Still more affected by his last words, Theodore turned from him and paced the room with quick steps: the entrance of Louis was a very seasonable relief to La Luc, who, taking a cordial he had brought, was soon sufficiently restored to discourse on the subject most interesting to him. Theodore tried to attain a command of his feelings, and succeeded. He conversed with tolerable composure for above an hour, during which La Luc endeavoured to elevate by religious hope the mind of his son, and to enable him to meet with fortitude the awful hour that approached. But the appearance of resignation which Theodore attained always vanished when he reflected that he was going to leave his father a prey to grief, and his beloved Adeline forever. When La Luc was about to depart, he again mentioned her. "Afflicting as an interview must be in our present circumstances," said he, "I cannot bear the thought of quitting the world without seeing her once again; yet I know not how to ask her to encounter for my sake the misery of a parting scene. Tell her that my thoughts never for a moment leave her, that"—— La Luc interrupted and assured him that since he so much wished it, he should see her, though a meeting could serve only to heighten the mutual anguish of a final separation.

"I know it—I know it too well," said Theodore; "yet I cannot resolve to see her no more, and thus spare her the pain this interview must inflict. O my father! when I think of those whom I must soon leave forever, my heart breaks. But I will indeed try to profit by your precept and example, and shew that your paternal care has not been in vain. My good Louis, go with my father—he has need of support. How much I owe this generous friend," added Theodore, "you well know, sir." —"I do in truth," replied La Luc, "and can never repay his kindness to you. He has contributed to support us all; but you require comfort more than myself—he shall remain with you—I will go alone."

This Theodore would not suffer; and La Luc no longer opposing him, they affectionately embraced and separated for the night.

When they reached the inn, La Luc consulted with Louis on the possibility of addressing a petition to the sovereign in time enough to save Theodore. His distance from Paris and the short interval before the period fixed for the execution of the sentence made this design difficult; but believing it was practicable, La Luc, incapable as he appeared of performing so long a journey, determined to attempt it. Louis, thinking that the undertaking would prove fatal to the father without benefiting the son, endeavoured, though faintly, to dissuade him from it—but his resolution was fixed.—"If I sacrifice the small remains of my life in the service of my child," said he, "I shall lose little; if I save him, I shall gain everything. There is no time to be lost—I will set off immediately."

He would have ordered post-horses, but Louis and Clara, who was now come from the bedside of her friend, urged the necessity of his taking a few hours repose. He was at length compelled to acknowledge himself unequal to the immediate exertion which parental anxiety prompted, and consented to seek rest.

When he had retired to his chamber, Clara lamented the condition of her father.—"He will not bear the journey," said she; "he is greatly changed within these few days."—Louis was so entirely of her opinion that he could not disguise it, even to flatter her with a hope. She added, what did not contribute to raise his spirits, that Adeline was so much indisposed by her grief for the situation of Theodore and the sufferings of La Luc that she dreaded the consequence.

It has been seen that the passion of young La Motte had suffered no abatement from time or absence; on the contrary, the persecution and the dangers which had pursued Adeline awakened all his tenderness and drew her nearer to his heart. When he had discovered that Theodore loved her, and was beloved again, he experienced all the anguish of jealousy and disappointment; for though she had forbidden him to hope, he found it too painful an effort to obey her, and had secretly cherished the flame which he ought to have stifled. His heart was, however, too noble to suffer his zeal for Theodore to abate because he was his favoured rival, and his mind too strong not to conceal the anguish this certainty occasioned. The attachment which Theodore had testified towards Adeline even endeared him to Louis, when he had recovered from the first shock of disappointment, and that conquest over jealousy which originated in principle and was pursued with difficulty, became afterwards his pride and his glory. When, however, he again saw Adeline—saw her in the mild dignity of sorrow more interesting than ever—saw her, though sinking beneath its pressure, yet tender and solicitous to soften the afflictions of those around her—it was with the utmost difficulty he preserved his resolution and forbore to express the sentiments she inspired. When he farther considered that her acute sufferings arose from the strength of her affection, he more than ever wished himself the object of a heart capable of so tender a regard, and Theodore in prison and in chains was a momentary object of envy.

In the morning, when La Luc arose from short and disturbed slumbers, he found Louis, Clara, and Adeline, whom indisposition could not prevent from paying him this testimony of respect and affection, assembled in the parlour of the inn to see him depart. After a slight breakfast, during which his feelings permitted him to say little, he bade his friends a sad farewell, and stepped into the carriage, followed by their tears and prayers.—Adeline immediately retired to her chamber, which she was too ill to quit that day. In the evening Clara left her friend, and conducted by Louis, went to visit her brother, whose emotions on hearing of his father's departure were various and strong.

CHAPTER XX

WE RETURN now to Pierre de la Motte, who after remaining some weeks in the prison of D——y, was removed to take his trial in the courts of Paris, whither the Marquis de Montalt followed to prosecute the charge. Madame La Motte accompanied her husband to the prison of the Chatelet. His mind sunk under the weight of his misfortunes, nor could all the efforts of his wife rouse him from the torpidity of despair which a consideration of his circumstances occasioned. Should he be even acquitted of the charge brought against him by the Marquis (which was very unlikely), he was now in the scene of his former crimes, and the moment that should liberate him from the walls of his prison would probably deliver him again into the hands of offended justice.

The prosecution of the Marquis was too well founded, and its object of a nature too serious, not to justify the terror of La Motte. Soon after the latter had settled at the abbey of St. Clair, the small stock of money which the emergency of his circumstances had left him being nearly exhausted, his mind became corroded with the most cruel anxiety concerning the means of his future subsistence. As he was one evening riding alone in a remote part of the forest, musing on his distressed circumstances, and meditating plans to relieve the exigencies which he saw approaching, he perceived among the trees at some distance a chevalier on horseback, who was riding deliberately along and seemed wholly unattended. A thought darted across the mind of La Motte that he might be spared the evils which threatened him by robbing this stranger. His former practices had passed the boundary of honesty—fraud was in some degree familiar to him—and the thought was not dismissed. He hesitated—every moment of hesitation increased the power of temptation—the opportunity was such as might never occur again. He looked round, and as far as the trees opened saw no person but the chevalier, who seemed by his air to be a man of distinction. Summoning all his courage, La Motte rode forward and attacked him. The Marquis de Montalt, for it was him, was unarmed, but knowing that his attendants were not far off, he refused to yield. While they were struggling for victory, La Motte saw several horsemen enter the extremity of the avenue, and, rendered desperate by opposition and delay, he drew from his pocket a pistol (which an apprehension of banditti made him usually carry when he rode to a distance from the abbey), and fired at the Marquis, who staggered and fell senseless to the ground. La Motte had time to tear from his coat a brilliant star, some diamond rings from his fingers, and to rifle his pockets, before his attendants came up. Instead of pursuing the robber, they all, in their first confusion, flew to assist their lord, and La Motte escaped.

He stopped before he reached the abbey at a little ruin, the tomb formerly mentioned, to examine his booty. It consisted of a purse containing seventy louis d'ors; of a diamond star, three rings of great value, and a miniature set with brilliants of the Marquis himself, which he had intended as a present for his favourite mistress. To La Motte, who but a few hours before had seen himself nearly destitute, the view of this treasure excited an almost ungovernable transport; but

it was soon checked when he remembered the means he
had employed to obtain it, and that he had paid for the
wealth he contemplated the price of blood. Naturally
violent in his passions, this reflection sunk him from the
summit of exultation to the abyss of despondency. He
considered himself a murderer, and startled as one awakened from a dream, would have given half the world,
had it been his, to have been as poor and, comparatively,
as guiltless as a few preceding hours had seen him.
On examining the portrait he discovered the resemblance, and believing that his hand had deprived the
original of life, he gazed upon the picture with unutterable anguish. To the horrors of remorse succeeded the
perplexities of fear. Apprehensive of he knew not what,
he lingered at the tomb, where he at length deposited
his treasure, believing that if his offence should awaken
justice, the abbey might be searched and these jewels
betray him. From Madame La Motte it was easy to
conceal his increase of wealth; for as he had never made
her acquainted with the exact state of his finances, she
had not suspected the extreme poverty which menaced
him, and as they continued to live as usual, she believed
that their expenses were drawn from the usual supply.
But it was not so easy to disguise the workings of remorse and horror. His manner became gloomy and
reserved, and his frequent visits to the tomb, where he
went partly to examine his treasure, but chiefly to
indulge in the dreadful pleasure of contemplating the
picture of the Marquis, excited curiosity. In the solitude of the forest, where no variety of objects occurred
to renovate his ideas, the horrible one of having committed murder was ever present to him.—When the
Marquis arrived at the abbey, the astonishment and
terror of La Motte, for at first he scarce knew whether
he beheld the shadow or the substance of a human form,

were quickly succeeded by apprehension of the punishment due to the crime he had really committed. When his distress had prevailed on the Marquis to retire, he informed him that he was by birth a chevalier; he then touched upon such parts of his misfortunes as he thought would excite pity, expressed such abhorrence of his guilt, and voluntarily uttered such a solemn promise of returning the jewels he had yet in his possession, for he had ventured to dispose only of a small part, that the Marquis at length listened to him with some degree of compassion. This favourable sentiment, seconded by a selfish motive, induced the Marquis to compromise with La Motte. Of quick and inflammable passions, he had observed the beauty of Adeline with an eye of no common regard, and he resolved to spare the life of La Motte upon no other condition than the sacrifice of this unfortunate girl. La Motte had neither resolution nor virtue sufficient to reject the terms—the jewels were restored, and he consented to betray the innocent Adeline. But as he was too well acquainted with her heart to believe that she would easily be won to the practice of vice, and as he still felt a degree of pity and tenderness for her, he endeavoured to prevail on the Marquis to forbear precipitate measures, and to attempt gradually to undermine her principles by seducing her affections. He approved and adopted this plan. The failure of his first scheme induced him to employ the stratagems he afterwards pursued, and thus to multiply the misfortunes of Adeline.

Such were the circumstances which had brought La Motte to his present deplorable situation. The day of trial was now come, and he was led from prison into the court, where the Marquis appeared as his accuser. When the charge was delivered, La Motte, as is usual, pleaded not guilty, and the Advocate Nemours, who had undertaken to plead for him, afterwards endeavoured to make it appear that the accusation on the part of the Marquis de Montalt was false and malicious. To this purpose he mentioned the circumstance of the latter having attempted to persuade his client to the murder of Adeline; he farther urged that the Marquis had lived in habits of intimacy with La Motte for several months immediately preceding his arrest and that it was not till he had disappointed the designs of his accuser by conveying beyond his reach the unhappy object of his vengeance, that the Marquis had thought proper to charge La Motte with the crime for which he stood indicted. Nemours urged the improbability of one man's keeping up a friendly intercourse with another from whom he had suffered the double injury of assault and robbery; yet it was certain that the Marquis had observed a frequent intercourse with La Motte for some months following the time specified for the commission of the crime. If the Marquis intended to prosecute, why was it not immediately after his discovery of La Motte? and if not then, what had influenced him to prosecute at so distant a period?

To this nothing was replied on the part of the Marquis; for as his conduct on this point had been subservient to his designs on Adeline, he could not justify it but by exposing schemes which would betray the darkness of his character and invalidate his cause. He therefore contented himself with producing several of his servants as witnesses of the assault and robbery, who swore without scruple to the person of La Motte, though not one of them had seen him otherwise than through the gloom of evening and riding off at full speed. On a cross examination most of them contradicted each other; their evidence was of course rejected; but as the Marquis had yet two other witnesses

to produce, whose arrival at Paris had been hourly expected, the event of the trial was postponed and the
court adjourned.

La Motte was reconducted to his prison under the
same pressure of despondency with which he had quitted
it. As he walked through one of the avenues he passed
a man who stood by to let him proceed, and who regarded him with a fixed and earnest eye. La Motte
thought he had seen him before, but the imperfect view
he caught of his features through the duskiness of the
place made him uncertain as to this, and his mind was
in too perturbed a state to suffer him to feel an interest
on the subject. When he was gone, the stranger inquired of the keeper of the prison who La Motte was;
on being told, and receiving answers to some farther
questions he put, he desired he might be admitted to
speak with him. The request, as the man was only a
debtor, was granted; but as the doors were now shut
for the night, the interview was deferred till the
morrow.

La Motte found Madame in his room, where she had
been waiting for some hours to hear the event of the
trial. They now wished more earnestly than ever to
see their son, but they were, as he had suspected, ignorant of his change of quarters, owing to the letters
which he had as usual addressed to them under an assumed name, remaining at the post-house of Auboine.
This circumstance occasioned Madame La Motte to address her letters to the place of her son's late residence,
and he had thus continued ignorant of his father's misfortunes and removal. Madame La Motte, surprised at
receiving no answers to her letters, sent off another containing an account of the trial as far as it had proceeded, and a request that her son would obtain leave
of absence and set out for Paris instantly. As she

was still ignorant of the failure of her letters, and had it been otherwise, would not have known whither to have sent them, she directed this as usual.

Meanwhile his approaching fate was never absent for a moment from the mind of La Motte, which, feeble by nature, and still more enervated by habits of indulgence, refused to support him at this dreadful period.

While these scenes were passing at Paris, La Luc arrived there without any accident, after performing a journey during which he had been supported almost entirely by the spirit of his resolution. He hastened to throw himself at the feet of the sovereign, and such was the excess of his feeling on presenting the petition which was to decide the fate of his son, that he could only look silently up, and then fainted. The king received the paper, and giving orders for the unhappy father to be taken care of, passed on. He was carried back to his hotel, where he awaited the event of this his final effort.

Adeline, meanwhile, continued at Vaceau in a state of anxiety too powerful for her long-agitated frame, and the illness in consequence of this confined her almost wholly to her chamber. Sometimes she ventured to flatter herself with a hope that the journey of La Luc would be successful, but these short and illusive intervals of comfort served only to heighten by contrast the despondency that succeeded, and in the alternate extremes of feeling she experienced a state more torturing than that produced either by the sharp sting of unexpected calamity or the sullen pain of settled despair.

When she was well enough she came down to the parlour to converse with Louis, who brought her frequent accounts of Theodore, and who passed every moment he could snatch from the duty of his profession in endeavours to support and console his afflicted friends. Adeline and Theodore both looked to him for the little comfort allotted them, for he brought them intelligence of each other, and whenever he appeared a transient melancholy kind of pleasure played round their hearts. He could not conceal from Theodore Adeline's indisposition, since it was necessary to account for her not indulging the earnest wish he repeatedly expressed to see her again. To Adeline he spoke chiefly of the fortitude and resignation of his friend, not however forgetting to mention the tender affection he constantly expressed for her. Accustomed to derive her sole consolation from the presence of Louis, and to observe his unwearied friendship towards him whom she so truly loved, she found her esteem for him ripen into gratitude and her regard daily increase.

The fortitude with which he had said Theodore supported his calamities was somewhat exaggerated. He could not forget those ties which bound him to life sufficiently to meet his fate with firmness; but though the paroxysms of grief were acute and frequent, he sought, and often attained in the presence of his friends, a manly composure. From the event of his father's journey he hoped little, yet that little was sufficient to keep his mind in the torture of suspense till the issue should appear.

On the day preceding that fixed for the execution of the sentence, La Luc reached Vaceau. Adeline was at her chamber window when the carriage drew up to the inn; she saw him alight and with feeble steps, supported by Peter, enter the house. From the languor of his air she drew no favourable omen, and almost sinking under the violence of her emotion, she went to meet him. Clara was already with her father when Adeline entered the room. She approached him, but dreading to receive from his lips a confirmation of the misfortune his countenance seemed to indicate, she looked expressively at him and sat down, unable to speak the question she would have asked. He held out his hand to her in silence, sunk back in his chair, and seemed to be fainting under oppression of heart. His manner confirmed all her fears; at this dreadful conviction her senses failed her, and she sat motionless and stupified. La Luc and Clara were too much occupied by their own distress to observe her situation. After some time she breathed a heavy sigh and burst into tears. Relieved by weeping, her spirits gradually returned, and she at length said to La Luc, "It is unnecessary, sir, to ask the success of your journey, yet when you can bear to mention the subject, I wish ———"

La Luc waved his hand—"Alas!" said he, "I have nothing to tell but what you already guess too well. My poor Theodore!"—His voice was convulsed with sorrow, and some moments of unutterable anguish followed.

Adeline was the first who recovered sufficient recollection to notice the extreme languor of La Luc and attend to his support. She ordered him refreshments, and entreated he would retire to his bed and suffer her to send for a physician, adding that the fatigue he had suffered made repose absolutely necessary. "Would that I could find it, my dear child," said he; "it is not in this world that I must look for it, but in a better, and that better I trust I shall soon attain. But where is our good friend, Louis La Motte? He must lead me to my son."—Grief again interrupted his utterance, and the entrance of Louis was a very seasonable relief to them all. Their tears explained the question he would have asked; La Luc immediately inquired for his son, and thanking Louis for all his kindness to him, desired to be conducted to the prison. Louis endeavoured to persuade him to defer his visit till the morning, and Adeline and Clara joined their entreaties with his, but

La Luc determined to go that night.—"His time is short," said he; "a few hours and I shall see him no more, at least in this world; let me not neglect these precious moments. Adeline! I had promised my poor boy that he should see you once more; you are not now equal to the meeting. I will try to reconcile him to the disappointment; but if I fail, and you are better in the morning, I know you will exert yourself to sustain the interview."—Adeline looked impatient, and attempted to speak. La Luc rose to depart, but could only reach the door of the room, where, faint and feeble, he sat down in a chair. "I must submit to necessity," said he; "I find I am not able to go farther to-night. Go to him, La Motte, and tell him I am somewhat disordered by my journey, but that I will be with him early in the morning. Do not flatter him with a hope; prepare him for the worst."—There was a pause of silence; La Luc, at length recovering himself, desired Clara would order his bed to be got ready, and she willingly obeyed. When he withdrew, Adeline told Louis, what was indeed unnecessary, the event of La Luc's journey. "I own," continued she, "that I had sometimes suffered myself to hope, and I now feel this calamity with double force. I fear too that M. La Luc will sink under its pressure; he is much altered for the worse since he set out for Paris. Tell me your opinion sincerely."

The change was so obvious that Louis could not deny it, but he endeavoured to soothe her apprehension by ascribing this alteration in a great measure to the temporary fatigue of travelling. Adeline declared her resolution of accompanying La Luc to take leave of Theodore in the morning. "I know not how I shall support the interview," said she; "but to see him once more is a duty I owe both to him and myself. The remembrance of having neglected to give him this last proof of affection would pursue me with incessant remorse."

After some farther conversation on this subject, Louis withdrew to the prison, ruminating on the best means of imparting to his friend the fatal intelligence he had to communicate. Theodore received it with more composure than he had expected, but he asked with impatience why he did not see his father and Adeline, and on being informed that indisposition withheld them, his imagination seized on the worst possibility and suggested that his father was dead. It was a considerable time before Louis could convince him of the contrary, and that Adeline was not dangerously ill; when, however, he was assured that he should see them in the morning, he became more tranquil. He desired his friend would not leave him that night. "These are the last hours we can pass together," added he; "I cannot sleep! Stay with me and lighten their heavy moments. I have need of comfort, Louis. Young as I am, and held by such strong attachments, I cannot quit the world with resignation. I know not how to credit those stories we hear of philosophic fortitude; wisdom cannot teach us cheerfully to resign a good, and life in my circumstances is surely such."

The night was passed in embarrassed conversation, sometimes interrupted by long fits of silence and sometimes by the paroxysms of despair; and the morning of that day which was to lead Theodore to death at length dawned through the grates of his prison.

La Luc meanwhile passed a sleepless and dreadful night. He prayed for fortitude and resignation both for himself and Theodore; but the pangs of nature were powerful in his heart, and not to be subdued. The idea of his lamented wife, and of what she would have suf-

fered had she lived to witness the ignominious death
which awaited her son, frequently occurred to him.

It seemed as if a destiny had hung over the life of
Theodore, for it is probable that the king might have
granted the petition of the unhappy father, had it not
happened that the Marquis de Montalt was present at
court when the paper was presented. The appearance
and singular distress of the petitioner had interested the
monarch, and instead of putting by the paper, he opened
it. As he threw his eyes over it, observing that the
criminal was of the Marquis de Montalt's regiment, he
turned to him and inquired the nature of the offence
for which the culprit was about to suffer. The answer
was such as might have been expected from the Marquis,
and the king was convinced that Theodore was not a
proper object of mercy.

But to return to La Luc, who was called according
to his order at a very early hour. Having passed some
time in prayer, he went down to the parlour, where
Louis, punctual to the moment, already waited to conduct him to the prison. He appeared calm and collected, but his countenance was impressed with a fixed
despair that sensibly affected his young friend. While
they waited for Adeline he spoke little, and seemed
struggling to attain the fortitude necessary to support
him through the approaching scene. Adeline not appearing, he at length sent to hasten her, and was told
she had been ill, but was recovering. She had indeed
passed a night of such agitation that her frame had
sunk under it, and she was now endeavouring to recover
strength and composure sufficient to sustain her in this
dreadful hour. Every moment that brought her nearer
to it had increased her emotion, and the apprehension
of being prevented seeing Theodore had alone enabled

her to struggle against the united pressure of illness and grief.

She now, with Clara, joined La Luc, who advanced as they entered the room, and took a hand of each in silence. After some moments he proposed to go, and they stepped into a carriage which conveyed them to the gates of the prison. The crowd had already began to assemble there, and a confused murmur arose as the carriage moved forward; it was a grievous sight to the friends of Theodore. Louis supported Adeline when she alighted; she was scarcely able to walk, and with trembling steps she followed La Luc, whom the keeper led towards that part of the prison where his son was confined. It was now eight o'clock. The sentence was not to be executed till twelve, but a guard of soldiers was already placed in the court, and as this unhappy party passed along the narrow avenues, they were met by several officers who had been to take a last farewell of Theodore. As they ascended the stairs that led to his apartment, La Luc's ear caught the clink of chains, and heard him walking above with a quick irregular step. The unhappy father, overcome by the moment which now pressed upon him, stopped, and was obliged to support himself by the bannister. Louis fearing the consequence of his grief might be fatal, shattered as his frame already was, would have gone for assistance, but he made a sign to him to stay. "I am better," said La Luc; "O God! support me through this hour!" and in a few minutes he was able to proceed.

As the warder unlocked the door, the harsh grating of the key shocked Adeline, but in the next moment she was in the presence of Theodore, who sprung to meet her, and caught her in his arms before she sunk to the ground. As her head reclined on his shoulder, he again viewed that countenance so dear to him, which had so often lighted rapture in his heart, and which though pale and inanimate as it now was, awakened him to momentary delight. When at length she unclosed her eyes, she fixed them in long and mournful gaze upon Theodore, who, pressing her to his heart, could answer her only with a smile of mingled tenderness and despair. The tears he endeavoured to restrain trembled in his eyes, and he forgot for a time everything but Adeline. La Luc, who had seated himself at the foot of the bed, seemed unconscious of what passed around him and entirely absorbed in his own grief, but Clara, as she clasped the hand of her brother and hung weeping on his arm, expressed aloud all the anguish of her heart, and at length recalled the attention of Adeline, who in a voice scarcely audible entreated she would spare her father. Her words roused Theodore, and supporting Adeline to a chair, he turned to La Luc. "My dear child!" said La Luc, grasping his hand and bursting into tears, "my dear child!" They wept together. After a long interval of silence he said, "I thought I could have supported this hour, but I am old and feeble. God knows my efforts for resignation, my faith in his goodness."

Theodore by a strong and sudden exertion assumed a composed and firm countenance, and endeavoured by every gentle argument to soothe and comfort his weeping friends. La Luc at length seemed to conquer his sufferings; drying his eyes, he said, "My son, I ought to have set you a better example and have practised the precepts of fortitude I have so often given you. But it is over; I know, and will perform, my duty." Adeline breathed a heavy sigh, and continued to weep. "Be comforted, my love; we part but for a time," said Theodore as he kissed the tears from her cheek; and uniting her hand with that of his father's, he earnestly recommended her to his protection. "Receive her," added he, "as the most precious legacy I can bequeath; consider her as your child. She will console you when I am gone; she will more than supply the loss of your son." La Luc assured him that he did now, and should continue to regard Adeline as his daughter. During those afflicting hours he endeavoured to dissipate the terrors of approaching death by inspiring his son with religious confidence. His conversation was pious, rational, and consolatory; he spoke not from the cold dictates of the head, but from the feelings of a heart which had long loved and practised the pure precepts of christianity, and which now drew from them a comfort such as nothing earthly could bestow.

"You are young, my son," said he, "and are yet innocent of any great crime; you may therefore look on death without terror, for to the guilty only is his approach dreadful. I feel that I shall not long survive you, and I trust in a merciful God that we shall meet in a state where sorrow never comes, *where the Son of Righteousness shall arise with healing in his wings!*" As he spoke he looked up; the tears still trembled in his eyes, which beamed with meek yet fervent devotion, and his countenance glowed with the dignity of a superior being.

"Let us not neglect the awful moments," said La Luc, rising; "let our united prayers ascend to Him who alone can comfort and support us!" They all knelt down, and he prayed with that simple and sublime eloquence which true piety inspires. When he rose, he embraced his children separately, and when he came to Theodore, he paused, gazed upon him with an earnest, mournful expression, and was for some time unable to speak. Theodore could not bear this; he drew his hand before his eyes and vainly endeavoured to stifle the deep sobs which convulsed his frame. At length recovering his voice, he entreated his father would leave him. "This misery is too much for us all," said he; "let us not prolong it. The time is now drawing on— leave me to compose myself. The sharpness of death consists in parting with those who are dear to us; when that is passed, death is disarmed."

"I will not leave you, my son," replied La Luc; "my poor girls shall go, but for me, I will be with you in your last moments." Theodore felt that this would be too much for them both, and urged every argument which reason could suggest to prevail with his father to relinquish his design. But he remained firm in his determination. "I will not suffer a selfish consideration of the pain I may endure," said La Luc, "to tempt me to desert my child when he will most require my support. It is my duty to attend you, and nothing shall withhold me."

Theodore seized on the words of La Luc—"As you would that I should be supported in my last hour," said he, "I entreat that you will not be witness of it. Your presence, my dear father, would subdue all my fortitude—would destroy what little composure I may otherwise be able to attain. Add not to my sufferings the view of your distress, but leave me to forget, if possible, the dear parent I must quit for ever." His tears flowed anew. La Luc continued to gaze on him in silent agony; at length he said, "Well, be it so. If indeed my presence would distress you, I will not go." His voice was broken and interrupted. After a pause of some moments he again embraced Theodore—"We must part," said he, "we *must* part, but it is only for a time —we shall soon be reunited in a higher world!—O God! thou seest my heart—thou seest all its feelings in this bitter hour!"—Grief again overcame him. He pressed Theodore in his arms, and at length, seeming to summon all his fortitude, he again said, "We *must* part. —Oh! my son, farewell for ever in this world!—The mercy of Almighty God support and bless you!"

He turned away to leave the prison, but quite worn out with grief, sunk into a chair near the door he would have opened. Theodore gazed with a distracted countenance alternately on his father, on Clara, and on Adeline, whom he pressed to his throbbing heart, and their tears flowed together. "And do I then," cried he, "for the last time look upon that countenance!—Shall I never—never more behold it?—O! exquisite misery! Yet once again—once more," continued he, pressing her cheek, but it was insensible and cold as marble.

Louis, who had left the room soon after La Luc arrived, that his presence might not interrupt their farewell grief, now returned. Adeline raised her head, and perceiving who entered, it again sunk on the bosom of Theodore.

Louis appeared much agitated. La Luc arose. "We must go," said he; "Adeline, my love, exert yourself— Clara—my children, let us depart.—Yet one last—last embrace, and then!"——Louis advanced and took his hand: "My dear sir, I have something to say; yet I fear to tell it."—"What do you mean?" said La Luc, with quickness; "no new misfortune can have power to afflict me at this moment. Do not fear to speak."—"I rejoice that I cannot put you to the proof," replied Louis; "I have seen you sustain the most trying affliction with fortitude. Can you support the transports of hope?"—La Luc gazed eagerly on Louis—"Speak!" said he, in a faint voice. Adeline raised her head, and, trembling between hope and fear, looked at Louis as if she would have searched his soul. He smiled cheerfully upon her. "Is it—O! is it possible!" she ex-

claimed, suddenly reanimated—"He lives! He lives!"
—She said no more, but ran to La Luc, who sunk fainting in his chair, while Theodore and Clara with one
voice called on Louis to relieve them from the tortures
of suspense.

He proceeded to inform them that he had obtained
from the commanding officer a respite for Theodore till
the king's farther pleasure could be known, and this in
consequence of a letter received that morning from his
mother, Madame La Motte, in which she mentioned
some very extraordinary circumstances that had appeared in the course of a trial lately conducted at Paris,
and which so materially affected the character of the
Marquis de Montalt as to render it possible a pardon
might be obtained for Theodore.

These words darted with the rapidity of lightning
upon the hearts of his hearers. La Luc revived, and
that prison so lately the scene of despair now echoed
only to the voices of gratitude and gladness. La Luc,
raising his clasped hands to heaven, said, "Great God!
support me in this moment as thou hast already supported me!—If my son lives, I die in peace."

He embraced Theodore, and remembering the anguish of his last embrace, tears of thankfulness and joy
flowed to the contrast. So powerful indeed was the
effect of this temporary reprieve and of the hope it
introduced, that if an absolute pardon had been obtained, it could scarcely for the moment have diffused
a more lively joy. But when the first emotions were
subsided, the uncertainty of Theodore's fate once more
appeared. Adeline forbore to express this, but Clara
without scruple lamented the possibility that her brother
might yet be taken from them, and all their joy be
turned to sorrow. A look from Adeline checked her.
Joy was, however, so much the predominant feeling of

the present moment that the shade which reflection threw upon their hopes passed away like the cloud that is dispelled by the strength of the sun-beam, and Louis alone was pensive and abstracted.

When they were sufficiently composed, he informed them that the contents of Madame La Motte's letter obliged him to set out for Paris immediately, and that the intelligence he had to communicate intimately concerned Adeline, who would undoubtedly judge it necessary to go thither also as soon as her health would permit. He then read to his impatient auditors such passages in the letter as were necessary to explain his meaning; but as Madame La Motte had omitted to mention some circumstances of importance to be understood, the following is a relation of the occurrences that had lately happened at Paris.

It may be remembered that on the first day of his trial, La Motte, in passing from the courts to his prison, saw a person whose features, though imperfectly seen through the dusk, he thought he recollected, and that this same person, after inquiring the name of La Motte, desired to be admitted to him. On the following day the warder complied with his request, and the surprise of La Motte may be imagined when in the stronger light of his apartment he distinguished the countenance of the man from whose hands he had formerly received Adeline.

On observing Madame La Motte in the room, he said he had something of consequence to impart, and desired to be left alone with the prisoner. When she was gone he told La Motte that he understood he was confined at the suit of the Marquis de Montalt. La Motte assented.—"I know him for a villain," said the stranger boldly.—"Your case is desperate. Do you wish for life?"

"Need the question be asked!"

"Your trial, I understand, proceeds to-morrow. I am now under confinement in this place for debt, but if you can obtain leave for me to go with you into the courts, and a condition from the judge that what I reveal shall not incriminate myself, I will make discoveries that shall confound that same Marquis. I will prove him a villain, and it shall then be judged how far his word ought to be taken against you."

La Motte, whose interest was now strongly excited, desired he would explain himself, and the man proceeded to relate a long history of the misfortunes and consequent poverty which had tempted him to become subservient to the schemes of the Marquis, till he suddenly checked himself and said, "When I obtain from the court the promise I require, I will explain myself fully; till then I cannot say more on the subject."

La Motte could not forbear expressing a doubt of his sincerity and a curiosity concerning the motive that had induced him to become the Marquis's accuser.—"As to my motive, it is a very natural one," replied the man: "it is no easy matter to receive ill usage without resenting it, particularly from a villain whom you have served."—La Motte, for his own sake, endeavoured to check the vehemence with which this was uttered. "I care not who hears me," continued the stranger, but at the same time he lowered his voice; "I repeat it—the Marquis has used me ill—I have kept his secret long enough. He does not think it worth while to secure my silence, or he would relieve my necessities. I am in prison for debt, and have applied to him for relief. Since he does not choose to give it, let him take the consequence. I warrant he shall soon repent that he has provoked me, and 'tis fit he should."

The doubts of La Motte were now dissipated; the

prospect of life again opened upon him, and he assured Du Bosse (which was the stranger's name) with much warmth that he would commission his advocate to do all in his power to obtain leave for his appearance on the trial and to procure the necessary condition. After some farther conversation they parted.

CHAPTER XXI

Leave was at length granted for the appearance of Du Bosse, with a promise that his words should not criminate him, and he accompanied La Motte into court.

The confusion of the Marquis de Montalt on perceiving this man was observed by many persons present, and particularly by La Motte, who drew from this circumstance a favourable presage for himself.

When Du Bosse was called upon, he informed the court that on the night of the twenty-first of April in the preceding year, one Jean d'Aunoy, a man he had known many years, came to his lodging. After they had discoursed for some time on their circumstances, d'Aunoy said he knew a way by which Du Bosse might change all his poverty to riches, but that he would not say more till he was certain he would be willing to follow it. The distressed state in which Du Bosse then was made him anxious to learn the means which would bring him relief; he eagerly inquired what his friend meant, and after some time d'Aunoy explained himself. He said he was employed by a nobleman, (whom he afterwards told Du Bosse was the Marquis de Montalt) to carry off a young girl from a convent, and that she was to be taken to a house a few leagues distant from Paris. "I knew the house he described well," said Du

Bosse, "for I had been there many times with d'Aunoy, who lived there to avoid his creditors, though he often passed his nights at Paris. He would not tell me more of the scheme, but said he should want assistants, and if I and my brother, who is since dead, would join him, his employer would grudge no money and we should be well rewarded. I desired him again to tell me more of the plan, but he was obstinate, and after I had told him I would consider of what he said and speak to my brother, he went away.

"When he called the next night for his answer, my brother and I agreed to engage, and accordingly we went home with him. He then told us that the young lady he was to bring thither was a natural daughter of the Marquis de Montalt and of a nun belonging to a convent of Ursulines, that his wife had received the child immediately on its birth, and had been allowed a handsome annuity to bring it up as her own, which she had done till her death. The child was then placed in a convent and designed for the veil, but when she was of an age to receive the vows, she had steadily persisted in refusing them. This circumstance had so much exasperated the Marquis that in his rage he ordered that if she persisted in her obstinacy she would be removed from the convent, and got rid of any way, since if she lived in the world her birth might be discovered, and in consequence of this her mother, for whom he had yet a regard, would be condemned to expiate her crime by a terrible death."

Du Bosse was interrupted in his narrative by the counsel of the Marquis, who contended that the circumstances alleged tending to criminate his client, the proceeding was both irrelevant and illegal. He was answered that it was not irrelevant, and therefore not illegal, for that the circumstances which threw light upon the character of the Marquis affected his evidence against La Motte. Du Bosse was suffered to proceed.

"D'Aunoy then said that the Marquis had ordered him to dispatch her, but that as he had been used to see her from her infancy, he could not find in his heart to do it, and wrote to tell him so. The Marquis then commanded him to find those who would, and this was the business for which he wanted us. My brother and I were not so wicked as this came to, and so we told d'Aunoy, and I could not help asking why the Marquis resolved to murder his own child rather than expose her mother to the risque of suffering death. He said the Marquis had never seen his child, and that therefore it could not be supposed he felt much kindness towards it, and still less that he could love it better than he loved its mother."

Du Bosse proceeded to relate how much he and his brother had endeavoured to soften the heart of d'Aunoy towards the Marquis's daughter, and that they prevailed with him to write again and plead for her. D'Aunoy went to Paris to await the answer, leaving them and the young girl at the house on the heath, where the former had consented to remain, seemingly for the purpose of executing the orders they might receive, but really with a design to save the unhappy victim from the sacrifice.

It is probable that Du Bosse, in this instance, gave a false account of his motive, since if he was really guilty of an intention so atrocious as that of murder, he would naturally endeavour to conceal it. However this might be, he affirmed that on the night of the twenty-sixth of April he received an order from d'Aunoy for the destruction of the girl, whom he had afterwards delivered into the hands of La Motte.

La Motte listened to this relation in astonishment.

When he knew that Adeline was the daughter of the
Marquis, and remembered the crime to which he had
once devoted her, his frame thrilled with horror. He
now took up the story, and added an account of what
had passed at the abbey between the Marquis and himself concerning a design of the former upon the life of
Adeline, and urged as a proof of the present prosecution originating in malice, that it had commenced immediately after he had effected her escape from the
Marquis. He concluded, however, with saying that as
the Marquis had immediately sent his people in pursuit
of her, it was possible she might yet have fallen a victim to his vengeance.

Here the Marquis's counsel again interfered, and
their objections were again overruled by the court. The
uncommon degree of emotion which his countenance
betrayed during the narrations of Du Bosse and La
Motte was generally observed. The court suspended
the sentence of the latter, ordered that the Marquis
should be put under immediate arrest, and that Adeline
(the name given by her foster mother) and Jean
d'Aunoy should be sought for.

The Marquis was accordingly seized at the suit of
the crown, and put under confinement till Adeline
should appear or proof could be obtained that she died
by his order, and till d'Aunoy should confirm or destroy the evidence of La Motte.

Madame, who at length obtained intelligence of her
son's residence from the town where he was formerly
stationed, had acquainted him with his father's situation and the proceedings of the trial; and as she believed that Adeline, if she had been so fortunate as to
escape the Marquis's pursuit, was still in Savoy, she
desired Louis would obtain leave of absence and bring
her to Paris, where her immediate presence was requi-

site to substantiate the evidence and probably to save the life of La Motte.

On the receipt of her letter, which happened on the morning appointed for the execution of Theodore, Louis went immediately to the commanding officer to petition for a respite till the king's further pleasure should be known. He founded his plea on the arrest of the Marquis, and shewed the letter he had just received. The commanding officer readily granted a reprieve, and Louis, who on the arrival of this letter had forborne to communicate its contents to Theodore, lest it should torture him with false hope, now hastened to him with this comfortable news.

CHAPTER XXII

On learning the purpose of Madame La Motte's letter, Adeline saw the necessity of her immediate departure for Paris. The life of La Motte, who had more than saved hers, the life, perhaps, of her beloved Theodore, depended on the testimony she should give. And she who had so lately been sinking under the influence of illness and despair, who could scarcely raise her languid head, or speak but in the faintest accents, now reanimated with hope and invigorated by a sense of the importance of the business before her, prepared to perform a rapid journey of some hundred miles.

Theodore tenderly entreated that she would so far consider her health as to delay this journey for a few days, but with a smile of enchanting tenderness she assured him that she was now too happy to be ill, and that the same cause which would confirm her happiness would confirm her health. So strong was the effect of hope upon her mind, now that it succeeded to the misery of despair, that it overcame the shock she suffered on believing herself a daughter of the Marquis, and every other painful reflection. She did not even foresee the obstacle that circumstance might produce to her union with Theodore, should he at last be permitted to live.

It was settled that she should set off for Paris in a few hours with Louis, and attended by Peter. These hours were passed by La Luc and his family in the prison.

When the time of her departure arrived, the spirits of Adeline again forsook her and the illusions of joy disappeared. She no longer beheld Theodore as one respited from death, but took leave of him with a mournful presentiment that she should see him no more. So strongly was this presage impressed upon her mind, that it was long before she could summon resolution to bid him farewell; and when she had done so, and even left the apartment, she returned to take of him a last look. As she was once more quitting the room, her melancholy imagination represented Theodore at the place of execution, pale, and convulsed in death; she again turned her lingering eyes upon him; but fancy affected her sense, for she thought as she now gazed that his countenance changed and assumed a ghastly hue. All her resolution vanished, and such was the anguish of her heart that she resolved to defer her journey till the morrow, though she must by this means lose the protection of Louis, whose impatience to meet his father would not suffer the delay. The triumph of passion, however, was transient; soothed by the indulgence she promised herself, her grief subsided, reason resumed its influence; she again saw the necessity of her immediate departure and recollected sufficient resolution to submit. La Luc would have accompanied her for the purpose of again soliciting the king in behalf of his son, had not the extreme weakness and lassitude to which he was reduced made travelling impracticable.

At length Adeline with a heavy heart quitted Theodore, notwithstanding his entreaties that she would not undertake the journey in her present weak state, and was accompanied by Clara and La Luc to the inn. The former parted from her friend with many tears, and much anxiety for her welfare, but under a hope of soon meeting again. Should a pardon be granted to Theodore, La Luc designed to fetch Adeline from Paris; but should this be refused, she was to return with Peter. He bade her adieu with a father's kindness, which she repaid with a filial affection, and in her last words conjured him to attend to the recovery of his health: the languid smile he assumed seemed to express that her solicitude was vain, and that he thought his health past recovery.

Thus Adeline quitted the friends so justly dear to her, and so lately found, for Paris, where she was a stranger almost without protection, and compelled to meet a father who had pursued her with the utmost cruelty, in a public court of justice. The carriage in leaving Vaceau passed by the prison; she threw an eager look towards it as she passed; its heavy black walls, and narrow-grated windows, seemed to frown upon her hopes—but Theodore was there, and leaning from the window she continued to gaze upon it till an abrupt turning in the street concealed it from her view. She then sunk back in the carriage, and yielding to the melancholy of her heart, wept in silence. Louis was not disposed to interrupt it; his thoughts were anxiously employed on his father's situation, and the travellers proceeded many miles without exchanging a word.

At Paris, whither we shall now return, the search

after Jean d'Aunoy was prosecuted without success. The house on the heath described by Du Bosse was found uninhabited, and to the places of his usual resort in the city, where the officers of the police awaited him, he no longer came. It even appeared doubtful whether he was living, for he had absented himself from the houses of his customary rendezvous some time before the trial of La Motte; it was therefore certain that his absence was not occasioned by anything which had passed in the courts.

In the solitude of his confinement the Marquis de Montalt had leisure to reflect on the past and to repent of his crimes, but reflection and repentance formed as yet no part of his disposition. He turned with impatience from recollections which produced only pain, and looked forward to the future with an endeavour to avert the disgrace and punishment which he saw impending. The elegance of his manners had so effectually veiled the depravity of his heart that he was a favourite with his sovereign, and on this circumstance he rested his hope of security. He however severely repented that he had indulged the hasty spirit of revenge which had urged him to the prosecution of La Motte, and had thus unexpectedly involved him in a situation dangerous—if not fatal—since if Adeline could not be found he would be concluded guilty of her death. But the appearance of d'Aunoy was the circumstance he most dreaded, and to oppose the possibility of this, he employed secret emissaries to discover his retreat and to bribe him to his interest. These were, however, as unsuccessful in their research as the officers of police, and the Marquis at length began to hope the man was really dead.

La Motte meanwhile awaited with trembling impatience the arrival of his son, when he should be relieved

in some degree from his uncertainty concerning Adeline.
On her appearance he rested his only hope of life, since
the evidence against him would lose much of its validity
from the confirmation she would give of the bad character of his prosecutor; and if the Parliament even condemned La Motte, the clemency of the king might yet
operate in his favour.

Adeline arrived at Paris after a journey of several
days, during which she was chiefly supported by the
delicate attentions of Louis, whom she pitied and esteemed, though she could not love. She was immediately visited at the hotel by Madame La Motte. The
meeting was affecting on both sides. A sense of her
past conduct excited in the latter an embarrassment
which the delicacy and goodness of Adeline would willingly have spared her; but the pardon solicited was
given with so much sincerity that Madame gradually
became composed and reassured. This forgiveness,
however, could not have been thus easily granted had
Adeline believed her former conduct was voluntary. A
conviction of the restraint and terror under which Madame had acted alone induced her to excuse the past.
In this first meeting they forbore dwelling on particular
subjects; Madame La Motte proposed that Adeline
should remove from the hotel to her lodgings near the
Chatelet, and Adeline, for whom a residence at a public
hotel was very improper, gladly accepted the offer.

Madame there gave her a circumstantial account of
La Motte's situation, and concluded with saying that
as the sentence of her husband had been suspended till
some certainty could be obtained concerning the late
criminal designs of the Marquis, and as Adeline could
confirm the chief part of La Motte's testimony, it was
probable that now she was arrived, the Court would
proceed immediately. She now learnt the full extent

of her obligation to La Motte, for she was till now ignorant that when he sent her from the forest he saved
her from death. Her horror of the Marquis, whom she
could not bear to consider as her father, and her gratitude to her deliverer, redoubled, and she became impatient to give the testimony so necessary to the hopes
of her preserver. Madame then said she believed it was
not too late to gain admittance that night to the Chatelet, and as she knew how anxiously her husband
wished to see Adeline, she entreated her consent to go
thither. Adeline, though much harassed and fatigued,
complied. When Louis returned from M. Nemours, his
father's advocate, whom he had hastened to inform of
her arrival, they all set out for the Chatelet. The view
of the prison into which they were now admitted so
forcibly recalled to Adeline's mind the situation of
Theodore that she with difficulty supported herself to
the apartment of La Motte. When he saw her a gleam
of joy passed over his countenance, but again relapsing
into despondency, he looked mournfully at her and then
at Louis, and groaned deeply. Adeline, in whom all
remembrance of his former cruelty was lost in his subsequent kindness, expressed her thankfulness for the
life he had preserved and her anxiety to serve him, in
warm and repeated terms. But her gratitude evidently
distressed him; instead of reconciling him to himself,
it seemed to awaken a remembrance of the guilty designs he had once assisted and to strike the pangs of
conscience deeper in his heart. Endeavouring to conceal his emotions, he entered on the subject of his present danger and informed Adeline what testimony would
be required of her on the trial. After above an hour's
conversation with La Motte, she returned to the lodgings of Madame, where, languid and ill, she withdrew

to her chamber and tried to obliviate her anxieties in sleep.

The Parliament which conducted the trial reassembled in a few days after the arrival of Adeline, and the two remaining witnesses of the Marquis, on whom he now rested his cause against La Motte, appeared. She was led trembling into the Court, where almost the first object that met her eyes was the Marquis de Montalt, whom she now beheld with an emotion entirely new to her, and which was strongly tinctured with horror. When Du Bosse saw her he immediately swore to her identity; his testimony was confirmed by her manner, for on perceiving him she grew pale and a universal tremor seized her. Jean d'Aunoy could nowhere be found, and La Motte was thus deprived of an evidence which essentially affected his interest. Adeline, when called upon, gave her little narrative with clearness and precision; and Peter, who had conveyed her from the abbey, supported the testimony she offered. The evidence produced was sufficient to criminate the Marquis of the intention of murder, in the minds of most people present; but it was not sufficient to affect the testimony of his two last witnesses, who positively swore to the commission of the robbery and to the person of La Motte, on whom sentence of death was accordingly pronounced. On receiving this sentence the unhappy criminal fainted, and the compassion of the assembly, whose feelings had been unusually interested in the decision, was expressed in a general groan.

Their attention was quickly called to a new object— it was Jean d'Aunoy who now entered the Court. But his evidence, if it could ever, indeed, have been the means of saving La Motte, came too late. He was reconducted to prison; but Adeline, who, extremely shocked by his sentence, was much indisposed, received orders to remain in the court during the examination of d'Aunoy. This man had been at length found in the prison of a provincial town, where some of his creditors had thrown him, and from which even the money which the Marquis had remitted to him for the purpose of satisfying the craving importunities of Du Bosse had been insufficient to release him. Meanwhile the revenge of the latter had been roused against the Marquis by an imaginary neglect, and the money which was designed to relieve his necessities, was spent by d'Aunoy in riotous luxury.

He was confronted with Adeline and with Du Bosse, and ordered to confess all he knew concerning this mysterious affair, or to undergo the torture. D'Aunoy, who was ignorant how far the suspicions concerning the Marquis extended, and who was conscious that his own words might condemn him, remained for some time obstinately silent, but when the *question* was administered his resolution gave way, and he confessed a crime of which he had not even been suspected.

It appeared, that in the year 1642 d'Aunoy, together with one Jaques Martigny, and Francis Balliere, had waylaid and seized Henri, Marquis de Montalt, half brother to Philippe; and after having robbed him and bound his servant to a tree, according to the orders they had received they conveyed him to the abbey of St. Clair, in the distant forest of Fontanville. Here he was confined for some time till farther directions were received from Philippe de Montalt, the present Marquis, who was then on his estates in a northern province of France. These orders were for death, and the unfortunate Henri was assassinated in his chamber in the third week of his confinement at the abbey.

On hearing this Adeline grew faint; she remembered the MS. she had found, together with the extraordinary circumstances that had attended the discovery. Every nerve thrilled with horror, and raising her eyes, she saw the countenance of the Marquis overspread with the livid paleness of guilt. She endeavoured, however, to arrest her fleeting spirits while the man proceeded in his confession.

When the murder was perpetrated, d'Aunoy had returned to his employer, who gave him the reward agreed upon, and in a few months after delivered into his hands the infant daughter of the late Marquis, whom he conveyed to a distant part of the kingdom, where assuming the name of St. Pierre, he brought her up as his own child, receiving from the present Marquis a considerable annuity for his secrecy.

Adeline, no longer able to struggle with the tumult of emotions that now rushed upon her heart, uttered a deep sigh and fainted away. She was carried from the court, and when the confusion occasioned by this circumstance subsided, Jean d'Aunoy went on. He related that on the death of his wife, Adeline was placed in a convent, from whence she was afterwards removed to another, where the Marquis had destined her to receive the vows; that her determined rejection of them had occasioned him to resolve upon her death, and that she had accordingly been removed to the house on the heath. D'Aunoy added that by the Marquis's order he had misled Du Bosse with a false story of her birth. Having after some time discovered that his comrades had deceived him concerning her death, d'Aunoy separated from them in enmity; but they unanimously determined to conceal her escape from the Marquis, that they might enjoy the recompense of their supposed crime.

Some months subsequent to this period, however, d'Aunoy received a letter from the Marquis charging him with the truth and promising him a large reward if he would confess where he had placed Adeline. In consequence of this letter he acknowledged that she had been given into the hands of a stranger; but who he was or where he lived was not known.

Upon these depositions Philippe de Montalt was committed to take his trial for the murder of Henri, his brother; D'Aunoy was thrown into a dungeon of the Chatelet, and Du Bosse was bound to appear as evidence.

The feelings of the Marquis, who in a prosecution stimulated by revenge had thus unexpectedly exposed his crimes to the public eye and betrayed himself to justice, can only be imagined. The passions which had tempted him to the commission of a crime so horrid as that of murder—and what, if possible, heightened its atrocity, the murder of one connected with him by the ties of blood, and by habits of even infantine association—the passions which had stimulated him to so monstrous a deed were ambition and the love of pleasure. The first was more immediately gratified by the title of his brother; the latter by the riches which would enable him to indulge his voluptuous inclinations.

The late Marquis de Montalt, the father of Adeline, received from his ancestors a patrimony very inadequate to support the splendour of his rank, but he had married the heiress of an illustrious family, whose fortune amply supplied the deficiency of his own. He had the misfortune to lose her, for she was amiable and beautiful, soon after the birth of a daughter, and it was then that the present Marquis formed the diabolical design of destroying his brother. The contrast of their characters prevented that cordial regard between them which their near relationship seemed to demand. Henri was benevolent, mild, and contemplative. In his heart reigned the love of virtue; in his manners the strictness of justice was tempered, not weakened, by mercy; his mind was enlarged by science and adorned by elegant literature. The character of Philippe has been already delineated in his actions; its nicer shades were blended with some shining tints, but these served only to render more striking by contrast the general darkness of the portrait.

He had married a lady who by the death of her brother inherited considerable estates, of which the abbey of St. Clair and the villa on the borders of the forest of Fontanville were the chief. His passion for magnificence and dissipation, however, soon involved him in difficulties, and pointed out to him the conveniency of possessing his brother's wealth. His brother and his infant daughter only stood between him and his wishes; how he removed the father has been already related; why he did not employ the same means to secure the child, seems somewhat surprising, unless we admit that a destiny hung over him on this occasion and that she was suffered to live as an instrument to punish the murderer of her parent. When a retrospect is taken of the vicissitudes and dangers to which she had been exposed from her earliest infancy, it appears as if her preservation was the effect of something more than human policy, and affords a striking instance that justice, however long delayed, will overtake the guilty.

While the late unhappy Marquis was suffering at the abbey, his brother, who to avoid suspicion remained in the north of France, delayed the execution of his horrid purpose from a timidity natural to a mind not yet in-

ured to enormous guilt. Before he dared to deliver his
final orders he waited to know whether the story he
contrived to propagate of his brother's death would veil
his crime from suspicion. It succeeded but too well, for
the servant whose life had been spared that he might
relate the tale, naturally enough concluded that his lord
had been murdered by banditti; and the peasant who a
few hours after found the servant wounded, bleeding,
and bound to a tree, and knew also that this spot was
infested by robbers, as naturally believed him and
spread the report accordingly.

From this period the Marquis, to whom the abbey of
St. Clair belonged in right of his wife, visited it only
twice, and that at distant times, till after an interval of
several years he accidentally found La Motte its inhabitant. He resided at Paris and on his estate in the
north, except that once a year he usually passed a month
at his delightful villa on the borders of the forest. In
the busy scenes of the court and in the dissipations of
pleasure he tried to lose the remembrance of his guilt,
but there were times when the voice of conscience would
be heard, though it was soon again lost in the tumult
of the world.

It is probable that on the night of his abrupt departure from the abbey, the solitary silence and gloom
of the hour, in a place which had been the scene of his
former crime, called up the remembrance of his brother
with a force too powerful for fancy, and awakened
horrors which compelled him to quit the polluted spot.
If it was so, it is however certain that the spectres of
conscience vanished with the darkness; for on the following day he returned to the abbey, though it may be
observed, he never attempted to pass another night
there. But though terror was roused for a transient

moment, neither pity or repentance succeeded, since when the discovery of Adeline's birth excited apprehension for his own life, he did not hesitate to repeat the crime, and would again have stained his soul with human blood. This discovery was affected by means of a seal bearing the arms of her mother's family, which was impressed on the note his servant had found and had delivered to him at Caux. It may be remembered that having read this note, he was throwing it from him in the fury of jealousy, but that after examining it again, it was carefully deposited in his pocket-book. The violent agitation which a suspicion of this terrible truth occasioned, deprived him for a while of all power to act. When he was well enough to write, he dispatched a letter to d'Aunoy the purport of which has been already mentioned. From d'Aunoy he received the confirmation of his fears. Knowing that his life must pay the forfeiture of his crime should Adeline ever obtain a knowledge of her birth, and not daring again to confide in the secrecy of a man who had once deceived him, he resolved after some deliberation on her death. He immediately set out for the abbey and gave those directions concerning her which terror for his own safety, still more than a desire of retaining her estates, suggested.

As the history of the seal which revealed the birth of Adeline is rather remarkable, it may not be amiss to mention that it was stolen from the Marquis, together with a gold watch, by Jean d'Aunoy. The watch was soon disposed of, but the seal had been kept as a pretty trinket by his wife, and at her death went with Adeline among her clothes to the convent. Adeline had carefully preserved it because it had once belonged to the woman whom she believed to have been her mother.

CHAPTER XXIII

WE NOW return to the course of the narrative, and to Adeline, who was carried from the court to the lodging of Madame La Motte. Madame was, however, at the Chatelet with her husband, suffering all the distress which the sentence pronounced against him might be supposed to inflict. The feeble frame of Adeline, so long harassed by grief and fatigue, almost sunk under the agitation which the discovery of her birth excited. Her feelings on this occasion were too complex to be analyzed. From an orphan, subsisting on the bounty of others, without family, with few friends, and pursued by a cruel and powerful enemy, she saw herself suddenly transformed to the daughter of an illustrious house, and the heiress of immense wealth. But she learned also that her father had been murdered—murdered in the prime of his days—murdered by means of his brother, against whom she must now appear, and in punishing the destroyer of her parent doom her uncle to death.

When she remembered the manuscript so singularly found, and considered that when she wept to the sufferings it described her tears had flowed for those of her father, her emotion cannot easily be imagined. The circumstances attending the discovery of these papers no longer appeared to be a work of chance, but of a Power whose designs are great and just. "O my father!" she would exclaim, "your last wish is fulfilled—the pitying heart you wished might trace your sufferings shall avenge them."

On the return of Madame La Motte, Adeline endeavoured as usual to support her own emotions, that she might soothe the affliction of her friend. She related what had passed in the courts after the departure of La Motte, and thus excited even in the sorrowful heart of Madame a momentary gleam of satisfaction. Adeline determined to recover, if possible, the manuscript. On inquiry she learned that La Motte in the confusion of his departure had left it among other things at the abbey. This circumstance much distressed her, the more so because she believed its appearance might be of importance on the approaching trial: she determined, however, if she should recover her rights, to have the manuscript sought for.

In the evening Louis joined this mournful party. He came immediately from his father, whom he left more tranquil than he had been since the fatal sentence was pronounced. After a silent and melancholy supper, they separated for the night, and Adeline in the solitude of her chamber had leisure to meditate on the discoveries of this eventful day. The sufferings of her dead father, such as she had read them recorded by his *own hand,* pressed most forcibly to her thoughts. The narrative had formerly so much affected her heart and interested her imagination that her memory now faithfully reflected each particular circumstance there disclosed. But when she considered that she had been in the very chamber where her parent had suffered, where even his life had been sacrificed, and that she had probably seen the very dagger, seen it stained with rust, the rust of blood! by which he had fallen, the anguish and horror of her mind defied all control.

On the following day Adeline received orders to prepare for the prosecution of the Marquis de Montalt, which was to commence as soon as the requisite witnesses could be collected. Among these were the abbess of the convent who had received her from the hands of d'Aunoy, Madame La Motte, who was present when Du Bosse compelled her husband to receive Adeline, and Peter, who had not only been witness to this circumstance, but who had conveyed her from the abbey that she might escape the designs of the Marquis. La Motte and Theodore La Luc were incapacitated by the sentence of the law from appearing on the trial.

When La Motte was informed of the discovery of Adeline's birth, and that her father had been murdered at the abbey of St. Clair, he instantly remembered and mentioned to his wife the skeleton he found in the stone room leading to the subterranean cells. Neither of them doubted from the situation in which it lay, hid in a chest in an obscure room strongly guarded, that La Motte had seen the remains of the late Marquis. Madame, however, determined not to shock Adeline with the mention of this circumstance till it should be necessary to declare it on the trial.

As the time of this trial drew near, the distress and agitation of Adeline increased. Though justice demanded the life of the murderer, and though the tenderness and pity which the idea of her father called forth urged her to revenge his death, she could not without horror consider herself as the instrument of dispensing that justice which would deprive a fellow being of existence; and there were times when she wished the secret of her birth had never been revealed. If this sensibility was in her peculiar circumstances a weakness, it was at least an amiable one, and as such deserves to be reverenced.

The accounts she received from Vaceau of the health of M. La Luc did not contribute to tranquillize her mind. The symptoms described by Clara seemed to say that he was in the last stage of a consumption, and the grief of Theodore and herself on this occasion was expressed in her letters with the lively eloquence so natu-

ral to her. Adeline loved and revered La Luc for his
own worth, and for the parental tenderness he had
shewed her, but he was still dearer to her as the father
of Theodore, and her concern for his declining state
was not inferior to that of his children. It was increased by the reflection that she had probably been the
means of shortening his life, for she too well knew that
the distress occasioned him by the situation in which it
had been her misfortune to involve Theodore, had shattered his frame to its present infirmity. The same cause
also withheld him from seeking in the climate of Montpellier the relief he had formerly been taught to expect
there. When she looked around on the condition of her
friends, her heart was almost overwhelmed with the
prospect; it seemed as if she was destined to involve
all those most dear to her in calamity. With respect to
La Motte, whatever were his vices, and whatever the
designs in which he had formerly engaged against her,
she forgot them all in the service he had finally rendered her, and considered it to be as much her duty as
she felt it to be her inclination to intercede in his behalf. This, however, in her present situation she could
not do with any hope of success; but if the suit upon
which depended the establishment of her rank, her fortune, and consequently her influence, should be decided
in her favour, she determined to throw herself at the
king's feet, and when she pleaded the cause of Theodore
ask the life of La Motte.

A few days preceding that of the trial, Adeline was
informed a stranger desired to speak with her, and on
going to the room where he was, she found M. Verneuil.
Her countenance expressed both surprise and satisfaction at this unexpected meeting, and she inquired,
though with little expectation of an affirmative, if he
had heard of M. La Luc. "I have seen him," said M.

Verneuil; "I am just come from Vaceau. But I am
sorry I cannot give you a better account of his health.
He is greatly altered since I saw him before."

Adeline could scarcely refrain from tears at the recollection these words revived of the calamities which had
occasioned this lamented change. M. Verneuil delivered her a packet from Clara. As he presented it he
said, "Besides this introduction to your notice, I have
a claim of a different kind, which I am proud to assert,
and which will perhaps justify the permission I ask of
speaking upon your affairs."—Adeline bowed, and M.
Verneuil, with a countenance expressive of the most
tender solicitude, added that he had heard of the late
proceeding of the parliament of Paris, and of the discoveries that so intimately concerned her. "I know
not," continued he, "whether I ought to congratulate
or condole with you on this trying occasion. That I
sincerely sympathize in all that concerns you I hope
you will believe, and I cannot deny myself the pleasure
of telling you that I am related, though distantly, to
the late marchioness, your mother, for that she *was your
mother* I cannot doubt.

Adeline rose hastily and advanced towards M. Verneuil; surprise and satisfaction reanimated her features.
"Do I indeed see a relation?" said she, in a sweet and
tremulous voice, "and one whom I can welcome as a
friend?" Tears trembled in her eyes; and she received
M. Verneuil's embrace in silence. It was some time before her emotion would permit her to speak.

To Adeline, who from her earliest infancy had been
abandoned to strangers, a forlorn and helpless orphan,
who had never till lately known a relation, and who
then found one in the person of an inveterate enemy;
to her this discovery was as delightful as unexpected.
But after struggling for some time with the various

emotions that pressed upon her heart, she begged
M. Verneuil's permission to withdraw till she could recover composure. He would have taken leave, but she
entreated him not to go.

The interest which M. Verneuil took in the concerns
of La Luc, which was strengthened by his increasing
regard for Clara, had drawn him to Vaceau, where he
was informed of the family and peculiar circumstances
of Adeline. On receiving this intelligence, he immediately set out for Paris to offer his protection and assistance to his newly discovered relation, and to aid, if
possible, the cause of Theodore.

Adeline in a short time returned and could then bear
to converse on the subject of her family. M. Verneuil
offered her his support and assistance if they should
be found necessary. "But I trust," added he, "to the
justice of your cause, and hope it will not require any
adventitious aid. To those who remember the late
marchioness, your features bring sufficient evidence
of your birth. As a proof that my judgment in this instance is not biassed by prejudice, the resemblance
struck me when I was in Savoy, though I knew the
marchioness only by her portrait; and I believe I mentioned to M. La Luc that you often reminded me of a
deceased relation. You may form some judgment of
this yourself," added M. Verneuil, taking a miniature
from his pocket. "This was your amiable mother."

Adeline's countenance changed; she received the picture eagerly, gazed on it for a long time in silence,
and her eyes filled with tears. It was not the resemblance she studied, but the countenance—the mild and
beautiful countenance of her parent, whose blue eyes,
full of tender sweetness, seemed bent upon hers, while a
soft smile played on her lips; Adeline pressed the picture to hers, and again gazed in silent reverie. At

length, with a deep sigh, she said, "This surely *was* my mother. Had she *but* lived, O my poor father! you had been spared." This reflection quite overcame her and she burst into tears. M. Verneuil did not interrupt her grief, but took her hand and sat by her without speaking till she became more composed. Again kissing the picture, she held it out to him with a hesitating look. "No," said he, "it is already with its true owner." She thanked him with a smile of ineffable sweetness, and after some conversation on the subject of the approaching trial, on which occasion she requested M. Verneuil would support her by his presence, he withdrew, having begged leave to repeat his visit on the following day.

Adeline now opened her packet, and saw once more the well-known characters of Theodore; for a moment she felt as if in his presence, and the conscious blush overspread her cheek. With a trembling hand she broke the seal, and read the tenderest assurances and solicitudes of his love; she often paused that she might prolong the sweet emotions which these assurances awakened, but while tears of tenderness stood trembling on her eyelids, the bitter recollection of his situation would return, and they fell in anguish on her bosom.

He congratulated her, and with peculiar delicacy, on the prospects of life which were opening to her; said everything that might tend to animate and support her, but avoided dwelling on his own circumstances, except by expressing his sense of the zeal and kindness of his commanding officer, and adding that he did not despair of finally obtaining a pardon.

This hope, though but faintly expressed, and written evidently for the purpose of consoling Adeline, did not entirely fail of the desired effect. She yielded to its enchanting influence, and forgot for a while the many subjects of care and anxiety which surrounded her. Theodore said little of his father's health; what he did say was by no means so discouraging as the accounts of Clara, who, less anxious to conceal a truth that must give pain to Adeline, expressed without reserve all her apprehension and concern.

CHAPTER XXIV

THE day of the trial so anxiously awaited, and on which the fate of so many persons depended, at length arrived. Adeline, accompanied by M. Verneuil and Madame La Motte, appeared as the prosecutor of the Marquis de Montalt; and d'Aunoy, Du Bosse, Louis de la Motte, and several other persons, as witnesses in her cause. The judges were some of the most distinguished in France; and the advocates on both sides men of eminent abilities. On a trial of such importance, the court, as may be imagined, was crowded with persons of distinction, and the spectacle it presented was strikingly solemn, yet magnificent.

When she appeared before the tribunal, Adeline's emotion surpassed all the arts of disguise, but adding to the natural dignity of her air an expression of soft timidity, and to her downcast eyes a sweet confusion, it rendered her an object still more interesting; and she attracted the universal pity and admiration of the assembly. When she ventured to raise her eyes, she perceived that the Marquis was not yet in the court, and while she awaited his appearance in trembling expectation, a confused murmuring rose in a distant part of the hall. Her spirits now almost forsook her; the certainty of seeing immediately and consciously the murderer of her father chilled her with horror, and she was with difficulty preserved from fainting. A low sound now ran through the court, and an air of confusion appeared which was soon communicated to the tribunal itself. Several of the members arose, some left the hall, the whole place exhibited a scene of disorder, and a report at length reached Adeline that the Marquis de Montalt was dying. A considerable time elapsed in uncertainty, but the confusion continued; the Marquis did not appear; and at Adeline's request M. Verneuil went in quest of more positive information.

He followed a crowd which was hurrying towards the Chatelet, and with some difficulty gained admittance into the prison; but the porter at the gate, whom he had bribed for a passport, could give him no certain information on the subject of his enquiry, and not being at liberty to quit his post, furnished M. Verneuil with only a vague direction to the Marquis's apartment. The courts were silent and deserted, but as he advanced, a distant hum of voices led him on till, perceiving several persons running towards a staircase which appeared beyond the archway of a long passage, he followed thither, and learned that the Marquis was certainly dying. The staircase was filled with people; he endeavoured to press through the crowd, and after much struggle and difficulty he reached the door of an anteroom which communicated with the apartment where the Marquis lay, and whence several persons now issued. Here he learned that the object of his enquiry was already dead. M. Verneuil, however, pressed through the ante-room to the chamber where lay the Marquis on a bed surrounded by officers of the law and two notaries, who appeared to have been taking down depositions. His countenance was suffused with a black and deadly hue and impressed with the horrors of death.

M. Verneuil turned away, shocked by the spectacle, and on enquiry heard that the Marquis had died by poison.

It appeared that, convinced he had nothing to hope from his trial, he had taken this method of avoiding an ignominious death. In the last hours of life, while tortured with the remembrance of his crime, he resolved to make all the atonement that remained for him, and having swallowed the potion, he immediately sent for a confessor to take a full confession of his guilt, and two notaries, and thus establish Adeline beyond dispute in the rights of her birth; and also bequeathed her a considerable legacy.

In consequence of these depositions she was soon after formally acknowledged as the daughter and heiress of Henri Marquis de Montalt, and the rich estates of her father were restored to her. She immediately threw herself at the feet of the king in behalf of Theodore and of La Motte. The character of the former, the cause in which he had risked his life, and the occasion of the late Marquis's enmity towards him, were circumstances so notorious and so forcible that it is more than probable the monarch would have granted his pardon to a pleader less irresistible than was Adeline de Montalt. Theodore La Luc not only received an ample pardon, but in consideration of his gallant conduct towards Adeline, he was soon after raised to a post of considerable rank in the army.

For La Motte, who had been condemned for the robbery on full evidence, and who had been also charged with the crime which had formerly compelled him to quit Paris, a pardon could not be obtained; but at the earnest supplication of Adeline, and in consideration of the service he had finally rendered her, his sentence was softened from death to banishment. This indulgence, however, would have availed him little, had not the noble generosity of Adeline silenced other prosecutions that were preparing against him and bestowed on him a sum more than sufficient to support his family in a foreign country. This kindness operated so powerfully upon his heart, which had been betrayed through weakness rather than natural depravity, and awakened so keen a remorse for the injuries he had once meditated against a benefactress so noble, that his former habits became odious to him and his character gradually recovered the hue which it would probably always have worn had he never been exposed to the tempting dissipations of Paris.

The passion which Louis had so long owned for Adeline was raised almost to adoration by her late conduct; but he now relinquished even the faint hope which he had hitherto almost unconsciously cherished, and since the life which was granted to Theodore rendered this sacrifice necessary, he could not repine. He resolved, however, to seek in absence the tranquillity he had lost, and to place his future happiness on that of two persons so deservedly dear to him.

On the eve of his departure La Motte and his family took a very affecting leave of Adeline. He left Paris for England, where it was his design to settle; and Louis, who was eager to fly from her enchantments, set out on the same day for his regiment.

Adeline remained some time at Paris to settle her affairs, where she was introduced by M. Verneuil to the few and distant relations that remained of her family. Among these were the Count and Countess D——, and the M. Amand who had so much engaged her pity and esteem at Nice. The lady whose death he lamented was of the family of de Montalt; and the resemblance which he had traced between her features and those of

Adeline, her cousin, was something more than the effect of fancy. The death of his elder brother had abruptly recalled him from Italy; but Adeline had the satisfaction to observe that the heavy melancholy which formerly oppressed him had yielded to a sort of placid resignation, and that his countenance was often enlivened by a transient gleam of cheerfulness.

The Count and Countess D——, who were much interested by her goodness and beauty, invited her to make their hotel her residence while she remained at Paris.

Her first care was to have the remains of her parent removed from the abbey of St. Clair and deposited in the vault of his ancestors. D'Aunoy was tried, condemned, and hanged, for the murder. At the place of execution he had described the spot where the remains of the Marquis were concealed, which was in the stone room already mentioned belonging to the abbey. M. Verneuil accompanied the officers appointed for the search, and attended the ashes of the Marquis to St. Maur, an estate in one of the northern provinces. There they were deposited with the solemn funeral pomp becoming his rank. Adeline attended as chief mourner, and this last duty paid to the memory of her parent, she became more tranquil and resigned. The MS. that recorded his sufferings had been found at the abbey and delivered to her by M. Verneuil, and she preserved it with the pious enthusiasm so sacred a relique deserved.

On her return to Paris, Theodore La Luc, who was come from Montpellier, awaited her arrival. The happiness of this meeting was clouded by the account he brought of his father, whose extreme danger had alone withheld him from hastening the moment he obtained his liberty to thank Adeline for the life she had preserved. She now received him as the friend to whom she was indebted for her preservation, and as the lover who deserved and possessed her tenderest affection. The remembrance of the circumstances under which they had last met, and of their mutual anguish, rendered more exquisite the happiness of the present moments, when no longer oppressed by the horrid prospect of ignominious death and final separation, they looked forward only to the smiling days that awaited them when hand in hand they should tread the flowery scenes of life. The contrast which memory drew of the past with the present frequently drew tears of tenderness and gratitude to their eyes, and the sweet smile which seemed struggling to dispel from the countenance of Adeline those gems of sorrow, penetrated the heart of Theodore and brought to his recollection a little song which in other circumstances he had formerly sung to her. He took up a lute that lay on the table, and touching the dulcet chords, accompanied it with the following words:

Song.

The rose that weeps with morning dew,
    And glitters in the sunny ray,
In tears and smiles resembles you,
    When Love breaks Sorrow's cloud away.

The dews that bend the blushing flow'r,
    Enrich the scent—renew the glow;
So Love's sweet tears exalt his pow'r,
    So bliss more brightly shines by woe!

Her affection for Theodore had induced Adeline to reject several suitors which her goodness, beauty, and wealth had already attracted, and who, though infinitely his superiors in point of fortune, were many of them inferior to him in family and all of them in merit.

The various and tumultuous emotions which the late events had called forth in the bosom of Adeline were now subsided; but the memory of her father still tinctured her mind with a melancholy that time only could subdue, and she refused to listen to the supplications of Theodore till the period she had prescribed for her mourning should be expired. The necessity of rejoining his regiment obliged him to leave Paris within the fortnight after his arrival; but he carried with him assurance of receiving her hand soon after she should lay aside her sable habit, and departed therefore with tolerable composure.

M. La Luc's very precarious state was a source of incessant disquietude to Adeline, and she determined to accompany M. Verneuil, who was now the declared lover of Clara, to Montpellier, whither La Luc had immediately gone on the liberation of his son. For this journey she was preparing when she received from her friend a flattering account of his amendment; and as some farther settlement of her affairs required her presence at Paris, she deferred her design and M. Verneuil departed alone.

When Theodore's affairs assumed a more favourable aspect, M. Verneuil had written to La Luc and communicated to him the secret of his heart respecting Clara. La Luc, who admired and esteemed M. Verneuil, and who was not ignorant of his family connections, was pleased with the proposed alliance. Clara thought she had never seen any person whom she was so much inclined to love, and M. Verneuil received an answer favourable to his wishes, and which encouraged him to undertake the present journey to Montpellier.

The restoration of his happiness and the climate of

Montpellier did all for the health of La Luc that his most anxious friends could wish, and he was at length so far recovered as to visit Adeline at her estate of St. Maur. Clara and M. Verneuil accompanied him, and a cessation of hostilities between France and Spain soon after permitted Theodore to join this happy party. When La Luc, thus restored to those most dear to him, looked back on the miseries he had escaped, and forward to the blessings that awaited him, his heart dilated with emotions of exquisite joy and gratitude; and his venerable countenance, softened by an expression of complacent delight, exhibited a perfect picture of happy age.

CHAPTER XXV

ADELINE, in the society of friends so beloved, lost the impression of that melancholy which the fate of her parent had occasioned; she recovered all her natural vivacity; and when she threw off the mourning habit which filial piety had required her to assume, she gave her hand to Theodore. The nuptials, which were celebrated at St. Maur, were graced by the presence of the Count and Countess D——, and La Luc had the supreme felicity of confirming on the same day the flattering destinies of both his children. When the ceremony was over, he blessed and embraced them all with tears of fatherly affection. "I thank thee, O God! that I have been permitted to see this hour," said he; "whenever it shall please thee to call me hence, I shall depart in peace."

"Long, very long, may you be spared to bless your children," replied Adeline. Clara kissed her father's hand and wept: "Long, very long," she repeated in a voice scarcely audible. La Luc smiled cheerfully, and turned the conversation to a subject less affecting.

But the time now drew nigh when La Luc thought it necessary to return to the duties of his parish, from which he had so long been absent. Madame La Luc too, who had attended him during the period of his danger at Montpellier, and hence returned to Savoy, complained much of the solitude of her life; and this was with her brother an additional motive for his speedy departure. Theodore and Adeline, who could not support the thought of a separation, endeavoured to persuade him to give up his château and to reside with them in France; but he was held by many ties to Leloncourt. For many years he had constituted the comfort and happiness of his parishioners; they revered and loved him as a father—he regarded them with an affection little short of parental. The attachment they discovered towards him on his departure was not forgotten either; it had made a deep impression on his mind, and he could not bear the thought of forsaking them now that heaven had showered on him its abundance. "It is sweet to live for them," said he, "and I will also die amongst them." A sentiment also of a more tender nature,—(and let not the stoic profane it with the name of weakness, or the man of the world scorn it as unnatural)—a sentiment still more tender attached him to Leloncourt,—the remains of his wife reposed there.

Since La Luc would not reside in France, Theodore and Adeline, to whom the splendid gaieties that courted them at Paris were very inferior temptations to the sweet domestic pleasures and refined society which Leloncourt would afford, determined to accompany La Luc and Mon. and Madame Verneuil abroad. Adeline arranged her affairs so as to render her residence in

France unnecessary; and having bid an affectionate adieu to the Count and Countess D—— and to M. Amand, who had recovered a tolerable degree of cheerfulness, she departed with her friends for Savoy.

They travelled leisurely, and frequently turned out of their way to view whatever was worthy of observation. After a long and pleasant journey they came once more within view of the Swiss mountains, the sight of which revived a thousand interesting recollections in the mind of Adeline. She remembered the circumstances and the sensations under which she had first seen them—when an orphan, flying from persecution to seek shelter among strangers, and lost to the only person on earth whom she loved—she remembered this, and the contrast of the present moment struck with all its force upon her heart.

The countenance of Clara brightened into smiles of the most animated delight as she drew near the beloved scenes of her infant pleasures; and Theodore, often looking from the windows, caught with patriotic enthusiasm the magnificent and changing scenery which the receding mountains successively disclosed.

It was evening when they approached within a few miles of Leloncourt, and the road winding round the foot of a stupendous crag presented them a full view of the lake and the peaceful dwelling of La Luc. An exclamation of joy from the whole party announced the discovery, and the glance of pleasure was reflected from every eye. The sun's last light gleamed upon the waters that reposed in "crystal purity" below, mellowed every feature of the landscape and touched with purple splendour the clouds that rolled along the mountain tops.

La Luc welcomed his family to his happy home, and sent up a silent thanksgiving that he was permitted thus to return to it. Adeline continued to gaze upon each well-known object, and again reflecting on the vicissitudes of grief and joy and the surprising change of fortune which she had experienced since last she saw them, her heart dilated with gratitude and complacent delight. She looked at Theodore, whom in these very scenes she had lamented as lost to her for ever, who when found again was about to be torn from her by an ignominious death, but who now sat by her side her secure and happy husband, the pride of his family and herself; and while the sensibility of her heart flowed in tears from her eyes, a smile of ineffable tenderness told him all she felt. He gently pressed her hand and answered her with a look of love.

Peter, who now rode up to the carriage with a face full of joy and of importance, interrupted a course of sentiment which was become almost too interesting. "Ah! my dear master!" cried he, "welcome home again. Here is the village, God bless it! It is worth a million such places as Paris. Thank St. Jacques, we are all come safe back again."

This effusion of honest Peter's joy was received and answered with the kindness it deserved. As they drew near the lake, music sounded over the water, and they presently saw a large party of the villagers assembled on a green spot that sloped to the very margin of the waves, and dancing in all their holiday finery. It was the evening of a festival. The elder peasants sat under the shade of the trees that crowned this little eminence, eating milk and fruits and watching their sons and daughters frisk it away to the sprightly notes of the tabor and pipe, which was joined by the softer tones of a mandolin.

The scene was highly interesting, and what added to its picturesque beauty was a group of cattle that stood some on the brink, some half in the water, and others reposing on the green bank, while several peasant girls dressed in the neat simplicity of their country were dispensing the milky feast. Peter now rode on first, and a crowd soon collected round him, who, learning that their beloved master was at hand, went forth to meet and welcome him. Their warm and honest expressions of joy diffused an exquisite satisfaction over the heart of the good La Luc, who met them with the kindness of a father and could scarcely forbear shedding tears to this testimony of their attachment. When the younger part of the peasants heard the news of his arrival, the general joy was such that, led by the tabor and pipe, they danced before his carriage to the château, where they again welcomed him and his family with the enlivening strains of music. At the gate of the château they were received by Madame La Luc, and a happier party never met.

As the evening was uncommonly mild and beautiful, supper was spread in the garden. When the repast was over, Clara, whose heart was all glee, proposed a dance by moonlight. "It will be delicious," said she; "the moonbeams are already dancing on the waters. See what a stream of radiance they throw across the lake, and how they sparkle round that little promontory on the left. The freshness of the hour too invites to dancing."

They all agreed to the proposal.—"And let the good people who have so heartily welcomed us home be called in too," said La Luc: "they shall *all* partake our happiness. There is devotion in making others happy, and gratitude ought to make us devout. Peter, bring more wine, and set some tables under the trees." Peter flew, and, while chairs and tables were placing, Clara ran for her favourite lute, the lute which had formerly afforded her such delight, and which Adeline had often touched with a melancholy expression. Clara's light hand now ran over the chords and drew forth tones of tender sweetness, her voice accompanying the following air:

> Now at Moonlight's fairy hour,
>   When faintly gleams each dewy steep,
> And vale and mountain, lake and bow'r,
>   In solitary grandeur sleep;
>
> When slowly sinks the evening breeze,
>   That lulls the mind in pensive care,
> And Fancy loftier visions sees,
>   Bid music wake the silent air.
>
> Bid the merry, merry tabor sound,
>   And with the Fays of lawn or glade,
> In tripping circlet beat the ground
>   Under the high trees' trembling shade.
>
> "Now at Moonlight's fairy hour"
>   Shall Music breathe her dulcet voice,
> And o'er the waves, with magic pow'r,
>   Call on Echo to rejoice!

Peter, who could not move in a sober step, had already spread refreshments under the trees, and in a short time the lawn was encircled with peasantry. The rural pipe and tabor were placed at Clara's request under the shade of her beloved acacias on the margin of the lake; the merry notes of music sounded; Adeline led off the dance, and the mountains answered only to the strains of mirth and melody.

The venerable La Luc, as he sat among the elder peasants, surveyed the scene—his children and people thus assembled round him in one grand compact of harmony and joy—the frequent tear bedewed his cheek, and he seemed to taste the fullness of an exalted delight.

So much was every heart roused to gladness that the morning dawn began to peep upon the scene of their festivity, when every cottager returned to his home blessing the benevolence of La Luc.

After passing some weeks with La Luc, M. Verneuil bought a château in the village of Leloncourt, and as it was the only one not already occupied, Theodore looked out for a residence in the neighbourhood. At the distance of a few leagues, on the beautiful banks of the lake of Geneva, where the waters retire into a small bay, he purchased a villa. The château was characterized by an air of simplicity and taste, rather than of magnificence, which however was the chief trait in the surrounding scene. The château was almost encircled with woods, which forming a grand amphitheatre, swept down to the water's edge, and abounded with wild and romantic walks. Here nature was suffered to sport in all her beautiful luxuriance, except where here and there the hand of art formed the foliage to admit a view of the blue waters of the lake, with the white sail that glided by, or of the distant mountains. In front of the château the woods opened to a lawn, and the eye was suffered to wander over the lake, whose bosom presented an ever-moving picture, while its varied margin sprinkled with villas, woods, and towns, and crowned beyond with the snowy and sublime Alps, rising point behind point in awful confusion, exhibited a scenery of almost unequalled magnificence.

Here, contemning the splendour of false happiness, and possessing the pure and rational delights of love refined into the most tender friendship, surrounded by the friends so dear to them, and visited by a select and enlightened society—here, in the very bosom of felicity, lived Theodore and Adeline La Luc.

The passion of Louis de la Motte yielded at length to the powers of absence and necessity. He still loved Adeline, but it was with the placid tenderness of friendship, and when, at the earnest invitation of Theodore, he visited the villa, he beheld their happiness with a satisfaction unalloyed by any emotions of envy. He afterwards married a lady of some fortune at Geneva, and resigning his commission in the French service, settled on the borders of the lake, and increased the social delights of Theodore and Adeline.

Their former lives afforded an example of trials well endured—and their present, of virtues greatly rewarded; and this reward they continued to deserve— for not to themselves was their happiness contracted, but diffused to all who came within the sphere of their influence. The indigent and unhappy rejoiced in their benevolence, the virtuous and enlightened in their friendship, and their children in parents whose example impressed upon their hearts the precepts offered to their understandings.

The End.